Bensarius squeezed Calopodius's shoulder. "The
tr_____, _____ _____. We've ____
on telegraph up here, b_____ ____
for everyone, and comm_____ ____
mess. My command bu_____ ____
at cross-purposes. I nee_____ ____
charge and organize the _____.

Cheerfully: "That's you, lad! Being blind won't be a
handicap at all for that work."

Calopodius wasn't certain if the general's cheer was
real, or simply assumed for the purpose of improving
the morale of a badly maimed subordinate. Even as
young as he was, Calopodius knew that the commander
he admired was quite capable of being as calculating
as he was cordial.

But . . .

Almost despite himself, he began feeling more cheerful.

"Well, there's this much," he said, trying to match
the general's enthusiasm. "My tutors thought highly of
my grammar and rhetoric. If nothing else, I'm sure I
can improve the quality of the messages."

The general laughed. The gaiety of the sound cheered
up Calopodius even more than the general's earlier
words. It was harder to feign laughter than words. A
blind man aged quickly, in some ways, and Calopodius
had become an expert on false laughter, in the weeks
since he lost his eyes.

This was real. This was—

Something he could do.

A future which had seemed empty began to fill with
color again.

"Yes," he said, with reborn confidence. "I can do that."

—from "Islands"

WORLDS

ERIC FLINT

WORLDS

Copyright © 2009 by Eric Flint

A Baen Books Original

Baen Publishing Enterprises
P.O. Box 1403
Riverdale, NY 10471
www.baen.com

ISBN: 978-1-4516-3751-9

Cover art by Tom Kidd

First Baen paperback printing, November 2011

Library of Congress Control Number: 2008049710

Distributed by Simon & Schuster
1230 Avenue of the Americas
New York, NY 10020

Pages by Joy Freeman (www.pagesbyjoy.com)
Printed in the United States of America

To the memory of my mother,

Mary Jeanne McCormick Flint

Born February 14, 1926
Died July 7, 2008

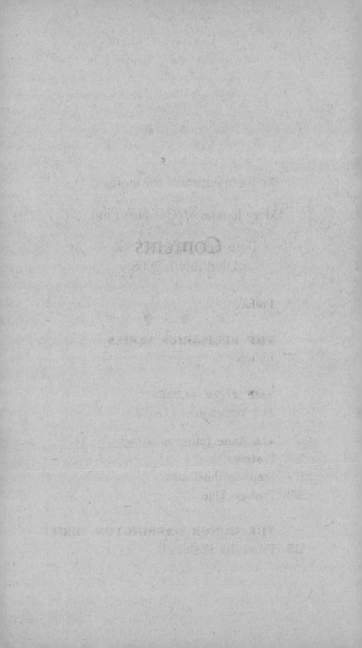

Contents

Preface

As an author, I'm almost a pure novelist. By good fortune, I happened to become a professional writer at a time when the market for science fiction and fantasy had become completely dominated by novels—and series, at that, not even stand-alone novels. That worked very nicely for me personally, since novels—especially series—are my natural inclination as a writer.

But that's not really why I work almost entirely in long-form writing, it's just good luck. I'd have done the same thing forty or fifty years ago when science fiction and fantasy was a predominantly short-form genre. Even though, in all likelihood, I'd never have been able to make a living as a writer, which I can do today.

It's just the way my brain works, that's all. When I first started writing fiction, like most aspiring authors, I tried to write short fiction. That's because I thought that it'd be much easier to get professionally published with short stories than with novels.

That's not actually true, today, as I discovered soon enough. If anything, there's *less* competition for novels than there is for short fiction. True enough, a typical novel publishing house will receive hundreds of manuscripts from unpublished authors every year, from which they will only select a literal handful. But a major commercial F&SF magazine will get that many submissions every *month*—from which they will select perhaps one or two from unpublished authors, if they select any at all.

The big drawback to launching a writing career with novels, or trying to, isn't actually the level of competition. It's that an aspiring writer obviously has to commit a far greater amount of time and effort to writing a novel than a short story. You can write a short story in days. Writing a novel, for all but the very fastest writers, takes several months—and can easily take a year or two, if you're working a full-time job.

The problem I always had with short fiction is that I simply couldn't start telling a story until I'd gotten the setting and background very well worked out. And once I'd done that and started writing, I invariably found myself writing a "short story" that was actually a novel in disguise—and would work far better as a novel in the first place. The only exceptions were a few short stories I wrote with a purely humorous purpose.

So, finally, I accepted the inevitable. I stopped trying to write short fiction and concentrated instead entirely on writing novels. And that's how my career got started. I'd published five novels and had several more under contract before I even tried to write short fiction again.

The reason I did, then, was because David Drake

commissioned me to write a novella for an anthology (*Foreign Legions,* published in 2001) that was based in his *Ranks of Bronze* setting. Any professional writer hates to turn down work, following the principle that a bird in the hand is worth two in the bush. So, despite my misgivings, I accepted the commission.

At that point, an interesting thing happened. I discovered that I didn't have any trouble writing that novella—"*Carthago Delenda Est,*" which is included in this volume—because David had *already* developed the setting and background. I found it quite easy to situate myself in an existing universe and simply figure out a story that would work just fine, despite being much shorter than my normal inclination.

A short time later, David Weber commissioned another story from me, this one to be included in an anthology of stories set in the universe of his very popular Honor Harrington series. In this instance, Dave wanted either a long novella or a short novel, not the short novella that Drake had commissioned.

The end result turned out to be the short novel "From the Highlands," which is also included in this volume. And, again, I made the same discovery. As long as the setting was *already* established, I had no trouble writing in any length from short story on up. Within a couple of years, I'd written several other pieces, most of them set in my own 1632 universe—the shortest of which is only three thousand words long. (That's "Portraits," also included herein.)

Once the logjam got broken, I wound up writing quite a bit of short fiction. Not as much, to be sure, as I wrote novels. But, eventually, I realized that I'd written enough short fiction to produce, if collected together, a very hefty anthology. So I proposed to Jim Baen that Baen Books produce such an anthology, and he accepted.

The result, you hold in your hand. This is something of an oddball collection of short fiction, I admit. The typical such collection is of a number of unrelated short stories, each of which stands entirely on its own. Whereas almost all of my short fiction is set in an existing universe—usually a series of my own, but sometimes that of another author—and many of the stories are related more directly still to novels or other stories in that series.

Still, I think every one of these stories can be read and enjoyed on its own. And it's my hope, of course, that if any reader of this anthology finds their interest being taken by one or another of the stories in it, they'll be inspired to investigate the novels in which that universe or universes are more fully developed.

So, welcome to my worlds.

Eric Flint
September 2008

THE
BELISARIUS
SERIES

Author's note:

This is the fourth version of this story. I originally wrote it as a novella to be included in the anthology *Warmasters*, published by Baen Books in 2002. After the hardcover edition appeared in May of that year, I decided that the story would be improved by adding a penultimate episode just before the existing ending. That episode was included in the version that was reissued in the mass market edition of *Warmasters*, which came out in February 2004.

In 2005, when I sat down to write the final novel in the Belisarius series, *The Dance of Time*, my original intention was to include "Islands" as an appendix to the novel, since the story serves in some respects as a bridge between the fifth volume *(The Tide of Victory)* and the last one. But my co-author Dave Drake convinced me that it would be better if I wove the various episodes of "Islands" into *The Dance of Time* as one of the subplots. So, I did so, polishing and slightly expanding the existing story. (In the novel subplot, I also continued the later adventures of Calopodius and Anna. But those events are not integral to this story, which stands on its own, so they're not included here.)

So that was the third version—and this is the fourth, which is the reassembly of the story as a stand-alone novella for this anthology, which I did by using the later and improved version I wrote for the novel.

When all is said and done, I still think the same thing I thought when I first wrote the story. It's probably the best piece of short fiction I've ever written—certainly in some respects—and it's one of the best things I've ever written in any length. The fact that the story can handle being shaped and re-shaped so often is simply a reflection of that. The one thing all good stories have in common is that they are very, very tough.

Islands

1

Bukkur Island, on the Indus river

He dreamed mostly of islands, oddly enough.

He was sailing, now, in one of his father's pleasure crafts. Not the luxurious barge-in-all-but-name-and-glitter which his father himself preferred for the family's outings into the Golden Horn, but in the phaselos which was suited for sailing in the open sea. Unlike his father, for whom sailing expeditions were merely excuses for political or commercial transactions, Calopodius had always loved sailing for its own sake.

Besides, it gave him and his new wife something to do besides sit together in stiff silence.

7

Calopodius' half-sleeping reverie was interrupted. Wakefulness came with the sound of his aide-de-camp Luke moving through the tent. The heaviness with which Luke clumped about was deliberate, designed to allow his master to recognize who had entered his domicile. Luke was quite capable of moving easily and lightly, as he had proved many times in the course of the savage fighting on Bukkur Island. But the man, in this as so many things, had proven to be far more subtle than his rough and muscular appearance might suggest.

"It's morning, young Calopodius," Luke announced. "Time to clean your wounds. And you're not eating enough."

Calopodius sighed. The process of tending the wounds would be painful, despite all of Luke's care. As for the other—

"Have new provisions arrived?"

There was a moment's silence. Then, reluctantly: "No."

Calopodius let the silence lengthen. After a few seconds, he heard Luke's own heavy sigh. "We're getting very low, truth to tell. Ashot hasn't much himself, until the supply ships arrive."

Calopodius levered himself up on his elbows. "Then I will eat my share, no more." He chuckled, perhaps a bit harshly. "And don't try to cheat, Luke. I have other sources of information, you know."

"As if my hardest job of the day won't be to keep half the army from parading through this tent," snorted Luke. Calopodius felt the weight of Luke's knees pressing into the pallet next to him, and, a moment later, winced as the bandages over his head began to be removed. "You're quite the soldiers' favorite, lad," added Luke softly. "Don't think otherwise."

In the painful time that followed, as Luke scoured and cleaned and rebandaged the sockets that had once been eyes, Calopodius tried to take refuge in that knowledge.

It helped. Some.

"Are there any signs of another Malwa attack coming?" he asked, some time later. Calopodius was now perched in one of the bastions his men had rebuilt after an enemy assault had overrun it—before, eventually, the Malwa had been driven off the island altogether. That had required bitter and ferocious fighting, however, which had inflicted many casualties upon the Roman defenders. His eyes had been among those casualties, ripped out by shrapnel from a mortar shell.

"After the bloody beating we gave 'em the last time?" chortled one of the soldiers who shared the bastion. "Not likely, sir!"

Calopodius tried to match the voice to a remembered face. As usual, the effort failed of its purpose. But he took the time to engage in small talk with the soldier, so as to fix the voice itself in his memory. Not for the first time, Calopodius reflected wryly on the way in which possession of vision seemed to dull all other human faculties. Since his blinding, he had found his memory growing more acute along with his hearing. A simple instinct for self-preservation, he imagined. A blind man had to remember better than a seeing man, since he no longer had vision to constantly jog his lazy memory.

After his chat with the soldier had gone on for a

few minutes, the man cleared his throat and said diffidently: "You'd best leave here, sir, if you'll pardon me for saying so. The Malwa'll likely be starting another barrage soon." For a moment, fierce good cheer filled the man's voice: "They seem to have a particular grudge against this part of our line, seeing's how their own blood and guts make up a good part of it."

The remark produced a ripple of harsh chuckling from the other soldiers crouched in the fortifications. That bastion had been one of the most hotly contested areas when the Malwa launched their major attack the week before. Calopodius didn't doubt for a moment that when his soldiers repaired the damage to the earthen walls they had not been too fastidious about removing all the traces of the carnage.

He sniffed tentatively, detecting those traces. His olfactory sense, like his hearing, had grown more acute also.

"Must have stunk, right afterward," he commented.

The same soldier issued another harsh chuckle. "That it did, sir, that it did. Why God invented flies, the way I look at it."

Calopodius felt Luke's heavy hand on his shoulder. "Time to go, sir. There'll be a barrage coming, sure enough."

In times past, Calopodius would have resisted. But he no longer felt any need to prove his courage, and a part of him—a still wondering, eighteen-year-old part—understood that his safety had become something his own men cared about. Alive, somewhere in the rear but still on the island, Calopodius would be a source of strength for his soldiers in the event of another Malwa onslaught. Spiritual strength, if not physical;

a symbol, if nothing else. But men—fighting men, perhaps, more than any others—live by such symbols.

So he allowed Luke to guide him out of the bastion and down the rough staircase which led to the trenches below. On the way, Calopodius gauged the steps with his feet.

"One of those logs is too big," he said, speaking firmly, but trying to keep any critical edge out of the words. "It's a waste, there. Better to use it for another fake cannon."

He heard Luke suppress a sigh. *And will you stop fussing like a hen?* was the content of that small sound. Calopodius suppressed a laugh. Luke, in truth, made a poor "servant."

"We've got enough," replied Luke curtly. "Twenty-odd. Do any more and the Malwa will get suspicious. We've only got three real ones left to keep up the pretense."

As they moved slowly through the trench, Calopodius considered the problem and decided that Luke was right. The pretense was probably threadbare by now, anyway. When the Malwa finally launched a full-scale amphibious assault on the island that was the centerpiece of Calopodius' diversion, they had overrun half of it before being beaten back. When the survivors returned to the main Malwa army besieging the city of Sukkur across the Indus, they would have reported to their own top commanders that several of the "cannons" with which the Romans had apparently festooned their fortified island were nothing but painted logs.

But how many? That question would still be unclear in the minds of the enemy.

Not all of them, for a certainty. When Belisarius took his main force to outflank the Malwa in the Punjab, leaving behind Calopodius and fewer than two thousand men to serve as a diversion, he had also left some of the field guns and mortars. Those pieces had savaged the Malwa attackers, when they finally grew suspicious enough to test the real strength of Calopodius' position.

"The truth is," said Luke gruffly, "it doesn't really matter anyway." Again, the heavy hand settled on Calopodius' slender shoulder, this time giving it a little squeeze of approval. "You've already done what the general asked you to, lad. Kept the Malwa confused, thinking Belisarius was still here, while he marched in secret to the northeast. Did it as well as he could have possibly hoped."

They had reached one of the covered portions of the trench, Calopodius sensed. He couldn't see the earth-covered logs which gave some protection from enemy fire, of course. But the quality of sound was a bit different within a shelter than in an open trench. That was just one of the many little auditory subtleties which Calopodius had begun noticing lately.

He had not noticed it in times past, before he lost his eyes. In the first days after Belisarius and the main army left Sukkur on their secret, forced march to outflank the Malwa in the Punjab, Calopodius had noticed very little, in truth. He had had neither the time nor the inclination to ponder the subtleties of sense perception. He had been far too excited by his new and unexpected command and by the challenge it posed.

Martial glory. The blind young man in the covered trench stopped for a moment, staring through sightless eyes at a wall of earth and timber bracing. Remembering, and wondering.

The martial glory Calopodius had sought, when he left a new wife in Constantinople, had certainly come to him. Of that, he had no doubt at all. His own soldiers thought so, and said so often enough—those who had survived—and Calopodius was quite certain that his praises would soon be spoken in the Senate.

Precious few of the Roman Empire's most illustrious families had achieved any notable feats of arms in the great war against the Malwa. Beginning with the top commander Belisarius himself, born into the lower Thracian nobility, it had been largely a war fought by men from low stations in life. Commoners, in the main. Agathius—the now-famous hero of Anatha and the Dam—had been born into a baker's family, about as menial a position as any short of outright slavery.

Other than Sittas, who was now leading Belisarius' cataphracts in the Punjab, almost no Greek noblemen had fought in the Malwa war. And even Sittas, before the Indus campaign, had spent the war commanding the garrison in Constantinople that overawed the hostile aristocracy and kept the dynasty on the throne.

Had it been worth it?

Reaching up and touching gently the emptiness which had once been his eyes, Calopodius was still not sure. Like many other young members of the nobility, he had been swept up with enthusiasm after the news came that Belisarius had shattered the Malwa in Mesopotamia. Let the adult members of the aristocracy whine and complain in their salons. The youth were burning to serve.

And serve they had . . . but only as couriers, in the beginning. It hadn't taken Calopodius long to realize that Belisarius intended to use him and his high-born fellows mainly for liaison with the haughty Persians, who were even more obsessed with nobility of bloodline than Greeks. The posts carried prestige—the couriers rode just behind Belisarius himself in formation—but little in the way of actual responsibility.

Standing in the bunker, the blind young man chuckled harshly. "He used us, you know. As cold-blooded as a reptile."

Silence, for a moment. Then, Calopodius heard Luke take a deep breath.

"Aye, lad. He did. The general will use anyone, if he feels it necessary."

Calopodius nodded. He felt no anger at the thought. He simply wanted it acknowledged.

He reached out his hand and felt the rough wall of the bunker with fingertips grown sensitive with blindness. Texture of soil, which he would never have noticed before, came like a flood of dark light. He wondered, for a moment, how his wife's breasts would feel to him, or her belly, or her thighs. Now.

He didn't imagine he would ever know, and dropped the hand. Calopodius did not expect to survive the war, now that he was blind. Not unless he used the blindness as a reason to return to Constantinople, and spent the rest of his life resting on his laurels.

The thought was unbearable. *I am only eighteen! My life should still be ahead of me!*

That thought brought a final decision. Given that his life was now forfeit, Calopodius intended to give it the full measure while it lasted.

"Menander should be arriving soon, with the supply ships."

"Yes," said Luke.

"When he arrives, I wish to speak with him."

"Yes," said Luke. The "servant" hesitated. Then: "What about?"

Again, Calopodius chuckled harshly. "Another forlorn hope." He began moving slowly through the bunker to the tunnel which led back to his headquarters. "Having lost my eyes on this island, it seems only right I should lose my life on another. Belisarius' island, this time—not the one he left behind to fool the enemy. The real island, not the false one."

"There was nothing false about this island, young man," growled Luke. "Never say it. Malwa was broken here, as surely as it was on any battlefield of Belisarius. There is the blood of Roman soldiers to prove it—along with your own eyes. Most of all—"

By some means he could not specify, Calopodius understood that Luke was gesturing angrily to the north. "Most of all, by the fact that we kept an entire Malwa army pinned here for two weeks—by your cunning and our sweat and blood—while Belisarius slipped unseen to the north. Two weeks. The time he needed to slide a lance into Malwa's unprotected flank—we gave him that time. We did. You did."

He heard Luke's almost shuddering intake of breath. "So never speak of a 'false' island again, boy. Is a shield 'false,' and only a sword 'true'? Stupid. The general did what he needed to do—and so did you. Take pride in it, for there was nothing false in that doing."

Calopodius could not help lowering his head. "No," he whispered.

But was it worth the doing?

The Indus river in the Punjab
Belisarius' headquarters
The Iron Triangle

"I know I shouldn't have come, General, but—"

Calopodius groped for words to explain. He could not find any. It was impossible to explain to someone else the urgency he felt, since it would only sound ... suicidal. Which, in truth, it almost was, at least in part. But ...

"May—maybe I could help you with supplies or—or something."

"No matter," stated Belisarius firmly, giving Calopodius' shoulder a squeeze. The general's large hand was very powerful. Calopodius was a little surprised by that. His admiration for Belisarius bordered on idolization, but he had never really given any thought to the general's physical characteristics. He had just been dazzled, first, by the man's reputation; then, after finally meeting him in Mesopotamia, by the relaxed humor and confidence with which he ran his staff meetings.

The large hand on his shoulder began gently leading Calopodius off the dock where Menander's ship had tied up.

"I can still count, even if—"

"Forget that," growled Belisarius. "I've got enough clerks." With a chuckle: "The quartermasters don't have that much to count, anyway. We're on very short rations here."

Again, the hand squeezed his shoulder; not with sympathy, this time, so much as assurance. "The truth

is, lad, I'm delighted to see you. We're relying on
telegraph up here, in this new little fortified half-
island we've created, to concentrate our forces quickly
enough when the Malwa launch another attack. But
the telegraph's a new thing for everyone, and keeping
the communications straight and orderly has turned
into a mess. My command bunker is full of people
shouting at cross-purposes. I need a good officer who
can take charge and organize the damn thing."

Cheerfully: "That's you, lad! Being blind won't be a
handicap at all for that work. Probably be a blessing."

Calopodius wasn't certain if the general's cheer was
real, or simply assumed for the purpose of improving
the morale of a badly maimed subordinate. Even as
young as he was, Calopodius knew that the commander
he admired was quite capable of being as calculating
as he was cordial.

But . . .

Almost despite himself, he began feeling more
cheerful.

"Well, there's this much," he said, trying to match
the general's enthusiasm. "My tutors thought highly of
my grammar and rhetoric, as I believe I mentioned
once. If nothing else, I'm sure I can improve the
quality of the messages."

The general laughed. The gaiety of the sound
cheered up Calopodius even more than the general's
earlier words. It was harder to feign laughter than
words. Calopodius was not guessing about that. A blind
man aged quickly, in some ways, and Calopodius had
become an expert on the subject of false laughter, in
the weeks since he lost his eyes.

This was real. This was—

Something he could do.

A future which had seemed empty began to fill with color again. Only the colors of his own imagination, of course. But Calopodius, remembering discussions on philosophy with learned scholars in far away and long ago Constantinople, wondered if reality was anything but images in the mind. If so, perhaps blindness was simply a matter of custom.

"Yes," he said, with reborn confidence. "I can do that."

For the first two days, the command bunker was a madhouse for Calopodius. But by the end of that time, he had managed to bring some semblance of order and procedure to the way in which telegraph messages were received and transmitted. Within a week, he had the system functioning smoothly and efficiently.

The general praised him for his work. So, too, in subtle little ways, did the twelve men under his command. Calopodius found the latter more reassuring than the former. He was still a bit uncertain whether Belisarius' approval was due, at least in part, to the general's obvious feeling of guilt that he was responsible for the young officer's blindness. Whereas the men who worked for him, veterans all, had seen enough mutilation in their lives not to care about yet another cripple. Had the young nobleman not been a blessing to them but rather a curse, they would not have let sympathy stand in the way of criticism. And the general, Calopodius was well aware, kept an ear open to the sentiments of his soldiers.

Throughout that first week, Calopodius paid little

attention to the ferocious battle which was raging beyond the heavily timbered and fortified command bunker. He traveled nowhere, beyond the short distance between that bunker and the small one—not much more than a covered hole in the ground—where he and Luke had set up what passed for "living quarters." Even that route was sheltered by soil-covered timber, so the continual sound of cannon fire was muffled.

The only time Calopodius emerged into the open was for the needs of the toilet. As always in a Belisarius camp, the sanitation arrangements were strict and rigorous. The latrines were located some distance from the areas where the troops slept and ate, and no exceptions were made even for the blind and crippled. A man who could not reach the latrines under his own power would either be taken there, or, if too badly injured, would have his bedpan emptied for him.

For the first three days, Luke guided him to the latrines. Thereafter, he could make the journey himself. Slowly, true, but he used the time to ponder and crystallize his new ambition. It was the only time his mind was not preoccupied with the immediate demands of the command bunker.

Being blind, he had come to realize, did not mean the end of life. Although it did transform his dreams of fame and glory into much softer and more muted colors. But finding dreams in the course of dealing with the crude realities of a latrine, he decided, was perhaps appropriate. Life was a crude thing, after all. A project begun in confusion, fumbling with unfamiliar tools, the end never really certain until it came—and then, far more often than not, coming as awkwardly as a blind man attends to his toilet.

Shit is also manure, he came to understand. A man does what he can. If he was blind...he was also educated, and rich, and had every other advantage. The rough soldiers who helped him on his way had their own dreams, did they not? And their own glory, come to it. If he could not share in that glory directly, he could save it for the world.

When he explained it to the general—awkwardly, of course, and not at a time of his own choosing—Belisarius gave the project his blessing. That day, Calopodius began his history of the war against the Malwa. The next day, almost as an afterthought, he wrote the first of the *Dispatches to the Army* which would, centuries after his death, make him as famous as Livy or Polybius.

The Iron Triangle

As always, the sound of Luke's footsteps awakened Calopodius. This time, though, as he emerged from sleep, he sensed that other men were shuffling their feet in the background.

He was puzzled, a bit. Few visitors came to the bunker where he and Luke had set up their quarters. Calopodius suspected that was because men felt uncomfortable in the presence of a blind man, especially one as young as himself. It was certainly not due to lack of space. The general had provided him with a very roomy bunker, connected by a short tunnel to the great command bunker buried near the small city that had emerged over the past months toward the southern tip of the Iron Triangle. The Roman army called that city "the Anvil," taking the name from the Punjabi civilians who made up most of its inhabitants.

"Who's there, Luke?" he asked.

His aide-de-camp barked a laugh. "A bunch of boys seeking fame and glory, lad. The general sent them."

The shuffling feet came nearer. "Begging your pardon, sir, but we were wondering—as he says, the general sent us to talk to you—" The man, whoever he was, lapsed into an awkward silence.

Calopodius sat up on his pallet. "Speak up, then. And who are you?"

The man cleared his throat. "Name's Abelard, sir. Abelard of Antioch. I'm the hecatontarch in charge of the westernmost bastion at the fortress of—"

"You had hot fighting yesterday," interrupted Calopodius. "I heard about it. The general told me the Malwa probe was much fiercer than usual."

"Came at us like demons, sir," said another voice. Proudly: "But we bloodied 'em good."

Calopodius understood at once. The hecatontarch cleared his throat, but Calopodius spoke before the man was forced into embarrassment.

"I'll want to hear all the details!" he exclaimed. "Just give me a moment to get dressed and summon my scribe. We can do it all right here, at the table there. I'll make sure it goes into the next dispatch."

"Thank you, sir," said Abelard. His voice took on a slightly aggrieved tone. "T'isn't true, what Luke says. It's neither the fame nor the glory of it. It's just . . . your Dispatches get read to the Senate, sir. Each and every one, by the Emperor himself. And then the Emperor—by express command—has them printed and posted all over the Empire."

Calopodius was moving around, feeling for his clothing. "True enough," he said cheerfully. "Ever since the old Emperor set up the new printing press in the Great Palace, everybody—every village, anyway—can get a copy of something."

"It's our families, sir," said the other voice. "They'll see our names and know we're all right. Except for those who died in the fighting. But at least..."

Calopodius understood. "Their names will exist somewhere, on something other than a tombstone."

They had approached Elafonisos from the south, because Calopodius had thought Anna might enjoy the sight of the great ridge which overlooked the harbor, with its tower perched atop it like a hawk. And she had seemed to enjoy it well enough, although, as he was coming to recognize, she took most of her pleasure from the sea itself. As did he, for that matter.

She even smiled, once or twice.

The trip across to the island, however, was the high point of the expedition. Their overnight stay in the small tavern in the port had been... almost unpleasant. Anna had not objected to the dinginess of the provincial tavern, nor had she complained about the poor fare offered for their evening meal. But she had retreated into an even more distant silence—almost sullen and hostile—as soon as they set foot on land.

That night, as always since the night of their wedding, she performed her duties without resistance. But also with as much energy and enthusiasm as she might have given to reading a particularly dull piece of hagiography. Calopodius found it all quite frustrating, the more so since his wife's naked body

*was something which aroused him greatly. As he had
suspected in the days before the marriage, his wife
was quite lovely once she could be seen. And felt.*

*So he performed his own duty in a perfunctory
manner. Afterward, in another time, he might have
spent the occasion idly considering the qualities he
would look for in a courtesan—now that he had a wife
against whose tedium he could measure the problem.
But he had already decided to join Belisarius' expedition to the Indus. So, before falling asleep, his thoughts
were entirely given over to matters of martial glory.
And, of course, the fears and uncertainties which any
man his age would feel on the eve of plunging into
the maelstrom of war.*

2

The Euphrates
Autumn, 533 AD

When trouble finally arrived, it was Anna's husband
who saved her. The knowledge only increased her fury.

Stupid, really, and some part of her mind understood
it perfectly well. But she still couldn't stop hating him.

Stupid. The men on the barge who were clambering
eagerly onto the small pier where her own little river
craft was tied up were making no attempt to hide
their leers. Eight of them there were, their half-clad
bodies sweaty from the toil of working their clumsy
vessel up the Euphrates.

A little desperately, Anna looked about. She saw
nothing beyond the Euphrates itself; reed marshes on
the other bank, and a desert on her own. There was

not a town or a village in sight. She had stopped at
this little pier simply because the two sailors she had
hired to carry her down to Charax had insisted they
needed to take on fresh water. There was a well here,
which was the only reason for the pier's existence. After
taking a taste of the muddy water of the Euphrates,
Anna couldn't find herself in disagreement.

She wished, now, that she'd insisted on continuing.
Not that her insistence would have probably done much
good. The sailors had been civil enough, since she'd
employed them at a small town in the headwaters of
the Euphrates. But they were obviously not overawed
by a nineteen-year-old girl, even if she did come from
the famous family of the Melisseni.

She glanced appealingly at the sailors, still working
the well. They avoided her gaze, acting as if they hadn't
even noticed the men climbing out of the barge. Both
sailors were rather elderly, and it was clear enough
they had no intention of getting into a fracas with
eight rivermen much younger than themselves—all
of whom were carrying knives, to boot.

The men from the barge were close to her, and
beginning to spread out. One of them was fingering
the knife in a scabbard attached to his waist. All of
them were smiling in a manner which even a sheltered
young noblewoman understood was predatory.

Now in sheer desperation, her eyes moved to the
only other men on the pier. Three soldiers, judging
from their weapons and gear. They had already been
on the pier when Anna's boat drew up, and their
presence had almost been enough to cause the sailors to pass by entirely. A rather vicious-looking trio,
they were. Two Isaurians and a third one whom Anna

thought was probably an Arab. Isaurians were not much better than barbarians; Arabs might or might not be, depending on where they came from. Anna suspected this one was an outright bedouin.

The soldiers were lounging in the shade of a small pavilion they had erected. For a moment, as she had when she first caught sight of them, Anna found herself wondering how they had gotten there in the first place. They had no boat, nor any horses or camels—yet they possessed too much in the way of goods in sacks to have lugged them on their own shoulders. Not through this arid country, with their armor and weapons. She decided they had probably traveled with a caravan, and then parted company for some reason.

But this was no time for idle speculation. The rivermen were very close now. The soldiers returned Anna's beseeching eyes with nothing more than indifference. It was clear enough they had no more intention of intervening than her own sailors.

Still—they could, in a way that two elderly sailors couldn't.

Pay them.

Moving as quickly as she could in her elaborate clothing—and cursing herself silently, again, for having been so stupid as to make this insane journey without giving a thought to her apparel—Anna walked over to them. She could only hope they understood Greek. She knew no other language.

"I need help," she hissed.

The soldier in the center of the little group, one of the Isaurians, glanced at the eight rivermen and chuckled.

"I'd say so. You'll be lucky if they don't kill you after they rob and rape you."

His Greek was fluent, if heavily accented. As he proceeded to demonstrate further. "Stupid noblewoman. Brains like a chicken. Are you some kind of idiot, traveling alone down this part of Mesopotamia? The difference between a riverman here and a pirate—"

He turned his head and spit casually over the leg of the other Isaurian. His brother, judging from the close resemblance.

"I'll pay you," she said.

The two brothers exchanged glances. The one on the side, who seemed to be the younger one, shrugged. "We can use her boat to take us out of Mesopotamia. Beats walking, and the chance of another caravan . . . But nothing fancy," he muttered. "We're almost home."

His older brother grunted agreement and turned his head to look at the Arab. The Arab's shrug expressed the same tepid enthusiasm. "Nothing fancy," he echoed. "It's too hot."

The Isaurian in the middle lazed to his feet. He wasn't much taller than Anna, but his stocky and muscular build made him seem to loom over her.

"All right. Here's the way it is. You give us half your money and whatever other valuables you've got." He tapped the jeweled necklace around her throat. "The rivermen can take the rest of it. They'll settle for that, just to avoid a brawl."

She almost wailed. Not quite. "I can't. I need the money to get to—"

The soldier scowled. "Idiot! We'll keep them from taking your boat, we'll leave you enough—just enough—to get back to your family, and we'll escort you into Anatolia."

He glanced again at the rivermen. They were standing some few yards away, hesitant now. "You've no business here, girl," he growled quietly. "Just be thankful you'll get out of this with your life."

His brother had gotten to his feet also. He snorted sarcastically. "Not to mention keeping your precious hymen intact. That ought to be worth a lot, once you get back to your family."

The fury which had filled Anna for months boiled to the surface. "I don't have a hymen," she snarled. "My husband did for that, the bastard, before he went off to war."

Now the Arab was on his feet. Hearing her words, he laughed aloud. "God save us! An abandoned little wife, no less."

The rivermen were beginning to get surly, judging from the scowls which had replaced the previous leers. One of them barked something in a language which Anna didn't recognize. One of the Aramaic dialects, probably. The Isaurian who seemed to be the leader of the three soldiers gave them another glance and an idle little wave of his hand. The gesture more or less indicated: *relax, relax—you'll get a cut.*

That done, his eyes came back to Anna. "Idiot," he repeated. The word was spoken with no heat, just lazy derision. "Think you're the first woman got abandoned by a husband looking to make his fortune in war?"

"He already has a fortune," hissed Anna. "He went looking for fame. Found it too, damn him."

The Arab laughed again. "Fame, is it? Maybe in

your circles! And what is the name of this paragon of martial virtue? Anthony the Illustrious Courier?"

The other three soldiers shared in the little laugh. For a moment, Anna was distracted by the oddity of such flowery phrases coming out of the mouth of a common soldier. She remembered, vaguely, that her husband had once told her of the poetic prowess of Arabs. But she had paid little attention, at the time, and the memory simply heightened her anger.

"He is famous," Anna insisted. A certain innate honesty forced her to add: "At least in Constantinople, after Belisarius' letter was read to the Senate. And his own dispatches."

The name Belisarius brought a sudden little stillness to the group of soldiers. The Isaurian leader's eyes narrowed.

"Belisarius? What's the general got to do with your husband?"

"And what's his name?" added the Arab.

Anna tightened her jaws. "Calopodius. Calopodius Saronites."

The stillness turned into frozen rigidity. All three soldiers' eyes were now almost slits.

The Isaurian leader drew a deep breath. "Are you trying to tell us that you are the wife of Calopodius the Blind?"

For a moment, a spike of anguish drove through the anger. She didn't really understand where it came from. Calopodius had always seemed blind to her, in his own way. But...

Her own deep breath was a shaky thing. "They say he is blind now, yes. Belisarius' letter to the Senate said so. He says it himself, in fact, in his letters. I—I guess it's true. I haven't seen him in many months. When he left..."

One of the rivermen began to say something, in a surly tone of voice. The gaze which the Isaurian now turned on him was nothing casual. It was a flat, flat gaze. As cold as a snake's and just as deadly. Even a girl as sheltered as Anna had been all her life understood the sheer physical menace in it. The rivermen all seemed to shuffle back a step or two.

He turned his eyes back to Anna. The same cold and flat gleam was in them. "If you are lying..."

"Why would I lie?" she demanded angrily. "And how do you expect me to prove it, anyway?"

Belatedly, a thought came to her. "Unless..." She glanced at the little sailing craft which had brought her here, still piled high with her belongings. "If you can read Greek, I have several of his letters to me."

The Arab sighed softly. "As you say, why would you lie?" His dark eyes examined her face carefully. "God help us. You really don't even understand, do you?"

She shook her head, confused. "Understand what? Do you know him yourself?"

The Isaurian leader's sigh was a more heartfelt thing. "No, lass, we didn't. We were so rich, after Charax, that we left the general's service. We—" he gestured at his brother "—I'm Illus, by the way, and he's Cottomenes—had more than enough to buy us a big farm back home. And Abdul decided to go in with us."

"I'm sick of the desert," muttered the Arab. "Sick of camels, too. Never did like the damn beasts."

The Arab was of the same height as the two Isaurian brothers—about average—but much less stocky in his frame. Still, in his light half-armor and with a spatha scabbarded to his waist, he seemed no less deadly.

"Come to think of it," he added, almost idly, "I'm sick of thieves, too."

The violence that erupted shocked Anna more than anything in her life. She collapsed in a squat, gripping her knees with shaking hands, almost moaning with fear.

There had been no sign; nothing, at least, that she had seen. The Isaurian leader simply drew his spatha—so quick, so quick!—took three peculiar little half steps and cleaved the skull of one of the rivermen before the man even had time to do more than widen his eyes. A second or two later, the same spatha tore open another's throat. In the same amount of time, his brother and the Arab gutted two other rivermen.

Then—

She closed her eyes. The four surviving rivermen were desperately trying to reach their barge. From the sounds—clear enough, even to a young woman who had never seen a man killed before—they weren't going to make it. Not even close. The sounds, wetly horrid, were those of a pack of wolves in a sheep pen.

Some time later, she heard the Isaurian's voice. "Open your eyes, girl. It's over."

She opened her eyes. Catching sight of the pool of blood soaking into the planks of the pier, she averted her gaze. Her eyes fell on the two sailors, cowering behind the well. She almost giggled, the sight was so ridiculous.

The Isaurian must have followed her gaze, because he began chuckling himself. "Silly looking, aren't they? As if they could hide behind that little well."

He raised his voice. "Don't be stupid! If nothing else, we need you to sail the boat. Besides—" He gestured at the barge. "You'll want to loot it, if there's anything in that tub worth looting. We'll burn whatever's left."

He reached down a hand. Anna took it and came shakily to her feet.

Bodies everywhere. She started to close her eyes again.

"Get used to it, girl," the Isaurian said harshly. "You'll see plenty more of that where you're going. Especially if you make it to the island."

Her head felt muzzy. "Island? What island?"

"The island, idiot. 'The Iron Triangle,' they call it. Where your husband is, along with the general. Right in the mouth of the Malwa."

"I didn't know it was an island," she said softly. Again, honesty surfaced. "I'm not really even sure where it is, except somewhere in India."

The Arab had come up in time to hear her last words. He was wiping his blade clean with a piece of cloth. "God save us." He half-chuckled. "It's not really an island. Not exactly. But it'll do, seeing as how the general's facing about a hundred thousand Malwa."

He studied her for a moment, while he finished wiping the blood off the sword. Then, sighed again. "Let's hope you learn something, by the time we get to Charax. After that, you'll be on your own again. At least—"

He gave the Isaurian an odd little look. The Isaurian shrugged. "We were just telling ourselves yesterday how stupid we'd been, missing out on the loot of Malwa itself. What the hell, we may as well take her the whole way."

His brother was now there. "Hell, yes!" he boomed.

He bestowed on Anna a very cheerful grin. "I assume you'll recommend us to the general? Not that we deserted or anything, but I'd really prefer a better assignment this time than being on the front lines. A bit dicey, that, when the general's running the show. Not that he isn't the shrewdest bastard in the world, mind you, but he does insist on fighting."

The other two soldiers seemed to share in the humor. Anna didn't really understand it, but for the first time since she'd heard the name of Calopodius—spoken by her father, when he announced to her an unwanted and unforeseen marriage—she didn't find it hateful.

Rather the opposite, in fact. She didn't know much about the military—nothing, really—but she suspected...

"I imagine my husband needs a bodyguard," she said hesitantly. "A bigger one than whatever he has," she added hastily. "And he's certainly rich enough to pay for it."

"Done," said the Isaurian leader instantly. "Done!"

Not long afterward, as their ship sailed down the river, Anna looked back. The barge was burning fiercely now. By the time the fire burned out, there would be nothing left but a hulk carrying what was left of a not-very-valuable cargo and eight charred skeletons.

The Isaurian leader—Illus—misunderstood her frown. "Don't worry about it, girl. In this part of Mesopotamia, no one will care what happened to the bastards."

She shook her head. "I'm not worrying about that. It's just—"

She fell silent. There was no way to explain, and one glance at Illus' face was enough to tell her that he'd never understand.

Calopodius hadn't, after all.

"So why the frown?"

She shrugged. "Never mind. I'm not used to violence, I guess."

That seemed to satisfy him, to Anna's relief. Under the circumstances, she could hardly explain to her rescuers how much she hated her husband. Much less why, since she didn't really understand it that well herself.

Still, she wondered. Something important had happened on that pier, something unforeseen, and she was not too consumed by her own anger not to understand that much. For the first time in her life, a husband had done something other than crush her like an insect.

She studied the surrounding countryside. So bleak and dangerous, compared to the luxurious surroundings in which she had spent her entire life. She found herself wondering what Calopodius had thought when he first saw it. Wondered what he had thought, and felt, the first time he saw blood spreading like a pool. Wondered if he had been terrified, when he first went into a battle.

Wondered what he thought now, and felt, with his face a mangled ruin.

Another odd pang of anguish came to her, then. Calopodius had been a handsome boy, even if she had taken no pleasure in the fact.

The Isaurian's voice came again, interrupting her musings. "Weird world, it is. What a woman will go through to find her husband."

She felt another flare of anger. But there was no way to explain; in truth, she could not have found the words herself. So all she said was: "Yes."

●   ●   ●

*The next day, as they sailed back to the mainland,
he informed Anna of his decision. And for the first time
since he met the girl, she came to life. All distance and
ennui vanished, replaced by a cold and spiteful fury
which completely astonished him. She did not say much,
but what she said was as venomous as a serpent's bite.*

*Why? he wondered. He would have thought, com-
ing from a family whose fame derived from ancient
exploits more than modern wealth, she would have
been pleased.*

*He tried to discover the source of her anger. But
after her initial spate of hostile words, Anna fell
silent and refused to answer any of his questions.
Soon enough, he gave up the attempt. It was not as
if, after all, he had ever really expected any intimacy
in his marriage. For that, if he survived the war, he
would find a courtesan.*

Charax, on the Persian Gulf

"I can't," said Dryopus firmly. Anna glared at him,
but the Roman official in charge of the great port
city of Charax was quite impervious to her anger. His
next words were spoken in the patient tone of one
addressing an unruly child.

"Lady Saronites, if I allowed you to continue on
this—" He paused, obviously groping for a term less
impolite than *insane*. "—headstrong project of yours,
it'd be worth my career."

He picked up a letter lying on the great desk in
his headquarters. "This is from your father, demanding
that you be returned to Constantinople under guard."

"My father has no authority over me!"

"No, he doesn't." Dryopus shook his head. "But your husband Calopodius does. Without his authorization, I simply can't allow you to continue. I certainly can't detail a ship to take you to Barbaricum."

Anna clenched her jaws. Her eyes went to the nearby window. She couldn't see the harbor from here, but she could visualize it easily enough. The Roman soldiers who had all-but-formally arrested her when she and her small party arrived in the great port city of Charax on the Persian Gulf had marched her past it on their way to Dryopus' palace.

For a moment, wildly, she thought of appealing to the Persians who were now in official control of Charax. But the notion died as soon as it came. The Aryans were even more strict than Romans when it came to the independence of women. Besides—

Dryopus seemed to read her thoughts. "I should note that all shipping in Charax is under Roman military law. So there's no point in your trying to go around me. No ship captain will take your money, anyway. Not without a permit issued by my office."

He dropped her father's letter back onto the desk. "I'm sorry, but there's nothing else for it. If you wish to continue, you will have to get your husband's permission."

"He's all the way up the Indus," she said angrily. "And there's no telegraph communication between here and there."

Dryopus shrugged. "No, there isn't—and it'll be some time before the new radio system starts working. But there is a telegraph line between Barbaricum and the Iron Triangle. And by now the new line

connecting Barbaricum and the harbor at Chabahari
may be completed. You'll still have to wait until I can
get a ship there—and another to bring back the answer.
Which won't be quickly, now that the winter monsoon
has started. I'll have to use a galley, whenever the
first one leaves—and I'm not sending a galley just for
this purpose."

Anna's mind raced through the problem. On their
way down the Euphrates, Illus had explained to her
the logic of travel between Mesopotamia and India.
He'd had plenty of time to do so. The river voyage
through Mesopotamia down to the port at Charax had
taken much longer than Anna had expected, mainly
because of the endless delays caused by Persian officials. She'd expected to be in Charax by late October.
Instead, they were now halfway into December.

During the winter monsoon season, which began in
November, it was impossible for sailing craft to make
it to Barbaricum. Taking advantage of the relatively
sheltered waters of the Gulf, on the other hand, they
could make it as far as Chabahari—which was the
reason the Roman forces in India had been working
so hard to get a telegraph line connecting Chabahari
and the Indus.

So if she could get as far as Chabahari . . . She'd
still have to wait, but if Calopodius' permission came
she wouldn't be wasting weeks here in Mesopotamia.

"Allow me to go as far as Chabahari then," she
insisted.

Dryopus started to frown. Anna had to fight to
keep from screaming in frustration.

"Put me under guard, if you will!"

Dryopus sighed, lowered his head, and ran his

fingers through thinning hair. "He's not likely to agree, you know," he said softly.

"He's my husband, not yours," pointed out Anna. "You don't know how he thinks." She didn't see any reason to add: *no more than I do.*

His head still lowered, Dryopus chuckled. "True enough. With that young man, it's always hard to tell."

He raised his head and studied her carefully. "Are you that besotted with him? That you insist on going into the jaws of the greatest war in history?"

"He's my husband," she replied, not knowing what else to say.

Again, he chuckled. "You remind me of Antonina, a bit. Or Irene."

Anna was confused for a moment, until she realized he was referring to Belisarius' wife and the Roman Empire's former head of espionage, Irene Macrembolitissa. Famous women, now, the both of them. One of them had even become a queen herself.

"I don't know either one," she said quietly. Which was true enough, even though she'd read everything ever written by Macrembolitissa. "So I couldn't say."

Dryopus studied her a bit longer. Then his eyes moved to her bodyguards, who had been standing as far back in a corner as possible.

"You heard?"

Illus nodded.

"Can I trust you?" he asked.

Illus' shoulders heaved a bit, as if he were suppressing a laugh. "No offense, sir—but if it's worth your career, just imagine the price we'd pay." His tone grew serious: "We'll see to it that she doesn't, ah, escape on her own."

Dryopus nodded and looked back at Anna. "All right, then. As far as Chabahari."

On their way to the inn where Anna had secured lodgings, Illus shook his head. "If Calopodius says 'no,' you realize you'll have wasted a lot of time and money."

"He's my husband," replied Anna firmly. Not knowing what else to say.

3

The Iron Triangle

After the general finished reading Anna's message, and the accompanying one from Dryopus, he invited Calopodius to sit down at the table in the command bunker.

"I knew you were married," said Belisarius, "but I know none of the personal details. So tell me."

Calopodius hesitated. He was deeply reluctant to involve the general in the petty minutiae of his own life. In the little silence that fell over them, within the bunker, Calopodius could hear the artillery barrages. As was true day and night, and had been for many weeks, the Malwa besiegers of the Iron Triangle were shelling the Roman fortifications—and the Roman gunners were responding with counter-battery fire. The fate of the world would be decided here in the Punjab, Calopodius thought, some time over the next year or so. That, and the whole future of the human race. It seemed absurd—grotesque, even—to waste the Roman commander's time...

"Tell me," repeated Belisarius. For all their softness, Calopodius could easily detect the tone of command in the words.

Still, he hesitated.

Belisarius chuckled. "Be at ease, young man. I can spare the time for this. In truth—" Calopodius could sense, if not see, the little gesture by which the general expressed a certain ironic weariness. "I would enjoy it, Calopodius. War is a means, not an end. It would do my soul good to talk about ends, for a change."

That was enough to break Calopodius' resistance.

"I really don't know her very well, sir. We'd only been married for a short time before I left to join your army. It was—"

He fumbled for the words. Belisarius provided them.

"A marriage of convenience. Your wife's from the Melisseni family."

Calopodius nodded. With his acute hearing, he could detect the slight sound of the general scratching his chin, as he was prone to do when thinking.

"An illustrious family," stated Belisarius. "One of the handful of senatorial families which can actually claim an ancient pedigree without paying scribes to fiddle with the historical records. But a family which has fallen on hard times financially."

"My father said they wouldn't even have a pot to piss in if their creditors ever really descended on them." Calopodius sighed. "Yes, General. An illustrious family, but now short of means. Whereas my family, as you know..."

"The Saronites. Immensely wealthy, but with a pedigree that needs a lot of fiddling."

Calopodius grinned. "Go back not more than three

generations, and you're looking at nothing but commoners. Not in the official records, of course. My father can afford a lot of scribes."

"That explains your incredible education," mused Belisarius. "I had wondered, a bit. Not many young noblemen have your command of language and the arts."

Calopodius heard the scrape of a chair as the general stood up. Then, heard him begin to pace about. That was another of Belisarius' habits when he was deep in thought. Calopodius had heard him do it many times, over the past weeks. But he was a bit astonished that the general was giving the same attention to this problem as he would to a matter of strategy or tactics.

"Makes sense, though," continued Belisarius. "For all the surface glitter—and don't think the Persians don't make plenty of sarcastic remarks about it—the Roman aristocracy will overlook a low pedigree as long as the 'nobleman' is wealthy and well educated. Especially—as you are—in grammar and rhetoric."

"I can drop three Homeric and biblical allusions into any sentence," Calopodius said, chuckling.

"I've noticed!" The general laughed. "That official history you're writing of my campaigns would serve as a Homeric and biblical commentary as well." He paused a moment. "Yet I notice that you don't do it in your *Dispatches to the Army*."

"It'd be a waste," said Calopodius, shrugging. "Worse than that, really. I write those for the morale of the soldiers, most of whom would just find the allusions confusing. Besides, those are really your dispatches, not mine. And you don't talk that way, certainly not to your soldiers."

"They're not my dispatches, young man. They're yours. I approve them, true, but you write them. And when they're read aloud by my son to the Senate, Photius presents them as Calopodius' dispatches, not mine."

Calopodius was startled into silence.

"You didn't know? My son is eleven years old, and quite literate. And since he is the Emperor of Rome, even if Theodora still wields the actual power, he insists on reading them to the Senate. He's very fond of your dispatches. Told me in his most recent letter that they're the only things he reads which don't bore him to tears. His tutors, of course, don't approve."

Calopodius was still speechless. Again, Belisarius laughed. "You're quite famous, lad." Then, more softly, almost sadly: "I can't give you back your eyes, Calopodius. But I can give you the fame you wanted when you came to me. I promised you I would."

The sound of his pacing resumed. "In fact, unless I miss my guess, those *Dispatches* of yours will someday—centuries from now—be more highly regarded than your official history of the war." Calopodius heard a very faint noise, and guessed the general was stroking his chest, where the jewel from the future named Aide lay nestled in his pouch. "I have it on good authority that historians of the future will prefer straight narrative to flowery rhetoric. And—in my opinion, at least—you write straightforward narrative even better than you toss off classical allusions."

The chair scraped as the general resumed his seat. "But let's get back to the problem at hand. In essence, your marriage was arranged to lever your family into greater respectability, and to provide the

Melisseni—discreetly, of course—a financial rescue. How did you handle the dowry, by the way?"

Calopodius shrugged. "I'm not certain. My family's so wealthy that a dowry's not important. For the sake of appearances, the Melisseni provided a large one. But I suspect my father loaned them the dowry—and then made arrangements to improve the Melisseni's economic situation by linking their own fortunes to those of our family." He cleared his throat. "All very discreetly, of course."

Belisarius chuckled dryly. "Very discreetly. And how did the Melisseni react to it all?"

Calopodius shifted uncomfortably in his chair. "Not well, as you'd expect. I met Anna for the first time three days after my father informed me of the prospective marriage. It was one of those carefully rehearsed 'casual visits.' She and her mother arrived at my family's villa near Nicodemia."

"Accompanied by a small army of servants and retainers, I've no doubt."

Calopodius smiled. "Not such a small army. A veritable host, it was." He cleared his throat. "They stayed for three days, that first time. It was very awkward for me. Anna's mother—her name's Athenais—barely even tried to disguise her contempt for me and my family. I think she was deeply bitter that their economic misfortunes were forcing them to seek a husband for their oldest daughter among less illustrious but much wealthier layers of the nobility."

"And Anna herself?"

"Who knows? During those three days, Anna said little. In the course of the various promenades which we took through the grounds of the Saronites estate—

God, talk about chaperones!—she seemed distracted to the point of being almost rude. I couldn't really get much of a sense of her, General. She seemed distressed by something. Whether that was her pending marriage to me, or something else, I couldn't say."

"And you didn't much care. Be honest."

"True. I'd known for years that any marriage I entered would be purely one of convenience." He shrugged. "At least my bride-to-be was neither unmannerly nor uncomely. In fact, from what I could determine at the time—which wasn't much, given the heavy scaramangium and headdress and the elaborate cosmetics under which Anna labored—she seemed quite attractive."

He shrugged again. "So be it. I was seventeen, General." For a moment, he hesitated, realizing how silly that sounded. He was only a year older than that now, after all, even if . . .

"You were a boy then; a man, now," filled in Belisarius. "The world looks very different after a year spent in the carnage. I know. But then—"

Calopodius heard the general's soft sigh. "Seventeen years old. With the war against Malwa looming ever larger in the life of the Roman Empire, the thoughts of a vigorous boy like yourself were fixed on feats of martial prowess, not domestic bliss."

"Yes. I'd already made up my mind. As soon as the wedding was done—well, and the marriage consummated—I'd be joining your army. I didn't even see any reason to wait to make sure that I'd provided an heir. I've got three younger brothers, after all, every one of them in good health."

Again, silence filled the bunker and Calopodius could

hear the muffled sounds of the artillery exchange. "Do you think that's why she was so angry at me when I told her I was leaving? I didn't really think she'd care."

"Actually, no. I think..." Calopodius heard another faint noise, as if the general were picking up the letters lying on the table. "There's this to consider. A wife outraged by abandonment—or glad to see an unwanted husband's back—would hardly be taking these risks to find him again."

"Then why is she doing it?"

"I doubt if she knows. Which is really what this is all about, I suspect." He paused; then: "She's only a year older than you, I believe."

Calopodius nodded. The general continued. "Did you ever wonder what an eighteen-year-old girl wants from life? Assuming she's high-spirited, of course—but judging from the evidence, your Anna is certainly that. Timid girls, after all, don't race off on their own to find a husband in the middle of a war zone."

Calopodius said nothing. After a moment, Belisarius chuckled. "Never gave it a moment's thought, did you? Well, young man, I suggest the time has come to do so. And not just for your own sake."

The chair scraped again as the general rose. "When I said I knew nothing about the details of your marriage, I was fudging a bit. I didn't know anything about what you might call the 'inside' of the thing. But I knew quite a bit about the 'outside' of it. This marriage is important to the Empire, Calopodius."

"Why?"

The general clucked his tongue reprovingly. "There's more to winning a war than tactics on the battlefield, lad. You've also got to keep an eye—always—on what

a future day will call the 'home front.'" Calopodius
heard him resume his pacing. "You can't be that naïve.
You must know that the Roman aristocracy is not very
fond of the dynasty."

"My family is," protested Calopodius.

"Yes. Yours—and most of the newer rich families.
That's because their wealth comes mainly from trade
and commerce. The war—all the new technology
Aide's given us—has been a blessing to you. But it
looks very different from the standpoint of the old
landed families. You know as well as I do—you must
know—that it was those families who supported the
Nika insurrection a few years ago. Fortunately, most
of them had enough sense to do it at a distance."

Calopodius couldn't help wincing. And what he
wasn't willing to say, the general was. Chuckling,
oddly enough.

"The Melisseni came that close to being arrested,
Calopodius. Arrested—the whole family—and all their
property seized. If Anna's father Nicephorus had been
even slightly less discreet ... The truth? His head
would have been on a spike on the wall of the Hip-
podrome, right next to that of John of Cappadocia's.
The only thing that saved him was that he was discreet
enough—barely—and the Melisseni are one of the
half-dozen most illustrious families of the Empire."

"I didn't know they were that closely tied ..."

Calopodius sensed Belisarius' shrug. "We were able
to keep it quiet. And since then, the Melisseni seem
to have retreated from any open opposition. But we
were delighted—I'm speaking of Theodora and Justinian and myself, and Antonina for that matter—when
we heard about your marriage. Being tied closely to

the Saronites will inevitably pull the Melisseni into the orbit of the dynasty. Especially since—as canny as your father is—they'll start getting rich themselves from the new trade and manufacture."

"Don't tell them that!" barked Calopodius. "Such work is for plebeians."

"They'll change their tune, soon enough. And the Melisseni are very influential among the older layers of the aristocracy."

"I understand your point, General." Calopodius gestured toward the unseen table, and the letters atop it. "So what do you want me to do? Tell Anna to come to the Iron Triangle?"

Calopodius was startled by the sound of Belisarius' hand slapping the table. "Damn fool! It's time you put that splendid mind of yours to work on this, Calopodius. A marriage—if it's to work—needs grammar and rhetoric also."

"I don't understand," said Calopodius timidly.

"I know you don't. So will you follow my advice?"

"Always, General."

Belisarius chuckled. "You're more confident than I am! But..." After a moment's pause: "Don't tell her to do anything, Calopodius. Send Dryopus a letter explaining that your wife has your permission to make her own decision. And send Anna a letter saying the same thing. I'd suggest..."

Another pause. Then: "Never mind. That's for you to decide."

In the silence that followed, the sound of artillery came to fill the bunker again. It seemed louder, perhaps. "And that's enough for the moment, young man. I'd better get in touch with Maurice. From the sound of things, I'd say the Malwa are getting ready for another probe."

Calopodius wrote the letters immediately thereafter, dictating them to his scribe. The letter to Dryopus took no time at all. Neither did the one to Anna, at first. But Calopodius, for reasons he could not determine, found it difficult to find the right words to conclude. Grammar and rhetoric seemed of no use at all.

In the end, moved by an impulse which confused him, he simply wrote:

Do as you will, Anna. For myself, I would like to see you again.

4

Chabahari, in the Straits of Hormuz

Chabahari seemed like a nightmare to Anna. When she first arrived in the town—city, now—she was mainly struck by the chaos in the place. Not so long ago, Chabahari had been a sleepy fishing village. Since the great Roman-Persian expedition led by Belisarius to invade the Malwa homeland through the Indus valley had begun, Chabahari had been transformed almost overnight into a great military staging depot. The original fishing village was now buried somewhere within a sprawling and disorganized mass of tents, pavilions, jury-rigged shacks—and, of course, the beginnings of the inevitable grandiose palaces the Persians insisted on putting anywhere that their grandees resided.

Her first day was spent entirely in a search for the

authorities in charge of the town. She had promised Dryopus she would report to those authorities as soon as she arrived.

But the search was futile. She found the official headquarters easily enough—one of the half-built palaces being erected by the Persians. But the interior of the edifice was nothing but confusion, a mass of workmen swarming all over, being overseen by a handful of harassed-looking supervisors. Not an official was to be found anywhere, neither Persian nor Roman.

"Try the docks," suggested the one foreman who spoke Greek and was prepared to give her a few minutes of his time. "The noble sirs complain about the noise here, and the smell everywhere else."

The smell was atrocious. Except in the immediate vicinity of the docks—which had their own none-too-savory aroma—the entire city seemed to be immersed in a miasma made up of the combined stench of excrement, urine, sweat, food—half of it seemingly rotten—and, perhaps most of all, blood and corrupting flesh. In addition to being a staging area for the invasion, Chabahari was also a depot where badly injured soldiers were being evacuated back to their homelands.

Those of them who survive this horrid place, Anna thought angrily, as she stalked out of the "headquarters." Illus and Cottomenes trailed behind her. Once she passed through the aivan onto the street beyond—insofar as the term "street" could be used at all for a simple space between buildings and shacks, teeming with people—she spent a moment or so looking south toward the docks.

"What's the point?" asked Illus, echoing her thoughts. "We didn't find anyone there when we disembarked."

He cast a glance at the small mound of Anna's luggage piled up next to the building. The wharf boys whom Anna had hired to carry her belongings were lounging nearby, under Abdul's watchful eye.

"Besides," Illus continued, "it'll be almost impossible to keep your stuff from being stolen, in that madhouse down there."

Anna sighed. She looked down at her long dress, grimacing ruefully. The lowest few inches of the once-fine fabric, already ill-used by her journey from Constantinople, was now completely ruined. And the rest of it was well on its way—as much from her own sweat as anything else. The elaborate garments of a Greek noblewoman, designed for salons in the Roman Empire's capital, were torture in this climate.

A glimpse of passing color caught her eye. For a moment, she studied the figure of a young woman moving down the street. Some sort of Indian girl, apparently. Since the war had erupted into the Indian subcontinent, the inevitable human turbulence had thrown people of different lands into the new cauldrons of such cities as Chabahari. Mixing them up like grain caught in a thresher. Anna had noticed several Indians even in Charax.

Mainly, she just envied the woman's clothing, which was infinitely better suited for the climate than her own. By her senatorial family standards, of course, it was shockingly immodest. But she spent a few seconds just imagining what her bare midriff would feel like, if it didn't feel like a mass of spongy, sweaty flesh.

Illus chuckled. "You'd peel like a grape, girl. With your fair skin?"

Anna had long since stopped taking offense at her

"servant's" familiarity with her. That, too, would have outraged her family. But Anna herself took an odd little comfort in it. Much to her surprise, she had discovered over the weeks of travel that she was at ease in the company of Illus and his companions.

"Damn you, too," she muttered, not without some humor of her own. "I'd toughen up soon enough. And I wouldn't mind shedding some skin, anyway. What I've got right now feels like it's gangrenous."

It was Illus' turn to grimace. "Don't even think it, girl. Until you've seen real gangrene..."

A stray waft of breeze from the northwest illustrated his point. That was the direction of the great military "hospital" that the Roman army had set up on the outskirts of the city. The smell almost made Anna gag.

The gag brought up a reflex of anger, and, with it, a sudden decision.

"Let's go there," she said.

"Why?" demanded Illus.

Anna shrugged. "Maybe there'll be an official there. If nothing else, I need to find where the telegraph office is located."

Illus' face made his disagreement clear enough. Still—for all that she allowed familiarity, Anna had also established over the past weeks that she was his master.

"Let's go," she repeated firmly. "If nothing else, that's probably the only part of this city where we'd find some empty lodgings."

"True enough," said Illus, sighing. "They'll be dying like flies, over there." He hesitated, then began to speak. But Anna cut him off before he got out more than three words.

"I'm not insane, damn you. If there's an epidemic,

we'll leave. But I doubt it. Not in this climate, this time of year. At least . . . not if they've been following the sanitary regulations."

Illus' face creased in a puzzled frown. "What's that got to do with anything? What regulations?"

Anna snorted and began to walk off to the north-west. "Don't you read anything besides those damned *Dispatches*?"

Cottomenes spoke up. "No one does," he said. Cheerfully, as usual. "No soldier, anyway. Your hus-band's got a way with words, he does. Have you ever tried to read official regulations?"

Those words, too, brought a reflex of anger. But, as she forced her way through the mob toward the military hospital, Anna found herself thinking about them. And eventually came to realize two things.

One. Although she was a voracious reader, she hadn't ever read any official regulations. Not those of the army, at any rate. But she suspected they were every bit as turgid as the regulations that officials in Constantinople spun out like spiders spinning webs.

Two. Calopodius *did* have a way with words. On their way down the Euphrates—and then again, as they sailed from Charax to Chabahari—the latest *Dispatches* and the newest chapters from his *History of Belisarius and the War* had been available constantly. Belisarius, Anna had noted, seemed to be as adamant about strewing printing presses behind his army's pas-sage as he was about arms depots.

The chapters of the *History* had been merely perused on occasion by her soldier companions. Anna could appreciate the literary skill involved, but the constant allusions in those pages were meaningless to Illus and his brother, much less the illiterate Abdul. Yet they pored over each and every *Dispatch*, often enough in the company of a dozen other soldiers, one of them reading it aloud, while the others listened with rapt attention.

As always, her husband's fame caused some part of Anna to seethe with fury. But, this time, she also thought about it. And if, at the end, her thoughts caused her anger to swell, it was a much cleaner kind of anger. One which did not coil in her stomach like a worm, but simply filled her with determination.

The hospital was even worse than she'd imagined. But she did, not surprisingly, find an unused tent in which she and her companions could make their quarters. And she did discover the location of the telegraph office—which, as it happened, was situated right next to the sprawling grounds of the "hospital."

The second discovery, however, did her little good. The official in charge, once she awakened him from his afternoon nap, yawned and explained that the telegraph line from Barbaricum to Chabahari was still at least a month away from completion.

"That'll mean a few weeks here," muttered Illus. "It'll take at least that long for couriers to bring your husband's reply."

Instead of the pure rage those words would have brought to her once, the Isaurian's sour remark simply caused Anna's angry determination to harden into something like iron.

"Good," she pronounced. "We'll put the time to good use."

"How?" he demanded.

"Give me tonight to figure it out."

●   ●   ●

It didn't take her all night. Just four hours. The first hour she spent sitting in her screened-off portion of the tent, with her knees hugged closely to her chest, listening to the moans and shrieks of the maimed and dying soldiers who surrounded it. The remaining three, studying the books she had brought with her—especially her favorite, Irene Macrembolitissa's *Commentaries on the Talisman of God*, which had been published just a few months before Anna's precipitous decision to leave Constantinople in search of her husband.

Irene Macrembolitissa was Anna's private idol. Not that the sheltered daughter of the Melisseni had ever thought to emulate the woman's adventurous life, except intellectually. The admiration had simply been an emotional thing, the heroine-worship of a frustrated girl for a woman who had done so many things she could only dream about. But now, carefully studying those pages in which Macrembolitissa explained certain features of natural philosophy as given to mankind through Belisarius by the Talisman of God, she came to understand the hard practical core which lay beneath the great woman's flowery prose and ease with classical and biblical allusions. And, with that understanding, came a hardening of her own soul.

Fate, against her will and her wishes, had condemned her to be a wife. So be it. She would begin with that practical core; with concrete truth, not abstraction. She would steel the bitterness of a wife into the driving will of *the* wife. The wife of Calopodius the Blind, Calopodius of the Saronites.

The next morning, very early, she presented her proposition.

"Do any of you have a problem with working in trade?"

The three soldiers stared at her, stared at each other, broke into soft laughter.

"We're not senators, girl," chuckled Illus.

Anna nodded. "Fine. You'll have to work on speculation, though. I'll need the money I have left to pay the others."

"What 'others'?"

Anna smiled grimly. "I think you call it 'the muscle.'"

Cottomenes frowned. "I thought we were 'the muscle.'"

"Not any more," said Anna. "You're promoted. All three of you are now officers in the hospital service."

"What 'hospital service'?"

Anna realized she hadn't considered the name of the thing. For a moment, the old anger flared. But she suppressed it easily enough. This was no time for pettiness, after all.

"We'll call it 'Calopodius' Wife's Service.' How's that?"

The three soldiers shook their heads. Clearly enough, they had no understanding of what she was talking about.

"You'll see," she predicted.

It didn't take them long. Illus' glare was enough to cow the official commander of the hospital, who was as sorry-looking a specimen of "officer" as Anna could imagine. And if the man might have wondered at the oddness of such glorious ranks being borne by such as Illus and his two companions—Abdul looked as far removed from a tribune as could be imagined—he was wise enough to keep his doubts to himself.

The dozen or so soldiers whom Anna recruited into the Service in the next hour—"the muscle"—had no trouble at all believing that Illus and Cottomenes and Abdul were, respectively, the chiliarch and two tribunes of a new army "service" they'd never heard of. First, because they were all veterans of the war and could recognize others—and knew, as well, that Belisarius promoted with no regard for personal origin. Second—more importantly—because they were wounded soldiers cast adrift in a chaotic "military hospital" in the middle of nowhere. Anna—Illus, actually, following her directions—selected only those soldiers whose wounds were healing well. Men who could move around and exert themselves. Still, even for such men, the prospect of regular pay meant a much increased chance at survival.

Anna wondered, a bit, whether walking-wounded "muscle" would serve the purpose. But her reservations were settled within the next hour after four of the new "muscle," at Illus' command, beat the first surgeon into a bloody pulp when the man responded to Anna's command to start boiling his instruments with a sneer and a derogatory remark about meddling women.

By the end of the first day, eight other surgeons were sporting cuts and bruises. But, at least when it came to the medical staff, there were no longer any doubts—none at all, in point of fact—as to whether this bizarre new "Calopodius' Wife's Service" had any actual authority.

Two of the surgeons complained to the hospital's commandant, but that worthy chose to remain inside his headquarters' tent. That night, Illus and three of

his new "muscle" beat the two complaining surgeons
into a still bloodier pulp, and all complaints to the
commandant ceased thereafter.

Complaints from the medical staff, at least. A body
of perhaps twenty soldiers complained to the hospital
commandant the next day, hobbling to the HQ as best
they could. But, again, the commandant chose to remain
inside; and, again, Illus—this time using his entire corps
of "muscle," which had now swollen to thirty men—
thrashed the complainers senseless afterward.

Thereafter, whatever they might have muttered
under their breath, none of the soldiers in the hospital protested openly when they were instructed to
dig real latrines, away from the tents—and use them.
Nor did they complain when they were ordered to
help completely immobilized soldiers use them as well.

By the end of the fifth day, Anna was confident
that her authority in the hospital was well enough
established. She spent a goodly portion of those days
daydreaming about the pleasures of wearing more
suitable apparel, as she made her slow way through
the ranks of wounded men in the swarm of tents.
But she knew full well that the sweat that seemed
to saturate her was one of the prices she would have
to pay. Lady Saronites, wife of Calopodius the Blind,
daughter of the illustrious family of the Melisseni, was
a figure of power and majesty and authority—and had
the noble gowns to prove it, even if they were soiled
and frayed. Young Anna, all of nineteen years old,
wearing a sari, would have had none at all.

By the sixth day, as she had feared, what was
left of the money she had brought with her from

Constantinople was almost gone. So, gathering her now-filthy robes in two small but determined hands, she marched her way back into the city of Chabahari. By now, at least, she had learned the name of the city's commander.

It took her half the day to find the man, in the taberna where he was reputed to spend most of his time. By the time she did, as she had been told, he was already half-drunk.

"Garrison troops," muttered Illus as they entered the tent that served the city's officers for their entertainment. The tent was filthy, as well as crowded with officers and their whores.

Anna found the commandant of the garrison in a corner, with a young half-naked girl perched on his lap. After taking half the day to find the man, it only took her a few minutes to reason with him and obtain the money she needed to keep the Service in operation.

Most of those few minutes were spent explaining, in considerable detail, exactly what she needed. Most of that, in specifying tools and artifacts—*more shovels to dig more latrines; pots for boiling water; more fabric for making more tents, because the ones they had were too crowded.* And so forth.

She spent a bit of time, at the end, specifying the sums of money she would need.

"Twenty solidi—a day." She nodded at an elderly wounded soldier whom she had brought with her along with Illus. "That's Zeno. He's literate. He's the Service's accountant in Chabahari. You can make all the arrangements through him."

The garrison's commandant then spent a minute explaining to Anna, also in considerable detail—mostly anatomical—what she could do with the tools, artifacts and money she needed.

Illus' face was very strained, by the end. Half with fury, half with apprehension—this man was no petty officer to be pounded with fists. But Anna herself sat through the garrison commander's tirade quite calmly. When he was done, she did not need more than a few seconds to reason with him further and bring him to see the error of his position.

"My husband is Calopodius the Blind. I will tell him what you have said to me, and he will place the words in his next *Dispatch*. You will be a lucky man if all that happens to you is that General Belisarius has you executed."

She left the tent without waiting to hear his response. By the time she reached the tent's entrance, the garrison commander's face was much whiter than the tent fabric and he was gasping for breath.

The next morning, a chest containing a hundred solidi was brought to the hospital and placed in Zeno's care. The day after that, the first of the tools and artifacts began arriving.

Four weeks later, when Calopodius' note finally arrived, the mortality rate in the hospital was less than half what it had been when Anna arrived. She was almost sorry to leave.

In truth, she might not have left at all, except by then she was confident that Zeno was quite capable of managing the entire service as well as its finances.

"Don't steal anything," she warned him, as she prepared to leave.

Zeno's face quirked with a rueful smile. "I wouldn't dare risk the Wife's anger."

She laughed, then; and found herself wondering through all the days of their slow oar-driven travel to Barbaricum why those words had brought her no anger at all.

And, each night, she took out Calopodius' letter and wondered at it also. Anna had lived with anger and bitterness for so long—"so long," at least, to a nineteen-year-old girl—that she was confused by its absence. She was even more confused by the little glow of warmth which the last words in the letter gave her, each time she read them.

"You're a strange woman," Illus told her, as the great battlements and cannons of Barbaricum loomed on the horizon.

There was no way to explain. "Yes," was all she said.

The first thing she did upon arriving at Barbaricum was march into the telegraph office. If the officers in command thought there was anything peculiar about a young Greek noblewoman dressed in the finest and filthiest garments they had ever seen, they kept it to themselves. Perhaps rumors of "the Wife" had preceded her.

"Send a telegram immediately," she commanded. "To my husband, Calopodius the Blind."

They hastened to comply. The message was brief:

```
ADDRESS  MEDICAL  CARE  AND
SANITATION  IN  NEXT  DISPATCH
STOP  FIRMLY  STOP
```

The Iron Triangle

When Calopodius received the telegram—and he received it immediately, because his post was in the Iron Triangle's command and communication center—the first words he said as soon as the telegraph operator finished reading it to him were:

"God, I'm an idiot!"

Belisarius had heard the telegram also. In fact, all the officers in the command center had heard, because they had been waiting with an ear cocked. By now, the peculiar journey of Calopodius' wife was a source of feverish gossip in the ranks of the entire army fighting off the Malwa siege in the Punjab. *What the hell is that girl doing, anyway?* being only the most polite of the speculations.

The general sighed and rolled his eyes. Then, closed them. It was obvious to everyone that he was reviewing all of Calopodius' now-famous *Dispatches* in his mind.

"We're both idiots," he muttered. "We've maintained proper medical and sanitation procedures *here*, sure enough. But..."

His words trailed off. His second-in-command, Maurice, filled in the rest.

"She must have passed through half the invasion staging posts along the way. Garrison troops, garrison officers—with the local butchers as the so-called 'surgeons.' God help us, I don't even want to think..."

"I'll write it immediately," said Calopodius.

Belisarius nodded. "Do so. And I'll give you some choice words to include." He cocked his head at

Maurice, smiling crookedly. "What do you think? Should we resurrect crucifixion as a punishment?"

Maurice shook his head. "Don't be so damned flamboyant. Make the punishment fit the crime. Surgeons who do not boil their instruments will be boiled alive. Officers who do not see to it that proper latrines are maintained will be buried alive in them. That sort of thing."

Calopodius was already seated at the desk where he dictated his *Dispatches* and the chapters of the *History*. So was his scribe, pen in hand.

"I'll add a few nice little flourishes," his young voice said confidently. "This strikes me as a good place for grammar and rhetoric."

5

Barbaricum, on the Indian coast

Anna and her companions spent their first night in India crowded into the corner of a tavern packed full with Roman soldiers and all the other typical denizens of a great port city—longshoremen, sailors, petty merchants and their womenfolk, pimps and prostitutes, gamblers, and the usual sprinkling of thieves and other criminals.

Like almost all the buildings in Barbaricum, the tavern was a mudbrick edifice that had been badly burned in the great fires that swept the city during the Roman conquest. The arson had not been committed by Belisarius' men, but by the fanatic Mahaveda priests who led the Malwa defenders. Despite the still obvious reminders of that destruction, the tavern was in use for the simple reason that, unlike so many buildings in the city, the walls were still standing and there was even a functional roof.

When they first entered, Anna and her party had been assessed by the mob of people packed in the tavern. The assessment had not been as quick as the one which that experienced crowd would have normally made. Anna and her party were . . . odd.

The hesitation worked entirely to her advantage, however. The tough-looking Isaurian brothers and Abdul were enough to give would-be cutpurses pause, and in the little space and time cleared for them, the magical rumor had time to begin and spread throughout the tavern. Watching it spread—so obvious, from the curious stares and glances sent her way—Anna was simultaneously appalled, amused, angry, and thankful.

It's her. Calopodius the Blind's wife. Got to be.

"Who started this damned rumor, anyway?" she asked peevishly, after Illus cleared a reasonably clean spot for her in a corner and she was finally able to sit down. She leaned against the shelter of the walls with relief. She was well-nigh exhausted.

Abdul grunted with amusement. The Arab was frequently amused, Anna noted with exasperation. But it was an old and well-worn exasperation, by now, almost pleasant in its predictability.

Cottomenes, whose amusement at life's quirks was not much less than Abdul's, chuckled his agreement. "You're hot news, Lady Saronites. Everybody on the docks was talking about it, too. And the soldiers outside the telegraph office." Cottomenes, unlike his older brother, never allowed himself the familiarity of calling her "girl." In all other ways, however, he showed her a lack of fawning respect that would have outraged her family.

After the dockboys whom Anna had hired finished stacking her luggage next to her, they crowded themselves against a wall nearby, ignoring the glares directed their way by the tavern's usual habitués. Clearly enough, having found this source of incredible largesse, the dockboys had no intention of relinquishing it.

Anna shook her head. The vehement motion finished the last work of disarranging her long dark hair. The elaborate coiffure under which she had departed Constantinople, so many weeks before, was entirely a thing of the past. Her hair was every bit as tangled and filthy as her clothing. She wondered if she'd ever feel clean again.

"Why?" she whispered.

Squatting next to her, Illus studied her for a moment. His eyes were knowing, as if the weeks of close companionship and travel had finally enabled a half-barbarian mercenary soldier to understand the weird torments of a young noblewoman's soul.

Which, indeed, perhaps they had.

"You're different, girl. What you do is *different*. You have no idea how important that can be, to a man who does nothing, day after day, but toil under a sun. Or to a woman who does nothing, day after day, but wash clothes and carry water."

She stared up at him. Seeing the warmth lurking somewhere deep in Illus' eyes, in that hard tight face, Anna was stunned to realize how great a place the man had carved for himself in her heart. Friendship was a stranger to Anna of the Melisseni.

"And what is an angel, in the end," said the Isaurian softly, "but something different?"

Anna stared down at her grimy garments, noting all the little tears and frays in the fabric.

"In *this*?"

The epiphany finally came to her, then. And she wondered, in the hour or so that she spent leaning against the walls of the noisy tavern before she finally drifted into sleep, whether Calopodius had also known such an epiphany. Not on the day he chose to leave her behind, all her dreams crushed, in order to gain his own; but on the day he first awoke, a blind man, and realized that sight is its own curse.

And for the first time since she'd heard Calopodius' name, she no longer regretted the life that had been denied to her. No longer thought with bitterness of the years she would never spend in the shelter of the cloister, allowing her mind to range through the world's accumulated wisdom like a hawk finally soaring free.

When she awoke the next morning, the first thought that came to her was that she finally understood her own faith—and never had before, not truly. There was some regret in the thought, of course. Understanding, for all except God, is also limitation. But with that limitation came clarity and sharpness, so different from the froth and fuzz of a girl's fancies and dreams.

In the gray light of an alien land's morning, filtering into a tavern more noisome than any she would ever have imagined, Anna studied her soiled and ragged clothing. Seeing, this time, not filth and ruin but simply the carpet of her life opening up before her. A life she had thought closeted forever.

"Practicality first," she announced firmly. "It is not a sin."

The words woke up Illus. He gazed at her through slitted, puzzled eyes.

"Get up," she commanded. "We need uniforms."

A few minutes later, leading the way out the door with her three-soldier escort and five dock urchins toting her luggage, Anna issued the first of that day's rulings and commandments.

"It'll be expensive, but my husband will pay for it. He's rich."

"He's not here," grunted Illus.

"His name is. He's also famous. Find me a banker."

It took a bit of time before she was able to make the concept of "banker" clear to Illus. Or, more precisely, differentiate it from the concepts of "pawnbroker," "usurer" and "loan shark." But, eventually, he agreed to seek out and capture this mythological creature— with as much confidence as he would have announced plans to trap a griffin or a minotaur.

"Never mind," grumbled Anna, seeing the nervous little way in which Illus was fingering his sword. "I'll do it myself. Where's the army headquarters in this city? They'll know what a 'banker' is, be sure of it."

That task was within Illus' scheme of things. And since Barbaricum was in the actual theater of Belisarius' operations, the officers in command of the garrison were several cuts of competence above those at Chabahari. By midmorning, Anna had been steered to the largest of the many new moneylenders who had fixed themselves upon Belisarius' army.

An Indian himself, ironically enough, named Pulinda. Anna wondered, as she negotiated the terms, what secrets—and what dreams, realized or stultified—lay behind the life of the small and elderly man sitting across from her. How had a man from the teeming Ganges valley eventually found himself, awash with wealth obtained in whatever mysterious manner, a paymaster to the alien army which was hammering at the gates of his own homeland?

Did he regret the life which had brought him to this place? Savor it?

Most likely both, she concluded. And was then amused, when she realized how astonished Pulinda would have been had he realized that the woman with whom he was quarreling over terms was actually awash in good feeling toward him.

Perhaps, in some unknown way, he sensed that warmth. In any event, the negotiations came to an end sooner than Anna had expected. They certainly left her with better terms than she had expected.

Or, perhaps, it was simply that magic name of Calopodius again, clearing the waters before her. Pulinda's last words to her were: "Mention me to your husband, if you would."

By mid-afternoon, she had tracked down the tailor reputed to be the best in Barbaricum. By sundown, she had completed her business with him. Most of that time had been spent keeping the dockboys from fidgeting as the tailor measured them.

"You also!" Anna commanded, slapping the most obstreperous urchin on top of his head. "In the Service, cleanliness is essential."

The next day, however, when they donned their new uniforms, the dockboys were almost beside themselves with joy. The plain and utilitarian garments were, by a great margin, the finest clothing they had ever possessed.

The Isaurian brothers and Abdul were not quite as demonstrative. Not quite.

"We look like princes," gurgled Cottomenes happily.

"And so you are," pronounced Anna. "The highest officers of the Wife's Service. A rank which will someday"—she spoke with a confidence far beyond her years—"be envied by princes the world over."

The Iron Triangle

"Relax, Calopodius," said Menander cheerfully, giving the blind young officer a friendly pat on the shoulder. "I'll see to it she arrives safely."

"She's already left Barbaricum," muttered Calopodius. "Damnation, why didn't she *wait*?"

Despite his agitation, Calopodius couldn't help smiling when he heard the little round of laughter which echoed around him. As usual, whenever the subject of Calopodius' wife arose, every officer and orderly in the command bunker had listened. In her own way, Anna was becoming as famous as anyone in the great Roman army fighting its way into India.

Most husbands, to say the least, do not like to discover that their wives are the subject of endless army gossip. But since, in this case, the cause of the gossip was not the usual sexual peccadilloes, Calopodius was not certain how he felt about it. Some part of him, ingrained with custom, still felt a certain dull outrage. But, for the most part—perhaps oddly—his main reaction was one of quiet pride.

"I suppose that's a ridiculous question," he admitted ruefully. "She hasn't waited for anything else."

When Menander spoke again, the tone in his voice was much less jovial. As if he, too, shared in the concern which—much to his surprise—Calopodius had found engulfing him since he learned of Anna's journey. Strange, really, that he should care so much about the well-being of a wife who was little but a vague image to him.

But... Even before his blinding, the world of literature had often seemed as real to Calopodius as any other. Since he lost his sight, it had become all the more so—despite the fact that he could no longer read or write himself, but depended on others to do it for him.

Anna Melisseni, the distant girl he had married and had known for a short time in Constantinople, meant practically nothing to him. But *the Wife of Calopodius the Blind*, the unknown woman who had been advancing toward him for weeks now, she was a different thing altogether. Still mysterious, but not a stranger. How could she be, any longer?

Had he not, after all, written about her often enough in his own *Dispatches*? In the third person, of course, as he always spoke of himself in his writings. No subjective mood was ever inserted into his *Dispatches*, any more than into the chapters of his massive *History of the War*. But, detached or not, whenever he received news of Anna he included at least a few sentences detailing for the army her latest adventures. Just as he did for those officers and men who had distinguished themselves. And he was no longer surprised to discover that most of the army found a young wife's exploits more interesting than their own.

She's different.

"Difference," however, was no shield against life's misfortunes—misfortunes which are multiplied several times over in the middle of a war zone. So, within seconds, Calopodius was back to fretting.

"Why didn't she wait, damn it all?"

Again, Menander clapped his shoulder. "I'm leaving with the *Victrix* this afternoon, Calopodius. Steaming with the riverflow, I'll be in Sukkur long before Anna gets there coming upstream in an oared river craft. So I'll be her escort on the last leg of her journey, coming into the Punjab."

"The Sind's not *that* safe," grumbled Calopodius, still fretting. The Sind was the lower half of the Indus river valley, and while it had now been cleared of Malwa troops and was under the jurisdiction of Rome's Persian allies, the province was still greatly unsettled. "Dacoits everywhere."

"Dacoits aren't going to attack a military convoy," interrupted Belisarius. "I'll make sure she gets a Persian escort of some kind as far as Sukkur."

One of the telegraphs in the command center began to chatter. When the message was read aloud, a short time later, even Calopodius began to relax.

"Guess not," he mumbled—more than a little abashed. "With that escort."

6

The Lower Indus
Spring, 534 AD

"I don't believe this," mumbled Illus—more than a little abashed. He glanced down at his uniform. For all the finery of the fabric and the cut, the garment seemed utterly drab matched against the glittering costumes which seemed to fill the wharf against which their river barge was just now being tied.

Standing next to him, Anna said nothing. Her face was stiff, showing none of the uneasiness she felt herself. Her own costume was even more severe and plainly cut than those of her officers, even if the fabric itself was expensive. And she found herself wishing desperately that her cosmetics had survived the journey from Constantinople. For a woman of her class, being seen with a face unadorned by anything except nature was well-nigh unthinkable. In any company, much less...

The tying-up was finished and the gangplank laid. Anna was able to guess at the identity of the first man to stride across it.

She was not even surprised. Anna had read everything ever written by Irene Macrembolitissa—several times over—including the last book the woman wrote just before she left for the Hindu Kush on her great expedition of conquest. *The Deeds of Khusrau*, she thought, described the man quite well. The Emperor of Persia was not particularly large, but so full of life and energy that he seemed like a giant as he strode toward her across the gangplank.

What am I doing here? she wondered. *I never planned on such as this!*

"So! You are the one!" were the first words he boomed. "To live in such days, when legends walk among us!"

In the confused time that followed, as Anna was introduced to a not-so-little mob of Persian officers and officials—most of them obviously struggling not to frown with disapproval at such a disreputable woman—she pondered on those words.

The words seemed meaningless to her. Khusrau Anushirvan—"Khusrau of the Immortal Soul"—was a legend, not she.

So why had he said that?

By the end of that evening, after spending hours sitting stiffly in a chair while Iran's royalty and nobility wined and dined her, she had mustered enough courage to lean over to the emperor—sitting next to her!—and whisper the question into his ear.

Khusrau's response astonished her even more. He grinned broadly, white teeth gleaming in a square-cut Persian beard. Then, he leaned over and whispered in return:

"I am an expert on legends, wife of Calopodius. Truth be told, I often think the art of kingship is mainly knowing how to make the things."

He glanced slyly at his assembled nobility, who had not stopped frowning at Anna throughout the royal feast—but always, she noticed, under lowered brows.

"But keep it a secret," he whispered. "It wouldn't do for my noble sahrdaran and vurzurgan to discover that their emperor is really a common manufacturer. I don't need another rebellion this year."

She managed to choke down a laugh, fortunately. The effort, however, caused her hand to shake just enough to spill some wine onto her long dress.

"No matter," whispered the emperor. "Don't even try to remove the stain. By next week, it'll be the blood of a dying man brought back to life by the touch of your hand. Ask anyone."

She tightened her lips to keep from smiling. It was nonsense, of course, but there was no denying the emperor was a charming man.

But, royal decree or no, it was still nonsense. Bloodstains aplenty there had been on the garments she'd brought from Constantinople, true enough. Blood and pus and urine and excrement and every manner of fluid produced by human suffering. She'd gained them in Chabahari, and again at Barbaricum. Nor did she doubt there would be bloodstains on this garment also, soon enough, to match the wine stain she had just put there.

Indeed, she had designed the uniforms of the Wife's Service with that in mind. That was why the fabric had been dyed a purple so dark it was almost black.

But it was still nonsense. Her touch had no more magic power than anyone's. Her knowledge—or rather, the knowledge which she had obtained by reading everything Macrembolitissa or anyone else had ever written transmitting the Talisman of God's wisdom—now, that was powerful. But it had nothing to do with her, except insofar as she was another vessel of those truths.

Something of her skepticism must have shown, despite her effort to remain impassive-faced. She was only nineteen, after all, and hardly an experienced diplomat.

Khusrau's lips quirked. "You'll see."

The next day she resumed her journey up the river toward Sukkur. The emperor himself, due to the pressing business of completing his incorporation of the Sind into the swelling empire of Iran, apologized for not being able to accompany her personally. But he detailed no fewer than four Persian war galleys to serve as her escort.

"No fear of dacoits," said Illus, with great satisfaction. "Or deserters turned robbers."

His satisfaction turned a bit sour at Anna's response.

"Good. We'll be able to stop at every hospital along the way then. No matter how small."

And stop they did. Only briefly, in the Roman ones. By now, to Anna's satisfaction, Belisarius' blood-curdling threats had resulted in a marked improvement in medical procedures and sanitary practices.

But most of the small military hospitals along the way were Persian. The "hospitals" were nothing more than tents pitched along the riverbank—mere staging posts for disabled Persian soldiers being evacuated back to their homeland. The conditions within them had Anna seething, with a fury that was all the greater because neither she nor either of the Isaurian officers could speak a word of the Iranian language. Abdul could make himself understood, but his pidgin was quite inadequate to the task of convincing skeptical— even hostile—Persian officials that Anna's opinion was anything more than female twaddle.

Anna spent another futile hour trying to convince the officers in command of her escort to send a message to Khusrau himself. Clearly enough, however, none of them were prepared to annoy the emperor at the behest of a Roman woman who was probably half-insane to begin with.

Fortunately, at the town of Dadu, there was a telegraph station. Anna marched into it and fired off a message to her husband.

```
WHY  TALISMAN  MEDICAL  PRECEPTS
NOT  TRANSLATED  INTO  PERSIAN
STOP  INSTRUCT  EMPEROR  IRAN
DISCIPLINE  HIS  IDIOTS  STOP
```

"Do it," said Belisarius, after Calopodius read him the message.

The general paused. "Well, the first part, anyway. The Persian translation. I'll have to figure out a somewhat more diplomatic way to pass the rest of it on to Khusrau."

Maurice snorted. "How about hitting him on the head with a club? That'd be somewhat more diplomatic."

By the time the convoy reached Sukkur, it was moving very slowly.

There were no military hospitals along the final stretch of the river, because wounded soldiers were kept either in Sukkur itself or had already passed through the evacuation routes. The slow pace was now due entirely to the native population.

By whatever mysterious means, word of the Wife's passage had spread up and down the Indus. The convoy was constantly approached by small river boats bearing sick and injured villagers, begging for what was apparently being called "the healing touch."

Anna tried to reason, to argue, to convince. But it was hopeless. The language barrier was well-nigh impassable. Even the officers of her Persian escort could do no more than roughly translate the phrase "healing touch."

In the end, not being able to bear the looks of anguish on their faces, Anna laid her hands on every villager brought alongside her barge for the purpose. Muttering curses under her breath all the while— curses which were all the more bitter since she was quite certain the villagers of the Sind took them for powerful incantations.

At Sukkur, she was met by Menander and the entire crew of the *Victrix*. Beaming from ear to ear.

The grins faded soon enough. After waiting impatiently for the introductions to be completed, Anna's next words were: "Where's the telegraph station?"

```
URGENT  STOP  MUST  TRANSLATE
TALISMAN  PRECEPTS  INTO
NATIVE  TONGUES  ALSO  STOP
```

Menander fidgeted while she waited for the reply.

"I've got a critical military cargo to haul to the island," he muttered. "Calopodius may not even send an answer."

"He's my husband," came her curt response. "Of course he'll answer me."

Sure enough, the answer came very soon.

```
CANNOT  STOP  IS  NO  WRITTEN
NATIVE  LANGUAGE  STOP  NOT
EVEN  ALPHABET  STOP
```

After reading it, Anna snorted. "We'll see about that."

```
YOU  SUPPOSEDLY  EXPERT
GRAMMAR  AND  RHETORIC  STOP
INVENT  ONE  STOP
```

"You'd best get started on it," mused Belisarius. The general's head turned to the south. "She'll be coming soon."

"Like a tidal bore," added Maurice.

7

The Iron Triangle

That night, he dreamed of islands again.

First, of Rhodes, where he spent an idle day on his journey to join Belisarius' army while his ship took on supplies.

Some of that time he spent visiting the place where, years before, John of Rhodes had constructed an armaments center. Calopodius' own skills and interests were not inclined in a mechanical direction, but he was still curious enough to want to see the mysterious facility.

But, in truth, there was no longer much there of interest. Just a handful of buildings, vacant now except for livestock. So, after wandering about for a bit, he spent the rest of the day perched on a headland staring at the sea.

It was a peaceful, calm, and solitary day. The last one he would enjoy in his life, thus far.

Then, his dreams took him to the island in the Strait of Hormuz where Belisarius was having a naval base constructed. The general had sent Calopodius over from the mainland where the army was marching its way toward the Indus, in order to help resolve one of the many minor disputes which had erupted between the Romans and Persians who were constructing the facility. Among the members of the small corps of noble couriers who served Belisarius for liaison with the Persians, Calopodius had displayed a great deal of tact as well as verbal aptitude.

*It was something of a private joke between him
and the general. "I need you to take care of another
obstreperous aunt," was the way Belisarius put it.*

*The task of mediating between the quarrelsome
Romans and Persians had been stressful. But Calopodius had enjoyed the boat ride well enough; and, in
the end, he had managed to translate Belisarius' blunt
words into language flowery enough to slide the command through—like a knife between unguarded ribs.*

*Toward the end, his dreams slid into a flashing
nightmare image of Bukkur Island. A log, painted
to look like a field gun, sent flying by a lucky cannon ball fired by one of the Malwa gunships whose
bombardment accompanied that last frenzied assault.
The Romans drove off that attack also, in the end.
But not before a mortar shell had ripped Calopodius'
eyes out of his head.*

*The last sight he would ever have in his life was
of that log, whirling through the air and crushing the
skull of a Roman soldier standing in its way. What
made the thing a nightmare was that Calopodius
could not remember the soldier's name, if he had
ever known it. So it all seemed very incomplete, in a
way that was too horrible for Calopodius to be able
to express clearly to anyone, even himself. Grammar
and rhetoric simply collapsed under the coarse reality,
just as fragile human bone and brain had collapsed
under hurtling wood.*

The sound of his aide-de-camp clumping about
in the bunker awoke him. The warm little courtesy
banished the nightmare, and Calopodius returned to
life with a smile.

"How does the place look?" he asked.

"It's hardly fit for a Melisseni girl. But I imagine it'll do for *your* wife."

"Soon, now."

"Yes." Calopodius heard Luke lay something on the small table next to the cot. From the slight rustle, he understood that it was another stack of telegrams. Private ones, addressed to him, not army business.

"Any from Anna?"

"No. Just more bills."

Calopodius laughed. "Well, whatever else, she still spends money like a Melisseni. Before she's done, that banker will be the richest man in India."

Luke said nothing in response. After a moment, Calopodius' humor faded away, replaced by simple wonder.

"Soon, now. I wonder what she'll be like?"

The Indus

The attack came as a complete surprise. Not to Anna, who simply didn't know enough about war to understand what could be expected and what not, but to her military escort.

"What in the name of God do they think they're doing?" demanded Menander angrily.

He studied the fleet of small boats—skiffs, really—pushing out from the southern shore. The skiffs were loaded with Malwa soldiers, along with more than the usual complement of Mahaveda priests and their mahamimamsa "enforcers." The presence of the latter was a sure sign that the Malwa considered this project so near-suicidal that the soldiers needed to be held in a tight rein.

"It's an ambush," explained his pilot, saying aloud the conclusion Menander had already reached. The man pointed to the thick reeds. "The Malwa must have hauled those boats across the desert, hidden them in the reeds, waited for us. We don't keep regular patrols on the south bank, since there's really nothing there to watch for."

Menander's face was tight with exasperation. "But what's the *point* of it?" For a moment, his eyes moved forward, toward the heavily shielded bow of the ship where the *Victrix*'s fire-cannon was situated. "We'll burn them up like so many piles of kindling."

But even before he finished the last words, even before he saw the target of the oncoming boats, Menander understood the truth. The fact of it, at least, if not the reasoning.

"*Why?* They're all dead men, no matter what happens. In the name of God, she's just a woman!"

He didn't wait for an answer, however, before starting to issue his commands. The *Victrix* began shuddering to a halt. The skiffs were coming swiftly, driven by almost frenzied rowing. It would take the *Victrix* time to come to a halt and turn around; time to make its way back to protect the barge it was towing.

Time, Menander feared, that he might not have.

"What should we do?" asked Anna. For all the strain in her voice, she was relieved that her words came without stammering. A Melisseni girl could afford to scream with terror; she couldn't. Not any longer.

Grim-faced, Illus glanced around the barge. Other than he and Cottomenes and Abdul, there were only five Roman soldiers on the barge—and only two of those were armed with muskets. Since Belisarius and Khusrau had driven the Malwa out of the Sind, and established Roman naval supremacy on the Indus with the new steam-powered gunboats, there had been no Malwa attempt to threaten shipping south of the Iron Triangle.

Then his eyes came to rest on the vessel's new feature, and his tight lips creased into something like a smile.

"God bless good officers," he muttered.

He pointed to the top of the cabin amidships, where a shell of thin iron was perched. It was a turret, of sorts, for the odd and ungainly looking "Puckle gun" that Menander had insisted on adding to the barge. The helmeted face and upper body of the gunner was visible, and Illus could see the man beginning to train the weapon on the oncoming canoes.

"Get up there—now. There's enough room in there for you, and it's the best armored place on the barge." He gave the oncoming Malwa a quick glance. "They've got a few muskets of their own. Won't be able to hit much, not shooting from skiffs moving that quickly— but keep your head down once you get there."

It took Anna a great deal of effort, encumbered as she was by her heavy and severe gown, to clamber atop the cabin. She couldn't have made it at all, if Abdul hadn't boosted her. Climbing over the iron wall of the turret was a bit easier, but not much. Fortunately, the gunner lent her a hand.

After she sprawled into the open interior of the

turret, the hard edges of some kind of ammunition containers bruising her back, Anna had to struggle fiercely not to burst into shrill cursing.

I have got to design a new costume. Propriety be damned!

For a moment, her thoughts veered aside. She remembered that Irene Macrembolitissa, in her *Observations of India*, had mentioned—with some amusement—that Empress Shakuntala often wore pantaloons in public. Outrageous behavior, really, but...when you're the one who owns the executioners, you can afford to outrage public opinion.

The thought made her smile, and it was with that cheerful expression on her lips that she turned her face up to the gunner frowning down at her.

"Is there anything I can do to help?"

The man's face suddenly lightened, and he smiled himself.

"Damn if you aren't a prize!" he chuckled. Then, nodding his head. "Yes, ma'am. As a matter of fact, there is."

He pointed to the odd-looking objects lying on the floor of the turret, which had bruised Anna when she landed on them. "Those are called cylinders." He patted the strange looking weapon behind which he was half-crouched. "This thing'll wreak havoc, sure enough, as long as I can keep it loaded. I'm supposed to have a loader, but since we added this just as an afterthought..."

He turned his head, studying the enemy vessels. "Better do it quick, ma'am. If those skiffs get alongside, your men and the other soldiers won't be enough to beat them back. And they'll have grenades anyway, they're bound to. If I can't keep them off, we're all dead."

Anna scrambled around until she was on her knees, then seized one of the weird-looking metal contraptions. It was not as heavy as it looked. "What do you need me to do? Be precise!"

"Just hand them to me, ma'am, that's all. I'll do the rest. And keep your head down—it's you they're after."

Anna froze for a moment, dumbfounded. "Me? Why?"

"Damned if I know. Doesn't make sense."

But, in truth, the gunner did understand. Some part of it, at least, even if he lacked the sophistication to follow all of the reasoning of the inhuman monster who commanded the Malwa empire. The gunner had never heard—and never would—of a man named Napoleon. But he was an experienced soldier, and not stupid even if his formal education was rudimentary. "The moral is to the material in war as three-to-one" was not a phrase the man would have ever uttered himself, but he would have had no difficulty understanding it.

Link, the emissary from the new gods of the future who ruled the Malwa in all but name and commanded its great army in the Punjab, had ordered this ambush. The "why" was self-evident to its superhuman intelligence. Spending the lives of a few soldiers and Mahaveda priests was well worth the price, if it would enable the monster to destroy the Wife whose exploits its spies reported. Exploits which, in their own peculiar way, had become important to Roman morale.

Cheap at the price, in fact. Dirt cheap.

The Iron Triangle

The battle on the river was observed from the north bank by a patrol of light Arab cavalry in Roman service. Being Beni Ghassan, the cavalrymen were far more sophisticated in the uses of new technology than most Arabs. Their commander immediately dispatched three riders to bring news of the Malwa ambush to the nearest telegraph station, which was but a few miles distant.

By the time Belisarius got the news, of course, the outcome of the battle had already been decided, one way or the other. So he could do nothing more than curse himself for a fool, and try not to let the ashen face of a blind young man sway his cold-blooded reasoning.

"I'm a damned fool not to have foreseen the possibility. It just didn't occur to me that the Malwa might carry boats across the desert. But it should have."

"Not your fault, sir," said Calopodius quietly.

Belisarius tightened his jaws. "Like hell it isn't."

Maurice, standing nearby, ran fingers through his bristly iron-gray hair. "We all screwed up. I should have thought of it, too. We've been so busy just being entertained by the episode that we didn't think about it. Not seriously."

Belisarius sighed and nodded. "There's still no point in me sending the *Justinian*. By the time it got there, it will all have been long settled—and there's always the chance Link might be trying for a diversion."

"You can't send the *Justinian*," said Calopodius, half-whispering. "With the *Victrix* gone—and the *Photius*

down at Sukkur—the Malwa might try an amphibious
attack on the Triangle. They could get past the mine
fields with a lot of little boats, where they couldn't
with just their few ironclads."

He spoke the cold truth, and every officer in the
command center knew it. So nothing further was said.
They simply waited for another telegraph report to
inform them whether Calopodius was a husband or
a widower.

The Indus

Before the battle was over, Anna had reason to be
thankful for her heavy gown.

As cheerfully profligate as he was, the gunner soon
used up the preloaded cylinders for the Puckle gun.
Thereafter, Anna had to reload the cylinders manually
with the cartridges she found in a metal case against
the shell of the turret. Placing the new shells into a
cylinder was easy enough, with a little experience.
The trick was taking out the spent ones. The brass
cartridges were hot enough to hurt her fingers, the
first time she tried prying them out.

Thereafter, following the gunner's hastily shouted
instructions, she started using the little ramrod provided
in the ammunition case. Kneeling in the shelter of
the turret, she just upended the cylinders—carefully
holding them with the hem of her dress, because
they were hot also—and smacked the cartridges loose.

The cartridges came out easily enough, that way—
right onto her lap and knees. In a lighter gown, a
less severe and formal garment, her thighs would

soon enough have been scorched by the little pile
of hot metal.

As it was, the heat was endurable, and Anna didn't
care in the least that the expensive fabric was being
ruined in the process. She just went about her business,
brushing the cartridges onto the floor of the turret,
loading and reloading with the thunderous racket of
the Puckle gun in her ears, ignoring everything else
around her.

Throughout, her mind only strayed once. After
the work became something of a routine, she found
herself wondering if her husband's mind had been
so detached in battles. Not whether he had ignored
pain—of course he had; Anna had learned that much
since leaving Constantinople—but whether he had
been able to ignore his continued existence as well.

She suspected he had, and found herself quite
warmed by the thought. She even handed up the next
loaded cylinder with a smile.

The gunner noticed the smile, and that too would
become part of the legend. He would survive the war,
as it happened; and, in later years, in taverns in his
native Anatolia, whenever he heard the tale of how the
Wife smote down Malwa boarders with a sword and
a laugh, he saw no reason to set the matter straight.
By then, he had come to half-believe it himself.

Anna sensed a shadow passing, but she paid it very
little attention. By now, her hands and fingers were
throbbing enough to block out most sensation beyond
what was necessary to keep reloading the cylinders.
She barely even noticed the sudden burst of fiery light

and the screams that announced that the *Victrix* had arrived and was wreaking its delayed vengeance on what was left of the Malwa ambush.

Which was not much, in truth. The gunner was a very capable man, and Anna had kept him well supplied. Most of the skiffs now drifting near the barge had bodies draped over their sides and sprawled lifelessly within. At that close range, the Puckle gun had been murderous.

"Enough, ma'am," said the gunner. "It's over."

Anna finished reloading the cylinder in her hands. Then, when the meaning of the words finally registered, she set the thing down on the floor of the turret. Perhaps oddly, the relief of finally not having to handle hot metal only made the pain in her hands—and legs, too, she noticed finally—all the worse.

She stared down at the fabric of her gown. There were little stains all over it, where cartridges had rested before she brushed them onto the floor. There was a time, she could vaguely remember, when the destruction of an expensive garment would have been a cause of great concern. But it seemed a very long time ago.

"How is Illus?" she asked softly. "And the others? The boys?"

The gunner sighed. "One of the boys got killed, ma'am. Just bad luck—Illus kept the youngsters back, but that one grenade..."

Vaguely, Anna remembered hearing an explosion. She began to ask which boy it was, whose death she had caused, of the five urchins she had found on the docks of Barbaricum and conscripted into her Service. But she could not bear that pain yet.

"Illus?"

"He's fine. So's Abdul. Cottomenes got cut pretty bad."

Something to do again. The thought came as a relief. Within seconds, she was clambering awkwardly over the side of the turret again—and, again, silently cursing the impractical garment she wore.

Cottomenes was badly gashed, true enough. But the leg wound was not even close to the great femoral artery, and by now Anna had learned to sew other things than cloth. Besides, the *Victrix*'s boiler was an excellent mechanism for boiling water.

The ship's engineer was a bit outraged, of course. But, wisely, he kept his mouth shut.

The Iron Triangle

The telegraph started chattering. Everyone in the command bunker froze for a moment. Then, understanding the meaning of the dot-dashes faster than anyone—even the operator jotting down the message—Calopodius slumped in his chair with relief. The message was unusually long, with two short pauses in the middle, and by the time it was completed Calopodius was even smiling.

Belisarius, unlike Calopodius, could not quite follow the message until it was translated. When he took the message from the hand of the operator and scanned it quickly, he understood the smile on the face of the blind young officer. He grinned himself.

"Well, I'd say she's in good form," he announced to the small crowd in the bunker. Then, quoting:

```
"ALL   FINE   EXCEPT   COTTOMENES
INJURED   AND   RAFFI   DEAD.   RAFFI
ONLY   TWELVE   YEARS   OLD.   FEEL
HORRIBLE   ABOUT   IT.   MENTION
HIM   IN   DISPATCHES.   PLEASE.
ALSO   MENTION   PUCKLE   GUNNER
LEO   CONSTANTES.   SPLENDID
MAN.   ALSO   INSTRUCT   GENERAL
BELISARIUS   MAKE   MORE   PUCKLE
GUNS.   SPLENDID   THINGS.   ALSO—"
```

"Here's where the pause was," explained the general. His grin widened. "It goes on:

```
"OPERATOR   SAYS   MESSAGE   TOO
LONG.   OPERATOR   REFUSES   GIVE
HIS   NAME.   MENTION   NAMELESS
OPERATOR   IN   DISPATCHES.   STUPID
OFFICIOUS   ASININE   OBNOXIOUS
WORTHLESS   FELLOW."
```

"Why do I think someone in that telegraph station has a sword at his throat?" mused Maurice idly. "Her bodyguards are Isaurians, right? Stupid idiot." He was grinning also.

```
"MENANDER   SAYS   WILL   ARRIVE
SOON.   WILL   NEED   NEW   CLOTHES."
```

Belisarius' grin didn't fade, exactly, but it became less purely jovial. His last words were spoken softly, and addressed to Calopodius rather than to the room at large.

"Here was the second pause. The last part of the message reads:

```
"AM  EAGER  TO  SEE  YOU  AGAIN.
MY  HUSBAND."
```

8

The Iron Triangle

There was no reception for Anna at the docks, when she arrived at the Iron Triangle. Just a small gang of men hurrying out from the bunker to catch the lines thrown from the *Victrix* and the barge.

She was a bit surprised. Not disgruntled, simply... Surprised.

Menander seemed to understand. "We do this as quickly as possible these days," he explained apologetically. "The Malwa have spotters hidden in the reeds, and they often fire rocket volleys at us whenever a convoy arrives."

As if his words were the cue, Anna heard a faint sound to the north. Vaguely, like a snake hissing. Looking up, she saw several rockets soaring up into the sky.

After a moment, startled, she realized how far away they were. "I didn't know they were so big."

"They have to be. Those are fired from the Malwa lines, miles to the north. At first, the spotters would fire small ones from the reeds. But that's just pure suicide for them. Even the Malwa, after a while, gave it up."

Too uncertain to know whether she should be worried or not, Anna watched the rockets climb higher into the sky.

"They're headed our way, girl," Illus said gruffly. He pointed toward the low bunker toward which they were being towed. The roof of the bunker was just tall enough for the *Victrix* to pass underneath. "I'd feel better if you moved into the bow. That'll reach the shelter first."

"Yes. I suppose." Anna gathered up the heavy skirts and began moving forward. Illus followed her, with Abdul helping Cottomenes limp along. Behind them came the four boys.

Glancing back, she saw that Menander had remained in his place. He was still watching the rockets. From his apparent lack of concern, she realized they must be veering off.

"Keep moving, girl," Illus growled. "Yes, the damn things are completely inaccurate. But they don't always miss—and any rocket that big is going to have a monster of a warhead."

She didn't argue the point. Illus was usually cooperative with her, after all, and this was his business.

Still, most of her mind was concentrated on the sound of the coming rockets. Between that, the deep gloom of the approaching bunker, and the need to watch her feet moving across the cluttered deck, she was caught completely by surprise when the fanfare erupted.

That happened as soon as the bow passed under the overhang of the ship bunker.

Cornicens, a lot of them, and some big drums. She wasn't very familiar with cornicens. They were almost entirely a military instrument.

"Oh," she said. "Oh."

Illus was grinning from ear to ear. "I was starting to wonder. Stupid, that. When you're dealing with the general."

By the time the fanfare ended and the bow of the ship bumped gently against the wharf inside the bunker, Anna thought she might be growing deaf. Cornicens were loud. Especially when the sound was reflected from such a low ceiling.

The cheers of the soldiers even seemed dim, in her ears. They couldn't be, of course. Not with that many soldiers. Especially when they started banging the hilts of their swords on their shields as well.

She was startled by that martial salute almost as much as she'd been by the cornicens.

She glanced at Illus. He had a peculiar look on his face. A sort of fierce satisfaction.

"Do they always do that?" she asked, almost shouting the words.

He shook his head. That gesture, too, had the air of satisfaction. "No, girl. They almost never do that."

When she saw the first man who came up the gangplank, after it was laid, Anna was startled again. She'd learned enough of Roman uniforms and insignia to realize that this had to be Belisarius. But she'd never pictured him so. The fact that he was tall and broadshouldered fit her image well enough. But the rest . . .

She'd read all of Macrembolitissa's work, so she knew a great deal about the general. Despite that knowledge—or perhaps because of it—she'd imagined some sort of modern Nestor. Wise, in a grim sort of way; not old, certainly—abstractly, she knew he was a young man—but still somehow middle-aged. Perhaps a bit of gray in his hair.

She'd certainly never thought he would be so handsome. And so very young, to have done all that he had.

Finally, as he neared, she found an anchor. Something that matched the writings.

The general's smile was crooked. She'd always thought that was just Macrembolitissa, indulging herself in poetic license.

She said as much.

Belisarius smiled more crookedly still. "So I'm told. Welcome to the Iron Triangle, Lady Saronites."

The general escorted her off the *Victrix*. Anna was relieved that he didn't offer her a hand, though. She'd be in far more danger of tripping over the long and ragged skirts without both hands to hold them.

She had to concentrate so much on that task that she wasn't really looking at anything else.

They reached the relatively safe footing of the wharf.

"Lady Saronites," said the general, "your husband."

She looked up, startled again.

"Oh," she said. "Oh."

There came, then, the most startling thing of all that day. For the first time in years, Anna was too shy to say a word.

"It's not much," said Calopodius apologetically.

Anna's eyes moved over the interior of the little bunker where Calopodius lived. Where she would now live also. She did not fail to notice all the little touches here and there—the bright, cheery little cloths; the crucifix; even a few native handcrafts—as well as the relative cleanliness of the place. But...

No, it was not much. Just a big pit in the ground, when all was said and done, covered over with logs and soil.

"It's fine," she said. "Not a problem."

She turned and stared at him. Her husband, once a handsome boy, was now a hideously ugly man. She had expected the empty eye sockets, true enough. But even after all the carnage she had witnessed since she left Constantinople, she had not once considered what a mortar shell would do to the rest of his face.

Stupid, really. As if shrapnel would obey the rules of poetry, and pierce eyes as neatly as a goddess at a loom. The upper half of his face was a complete ruin. The lower half was relatively unmarked, except for one scar along his right jaw and another pucker-like mark on his left cheek.

His mouth and lips, on the other hand, were still as she vaguely remembered them. A nice mouth, she decided, noticing for the first time.

"It's fine," she repeated. "Not a problem."

A moment later, Illus and Abdul came into the bunker hauling her luggage. What was left of it. Until they were gone, Anna and Calopodius were silent. Then he said, very softly:

"I don't understand why you came."

Anna tried to remember the answer. It was difficult. And probably impossible to explain, in any event. *I wanted a divorce, maybe* ... seemed ... strange. Even stranger, though closer to the truth, would be: *or at least to drag you back so you could share the ruins of my own life.*

"It doesn't matter now. I'm here. I'm staying."

For the first time since she'd rejoined her husband, he smiled. Anna realized she'd never really seen him smile before. Not, at least, with an expression that was anything more than politeness.

He reached out his hand, tentatively, and she moved toward him. The hand, fumbling, stroked her ribs.

"God in Heaven, Anna!" he choked. "How can you stand something like that—in this climate? You'll drown in sweat."

Anna tried to keep from laughing; and then, realizing finally where she was, stopped trying. Even in the haughtiest aristocratic circles of Constantinople, a woman was allowed to laugh in the presence of her husband.

When she was done—the laughter was perhaps a bit hysterical—Calopodius shook his head. "We've got to get you a sari, first thing. I can't have my wife dying on me from heat prostration."

Calopodius matched deed to word immediately. A few words to his aide-to-camp Luke, and, much sooner than Anna would have expected, a veritable horde of Punjabis from the adjacent town were packed into the bunker.

Some of them were actually there on business, bringing piles of clothing for her to try on. Most of them, she finally understood, just wanted to get a look at her.

Of course, they were all expelled from the bunker while she changed her clothing—except for two native women whose expert assistance she required until she mastered the secrets of the foreign garments. But once the women announced that she was suitably attired, the mob of admirers was allowed back in.

In fact, after a while Anna found it necessary to leave the bunker altogether and model her new clothing on the ground outside, where everyone could get a good look at her new appearance. Her husband insisted, to her surprise.

"You're beautiful," he said to her, "and I want everyone to know it."

She almost asked how a blind man could tell, but he forestalled the question with a little smile. "Did you think I'd forget?"

But later, that night, he admitted the truth. They were lying side by side, stiffly, still fully clothed, on the pallet in a corner of the bunker where Calopodius slept. "To be honest, I can't remember very well what you look like."

Anna thought about it, for a moment. Then:

"I can't really remember myself."

"I wish I could see you," he murmured.

"It doesn't matter." She took his hand and laid it on her bare belly. The flesh reveled in its new coolness. She herself, on the other hand, reveled in the touch. And did not find it strange that she should do so.

"Feel."

His hand was gentle, at first. And never really stopped being so, for all the passion that followed. When it was all over, Anna was covered in sweat again. But she didn't mind at all. Without heavy and proper fabric to cover her—with nothing covering her now except Calopodius' hand—the sweat dried soon enough. That, too, was a great pleasure.

"I warn you," she murmured into his ear. "We're not in Constantinople any more. Won't be for a long time, if ever. So if I catch you with a courtesan, I'll boil you alive."

"The thought never crossed my mind!" he insisted. And even believed it was true.

THE
1632
SERIES

Author's note:

The 1632 series is, so far at least, my "magnum corpus." The novels and anthologies which comprise this series are my most popular works, and I've written more of them than I have of anything else. As of today, nine novels and nine anthologies have appeared in the series—see the appendix for a list of all the titles—with a lot more coming.

Most of what I write in this series are novels, but I've also written some short fiction. Included here is the first short piece I wrote, "The Wallenstein Gambit," which was my story for the anthology entitled *Ring of Fire*, which basically serves as the third book in the series. I use the word "short" advisedly, since "The Wallenstein Gambit" is long enough to be considered technically a short novel.

The other three stories are much shorter. They are the first of the Anne Jefferson stories, which I write for the paper editions of the *Grantville Gazette* anthologies. A fourth Anne Jefferson story, not included in this anthology, is contained in the paper edition of *Grantville Gazette IV*, which came out in June 2008.

These stories began as something of a joke between me and my publisher, Jim Baen. Jim designed the cover for the paper edition of the first *Grantville Gazette* in blithe disregard for any of the stories that were in the volume. When I pointed that out to him, after he showed me the cover, he very cheerily told me that he figured it was my job to fix that problem.

So, grumbling a bit, I did. The result was "Portraits."

So it went, from there. Jim would design a cover and have an artist do it—that's Tom Kidd, who has done most of the covers for the series—and then it would be up to me to write a story that illustrated it. It was quite a challenge, because I had to work within very tight constraints. The same model was used for all the covers, which meant that I had to use the same character, once I established her as Anne Jefferson in the first story.

So why would Anne Jefferson in a white dress be included as part of the night watch? Well, you'll find out in "Steps in the Dance," the story I wrote for the second volume. Why would she be posing for another and different portrait with an artist also on the cover—his hands, anyway? You'll find out in "Postage Due," the story for the third volume.

As time went on, I found myself enjoying the challenge. Alas, with the fourth volume, it's now over. Jim died in June of 2006, and he'll no longer be around to play his side of the game. So, I'll have to do the best I can on my own, trying to figure what sort of perverse cover would have tickled his fancy, partly for its own sake and partly to goose his author.

If you'd like to see the original covers for which these three stories were written, by the way, you can see them on Baen's web site www.baen.com. Select "Catalog" from the menu, then select "F" from the alphabet of authors, then select "Eric Flint."

Better yet, you can buy them.

The Wallenstein Gambit

CHAPTER I: *The Bohemian Opening*

March 1633

1

"So what's this all about, Mike?" asked Morris Roth, after Mike Stearns closed the door behind him. "And why did you ask me to meet you in Edith's home?"

Grantville's jeweler looked around the small living room curiously. That was the part of Mike's request that Morris had found most puzzling. By the early spring of 1633, Stearns was usually so busy with political affairs that people came to see him in his office downtown.

As soon as he spotted the young man sitting in an armchair in the corner, Morris' curiosity spiked—and, for the first time, a trace of apprehension came into his interest. He didn't know the name of the young man, but he recognized him even though he wasn't in uniform.

He was a German mercenary, captured in the short-lived battle outside Jena the year before, who'd since enrolled in the army of the United States. More to the point, Morris knew that he was part of Captain Harry Lefferts' unit—which, in reality if not in official parlance, amounted to Mike Stearns' combination of special security unit and commandos.

"Patience, patience," said Mike, smiling thinly. "I'd apologize for the somewhat peculiar circumstances, but as you'll see for yourself in a moment we have a special security problem to deal with." He glanced at the man sitting in the armchair. "I think the best way to make everything clear is just to introduce you to someone. Follow me."

Stearns turned and headed for the hallway, Morris trailing behind. Edith Wild's house wasn't a big one, so it only took a few steps before he came to a closed door. "We're keeping him in here, while he recovers from his latest round of surgery. Edith volunteered to serve as his live-in nurse."

Morris restrained his grimace. Edith Wild was capable enough as a nurse, so long as it didn't involve any real medical experience. Like many of Grantville's nurses since the Ring of Fire, she'd had no background in medical work. She'd been employed in a glass factory in Clarksburg.

Her main qualification for her new line of work, so far as Morris could tell, was that she was a very big woman, massive as well as tall, and had much the same temperament as the infamous Nurse Ratchett in a movie he'd once seen, *One Flew Over the Cuckoo's Nest.* Not the sadism, true. But the woman was a ferocious bully. She was normally engaged in enforcing Grantville's public health laws, a job which required a firm hand given the huge influx of immigrants who had a seventeenth-century conception of sanitation and prophylaxis.

A "firm hand," Edith Wild certainly had. Morris had, more than once, heard Germans refer to her as "the Tatar." When they weren't calling her something downright obscene.

And who is "he"? Morris wondered. But he said nothing, since Mike was already opening the door and ushering him into the bedroom beyond.

It was a room to fit the house. Small, sparsely furnished, and just as spick-and-span clean as everything else. But Morris Roth gave the room itself no more than a cursory glance. Despite the bandages covering much of the lower face, he recognized the man lying in the bed within two seconds.

That was odd, since he'd never actually met him. But, perhaps not so odd as all that. Like many residents of Grantville, Morris had a poster up in his jewelry store that portrayed the man's likeness. True, in the form of a painting rather than a photograph. But he could now see that it was quite a good likeness.

He groped for words and couldn't find any. They'd have been swear words, and Morris avoided profanity. The poster in his shop was titled: *Wanted, Dead or Alive.*

The man was studying him with dark eyes. Despite the obvious pain the man was feeling, his expression was one of keen interest.

Abruptly, the man raised a hand and motioned for Morris to approach him.

"Go ahead," said Mike, chuckling harshly. "He doesn't bite, I promise. He couldn't anyway, even if he wanted to. His jaw's wired shut."

Reluctantly, much as he'd move toward a viper, Morris came over to the side of the bed. There was a tablet lying on the covers—one of the now-rare modern legal tablets—along with a ballpoint pen.

The man in the bed took the pen in hand and, shakily, scratched out a message. Then, held it up for Morris to see.

The words were written in English. Morris hadn't known the man in the bed knew the language. He wasn't surprised, really. Whatever other crimes and faults had ever been ascribed to that man, lack of intelligence had never been one of them.

But Morris didn't give any of that much thought. His attention was entirely riveted on the message itself.

CHMIELNICKI
I CAN STOP IT

For a moment, it seemed to Morris Roth as if time stood still. He felt light-headed, as if everything was unreal. Since the Ring of Fire, when Morris came to understand that he was really stranded in the seventeenth century, in the early 1630s, not more than a week had ever gone by without his thoughts turning to the Chmielnicki Massacre of 1648. And wondering if there was something—anything—he could do to prevent it. He'd raised the matter with Mike himself, several times before. Only to be told, not to his surprise, that Mike couldn't think of any way a small town of Americans fighting for its own survival in war-torn Germany in the middle of the Thirty Years War could possibly do anything to stop a coming mass pogrom in the Ukraine.

"How?" he croaked.

Again, the man scrawled; and held up the tablet.

COMPLICATED
STEARNS WILL EXPLAIN
BUT I WILL NEED YOUR HELP

Morris looked at Stearns. Mike had come close and seen the message himself. Now, he motioned toward the door. "Like he says, it's complicated. Let's talk about it in the living room, Morris. After the extensive surgery done on him, the man needs his rest."

Morris followed Mike out of the bedroom, not looking back. He said nothing until they reached the living room. Then, almost choking out the words, could only exclaim:

"Wallenstein?"

Mike shrugged, smiling wryly, and gestured at the couch. He perched himself on an ottoman near the armchair where the soldier was sitting. "Have a seat, Morris. We've got a lot to discuss. But I'll grant you, it's more than a bit like having a devil come and offer you salvation."

After Morris was seated, he managed a chuckle himself.

"Make sure you use a long spoon."

Seeing the expression on Mike's face, Morris groaned. "Don't tell me!"

"Yup. I plan to use a whole set of very long-handled tableware, dealing with that man. And, yup, I've got you in mind for the spoon. The ladle, actually."

"He wants money, I assume." Morris scowled. "I have to tell you that I get awfully tired of the assumption that all Jews are rich. If this new venture of ours takes off, I might be. Faceted jewelry is unheard-of in this day and age, and we should get a king's ransom for them. But right now . . . Mike, I don't have a lot of cash lying around. Most of my money is invested in the business."

Mike's smile grew more lopsided still. "Wallenstein's no piker, like the rest of them. He wants a lot more than your money, Morris. He doesn't want the gold from the goose, he wants the goose himself."

Morris raised a questioning eyebrow.

"Figure it out. Your new jewel-cutting business looks to make a fortune, right? So where's that fortune going to pour into? Grantville—or Prague?"

Morris groaned again. "Mike, I'm over fifty years old! So's Judith. We're too old to be relocating to— to— A city that doesn't have modern plumbing," he finished, sounding a bit lame even to himself.

Stearns said nothing, for a moment. Then, harshly and abruptly: "You've asked me four times to think of a way to stop the coming massacres of Jews in the Ukraine. Probably the worst pogrom in Jewish history before the Holocaust, you told me. This is the best I can manage, Morris. *I* can't do it, but Wallenstein . . . maybe. But it's a hell of a gamble—and, frankly, one which has a lot more parameters than simply the Jewish problem in eastern Europe."

Morris' mind was finally starting to work clearly again. "To put it mildly. Am I right in assuming that Wallenstein came here secretly to propose an alliance? He'll break from the Austrian Habsburgs and take Bohemia out of Ferdinand's empire?"

Mike nodded. "That—and the best medical care in the world. Julie's bullets tore him up pretty good, Morris, and the man's health was none too good to begin with. The truth is, Doctor Nichols—he did most of the actual surgery—doesn't think Wallenstein's likely to live more than a few years."

"A few years . . ." Morris mused. "Do you think—?"

"Who knows, Morris? Immediately, the alliance is a godsend for us, as weird as it looks. I've discussed it with Gustav Adolf and he agrees. If Becky's mission to France can't get us a peace with Richelieu, we're looking to be at war again soon. A revolt in Bohemia—sure as hell with Wallenstein in charge—will at least take the Austrians out of the equation. As for the Ukraine . . ."

He shrugged. "We've got fifteen years, theoretically—assuming the butterfly effect doesn't scramble so-called 'future history' the way it usually does."

"It'll maybe scramble the timing," Morris said grimly, "but I doubt it'll do much to scramble what's coming. The Chmielnicki Massacre was centuries in the making, and the ingredients of it were pretty intractable."

Mike nodded. Morris knew that after the first time he'd raised the subject with Mike, Stearns had done some research on it. He'd been helped, of course, by his Jewish wife and father-in-law. By now, Morris thought, Mike probably knew more than he did about the situation of eastern European Jewry.

"Intractable is putting it mildly. If it were just a matter of religious or ethnic prejudices and hatreds, it'd be bad enough. But there's a vicious class factor at work, too. Polish noblemen are the landlords over Ukrainian peasants—whom they gouge mercilessly—and they use the Jews as their rent collectors and tax farmers. So when the Ukrainian peasants finally revolted under Cossack leadership—will revolt, I should say—it's not too hard to figure out why they immediately targeted the Jews."

Morris sighed. As much as he was naturally on the side of the Jews in the Ukraine, he knew enough about the situation not to think for a minute that there was any simple solution. In fact, he'd once gotten into a ferocious quarrel with one of the Abrabanel scions who, like a number of the young Jews who had gravitated into Grantville, had become something of a Jewish nationalist.

Arm the Ukrainian Jews! the young man had proclaimed.

"For what?" Morris had snarled in response. "So they can become even more ruthless rent collectors? You stupid idiot! Those Ukrainian peasants are people too, you know. You've got to find a solution that they'll accept also."

He stared at the large bookcase against one of the walls, where Edith kept her beloved collection of Agatha Christie novels. For a moment, he had a wild and whimsical wish that the great detective Hercule Poirot would manifest himself in the room and provide them all with a neat and tidy answer.

Neat and tidy . . . in the seventeenth century? Ha! We never managed "neat and tidy" even in our own world.

"All right," he said abruptly. "As long as Judith agrees, I'll do it. I'll try to talk Jason Gotkin into coming with us, too, since he was studying to be a rabbi before the Ring of Fire."

Having made the pronouncement, he was immediately overwhelmed by a feeling of inadequacy. "But—Mike—I don't . . ."

"Relax, Morris," said Mike, smiling. "You won't be on your own. Just for starters, Uriel Abrabanel has agreed to move to Prague also."

Morris felt an instant flood of relief. Rebecca's uncle was probably an even more accomplished spymaster and political intriguer than her father Balthazar. And if he was elderly, at least he didn't have Balthazar's heart problems. So far as anyone knew, anyway.

"Take those young firebrands around Dunash with you, also."

Morris grimaced. Dunash Abrabanel was the young man he'd had the quarrel with. "I'm not sure they'll listen to me, Mike. Much less obey me."

"Then let them stay here and rot," Mike said harshly. "If nothing else, Morris, I want to give those fellows something to do that'll keep them from haring off to the Holy Land in order to found the state of Israel. I do *not* need a war with the Ottoman Empire on top of everything else."

Morris chuckled. "Mike, not even Dunash is crazy enough to do that. It's just a pipedream they talk about now and then, usually after they've had way too much to drink."

"Maybe so. Then again, maybe not. They're frustrated, Morris, and I can't say I blame them for it. So let's give them something constructive to do. Let them go to Prague and see if they can convince Europe's largest Jewish community to throw its support behind Wallenstein."

Morris was already thinking ahead. "That won't be easy. The Jews in Prague are Ashkenazim and they're Sephardic. Not to mention that Prague's Jewry is orthodox, which they really aren't—well, they are, but they often follow different—and...Oh, boy," he ended lamely.

"I didn't say it would be easy, Morris."

"Dunash will insist on arming the Jews."

Mike shrugged. "So? I'm in favor of that anyway. As long as those guns aren't being used to help Polish noblemen gouge their peasants, I'm all for the Jewish population being armed to the teeth."

"Will Wallenstein agree to that? As it stands, Bohemian laws—like the laws of most European countries—forbid Jews from carrying weapons."

Mike jerked at thumb at the bedroom door. "Why ask me? The man's right in there, Morris. Negotiate with him."

After a moment's hesitation, Morris squared his shoulders and marched into the bedroom.

When he came back out, a few minutes later, he had a bemused expression on his face.

"Well?"

Mutely, Morris showed Mike a sheet of paper from Wallenstein's legal pad. When Mike looked down at it, he saw Wallenstein's shaky scrawl.

AGREED
JEWS MAY BE ARMED
BUT MUST SUPPORT ME
OR I WILL BURN DOWN THE GHETTO

"He's not the nicest guy in the world," Morris observed. He folded up the sheet and tucked it into his short pocket. "On the other hand..."

Mike finished the thought for him. "He's ambitious

as Satan and, whatever else, one of the most capable men in the world. Plus, he doesn't seem to share most of this century's religious bigotry. That doesn't mean he won't burn down the ghetto. He will, Morris, in a heartbeat. But he won't do it because you're Jews. He'll do it because you failed him."

Judith agreed more quickly than Morris would have thought. Indeed, his wife began packing the next morning. But the first thing she put in the trunk was the biggest ladle they had in the kitchen.

"We'll need it," she predicted.

2

"It looks a little weird without the statues," mused Len Tanner, adjusting his horn-rim glasses. He leaned over the stone railing of the Charles Bridge and looked first one way, then the other. The bridge was the main span across the Vltava river, and connected the two halves of the city of Prague. It had been built almost two centuries earlier, in the fourteenth century—though not finished until the early fifteenth, moving as slowly as medieval construction usually did—and had been named after the Holy Roman Emperor who commanded its erection. The *Karlüv most*, to use the proper Czech term, although Tanner said they hadn't given it that name until sometime in the nineteenth century. In this day and age, it was still just called the Stone Bridge.

Watching Tanner, Ellie Anderson almost laughed. Something in the little twitches Len was making with his lips made it clear that he'd have been chewing on his huge mustache, if he still had one.

But, he didn't—and wouldn't, as long as Ellie had anything to say about it. However many of Len Tanner's quirks and foibles she'd grown accustomed to and decided she could live with, that damned walrus mustache was not one of them. She preferred her men clean-shaven and always had, a quirk of her own she suspected came from memories of a great bearded lout of a father. Dim memories. He'd been killed in a car wreck when she was only seven years old, caused by a drunk driver. Him. It was a one-car accident and the only other casualty had been the oak tree at the sharp bend in the road near their house.

Fortunately, the oak tree had survived. Ellie's memories of the oak tree were a lot more extensive, and a lot fonder, than those of her father. Years later, she'd even built a treefort in it. The neighbors had been a little scandalized. Not so much by the implied disrespect for her father—truth be told, nobody in that little eastern Kentucky town had had much use for Dick Anderson—but because it was yet another display of the tomboy habits that had already made her the despair of the town's gentility.

"Gentility" as they saw themselves, anyhow. Ellie had thought then—still did—that the term was ludicrous applied to seven matrons, not one of whom had more than a high school education and only two of whom had ever been anything more than housewives and professional busybodies.

She wondered, for a moment, what had happened to any or all of them. She hadn't been back to her hometown in ten years, since her mother died of cancer and her two brothers had made it clear they'd just as soon not be burdened with her company. Since the feeling was mutual, she'd simply come in for the funeral and left the same evening.

And what do you care, anyway? she asked herself sarcastically. *They're a whole universe away, so it's a little late to be thinking about it now.*

But she knew the answer. Hers had been a self-sufficient life, and she was not sorry for it. Still, it had often been a lonely one, too.

It wasn't now, because of Len Tanner. Ten times more aggravating, often enough, but . . . not lonely.

"Looks weird," he repeated.

"Oh, for God's sake, Len! Doesn't it strike you as a little eccentric to call a city 'weird' because it doesn't have statues from three and half centuries later, in another universe, that only *you* remember because—far as I know—you're the only resident of Grantville weird enough to go to Prague on vacation?"

The jibe, not to Ellie's surprise, simply made Tanner look smug.

"Not my fault the rest of 'em are a bunch of hicks. 'Vacation,' ha! For most of 'em, that meant fishing somewhere within fifty miles or—ooh, how daring—a trip to the big city called Pittsburgh." Again, his lips made that *wish-there-was-a-mustache-here* twitch. "Ha! I remember, back when Mike Stearns went to Los Angeles for three years. Everybody else in Grantville—'cept me—thought he'd gone to Mars or something. The only 'furrin country' most of those boys had ever been to was Vietnam. And that was hardly what you'd call a sight-seeing trip."

It was one of the many odd little things about Len Tanner, Ellie reflected. To her surprise, she'd discovered that he was probably the most widely traveled man she'd ever known. Tourism was one of Len's passions. His main passion, probably, leaving aside that grotesque mustache. For his entire adult life, every vacation he'd gotten—and he'd always been willing to work extra hours to pile up vacation time—Tanner had gone somewhere outside the old United States. Some of them pretty exotic places, like China and—

Ellie chuckled. One of Tanner's little brags was that he was the only American veteran in Grantville who'd made it all the way to Hanoi. True, he was a veteran of the Grenadan conquest, which the Vietnam vets in town didn't consider a "real war." Still, they didn't begrudge him the boast. They even chuckled at it, themselves, partly because most people who got to know him tended to like Len Tanner, and partly because . . .

He was a lonely man, and, what was worse, a man who was uncomfortable in his loneliness. So, for years, his friends and drinking buddies had indulged his little oddities.

Loneliness had been at the heart of his compulsive traveling, Ellie suspected. Tanner had adopted tourism as a hobby, the way other lonely people adopt other things. And if it was a more expensive hobby than most, it had at least made Tanner less parochial-minded than most people of Ellie's acquaintance. He actually *had* seen the "big wide world," even if his ingrained awkwardness with learning foreign languages always kept him at a certain distance from the people whose countries he'd visited.

Now, Tanner was staring up at the Hradcany. The hill upon which Prague Castle was perched overlooked the entire city. It wasn't much of a hill, really, but it hardly mattered. The *Prazský hrad*—to use the Czech term for "Prague Castle"—seemed to dominate everything. It was an ancient edifice, begun in the ninth century CE by the rulers of the Slavic tribes who had migrated into the area a century or two earlier, and added to in bits and pieces as the centuries passed. But, always, whether the rulers of the area that eventually became known as Bohemia were Slavic princes or German Holy Roman Emperors, the seat of power was in Prague Castle.

"At least that's still pretty much the same," Tanner said. "Except for that stupid, boring façade they added in the eighteenth century. Good riddance—or riddance-never-come, I guess I should say." He exuded an air of satisfaction, studying the hill. "Even when I visited it, though, that gorgeous cathedral was the centerpiece. Now, even more so."

Ellie wouldn't have used the term "gorgeous" to describe St. Vitus Cathedral, herself. As far as she was concerned, the immense Gothic structure that loomed over the entire Hradcany belonged where everything Gothic belonged—in a romance novel, preferably featuring sexy vampires.

Womanfully, though, she restrained herself from calling it "ugly and grotesque." One of Tanner's many little quirks was that he invariably defended—ferociously—each and every architectural or artistic endeavor of the Roman Catholic Church. That was to make up, she'd once accused him, for the fact that he was never found in church more than once a year.

I ain't a "lapsed Catholic"! he'd responded hotly, at the time. *Just, y'know, not around as much as maybe I oughta be.*

Well, that's one way to put it, Ellie had retorted. *Is that why Father Mazzare greets you with "howdy, stranger"?*

Remembering that minor fight, she smiled a little. She and Tanner bickered a lot, but, truth be told, he really *was* a hard man to dislike. Once you got to know him, at least. Most of his vices and character flaws he wore on his sleeve. What lay underneath— assuming you could cut your way through that damn crust—was . . . really pretty nice and warm.

At least, Ellie Anderson thought so. More and more, in fact, as time went on.

As was her own nature, the surge of sentiment made her brusque.

"C'mon, Len! Let's quit gawking at the sights. We're supposed to be on a secret mission for Morris Roth, remember?"

Tanner gave her a sour look. Then, bestowed a look considerably more sour on the squad of men who were following them. Lounging along behind them, it might be better to say. The four mercenary soldiers in Pappenheim's pay somehow managed to make their way across a bridge as if they were loafing in an alehouse.

"Some 'secret' mission," he grumbled. "With those clowns in our wake. Why don't we just put on signs saying: *Attention! Dangerous furriners!*"

She took him by the arm and began leading him along the bridge, toward that part of Prague known as the *Staré Mesto*—which meant nothing fancier than "Old Town"—where the eastern end of the Charles Bridge abutted.

"Jesus! Were you just as suspicious of tourist guides, too, back in your globe-trotting days? You know damn good and well—ought to, anyway, as many briefings as we had to sit through—that nobody in this day and age thinks of anybody as 'furriners.' Well. Not the way you mean it. A 'furriner' is anybody outside of your own little bailiwick. So who cares if they're 'Czech' or 'German' or 'French' or 'English'—or even 'American,' for that matter? That's the business of the princes, not the townfolk."

By the end, she was almost grumbling the words herself. Tanner's quirks, harmless as they might be, *were* sometimes annoying.

"I never trusted guide books. They don't pay the guys who write 'em to tell the truth, y'know? They pay 'em to sucker in the tourists."

Her only response was to grip his arm tighter and march him a little faster across the bridge. And maybe tighten her lips a little.

Stubbornly, Ellie continued her little lecture. "So nobody—except you—gives a fuck about whether we're here on a 'secret mission' or not." She jerked her head backward a little, indicating the castle behind them. "Not even Don Balthasar de Marradas gives a damn what we're doing here. If he's even noticed us at all."

Len's good humor returned. "How's he supposed to? He's too busy squabbling with the Count of Solms-Baruth over which one of them is *really* the Emperor's chosen administrator for Prague. Gawd, there are times I love the butterfly effect."

Ellie grinned. Grantville's knowledge of central European history in the seventeenth century was spotty and erratic, as you'd expect from the records and

resources of a small town in West Virginia that had
neither a college nor a business enterprise with any
particular reason to develop a specialized knowledge
about central Europe, even in their own time much
less three or four centuries earlier. But, there were
occasional exceptions to that rule, little glimpses of
historical detail—like islands in a sea of obscurity—
usually engendered by some individual interest of one
or another of Grantville's residents.

And, as it happened, Prague in the middle of the
seventeenth century was one of them. That was because,
some years before the Ring of Fire, Judith Roth had
developed an interest in genealogy. She'd traced her
ancestors back to the large Jewish community which
had lived in Prague since the tenth century and had
enjoyed something of a "golden age" recently because of
the tolerant policies of the Austrian Habsburg Emperor
Rudolf II, who'd reigned from 1576 to 1612.

Judith's interest in genealogy had lapsed, eventually. But she'd never bothered to erase the data she'd
accumulated from her home computer's hard drive.
Eventually, some months after the Ring of Fire, it
had occurred to her to look at it again.

Melissa Mailey—for that matter, the entire executive branch of the U.S. government—had practically
jumped for joy. Most of the information, of course,
concentrated on Jewish genealogy and history. But,
as is invariably true when someone does a broad and
sweeping search for data on the internet, there was a
lot of other stuff mixed in with it, mostly disconnected
and often-useless items of information.

One of those little items—the one that was causing
Tanner and Anderson to enjoy a moment's humor as

they crossed the Charles Bridge—was that Johann Georg II, Count of Solms-Baruth and one of the Austrian emperor's top administrators, had died in the plague that swept Prague in the spring of 1632.

But that had been in a different universe. In this one, he was very much alive a year later, in the spring of 1633. Apparently, following Gustavus Adolphus' victory at the battle of Breitenfeld in September of 1631, the influence of the newly arrived Americans on events thereafter had been enough to send a multitude of ripples through "established history." Small ones, at the beginning, as was always true of the butterfly effect—so named after the notion that the flapping of a butterfly's wings could eventually cause a hurricane. But big enough, obviously, to allow one Count Johann Georg II to survive the disease that had felled him in another universe.

Good for him, of course—but now, also, good for those who were secretly scheming with Wallenstein to overthrow Austrian rule in Bohemia. Because the Count of Solms-Baruth was a stubborn man, and refused to concede pre-eminence in Bohemia's administrative affairs to the Emperor's favored courtier, Don Balthasar de Marradas. The enmity between Count Johann Georg and Don Balthasar went back to 1626, apparently, when Wallenstein had selected the count over the don as his chief lieutenant in the campaign against the Protestant mercenary Mansfeld.

Neither Tanner nor Ellie knew much of the details, which were as tangled as seventeenth-century aristocratic feuds and vendettas usually were. All that mattered to them was that Solms-Baruth was tacitly on Wallenstein's side, and he was doing his level best to interfere with

Marradas' ability to retain firm Austrian control over political developments in Prague and Bohemia. Which, among other things, meant that the two of them could carry out their special project in Prague—even go on side expeditions like the one that was taking them across the Charles Bridge—without any real fear of being stopped and investigated by Austrian soldiery.

In fact, the only soldiery in sight were the four men in the squad following them—who had been given the assignment personally by Wallenstein's general Pappenheim, and had an official-looking document signed by the count to establish their credentials should anyone think to object.

"There are times," Ellie mused, "when the 'Machiavellian' scheming and plotting of these fucking seventeenth-century princes and mercenary captains reminds me of the Keystone Kops more than anything else."

Tanner came to an abrupt halt. "Think so?" He pointed a finger ahead of them, and slightly to the left. "We'll be coming to it soon, on our way to the Josefov. The Old Town Square—'Starry-mesta,' the Czechs call it, or something like that. That's where Emperor Ferdinand—yup, the same shithead who's still sitting on the throne in Vienna—had twenty-seven Protestant leaders executed after the Battle of the White Mountain."

Now he swiveled, and pointed back toward the Hradcany. "The guy who did the executing was—still is—one of the most famous executioners in history. Jan Mydlar's his name. When I was here, I saw his sword hanging in one of the museums in the Castle. They say he could lop a man's head off with one stroke, every time."

The finger lowered slightly. "They stuck the heads

on spikes, right there, all along the Charles Bridge. They left them there to rot, for years. Only took the last down maybe a year ago."

He turned and they started walking again. In silence.

As they neared the end of the bridge, Ellie cleared her throat. "Whatever happened to that guy? The executioner, I mean. Jan Whazzisname."

Tanner shrugged. "Not sure. Maybe he's still alive."

Ellie gurgled something inarticulate. Tanner gave her a sly, sidelong glance.

"Hey, sweetheart, cheer up. The funny thing is, according to the story Mydlar was something of a Bohemian patriot himself. They say he wore a black hood that day—in mourning, so the story goes— instead of the flame-red hood he normally wore. So who knows? If he's still around, he might wind up working for us."

"Like I said," Ellie muttered. "The Keystone Kops. Okay, sure, on steroids."

CHAPTER II: *Pawn to King Four*

April 1633

1

By the time the expedition finally set out for Prague, three weeks after his meeting with Mike Stearns and Wallenstein, Morris was feeling a bit more relaxed about the prospect. A bit, not much.

What relaxation did come to him derived primarily from the presence in their party of Uriel Abrabanel. By temperament, Rebecca's uncle was less given to

sedentary introspection than his brother. True, Balthazar
Abrabanel had spent much of his life working as a spy
also. But he was a doctor by trade and a philosopher
by inclination—more in the nature of what the term
"spymaster" captures.

His brother Uriel had had no such side interests,
beyond the financial dealings that were part of being
a member of the far-flung Abrabanel clan and integral
to his espionage. He'd spent much of his earlier life
as a seaman—a "Portuguese" seaman, using the standard subterfuge of secret Jews anywhere the Spanish
Inquisition might be found—and, though now in his
sixties, he rode a horse as easily as he had once ridden a yardarm.

"Oh, yes," he said cheerfully, "they're a lot of hypo-
crites, the English. Jews have been officially banned
from the island for centuries, but they always let some
of us stay around, as long as we—what's that handy
American expression?—ah, yes: 'kept a low profile.'
Not only did their kings and queens and dukes and
earls always want Jewish doctors, but they also found
us *so* handy to spy on the Spanish for them."

Morris tried not to make a face. Even two years
after the Ring of Fire, with the attitudes and sensibilities of one born and raised in twentieth-century
America, he found it hard to accept the position of
Jews in the seventeenth century. What he found harder
to accept—and even more disturbing—was the readiness of Jews in his new universe to accommodate to
that seventeenth-century reality.

Uriel must have sensed some of his distaste. "Whatever else, Morris, we must survive. And the truth is
that, for all their hypocrisy, the English are no real

threat to us. Not the Stuarts, nor the Tudor dynasty before them. The real enemy…"

His voice trailed off, as Uriel studied the landscape ahead of him. His eyes were slitted, though there was really nothing in that central European countryside to warrant the hostility. By now, having skirted Saxony, they were through the low Erzgebirge mountains and beginning to enter the Bohemian plain.

"The *Habsburgs*," he said, almost hissing the words. "There is the source—well, the driving engine, anyway— of Europe's bigotry in this day and age. The Austrians as much as the Spanish."

"I would have thought you'd name the Catholic Church. From what I hear, the Austrian Emperor has treated the Jewish community in Prague rather well."

"That's because he needs their money to keep his war coffers full. As soon as the war's over, Ferdinand will treat the Jews in Prague just as savagely as he treated the Utraquists and the Unity of Brethren. Watch and see."

Uriel shrugged. "I am not fond of the Roman Catholic Church, to be sure. But then, I'm no fonder of most Protestant sects either. No pope ever fulminated as violently against the Jews as Martin Luther. Still, religious intolerance we can live with. Being fair, it's not as if there aren't a lot of Jews who are just as intolerant. The real problem is when that intolerance gets shackled to a dynasty driving for continental power. Which, for centuries now in Europe, has meant the Habsburgs first and foremost."

Morris glanced to his left, where a number of horsemen were escorting several large wagons. Uriel followed his gaze, and a slight smile came to his face.

"Ah, yes. The Unity of Brethren. It will certainly be interesting to see how they finally—"

Again, he groped for an American colloquialism. Uriel was very fond of the things.

"'Shape up,'" Morris provided.

"Indeed so! Such a splendid expression! 'Shape up', indeed."

Morris shook his head ruefully. The political situation he was about to plunge into in Prague was a genuine nightmare. Since the Habsburg armies had conquered Bohemia, after the short-lived period from 1618 to 1621 during which the Bohemians had tried to install a Protestant king against Ferdinand's wishes, the Austrian emperor had ruled the province tyrannically. In particular, he had introduced a level of brutality into religious persecution that had not been seen in Europe since the campaigns of the Spanish Duke of Alva during the first years of the Dutch revolt.

It was said that, upon hearing the news of the Catholic victory at the Battle of the White Mountain, a priest in Vienna had taken the pulpit to urge Emperor Ferdinand II to follow the Biblical precept: *Thou shalt break them with a rod of iron; thou shalt dash them into pieces like a potter's vessel.*

Ferdinand had needed no urging. He was a bigot by nature, who was a genuine Catholic fanatic, not simply a monarch using the established church to further his political ends. In point of fact, it was also rumored— apparently based on good information—that Pope Urban VIII had several times tried to rein in the Habsburg emperor's religious zeal. But, to no avail. Stalin's notorious wisecrack from a later century—*how many divisions has the Pope?*—would have been understood perfectly by rulers of the seventeenth century, the Catholic ones perhaps even better than the Protestants. Like Cardinal Richelieu in France, Emperor Ferdinand felt he was simply following Christ's advice to give unto Caesar that which was Caesar's.

And he was Caesar, and Bohemia was his, and he intended to make the most of it. Thus, he had:

—executed dozens of Protestant noblemen who'd led the short-lived revolt;

—banned the Utraquist and Calvinist and Hussite sects of the Protestant creed outright, and made it clear to the Lutherans that they were henceforth on a very short leash;

—abolished elective monarchy and made the Kingdom of Bohemia henceforth hereditary in the Habsburg line;

—had the Letter of Majesty, the Bohemians' much-cherished charter of religious liberty that had been captured in the sack of Prague, sent to him in Vienna, where he personally cut it into pieces;

—with his Edict of Restitution in 1629, seized Protestant churches and church property and given them to the Catholic church;

—seized the estates of "rebels," bringing into his dynasty's possession the property of over six hundred prominent Protestant families, fifty towns, and about half the entire acreage of the province;

—allowed his soldiery—mostly Bavarians in Bohemia and Cossacks in Moravia—to ravage and plunder the peasantry and the small towns, more or less at will, thereby saving himself much of the need to actually *pay* his mercenaries;

—ruined the economy of Bohemia and Moravia

by severely debasing the currency in order to buy up still more estates;

—transformed the once-prosperous peasantry and urban commoners of the region into paupers, and created a handful of great landowners to rule over them (of whom none was greater and richer than Wallenstein, ironically enough in light of current developments);

—and...

Oh, it went on and on. True, Morris would admit— even Uriel would—Emperor Ferdinand II of Austria did not really make the roster of Great Evil Rulers of History. He just wasn't on a par with such as Tamerlane and Hitler and Stalin. But he was certainly a contender for the middleweight title of Rulers You'd Like to See Drop Dead. A narrow-minded, not overly intelligent man, who could invariably be counted on to follow the stupidest and most brutal policy offered to him by his multitude of advisers and courtiers.

Yes, stupid as well as brutal. A stupidity that was evidenced in the fact that the mission Morris was on was designed to break Bohemia away from the Habsburg empire again—permanently, this time, if all went well—and the instrument of that break would be the very man whom Ferdinand himself had raised up from obscure origins because he was the most brutally capable mercenary captain of the day and age.

Albrecht Wenzel Eusebius von Wallenstein. Born in the year 1583 into a family of the minor Protestant Bohemian nobility, and orphaned at the age of thirteen. Today he was the greatest landowner in Bohemia—possibly in the entire Austrian empire except for Ferdinand himself—as well as the duke of Friedland, a member of the Estate of Princes of the Empire, recognized as the duke of Mecklenburg by the Habsburgs (if not, of course, by the Swedish king Gustav Adolf who today actually controlled Mecklenburg), and prince of Sagan.

Thinking about Wallenstein—and the big ladle Judith had stuffed into one of their trunks—Morris grunted.

"What do you think of him, Uriel?"

Abrabanel had no difficulty understanding the subject. "Wallenstein? Hard to say." He paused for a moment, marshalling his thoughts.

"On the one hand, he is probably the most completely amoral man in the world. I doubt if there is any crime he would shrink from, if he felt it would advance his purposes."

"No kidding." Morris scowled. "He's the stinking bastard who ordered his Croat cavalry to attack our school last year. Tried to slaughter all of our children!"

Uriel nodded. "Indeed. On the other hand... There is a lot to be said for him, as well. It's no accident, you know, that he wound up becoming something of a folk hero in German legend."

He barked a little laugh. "Not an unmixed admiration, of course! Still, what I can tell of reading your books from the future, the Germans came to grudgingly admire the man in the decades and centuries after his death, much as the French never stopped grudgingly admiring Napoleon. The German poet and playwright Schiller even wrote several plays—in the next century, that would be—about him. Odd, really—a Corsican folk hero for the French, and a Bohemian one for the Germans."

The scowl was still on Morris' face. "Big deal," he

said, adding somewhat unkindly: "That's just because the Frogs and the Krauts don't have too many genuine heroes to pick from."

Uriel's easy smile came. "Such terrible chauvinism! Of course, that term does come from a French word, so I suppose there's some truth to your wisecrack. Still—"

The smile didn't fade, but the old spy's dark eyes seem to darken still further. "Do not let your animosities get the best of you, Morris. This much is also true of Wallenstein: a peasant on one of his estates is in a better situation than peasants anywhere else in the Austrian empire. Wallenstein is shrewd enough to know when *not* to gouge, and he even fosters and encourages what you would call scientific farming. He opposed the Edict of Restitution and, by all accounts, is not much given—if at all, beyond the needs of diplomacy—to religious persecution. If he is amoral, he is not *im*-moral."

"They say he believes in astrology," grumbled Morris.

"Indeed, he is quite superstitious." Uriel's smile broadened, becoming almost sly. "On the other hand, they also say he treats his wife very well."

Morris grunted again. "Um. Well, okay. That's something, I guess."

They heard the sounds of a horse nearing and twisted in their saddles to look backward. The motions were easy and relaxed, since both men were experienced riders. In Morris' case, from an adult lifetime of being an enthusiast for pack-riding; in Uriel's, from an adult lifetime that had had more in the way of rambunctious excitement—including several desperate flights on horseback across the countryside—than most city-dwelling Jews of the time ever experienced.

The same could not be said for the man approaching them, and neither Morris nor Uriel could restrain themselves from smiling. Jason Gotkin, though in his early twenties, was not at all comfortable on horseback—and showed it. He rode his mount as gingerly, and with the same air of uncertainty, as an apprentice liontamer enters a lion's cage.

Seeing their expressions, Jason flushed a little. When he finally came alongside—it might be better to say, edged his horse alongside with all the sureness of a cadet docking a boat—his words were spoken in something of a hiss.

"Look, I was getting a degree in computer science and was trying to decide between a life spent as a software engineer or a rabbi. I was *not* planning to become a cowboy."

Uriel's smile widened into a grin. Among the uptime hobbies that Uriel had adopted since the Ring of Fire, reading westerns was one of them. He was particularly fond of Donald Hamilton, Luke Short and Louis L'Amour.

"I should hope not! Leaving aside your pitiful manner on horseback, you can't—what's that expression?—hit the broadside of a barn. With a rifle, much less a revolver."

"Software engineer," Jason hissed again. "*Rabbi.*" He scowled faintly. "The average rabbi does not pack a gun. Not even in New York—and wouldn't, even if it weren't for the Sullivan Act."

Morris' gaze slid away from Jason and drifted back toward the rear of the not-so-little caravan. There, almost at the very end, was the small group of horsemen centered around the figure of young Dunash Abrabanel. None of them rode a horse any better than Jason. But, unlike Jason, all of them were armed to the teeth. They looked like a caricature of highwaymen, in fact, they had so many firearms festooned upon their bodies and saddles.

Morris sighed. "We're nearing Bohemian territory, if we're not already in it. They're going to have to hide the guns, Jason. Whatever Wallenstein's promises, until he carries out his rebellion Imperial law still applies."

"Either that or agree to pretend they aren't Jews," grunted Uriel. The humor that had been on his face was gone, now. This was a sore subject with him, and one on which he and Dunash's little group had already clashed several times. Many times in his life, Uriel had passed himself off as a gentile of one sort or another. Once, he'd even successfully passed himself off as a Spanish hidalgo.

"Stupid!" he said, almost snarling. "They are no more observant—not any longer—than I am. Much less my brother Balthazar. And even in the days when we were, neither of us hesitated to do what was necessary. So why do they insist on flaunting their Jewishness, when it is pointless?"

Morris started to sigh again, but managed to restrain himself. Jason was apprehensive enough as it was, without Morris making his own nervousness about their project apparent.

It was hard. Even in the age from which Morris had come, the urbane and cosmopolitan world of America at the turn of the twenty-first century, there had been divisions between observant and non-observant Jews, leaving aside the disagreements between the various branches of Judaism. In the seventeenth century, those tensions were far more extreme.

Not, perhaps, for the Ashkenazim of central and eastern Europe, cloistered as they were—corralled by the gentiles surrounding them, more properly speaking—into their tight ghettos and shtetls. There, rabbinical influence and control was powerful. Even enforced by law, since in most places—Prague being no exception—the gentile authorities gave the rabbinate jurisdiction over the members of the Jewish ghettos. But for the Sephardim, since the expulsion from Iberia, it was far more difficult. The Sephardic Jews had been scattered to the winds, and although many of them had managed to retain their traditions and customs and ritual observances, many others had not. So, the issue of how to handle nonobservant Jews—any number of whom had even officially converted to Christianity—was always difficult. In practice, Amsterdam being one of the major exceptions, most Sephardic rabbis and observant communities had adopted a fairly tolerant and patient attitude.

Morris and Judith Roth were themselves Ashkenazim, but their attitudes had far more in common with the cosmopolitan Sephardim they'd encountered since the Ring of Fire than the Ashkenazim of this day and age. And now, unwittingly, the arrival of a half-dozen modern Jews into the seventeenth century had introduced a new element into the equation: the twentieth-century ideology of Zionism.

"Zionism," at least, using the term loosely. Not even Dunash proposed to launch a campaign to create the state of Israel in the middle of the seventeenth century. His own Abrabanel clan would squash any such notion instantly, since their own survival and well-being depended largely on the tolerance of the Ottoman Empire. Murad IV, the current sultan ruling in Istanbul, bore not the slightest resemblance to Lord Balfour. "Murad the Mad," they called him, and for good reason. Though astonishingly capable for a ruler who was obviously a sociopath, one of his principal amusements was wandering about Istanbul personally executing inhabitants he discovered violating his recently decreed hardcore Islamic regulations.

So, the zeal of Dunash and his young comrades had been turned elsewhere. Toward the great mass of Jews living in eastern Europe, and the alleviation of their plight. They had been more enthusiastic about Wallenstein's scheme than anyone. Even Wallenstein himself, Morris suspected. If a Jewish homeland could not be created in the Levant, who was to say that somewhere in eastern Europe...

It was a tangled mess. Morris had supported the state of Israel, was a U.S. army veteran himself, and had no philosophical attachment to pacifism. But he also did not share Dunash's simple faith in the efficacy of violence as a way of solving political problems. In the end, he thought tolerance and a willingness to accept a compromise were far more practical methods than shooting a gun.

Not, admittedly, that shooting a gun isn't sometimes necessary to get the other guy to accept a compromise, he reminded himself.

He put the thought into words. "Look at it this way. Maybe having them along will help the others involved see things the right way."

Uriel looked skeptical. *"Pappenheim? And what do you propose for our next trick? Intimidate a wolf with a stick?"*

Pappenheim himself came out to meet them, as they neared the outskirts of Prague. Wallenstein's chief general rode down the line of the little caravan, inspecting them coldly. Looking every bit, Morris thought . . .

Like a wolf on horseback.

There was no other way to describe him. Pappenheim was just plain scary. Melissa Mailey had a copy of C.V. Wedgwood's classic *The Thirty Years War*, and Morris had read the passage in it describing Pappenheim. In fact, he'd reread the passage in the copy of the book which he now owned himself, produced by a seventeenth-century printing press, just before leaving on this expedition. Morris had an excellent memory, and now, watching Pappenheim trotting down the line, he called it up:

The heaviest loss Wallenstein had suffered at Lützen was that of Pappenheim. Reckless of his men, arrogant and insubordinate, Pappenheim was nevertheless the soldier's hero: tireless, restless, the first in attack, the last in retreat. Stories of his fantastic courage were told round the camp fires and he had a legend before he was dead—the hundred scars that he boasted, the birthmark like crossed swords which glowed red when he was angry. He flashes past against that squalid background, the Rupert of the German war. His loyalty to Wallenstein, his affection and admiration, had been of greater effect in inspiring the troops than Wallenstein probably realized. The general owed his power to his control over the army alone, and the loss of Pappenheim was irreparable.

But Pappenheim hadn't died at the battle of Lützen in this universe, because that battle had never been fought. He was still alive, still as vigorous as ever—and still Wallenstein's right hand man. Come out to meet Wallenstein himself, who was hidden in one of the covered wagons since his trip to Grantville had been kept a secret.

Morris watched as Pappenheim exchanged a few words with Wallenstein, who had pushed aside for a moment the coverings of his wagon. Then, watched as Pappenheim inspected the rest of the caravan, examining the peculiar new allies whom Wallenstein had brought with him.

Pappenheim spent not much time studying the men from the Unity of Brethren. Those, he was familiar with. Though now defeated and scattered, the spiritual descendants of Huss and Jan Zizka were a force to be reckoned with. One which had often, in times past, proven their capacity to break aristocratic forces on the field of battle.

He spent more time studying Dunash Abrabanel and his little band of Jewish would-be liberators. Pappenheim wasn't exactly sneering, but there was enough in the way of arrogant condescension in his face to cause Dunash and his followers to glare at him.

Morris decided he'd better go back there and defuse the situation. With the ease of an experienced horseman, he was soon at Pappenheim's side.

"Is there a problem, General?" he asked, keeping his tone level and mild.

Pappenheim swiveled to gaze at him. Up close,

Morris could see the famous birthmark. It didn't really look like crossed swords, he thought. Just like another scar.

"You are the jeweler, yes?" Since it wasn't really a question, Morris didn't reply.

Pappenheim grunted. "There are times I think the Duke of Friedland is mad. Nor do I have his faith in astrologers. Still . . ."

Suddenly, his face broke into a grin. It was a cold sort of grin, without much in the way of humor in it.

"Who is to say? It is a mad world, after all."

2

"Well, will it do?" asked Len, a bit gruffly.

"It will do splendidly," Uriel assured him. He cocked an eye at Morris and Jason. "Yes?"

"Oh, sure," said Morris, looking around the cavernous room that served the—small palace? mansion? it was hard to say—as something of a combination between an entry hall and a gathering place. Not for the first time, he was struck by the conspicuous consumption that was so typical of Europe's nobility of the time.

He reminded himself that there had been plenty of conspicuous consumption by rich people in the universe they came from, also. But at least they didn't—well, not usually—have people living in hovels next door. Not to mention—

He moved over to one of the windows and gazed out at the street beyond, almost glaring. Across the narrow passageway rose the wall of Prague's ghetto, sealing off the Jewish inhabitants from the rest of the city. The *Josefov*, that ghetto was called. Somewhere around fifteen thousand people teemed in its cramped quarters, the largest ghetto in Europe. It was quite possibly the largest urban concentration of Jews anywhere in the world, in the year 1633, except maybe Istanbul.

Jason came to stand next to him. The young man's gaze seemed filled with more in the way of dread—anxiety, at least—than Morris' anger.

Morris smiled crookedly. It was hard to blame Jason, of course. Morris could glare at the injustice embodied in that ghetto wall till the cows came home. *He* wasn't the one he was trying to wheedle and cajole and finagle into becoming a new rabbi for its inhabitants. A Reform rabbi-to-be, with precious little in the way of theological training, for a community that was solidly orthodox and had a long tradition of prestigious rabbis to guide them. Rabbi Loew, in fact—the one reputed by legend to have invented the golem—had been Prague's chief rabbi not so long ago. He'd died only a quarter of a century earlier.

"They don't even *use* the term 'Orthodox,'" Jason muttered. "In this day and age, there's nothing 'unorthodox' to give the term any meaning. In our universe, the term didn't come into existence until after the Reform movement started in the nineteenth century. In the here and now, Jews are Jews. Period."

He gave Morris a look of appeal. "They'll just declare me a heretic, Morris, and cast me out. So what's the point?"

Morris jabbed a stiff finger at the street separating their building from the ghetto. "You're *already* out of the ghetto, Jason. So how can they 'cast' you out?" He glanced at the two gentiles in the room. "That's why I asked Len and Ellie to find us a place just outside of the Josefov."

Jason gave the two people mentioned a questioning look. "Is there going to be any kind of . . . you, know. Trouble about this?"

Len shrugged. "From who? Don Balthasar de Marradas? Yeah, sure, he's officially in charge here in Prague—so he says, anyway. But most of the soldiers and officials in the city are Wallenstein's people, from what Ellie and I can tell. And the ones who aren't are too pre-occupied dealing with Wallenstein to be worrying about whether a few Jews are living outside the ghetto."

"They wouldn't know the difference anyway," added Ellie. "Not with you guys."

She hooked a thumb in the direction of the Hradcany. "Don't think they won't learn soon enough that some more Americans have arrived. They're not *that* preoccupied. Whatever else is backward about the seventeenth century, spying sure as hell isn't. By the end of the week—latest—Marradas will have his fucking stoolies watching you, just like they do us."

Morris found Ellie's coarse language refreshing, for some odd reason. He was one of the few people in Grantville who'd always liked Ellie Anderson, and had never found her brash and vulgar personality off-putting. And, in their current circumstances, he thought her *go-fuck-yourself* attitude toward the world was probably . . .

Dead on the money.

"Dead on the money," he murmured, repeating the thought aloud. "Stop worrying, Jason. Ellie's right. They'll spy on us, but what they'll see is Americans, not Jews."

"What about Dunash and the others?"

Morris shrugged. "What about them? The plan is for them to find quarters in the ghetto anyway, as soon as possible. They'll be officially coming here every day to work in my new jewelry establishment. Even in the here and now, Jews are allowed out of the ghetto on legitimate business."

"Especially when the soldiers stationed in the area to check stuff like that are handpicked by Pappenheim," Ellie added cheerfully. "Nobody fucks with Pappenheim. I mean, *nobody*. The one and only time a Habsburg official gave Pappenheim a hard time since he arrived here, Pappenheim beat him half to death. The way the story goes, he dumped the fuckhead out of his chair, broke up the chair and used one of the legs to whup on him."

Morris couldn't help smiling. Pappenheim was scary, true enough. But if there was one lesson Morris had drawn from his studies of history, it was that bureaucrats, in the end, killed more people than soldiers. Way more. If Morris had to make a choice between this century's equivalents of General Heinz Guderian and Adolf Eichmann, he'd pick Guderian any day of the week.

No "if" about it, really. He *had* been given the choice, and he'd made it. Whatever new world Wallenstein and his ruthless generals made out of Bohemia and eastern Europe, Morris didn't think it could be any worse than the world the Habsburgs and their officials had made—not to mention the Polish *szlachta* and the Russian *boyars*.

Wallenstein, whatever else, was looking to the future. He'd get rid of the second serfdom that was engulfing

eastern Europe and its accompanying oppression of
Jews, if for no other reason, because he wanted to
build a powerful empire for himself. Of that, Mike
Stearns was sure—and Morris agreed with him. Wallenstein had said nothing to Stearns—or Torstensson,
Gustav Adolf's emissary in the negotiations—about his
plans beyond seizing power in Bohemia and Moravia. But neither of them doubted that Wallenstein
had further ambitions. He'd try to take Silesia, for a
certainty—he was already the ruler of Sagan, one of
the Silesian principalities—and probably other parts
of Poland and the Ukraine.

In short, he was—or hoped to be—a seventeenth-
century Napoleon in the making. That could obviously
pose problems in the future. But for Morris, as for
most Jews, Napoleon hadn't simply been a conqueror
and a tyrant. He'd also been the man who broke
Germany's surviving traits of medievalism, had granted
civil rights to the Jews—and had had a short way with
would-be pogromists.

Jason was still worrying. "If they know we're
Americans—even if they don't realize we're Jews—
won't that cause trouble in its own right?"

Ellie's grin was lopsided and a tad sarcastic. "Where
the hell have you been for the last two years? In
the here and now, people don't give a fuck about
'patriotism.' Ain't no such animal. You're loyal to a
dynasty—or work for one, at least—not a country.
Wallenstein's paying us the big bucks—he is, too, don't
think Len and me didn't stick it to him good—and
so everybody assumes we're his people."

Morris nodded. "I don't think the word 'patriotism'

has even been invented yet. She's got the right of it, Jason. The Habsburgs will be suspicious of anyone connected with Wallenstein, right now, because of the strains between them. But until and unless they're ready to move against him, they won't meddle much with us."

"Nothing dramatic and open, anyway," added Uriel. "Though I'd keep an eye out for a stiletto in the back in dark corners. And we need to make sure we hire a trustworthy cook or we'll need to hire a food-taster." He grimaced. "Food-tasters are expensive."

Jason gave Morris a meaningful look. Morris sighed. "Oh, all right, Jason. We'll start eating kosher."

He wasn't happy about it. Still . . .

The dietary restrictions of Orthodox Judaism irritated Morris, but they weren't ultimately that important to him. Compared to such things as separate seating for women in the synagogue, no driving on Shabbat, family purity laws, women not being allowed to participate in the service, the divinity of the oral law—oh, it went on and on—keeping kashrut barely made the list.

"It's a good idea, Morris," said Jason softly. "At least that'll remove one obstacle. And the truth is, it's a safer way to eat anyway, in a time when nobody's ever heard of FDA inspectors."

Then, he looked faintly alarmed. Morris chuckled harshly. "Yeah, I know. You can't cook worth a damn, kosher or not. Neither can I."

Morris looked toward the bank of windows on a far wall. Somewhere beyond, over one hundred and fifty miles as the crow flies, lay Grantville—where his wife was getting ready to join him with the rest of the workforce that was moving to Prague.

"Judith is gonna kill me," he predicted gloomily.

"Nonsense," pronounced Uriel. "Hire cooks from the ghetto. You have no choice anyway, under existing law. It is illegal for a Jew to hire Christian servants—and you'll need servants also, living in this almost-a-palace. Or Judith will *surely* murder you."

"That's a good idea," Jason chimed in eagerly. "It'll help dispel suspicions of us, too, if people from the ghetto get to know us better. If you have cooks and servants coming in and out of the house every day, as well as jewelers and gemcutters coming to the workplace..."

That just made Morris feel gloomier. "Great. So now I've got to be an exhibit in a zoo, too?"

"Yes," said Uriel firmly.

CHAPTER III: *Fianchetto*

June 1633

1

"Please come in, Bishop Comenius, all of you." Morris waved his hand toward the many armchairs in the very large living room.

Morris still thought of it as a "living room," even though he suspected that "salon" was a more appropriate term. Despite having now lived in this mansion in Prague for a number of weeks, Morris was still adjusting mentally to the reality of his new situation. Three months ago, by the standards of the seventeenth century, he had been a well-off man. Today, after the results reported by his partners Antonio

Nasi and Gerhard Rueckert in the letter Morris had received two days earlier, he was a wealthy man—by the standards of any century.

Seeing the entourage Comenius had brought with him and who were now filing into the room—a room that was already occupied by a large number of people—Morris was glad that the room was so enormous. It was a very proper-looking room, too, since he and Judith never used it as a "living room"—for that, they maintained a much smaller and more comfortable room on the second floor of the mansion—and the small army of servants they had recently acquired kept it spotlessly clean.

That was another thing Morris was still trying to get accustomed to. Servants. And not just a cleaning lady who came in once a week, either, but a dozen people who came and went every day. In fact, they would have *lived* in the mansion except that, following Uriel and Jason's advice—which was the law, anyway—Morris had hired exclusively Jewish cooks and servants. By the laws still in force in Prague, they were required to return to the ghetto every night, just as they were required to wear distinctive insignia identifying themselves as Jews whenever they left the ghetto.

Morris did not share the ferocious egalitarianism of such people as Gretchen Richter and her Committees of Correspondence, although he was, quietly, one of her chief financial backers. He wasn't even as egalitarian as some of the more diehard members of the United Mine Workers and their growing number of spin-off unions. Still, he found the situation somewhat embarrassing—and was growing angrier all the time at the restrictions placed on Jews in his new day and age. The restrictions were being ignored in his case, true, since Morris fell into the informal category of a "court Jew." But they still left a smoldering resentment.

Seeing the last man filing into the salon after Bishop Comenius, Morris felt the resentment vanish.

"Hey, Red! Long time. I was wondering if you were still alive."

Red Sybolt squinted at him. "Hi, Morris. Oh, yeah, I'm still around. Still kicking, too." He jerked a thumb at the very large man by his side. "Hell, even Jan here is still alive, which is a real miracle given how crazy he is. Things got hairy now and then, especially in Saxony, but the worst that happened is my glasses got busted. I still haven't managed to scrounge up a new pair."

Morris had always liked Bobby Gene "Red" Sybolt. He wasn't sure why, exactly, since on the face of it Red and he shouldn't have gotten along all that well. Just for starters, Red was one of those union activists who, though not really a socialist himself, had been influenced by socialists he'd run across in the course of his activities before the Ring of Fire. In his case, by the Socialist Workers Party, which had, off and on, had a certain presence in northern West Virginia going back to the late 1940s. One of the things Red had picked up from the SWP was a hostility toward Zionism. And while Morris had been uneasy about some of the policies of the state of Israel toward Palestinians, both he and his wife Judith had always been supporters of Israel.

But Red was such a friendly man that it was hard for anyone to dislike him. Even Quentin Underwood, the hardnosed manager of the mine Red had worked in for a while, was known to allow that "the damn commie" was personally a decent enough fellow. And Morris knew that Red's anti-Zionism was not a veiled form of anti-Semitism. It was simply a political opposition to what Red considered a colonial-settler state. As he'd once put it to Morris:

"Where the hell did Europe get off exporting its anti-Semitism problem onto the backs of the Arabs? I got no problem with the Jews having a homeland. Since it was the Germans massacred 'em, they should have been given Bavaria. Or Prussia. Instead, the British offered them a choice between Palestine, Kenya and Madagascar. Guess what those all have in common? Natives of the swarthy persuasion, that's what. Typical British imperialism! Lord Balfour said it all: 'We will create for ourselves a loyal Jewish Ulster in the Middle East.'"

Morris had disagreed, of course. But it had been a friendly enough argument, as his arguments with Red usually were. And, besides, in one of those odd quirks of human personality which made the real world such an interesting place, the radical Red Sybolt had also been the only inhabitant of Grantville before the Ring of Fire except Morris himself who had been genuinely interested and knowledgeable about gems and jewelry.

Red claimed that was due to the residual bad influence of his ex-wife; Morris suspected it was due to the residual regrets Red had concerning the life style he'd chosen for himself. The life of an itinerant union organizer and "hell-raiser" did not lead to expansive bank accounts. Red had spent many hours in Morris' jewelry store discussing gemstones, but he'd never bought so much as a single gold chain.

"Did the faceted jewelry make as big of a splash as I told you they would?"

Morris smiled wryly. In another of those little ironies of life, it had been Red Sybolt who brought to his attention the fact that faceted jewelry was first introduced into the world in the *second* half of the seventeenth century. Simple faceting and polishing had been done for a long time, to be sure—which meant that the needed tools and experienced workers would be available—but the art of gemcutting had not advanced much in almost two centuries. People in 1633 were still accustomed to nothing fancier than polished stones and, at most, the simple design of the "Old Single Cut," which dated back to the fifteenth century. The first real advance in gemcutting wouldn't come until the middle of the seventeenth century, with the introduction of the Mazarin Cut.

In short, Red pointed out, Morris had had the great luck of arriving in the right place at the right time— riding just ahead of the wave. The tools and skills were in place, all that was needed was the addition of Morris' knowledge. For a few years, if he played it right, Morris and his two new partners would be in a position to make a fortune.

So it had proved—as the letter upstairs verified. It had taken Morris and his partners a year before they could begin producing modern-style faceted gems. Morris knew the theory, yes; but he had the skills of an uptime jeweler, which was not the same thing as an experienced gemcutter. They'd had to hire and train seventeenth-century jewelers, which had taken time. Fortunately, two of the jewelers they'd taken on had turned out to be very adept at grasping the new ideas. So adept that both of them had been given hefty shares of stock in the company, lest they become disgruntled and take their skills elsewhere.

"Yes, you were right." Morris grinned. "Sure you don't want some stock? My offer's still good."

Red shook his head fiercely. "Get thee behind me, Satan! Me? What kind of respectable agitator owns stock in a company which is no doubt plunderin' the poor?" But he was smiling as he said it, and, after seating himself in one of the expensive armchairs, luxuriated visibly in its comfort.

"Okay," he admitted, "plunderin' the idle rich is probably more accurate. Still, I wouldn't feel comfortable with it." He gave Morris a nearsighted squint. "Mind you, I *will* expect some hefty donations to the cause."

Morris looked around the room, all of whose inhabitants except him were now seated. "*Which* cause, Red?" he asked mildly. "I see at least... what is it? Four or five present."

Red's smile widened. "Bit of a problem, isn't it?" His own eyes moved across the room, and if he was nearsighted and without glasses, he seemed to have no problem at all assessing its occupants.

"Yup, quite a collection. You got your Committees of Correspondence—that's me—your Brethren, and I figure at least three different varieties of Zionism. Not to mention the other budding exploiters of the downtrodden—hey, Len, Ellie, how's it going?—and, lounging just outside the front door, I figure at least two flavors of military dictatorship we poor lambs seem to have allied ourselves with. Three, if you count that pig Holk, even though he's too stupid to even make a respectable fascist."

At the mention of Holk, Morris grimaced. So did Jan Billek.

"His troops have been ravaging northern Bohemia just as badly as they did Saxony," Jan growled, in his heavily accented English. "Even though they are supposed to be 'protecting' it."

Morris had no trouble believing him. In preparation for his relocation to Prague, he'd studied what he could find in Grantville's libraries as well as Judith's genealogical data. One of Grantville's bibliophiles had donated a copy of some plays written by the eighteenth-century German writer Schiller. Morris had read the following passage in one of them, *Wallenstein's Camp*:

> *In Bayreuth, in the Vogtland, in*
> *Westphalia;*
> *Wherever we have survived—*
> *Our children and grandchildren,*
> *Will still be telling stories,*
> *After hundreds and hundreds of years,*
> *About Holk and his hordes.*

Heinrich Holk was one of the major military commanders of the Habsburg forces now stationed in Bohemia. He was the worst type of condottiere in the Thirty Years War—a breed of men who were none too savory to begin with. A one-eyed, primitive, drunken mass murderer; a scourge who persecuted and mistreated the people he was charged with protecting; and a dishonor to the imperial army. Holk, born into the family of a Danish Protestant official, had not only changed his allegiance several times during the course of the Thirty Years War, but also his faith—which, admittedly, was nothing especially unusual for the time. Wallenstein had done the same, early in his career, converting from his native Protestantism to Catholicism in order to ingratiate himself with the Habsburgs.

Unlike Wallenstein or such men as Tilly and Pappenheim, however, Holk did not have any significant victories to his credit. His military prowess was demonstrated only by raids, plundering and atrocities, and he had been defeated on several occasions—by Wilhelm Christian of Brandenburg near Magdeburg, in 1630; later the same year by the Swedes near Demmin; and again by the Swedes at Werben in 1631. Not to mention that Holk had failed to bring his troops to meet Tilly's in time for the battle of Breitenfeld, which had been partly responsible for Tilly's defeat there at the hands of Gustavus Adolphus.

Unfortunately, Holk's services were much in demand, because whatever his multitude of faults Holk was also a thoroughly competent commander in the major criterion by which that was usually judged in the Thirty Years War: he could hold together a random heap of mercenaries with consistent firmness. But he did so by making his army a refuge for the dregs of loot-hungry, brutal soldiery.

Morris was still a bit mystified why Wallenstein accepted the crude Holk as one of his top subordinates. As a rule, Wallenstein was a better judge of men—at least their capabilities, if not their morality. Morris thought it was probably due to the simple fact that Holk seemed to admire Wallenstein, which he demonstrated by imitating his master in Holk's own gross and coarse manner. Like Wallenstein, he threatened to punish people "through taking them by the head"—which meant hanging them, in the slang of the time. And when a subordinate reacted sluggishly to orders, Holk accused him of having the "inborn speed of Saturn"—another one of Wallenstein's favorite expressions.

Morris knew that in the history of the universe they had come from, after Pappenheim's death at the battle of Lützen, Holk had become Wallenstein's prime factotum. Whatever else, Wallenstein had been able to assign tasks to Holk with the certain knowledge that whatever could be done by harshness and brutality would be done well. Or thoroughly, at least. But without Pappenheim's ability to generate genuine loyalty in the army, and Pappenheim's sense of strategy, Wallenstein had soon fallen foul of the Byzantine factionalism within the Habsburg forces. Not that Wallenstein hadn't been guilty of the same factionalism himself, of course—but with Holk instead of Pappenheim to rely on, he had been outmatched.

"What's Wallenstein going to do about him?" demanded Red. "If this keeps up, Morris, there won't be much left of northern Bohemia. Wallenstein—there, at least—will be 'King of Nothing.'"

Morris almost snarled: *Why ask ME?*

But he didn't, because he knew the answer, as much as it discomfited him. In the months since he'd arrived, Morris had indeed become Wallenstein's "court Jew." It was an odd and informal position, but one which was not all that uncommon in the Europe of the day. Despite all the restrictions and sometimes-savage persecution of Jews, most of the European courts had a few wealthy and prominent Jews in their entourage.

For the most part, of course, that was because Jewish money and medical skill was wanted by Europe's monarchs and high nobility. But there was more to it than that, at least for some of Europe's Christian rulers, especially the smartest ones. Being "outside the loop," their Jewish courtiers could often be relied upon for better and more objective advice. Queen Elizabeth of England, when she'd been on the throne, had often consulted with her Jewish doctor Roderigo Lopez on her diplomatic as well as medical affairs.

And . . . from what Morris could tell, Wallenstein even seemed to *like* him. It was hard to be sure, of course, with a man like Wallenstein. But Edith Wild had told Morris that Wallenstein spoke well of him in private. And Edith—talk about miracles!—had somehow managed to become one of the few people whom Wallenstein trusted. Edith herself thought that was because, after an initial period of hesitation—even veiled hostility—Wallenstein's wife had taken a liking to her. If not for her own sake, then because Edith was keeping her husband alive. And, in fact, under Edith's bullying regimen, Wallenstein's shaky health had improved. Rather dramatically, in fact. Edith even managed to intimidate Wallenstein's pestiferous astrologers into not contradicting her medical and dietary advice. (And there was a true miracle. Seventeenth-century astrologers, as a rule, made the "snake-oil salesmen" of Morris' time look like downright saints and wise men.) Finally—oh, the world was a wondrous place—it had turned out that Wallenstein had developed a fanatic enthusiasm for the multitude of Agatha Christie mysteries that Edith had brought with her to Prague. *All that keeps me alive!* he'd once sworn to Morris, to all appearances dead seriously.

"I'll talk to him," Morris said gruffly. "Though I'm not sure if he'll listen."

"What *is* he up to, anyway?" Red asked. "There are rumors flying all over, but nobody really knows what he's planning."

Morris shrugged. "Don't ask me. Uriel might be able to give you a good educated guess, but he had to go back to Grantville on mysterious business of his own. Whenever I ask—very diffidently, let me tell you—Wallenstein just gets grimmer than usual and more or less tells me to mind my own business. 'Soon,' is all he'll say."

Morris had been about to sit down himself, but instead he moved over to one of the windows and gazed up at the Hradcany across the river. He couldn't see Wallenstein's own palace, from here, since it was perched in the Malá Strana at the bottom of the hill instead of the summit. But St. Vitus Cathedral, which dominated the Hradcany, always reminded him of Wallenstein. For all of Wallenstein's forward-looking temperament, there was ultimately something Gothic about the man.

Ellie Anderson seemed to be sharing his thoughts. "Fucking vampire," he heard her mutter.

For some odd reason, the image of Wallenstein lurking in his palace like Count Dracula cheered Morris up. Granted, Dracula was a monster. But at least he wasn't *stupid*.

Morris turned away from the window. "Enough of that. Wallenstein will do whatever he'll do, and whenever he chooses to do it. We have no control over that, so let's concentrate on what we can control. Influence, at least."

He knew why Comenius and Billek had come. Comenius, to pay his official regards, since the central figure in the Church of the Brethren had just arrived in Prague. But he was really here to lend his authority to Jan Billek—and Red's—long-standing proposal with regard to the paramilitary forces that were being quietly organized to support Wallenstein when the time came.

Morris had wrestled with his decision for days. More precisely, he had wrestled with his reluctance to have a confrontation with his own people. But, now, the decision came into clear and hard focus. He braced himself for a brawl.

"Red and Billek are right, Dunash. Your people and those of the Brethren should form a joint unit. It's stupid to do otherwise."

Dunash Abrabanel shot to his feet. "Our interests will be pushed aside—as always!"

"Shut up, you—" Morris caught himself, almost laughing, before he added: *young whippersnapper!*

Still, his jaws were tight. "What the hell do *you* know about it, Abrabanel?" He glared at Dunash and the young Jews sitting around him—all except Jason Gotkin, the only young up-time Jew in their midst, who was seated off to the side, a bit isolated from the others.

"What do *any* of you know about military affairs?" Morris demanded. "In the world I came from, the worst enemy the Jewish people ever faced was not defeated by Israel. Nor could he have been, even if Israel had existed at the time. He was defeated by the great armies of the United States, England and Russia—all of whom had Jews serving in them. The

Russians, especially. There were over two hundred Jewish generals in the Red Army. Berlin was first penetrated by Russian soldiers under the command of one of them—and Auschwitz was liberated by another."

He lapsed into one of his rare uses of profanity. "*So shut the fuck up!* Not one of you has any real idea what to do with those guns you festoon yourselves with, like a bunch of would-be bandidos. I leave aside what Pappenheim had to say."

The one and only time that Pappenheim had observed Dunash's band of youngsters attempting what they called a "military exercise," his comments had been vulgar, brief and to the point. Most of which he had uttered as he trotted his horse away, shaking his head in disgust.

"Look, Dunash, he's right," said Red mildly. "The truth is, the Brethren aren't really what you'd call 'seasoned soldiers,' either. But at least they're familiar with firearms, and a lot of them have seen some actual fighting. Most of all—" He hesitated a moment, gauging Dunash's temper. "Most of all, they aren't arrogant."

He left unspoken the obvious implication: *like you are.* "That's why they've agreed to let some of Wallenstein's officers train them."

Dunash said nothing, but his jaws were even tighter than Morris' felt. Red kept on, talking smoothly. Morris decided to let him handle it. Whatever Morris sometimes thought of Red's political opinions, the fact remained that Red—not Morris—was the experienced organizer in the group.

"Look, I'm not too fond of the situation either. Neither is Jan or any of the Brethren. But the truth is that Wallenstein—probably Pappenheim, actually—seems to have been careful in their selection of officers. They're really not too bad."

Jan Billek nodded. "Two are quite good. I even have hopes of converting one of them."

"And look on the bright side," Red continued. "Officers be damned. We'll be the grunts with the actual guns in our hands, if push comes to shove. Neither Wallenstein nor Pappenheim—sure as hell not the officers directly over us—have any doubt at all what'll happen if they order us to do something we don't want to do."

He and Jan exchanged a meaningful glance. Morris' anger faded, replaced by his earlier good humor. "Ha!" he barked. "Red, should I start calling you 'commissar'?"

Red smiled a little sheepishly. "Well...the word doesn't mean anything, in the here and now. But, yeah." He gave Billek another glance. "Actually, you oughta apply the title to Jan. He's really the one all the Brethren soldiers listen to."

Jan's face was stolid, but Morris thought he detected a little gleam somewhere in the back of his eyes. "Indeed," he said. "And why should they not? Good Brethren, so they understand the difference between 'orders' and 'what should be done.'"

Suddenly, to Morris' surprise, Jason Gotkin spoke up. "Do it, Dunash. They're right and you're wrong—and the truth is, I think it'll help you recruit more Jews from the ghetto, anyway."

Dunash seemed to be even more surprised that Morris was.

"How so? An exclusively Jewish force—"

astonished by Comenius' accurate asses[s]
[th]e American strangers whom he had neve[r]
[me]re. Obviously, the Brethren (with Red's help[)]
[had a]n excellent espionage service in all but nam[e.]
[Still], it wasn't *quite* accurate. Except for a few place[s]
[lik]e Amsterdam, most rabbis were loath to proclai[m]
[s]omeone an actual "heretic," since Jews didn't plac[e]
[on] the same emphasis that Christians did on doctrina[l]
purity. What most of them would have said abou[t]
Morris was that he was "practically an apikoros"—a[n]
uncomplimentary term indicating someone who wa[s]
much too loose and self-willed in his interpretatio[n]
and application of customs and observances.

"Yet in the world they came from," Comenius con[-]
tinued, "it was people such as this who built a natio[n]
which, in the fullness of time, provided a sanctuar[y]
for my people as well as yours. Most of the world'[s]
Brethren wound up living in that 'United States,' a[s]
did the single largest grouping of the world's Jews[.]
There is a lesson there for any of God's children, i[n]
[w]hatever manner they see that God. Unless you are
[b]lind. Which I am not. Freedom of religion must be [a]
[th]e banner for both of us—a banner which, by its [na-]
[t]ure, must be held jointly."

[H]e sat down. "That is my pledge—and the pledge [of]
[th]e Unity of Brethren. You will not be 'buried.' [Un-]
[les]s you are buried by our enemies, along with [our-]
[sel]ves."

[The] decision hung in the balance. Then—and this
[surprised] Morris more than anything that happened
[that even]ing—Dunash turned to Jason.

[You'l]l be our rabbi, if anyone is to be. You are
[willing]?"

"Will seem crazy to them," Jason interrupted forcefully. "Cut it out, Dunash. How many have you managed to recruit so far, since you've been here? All of five, I believe—three of whom are orphans, two of those too young to use a gun—and of the other two, one of them is not much more than the village idiot. You know as well as I do that the only recruit you've gotten in three months who'll be any use is Bezalel Pitzkler."

Jason's eyes examined the eight young men sitting around Dunash. "At that rate—one real recruit every three months—you won't be able to field more than a squad when the balloon goes up. What's the point?"

"We have special weapons!" one of Dunash's followers said stoutly.

Morris had to fight down a sneer. Red didn't even bother. "Oh, swell. 'Special weapons.' Which translates to: maybe three dozen rockets you got smuggled into Prague, supplied by sympathizers in Grantville—do notice that I'm not inquiring as to the particulars, but I somehow doubt that Mike Stearns or Frank Jackson authorized that—and none of which you really know how to use."

"Do you?" demanded Dunash.

"Me? Don't be silly. Rockets are dangerous. Besides, I'm a man of peace. Well, a man of words, anyway. But I know someone who *does* know how to use them, and he happens to be a friend of mine—well, associate—and he's willing to come here for a bit and teach us. I hope you noticed the functioning pronoun there. *Us.*"

Red leaned back in his seat, spreading his hands in something of a placating gesture. "Dunash, if it'll make you feel better, you and your guys can stay in charge of the rockets. As well as that pickup truck that you've also managed to smuggle into this city, piece by piece, to use as a jury-rigged katyusha—a truck which you have no fricking idea in the world how to assemble. Or drive, even if you did manage by some kinda miracle to put it back together in working order."

Red looked smug. "I, on the other hand, am a crackerjack auto mechanic. I've rebuilt more cars and trucks than I can remember. And I *do* know how to drive."

"In a manner of speaking," Morris muttered under his breath. He'd driven with Red, on two occasions in the past. And while the union organizer wasn't quite as reckless as the now-infamous Hans Richter, riding in the passenger seat of a vehicle driven by Red Sybolt was no pleasure for anyone other than a daredevil. Or teenagers, among whom Red had always been surprisingly popular for a man in his forties.

"That's the deal, Dunash," Red went on. "You can keep the rockets, and I'll volunteer to show you how to put together the truck—even get you some fuel, which you haven't given any thought to at all. And I'll drive it for you when the time comes. But you give up the idea of a separate Jewish combat unit and integrate yourselves with us."

Dunash was still looking stubborn, but his cousin Yehuda spoke up. "Who is 'us,' exactly?"

Red hooked a thumb at Billek. "The Brethren, mostly, other than some people from the CoC we've managed to get started here in Prague. By now, me and Jan—mostly him—have managed to recruit about four

thousand volunteers from the [...] are already in Prague, with t[...]

Four thousand. Red let th[...] for a moment. Four thousan[...] Abrabanel's handful. For [...] doubt for a minute that [...] people from his newly organize[...] had following him. Say what you would a[...] Sybolt, the man was a superb organizer.

"We will be buried," hissed Dunash.

For the first time since he'd entered the room, Bishop Comenius spoke. "No, you will not be 'buried,' young man. I give you my word on that. My oath before God, if you will accept it."

Comenius was, by nature, an immensely dignified man, and even Dunash was visibly affected by his words. The more so after the bishop rose to his feet.

"I am recognized by all the Brethren as the fore- most religious authority in our church." To the si[...] Deacon Billek nodded firmly. "Tolerance was on[...] our watchwords from the beginning of our faith[...] now that I have had a chance to study wh[...] have happened in the world of our future[...] has been fortified."

He turned and pointed to Len Ta[...] Anderson. Then, to Morris himself[...] and finally, to Red Sybolt. "Conside[...] five people. One, a Catholic note[...] a man and a woman who bel[...] one, a Jew who is considere[...] Jews living today; the last,[...] to decide whether he can be[...] because he is no longer sure exact[...]

Morris wa[...] ment of fi[...] met befo[...] had a[...] Tru[...] li[...]

b[...] th[...] na[...]

of t[...] Unles[...] us our[...] The[...] surprise[...] that mor[...] sure of th[...] "You w[...] sure of thi[...]

Jason was obviously as startled as Morris was. But he still managed to nod as firmly as Billek.

"Yes, Dunash. It's—ah—kosher."

2

Over dinner, Comenius raised the subject that Morris had suspected was his primary reason for coming. Normally, he would have had to suppress a sigh, but in this instance . . .

Rich, remember. You are now stinking rich, Morris Roth, so stop thinking like a small town jeweler. Judging from the letter I got from Antonio and Gerhard—and I think they're right—within five years I'll be one of the richest men in Europe. Especially if I divest and diversify intelligently. Our monopoly on faceted jewelry will bring us a fortune for a few years, but it won't last.

"Yes, Bishop, I will finance your proposed university."

The words came out more abruptly—even curtly— than Morris had intended. The thought of his new wealth still made him feel awkward and out of place. The last thing Morris Roth had ever expected, in all the years he'd spent as the jeweler for a small town in northern West Virginia, was that someday, in another universe, he'd become the equivalent of the founder of a new house of Rothschild.

Comenius looked a bit startled. "How big—I mean . . ."

Morris smiled wryly. "How big a donation? If you give me two months—let's say three, to be on the safe side—to have the funds transferred, I can finance the entire thing. Enough to get it started, at least. I assume you intend to locate the new university here in Prague, yes?" He shifted in his seat, feeling awkward again. "There will be some conditions, however."

"Of course." Comenius inclined his head, inviting Morris to elaborate.

"First. I'll agree to have theological schools attached to the university, so long as there are no restrictions with regard to creed. That will include a Jewish rabbinical seminary."

He looked over at Jason, whose expression was a little strained. Forcefully, Morris added: "Yes, I know the rabbis currently in Prague will probably want no part of it. That's their problem, not mine. If they want to stick to their yeshivahs, so be it. Even if it's nothing more than a plaque on a door, with nothing behind the door, I want some building in the university—or part of one, anyway—set aside for that purpose."

He turned back to Comenius. "But the university itself will be secular. Open to anyone, regardless of creed, and unaffiliated to any religion. Agreed?"

Comenius nodded. "Yes. But that still leaves the question of how the theological schools themselves will be regulated. Herr Roth—"

"Please, call me Morris."

"Ah, Morris. You will find it difficult—perhaps not impossible, but difficult—to find anyone who can serve as the regulating authority of this university who is *not* affiliated, in one manner or another, with an existing creed. Most of the scholars in—ah, how strange the thought—in 'this day and age' are religious figures." Comenius hesitated a moment. "Unless you choose to select someone from your own people."

Morris chewed on the problem, for a moment. He considered, and then discarded, various possibilities from the American uptimers. The problem was that any of them he could think of who'd be qualified, even remotely, to become a university president—or "rector," to use the seventeenth-century term—were overwhelmed already with other responsibilities. And if any of them were available, the top priority anyway would be the new university that was taking shape in Jena, which was, after all, part of the CPE rather than a foreign country.

"No . . ." he said slowly. "It'll have to be someone from this day and age."

Comenius nodded again. "So I thought. But, as I said, such a person will most likely be affiliated already with one or another creed. If they have authority over the theological schools . . ."

Morris grunted. "Yes, I understand the problem. Fine. We'll set it up so that the religious schools have complete control over their own curriculum and methods of instruction. They'll also have complete control over hiring and firing their teachers. The only authority the university will have over them will involve such things as the building code, fire regulations, sanitation, and so forth. How's that?"

Comenius looked a bit dubious. "Workable, perhaps. There will still be a great deal of suspicion."

Morris had to restrain himself from slapping his hand on the table. There were things he liked about seventeenth-century Europeans. Most of them, anyway. There were also some things he detested. One of them was their seemingly inveterate and obsessive religious sectarianism.

"Let them be suspicious," he growled. "The way I look at it, Bishop, the main point of this university—one of them, at least—is to start overcoming those suspicions. In practice, which is always the best way to do it."

He gave Comenius something just barely short of a glare. "Understand something, Bishop. I *know* a secular university will work—and way better than the alternatives you have today. *I know it*—because I've seen it. My own kids went to West Virginia University, which was a far better university than anything you've got in Europe today. And in the world I come from, WVU was just considered a middling-rate university."

Judith interjected herself. "Morris, don't be so hardnosed. A lot of those universities got started as religious ones, remember. Including Harvard and the University of Chicago, if I remember right."

Morris suspected he was looking mulish, and the suspicion made him still more mulish. "Yeah, I know. I also know how long it took to haul them kicking and screaming into the modern world. Harvard didn't even go coeducational until—"

He broke off, rubbing his face. "Oh, hell, don't tell me."

Comenius' brow was creased with a frown of confusion. "I am afraid my English is perhaps not as good as it should be. What does that term mean? 'Coeducational,' I think it was."

Morris glared at the table. "Well, that's the second thing . . ."

Eventually, they got past that hurdle. But only because Morris finally agreed—under Judith's coaxing—that the university would have two colleges, one for men and one for women, with separate faculties. He did manage to hold the line on a common curriculum—"I want women *educated,* damn it; I'm not shelling out money for a lousy finishing school"—as well as a common library. And he took a certain sly pleasure in having gotten Comenius to agree to a coeducational "student union"—mostly, he suspected, because Comenius didn't quite understand what was involved.

That would be a fight in the future, he was sure, but Morris was willing to deal with that when the time came. Somewhere in the middle of construction, he suspected, once Comenius finally realized that Morris proposed to have young men and women socializing and dining together at all hours of the day and night with no real supervision or chaperonage. But since Morris would control the purse strings, he imagined the construction workers would obey him.

The rest of it went smoothly enough. They settled on the name "University of Prague," which wasn't a problem since the only existing university in the city was named the Karolinum—or "Charles University"—founded in the fourteenth century by the same Emperor Charles who'd had the city's great bridge erected. The Karolinum was located in the southern part of Staré Mesto, so they agreed to find land for the new university somewhere in the northern part of Old Town, even though that would be somewhat more expensive. Morris was pretty sure that a certain amount of friction between the two universities was bound to happen. The Karolinum was no "cow college." Even after the ravages of the past fifteen years, it was still considered one of the premier universities in Europe. In the long run, he thought having two major universities in Prague would simply enhance the city's prestige—and its prospects. But in the short run, competition between the two universities was likely to be a source of trouble. He saw no reason to aggravate the situation by placing them cheek-to-jowl.

Besides, a location in the northern part of Old Town would have the further advantage, to his way of thinking, of being close to the Josefov. Already, in the few short months since he'd become resident in Prague, Morris had come to realize that the Jewish inhabitants were going to be at least as resistant to change as the gentile ones. In some ways, more so, even in ways that objectively benefited them. Morris thought that having a university open to Jewish students just a short walk from the ghetto would have a nicely subversive effect.

Of all the things he missed about the universe they'd lost forever, the thing he missed the most was the atmosphere in his old synagogue and the Hillel House attached to the campus at WVU. That relaxed, sophisticated, cosmopolitan modern Judaism that he'd grown up with and cherished. He knew that Jason had come to have a real respect for some of the orthodox rabbis he'd encountered in Prague's ghetto. But, to Morris, they were as much a part of the problem as the Cossack butchers who would soon enough be slaughtering tens of thousands of Jews in the Ukraine. Their stiff necks bent over, endlessly studying the complexities of the Torah and the Talmud and the midrash, completely oblivious to the disaster that was beginning to curl over them. Morris had every intention of undermining their control and authority over the largest Jewish community in Europe, as best he could, using any legitimate means at his disposal.

● ● ●

Comenius had tentatively advanced the idea of naming it "Roth University," but Morris declined the honor immediately. He said that was because he thought it would create unnecessary problems by having the university too closely associated with its Jewish founder. But the real reason was simply that he found the idea too self-aggrandizing and presumptuous. In times past, in the universe he'd come from, he'd been known to make wisecracks about the swelled egos of the men who'd founded "Carnegie-Mellon Institute."

Judith had given him something of an odd look, then. Morris wasn't sure—he'd find out soon enough, of course, once they were alone—but he thought he was probably in for a little lecture on the subject of false modesty.

So be it. In times to come, he might get comfortable enough with his new status to consider the possibility. Morris had a feeling this was not going to be the last university he provided the financial backing for— assuming, of course, he and Judith survived the years to come. If this new world had greater opportunities than his old one, it also had much greater dangers.

The last item remaining was the first: who would they find to become the rector of the new university?

By the end of the evening—quite a bit early on, in fact—Morris had already made up his own mind. So as soon as Comenius raised the subject again, he had his answer ready.

"I think it should be you, Bishop."

Comenius, startled, began to say something by way of protest. Morris raised his hand.

"Hear me out, please. Yes, I know you're the central leader of the Unity of Brethren, recognized as such all over Europe. You're also famous for being an advocate of educational reform. To the best of my knowledge, you're the only person in this day and age who's actually written books on the subject. Well, okay, outside of the Jesuits. But while I'm perfectly willing for the new university to have Catholic students—Jesuit teachers, for that matter—there's no way I want a Jesuit in charge of it. Not in today's political climate, anyway. So I think it makes perfect sense for you to do it. As far as the religious issue goes..."

Morris shrugged. "You said it yourself, Bishop—we'll face that with almost anyone we select. The advantage to it being you is twofold. First, you've become just about as well-known for advocating religious tolerance. And second—not to put too fine a point on it—the Brethren are a relatively small church. Certainly compared to the Catholics or the Lutherans or the Calvinists. So you won't seem as much of a threat to anyone, even leaving aside your own views on toleration."

Comenius was still hesitant. Morris regarded him for a moment, and then added: "And, finally. I think you and I can get along pretty well. Better than I think I'd get along with anyone else."

Comenius stared at him for a moment. Then, with a wry little smile, inclined his head. "So be it, then. I can hardly refuse, since without you none of this would be possible at all."

Judith was giving Morris that same odd little look. This time, he understood it completely.

Okay, fine. Yes, I'll have to get used to it. But I draw the line at the "Baron" business. I am NOT a Rothschild. Just a Roth.

3

After dinner, most of the guests left. The only ones who remained behind, at Morris' quietly spoken request, were Ellie Anderson and Len Tanner.

"So. Why'd you ask us to stay, Morris?" Ellie's question was asked with a tone of voice that indicated a certain suspicion on her part. Of course, Ellie was usually a little suspicious of most things.

In this case, however, with good reason.

"*That's* why I asked, as a matter of fact. I'm hoping to talk you into staying."

For a moment, both Len and Ellie looked a little confused. Then, as his meaning registered, Ellie gave Len a quick, hostile little glance.

"Did you put him up to this?" she demanded.

Len looked aggrieved. "I had nothing to do with it! This is the first time Morris has ever raised the subject."

Morris found the interchange both interesting and heartening. He'd had no idea that Len had given some thought himself to remaining in Prague.

"He's telling the truth, Ellie. This is the first time I've ever brought it up."

Ellie transferred the hostile look to him. "The answer's 'no.' Prague's okay, I guess, but I have no intention of staying here after we get this job done."

"Why not?" Judith asked. "It's not as if you have any family in Grantville." Diplomatically, she did not add what she could have: *or all that many friends either, when you get right down to it*. Ellie's abrasive manner didn't bother either of the Roths, but the woman's temperament was not one that had ever made her very popular.

Diplomacy, as usual, was wasted with Ellie. "Or any friends either," she snorted, half-barking the words. "So what? Grantville has toilet paper."

Len made a face. Ellie scowled. "Okay, fine. It's that crappy stuff that they're starting to make in Badenburg, which is all there is since the modern stuff ran out. So what? It's still toilet paper and it still beats the alternatives."

She raised her left hand and began ticking off fingers. "Two. It's got modern plumbing. Fuck squatting over a hole. Here, even in Wallenstein's palace, that's about all you've got. Three. It's got electricity—I am *so* sick and tired of reading by lamplight at night."

"Prague will have all of those things before too long, Ellie," Morris said mildly. "And if it really bothers you that much, import what you need in the meantime."

"With what money?" she demanded. "AT&L is still scraping by and will be for at least another year. We can't even afford to pay Dougie to start running the company full time, which is a fucking waste because he'd be great at it. Instead, half the time he's galloping off into the countryside somewhere running messages for the king of Sweden. He'll get killed, you watch. If Wallenstein hadn't come up with the dough for this special project here in Prague, I'm not sure we wouldn't have had to close our doors. That's the only reason Len and I agreed to come here at all. We didn't have any choice."

"With what money? With the sudden influx of money you'll get from *me*. From the new company—or subsidiary, if you prefer—that I propose to form here in

Prague. Call it AT&L Bohemia, if you want. I'll put up all the capital and you give me forty-nine percent of the stock—you can remain in control of it, I don't care—and agree to live here for another, say, five years. If you're still unhappy five years from now, fine. You go back to Grantville, if you want. No hard feelings."

Ellie and Len stared at him. Morris found himself swallowing. "Me and Judith would miss you guys. We really would. Right now, except for the two of you and Jason, we really don't have anybody to talk to here in Prague who...You know. Understands us."

"How long do *you* plan on being here, Morris?" asked Len.

Morris and Judith looked at each other. Judith shrugged. "Who knows?" she mused. "Either a very short time—if Wallenstein's plans go sour and we wind up having to run for it—or...probably the rest of our lives. Except for trips."

Morris rose from the table and went over to one of the windows. Pushing aside the heavy drapes, he stared out over the city. At night, in the seventeenth century, even a large town like Prague was eerily dark to someone accustomed to American cities at the turn of the twenty-first century. A few lamps in windows, here and there, one or two small bonfires in open areas, not much more than that. The Hradcany, at a distance, was just a formless lump of darkness, with the towers of the cathedral barely visible against the night sky.

"We've got fifteen years to prevent one of the worst massacres ever perpetrated on my people," Morris said quietly. "And I'm just a small-town jeweler who really doesn't have any idea how to do it—except, maybe, do what I can to turn Bohemia into a country that can start drawing those Jews—some of them, anyway—out of the line of fire. And, maybe—most of this is completely out of our control—help build this into a nation that can intervene ahead of time."

"You're talking about *Wallenstein,* Morris," Ellie pointed out harshly.

Morris' lips twisted into something that was half a grin, half a grimace. "Ah, yes. Wallenstein. Actually, this was his idea in the first place. Trying to get you to stay here and set up a telephone company, I mean. Just like I know when I go talk to him tomorrow about the new university the bishop and I want to establish that he'll agree immediately. That's an idea he's also raised with me, on several occasions."

He turned away from the window. "In fact, I won't be surprised if he provides the land and the building for both projects, free of charge—assuming you agree to stay."

Len and Ellie were back to staring at him. "Look," Morris said abruptly, "Wallenstein wants it all—a modern nation that will give him the power he needs to become the historical figure he thinks he deserves to be. In some ways, he's a raving egotist, sure enough. But he's *smart.* Bohemia is not big enough for him, unless he modernizes it. That means the whole works. An electrified capital city, one of the world's premier universities, factories, you name it—yes, and toilet paper. Why else do you think he's agreed to remove all religious restrictions, even on Jews? The goodness of his heart? Not hardly. It's because—I'm as sure of this as I am of anything—he plans on grabbing most of the Ukraine and probably a good chunk of Poland and the Balkans. Maybe even part of Russia, who knows? And the only way he can do that, starting with little Bohemia as his power base, is to make Bohemia the Japan of eastern Europe. And he can't do that without stripping away all the medieval customs and traditions that get in the way."

Morris barked a laugh. "He spent a lot of time in Edith Wild's house in Grantville himself, you know. I've heard him complain about the lack of toilet paper here in Prague several times."

"So have I," muttered Len, giving Ellie a glance. "I also heard him pissing and moaning about no electricity, too."

Ellie's face looked pinched. She'd undoubtedly heard the same thing from him. Morris knew that Wallenstein spent a lot of time with Ellie and Len, watching them as they set up a telephone center in his palace. Not so much because he was trying to oversee the work, about which he knew effectively nothing, but simply because he was interested. Wallenstein was a curious man, interested in many things. Except when his shaky health was acting up, or he was distracted by his obsession with astrology, Wallenstein's mind was always alert and active.

The pinched look on Ellie's face went away, replaced by... something else. She cocked her head sideways a bit.

"I'm curious about something. It sounds like—no offense—you're almost planning to set up Bohemia as a counterweight to the CPE. Even a rival. Doesn't that bother you any?"

Morris shrugged. "Some, sure. But I talked to Mike about it before we left Grantville, and he agrees that it's the only way to do it. That's not just because of the Jewish question, either. Mike's thinking about the whole picture."

"What Wallenstein *wants* is one thing," Judith chipped in. "What he winds up with . . . well, that's something else. He's not the only player in the game."

Mention of the word *game* jogged Morris' mind. Like him, Len was a chess enthusiast. "Think of it as a *fianchetto*, Len. You move up knight's pawn one rank, creating a little pocket for the bishop. Then the bishop sits there, protected, but ready to attack at a diagonal."

"Yeah, I know. I like the maneuver myself. But what's the—oh."

"'Oh,' is right. And that's just what Wallenstein might be saying, one of these days. Chess is just a game, so it has firm and hard rules. Real life doesn't. A bishop can take out its own queen, in the real world, if that ever proves necessary. Try to, anyway."

While Len chewed on the analogy, Morris returned to the table and sat down again. "It's a race, really. That how Mike puts it. A strange kind of race, because we're trying to beat the same man we're allied with—without ever attacking him directly. He'll try for one thing, but the means he has to use for his ends can turn around and bite him on the ass. In our world, the Japanese wound up being saddled by a military dictatorship as they modernized. But who's to say the same thing has to happen here? Maybe it will. Then, again, maybe it won't."

Honesty forced him to say the next words. "It'll be dangerous, I admit. You'd be a lot safer staying back in Grantville."

Oddly, that did it. Ellie sat up straight. "You think I'm *afraid* of these assholes? Bullshit. Len, we're staying."

"Yes, dear," he murmured.

"And stop smirking."

"Hey, look, they got the best beer in the world here, just like they did four hundred years from now. You admitted it yourself, just the other day."

"I said, stop smirking."

The last conversation Morris Roth had that day was the one he hadn't foreseen or planned on. After everyone had left and he and Judith were getting ready for bed, his wife said to him:

"There's one last thing, O great Machiavellian prince of the Jewish persuasion."

"Yes?"

"I want you to stop bullying Jason."

Morris stared at her. Judith was busy turning down the covers, but she looked up at him squarely.

"Yes, you *are*," she said firmly. "He's just a young man who wants to become a rabbi, Morris. That's *all*. There's at least one of those rabbis in the ghetto whom he likes a lot, and wants to study with. So let him do what he wants, instead of trying to force him to be your Reform champion who'll slay the dragon of Orthodoxy. Let him study and decide for himself what he thinks. And if he winds up becoming an Orthodox rabbi, so be it."

Morris felt his jaws tighten. "You really want to listen to him at prayer, thanking God for not making him a woman?"

Judith shook her head. "That's neither here nor there, Morris. No, of course I don't. So what? I know how much you miss Rabbi Stern and our old synagogue and Hillel House. So do I. But you can't force Jason to become something he isn't. He's not even twenty-three years old, for Pete's sake. Steve Stern was a middle-aged man with all the confidence of someone who'd studied the Torah and the Talmud for years and was an experienced rabbi. How can you possibly expect Jason to substitute for him? Just because *you* want to launch a Reform movement two hundred years ahead of schedule? Well, then, why don't you do it yourself, big shot? Instead of trying to jam a kid into it, while you turn yourself into another Rothschild."

Morris winced. That struck . . . a little close to home. As much as Morris prized his Reform beliefs, he knew perfectly well that he'd be completely overmatched if he tried to cross theological lances with Orthodox rabbis.

Judith smiled. "Thought so. You chicken."

She straightened up from the bed. "Has it ever occurred to you, even once—because I know it has to Jason—that maybe, just maybe, you ought to apply your fancy chess terms to this situation also? Who is to say, Morris Roth, how Judaism will develop in *this* universe? They don't even use the term 'Orthodoxy' in the here and now. Maybe . . ."

She waved her hand, half-irritably. "I don't know. Maybe everything will shape up differently. Maybe it won't. What I *do* know is that you've got one unhappy kid on your hands, and you're driving him away with your pressure and your demands. Leave him alone, Morris. Let Jason Gotkin do whatever Jason Gotkin winds up doing. You never treated our own kids the way you're treating him. So why are you doing it to someone who's become something of an adopted son?"

Morris thought about it, for a moment. Then, heaved a deep sigh. She was right, and he knew it.

"Okay. I guess I look a little silly parading around as 'Baron Roth,' huh?"

His wife looked at him calmly. "No, actually, that's not true. Give it a few more years, and I think you'll have the role down pat. Come as naturally to you as breathing. Surprises the hell out of me, I admit, being married to you for over thirty years. But . . . there it is. Morris, if we survive, you will—we will, I guess— become the new Rothschilds of this universe. So what do you say we don't screw it up? I'd hate to be remembered as a pack of overbearing bullies. I really would."

4

"We cannot postpone a decision on this matter forever, Isaac." Mordechai Spira spoke softly, as was his habit, but firmly nonetheless.

His friend and fellow rabbi sighed and looked out the window of his domicile. Beyond, the narrow and crooked street was as crowded as it usually was at that time of the morning. Prague's Jewish population was really too big for the Josefov's cramped quarters, and it showed. People were almost living on top of each other.

"Things are still very tense, Mordechai," Isaac Gans pointed out. "Between the mess with Heller and then—just what was needed—the strains with Auerbach . . ."

Mordechai nodded, understanding the point. Prague's last two chief rabbis had been something of a disaster for the Jewish community. Heller had fallen afoul of the Habsburgs and had wound up being cast into prison in Vienna. Mordechai thought Heller was personally blameless in the matter, having simply had the misfortune of being politically inept in a tense political situation. The Habsburgs had imposed a harsh tax on Prague's Jewish community in order to help fund their military activities in the savage war that had been rolling across Europe for over a decade. Forty thousand thalers! Heller had tried to resist, and then, when resistance proved futile, had done his best to collect the tax fairly.

But... he had enemies, and they had taken advantage of the situation to lay accusations against him before the emperor. In the end, his supporters in the Jewish community had been able to get his death sentence commuted, though only because Ferdinand II's greed was such that he had been willing to ransom him for another 12,000 thalers. Still—and probably for the best, all things considered—Heller had not been able to return to Prague. He'd accepted instead a position in the rabbinate of far-off Nemirow.

Probably for the best, Mordechai reflected. It was hard to say. Alas, he'd been replaced by Simon Auerbach, who, if he had better political skills had been a much harder man for Mordechai and other rabbis to get along with. Auerbach had been a renowned Talmudist, true enough. But he was one of those men whose great learning was coupled to a harsh and inflexible temperament. Throughout his career he had clashed with those around him—at Lublin, with Meïr ben Gedaliah, another famous Talmudist; later, at Posen, with the city's rosh yeshivah, Benjamin of Morawczyk; and, soon after his arrival at Prague, he'd had a quarrel with Heller himself.

Auerbach had died, a year and a half earlier. But he'd done enough damage in the two short years he'd been at Prague that it was still felt, especially coming on top of the continuing strains in the community over the Heller imbroglio.

The current chief rabbi was a mild-mannered sort of fellow, thankfully. Alas, he was one of those people whose mild manner was principally due to his reluctance to make any decisions. Not a good characteristic for the chief rabbi of the largest Jewish community in Europe—at any time, much less these.

"Still," Mordechai said abruptly, "a decision must be made. We cannot continue to simply ignore Jason Gotkin."

"We haven't *ignored* him, Mordechai," protested Gans.

Spira waved his hand. "Stop avoiding the issue. First of all, even in social matters we've avoided him. And the Roths, even more so. Yes, we speak to Jason in the street. But have you invited him to your home for Shabbat dinner? No. Neither have I. Neither has anyone. It's grotesque. A *schande!*"

He waited a moment; Issac looked away.

"No," Mordechai repeated. "A complete breach with our customs. And, as I said, neither have I—despite the fact that I like Jason Gotkin. Quite a bit, in fact." He chuckled softly. "And don't forget that *I* have three unmarried daughters."

Gans started to grimace; but, then, as his innate fairness and good humor rallied, the grimace shifted into something of a sly smile. "Well, true. And I imagine Sarah in particular would take a fancy to him."

Mordechai must have looked somewhat alarmed, because Issac's sly smile started bordering on a grin. "Yes, I know she's your favorite, even if you'll never admit it. But that's because she's sprightly. Just the sort of girl to find an exotic fellow like Gotkin of interest. He's a rather handsome boy, too, you know. To be sure, his Yiddish is somewhat pathetic."

"His Hebrew isn't," Mordechai pointed out, forcefully. "In fact—spoken, at least—I suspect it's better than yours or mine. Or any other Jew's in the world today."

Isaac rubbed his forehead. "Do you really believe it, Mordechai?"

"Say better: is there any way to *doubt* it, any longer?" Spira's eyes moved to a table in the corner of the room, atop which sat a book whose appearance was unlike that of any other Mordechai had ever seen. He'd lent it to his friend Isaac a week earlier, after Jason Gotkin had lent it to him.

On one level, the book was simply another edition of the Tanakh—the Jewish version of the ancient holy texts which, in a slightly different variant, Christians called "the Old Testament." Jason had told Mordechai that he'd had it in his possession when the mysterious event had taken place which had brought him and his town into the world from . . . somewhere else. "In my bags in the trunk of my car," as he'd put it, whatever that meant.

Mordechai rose and went over to the table. He opened the book and began fingering the pages. He'd lent it to Isaac, in part, because Isaac knew how to read English—a language of which Mordechai himself was completely ignorant.

"Leave aside the pages and the printing, Isaac— though I know you've never seen anything like it." He swiveled his head around, to regard his friend. "It *is* the Tanakh, yes?"

Gans nodded.

"The Tanakh. In *English*. At a guess, Isaac, how many copies of an English Tanakh—in any edition, much less one so fine as this—do you think exist in the world?"

Gans looked away, staring back out the window. "I suspect that is the only Tanakh anywhere in the world, printed in English."

"The world *today*, Isaac. Our world. This one. Which means—to me at least—that the boy must be telling the truth. The rest—"

He waved his hand at the window. "—all of it, this new Confederated Principalities of Europe, Gustavus Adolphus grown so mighty, Wallenstein's disaster at the Alte Veste, the political turmoil. All of that I might possibly ascribe to something else. Those are things of the *goyishe* princes." Then, softly: "But how can I explain such a fine edition of the Tanakh, printed in a language which very few Jews in the world today use? Except some Sephardim, and they would have no more use for an English Tanakh than we do."

He closed the book and returned to his chair. "We are rabbis, Isaac, not princes. All that faces us, right now, is that a Jewish boy who is—in any manner that you or I can determine—qualified to do so, wishes to join the yeshivah. He does not even ask for financial support, though he is entitled to it. On what grounds can we deny him that wish? For weeks now, I have searched the Talmud and as much of the commentaries as I could, and found nothing."

"Nothing? He is probably a heretic, Mordechai."

"Be careful, Isaac," replied Spira softly. "Yes, he comes *from* what appears to be heresy—to me as well as to you. *Appears* to be, I remind you. Heresy is not that simple to judge, as you well know. And so what? Has he told us he wishes to advocate heresy? No. He simply wishes to study. On what grounds can we refuse him—without, ourselves, abandoning the traditions we would accuse him of having abandoned?"

Isaac went back to his window-watching.

"And what is so fascinating out there?" demanded Mordechai. "Besides too many Jews in too little space, as always. Stop avoiding this, Isaac. In the end, it is our souls that are being tested here, not the soul of Jason Gotkin."

Gans sighed. "True enough. Very well, Mordechai. I will support you in this. But I warn you, I do not think we will be able to convince the rosh yeshivah."

Spira shrugged. "No, I don't expect we will. But with your support, no one will oppose me if I begin instructing the boy myself. And I already have a chevrusah for him."

Gans burst out laughing. "Mordechai, you schemer! I assume you asked young Hoeschel. I think that boy would accept any challenge."

"Schmuel is a bold one, true enough," allowed Spira, smiling. "But he's met Gotkin, you know, several times. He likes him and tells me he would be quite happy to become Jason's study partner."

Now that he'd finally made his decision, Gans seemed to relax. That was his usual pattern, Mordechai knew—and the reason he'd begun with him. Isaac Gans was perhaps the best scholar among the rabbis in Prague; careful and deliberate in coming to a conclusion, but firm and confident about it thereafter. His support would mean a great deal.

"And why shouldn't he?" said Isaac. "He *is* a nice boy, whatever else may be said about him."

He was smiling slyly again. "You watch. The first time you invite him to Shabbat dinner, Sarah will start pestering you the next day. As sprightly as she is, she'll be hard to resist, too. Especially after she enlists your wife—which she will. You watch."

Mordechai Spira did his best to look stern and patriarchal. Master of his house. But Isaac's smile just kept widening.

5

That same morning, in Vienna, a prince of the goyim came to a decision.

"Very well. I agree. We have no choice, any longer."

Emperor Ferdinand II eyed General Piccolomini skeptically. He didn't trust the mercenary, though he understood the man's reasons for refusing to remain in Prague. Piccolomini had once been one of Wallenstein's closest subordinates. But had he remained within Wallenstein's reach, after the Alte Veste, the Bohemian magnate would surely have had him assassinated. By now, the emperor was sure—so was Piccolomini—Wallenstein had obtained his own copies of books from Grantville. In another universe, Piccolomini had been one of the chief conspirators in the plot that had resulted in Wallenstein's assassination.

As he still was in *this* universe, to be sure—but now he proposed to keep his distance.

"It will work, Your Majesty," Piccolomini assured him. "Wallenstein is on his guard, yes. But he also listens to his astrologers—and two of them are now

on the imperial payroll. With their influence, Rossbach
has ingratiated himself with Wallenstein. He assures
me he can manage it."

"How much?" the emperor grunted.

Piccolomini understood the terse question. "He
wants thirty thousand thalers—but he will settle for
twenty, I think, if your Majesty makes him a Freiherr."

Ferdinand grunted again. Then, decided he could
live with it. If the imperial purse was too straitened,
when the time came, he could always simply refuse to
pay the full amount. What could Rossbach do, after all?

"And Pappenheim?"

"Rossbach says he will do his best, but—" Piccolomini
made a face. "Assassinating Pappenheim is a different
matter. Risky, much riskier. Unfortunately, Pappenheim
doesn't listen to astrologers. And, up close . . ."

He shrugged. So did the emperor—although, in his
case, the gesture was one of a man relieving himself
of a load. Who was to say? If Rossbach made the
attempt on Pappenheim, either he would succeed or
he would fail. Mostly likely, he would fail.

So be it. Wallenstein would still be dead, which was
the key thing. And the emperor would be relieved of
the burden of paying 20,000 thalers to his assassin.

"Let it be done, then," he commanded.

"He won't *listen* to me, Edith," complained Isabella
Katharina. Wallenstein's wife shook her head. "Those
damned astrologers! All he listens to! And they are
telling him he has nothing to fear in the year ahead."

Edith Wild scowled and glanced at the door. Her
bedroom directly adjoined the suite that served Wallenstein and his wife as their living quarters in the

palace. That was due to Isabella Katharina's insistence
that Wallenstein's nurse be readily available in the event
his poor health suddenly deteriorated. In the months
since she'd arrived in Prague, Isabella had come to
trust Edith's advice far more than she did those of
her husband's doctors. Much less his astrologers.

Smart woman, thought Edith. "What does Pappenheim say?"

"My husband won't listen to him either. I spoke
to Gottfried myself, and he says he can do nothing
beyond make sure that a guard is always stationed
at the entrance."

"Well, that's true enough. He can't very well force
the Duke to accept guards in his own suite."

Isabella seemed close to tears. Edith patted her on
the shoulder. "All right, then, you'll just have to rely
on me, if something happens."

As much as Isabella trusted her, the look she gave
Edith now was definitely on the skeptical side.

Edith sniffed, and marched over to the chest in
the corner that held her clothes. After rummaging in
the bottom for a moment, she brought out something
and showed it to Isabella.

"This'll do the trick."

Now more intrigued than anything else, Isabella
came over and stared at the thing.

"Is that one of your American pistols?"

Edith grunted. "Don't call it a 'pistol.' It's a revolver.
Smith and Wesson .357 Magnum Chief Special. Holds
five rounds, 125 grain. Kicks like a mule and it'll
damn near blow your eardrums, but it'll drop an ox.
I wouldn't have bought it myself, it's my son's. But
he gave it to me after the first time he fired it on

the shooting range." She sniffed again. "I hate to say it, but he's something of a sissy—even if he does like to hang out with those bums at the Club 250, pretending otherwise."

She was wearing seventeenth-century-style heavy skirts with a separate pocket underneath, attached by a drawstring. Using a slit in the skirts designed for the purpose, she slipped the revolver into the pocket. "Anyway, relax. If anybody gets into the Duke's rooms, I'll see to it they don't leave. Except in a coffin."

Isabella gazed up admiringly at the large American woman. "What would we do without you?"

"I don't know," grunted Edith.

It was the truth, too. There were ways in which taking care of Wallenstein and his wife was like taking care of children. Still, she'd grown very fond of the two of them. The Duke himself was always courteous to her—far more courteous than any "fellow American" had ever been, she thought sarcastically—and Isabella had become a real friend.

Edith Wild hadn't had many friends in her life. That was her own harsh personality at work, she understood well enough. She'd never really been sure how much she'd like *herself*, if she had any choice in the matter. So it was nice to have a place again in life, and people who treated her well.

"Don't worry about it," she gruffed. "I like it here in Prague, and I plan on staying. Anybody tries to fuck with the Duke, they're fucking with me."

"You shouldn't swear so much," chided Isabella. The reproof was then immediately undermined by a childish giggle. "But I'm *so* glad you're here."

CHAPTER IV: *En passant*

July 1633

1

"I feel silly in this getup," Morris grumbled, as Judith helped him with the skirted doublet. "Are you sure? I mean, I've gotten used to wearing it—sort of—when I go visit Wallenstein in his palace. He dresses like a peacock himself and insists everyone does at his little courts. But I'm just going next door!"

"Stop whining, Morris," his wife commanded. She stepped back and gave him an admiring look. "*I* think you look terrific, myself. This outfit looks a lot better on you than a modern business suit ever did."

She was telling him nothing more than the truth, actually. Judith thought he *did* look terrific. Her husband had the kind of sturdy but unprepossessing face and figure that a drab up-time business suit simply emphasized. Whereas that same figure, encased in the clothing worn by seventeenth-century courtiers, looked stately rather than somewhat plump—and it was the shrewdness and intelligence in his face that was brought forward, rather than the plain features, when framed by a lace-fringed falling collar spilling across his shoulders and capped by a broad-brimmed hat.

"The plume, too?" he whined.

"I said, 'stop whining.' Yes, the plume too." She took him by the shoulders, turned him around, and began gently pushing him toward the door of their suite. "Look at it this way, Morris. For years I had to listen to you crab and complain about how much you hated wearing a tie. Now—no ties."

He hadn't quite given up. "Damnation, I'm just going across the street—barely inside the ghetto—to visit Jason in the new community center."

They were outside the suite that served them as their private quarters, and moving down the hallway toward the great staircase. Judith was no longer actually pushing him ahead of her, but she was crowding him closely enough to force him forward.

"Which you have never yet visited," she pointed out. "Not once in the two weeks since it was finished and Jason started working out of it. Even though you paid for the whole thing—buying the building, refurbishing it, and stocking it with what's becoming a very fine library as well as a kitchen for the poor."

Now, they were starting down the stairs. Judith wasn't crowding him quite as closely any longer. Not quite.

"I won't feel comfortable there," he predicted. "Especially not wearing this damn getup. When I went to Hillel House—"

"This is *not* Hillel House in Morgantown, Morris," Judith pointed out firmly. "And this is *not* the twenty-first century. Everybody in the ghetto knows you're the benefactor who financed the new community center—just like they know you're the source of the not-so-anonymous funds that went to help refurbish the Rathhaus and improve the Old-New Synagogue."

They'd reached the bottom of the stairs. Morris turned around and planted his hands on his hips, almost glaring at his wife.

"Yes? And did they use the money the way I wanted?"

Judith gave him a level look, for a moment, before responding. "Yes, as a matter of fact, they did. Avigail and Hirshele thanked me for it just yesterday. They say the seats in the womens' section of the synagogue are much improved—and the air circulation even more so."

That only made Morris look more sour yet. "Swell. So I'm aiding and abetting 'separate but equal'—which it never is."

It was Judith's turn to plant her hands on her hips. It was a gesture she did a lot more authoritatively than he did.

"Morris, cut it out. You're fifty-three years old and I'm only a year younger than you are. Neither one of us is going to live long enough to see a tenth of the changes you'd like to see—and you know it as well as I do. So what do you say we keep our eyes focused on what's really critical?"

She was actually a little angry, she realized, not just putting on an act. "What do you think those Jews are, over there in the Ukraine, whose lives you want to save? A bunch of Mendelssohns and Einsteins and Oppenheimers? Hundreds of thousands of budding Stephen Jay Goulds, champing at the bit to study evolution and biology? They're every bit as set in their ways and customs as the crankiest rabbi here in Prague—a lot more so, in fact. So?"

He looked away. "I just don't like it," he murmured.

Judith shook her head. "Husband, I love you dearly but sometimes you are purely maddening. What's *really* going on here is that you just have a bad conscience because you know you've hurt Jason's feelings by not showing up sooner at the community center. And now—*men!*—you're taking it out on everybody else.

Starting with me. So cut it out. Just do your duty and march over there. Wearing your Jewish prince outfit."

She took him by the shoulders and spun him around, facing the door to the street. A servant was standing by, ready to open it. Judith was a bit startled to see him, only realizing now that he would have heard the whole conversation.

How much of it he would have understood, of course, was another question. So far as she knew, Fischel spoke no English at all.

So far as she knew—but she'd never asked. Mentally, she shrugged her shoulders. Nothing had been said that would come as any surprise to anyone, after all. Unlike Morris, Judith never let her own attitudes blind her to the fact that seventeenth-century traditional Jews—and certainly their rabbis—were no dummies. By now, months after the Roths had arrived in Prague with a big splash, the people of the ghetto would have made their own assessment of these exotic foreign Jews.

Well, perhaps not "assessment." Not yet, anyway. But Judith was quite sure that she and Morris had been studied very carefully by their servants—and their observations faithfully reported to their rabbis.

"Go," she commanded.

After Morris left, Judith went to the kitchen—insofar as the term "kitchen" could be used to describe a huge suite of interconnected rooms on the lowest floor devoted to the storing, preparation and serving of food for the inhabitants of a small palace. And not just food for the lord and lady of the mansion, either, and the guests who came to their now-frequent dinners and soirees. Judith was well aware that the midday meal that the cooks and servants made for themselves was their biggest meal of the day—and that they quietly smuggled food out every night, for their families back in the ghetto. Quietly, but not particularly surreptitiously. Judith had made clear to them, long since, that whatever disputes she might have with aspects of their beliefs and customs, she was a firm believer in the Biblical precept about not muzzling the kine that tread the grain.

Avigail, as usual, was tending the big hearth in which the actual cooking was done. Even after the months she'd been in Prague, Judith was still always a little startled to see that hearth, and the profusion of kettles hanging over it and smaller skillets nestled directly in the coals. It was such homely things as the absence of stoves that really drove home to her, more than anything else, that she was now living in a different universe.

Avigail straightened up and smiled at her. "Good morning, gracious lady."

Avigail spoke Yiddish, not German, but Judith had no trouble understanding her. Except for some loan words, the languages were almost identical. The spoken languages, that is. Yiddish was written in Hebrew characters, which Judith couldn't read at all. One of the reasons Judith had hired Avigail was because the woman could read German also, which allowed Judith to leave notes for her when need be.

Now, she wondered what *other* languages Avigail might speak. Judith knew the woman was fluent in Czech also. But—

She blurted it out. In English. A language she had just assumed—without ever asking—would be completely foreign to the cook.

"Avigail, do you speak English?"

The cook hesitated for a moment. Then, her face a bit stiff, replied in heavily accented but quite understandable English: "Yes, gracious lady. I do."

Judith suddenly realized that the normally-bustling and busy kitchen had fallen very quiet. She scanned the room and saw that all five of the cooks and helpers present were staring at her. All of them with that same, slightly stiff expression.

"Do *all* of you speak English?"

Again, that hesitation. Then, again, nodding heads. For a moment, Judith wavered between anger and... Well...

She burst out laughing. "Does *every* servant in this house speak English?"

Nods. A bit hastily, Avigail said: "Young Jacob upstairs, not so well." She pointed with a ladle at a teenage girl standing in a corner near the pantry. "And little Rifka over there, even worse. Lazy youngsters, they don't do their studies like they should."

Judith had to fight to bring her laughter under control. "Their 'studies,' no less!"

She shook her head, grinning. "They must have scoured the ghetto to find this many English-speakers. Avigail, if you have any questions—or if the rabbis do—you need only ask. I really have no secrets. Neither does my husband."

There didn't seem anything else to say. Still grinning, she left the room.

After she was gone, Avigail and the three women who'd been employed since the first days after the Roths arrived, turned their heads to regard Rifka.

The young woman was new to the household, having only started working there the week before. Their expressions were identical: that of older women finally and fully vindicated in front of skeptical and callow striplings.

"You see?" demanded Avigail. "Did we not tell you?"

"I will study harder," Rifka said meekly.

"That's not what I meant!" snapped Avigail. "And you know it perfectly well."

She sniffed, turned away, and went back to work with her ladle. It had a very long handle, because the hearth was large and the fire was hot. But the ladle in Avigail's mind had just grown shorter still. By now, it was not much longer than a spoon.

2

The first thing Morris saw when he entered the community center—the first thing he really noticed, at least, because of his nervousness—was the rabbi standing next to Jason and another young man.

He assumed he was a rabbi, at least. Partly from the clothing the man was wearing, but mostly from certain indefinable things about the way he carried himself—and the very evident respect with which Jason and the other youngster were listening to what he had to say.

Morris found himself almost gritting his teeth. He had a better knowledge of history, in general, than most residents of Grantville. And because he'd always been especially interested in Jewish history, he had a particularly good knowledge of that subject. He felt like shouting at the three of them: *Your damn rabbinate didn't start running the show until not much more than a thousand years ago! Those old men in Babylon who started throwing their weight around after the destruction of the Second Temple. Our history goes back at least two thousand years earlier than that. Ask David and Solomon—or Abraham and Moshe—if they kowtowed to a bunch of old men with long beards and stupid hats!*

But, he didn't. It would have been unfairly one-sided, as well as rude and pointless. And, besides...

Well, the fact was that the rabbi in question was not particularly old. In fact, he looked to be younger than Morris himself.

Nothing for it, then. Morris took a deep breath and marched over.

Seeing him come, Jason smiled widely. It was the biggest smile Jason had given Morris in at least two months, and Morris felt himself warming. As Judith had said, since the Ring of Fire Morris had come to look upon young Gotkin as something of an adopted son. The estrangement that had grown between them since their arrival in Prague had been painful.

The rabbi turned his head and regarded Morris. He obviously knew who he was, even though they'd never met. Morris was not surprised. This was not the first time, by any means, that Morris had entered the ghetto. He'd made a number of trips—right into the center of the Josefov—to meet with Dunash and his people. And, every time, although people had not been rude about it, Morris had been quite aware that he'd been carefully and closely observed everywhere he went. And was just as sure that the people who watched him passed on their observations to their rabbis.

As he neared, the rabbi smiled politely and addressed

him. "Good morning, Don Morris. Since I have never had the opportunity, let me take it now to thank you for your generosity in providing for this center. And your many other generosities."

The rabbi's German was excellent, if oddly accented to Morris' ear. By now, Morris' own German was almost fluent. What he found more interesting, though, was the way the rabbi had addressed him. *Don Morris*—as if Morris were a Sephardic hidalgo. True, it made a certain sense, because most court Jews in the first half of the seventeenth century were still Sephardic rather than Ashkenazi. Still...

Morris decided it was a workable compromise, for him as much as the rabbi. Although there were some differences in the way Sephardim and Ashkenazim observed their faith, which resulted in friction and even occasional clashes, neither one of the branches of Judaism considered the other to be heretics. Not to mention that Italian Jews, in this day and age, constituted something of a third tradition of their own.

Truth be told, the friction between Ashkenazim and Sephardim was due more to social factors than religious ones. Sephardim, as a rule, were more comfortable with cultural accommodation to gentile society—and, as a rule, considerably wealthier than most Ashkenazim. So, they tended to look down on Ashkenazim as the equivalent of "country rubes"—a disdain which the Ashkenazim returned in kind, much as Morris' hillbilly neighbors made wisecracks about city slickers. But, since he'd arrived in his new universe, Morris had discovered that the interaction between the two—and with the Judaeo-Italians—was quite a bit more extensive than his study of history had led him to suspect.

Besides, the man was being courteous. Whatever his underlying attitudes, Morris had never found it possible to be rude to someone who was not being rude to him.

He nodded. Graciously, he hoped. "My pleasure, rabbi. Ah—"

"This is Rabbi Spira," Jason said promptly, almost eagerly.

So. This is the one.

Morris had to fight down a momentary surge of jealousy. Although Jason had been veiled about it, Morris was well aware that the young man had come to develop a deep admiration for Mordechai Spira—and something that bordered on filial respect.

Now that Morris had finally met the man, he could understand that better. As much as Morris was inclined to dislike zealots—and he considered all Orthodox rabbis to be zealots, by their nature—he couldn't miss the intelligence in Spira's eyes. Nor the quite evident warmth and kindliness in them, either. Jason had told him, more than once, that even when Rabbi Spira corrected him for his errors, he invariably did so with good humor. Even wit.

For Morris Roth, "witty Orthodox rabbi" had always been something of an oxymoron. Unlike Jason, who'd lived in Israel for a year as a student, Morris and Judith had never done more than visit the country for a couple of weeks at a time. Morris had not had much contact with Orthodox Judaism in the United States he'd come from, since his area of the country was dominated by Reform Judaism. So his main personal impression of Orthodox rabbis came from what he'd seen in Israel—which, to him, had been their constant interference in Israel's politics, their narrow-minded obsessions, the readiness with which they threw their political weight around. He'd been particularly angry at their refusal—well, some of them—to allow their adherents to serve in Israel's armed forces, at the same time that they demanded those armed forces be used to carry out policies *they* wanted.

He had to remind himself—as Judith reminded him constantly—that they'd left that world behind. There was no Israel in this universe. Not yet, at least; and not for some time to come, if ever. The rabbinate that existed here was one that had been shaped by the life of Jews in central and eastern Europe's ghettos and shtetls. It simply wasn't fair for Morris Roth to pile atop Mordechai Spira's head all the sins of a rabbinate in a different time, in a different universe.

He began to say some words that would have been simply friendly. But he'd barely begun before he heard noises coming from the entrance. The sounds were very faint, seeming to come from a great distance, but Morris thought he recognized them.

Gunshots. Then, a moment later—

Lots of gunshots.

"It's starting," he said. "Finally."

3

Ellie leaned back in the chair before the console, and took a deep breath.

"Well, Duke, there it is. Finished. Finally."

Wallenstein examined the telephone center, his eyes bright with interest. "And you have the people trained to operate it, yes?"

Ellie nodded. "Three, so far. Enough to keep shifts going round the clock—for a while, anyway. You'll need to give them some time off, though, now and then."

Wallenstein was frowning a little, as he often did listening to Ellie's idiosyncratic blend of German and English. Belatedly, she realized that the expression "round the clock" wouldn't have meant much to him. True, they had clocks in the seventeenth century. But the devices were rare and expensive, too much so for their habits to have entered popular idiom yet.

Wallenstein shrugged irritably. "I see no problem." He jerked his head toward a door. "They will sleep here, anyway."

The new telephone center, at Wallenstein's insistence, had been built directly adjoining his personal suite in the palace. He'd even had living quarters connected to it prepared for the eventual telephone operators. Ellie thought that was an odd arrangement. But, given Wallenstein's shaky health—not to mention the terrible wounds that Julie Mackay had inflicted upon him at the Alte Veste, which he would never fully recover from even with the help of American medical care—she could understand it. Wallenstein had to spend a lot of his time, now, resting in his bed. But with a telephone literally at his fingertips, he would have the wherewithal to continue managing the empire he intended to build for himself. Ellie and Len had already built and put in place a direct phone connection between Wallenstein's bed in his private room and the telephone center itself.

By now, Ellie had gotten to know Wallenstein well enough not to be afraid to contradict him. The Duke of Friedland was insistent upon his privileges, and had a very harsh way with anyone who was impolite to him. But he did not bridle at being opposed over a matter of substance, as long as it was done respectfully and not too insistently. And, fortunately, he cut more slack for Ellie than he did for just about anyone else except his wife Isabella and his nurse, Edith Wild. And Pappenheim, of course.

Ellie shook her head. "Duke, this is not that simple a system to operate. It takes a lot of mental alertness—at least, assuming you wind up using it as often as you think you will. What I mean is—"

There was an interruption at the door. More precisely, in the large room beyond that served Wallenstein's private suite as an entry salon. A man was pushing his way in, overriding the protests of the guard stationed at the entrance to the suite. There seemed to be several men standing in the corridor beyond, as well.

Ellie recognized him. It was Eugen Rossbach— *Ritter* Rossbach, as he insisted on being called—one of the mercenary captains who had attached himself to Wallenstein's service. Wallenstein was rather partial to the man. Ellie despised him, herself—but then, admittedly, Ellie despised most of the mercenaries who surrounded the Duke of Friedland. Perhaps oddly, Pappenheim—in some ways the most frightening of them all—was the one she disliked the least.

Wallenstein, now frowning fiercely, stepped out of the small telephone center into the main salon. "What is it, Rossbach? I am occupied at the moment."

Rossbach, still fending off the protesting guard with one hand, waved a document with the other. "Yes, my apologies—but you must see this immediately! It's from the emperor!"

Ellie rose and came to the doorway. Wallenstein took

a step forward to take the message, which Rossbach extended toward him.

It suddenly dawned on Ellie that the three men with Rossbach were coming into the main salon, now that the guard was distracted. *Why?*

One of them—then the other two—reached for their swords. Without thinking, Ellie grabbed Wallenstein by his collar and yanked him backward.

The Duke cried out in protest. Rossbach snarled. Then—Ellie never saw the stabbing itself—the guard suddenly screamed and staggered forward. Behind him, as he fell to his knees, she could see one of Rossbach's companions with his sword now in his hand. The tip of it was covered in blood.

Wallenstein cried out again. A curse of some sort, Ellie thought. Rossbach shouted something, dropped the document and drew his own sword.

Ellie hauled Wallenstein back into the telephone room. He stumbled on the way and fell backward, landing on his rump. She just had time to slam the door shut in Rossbach's face.

Then, fumbled to find the lock which—

Didn't exist.

Goddamit! There'd been no reason, after all, to put a lock on that door. In fact, Wallenstein would have been furious if they'd done so. It was *his* telephone center, not that of the men who would be operating it for him.

She heard Rossbach's fist slamming the door. Then, a moment later, a much heavier *wham* as his boot slammed into it.

Ellie's fear and fury were, for a moment, penetrated by an absurd impulse to cackle with laughter. *That idiot Rossbach thinks the door IS locked.*

But it probably wouldn't take him long to figure it out. And besides—another *wham*—even if he didn't, that door wasn't really that solid. He'd be able to kick it in easily enough.

Wallenstein was now rising to his feet. Unfortunately, in his own personal suite, the Duke wasn't carrying his sword. They were both unarmed.

"Bullshit!" Ellie snarled. She stooped over and rummaged through the big tool chest that had been in the room for weeks now. An instant later, she came up with a modern Crescent wrench—Len's 12-incher—as well as the two-foot cheater pipe he used for extra leverage when he needed it.

She tossed the pipe to Wallenstein and hefted the wrench. It wasn't much, but it would have to do.

Wham!

Wham!—and the door came off the hinges. Rossbach and another man started pushing through the doorway, their swords level.

WHAM! WHAM!

Both of them sailed through the opening, as if shot from a cannon, their swords flying out of their hands. Wallenstein clubbed Rossbach down, but Ellie missed the other man. Her swing had been wild, accompanied by a shriek of fear as she dodged the sword sailing ahead of him. Now it was her turn to fall on her ass.

It didn't matter, though. The swing had been more of a reflex than anything else. She'd seen the erupting exit wound on the man's belly. That *WHAM* had been a gunshot.

She stared through the open, shattered doorway. She could see Edith Wild standing in the salon, now. The big woman's face was contorted with anger and she was holding a modern-style revolver in both hands. The two remaining assassins were out of Ellie's range of view. But she could just imagine how astonished they were. Ellie was astonished herself.

WHAM! WHAM!

Now that Ellie wasn't completely overwhelmed by adrenalin, the sound of the gunshots seemed ten times louder. Edith must have been nearly deafened. Each shot from the short-barreled revolver was accompanied by a bright yellow muzzle flash. The gun bucked in Edith's big hands—so badly that Ellie was pretty sure the second shot had gone wild.

But Edith didn't seemed fazed at all. The snarl stayed on her face and she brought the gun back into line.

"The Tatar," indeed. *Don't fuck with Nurse Ratchett.*

Ellie heard a man shout something. A protest of some kind, perhaps, or a plea for mercy.

Fat lot of good it did him. *WHAM!*

Ellie shook her head to clear it. When she looked up again, Edith was no longer in sight. Hearing some sort of noise—she couldn't really tell what it was, her ears were ringing so badly—Ellie scrambled over on her hands and knees and stuck her head out the door.

Edith's last shot had gone a little wild too, it seemed. The man had only been wounded in the shoulder— from what Ellie could tell, nothing more than a flesh wound—and Edith's gun was out of ammunition.

Fat lot of good it did him. *Don't fuck with Nurse Ratchett.* Edith had wrestled him to the floor and was now clubbing his head with her revolver.

Thump. Thump. Thump. Thump.

Wallenstein stuck his own head out the door, crouched a little higher than Ellie. "Rossbach is dead," he announced.

He studied Edith at her work for a moment, then straightened and helped Ellie to her feet. When she looked at him again, to her surprise, Wallenstein was smiling thinly and stroking his badly scarred jaw.

"A pity there are so few American women," he announced. "If I had an army of you mad creatures, I could conquer the world."

Pappenheim charged into the salon, his sword in his hand. Behind him came at least half a dozen soldiers. When he saw Wallenstein, obviously unhurt, the relief on his face was almost comic. It was odd, really—not for the first time, the thought came to Ellie—how much devotion a man like Wallenstein could get from a man like Pappenheim. She didn't think she'd ever really understand it.

But, she didn't need to. The fact itself was enough. Wallenstein was still alive and kicking and now Pappenheim was on the scene. Which meant that—finally—all hell was about to break loose.

"Best stop her, Gottfried," said Wallenstein, pointing to Edith. The nurse was still clubbing the would-be assassin, though he was now completely limp and lying on the floor. "It would help if we could get him to talk."

Even ferocious Pappenheim seemed a little daunted by the project. After a moment's hesitation, he sheathed his word and walked over, taking care to remain outside of Edith's reach.

He knelt to bring himself into her field of view and gave Edith his most winning smile. Which, on

Pappenheim's face, looked about as out of place as anything Ellie could imagine.

He extended his hand in a carefully nonthreatening plea for restraint. "*Bitte*, Frau. We need the man to talk."

Edith let up on her thumping and glared at Pappenheim. Then, gave the assassin one final thump and rose heavily to her feet. "All right. But he better never try it again."

Pappenheim studied the man's bloody head. "No fear of that, I think."

Now Isabella came piling into the room, shrieking with fear, and practically leaped into her husband's arms. As he comforted her, Wallenstein gave Ellie a meaningful glance.

"Yes, boss," she muttered. She went back into the telephone center and started making the connections.

As Ellie expected, it wasn't long before Wallenstein came in. He was a considerate husband, but some things that man would always insist on doing himself.

"The first time it is used," he confirmed. "I will do so, and no other."

Ellie had already made the connection to the barracks adjoining Wallenstein's palace where he kept his trusted officers and troops. (Except Pappenheim and the *most* trusted ones—they lived in the palace.) Len was handling the phone center in the barracks itself, and they'd had time to exchange a few words.

Wallenstein leaned over and spoke into the tube. "Do it," was all he commanded.

Pappenheim crowded in, giving the telephone equipment no more than an interested glance. "I will see to Marradas myself."

"Make sure there's not another miracle, Gottfried."

The smile that now came to Pappenheim's face didn't look out of place at all.

Ellie never saw it herself, since she spent the next many hours closeted in the telephone center. But she heard about it. In the famous "defenestration of Prague" that had been the incident usually cited as the trigger for the Thirty Years War, the Catholic Habsburg envoys thrown out of a high window in Prague Castle by rebellious Protestant noblemen had landed in a pile of manure. Their survival had been acclaimed as a miracle by the Catholic forces and had been disheartening to the Protestant rebels.

Marradas fell about the same distance—seventy feet—after Pappenheim threw him out of a window in the castle. But, as commanded, there was no second miracle. Marradas landed on a pile of stones on the street below—placed there by Pappenheim's soldiers at his command, while Pappenheim kept the screaming and struggling Spanish don pinned in his grip for ten minutes until the work was finished.

4

Ellie heard about it from Morris Roth, who had watched it happen—at a distance, through binoculars, from the room in the uppermost floor of his mansion that gave him the best vantage point.

Morris had gone back to his mansion as soon as he realized the coup was underway. Jason had followed him along with, somewhat to Morris' surprise, Mordechai Spira. The rabbi had not even taken the precaution of wearing the special badge that Jews were required to wear under Habsburg law whenever they left the ghetto.

For the first few hours, it was hard to tell exactly what was happening. Morris had tried to reach Len and Ellie with the CB radios they'd brought with them to Prague, but there was no answer. That meant neither of them were in their private rooms in Wallenstein's palace. They always left their CB there, hidden in one of their chests, since the existence of the radios was supposed to be a secret from their new allies. None of them really thought that Wallenstein was fooled any, but since he also never raised the issue, they'd decided that maintaining discretion was the best policy. Soon enough, no doubt, now that the conflict was out in the open, Wallenstein would start pressuring his American allies to provide him with more in the way of technological advancement.

But their protracted failure to answer was enough by itself to confirm Morris' guess. That had to mean that both of them were busy in the new phone centers, which Wallenstein would be using to coordinate the first stages of his coup d'etat.

The defenestration of Marradas took place early in the afternoon. A few short minutes later, a new standard began appearing, draped over the walls of every prominent building on the Hradcany—even the cathedral. Morris didn't recognize it, but he was sure it was the new coat of arms that Wallenstein had designed for himself.

Duke of Friedland, Prince of Sagan—and now, King of Bohemia and Moravia.

Morris lowered the binoculars. "Well, that's it. For the moment, anyway."

He heard Mordechai Spira clear his throat. "We will not take sides in this, Don Morris. None of us have any love for the Habsburgs, but . . . Wallenstein . . . It was he, you know, who had poor Jacob Stein guarded by dogs under the gallows while he extorted eleven thousand florins from us."

"Yes, I know. But the fact was that Stein had broken the law—even if unwittingly—and there are plenty of goyishe princes who would have executed him *after* squeezing the silver from us. And it is also a fact that Wallenstein eventually exonerated Hanok ben Mordechai Altschul, who had also been accused, when many a goyishe prince—most of them—would never have bothered distinguishing a guilty Jew from an innocent."

He turned his head and looked at Spira. The rabbi's eyes were a little wide. "You know the history of it?" he asked, obviously surprised.

"I know a great deal of history," Morris said harshly. He was on the verge of uttering some bitter phrases— more than phrases, entire paragraphs—on the ineffectual role generally played by Orthodox rabbis when the Nazi Holocaust swept over eastern Europe's Jewry.

But, thankfully, he managed to swallow them. Mordechai Spira seemed a well-meaning man, and young Jason liked and admired him—and, most of all, it was simply unfair to blame a man or even a group of men for the faults and failures of other men in a completely different time and place.

"I know a great deal of history," Morris repeated, but this time softly, almost sighing the words. "I only wish I knew what to do with that knowledge."

Inadvertently, his eyes drifted eastward. Spira's eyes followed his gaze.

"You are worried about the Ukraine, I know. Jason has told me."

"Will you help me, then?"

The rabbi hesitated, but not for more than a second or two. "I will do everything I can, Don Morris, which I feel I can do in good conscience."

Morris thought about it. "I guess I can live with that."

He went back to studying the city with his binoculars. "I do not know what is going to happen now, Rabbi. But you are not pacifists."

"No, we are not."

"You will defend the ghetto, whether or not you take sides in this business." It was a command, not a question. "I do not know if there will be trouble, but there may be. Not from Wallenstein or Pappenheim, but the Habsburgs. Or, for that matter, who knows what Holk and his butchers will do, when they get the news."

"Yes," replied Spira. "We will do our best, at least. Though we have no weapons beyond tools and kitchen knives."

Morris chuckled, and lowered the binoculars. "That's what you think. Show him, Jason."

Ten minutes later, Mordechai Spira's eyes were wider yet. Jason and Dunash's people—who'd arrived at the Morris mansion just moments earlier—were hauling the muskets out of the crates in the basement and stacking them against the walls.

"I was able to bring two hundred, which was all Mike Stearns told me he could spare," Morris explained. "These are the new flintlocks. You'll need to have Jason explain how they work. They're not really much different from matchlocks, just better. I assume that in a ghetto of some fifteen thousand people, there have to be at least a few hundred who've handled firearms before."

Spira nodded. "Oh, yes. Many are here from the small villages, where things are less regulated. And there are at least a few dozen former seamen."

"We can help too!" Dunash said eagerly.

Morris glared at him. "You *are* taking sides in this business, young man—and you have commitments already. Red and Billek are counting on you to man the katyusha. So get your ass out of here."

Dunash hesitated. But Jason spoke up, very firmly. "Do as he says, Dunash. All of you."

The young Abrabanel firebrands and their new recruits—there were almost twenty of them, now—immediately left. The rabbi turned his head to watch them go, before bringing his gaze to Jason. It was almost as he were examining him.

Then, he smiled. "I have great hopes for you, young man. I think you will make a splendid rabbi."

Now he looked at Jason's chevrusah. "Spread the word, Schmuel. We want only men who know how to use guns. No point in trying to teach complete novices."

After Schmuel raced out, Spira chuckled. "Such as myself. Tell me, Don Morris, are you familiar with guns?"

Before answering him—by way of answer, rather—Morris went to another crate and drew out a different weapon. This one, unlike the others, was encased in a fancy covering rather than simple cloth.

He unzipped the guncase and drew out the rifle.

"This is a much better gun than those flintlocks, Rabbi. I've owned it for many years. It is called—well, never mind. Yes, I know how to use it. I was a soldier in the American army, some years ago. In fact, I'm quite a good shot."

Spira seemed to be examining him, now. Morris shifted his shoulders uncomfortably. "Look, Rabbi, it's not just my military training. In the world I came from my wife and children and I were the only Jews in our town. And it's a mountain country town, where everybody hunts."

He looked down at the rifle, caressing the sleek stock. "The strange thing about it—perhaps—is that I never actually hunted myself. Hunting is not part of our traditions and customs."

Spira nodded. "No, it is not. We may only eat meat which has been properly slaughtered by a schohet."

Morris smiled wryly; almost bitterly. "Ah, yes, all those rules. Most of which I do not agree with but still often find it hard to ignore completely. Like hunting." He raised the rifle a bit, as if starting to bring it to his shoulder, and then lowered it again.

"But, you see, Rabbi . . . it would have been stand-offish for me not to join my friends in their favorite sport. So, I did, even though I never shot any deer. I just went along. I always enjoyed the outdoors anyway. And—I don't know—I suppose just in order to prove that the reason I didn't wasn't because—well—"

He shifted his shoulders again. "I was one of the best shots on the rifle range and everybody knew it. So my friends—yes, gentile friends, I had lots of them—still do—would tease me about it. But not much, and not hard, and only in fun."

He gave Spira something of a challenging stare. Spira looked away, but Morris didn't think it was because the rabbi was afraid of the challenge, or trying to avoid it.

"There are many wise and wonderful sayings in the midrash, Don Morris. 'When in a city, follow its customs' is one of them."

Morris swallowed. He'd heard that one before, from his rabbi Steve Stern, in a universe now impossible to reach.

Spira brought his gaze back. "But I think there is perhaps an even more apt saying—though not from the midrash. It is one of your American folk sayings, Jason tells me."

The rabbi gestured toward the west, where, faintly, the sounds of fighting could still be heard across the river. "We will not take sides in this affair. But, however it is settled, we will be guided by the wisdom of the ancient Babylonian sage Schmuel. *The law of the kingdom is the law.*' That will suffice for you, I think, in the immediate period."

"Yeah," Morris gruffed. "I can live with that. For a while, at least. So can Wallenstein."

Spira nodded. "And, in the meantime, Don Morris—"

"I prefer to be called just 'Morris,'" he stated abruptly.

Spira nodded again. "As you wish. And, in the meantime, Morris . . . don't be a stranger."

With that, smiling, the rabbi turned away and headed for the stairs. "Now," he said over his shoulder, "I'd best see after young Schmuel—who is no sage. Indeed, he can be excessively enthusiastic. Please come with me, Jason, I could use your help."

• • •

Morris stayed alone in the basement after they left, silent, for perhaps five minutes. Then he began loading the rifle.

"Did you think it was going to be simple?" he muttered to himself. "You dummy."

CHAPTER V: *Castling*

July 1633

1

For the next two days, while Wallenstein and Pappenheim fought a chaotic and swirling series of small battles in and around Prague with military units who opposed the rebellion—or simply wanted to remain neutral, which Wallenstein wasn't going to tolerate— Morris Roth remained in his mansion. He stayed on the uppermost floor most of the time, except for brief snatches of sleep; moving from window to window, rifle in his hands, keeping watch on the streets below. He hadn't planned it that way—certainly Len and Ellie hadn't, when they purchased the building on his behalf—but because of its location just outside one of the main gates in the ghetto wall, his mansion served the Josefov as something in the way of a ravelin. An exterior little fortress from which enfilade fire could be brought to bear on anyone attempting to assault the fortress itself.

He only used the rifle once, during those two days. That was on the evening of the first day, just before sundown, when a small band of ruffians—possibly

soldiers operating on their own, possibly just criminals; it was hard to tell—advanced toward the ghetto
brandishing a haphazard collection of swords, pikes and
arquebuses. Morris warned them off when they were
fifty yards away. When the only response he got was
a small volley of arquebus fire that did no damage at
all beyond making a few pockmarks in the thick walls
of the mansion, he shot three of them.

One round each, good center mass shots. Not hard
to do, at that range, especially for a good shot like
Morris. All of them fell in the street, in the space of
less than ten seconds. The rest promptly fled.

One man had been killed instantly; the other two
were mortally wounded, dying within minutes. One
of the men managed to crawl perhaps twenty feet
before he finally collapsed.

Morris slept hardly at all that night. Early in the
morning, Judith found him back at his post, rifle held
firmly in his grip. He avoided her eyes, though, when
she approached and placed her hand on his shoulder.

"Talk to me, Morris."

"What's there to say?" he asked, shrugging. "I'm
a small-town jeweler who hasn't even been in a fist
fight since I was a kid in boot camp. Over thirty years
ago. Yeah, sure, I was in Vietnam. Big deal. I spent
my whole tour of duty as a supply clerk in the big
army base at Long Binh, and I didn't get there until
long after the Tet Offensive."

While he spoke, his eyes kept ranging across the
streets below, looking for possible threats. He never
looked at Judith once. "I guess you could call it
'combat duty,' since I always knew that some of the
explosions and shots I heard during the night was stuff

aimed into the base rather than our own Harassment and Interdiction fire. But nothing ever landed close to me—and I never once had to fire my own weapon at any enemies I could see." Very softly: "I've never even shot a deer before, much less a man. Then stare at their bodies afterward, while they bleed to death."

Judith gave his shoulder a little squeeze; then, disappeared for a while. When she returned, she had Mordechai Spira in tow along with another rabbi who seemed to be a close friend of his. A man by the name of Isaac Gans. The two of them kept Morris company the rest of the day. There was little conversation, because Morris was not in a mood for talking. Still, he appreciated their presence. Not so much for anything they said or did, but just for the fact of it.

Neither Spira nor Gans was wearing Jewish insignia. During the afternoon of the day before, just a short time before Morris had his confrontation with the band of thugs, a small squad of soldiers led by a sub-officer had placed posters on buildings near the ghetto—as well as two posters flanking the entrance to the ghetto itself. The posters were proclamations by Wallenstein. The first proclamation announced that he was now the king of Bohemia—and Pappenheim was the duke of Moravia.

There were many proclamations on those posters. Among them, Wallenstein had kept the promise he'd made to Morris long months before, in a small house in Grantville. Freedom of religion was guaranteed. Distinctions between citizens (that was a new word, just in itself—*citizens*) would no longer take religious affiliation into account. And, specifically, all restrictions on Jews were abolished.

It was pretty impressive, actually. At least, the words were. A lot of the language was cribbed from texts of the American Revolution as well as the *Declaration of the Rights of Man* adopted in 1789 by the National Assembly during the French Revolution. One, in particular, was taken word-for-word from the French declaration:

No one shall be disquieted on account of his opinions, including his religious views, provided their manifestation does not disturb the public order established by law.

True enough, there was wiggle room there, if Wallenstein chose to exercise it. "Disturb the public order" could become a weasel phrase easily enough, in the hands of an autocrat.

Which Wallenstein would be. His proclamations, needless to say, did not include the *political* aspects of the French and American declarations. The rights and liberties of citizens would be respected—or so, at least, Wallenstein proclaimed. But political power would remain in the hands of the new king. There was a provision for the formation of a National Assembly, but it was obvious that Wallenstein intended it to remain purely advisory.

So be it. What Wallenstein intended was one thing; what eventually resulted, another. And, in the meantime, at least Jews no longer had to wear badges or distinctive yellow hats whenever they left the ghetto. They could build synagogues anywhere in Prague— in all of Bohemia and Moravia, in fact—and could henceforth own the guns to protect them, if need be.

There was one part of the proclamation that almost made Morris laugh. Wallenstein had also ordered the dismantling of the wall of the ghetto. And, sure enough,

Dunash and his firebrands immediately began eagerly tearing down one little section of the wall near the quarter of the ghetto where they lived—ignoring the protests of most of their neighbors.

Their *Jewish* neighbors, for whom the wall was something of a comfort as well as a curse. The neighbors had even gone to register a protest with the rabbis.

The chief rabbi had hemmed and hawed. But most of the other rabbis—led by Spira and Gans, according to Jason—decided soon enough that the wisdom of the ancient Babylonian sage still applied: *The law of the land is the law.*

So, Dunash and his men had been able to proceed in the work cheerfully and unmolested.

But only for two days. In midafternoon of the third day, having established their control of Prague itself, Wallenstein and Pappenheim took most of their soldiers out of the city, marching to the southwest, to meet an oncoming army dispatched by Ferdinand II.

There was to be a second Battle of the White Mountain, it seemed.

The day after Wallenstein and Pappenheim left, Holk—who had been ordered to guard the northern frontier against any possible Saxon interference—announced that he was marching into Prague instead. "To secure the city from disorders," he was reported to have said. Or words to that drunken effect.

Whether he had decided to throw his lot in with Emperor Ferdinand, or simply couldn't resist the opportunity to loot a major city, no one knew. To the inhabitants of Prague, it hardly mattered. Not even the still-considerable body of residents who were

Habsburg loyalists wanted Holk around. Nobody in their right mind, except his own thugs, wanted Holk anywhere nearby.

Morris got the news from Red Sybolt and Jan Billek. "Is it true?" he asked.

"Seems to be," said Billek. "There is already a small stream of refugees coming into the city from the north. They believe it, certainly—that is why they are trying to get out of Holk's path."

Morris leaned out the window, scowling toward the north. "What does Holk think he's doing? If Wallenstein wins, he's dead meat."

"Does Holk 'think' at all?" Red shrugged. "He's a drunk and a thug, Morris. For all we know, he didn't decide anything at all. Maybe his own soldiers put him up to it, and he doesn't dare refuse them. Sacking a big city like Prague when it's got no real army to defend it is the kind of opportunity every mercenary dreams about in the Thirty Years' War. Look at it from their point of view. At the very least, they'll have two or three days to plunder and pillage before Wallenstein and Pappenheim get back and they have to run for it. You think the average mercenary—sure as hell in Holk's army—thinks in the long run? 'Planning for the future' for guys like that means 'gimme what I want—now.'"

Morris brought his head back, still scowling. "All right. It'll be up to you and Jan, then. Wallenstein didn't leave more than a thousand soldiers here. Good thing he didn't take your Brethren volunteers with him, too."

Red smiled lopsidedly. "Pappenheim still doesn't trust us. Not our loyalty, just how much use we'd be in a battle. He's more set in his ways than Wallenstein, you know—and with Wallenstein in the shape he's in, Pappenheim will have to do the actual commanding on the battlefield."

Morris' smile was even more lopsided than Red's. "I never thought I'd say this, but I really wish—*really* wish—Wallenstein had stayed behind. What a world! To think I'd ever find Wallenstein's presence a comfort." He shook his head. "But . . . there it is. I surely would."

He glanced up at the Hradcany. "What about the soldiers he did leave behind?"

"Oh, I think we can count on them, well enough," Billek assured him. "Pappenheim left one of his protégés in charge—young Kastner, I do not think you know him. His unit is one of the best, actually. Wallenstein and Pappenheim want something to return to, assuming they win their battle. There are still plenty of Habsburg loyalists in the population, especially among the Catholics."

"Why'd they take almost everybody with them, then?"

"Morris, be realistic," said Sybolt. "If you were Wallenstein, you'd do the same thing. If he loses this upcoming battle against the Austrians, he's finished. He's burned all his bridges behind him, now. It's not as if he figured on Holk running wild, after all—and even if he did consider the possibility, so what? If Wallenstein whips the Austrians and comes back to a wrecked and plundered Prague, he's *still* the king of Bohemia. Cities can be rebuilt, too, you know. Look at Magdeburg."

Morris took a deep breath and let it out slowly. "True. Tough on the people living in the city, though."

"Yup. Unless they protect themselves. Speaking of which, what are your orders?"

"*My* orders?" Morris stared at him. "I'm not in charge here."

Red chuckled. "Morris, sometimes you're a real babe in the woods. What does 'in charge' have to do with anything? Nobody put Holk 'in charge' either—but he's still on his way."

Sybolt stepped up to the window and studied the Hradcany for a moment. "Kastner's just a youngster, Morris. He hasn't got the confidence to take charge of the whole city. What he'll do is fort up in the castle and the key buildings in the Malá Strana below the hill—including Wallenstein's palace, of course—and just be satisfied with fending Holk off."

"He is right," said Billek. "And Holk will make no real effort to take the Hradcany. He and his men are looking for loot, not a protracted siege." He came forward and joined Sybolt at the window, examining the city. "From the direction they are coming, they will strike Prague on the west bank of the Vltava first. Then, they will recoil from Kastner's men in the Hradcany and the Malá Strana and head for the Stone Bridge. Most of Prague is on this side of the river. Not the richest part, to be sure, but Holk and his men are not fussy looters. And this is the soft part of the city."

Billek glanced at the two rabbis standing not far away. The faces of both Spira and Gans were calm enough, but tight with worry. "Especially the Josefov. Jews are not armed and everyone knows it. They will begin their plunder and ravages in Old Town and move north to the ghetto."

Morris was no military man, but, as he studied the layout of the city, he decided that Red and Jan were right. Given the nature of Holk and his army, that was exactly what they'd do.

"We should try to trap them on the Stone Bridge," he said abruptly. "Never let them get across at all."

Then a bit startled by the sureness with which he'd spoken, Morris added: "I think."

"Well, so do I," said Red. "So does Jan—we talked about it on our way over here. Good thing we've got a smart boss."

"Who made me the 'boss'?" Morris demanded. "I still don't understand—"

Billek interrupted him. That was unusual, for the normally reserved and polite leader of the Brethren. "Do not be stupid, Morris," he said forcefully. "*Don Morris,* rather."

Billek nodded toward the two rabbis. "The only way this plan will work is if the Jews hold the eastern side of the bridge and keep Holk pinned on it. While we Brethren and Red's CoC volunteers hammer them from fortified positions in the Malá Strana. We have most of the guns and will do most of the killing. But the eastern end of the bridge *must* be held—and firmly."

Spira and Gans looked startled. Billek shook his head. "As Red says, we must be realistic here. Who else *except* the Jews will hold the eastern end of the bridge from Holk—hold it at all, much less firmly? Except for the Brethren, the Christian population on the east side of the river is still confused and uncertain. They won't fight—not most of them—not against such as Holk. They will simply flee the city."

Morris felt his jaws tighten. "Whereas the Jews don't have any place to run to. If they try to leave the city, in this chaos, they'd likely be plundered by"—he almost said *the stinking goyishe villagers on the way*, but didn't—"you know, everybody. Just about."

Billek said nothing. After a moment, to Morris' surprise, Red grinned cheerfully.

"Hey, Morris, look at it this way—it happened once before, didn't it? Well, in a manner of speaking."

Morris couldn't help but smile himself. *Talk about a topsy-turvy world!* In the universe they'd come from, in the year 1648, a Swedish army had marched into Prague and taken the Hradcany and the Malá Strana on the west bank of the river. Convinced that they'd do better even under the heavy hand of the Habsburgs than at the hands of a conquering Swedish army—by the end of the Thirty Years War, Swedish armies were no more disciplined than anybody's—the Jews of Prague's ghetto had joined with Catholic students and burghers to fight off the Swedes when they tried to cross the Stone Bridge and pillage the eastern half of the city. It had been the last major battle of the Thirty Years War, in fact. It didn't end until nine days after the Peace of Westphalia was signed—and the Swedes never did make it across the bridge.

Less than a hundred years later, under Empress Maria Theresa, the Habsburgs repaid the loyalty of Prague's Jewry by expelling them from the city.

"Right," Morris growled, his smile fading. "Let's do it again—and we'll hope, this time, it turns out better in the long run."

He turned away from the window and faced the two rabbis. "Will you agree?"

Spira and Gans looked at each other. Spira nodded. Gans shrugged. "Do we have a choice? Not that I can see. And I am sure all the other rabbis will agree."

"You will be in command, yes, Don Morris?" asked Spira. He gave Billek and Red a somewhat apologetic glance. "Our people will follow you. Not . . . others."

"See?" Red demanded, smiling wider than ever. "Like I said, you're the boss."

"Make sure you are on a horse," Billek added. "Biggest horse you can find. And wear something suitable."

2

Morris had been prepared for a brawl with Dunash. He was sure the young militant would try to insist that he and his men should remain with the other Jews on the east bank, rather than fighting with the Brethren as they were supposed to do.

But, to his surprise, Red Sybolt scuttled the problem before it could even emerge.

"We may as well keep me and Dunash and the katyusha on this side anyway, Morris. Those rockets are about as accurate as spitting in the wind. If we fire them at the bridge from the Malá Strana, we're as likely to kill our own people over here as Holk's people on the bridge."

Red pointed across the river. "The Brethren will be sheltered in fortified positions over there. At the beginning, for sure. So they'll be safe enough from friendly fire, since those warheads really aren't that powerful. We designed them as antipersonnel weapons. A small charge and a lot of shrapnel, basically."

"Jan's okay with that?"

"Yeah, he and I already talked it over." Red's easy grin was back. "Besides, the truck's in your basement, remember? That was the only place secret enough to assemble it under Wallenstein's nose. Well, under

Marradas' nose. I'm pretty sure Wallenstein knows we have the thing. It'll be hard enough to haul it out of there, much less try to get it across the river and under shelter. The Malá Strana doesn't have too much in the way of garages, you know."

After he thought it over, Morris decided Red was right. If nothing else, even if the katyusha proved ineffective in the battle, just having a fabled American war machine show up in the midst of the motley "army" assembling on the eastern end of the bridge would do wonders for morale. Especially with Jews manning the thing.

Besides, he was tiring of fighting with Dunash.

"Okay, done."

He had a bigger problem with the horse. Big enough that he even lapsed into profanity for a moment. "Where the hell did you get this thing? I didn't think Clydesdales even existed in this day and age." A little whine came into his voice. "And how am I supposed to even get onto it, anyway? Especially wearing this stupid getup. With a winch?"

He was coming to detest Red's grin. "Why not? According to a movie I saw once, that's how the old knights got lifted onto their horses." Red gave the horse in question an admiring look. "And quit exaggerating. It's not a Clydesdale, not even close. Just the second biggest horse Pappenheim owns. He took the biggest one with him."

Morris grimaced. "Oh, swell. Now I'll have Pappenheim furious with me, on top of everything else. Do they hang horse thieves in Bohemia? I'm sure they do."

Red shrugged. "If you keep Prague intact, I really don't think Pappenheim's going to mind much that you used one of his horses to do it. Look, Morris. Nobody ever said being a champion wasn't risky."

"Champion." *Oh, swell. Like I need a hole in the head.*

Gloomily, Morris went back to studying the horse. He was a good horseman, to be sure—within the limits of what "good horsemanship" meant for an American whose experience was almost entirely with the sort of horses one encountered on riding trails and pack stations. Whether that would translate into being able to control a seventeenth-century warhorse...

A bit to his surprise, it did. The warhorse was more spirited than Morris was accustomed to, but on the other hand it had been trained to remain steady in the middle of a battlefield. Once he got accustomed to it, in fact, he found himself enjoying the experience. It really was quite a horse.

And, there was no doubt of one thing: as silly as he felt, riding a horse while wearing the fancy garb of a seventeenth-century nobleman, his appearance before the crowd now erecting barricades at the eastern end of the Stone Bridge had an impact. He even got cheered. A very big cheer, in fact. Jason had told Judith that the story was already widely spread of how Don Morris had slain goyishe bandits seeking to victimize the ghetto, with his powerful American arquebus. As many as ten bandits, in one version of the story.

As big a cheer as it was, though, it was not as big as the cheer the katyusha received, when Red and

Dunash's people finally managed to get it out of the basement—they used dozens of people with ropes to just *lift* it out—and Red drove it slowly forward onto the little square abutting the bridge.

Morris was startled when the initial cheer evolved into a chant: *APC! APC!* He wouldn't have guessed that the population of far-off Prague—certainly not the Jews in its ghetto—would have ever heard of that acronym. It was ironic, of course, since the "APC" was nothing of the sort. True, Red had mounted some thin armor plate to protect the engine and the driver and gunner in the front seat. But the thing was no solid and heavy coal truck. It was just an old Dodge Ram with a jury-rigged and flimsy-looking rocket launcher fixed in the bed.

It didn't matter. None of Prague's civilians had ever seen an American war machine before, but they'd heard the rumors. For them, "APC" was more in the way of a spoken talisman than anything else. And this was an age when most common folk believed in the power of talismans and amulets. That was as true for the Jews as the Christians, although the forms were different. The so-called "Book of Raziel the Angel"—the *Sefer Raziel ha-Mal'akh*—hadn't been produced yet in printed form, but parts of the ancient manuscript went back to Babylonian Talmudic times. It had drifted around the world's Jewish communities for centuries, never really approved by the rabbinate but never banned either. Morris wouldn't have been surprised to discover that a goodly percentage of the Jews building the barricades had little metal or paper amulets under their clothes, using the formulas of the *Sefer Raziel*.

When Red finally brought the pickup-cum-katyusha

to a halt, after positioning it in the firing slot left open in the barricades, he rolled down the window and gave Morris an admiring look.

"I do declare, perched way up there on that great big horse—hell of a nice plume to the hat, too—you look like the spittin' image of a hidalgo. Damn near a conquistador, in fact."

"My family came from Krakow," Morris groused. "The closest I ever got to Spain was eating tapas once in a restaurant in Philadelphia."

"Don't knock it, Morris. All that matters is that you look and act the part. They've got a recognized leader now, instead of everybody fumbling around wondering who's in charge. That'll help steady everybody's nerves—a lot—as long as you don't get yourself shot."

For some odd reason, the warhorse had a delayed reaction to the Dodge Ram. It was accustomed to the sounds of gunfire, not internal combustion engines, to be sure. But Morris never did figure out why the blasted critter chose the moment when Red turned *off* the motor to start getting jittery.

Very jittery. Morris had a few tense and interesting moments, though he managed to stay in the saddle. He did lose the hat, though.

"Or fall off the horse," Red added sarcastically.

3

That evening, after looking for Len all over the Hradcany, Ellie finally figured out where he'd be. She realized it within seconds after she returned to the rooms in the castle that the young commander Kastner had assigned to them. Kastner, worried lest Wallenstein's precious American technical experts might get hurt in the fighting, had insisted that Ellie and Len move from Wallenstein's palace into the greater safety of the fortress above.

There'd been no point arguing with him. Kastner had no idea how the telephones worked, so he had no intention of trying to use them. In what was coming, Len and Ellie would just be fifth wheels on a cart. So, Len grumbling the whole time, they'd spent the morning hauling their belongings up the hill. Then, having made the last trip alone for a few final items while Len stayed behind in order to arrange their new living quarters, she'd come back to find him gone.

She'd spent most of the afternoon searching for him, growing increasingly worried. But when she finally returned, half-exhausted from endless hiking, she noticed that the lid to one of the chests was cracked open. That chest was normally kept locked, because it was the one where they kept their personal weapons.

She opened the chest and looked. Len's 12-gauge was missing.

What could he possibly—?

—I'll kill him if the idiot—!

Oh.

It all fell into place. Not sure whether she was more relieved than exasperated, Ellie closed the chest and sat down on it. For a moment, half-slumped, she tried to decide what to do. For that matter, what to think.

Then, shrugging, she got up and left. That was her man, when it was said and done. Quirks and foibles and all.

Although even for Len, this is a doozy.

●　　　●　　　●

She found him where she'd thought she would—the one place it had never occurred to her to look the entire afternoon. The place she must have circled at least four times while she searched for him. Impossible not to, of course, since it dominated the Hradcany.

Len was sitting in one of the rear pews in the huge Gothic cathedral. Just staring at the altar, his shotgun across his knees. Ellie was sure he'd been there the whole afternoon. The handful of priests watching him were still nervous, clearly enough, but it was the kind of nervousness that had worn itself down after a few hours. A few hours while the bizarre intruder—monster from another world, with a monstrous weapon—just sat there and did nothing.

She slid into the seat next to him. "You might have left me a note, dammit!"

Len looked uncomfortable. "I started to write one, but... I don't know. I didn't know what to say. How to explain it."

Ellie sighed. Then, felt all her exasperation going away. That was the nature of the man, after all. She reached out her hand and stroked the back of his neck.

"'S okay. I shoulda figured you'd unlapse your own way. You weird duck. What? You figure on protecting the cathedral all by your lonesome?"

She gave the priests a skeptical glance. "I don't think they'd be much help, if Holk's hordes came pouring in. Not that they will, without taking the Hradcany from Kastner. Which they won't."

Len flushed. "It's the principle of the thing, Ellie. Kastner's people didn't want me underfoot anyway, so I figured... Look, religious freedom's for everybody. That means Catholics too, even if the bums running the show here screwed up. And this cathedral's ancient. It's a *holy* place, even if I don't think much of the current tenants."

His hand tightened on the stock of the shotgun. "So anybody tries anything..."

"Ha! Saint Len and the Dragon, is it?"

Len's flush deepened. His eyes now seemed riveted on the altar.

"Will you marry me?" he asked abruptly. "I've been thinking about it all afternoon."

She studied him for a moment. "I'm not getting married in a fucking church, Len."

"You shouldn't swear in here."

"*Not* in a fucking church. I can't stand churches."

Len took a deep breath, sighed. His hand finally left the stock of the shotgun and came up as if to stroke his absent mustache.

Feeling the bare skin, he sighed again. "You are one hard woman, Ellie Anderson."

There was nothing much she could say, since that was true enough. So she said nothing.

Neither did he, for maybe five minutes. Then, finally, he looked at her.

"Was that a 'yes'?"

Ellie chuckled and went back to stroking his neck. "Yes, Len, that was a 'yes.' Just not in a fucking church. If you can't live with that, you can't live with me."

She looked at the altar, then at the priests. "But I don't mind if you decide to pull crazy stunts like this, now and then. So I figure we're square."

"Okay." He stroked his nonexistent mustache. "I can live with that."

4

The first detachments from Holk's army started showing up in the outskirts of the city early the next morning. By midmorning, they were exchanging shots with Kastner's men forted up in the Hradcany; by noon, with his men forted up in the Malá Strana. By mid-afternoon, most of Holk's ragtag army had poured into the city's west bank—as undisciplined as you could ask for—and decided they'd had enough of cracking their heads against Kastner's troops.

Holk himself showed up then, on his own big warhorse, and led the charge. He waved his sword to the east, very dramatically. *That way! To the Stone Bridge!*

Tanner stayed in the cathedral the whole time, Saint Len faithfully at his post in case the dragon showed up.

Ellie, on the other hand, joined the soldiers on the walls of the Hradcany. She had a better vantage point to see what was happening than Morris and Red did, across the river. So, using her CB, she kept them informed all day of the movements of Holk and his men. Insofar as that rabble could be said to have "maneuvers" at all, other than the mercenary equivalent of Brownian motion.

When Holk showed up, though, waving his stupid sword, she put down the CB and drew her pistol. Then, cursing a blue streak, clambered up on the wall and emptied the entire clip at him.

"Where'd you go?" Red asked her, when she got back on the CB. Ellie explained in a few curt sentences, about every other word of which was short and had an Anglo-Saxon pedigree.

"Fer chrissake, Ellie—with a 9mm automatic? What're you, nuts? That's gotta be at least six hundred yards. You'd be lucky to hit the river at that range."

"It's the principle of the thing," she stoutly insisted.

CHAPTER VI: *Discovered Check*

July 1633

1

By the time Holk finally got his men organized—using the term loosely—it was almost sundown. He began to send men onto the Stone Bridge, but the small detachments retreated quickly once they started getting peppered by shots fired from the flintlock-armed men now perched behind the barricade.

So far as Ellie could tell, looking down on the bridge from the distance of the Hradcany without binoculars, that initial volley—using the term loosely—didn't do more than scare off the thugs. She didn't think a single one of them had even been wounded.

Ellie was sure Morris hadn't ordered the volley. The Stone Bridge had a span of some five hundred yards, with a little dogleg in it about one-third of the way across from the west bank. The flintlocks had started firing as soon as Holk's men made it to the dogleg and came in sight of the barricades—a range of well over three hundred yards. Maybe James Fenimore Cooper's fictional marksman Natty Bumppo could hit something with a flintlock at that range, but ghetto-dwellers with meager experience with firearms hadn't much more chance than Ellie had with her 9mm.

Red confirmed her assessment. "Naw, just buck fever. Morris is fit to be tied. Good thing he ain't a cursing man. He's doing a pretty good job right now of flaying them alive with proper language. He's even waving his sword around."

Ellie stared at the now-darkening western bank, dumbfounded. "Morris has a *sword*? Where the fuck did he get a sword?"

Red's chuckle crackled in the CB. "Judith had it made up for him, believe it or not. Presented it to him this morning, scabbard and everything. She even had a special scabbard made up so he could sling his rifle on the horse."

Ellie burst out laughing. "Judith Roth—the gray eminence. It's like they say: 'behind every successful man there's a woman.'"

"No shit. And you should see the collection of women she's got around her, right here on this end of the bridge. Every prestigious matron in the ghetto, near as I can tell. Oh, sure, they're all being proper as you could ask for—but you can't fool me. Patriarchy be damned. That's the biggest collection of political clout in one city this side of old Mayor Daley's grave."

A moment later he added, in the satisfied tones of an longtime union agitator: "We're pretty well organized over here, actually. If Morris can just keep those eager beavers from wasting all the ammunition. And if he can keep from stabbing himself with the sword. He handles it like a butcher knife. Except he ain't an experienced butcher. Personally, I wish he'd start swinging the rifle around. THAT he knows what he's doing with."

Ellie shook her head firmly, even though Red

couldn't possibly see the gesture. He was perched in the cab of the Dodge Ram, over half a mile away. "It's the principle of the thing, fella. You don't rally troops with a rifle. You do it with a sword. Haven't you ever seen any movies?"

Had Judith Roth heard the exchange, she would have disagreed. She was watching Morris also, and while she'd have admitted that he wasn't exactly handling the sword with panache, he was doing a fair job with it nonetheless. There was certainly no danger that he'd stab himself. Cut himself, maybe. Judith had made sure that the sword's tip had been blunted when she ordered it made.

Still and all, everything considered, she thought he looked superb. The horse was magnificent, Morris himself looked very distinguished in his nobleman's garb—the big plumed hat helped a lot—and nobody watching on this side of the river really had any more idea than Morris did how a sword should properly be held anyway. It was enough that he had one and was swinging it around authoritatively while bellowing authoritative-sounding orders.

Most of all, he didn't look afraid. Not in the least. In fact, he looked downright fearless.

And that was such an odd sensation, for Judith. That her husband was a brave enough man, in those myriad little ways with which people confront the challenges of daily life, Judith had known for many years. But that was the quiet courage of a husband and a father and a countryman, not the same thing at all as the dramatic valor of a commander on the battlefield.

She wasn't really that surprised that Morris could *do* it. But she was well-nigh astonished that he could do it so well in public.

One of the women standing next to her, on the far side of the little square where the barricades had been erected, spoke softly in her ear. "I am very glad your husband is here, gracious lady. And you also."

That was Eva Bacharach, a woman just about Judith's age. Her brothers Chaim and Napthali were noted rabbis, and Eva herself was the widow of a rabbi who had died almost twenty years earlier. Since her husband Abraham had died, Eva had raised their three daughters and one son, somehow managing at the same time to gain quite a reputation in the ghetto as a noted Hebraist and a scholar in her own right. Even the rabbis were known to consult with her on difficult textual problems.

When Judith first learned that, from another woman in the ghetto, she'd been so surprised that her expression must have shown it. The woman had chuckled and said dryly: "Gracious lady, we are in Prague, not Amsterdam."

That short phrase had crystallized Judith's growing conviction that her husband's projected head-on collision with orthodox Judaism needed to be sidetracked before the inevitable train wreck ensued.

Prague, not Amsterdam.

Amsterdam's rabbinate was notorious all over Europe for pigheadedness, intolerance and authoritarianism. Whereas the rabbinate of Prague had been shaped, in the previous century, by one of the few rabbis of the era whose name would be remembered for centuries: Judah Loew ben Bezalel, also known as the Maharal. A man who became a legend in his own time for his learning and wisdom—a legend which only grew after his death. One of the great rabbis of the early modern era, a shaper of the orthodox tradition—yet also conversant with the scientific knowledge of the time and on friendly terms with many of its great scientists. One of his disciples, David Gans—a cousin of Mordechai Spira's friend Isaac—had studied for a time with Tycho Brahe.

The Maharal. Eva's grandfather, as it happened. And one of Judith's own ancestors.

Judith turned to look at Eva. "I am very glad we are here also. And will be staying. But—please—call me Judith. We are related, you know."

Eva's eyebrows went up. "Oh, yes," Judith said. "I am one of your descendants, Eva Bacharach. Very distant, of course. And also a descendant of your grandfather—I can remember how excited I was when I learned *that.*"

Judith laughed softly. "In the world I came from, they even made what we call a 'movie' about him. True, it was because of the legend that grew up that he created the golem. But I knew enough to understand how much more important he was for all his other work."

"The golem!" Eva choked. "That silly story! Do you mean to tell me that—that—in some other world, wherever that may be—people actually *believe* it?"

Judith wagged her head in a semi-jocular manner. "Maybe yes, maybe no. It's one of those stories that people want to believe, even if they really don't."

Now Eva was laughing softly also. "My grandfather would have been mortified! Ha! The golem!"

When the laughter ebbed, Eva cocked her head and regarded Judith a bit sideways. "The rabbis will probably need to spend a hundred years—maybe two hundred—chewing on the significance of that other world of yours and what we should think about it all. But since we are women, we are not under their obligations. Much easier for us."

"Yes, I agree. Much easier. Quicker, too."

Eva nodded sagely. "Yes. Much quicker."

Perhaps twenty yards away, on the same side of the square as Judith and Eva, Mordechai Spira and Isaac Gans were also watching Morris.

"We will not be able to ignore this man," Mordechai stated, quietly but firmly. "Never think it, Isaac."

His friend and fellow rabbi made a little snorting sound. "I didn't think we would. Or should, for that matter. By now, I don't think even Joseph ben Abraham Khalmankhes retains that delusion. Certainly none of the other rabbis do."

Mordechai nodded. "Good. The beginning of wisdom is like everything else. Always the hardest part."

"It won't be so bad," Issac predicted. "In some ways, even good. Complicated, though, yes."

Spira chuckled. " 'Complicated,' applied to this problem, is like saying the sun is bright. Just for a start, do we decide to accept or not those books of young Jason's? It is one thing to respect wisdom. But are we also obliged to respect the wisdom of another universe altogether?"

"You know my opinion. Does not the midrash say that the Holy One, Blessed be He, created many universes before this one? Could He not continue to do so?" Gans shrugged. "How can it matter how many universes there are? There is still only one God."

"Yes, I know your opinion—and I am inclined to share it. Still..."

Mordechai Spira shook his head. "I am not one of those Amsterdam blockheads who finds heresy everywhere he looks. But I started reading that translation you made for me of that one book of Jason's—the one by Mordechai Kaplan—and..."

Gans smiled slyly. "It's interesting, though, admit it."

"Oh, yes. 'Reconstructionist' Judaism, if you will! The number of schisms our descendants seem to have managed to find." Again, he shook his head. "Almost as bad as Christians."

"On the other hand, there is a lot to admire also. And, whatever else, if Jason's commentaries add to our understanding of Him and his Holy Torah, we must respect them. Subject them to searching analysis and criticism, to be sure, as Rabbi Moshe Ben Nachman did to even Maimonides' work. But respect them nonetheless." Isaac's smile widened. "And the truth is, I am particularly taken by the works of the Chasidim that Jason had with him."

Mordechai cocked a questioning eyebrow. Isaac made a little apologetic gesture with his hand. "Sorry, I haven't had time to translate those yet. But—"

He was interrupted by a commotion on the southern side of the square. As the crowd there parted, Mordechai and Isaac could see that a large group of young men was advancing—somewhat tentatively, almost diffidently—toward the Stone Bridge. All of them were armed, though only a few of them with firearms.

They were all gentiles, clearly enough. After a moment, Isaac identified them.

"Christian students. From the Karolinum."

Mordechai brought his eyes back to Morris Roth. The American don was now trotting his horse toward the oncoming students. He had sheathed his sword and was not projecting an aura of menace. But he nonetheless managed to look authoritative. Very authoritative, in fact.

Spira found himself quite thankful that Don Morris was handling the situation, which could easily become tense. Then, found himself pondering his own reaction.

Indeed, it was so. Don Morris could not be ignored. Nor should he be, even if it were possible. For good or ill, Spira was quite sure that the man would bestride their world in the years to come. Whether as a champion or a menace—or both—remained to be seen. Supported, perhaps; combated, perhaps. Most likely both, Mordechai suspected, at different times. But whatever else, never ignored.

Mordechai and Isaac were too far away to hear the exchange between Don Morris and the Christian students from the Karolinum. But, within a short time, the resolution was obvious. With Don Morris on his warhorse prancing in their lead, the students came to join the Jews already on the barricade.

"So it is," Mordechai stated. "It will be complicated. But you were saying something?"

As he watched the students begin intermingling with the fighters on the barricade, Isaac spoke softly. "There is a lot of wisdom in those pages Jason brought to us, Mordechai. The wisdom of the Chasidic folktales, in particular, I think will serve us well in the time to come."

"And what do those stories relate?"

"I will give you two. In the first, a simple wagon-driver stops his cart at the side of the road to speak the

Hebrew alphabet, one letter at a time. 'God,' he cries out, 'I don't know the prayers, so I am sending you the alphabet. You must know the prayers. Make them up out of the letters I am sending.'"

Mordechai barked a laugh. "Oh, I like that! And the other?"

"Ah, that one is my favorite. It seems one day a disciple came to complain to his teacher. 'Rabbi, some of the congregants are gossiping in the midst of prayer!'"

Spira smiled crookedly. "Not such a different world after all, then. And the rabbi's response?"

"'O God,' said the rabbi. 'How wonderful are your people! Even in the midst of gossip, they devote a few moments to prayer!'"

Shortly thereafter, the first campfires began springing up on the opposite bank of the river. Holk and his men were settling in for the night, it seemed, and would make no further attempt to storm the bridge until the next morning.

At sundown, Mordechai Spira returned to his home in the ghetto. The fighters would remain on the barricades, keeping watch through the night, with Don Morris there to lead them and keep them steady. But there was no reason for him to remain. Mordechai would return before daybreak, to do what he could. But he wanted to spend this night—perhaps their last—with his family.

Over the dinner, he told the stories to his wife and children. And was still smiling himself when he finally went to bed.

●   ●   ●

The rabbi slept soundly that night, but Holk and his mercenaries did not. Jan Billek took advantage of the darkness to move his Brethren forward, from the positions they'd initially taken farther south in the Malá Strana. From their new positions, skirmishers were able to harass Holk's mercenaries all through the night. Occasionally with gunfire, but usually with grenades and swords, in constant probing sallies.

It was a bitter, nasty sort of fighting. And if none of the Brethren were as nasty as Holk's men, they were considerably more bitter. They had been victimized for years by such men, and were finally able to take some revenge.

They were also a lot more determined and resolute. Holk's ruffians had come into Prague expecting an easy and pleasant few days of murder, rape, arson and looting. They had not expected to spend their first night in the city worrying about getting their throats cut by dimly seen figures lunging from the darkness—or getting shredded by bomblets suddenly launched into their campfires.

Not all that many of Holk's men were actually killed or wounded that night. Less than a hundred. But none of them slept well, and a considerable number didn't sleep at all.

Except Holk himself. He was drunk by sundown, and comatose by midnight.

2

"Okay, Red. Tell Morris they'll be coming any minute. Holk's done with the cursing and he's starting to threaten people with his sword. No, I take it back.

I can't see too well from here, but I think he's put the sword away and now he's threatening them with a wheel-lock pistol."

"Thanks, Ellie, I'll tell him." Sybolt leaned out of the cab window and hollered the news to Morris. Then, quipped to Dunash in the passenger seat: "It's the old story. 'Go get 'em, boys! You first!'"

Dunash was too nervous to appreciate the jest. The young man was doing his best to retain his composure—and doing quite well at it—but only by adopting a stern and stiff demeanor. Butter wouldn't melt in his mouth. In fact, Red thought, you could probably use it for an icebox.

"Relax, old son. This is gonna be a cakewalk. Trust me."

Dunash made no reply for perhaps half a minute. Then, abruptly, almost harshly: "Why would anyone walk on a cake? And what does that mean, anyway?"

Red shook his head ruefully. "Gawd, all the work it's going to take me to recover my reputation as an endless source of wit and wisdom. Oh, well. What it means, Dunash, is that we're going to win this battle. Easily."

"Why do you think that?"

Red pointed at the roof of the cab. "Because of this thing. Mind you—in general, that is—I think it's about as useless a gadget on the battlefield as you could imagine. I guess the Russians did pretty well with katyushas in the Second World War, but they used jillions of 'em. Just one? Pointless."

Dunash was inordinately proud of the katyusha. "Why?" he asked, in a very aggrieved tone.

"It's an area effect weapon, Dunash. Rockets—sure as hell these—aren't that accurate. If you've got a ton of them the way the Russkies did, that's one thing. Saturation bombardment, they call it. But just one? Pointless. On a battlefield, that is."

"Then why did you—"

"On a *battlefield,* I said." Red jabbed his finger at the quarter-inch steel plate that covered the windshield except for small viewing slits left for the driver and the gunner. "But that's a bridge, not a battlefield. A bridge that's the only way to cross the Vltava without boats—which Holk didn't think to bring with him, and he can't round up now that he's here because Jan and his boys made sure all the ones in Prague were taken up the river."

Red leaned forward over the steering wheel and peered through the viewing slit. "A bridge that I figure is not more than fifty feet wide and at least five hundred yards long. With no cover on it anywhere—not even the statues that Len says used to be on it hundreds of years from now—and only that one little dogleg way over to the other side of the span. Oh, those poor bastards. They've gotta cross about a quarter of a mile in plain sight with only maybe fifteen of them—okay, make it twenty with that mob—in the front line."

He leaned back, very satisfied. "Would *you* want to be one of those fifteen or twenty guys? I sure as hell wouldn't. Not with two hundred flintlocks and a fair number of old-style arquebuses banging away at me." He rapped the roof of the cab with his knuckles. "Not to mention after this baby cuts loose."

"Morris won't let them fire until they get within a hundred yards," Dunash pointed out. "So what does the rest of that distance mean?" Sourly, he looked at the firing switches mounted on the dashboard in front of him: "And you won't let me fire this until they get within *fifty* yards."

"All it'll take, boy. You watch." He opened the door to the cab and began climbing out. "But now that you bring it up, I better make sure those hotshots of yours didn't fiddle with my instructions."

They hadn't, although Red was sure they'd been tempted to. Most down-timers, in his experience, even ones with considerable military experience, tended to exaggerate the capabilities of American weapons. Enthusiasts like Dunash's followers, even more so. But the young men tending the rocket launcher in the bed of the pickup had left the settings alone. Even though it must have aggravated them to see that Red had lowered the elevation until the rockets were pointed at the ground right in front of the truck.

Well, almost. Red estimated that the rockets would hit somewhere between fifty and a hundred yards ahead. Exactly what he wanted.

"Those rockets could hit the Hradcany from here!" one of them complained, as Red started to clamber down out of the bed.

Once he was back on the ground, Red squinted at the fortress in question. He was still without glasses, so it wasn't much more than a blur to him.

"Oh, sure, they can fly that far. But *hit* it? Be a pure accident." He pointed toward the Malá Strana. "They'd be just as likely to hit Wallenstein's palace. Just do it my way, boys. Holk's got as much chance of getting across this bridge as a pig does of flying. You watch."

After he got back into the truck and closed the door, Red cocked his head and smiled at Dunash. "Pigs *can* fly, you know."

Dunash frowned; as often, not sure whether Red was kidding or not.

"Sure they can," Red insisted. "Throw one off the highest wall in Prague Castle sometime and see for yourself."

The CB squawked. "They're starting the charge, Red! They're on their way!"

His eyes came back to the firing slit, as he reached for the CB. "Yup, that pig'll fly. All the way to the ground."

Only seconds thereafter, Morris could see the first ranks himself, charging across the bridge. Using the term "ranks" very loosely, of course. Holk's men just looked like a mob.

For a moment, he reached for the sword, ready to start swinging it around again as he bellowed meaningless but reassuringly martial words. But, as if it had a mind of its own, his hand went to the stock of his rifle instead.

He decided his hand was smarter than his brain. So, he drew the rifle out of the saddle holster his wife had had made for him. Then, with motions than were much surer than those with which he held a sword, jacked a round into the chamber and propped the butt of the rifle on his hip.

And said nothing. He just couldn't think of anything to say, since it was all too obvious. The brigands were coming and he intended to shoot them down. Simple as that. What was there to say about it?

His hand *was* smarter than his brain. Morris Roth had no way of knowing it—and never would—but the easy and assured motion, and the silence that followed, had precisely the right effect on the men on the barricades. Almost all of whom had been nervously watching him, once they realized the fight was finally underway.

In truth, it had a much more profound effect than any amount of sword-waving and speechifying could have had, at least with that assemblage of warriors-that-weren't. Shopkeepers, butchers, bakers, students—rabbinical students, some of them. With the exception of a few of the former seamen, who'd dealt with pirates, almost none of them had ever been in a battle before of any kind—much less a pitched battle against an army with as ferocious a reputation as Holk's. True, the tactical situation was completely in their favor, but they didn't really have the experience to know that.

But Don Morris did—or so, at least, they blithely assumed. He'd *told* them they could win, hadn't he? In speech after speech given the day before. And, now that the fury was finally about to fall on their heads, wasn't Don Morris sitting on his saddle not more than ten yards behind the barricade, as calm as could be? Not even bothering with his sword—not even *aiming* his rifle. Just...

Waiting.

He didn't speak until Holk's forces were within two hundred yards. "Fire when I do!" he commanded. Quite sure, this time, that he would be obeyed.

Red glanced into the side mirror of the pickup. "Shit," he snarled. "Dunash, tell—"

He opened the door. "Never mind, I'll do it myself."

Hopping out of the truck, Red took several steps toward the rear, making broad shooing motions with his arms. "All of you get the hell out of the way!" he bellowed. "The backblast on these rockets is fierce!"

A number of women and children and old men had started crowding in behind the pickup to get a better look at the oncoming soldiers. They didn't really understand what Red was shouting at them, but they got the gist of it well enough. A moment later, Red had a clear firing lane again.

He clambered back into the truck.

"They're almost here!" Dunash hissed.

Red squinted through the slit. "Oh, bullshit. I can't see the whites of their eyes."

He glanced over and saw that Dunash's hands were twitching, as if they couldn't wait to flip the firing switches.

"Whites of their eyes," he growled. "You don't flip those switches till I say so."

The day before, just to be sure there wouldn't be a problem, Morris had fired the rifle while in the saddle. The warhorse hadn't even flinched.

When the first of Holk's men was within one hundred yards, Morris brought the rifle butt to his shoulder. He'd removed the telescopic sight the day before, seeing no use for it in the coming fray. Peering over the iron sights, he saw that his guess had been correct. At that range, firing into that mob, he could hardly miss with a blindfold on.

He squeezed the trigger. Oddly, as he did so, thinking only of the horse.

I wonder if Pappenheim would sell it to me?

3

The stern control Morris had managed to gain over his motley troops had its effect. This time, the first volley was actually that—a volley. A single, hammering blow at the enemy, shocking men with its power even more than the actual casualties inflicted.

The casualties themselves were . . . not as good as they could have been, had experienced troops fired that volley. Many of the shots went wild, more than usual with such inaccurate firearms.

So, Holk's men reeled and staggered, but they came on nonetheless, almost without breaking stride. Granted, these weren't men of the caliber of the great armies of Tilly or Gustavus Adolphus. Holk had known what he was doing when he delayed his arrival at Breitenfeld. On *that* battlefield, his thugs would have been coyotes at a wolf party. Still, they were mercenary soldiers with fifteen years of the Thirty Years War under their belts. They'd charged into gunfire before, and knew that the only way to get through it was just to plunge ahead, pikes leveled.

They were all pikemen in the front ranks. The clumsy arquebuses of the seventeenth century would have been almost useless in this kind of charge across a long and narrow bridge. And pikes always had the advantage of sheer terror, in a frontal assault. Outside of a cavalry charge, there was perhaps nothing quite as intimidating as the sight of hundreds of pikes, each of them almost twenty feet long and tipped with a cruel foot-long blade, charging directly at you.

Of course, it would have helped if Holk's men had

been able to level the pikes. But, in that pressing mob, with no ranks being maintained, that was impossible for all but the very foremost. The first thing a pikeman learned was that a pike could easily kill or main the man in front of him, if not handled carefully. Those who didn't learn it—and quickly—found themselves out of the army. Sometimes, in a coffin. The term "fragging" didn't exist yet, but nobody had to teach seventeenth-century mercenaries how to deal with a fellow soldier who was a danger to his mates—or a sub-officer, for that matter.

The second volley was more ragged, but it struck even harder. The range was shorter. Fifty yards. Holk's men were definitely staggering, but still they came on. They had no choice, really, since by now there were thousands of men behind them on the bridge, pushing them forward.

"Okay, shoot," Red said quietly.

Dunash's fingers flew to the firing switches.

That volley broke the charge. To Holk and his men, it seemed as if a dragon had suddenly belched. Licking down the bridge with a tongue of fire that just seemed to engulf men whole. Swallow entire *ranks* of them.

The katyusha was firing the second generation of rockets that Grantville had been able to manufacture in quantity. It was a variation on the old nineteenth-century Hale 24-pounder rotary rocket—2.4 inches in diameter, slightly less than two feet long, with a maximum range of 4000 yards. The propellant as well as the warhead were black powder. The rockets were fired from a single-level rack, twelve tubes mounted side by side on an adjustable framework fixed into the bed of the Dodge Ram.

Red had foreseen the impact of the rockets fired at such close range on such a narrow target. The maximum flight time for a Hale rocket was about twenty seconds, most of it ballistic. At that point-blank range, the Hale rockets struck the advancing troops in split-seconds. But what he hadn't foreseen—was almost aghast when he witnessed it—was the effect of the stone retaining walls on either side of the bridge.

The rockets struck the paving of the bridge, just as Red had foreseen, between fifty and a hundred yards ahead. Some of them exploded instantly, but not most of them. Red had chosen to use contact fuses for this battle instead of the self-lit fuse that had been the standard for the old Hale rockets. But since the somewhat jury-rigged contact fuses available in this day and age made him nervous, he'd adjusted them to fire only in the event they made a direct hit.

Which most of them didn't. They struck the stones at a low glancing angle and kept on, sailing and skidding down the bridge—caroming off the low walls—until they finally ran out of fuel and momentum or hit something solid enough to explode. The narrowness of the bridge concentrated the impact, but it was the walls that channeled it into sheer havoc.

Without uptime propellant the black powder rockets were occasionally prone to explosion—CATO, as the rocket club kids called it ("Catastrophe At Take Off")—caused by an unforeseen bounce or bump that cracked the grain. Then the rockets were little more than large bombs, more black powder burning than could be safely ejected as the pressure rose. Red preferred not to have twenty pounds of black powder exploding near his head, so he'd inspected them carefully. One of them did burst, nonetheless. But that fact didn't make the charging enemy infantry any happier. The rocket exploded some fifty feet in front of the truck and became a huge ball of fire and flying debris hurtling towards Holk's troops at hundreds of miles per hour. A shot of grape from a six-pounder couldn't have been more effective. Grape didn't set the recipient on fire.

Two of the rockets, on the other hand, never exploded at all. Red later found one of them lying on the stones not more than fifty yards from the other end of the bridge. But that didn't matter, either. All twelve of the rockets in that volley did their damage, even those two—and far more damage than Red had foreseen. It was as if the dragon had a dozen serpent tongues, licking down the great Stone Bridge for hundreds of yards, racing the length of the span up to the dogleg in less than two seconds. Hissing with fury, belching smoke, upending dozens of terrified men for every one they killed or wounded—which meant dozens of pikes flailing about, gashing and bashing and wounding still more.

The sheer weight of the charge would probably have kept it going, struck only by bullets. Men at the front being shoved forward willy-nilly by those at the rear. But the dragon-tongues ravaged the men in the first hundred yards, paralyzed and confused those behind them—and gave those at the very rear the time to do what soldiers rarely have in a frontal assault.

Time to think things over.

Even the best mercenary soldiers are not given to mindless obedience to orders. And Holk's men were far from the best. The charge staggered to a halt, and the men at the rear began coming back off the bridge. That relieved the pressure on those ahead of them; and, inchoate rank after rank, Holk's charge started disintegrating.

It took time, of course. Perhaps fifteen minutes, in all. But the critical furious momentum of the initial charge had been lost, and Holk's officers were neither good enough nor respected enough to rally the army. They did manage, four times, to paste together small charges from those men toward the front who could be convinced or cajoled or bullied into it. But the first three of those charges were driven off, easily enough, by the flintlocks and the arquebuses.

By then, Dunash's rocketeers had been able to reload the katyusha, and the dragon belched again. The fourth charge was shredded, and Holk's men had had *enough*. This was even worse than the Hradcany. They hadn't signed on to fight a damn dragon.

So, back they came, in a hurry, leaving hundreds of dead and dying and wounded behind them on the bridge. Two of the corpses were those of sub-officers, too stupid or inexperienced to understand when it was time to stop trying to force mercenary soldiers to do something they really, really, really didn't want to do any more. One of them bled to death from no fewer than five stab wounds.

4

"For Chrissake, Red, it's obvious even from here. Tell Morris to quit screwing around with his stupid modesty act and start waving his hat. And while he's

at it, do the Roy Rogers bit with the fucking horse. Y'know, rearing up on the hind legs. Whatever they call that silly stunt, I don't know. I can't stand big fucking animals. Damn things are dangerous. Even cats make me nervous, with their fangs and shit."

5

After Red whispered in his ear—well, shouted in his ear—Morris did take off his big, wide-brimmed plumed hat and wave it around, acknowledging the enthusiastic roars of approval from the crowd. He drew the line, though, at rearing the horse.

It didn't matter, really. Ellie was too nervous about a lot of things. After that sunny day in Prague, in July of the year 1633—as Christians counted it; for the Jews who made up most of the crowd it was the month of Av and the year was 5393—it wouldn't have mattered if Don Morris had fallen off the horse entirely—or lost his hat in the river.

Don Morris, he was; and Don Morris he would always remain. For them as well as their descendants who heard the tale. It had been a long time, after all—a very long time—since the Ashkenazim of central and eastern Europe had had a martial hero of their own. The ancient Hebrews had had a multitude, of course; and the Sephardim, in their Iberian heyday, more than a few. But for the Ashkenazim of Europe, for many centuries, heroism had been something that could only be measured by martyrs.

Martyrs were to be cherished, certainly. But it was nice—delightful, in fact—not to have to do it again. And who was to say? Perhaps never again. There

were those other men, after all, who would outlive
Don Morris. The much younger Jews who looked very
bold and handsome, perched up there on that strange
thing that was so much bigger and more deadly than a
mere horse. And didn't seem to be afraid of it at all.

Perhaps the golem was not simply a silly legend.
The Maharal had been a *very* wise man. One of the
wisest, even in a city of wise men like Prague.

6

As usually happens in history, the famous Battle of
the Bridge didn't have a neat ending. Holk and his
men never tried to charge across the bridge again. But
they did remain in Prague for days thereafter, burning
and plundering what they could in the Malá Strana.

One part of the plan had not worked. Billek and
his Brethren had tried—quite valiantly—to trap Holk's
army on the bridge and slaughter them wholesale. But
Holk had twice as many men in his army as he could
get onto the bridge in one charge, and if he was a
drunk and a brute he was not actually incompetent.
So, he'd stationed half his army to protect the western
entrance to the bridge, and the Brethren were unable
to drive them off. Indeed, they suffered fairly heavy
casualties in the attempt.

And continued to suffer them, the next day. The
crude fact, soon evident, was that Billek's inexperienced volunteers simply couldn't stand toe-to-toe with
Holk's toughs in a pitched battle. They tried, the next
morning, fighting in the open in the streets, but by
noon Billek realized his mistake and ordered a retreat.
Thereafter, in the days that followed, the Brethren

went back to their tactics of harassment and fighting from well-fortified positions.

At that, they were extremely capable—just as their Hussite ancestors, from the shelters of their armored wagons, had been very good at breaking noble cavalry. They couldn't defeat Holk—couldn't even drive him off—but they could certainly bleed him. And, what was most important, bleed the morale of his army.

Morris, during those same days, lapsed frequently into profanity. Understandably enough, having driven off the charge across the bridge on the first day and being in no real danger thereafter, the Jews of the ghetto were reluctant to get involved in the fighting still taking place in the Malá Strana. That was a goyishe battle in a goyishe part of the city where few of them had ever gone, and fewer still had ever lived. All of Morris' attempts to plead and convince and cajole them—even curse them, which he did more than once—had little effect.

But Dunash and his young firebrands came into their own, during those same days. They *did* participate in the fighting. First, at irregular intervals, by racing onto the bridge—almost all the way across, on one occasion—and firing rocket volleys at Holk's encampment. Then, racing off before Holk's cannons could retaliate. (Holk had finally brought in his artillery, three days too late to do any good.)

Secondly, perhaps more importantly, every day after sundown at least some of Dunash's men made their way across the river in a few small boats that they'd kept safely hidden away. Once there, they joined the Brethren in their nightly harassment of Holk's forces.

In purely military terms, they were not much of a factor. But the political effect was significant—and, by the fourth day, was starting to result in a steady trickle of recruits to Dunash's miniature army. In any population of fifteen thousand people, there are a fair number of bold youngsters who don't see things the way their sage elders do.

Most of the Malá Strana was in ruins, by the end, though civilian casualties were minimal. Fortunately, the inhabitants of that section of Prague had fled before Holk arrived. For that matter—much to the disgruntlement of Holk's troops—they'd taken their valuable belongings with them. The destruction wreaked by Holk's army during the week it spent in Prague was not so much due to looting, as such; it was simply the mindless destruction and arson visited upon a town by frustrated and angry troops. Who became even more frustrated, the more they wrecked and burned, because their own living quarters and rations got steadily worse as a result.

Holk would have tried to restrain them, had he not been Heinrich Holk. Being Holk, it never once occurred to him to do so.

Then, a week after the siege of Prague began, word came from the southwest. A second battle of the White Mountain had indeed been fought. Actually, the battle was fought a good twenty miles away from the White Mountain, but since victors get to name battles, "the Second Battle of the White Mountain" it was.

It seemed that Wallenstein thought it made a nice touch, to inaugurate the new kingdom of Bohemia and Moravia.

Oh, yes. He'd won. Pappenheim and his dreaded Black Cuirassiers had pursued the retreating Austrians for miles, slaughtering pitilessly.

"Practicing for Holk," Pappenheim was reported to have said afterward.

The news arrived in the morning. By late afternoon, Holk's army was out of Prague, racing for the north. Holk, it was said, had already opened negotiations with the Elector of Saxony, John George, looking for a new employer. And shelter from the coming storm.

7

But there was no storm on the day that Wallenstein and Pappenheim finally returned to Prague—other than a storm of applause from the residents of the city who greeted his victorious army, on both banks of the river. Whatever private reservations any of them had regarding the change of power, nobody was willing any longer to speak out in open opposition.

Not even the Catholics in the city. First, because the Jesuits dominated the Catholic church in Bohemia. Wallenstein had always been partial to the Jesuits, and had sent them a friendly private note assuring them that they would be able to remain in Prague unmolested—provided, of course, they agreed to cease and desist their activities against Protestants on behalf of the Austrian Habsburgs.

The Jesuits hadn't decided yet, how they would react to that last provision. But they didn't have to fear for their own lives in the immediate period.

The second reason they decided to stay, however,

and abide by Wallenstein's conditions—at least for the moment—would have amazed Ellie Anderson. Whatever she thought of Len Tanner's behavior during the siege, the Jesuits had reacted otherwise. Quirky—even foolish—he might have been. But, as the days passed and the pudgy American kept returning to his self-assigned post of duty in the cathedral, always with that bizarre weapon in his hands, the Jesuits came to the conclusion that whatever Wallenstein might think, his new American allies had their own opinions. And, whatever else, were clearly stubborn about them.

That was an interesting datum, with interesting possibilities for the future. The Jesuits in Prague duly recorded their impressions in several letters they sent to their Father General in Rome, Mutio Vitelleschi. They did so, of course, in the full knowledge that Vitelleschi was close to the Pope and would pass along their letters. The gist of them, in any event. So, the Jesuits would be patient. They were trained, and accustomed, to thinking in the long run.

Most of the crowd gathered to cheer Wallenstein's army, however, were Protestants of one sort or another—counting the Brethren and the Utraquists in their number, although they predated Martin Luther—and the Jews. Those people were far less ambivalent about the situation. Granted, Wallenstein was still an enigmatic figure, and a somewhat unsettling one. But the Habsburgs weren't enigmatic at all. Most of Prague's residents had had more than enough of the royal bigot Ferdinand II, sitting on his throne in Vienna.

And, finally, there was this: Wallenstein did not return alone. He had Pappenheim, of course, but he also brought with him tangible proof that his new regime had secured at least one redoubtable ally: the United States in Thuringia, if not perhaps the entire Confederated Principalities of Europe.

The proof came in the form of two APCs that Mike Stearns sent to Bohemia the minute he got word from Morris Roth—yes, there had been a long-distance radio stashed in that great mansion's basement, along with so many other treasures—that the political crisis had finally erupted and it was time for the United States to forego all secrecy. The APCs had not arrived in time to play any role at the second battle of the White Mountain, but they did arrive in time to join Wallenstein's triumphal procession back into Prague.

The only unfortunate episode in the day's celebrations—and that, only mildly unfortunate— was that the biggest cheer of all was not reserved for Wallenstein himself. That cheer erupted, quite spontaneously, when the two APCs from Grantville rumbled onto the Stone Bridge from the Malá Strana side and were met halfway by the katyusha coming from the east bank. Now that they could see what a *real* APC looked like, almost dwarfing the katyusha drawn up before it, Prague's citizens were greatly heartened. Their own little one had driven off Holk, no? Who knew what the big ones could do?

Best of all, perhaps—at least for fifteen thousand of the city's residents—was that the katyusha was festooned with banners. One—the largest, of course—was Wallenstein's new banner. But there was also, resting alongside it, the banner of the Josefov. The central image on the flag was that of a hexagram—a symbol that had, in another universe, evolved over the centuries into the Star of David.

There was something very fitting about it all, they thought. So far as anyone knew, Prague had been the first city in Europe whose Jews were given the right to fly their own flag. They had been given that right in the Christian year 1354—by the same Emperor Charles IV who had built the Stone Bridge it was now flying over, and which that katyusha had so valiantly defended.

Uriel Abrabanel had returned also, with the APCs. He'd come onto the bridge with the war machines, but he'd kept going, walking all the way across.

Morris came out of the crowd to greet him. "'Bout time you got back," he grumbled. "Where were you when all the dust was flying?"

Uriel grinned, quite unabashed. "I was busy. Never mind with what, I won't tell you. Besides, flying dust is no place for a proper spy. That's the business of princes and soldiers—and hidalgos, I hear."

"Just what I need. More rumors." Morris made a face. "So? Are you staying?"

"Certainly. Spies are all mercenaries at heart, you know. I also hear that the new hidalgo in Prague is a very generous patron."

Morris sighed. "Et tu, Brute? Soak the rich Jew, that's all anybody thinks about. Even other Jews."

"Stop whining. You need a good spy. Better yet, a good spymaster."

Morris thought about it. Not for very long. "Boy, isn't that the truth? Okay, Uriel, you're hired."

CHAPTER VII: *End Game*

August 1633

1

"That is a ridiculous price for that horse." Pappenheim was smiling when he said it, though. A rather cold and thin smile, true, but—

From Pappenheim, that was good enough.

"All I can afford," Morris insisted. "It's not the horse that's the problem, Gottfried, it's the cost of feeding the great brute."

"And that statement is even more ridiculous. Not about the horse's appetite—I know what that costs—but the rest of it."

Pappenheim's eyes ranged up and down Morris' figure, examining his apparel. "What, no pearls? They're quite in fashion, I'm told, in Paris and Vienna—and you needn't worry about the sumptuary laws any longer, because the King of Bohemia has abolished all of them."

Morris was tempted to state that was because Wallenstein was a clotheshorse himself, but he wisely refrained. It *was* an autocracy, after all, even if Morris Roth was about as well-respected and well-regarded a courtier—in Bohemia, at least—as any in Europe. And he didn't even have to fawn all over his monarch to maintain the status. Clotheshorse or not, Wallenstein was far more interested in results than flattery.

Pappenheim rose from his chair. "Oh, let's be done with it. Morris, I give you the horse as a gift. In fact, I'll even include a full set of cuirassier armor to go with it. In recognition of your valor at the bridge."

He grinned at Morris' startled expression. "Don't worry. I promise I won't hold it against you if you never wear it. Miserable heavy stuff, I'll be the first to admit."

"It's not you I'm worried about, Gottfried," Morris replied. "It's my wife. She'll never let me leave it stuffed safely away in a chest. You watch. The first big ceremonial occasion—eek."

How Pappenheim could manage a grin that wide, and that cold, Morris would never understand.

"Indeed so," said the Duke of Moravia. "The coronation is less than two weeks from now. Still, that's more than enough time for me to have the armor ready. Do try your best not to trip during the procession, Morris. You'll never get up again, not at your age. Without a winch."

2

That night, Jason came back from his first Shabbat dinner at the home of Mordechai Spira.

He seemed in a peculiar mood, and said very little before he went to bed. Morris didn't notice, but Judith did.

The next morning, she pressed Jason about it.

"I don't know. It's hard to explain. A lot of it I liked—a lot. The discussion was almost exhilarating at times. The rabbi was at his best, too. I learned a lot and I laughed a lot at the same time. But..."

He ran fingers through his hair, which had gotten very long. "I don't know if I'll ever get used to men dancing alone. And it was weird, having the women do all the serving and cooking as if they were menials.

Although I was even more surprised—pleased, but surprised—when the women participated in the Talmudic discussion after dinner. I didn't think they would."

Judith was surprised herself, hearing that. Although...

She reminded herself not to make the mistake her husband Morris was prone to making. People are not categories, not even categories to which they belong. Unusual rabbis were still rabbis, after all. So why should it really be that surprising—in the same city which had produced a woman like Eva Bacharach—that the wife and daughters of Mordechai Spira would be unusual women?

"One of the rabbi's daughters even made a joke in the course of it," Jason continued. "Pretty funny one, too."

His eyes got a little unfocused. Judith had to struggle not to smile.

"Tell me about her. The daughter, I mean."

Jason mumbled some vague phrases. The only ones that weren't hopelessly murky had to do with the girl's eyes—very bright, apparently—and the fact that her name was Sarah.

But Judith let it go. There was no reason to pursue the matter with Jason, at the moment, since it obviously made him uncomfortable. Eva Bacharach would be coming for a visit later that day. Judith could find out everything she needed to know from her.

"I just don't know what to think," he complained. "Everything seems gray, and complicated. It's confusing."

"And you think that'll change? It won't. Trust me. But for the moment—"

She gave the young man a very warm smile. "Welcome to your life, Jason Gotkin."

3

In late afternoon, Mordechai Spira visited his friend Isaac Gans.

After seeing Mordechai to a chair, Gans sat in his own.

"And?"

"You were quite wrong, Isaac. Sarah didn't start pestering me until after lunch."

"Ha!" Isaac chuckled. "That's because she spent the whole morning conspiring with your wife."

"I know," said Mordechai gloomily. His eyes moved to the books on Isaac's study table. "It's a puzzling and tangled problem, given who the fellow is. But I'm sure I can find something in the Talmud—perhaps the responsa—to guide me properly."

"Of course you can. Everything pertaining to proper conduct is contained somewhere in the Talmud or the midrash or the responsa. I'm more the scholar than you are, though I don't have your stature as a judge." Stoutly: "So I will be glad to help!"

Gans leaned forward, spreading his hands wide. "But we must begin by facing the truth, Mordechai my old friend. We're rabbis. Studying the sacred texts takes time—hours and hours, days and weeks, poring over the words—and we are dealing with women."

Spira grimaced ruefully. "They're quick."

"Indeed. And so, I think, are these new times. We will just have to do our best."

"Always."

The Anne Jefferson Stories

Portraits

"I still can't believe I did that," said Anne Jefferson, studying the painting. It was obvious that she was struggling not to erupt in a fit of giggles.

Pieter Paul Rubens looked at her, smiling faintly, but said nothing. He'd gotten a better sense of the way the woman's mind worked, in the days he'd spent doing a portrait of the American nurse, even to the point of understanding that for her the menial term "nurse" was a source of considerable personal pride. But he still didn't fool himself that he really understood all the subtleties involved. There was a chasm of three and half centuries separating them, after all, even leaving aside the fact that they were—at least officially—enemies in time of war. If not, admittedly, actual combatants.

The sound of siege cannons firing outside reminded him of that enmity. For a moment, the big guns firing at distant Amsterdam caused the windows in the house to rattle.

The Jefferson woman heard them also, clearly enough. Her grin was replaced by a momentary grimace. "And back to the real world..." he heard her mutter.

But the grin was back, almost immediately. "It's the pom-poms and the baton," Jefferson said. "Ridiculous! I never even tried out for the cheerleading squad."

Rubens examined the objects referred to. His depiction of them, rather. The objects themselves were now lying on a nearby table. They weren't really genuine American paraphernalia, just the best imitations that Rubens' assistants had been able to design based on the American nurse's description. But she'd told him earlier that he'd managed to capture the essence of the things in the portrait.

"Coupled with the American flag!" she half-choked. "If anybody back home ever sees this, I'll be lucky if I don't get strung up."

The English term *strung up* eluded Rubens, since his command of that language was rudimentary. He'd spent some months in England as an envoy for King Philip IV of Spain, true, during which time he'd also begun painting the ceiling of the Royal Banqueting House at Whitehall Palace. But he'd spent most of his time there in the entourage of the English queen, who generally spoke in her native French.

However, he understood the gist of it. Jefferson had spoken the rest of the sentence in the German which they'd been using as their common tongue. Jefferson's German was quite good, for someone who'd only first spoken the language three years ago. Rubens' own German was fluent, as was his French, Italian, Latin and Spanish. Not surprising, of course, for a man who was—and had been for several decades now—recognized by everyone as the premier court artist for Europe's Roman Catholic dynasties, as well as being a frequently used diplomat for those same dynasties.

"Do you really think they will be offended?" he asked mildly.

Jefferson rolled her eyes. "Well, if anyone ever sees it I'll probably get away with it just because it was done by Rubens. You know, *the* Rubens. But they don't call them 'hillbillies' for nothing. Seeing me half-naked, wrapped in an American flag and holding pom-poms and a cheerleader's baton..." She brought her eyes back to the portrait, and shook her head ruefully. "I still don't know what possessed me to agree to this."

"Indulging a confused old artist, shall we say?" Rubens smiled crookedly. "You have no idea what a quandary your books from the future pose to an artist. If you can see a painting you *would* have done, do you still do it? When every instinct in you rebels at the notion? On the other hand..."

He glanced over his shoulder. His young wife Hélèna Fourment was sitting on a chair nearby, looking out the window. "Who knows? I may still do the original portrait, with her as the model as she would have been. But this seemed to me an interesting compromise. Besides..."

His eyes moved to the portrait, then to the young American model. "I was trying to capture something different here. Hard to know whether I succeeded or not, of course. You are such a peculiar people, in many ways."

Hearing a small commotion in the corridor outside his studio, the artist cocked his head. "Ah. Apparently the day's negotiations are concluded. Your escort is here to return you to Amsterdam. It has been a pleasure, Miss Jefferson. Will I see you again some day?"

Anne went over to a side table and began gathering up her things. "Who knows, Master Rubens? We might none of us survive this war."

"True enough. Even for those of us not soldiers, there is always disease to carry us away. So—please. Take the portrait with you."

She stared back at him over her shoulder. Then, stared at the painting.

"You've got to be kidding. That's ... a *Rubens*." For a moment, her mouth worked like a fish gasping out of water. "The only place you find those in the world I came from is in museums. Each one of them is worth millions."

"You are no longer in that world," Rubens pointed out. "Please. In this world of mine, you will do me the favor. And—who knows?—perhaps the portrait will somehow help shorten the war."

He took it off the easel and presented it to her. Hesitantly, Anne took it.

"You're sure?"

"Oh, yes. Quite sure."

After Jefferson left, Rubens turned to his wife. "A pity she is such a skinny thing," he murmured. "Of course, she wouldn't let me portray her breasts properly anyway. Odd, the way their American modesty works."

Fourment simply smiled. It was a rather self-satisfied smile. She was even younger than Jefferson, had a bosom that no-one would describe as "skinny," and there was nothing at all odd about the way her modesty worked. In her world, she was a proper wife and always properly attired as such. In her husband's world, she was whatever he needed her to be.

"When are you going to do *The Three Graces*?" she asked. "Or *The Judgment of Paris*?"

He shrugged. "Perhaps never."

Fourment pouted. "I thought I looked *good* in those paintings!"

Rubens didn't know whether to laugh or scowl. In another universe, those paintings would have been done in the year 1638. Bad enough for an artist to be confronted with illustrations of his future work. Worse still, when the wife who served as the model for them began wheedling him about it!

In the end, he laughed.

Another man was scowling.

"I still don't like the idea," Jeff Higgins grumbled, as he and Anne Jefferson brought up the rear of the Dutch delegation returning from the parlay to Amsterdam. "And Gretchen'll be having a pure fit."

"She'll get over it," Anne said firmly. "Look, I had orders. So there's an end to it."

She gave Jeff a none-too-admiring sidelong glance. "How is it, three years after the Ring of Fire, that you *still* can't ride a horse?"

Jeff gave the horse he was mounted on a look that was even less admiring. "I don't *like* horses, dammit. I'm a country boy. The only breed of horse I recognize is Harley-Davidson."

"You own a Yamaha."

"Fine. I'm a traitor too."

"Give it a rest, Jeff!" Now Anne was scowling. "I had *orders*."

"Mike Stearns is too damn clever for his good," Jeff muttered.

"So run against him, the next election."

Jeff ignored the suggestion. His head was now turned to his left, where the Spanish batteries were located. "Well, at least it looks like they've stopped firing. I guess we'll get back into the city after all."

"Like we have every other time. You're paranoid. And what are you complaining about, anyway? *I'm* the one who has to ride a horse carrying a great big portrait. The only thing that's saved me so far is that he didn't have it framed."

Jeff looked at the portrait Anne was balancing precariously on her hip. He couldn't see the actual image, because it was wrapped in cloth.

"I can't believe it. A *Rubens*. When are you going to show it to us?"

Jefferson looked very uncomfortable. "Maybe never. I haven't decided yet."

"Like that, huh?" Jeff's scowl finally vanished, replaced by a grin. "Gretchen won't let you keep it under wraps, you know that. She'll insist on that much, at least."

When Rubens was ushered into the small salon which the Cardinal-Infante used for private interviews, Don Fernando rose to greet him. The courtesy was unusual, to say the least. The Cardinal-Infante was the younger brother of the King of Spain, in addition to being the prince in all but name who now ruled the Spanish Netherlands. People rose for him, not the other way around.

But he was a courteous young man, by temperament. And, even for him, Rubens was . . . Rubens.

"What is it, Pieter?" asked Don Fernando.

"Thank you for responding to my request so quickly, Your Highness." Rubens reached into his cloak and drew forth several folded pieces of paper. "After Miss Jefferson departed my studio and returned to Amsterdam, we discovered that she had left this behind. It was lying on the side table near the entrance."

The Cardinal-Infante frowned. "You wish me to have it returned to her? Forgive me, Pieter, but I'm very busy and this hardly seems important enough—"

"Your Highness—please. I would not pester you over a simple matter of formalities. Besides, I'm quite certain she left it behind deliberately." He gestured toward a desk in the corner. "May I show you?"

The Spanish prince nodded. Rubens strode over to the desk and flattened the papers onto it, spreading out the sheets as he did so.

"She is a nurse, you know—a term which, for the Americans, refers to someone very skilled in medical matters. But I'm quite sure she didn't draw these diagrams. That was done by a superb draftsman. Not to mention that the text is in Latin, a language I know she is unfamiliar with."

The Cardinal-Infante had come to his side, and was now bent over examining the papers. As was to be expected of a royal scion of Spain, Don Fernando's own Latin was quite good.

"God in Heaven," he whispered, after his eyes finished scanning the first page.

"Indeed," murmured Rubens. "It contains everything, Your Highness. The ingredients, the formulas, the steps by which to make it—even these marvelous diagrams showing the apparatus required."

The Cardinal-Infante's eyes went back to the lettering which served as a title for the papers. *How to Make Chloramphenicol.*

"But can we trust it?" he wondered.

Rubens tugged at his reddish beard. "Oh, I don't doubt it, Your Highness. I realize now that was why she agreed to pose for me, even though it obviously made her uncomfortable. That strange American modesty, you know. Scandalous clothing combined with peculiar fetishes regarding nudity."

The Spanish prince cocked his head. With his narrow face, the gesture was somehow birdlike. "I am not following you."

Rubens shrugged. "Over the days of a sitting, an artist gets to know his model rather well. Well enough, at least, to be able to tell the difference between a healer and a poisoner." He pointed to the papers on the desk. "You can trust this, Your Highness. And, in any event, what do you have to lose?"

"Nothing," grunted Don Fernando. "I'm losing a dozen men a day to disease now. Mostly typhus. We can test it on a few of them first. If we can make the stuff at all, that is."

"That's no problem, I assure you." Rubens hesitated a moment. "We're in the Low Countries, you know. Not—ah—"

"Benighted Spain?" The Cardinal-Infante laughed. "True enough. Outside of Grantville itself—maybe Magdeburg too, now—there is probably no place in Europe better supplied with craftsmen and artisans and workshops."

The two men fell silent, looking down at the papers.

"Why?" the Cardinal-Infante finally asked. "From

what you're saying, she could hardly have done this on her own."

The continent's greatest artist pondered the matter for a moment. Then, shrugged. "Perhaps we should just tell ourselves they also have peculiar notions of war. And leave it at that."

"That won't be good enough, I'm afraid." Don Fernando sighed. "I have no choice but to use it. But...why do I have the feeling I'm looking at a Trojan Horse here?"

Rubens' eyes widened. "It's just medicine, Your Highness."

The Spanish prince shook his head. "Horses come in many shapes."

Gretchen was, indeed, still in a steaming fury. "Why don't we hand them ammunition as well?" she demanded.

Anne was tired of the argument. "Take it up with Mike, dammit! I was just doing what he told me to do, if I ever got the chance."

Gretchen stalked over to the window of the house in Amsterdam where the American delegation was headquartered. Along the way, she took the time to glare at the wife of the man in question.

Rebecca just smiled. Diplomatic, as always. "It's not just the soldiers, you know."

Diplomacy was wasted on Gretchen. "You propose to tell *me* that? I am the one who was once a camp follower, not you!"

Gretchen was at the window now, and slapped her hand against the pane. Not, fortunately, quite hard enough to break it. "Yes, I know that three women

and children die from disease in a siege, for every
soldier who does. So what? It's the soldiers who do
the fighting."

Rebecca said nothing. Eventually, Gretchen turned
away from the window. To the relief of everyone else
in the room, her foul humor seemed to be fading. If
nothing else, Gretchen could always be relied upon
to accept facts as given.

"Enough," she stated. "What's done is done. And
now, Anne, show us this famous portrait."

Anne fidgeted. Not for long.

"Do it!" Gretchen bellowed. "I will have *that* much
satisfaction!"

After the portrait was unveiled and everyone stopped
laughing, Gretchen shook her head.

"You coward," she pronounced. "If we're to play at
this posing game, let us do it properly. I will show you."

The next morning, Rubens was summoned by the
Cardinal-Infante to that area of the siegeworks where
the Spanish prince was positioned every day.

Once he arrived atop the platform, the prince handed
him an eyeglass and pointed toward Amsterdam.

"This, you will want to see."

After peering through the eyeglass for a moment,
Rubens burst out laughing. "That must be the famous
Richter."

He lowered the eyeglass. "No odd modesty there.
What a brazen woman! And I see she's read the same
books I have. One of them, at least."

Don Fernando cocked his head. "Meaning?"

Rubens pointed toward the distant figure of Gretchen

Richter, posed atop the ramparts of the besieged city. "That's a painting that will be done—would have been done—two hundred years from now. By a French artist named Eugène Delacroix. It's called *Liberty Leading the People*. And now, Your Highness, with your permission, I *must* gather my materials. The opportunity is impossible to resist. What magnificent breasts!"

The Cardinal-Infante's eyes widened. "You will *not* give it the same title!" The words were half a command, half a protest. "Damnation, I don't care if she's naked from the waist up and waving a flag. She's still a rebel against my lawful authority!"

"Oh, certainly not, Your Highness. I'll think of something suitably archaic."

A moment later, Rubens was scampering off the platform, moving in quite a spry manner for a man in his mid-fifties.

The prince sighed, and gave in to the inevitable. "Tell the batteries not to fire on that portion of the city's defenses, until I say otherwise," he told one of his officers. He smiled ruefully. "Hell hath no fury like an artist thwarted."

After the officer left, Don Fernando went back to studying the distant tableau through the eyeglass. A magnificent pair of breasts, indeed.

By the time Rubens returned, with his needed paraphernalia, the prince of Spain had made his decision.

"You will call it *The Trojan Horsewoman*," he proclaimed. "That seems a suitable title, for a portrait depicting what has become the most peculiar siege in history."

Steps in the Dance

"Stop whining, Harry," said Anne Jefferson. "If I can do it, you can do it."

"No way am I posing half-nekkid," growled her male companion. He gripped the rifle with both hands, as if ready to deal with any threatening horde.

Any horde.

Mongols.

Huns.

Famous artists.

"Ha! The truth about Macho Man, exposed to the world at last! A coward. A craven." Anne swiveled her head to give him her best sneer, even if it was mostly wasted in the twilight. The lamps which were starting to be lit in front of the taverns on the street in Amsterdam didn't yet add much to the illumination.

"I'm *not* a coward," Harry Lefferts insisted stubbornly. "And I'm not cravin' anything at the moment except relief from pushy women."

He tried a lusty grin, directed at Anne. Alas, it was a pale version of her sneer.

"Not relief from all women, o' course. Just pushy ones. If you were to change your ways..."

"I'd call that a nice try, except it's so feeble." She tried to stride forward, but the combination of the absurd sorta-wedding dress she was wearing, the cobblestoned street, and her seventeenth century Dutch version of high heels caused her to stumble.

Fortunately, Adam Olearius was there to catch her arm and keep her standing, if not exactly steady. He'd been walking alongside her ever since they'd left the USE embassy, as he listened to the repartee between Anne and Harry.

Smiling, as he did so. By now, several weeks after Harry's arrival in Amsterdam, Adam had long since recognized that Harry was not a rival, despite the young American's seemingly irrepressible flirting. In fact, he'd rather come to like the man, even if he was a little scary at times.

Scary this time, too, in a way. Adam had been keeping an eye out for the possibility that Anne might stumble, which Harry had not. Adam had a very personal interest in the young woman, and was more familiar than either of his companions with the hazards of negotiating the streets of the era. The cobble-stones as such hadn't caused Anne to stumble. Rather, her shoe had skidded in the material covering one of the stones. There were unfortunate consequences to using horses for transport in cities.

Partly, too, because Adam Olearius was a more solicitous man by nature than Harry Lefferts was or ever would be. And finally—being honest—because he was not pre-occupied with the prospect of shortly becoming the model for one of the half-dozen most famous artists of the time. Of *all* times, actually, judging from the American history books Adam had read.

So, he'd been half-expecting the stumble, and was there almost instantly. But Harry was only a split-second behind him. Somehow, he managed to shift his grip on the rifle and his footing in order to seize Anne's other elbow, with such speed and grace that Adam was not really able to follow the motions.

In the three short years since the Ring of Fire, Harry Lefferts had become a rather notorious figure in certain European circles. For several reasons, one of which was his skill as a duelist. Seeing the way he moved, Adam had no trouble understanding the reason.

Yes, frightening, in its way, especially given the man's incredibly sanguine temperament. Fortunately for the world, Harry was also—as a rule—quite a good-natured fellow. He was not actually given to picking fights, Adam had concluded, after observing him for several weeks. He was simply very, very, very good at ending them—and instantly ready to do so if someone else was foolish enough to begin the affair.

That notoriety, of course, did not fit well with Harry's official role as a combination "secret" agent and what the Americans called a "commando." Anne Jefferson had teased him about it.

The other two women in the USE embassy in Amsterdam had not. Rebecca Abrabanel had subjected him to a long, solemn lecture on the subject. Gretchen Richter had subjected him to a short and blistering excoriation.

Blistering, indeed. Adam happened to have been there himself, to hear it. The expression one of the up-timers had used afterward struck him as most appropriate. *She really peeled the paint off the walls, didn't she?*

Had she been a man, her tirade might have led to a challenge.

Although . . . perhaps not. Adam was pretty sure that Gretchen Richter was one of the few people in the world who intimidated Harry Lefferts. If not as proficient as he was with weapons, she was every bit as ready to employ them—and with attitudes as sanguine as his, and then some.

There was more to it, though. Adam knew, at least in its general outlines, how Harry had first met the woman, very shortly after the Ring of Fire.

"Shithouse Gretchen," was the way Harry sometimes referred to her, when she'd done something to get on his nerves. But he never said it in front of her—and there was always more than a trace of grudging respect even when he did. In the end, for all his often-debonair manners and the way he was idolized by a number of young European gentry and noblemen, Harry Lefferts was a hillbilly and a former coal miner. Getting one's hand dirty, and being willing to do so, was something he deeply respected.

Oddly enough, Harry's thoughts seemed to have been running parallel to Adam's. After Anne's footing was steady again, Harry released her elbow and went back to his grumbling.

"And why me, anyway? Shithouse Gretchen's *built* like a damn brick shithouse. And *she's* willing to pose."

"Don't be vulgar, Harry," scolded Anne.

"Who's being vulgar? The truth is what it is. Those tits of hers would intimidate a Playboy bunny—and it's not as if she's kept them under wraps. Not hardly. Not after she posed for *Rubens*."

He barked a laugh that was half-sarcasm, and half genuine humor. "Ha! You watch, Anne! Give it a century or two and that damn painting will be hanging in the Louvre. Or the—what's it called?—that famous museum in Spain. The Pardo, I think. Lines of tourists a mile long all shuffling past to stare at the world's most famous tits."

Olearius suspected he was right. He'd seen the painting himself, on the two previous occasions when he'd visited the mansion where the Spanish had set up their headquarters for the siege of Amsterdam. The enemy commander, the cardinal-infante Don Fernando, had it prominently displayed in his salon.

A bit odd, that was, given that the painting romanticized Don Fernando's stubborn Dutch opponents. Rubens' whimsical version of the future painting by Eugène Delacroix which would have been called *Liberty Leading the People* depicted a bare-breasted Gretchen Richter holding a flag on the ramparts of Spanish-besieged Amsterdam.

Had the Spanish commander of that siege been a different sort of man, Olearius would have assumed nothing more was involved than any man's interest in such a remarkable female form. But...

No, that wasn't it. To be sure, for all his slender, red-headed boyish appearance, Don Fernando was a very vigorous man—and not one upon whom his official title as a cardinal weighed any too heavily. But he was no bumpkin, either, easily distracted by mere lust. Olearius was quite an experienced diplomat, and he'd already come to the conclusion than Don Fernando was as shrewd as any prince in the long and successful history of the Habsburg dynasty. If Don Fernando had chosen to have that painting prominently displayed in his headquarters, there was a political reason for it.

More likely, several reasons. Don Fernando could be surprisingly subtle for such a young man.

"Shit," Anne muttered. Olearius glanced over and saw that she'd finally spotted the cause of her mishap. They'd reached a well-illuminated corner and the contents smeared across the sole of her shoe and partway up the sides were now easily visible and quite evident.

"Yeah, sure is," said Harry cheerfully. "Look on the bright side, though. It's just horse-shit. Someday I'll tell you about the time Gurd and me had to wade through—naw, it's too disgusting."

He started to reach for the handkerchief he had in his pocket, but Adam had already drawn out his own and offered it to Anne.

"Thanks," she said, smiling at him warmly. But the smile vanished as soon as she spotted the men starting to spill out of the tavern on the corner. "Oh, damn, here they come. Stand in front of me, guys. Appearances Must Be Maintained."

Adam and Harry moved to block her from the sight of the night watchmen emerging from the tavern. Adam, with a solemn demeanor. Harry . . . not.

"Stop grinning, Harry," Anne hissed, as she stooped down to clean off her shoe.

"Can't help it," he insisted. "Besides, don't get paranoid. I'm not grinning at you, I'm grinning at the flag that guy is carrying."

Olearius had noticed it himself. Anne glanced up from her labor.

"Why is a Dutch soldier carrying a U.S. flag?" she wondered.

"It's a real one, too," Harry said. "Old one, I guess I oughta say. Not the NUS flag. Fifty stars."

He seemed genuinely aggrieved. "Damn. They musta got it from Grantville. Some bums will sell anything."

"They might have made it themselves," Adam pointed out. "Holland is a textile center, after all, and Amsterdam has plenty of seamstresses."

The mystery was solved, as soon as the night watch came up. One of them extended the flag to Harry. "You will need this," he explained, in heavily accented English.

"Why?" Harry asked, as he took the flag. He used the Dutch word. One of Harry's many talents was a proficiency with languages, and his Dutch had gone from non-existent to semi-passable in just a few short weeks.

Semi-passable, at least, for practical purposes like ordering beer and getting directions. There was not much chance he'd be able to argue pre-predestination with Dutch theologians, even assuming Harry had any desire to. A proposition about as unlikely as a wolverine becoming an opera enthusiast, in Adam's estimation.

The night watch soldier shrugged. "Word came from the Spanish to send one with you. The artist requires it, apparently."

That still left the mystery of where the flag came from. But the night watchman answered that also. Smiling, he added: "We took the one from the tavern wall. Make sure you bring it back. The owner had it made himself and he likes to keep it up. He thinks it's a good luck charm."

"Well, sure," replied Harry.

• • •

Getting through the walls of Amsterdam was easy, of course, with the night watch leading the way to the gate. Getting through the Spanish siege lines beyond to the cardinal-infante's headquarters...

Proved to be not much more difficult. Spanish officers were waiting to guide them through the maze of trenches and earthworks, all Castilian hidalgo courtesy. They were respectful toward Adam, even more respectful if openly curious toward Harry, and, of course, almost effusively gallant toward Anne.

There was no fear, here, that she might stumble on treacherous footing. The Spanish had even laid planks through the trenches, solely on her behalf. Even if she had stumbled, the press of officers around her would have prevented any undignified fall.

"Bunch of leches, you ask me," Harry muttered at one point to Adam. "You better keep your eye on them."

Olearius shook his head. "Even granted that the Castilian reputation is well-deserved, that's really not what's involved here. You forget, Harry. Anne is the one who gave them the chloramphenicol. The formula, at least. Someday, that might very well save their lives, and those of their families."

That brought a scowl to Harry's face. "I still think Mike was crazy to give it to them."

Adam couldn't resist. "Surely you won't vote for Quentin Underwood in the next election? He shares your opinion, I'm told."

The scowl deepened considerably. "Not a cold chance in hell. I don't care what fancy positions the bum occupies in the here and now. Far's I'm concerned, he's still the stinkin' manager of the stinkin' mine I used to work in. Sooner vote for the Devil."

He spread the scowl around. "Or one of these damn hidalgos, come down to it. Betcha *they* never heard of 'forced overtime.' Still . . . Mike was crazy," he concluded stubbornly.

There was a time when Adam Olearius might have agreed with him. But his experiences as a diplomat from the duchy of Holstein during the siege of Amsterdam had led him to develop a great respect for the acumen of Mike Stearns and his Sephardic wife. However much Stearns' surreptitious delivery of the formulas for antibiotics to the Spanish might violate the usual notions of strategy, Olearius had decided that the tactic was a splendid illustration of one of those up-time saws he'd become fond of: *crazy like a fox*.

Lesser statesmen simply thought to defeat their enemies. Stearns was seeking to shatter them into splinters, and turn half the splinters into his allies. Or, at least, sideline them into neutrality.

He might very well succeed, too, Adam thought. How else to explain this night's peculiar expedition except as one more step in an intricate diplomatic dance? A four-way dance, at that—Stearns, his wife, the Prince of Orange, and Don Fernando—and one being invented on the spot.

Five-way dance, really, since the cardinal-infante had to maintain his own sure-footed steps when it came to the reaction of the King of Spain and his notorious chief adviser, the Count-Duke of Olivares.

They arrived, finally. By now, the night had settled in, and all that illuminated the Spanish headquarters were sconces and lamps. A multitude of them—with what seemed like mirrors on every wall to enhance the lighting.

Amazingly, on the pristine flooring of the entrance salon, Anne stumbled again. But the cardinal-infante himself was there to catch her.

As gallant as any of his officers, he set her back upright with nothing more than a cheerful laugh. As if the younger brother of the Spanish king took assisting common women for granted.

He probably didn't look at it that way, however, Adam reflected. Whatever the Americans themselves might think, or say, or write—or even, astonishingly, practice at least most of the time—the aristocracy of Europe had generally come to the conclusion that they qualified as nobility.

Why not? In the end, if you stripped away all the trappings and the mythologies, the nobility of Europe owed its present exalted position to the crude fact that its ancestors had been the toughest men of their time. That, or the richest, or both. Today, three years after the Ring of Fire, only a handful of lunatic counts and the emperor of the Turks—who was known as Murad the Mad—tried to deny that the up-timers were both mighty and wealthy.

Hearing a little stir behind him, Adam turned and saw that four Spanish officers were clustered around Harry. They were frowning at him, and he was responding with a scowl of his own.

Harry had quite a formidable scowl, too. Fortunately, he was not stupid.

"I was *told* to bring the rifle," he said, almost snarling the words. In perfectly fluent Spanish, not to Olearius' surprise, albeit with an accent that had more in it of Italy than Castille. He'd originally picked up the language in the course of his journeys with Mazarini, Adam guessed.

"It's not loaded, you—" Fortunately, again, Harry left off the rest. He simply, with a quick and smooth motion that made his proficiency with the weapon obvious, drew the bolt and exposed the empty chamber.

The Spanish officers clustered around him still more closely. Now, however, with professional interest in the exotic up-time rifle, rather than suspicion. They began peppering Harry with technical questions, which he answered readily.

Much more readily than Olearius would have expected, in fact. He suspected that was another subtle step in the dance.

"This is the same sort of rifle that shot Wallenstein at the Alte Veste?" asked one of the Spaniards.

"Pretty much," Harry replied. "The caliber's slightly different. This is what we call a '30-06.' "

The four officers eyed him closely. "Could you make such a shot?"

Harry hesitated, for just a split second, before answering. Male pride at work, probably. Then, chuckling, he shook his head.

"No, I couldn't. I'm a very good shot, but Julie Sims—Mackay, now—is just plain out of my league."

"So it is true? It *was* a woman who fired that shot?"

"Sure was." Harry held up the rifle a moment, as if studying it. "With this, and me shooting it . . . I figure I could hit a target up to five hundred yards. Maybe six."

The cardinal-infante had come over himself to

follow the conversation. Olearius saw him frown for a moment, as he made the necessary mathematical translations into Spanish distances.

The frown was replaced by a look of keen interest. "*That* far? Our siege lines are within that range. Some of them, well within. Yet you have never shot any of my soldiers."

Harry gave him a look that Adam found it difficult to interpret. Complicated, it seemed to be. There was something in there of menace, something of calculation, something of cold amusement, and...

Yes, exasperation.

So. *Another* step in the dance—and, as with so many, one that the dancer found too fancy for his taste.

Luckily for Europe, Olearius mused, Mike Stearns and not Harry Lefferts was the choreographer here.

The cardinal-infante tossed his head a little. "Tomorrow morning, we will see."

Don Fernando called over his shoulder to the servants against the far wall. "Up in my chamber. There is a old hunting hat in the wardrobe. The one with the red stripe, not the blue one. Bring it down here."

One of the servants sped on his way. All graciousness, now, the cardinal-infante bowed slightly and waved his hand toward a wide door on the side of the salon. "Please, come. Rembrandt is waiting."

The sitting was the usual tedious business. The night watch was kept waiting, while Rembrandt concentrated on the portrait of Anne and Harry Lefferts. More precisely, the portrait of Anne, a slim and attractive figure in a white gown, gazing serenely at the flag draped over her lap. All that would ever be seen of

Harry was a grim and menacing figure standing guard with a rifle beside her and off to the side, but one whose face was mostly concealed by a "Caterpillar" cap.

Harry had insisted on the cap, as a condition. *Gotta keep my anomaly as a secret agent.*

Rebecca Abrabanel had burst into outright laughter, hearing that. Even Gretchen Richter had smiled.

"Okay, so I know I'm not pronouncing it right," Harry grumbled. "It's still true."

"It is not that!" Rebecca held a hand over her mouth to restrain any further laughter. "It is just..."

"Ridiculous," Gretchen finished for her. "Preposterous comes to mind, also."

Her smile was gone. She didn't quite glare at Harry. Not quite.

"Ridiculous," she repeated, almost hissing the word. "After the public duels you've fought—not to mention the bastards you've probably left scattered across half of Europe. Secret agent, ha!"

She began taking toddling little steps across the main salon of the USE embassy, waving her hands like a small child. "You will see! 'Mr. Secret Agent,' soon pursued by a horde of infants. 'Papa!' 'Papa!'"

That started Rebecca laughing again. Even Harry had smiled.

"Still," he insisted, after she was done. "It's the principle of the thing."

But perhaps it was just as well, Olearius concluded by the end of the evening. Rubens had managed to sketch enough of the portrait for the Holstein diplomat to get a sense of the thing.

Yes. Anne, in that white gown—the purpose for which was now clear—would be the center of it. Anne, with her pretty young face, and serene expression. Holding the flag the way a young expectant mother might hold a quilt she was making for her coming child. With that dark, grim, faceless, frightening figure in the background—all painted in dark colors, except for a gleaming flash from the rifle barrel—to serve the more observant eye as a reminder.

Yes, splendid. All the more so in that Olearius was quite certain that the cardinal-infante had commissioned the painting. Unlike *The Trojan Horsewoman*, this was not a project that Rubens had dreamed up himself and then foisted onto a reluctant patron.

A reminder—but to whom? The Spanish soldiers? The cardinal-infante himself?

Both?

Or, perhaps, someday he would send it to his older brother. As a way to ameliorate the anger that was already coming from Madrid; or, at least, provide himself with an excuse.

"Done, for tonight," Rubens pronounced. As courteous as ever—the great painter was an accomplished diplomat in his own right—he smiled at Anne and Harry. "Tomorrow evening, the same time?"

"Of course," said Anne cheerfully.

"Sure," muttered Harry. Finally, seeing that the damn artist had set aside his brushes, he removed the cap.

Don Fernando had left the studio, soon after ushering them into it. Patron of the arts or not, watching a sitting was a boring business. In any event, as commander of the Spanish army that had overrun most of the Netherlands, there were always pressing demands on his time.

But he was there, punctiliously, to see them off.

"Tomorrow morning," he said to Harry. He lifted his hand, holding a battered old hat. "I will have this placed somewhere visible on the siege lines."

"Sure," muttered Harry.

The first shot came just a few minutes after daybreak.

"He missed," said one of the cardinal-infante's officers, with great satisfaction.

"Wait," cautioned Miguel de Manrique. Unlike the officer who had spoken, the cardinal-infante's chief lieutenant had experience with the Americans. He'd been in command of the Spanish troops at the Wartburg.

Don Fernando gave him a questioning eye.

Manrique waved his hand. "The weapons are not magical, Your Highness. At this range, even the wind matters. Remember—all accounts we've gotten are agreed—the Sims woman missed her first shot at Wallenstein also. So let us wait."

Perhaps two seconds later, the hat went sailing off the wall it had been perched upon. A moment thereafter, they heard the sound of a distant gunshot.

An aide ran to retrieve the hat. When it was brought back to the cardinal-infante, he saw that a bullet hole had been added to the crown.

"Yes," he said. "A splendid painting. I shall have it hung in the main salon."

A few nights later, when the sittings were finally done, Don Fernando had a few last words with Harry.

"That peculiar request you made, two nights ago."

Harry inclined his head, smiling.

"I investigated. It is indeed true that you killed no one coming into the city."

The smile vanished. "Had orders," Harry growled. "Stupid as they might be."

"Yes." The cardinal-infante was smiling, now. "I suspected as much. Very well. When the time comes, send me word and I will see you—and your men— safely through our lines. To wherever else you might go—and do note that I neither ask nor make any conditions. Except a promise that you are not going to Spain."

"Nowhere near Spain. Ah, Your Highness. My word on it."

"That's done, then." Turning to Anne and Olearus, the cardinal-infante smiled still wider. "You look splendid in that gown, Mademoiselle Jefferson. May I hope to see you in it again, someday?"

The long hours of sitting seemed to have fixed serenity upon the young woman's face. She simply inclined her head toward Olearius and said, "Ask him."

"Ah . . ." said Adam.

Diplomacy was called for, here. An intricate dance, with steps of its own.

"I certainly hope so," he said.

Anne nodded, as serenely as ever. "Apparently, yes, then."

"Jesus," grumbled Harry. "Can't anybody around here do *anything* straight-up?"

As one person, a nurse from America and a diplomat from Holstein and a prince from Spain gave Harry Lefferts an identical look.

What a barbarian.

Postage Due

"You've got to be kidding."

Anne Jefferson looked around the table in the big dining room of the USE's embassy in Amsterdam, at each of the other people sitting there. Immediately to her left sat Rebecca Abrabanel, the ambassador of the United States of Europe to the United Provinces. Sitting next to her, at the end of the table, was her husband Mike Stearns. Mike was the prime minister of the USE, and had arrived in besieged Amsterdam only two days earlier, in a daring airlift that still had the entire city talking—as it did the Spanish army camped in the siege lines beyond.

He and Rebecca were holding hands, clasped on the table. To Mike's left sat Jeff Higgins and right next to him—directly across the table from Anne—sat Jeff's wife Gretchen Richter.

Finally, at the other end of the table facing Mike Stearns and just to Anne's right, sat Adam Olearius.

As of the day before, Anne Jefferson's new fiancé. He'd finally proposed, and she'd taken all of two seconds to accept.

"This is a joke, right?"

That was more in the way of a firm statement than a question.

Silence.

"This is a joke, right?" she repeated. Her voice rose with the last word, a firm statement transmuting into a real question.

"A *joke*. It's got to be."

Desperation was creeping into her voice.

Anne now glared at Mike Stearns, her glare almost instantly being transferred to the handclasp.

"Stop holding hands with your wife!" she snapped. "It's disgusting."

Mike's eyebrows went up a little. Rebecca's went up quite a bit more.

Anne's jaws tightened. "Fine," she said, through gritted teeth. "It's not disgusting, it's aggravating. But that expression on Mike's face *is* disgusting. We all know you're getting laid since you flew into Amsterdam in that reckless flying stunt of yours, Mike. You don't have to be so infuriatingly smug about it."

Rebecca's eyebrows came back down, and a very serene expression came to her face.

"You!" snarled Anne. "*That* expression is even worse!"

Rebecca smiled—very serenely—and replied:

"I will point out that I have also sat for a portrait, in the interests of the nation."

"Baloney! You just sat for that stupid portrait Mike keeps in his office in Magdeburg so he'd be able to keep admiring you after you left for Amsterdam.

Don't give me any crap about 'the national interest.' And—"

Her voice was rising again, as desperation returned.
"—*you* didn't pose half-naked."

Across the table from her, Gretchen Richter sniffed.
"Half-naked, nonsense. The proposal was clearly
explained. By the time the portraits are finished, you
will be modestly garbed in various banners. To be
sure, Rubens and Rembrandt and the Hals brothers
will see you half-naked while you pose, but so what?
They're artists. They don't count. Besides, Rubens
has already seen you half-naked, plenty of times.
Half, did I say? Nine-tenths naked."

Anne's glare at Gretchen made the one she'd
bestowed on Mike and Rebecca seem like a fleeting
glance of mild disapproval.

"So why don't you do it, then? The whole damn
world has seen *you* half-naked!"

Gretchen sniffed again. "Don't be ridiculous. Only
the Spanish army camped outside in the siege works
and maybe half of Amsterdam's residents."

"Pretty much all of the city's residents, sweetheart,"
said her husband mildly. "It was a very popular, ah,
tourist attraction while it lasted. I think the only
ones who didn't come for a look-see were some old
crones, and some of the preachers. Well, a few of
the preachers."

Jeff didn't seem aggrieved any, though, at the
thought of tens of thousands of people having gazed
upon his wife's naked breasts. Actually, he seemed a
little smug about it himself. Given Gretchen's bosom,
that was perhaps understandable.

"You didn't answer my question!"

Gretchen shrugged. "I offered. They turned me down." She gave Mike and Rebecca a dismissive glance. "They said I wouldn't be the appropriate model for the purpose."

"Not hardly," drawled Mike. "The Spanish would have had conniptions. So would the prince of Orange, for that matter."

His eyes grew a little unfocused, as if he were contemplating something in the distance. "Now that I think about, I doubt Gustav Adolf would have been any too pleased, either."

"Kings." Gretchen's tone was icy. "Wretches, all of them. That fat Swedish bastard is depending on the Committees of Correspondence to keep his new little empire for him when the fighting starts up again next spring. But God forbid he should admit it."

Rebecca cleared her throat. "As it happens, Gretchen, I did pass your offer on to the cardinal-infante. The reports I've received indicate that Don Fernando was rather intrigued by the idea. But, not surprisingly, his advisers were adamantly opposed."

Her eyes moved back to Anne Jefferson. "You, on the other hand, are most acceptable to all parties involved. Especially with Gretchen as the alternative. You are a nurse, after all, a healer. Not a revolutionary agitator with a reputation for being distressingly quick with her revolver."

"Nine millimeter automatic," corrected Gretchen. "I don't like revolvers. Rate of fire is too slow."

"It's a conspiracy!" wailed Anne.

"Well, sure," said Mike. "How else would you pull off a stunt like this?"

In a tavern not far away, four men sat around a small table in the corner, hunching their upper bodies forward in the way men will when they conspire.

"So he's agreed, then?" asked Harry Lefferts, the leader of the little group.

The man to his left nodded. Donald Ohde, that was, the Scot-born German who served as the financier for Harry's special team. Or the "dog robber," as Harry called him.

"Oh, sure. He's always short of money, and his brother Frans even more so."

"It'll take everything we've got in the way of specie," cautioned the man across the table from Harry. That was Paul Maczka. Like most of the men in Harry's team, he was of hybrid origin: in his case, part-Swede, part-Saxon. And, like every single one of them, an adrenaline junkie addicted to adventures. But he tended to be very conservative whenever financial matters arose.

Harry waved his hand. "It's only money. We're not giving up any of the essentials."

Ohde nodded. "I told Hals. No up-time guns, no dynamite, nothing. Just money." He sneered, slightly. "Artist. Didn't even know what dynamite was, I think."

But Paul was not one to give up easily. "You can't get food, shelter and transport with weapons," he pointed out. "Not unless we're going to rob our way across to England, which would be stupid. We need *some* money."

The fourth man at the table spoke up. "We'll have lots of money once the deal closes. Ten times what we've got now. More than that. Enough to turn this shoestring operation into something out of a James Bond movie. Too bad they haven't invented jet skis yet. We could afford enough for all of us."

Gerd beamed. "Imagine the sight we'd make! Blowing our way up the Thames thumbing our noses at King Charles' soldiers."

Gerd went all the way back to the formation of Harry's special team. So, of all the down-timers there, he more than any of them could claim to be an "old Grantville hand." But it hardly mattered. By now, all of Harry's commandos had seen plenty of up-time films.

James Bond movies were very popular with them. Almost as popular as *The Terminator.*

Maczka was still skeptical. "That stuff is hardly what you can call liquid assets."

Ohde shook his head. "I've already got the buyer. Three of them, in fact, but it'll be the Frenchman who outbids the others. Stop fretting, Paul. Two days after it's all over, we'll be rich and on our way to the Tower."

He paused a moment. "Well, *we* won't be rich. But the cause will."

He even meant it, and quite sincerely. Of all the odd things about Harry Lefferts' special unit, perhaps the oddest was their code of honor. Very flexible and fuzzy at the edges, but hard as iron at the center.

Mike Stearns had once remarked that it was all that kept them from being the most frightening pack of bandits in Europe. He'd made the remark to his wife Rebecca after one of his meetings with Harry, where he'd given Lefferts another "special assignment."

Mike had shaken his head ruefully, his hands cradling a cup of coffee. "Harry Lefferts. I swear. I told him to be a little careful about the way he raised funds for the operation. I didn't want any CIA drug-dealing scandals."

Rebecca sipped from her own coffee cup. "What did he say in response?"

Mike chuckled. "Harry Lefferts. What do you think? 'Can't, Mike,' he said. 'Drugs ain't illegal in this day and age.'"

Rebecca nodded. "True. That must have been a bit of a relief for you."

Mike shook his head. "No, not really. Not when the next words out of Harry's mouth were: 'More's the pity. We'll have to figure out something else.'"

"Oh."

On their way back to Anne's residence, her hand tucked into the crook of Adam's elbow, she gave her brand-new fiancé an uncertain look.

"You sure you won't mind?"

"Oh, no," he said, smiling. "Leaving aside her indelicate phrasing, Gretchen was quite right. You'll be wearing a pair of shorts and a halter in this pose. Which is considerably more than you wore for Rubens in your previous sessions."

Anne's mouth twisted into a grimace. "'Pair of shorts.' Pair of hot pants, is what they actually are. And that so-called halter they want me to wear is what plenty of people would call a bikini top."

After a moment: "Okay. Not on the Riviera, I guess. But they sure would have called it that back in West Virginia."

Her expression grew a bit grumpy. "The *real* West Virginia, I mean. Not this screwy wild-ass version of it we've somehow turned into since the Ring of Fire."

After a few more seconds, she said: "Well, okay. I'll do it, then."

● ● ●

The sessions started two days later. As agreed, in a house in Amsterdam, this time, instead of the Spanish camp where Anne had posed for Rubens on previous occasions. Three out of the four artists were Dutch, after all. Easier for Rubens to join them, than the other way around.

Rubens didn't mind. He was a very experienced diplomat as well as an artist, who'd often served the Habsburgs in their foreign affairs.

He'd always liked Amsterdam, in any event. And, who was to say? If this latest of many complicated steps in the dance of state affairs advanced matters still further, he might someday be able to buy a house of his own in the city.

"Let's begin," he said. Without there having been any discussion, Rubens had assumed leadership of the little project. It seemed natural enough. Not only was he slightly older than the two Hals brothers, he was considerably better known and more successful. The chaotic habits of the Hals family left them usually just two steps ahead of the debt-collectors.

Rembrandt might have challenged the matter. By now, they all knew that in the future world Grantville came from, Rembrandt would be an even more famous artist than Rubens. In many peculiar and subtle little ways, knowledge of what *would* have happened was modifying social status all across Europe. Rembrandt was still very young—only twenty-eight—and had not yet created the masterpieces that would, three and half centuries later, rank him among the greatest artists of all time. But everyone knew he *would* be—or had been, at least, in another world, since there was no telling what would happen in this one. So, he already had most of the prestige of a master.

He'd confided to Rebecca once that it made him very uncomfortable. And he handled the problem by maintaining a stance of modesty that was sometimes almost comical.

So, he made no objection. In this day and age, Rubens was preeminent among them.

"Let's begin," Rubens repeated. "Anne, if you would be so good as to remain still and steady."

"Still and steady ain't the problem," replied Anne, somehow managing to talk clearly while barely moving her lips. "It's keeping this stupid fucking bimbo smile plastered on my face that's the problem."

There had been a time when the thought of using foul language in front of great artists would have appalled Anne Jefferson. But now that she'd come to know them, in their own time and place, she didn't think much of the matter. All things considered, West Virginians and seventeenth-century Europeans got along quite well. It was an earthy age, whose people were at least as rowdy and raucous as Appalachian hillbillies.

Standing at his easel, Rembrandt smiled and went to work. The Hals brothers had already started.

Not a word was spoken in the salon for over an hour. Then Dirck Hals paused at his labor, frowned, and muttered to his older brother.

"It's slipped my mind. Which banner am *I* supposed to be portraying?"

"You idiot," came the toneless response. Frans Hals lifted the brush from his canvas and pointed at one of the flags hanging from the far wall. "That one."

●   ●   ●

Three days later, it was done. The salon of the house was now crowded with people gazing admiringly at the four portraits displayed to one side.

Anne Jefferson was the model for all of them, a fact which was obvious at a glance. The American was most attractive, in the way that young women who are pretty but not beautiful are. Pleasing to the eye, but not threatening or intimidating, and with just enough in the way of irregularity of features to make her face distinctive and easily remembered.

"Perfect," murmured the cardinal-infante. The commander of the Spanish army and his aides had been given a safe-conduct for the day, so they could cross the lines and come into Amsterdam to see the portraits. By now, after the long weeks of what had become a very peculiar siege, not even his advisers had raised much of a protest.

A bit, of course. Don Fernando was, after all, the younger brother of the king of Spain as well as a cardinal and an army commander. From the standpoint of a hostage, as good as you could ask for.

But the man across the room had given his word, and he was the prince of Orange. Enemies they might be, but by this point in time there was also a great deal in the way of trust between Don Fernando and Fredrik Hendrik.

There had been many negotiations and diplomatic advances, after all, of which this was only the latest. More to the point, the days of the duke of Alva and his massacres and the equally bloody Dutch responses to them were thankfully many decades in the past. Even the sturdiest Calvinist in Amsterdam, except for diehard Counter-Remonstrants, would allow that Don Fernando was a good enough sort, for a papist and a Spaniard. And most of the soldiers in the cardinal-infante's army would reciprocate the sentiment, with regard to the House of Orange. It had been a hard-fought war, but not a savage one.

Don Fernando's eyes lifted from the canvas he was particularly interested in, and met Fredrik Hendrik's gaze. "I might need a bit of help with the printing," he said, "once we're ready to begin producing large quantities. I fear that siege lines tend to be short of printing presses."

"Not a problem," said the prince of Orange. "I shall see to it you have the services of some of the printers in the city."

Graciously, he left unsaid the fact that only *Spanish* siege lines would be short of printing presses. Dutchmen would have plenty, anywhere they went, not being semiliterate jumped-up sheepherders who called themselves "hidalgos."

Don Fernando nodded and made a little gesture to his aides. Two of them stepped forward and took up one of the portraits.

"We'll be off, then. I think we can safely expect the service to begin . . . in a month?"

Fredrik Hendrik pursed his lips, considering. "In the United Provinces, certainly." A bit wryly: "There's not much left of them, after all, since you arrived. I imagine you'll be able to do the same in the Spanish Netherlands. For the rest—"

He shrugged. "No telling what Gustavus Adolphus will decide."

"No, not yet," agreed the cardinal-infante. "The

great test of arms is still ahead of us, in the spring. But what about the other small principalities?"

"I've already raised the matter with De Geer, and I think Essen will certainly agree. Probably Duke Anton of Oldenburg, also. You'll have to deal with the archbishop of Cologne, of course. As for Cleves..."

He rolled his eyes, the Spanish commander almost immediately doing the same. Since the death of Duke Johann Wilhelm in 1609, and the passing of the inheritance to his sisters, Cleves had splintered badly.

"We'll manage something," said Fredrik Hendrik.

A week later, the end result began appearing. In Amsterdam first, of course.

"Marvelous," said the dye-maker, examining the sheets of paper with their many small portraits. "And you guarantee they will be accepted anywhere in the Low Countries? These in Brussels, for instance?"

The agent from the new postal service nodded. "And those from Brussels will be accepted here. As long as the blonde is portrayed, it doesn't matter which flag she's got wrapped around her. House of Orange colors, the cardinal-infante's colors, it doesn't matter. The stamps are all good anywhere that either Fredrik Hendrik or Don Fernando's authority reaches. That, for sure, right from the start. Soon enough, we expect other principalities to join in. Who knows? Within a year, perhaps even the USE and Denmark and France."

The dye-maker chuckled. "That'll depend a lot on who wins the war. Still..."

The dye-maker's wife intervened. She'd been silent up to now, standing next to her husband and squinting suspiciously at the sheets of paper. "We want some of the glue thrown in. And a brush to apply it. Brushes are expensive."

"Not a problem. A pot of glue and a small brush comes with every purchase of a sheet. One hundred stamps to a sheet."

The postal agent pointed to one of the sheets spread out across the dye-maker's table. "They're already creased, as you can see. Easy to cut them out. We're hoping, within possibly a year, to provide them with some gum already pasted to the back surface. Just wet them a little—a tongue-licking will do it—and the stamps will adhere to the parcel on their own. No glue needed at all."

The dye-maker pondered the matter, for a moment. But not for long. The established method for using postage worked, yes. But it was time-consuming, for a busy artisan, to have to go to a postal agent and have him manually stamp the parcel with a seal and sign it. Something of a nuisance. This way, with pre-paid postage, it would be much simpler.

And less costly, too. Not only were the new "stamps" slightly less expensive than the existing postal rates, simply in terms of money, but they were also much less expensive in terms of labor lost. If the postal agent could be believed, and the dye-maker thought he could, there would soon be special boxes in place all over the city where a pre-posted parcel could simply be dropped off for delivery. Fifteen minutes work for an artisan's wife or apprentice—perhaps only five or ten—instead of two hours or more.

"I'll buy a sheet, then."

"Splendid. Which one would you like?"

The dye-maker's eyes widened. "I have a choice?"

"Certainly," said the postal agent. "I told you. Any of the portraits is valid. All that matters is that it's the same blonde. She's the nurse, you know."

The dye-maker and his wife nodded. Anne Jefferson was quite well known in the city. Almost as well known as Gretchen Richter, in fact.

"Well..." The dye-maker stood up a bit straighter. "We should take the colors of Orange," he said stoutly.

"No," said his wife. "That portrait, she's showing too much skin. And who's Rembrandt, anyway? Never heard of him."

She pointed to the sheet with Rubens' version. "That one. He's famous and most of our trade is with the south, anyway. The cardinal-infante's colors are sure to be welcome in Brussels. Catholic or not, the linen-makers there are better business for us than these tight-fisted bastards in Amsterdam."

"Done," said the postal agent, reaching into his parcel and hauling out a pot of glue and a brush. "Oh, yes, I failed to mention that the pots and brushes all come with the initials of the artists. Whichever one you'd like."

"Rubens, of course," sniffed the dye-maker's wife. "The Hals brothers are drunkards and ne'er-do-wells. And nobody's ever heard of this Rembrandt fellow, whoever he is."

"Rubens it is, then."

"You're feeling better about the whole thing, I see," said Adam Olearius.

Anne smiled. "Well, yeah. From what I hear, the stamps are selling like crazy. Hands across the border, and all that." Then, quietly: "If it'll keep a few more people from getting killed, it was worth it."

"Might keep a lot of people from getting killed," her fiancé mused, sitting on the divan next to her. "Well, not by itself, of course. But along with all the rest..."

He lifted his shoulder in a little shrug. "Hard to know, of course, as it so often is with diplomacy. It's always a gamble."

"God *damn*," hissed Harry Lefferts. "Talk about a long shot paying off!"

He and Thorsten and Gerd stared at the pile of coins Donald Ohde has spilled onto the tavern table. Spanish silver, most of it, the best currency in Europe. But there were plenty of gold pieces mixed in with the lot. Some of them were probably adulterated, but with *that* big a pile it hardly mattered.

They did not bother casting glances around the tavern to make sure that no one was observing them. No doubt there was a footpad or two among the crowd in the tavern. But by now, weeks after their arrival in Amsterdam, no footpad or cutpurse in his right mind—no gang of them, either—would even think of crossing Harry Lefferts and his wrecking crew. The only difference between the way they gauged the matter and Mike Stearns did, was that professional cutthroats knew that Harry & Company *were* the most frightening pack of bandits on the continent. That they might be something else as well was irrelevant, from a criminal's standpoint.

"Time to get out of town, then," said Harry. "Before the storm hits."

Ohde frowned. "There will be no 'storm,' Harry. I

can assure you that the Frenchman was most satisfied with the transaction."

"Who cares about him? Sooner or later, Anne Jefferson's going to wonder what happened to the *originals*. We don't want to be anywhere within miles when that happens. Trust me."

Paul Maczka looked skeptical. "Come on, Harry. She's just a nurse. Gretchen, yes, we'd be in real trouble."

"'Just a nurse,'" Harry mimicked. "Yeah, fine—but she's a *West Virginia* nurse. She's Willie Ray Hudson's granddaughter, fer chrissake. Got cousins—first, second, third, you name it—all over the hills and hollers. At least two of them are serving in the Thuringian Rifles and another one is downright crazy. Marcus Acton, Jr. Got in a fight with him once. I won, but it was touch-and-go. Just as soon not do it again."

He started scooping coins and shoveling them into his money pouch. "Come on, guys, fill 'em up. I want to be halfway to the Channel ports before Anne figures it out, and we find ourselves in the middle of a down-time version of the Hatfield-McCoy feud."

"They did *what?*" shrieked Anne.

Mike Stearns flinched from the blast. "Just what I said. They finagled three out of the four originals and sold them to someone. For a small fortune, what I hear."

Anne's face was pale, her expression a combination of shock, outrage and fury. "*How did they get them?*"

Mike grimaced. "They just bought them outright from the Hals brothers. Those two are always strapped for cash. Rembrandt told me he let them have his for free, once they explained what they wanted it for."

"That stinking bastard!"

"It *is* a good cause, Anne. The one thing about Harry is that you can trust him to be honest. Well, okay, in a Robin Hood and Jesse James sort of way. He's not really what you could call an upstanding citizen. But he's not a thief, either. That money *will* go to spring our people out of the Tower."

The last sentence put something of a damper on Anne's gathering fury. She knew all of the people imprisoned in the Tower of London herself, after all. Two of them were friends of hers.

"Well, yeah, fine. But. Still."

After a few seconds' silence, she hissed: "One of these days, I swear I will kill that son of a bitch."

Mike pursed his lips. "You'll have to take a number. By now, the line's probably up to a hundred or so."

After Mike left, Anne turned to Olearius and he gave her a comforting embrace.

"At least Rubens didn't sell his," she whispered. "I'm glad for that. He's always been my favorite."

Adam said nothing, judging it to be an unwise time to explain that Rubens *had* sold his original. He'd sold it to Olearius himself, and for a token sum, once Adam explained his purpose.

But now was not the time to get into that. The portrait was safely stowed away, in a place Anne would never think to look.

There was no hurry, after all, given his purpose. Adam would tell her in a few years, when the whole incident had faded into one of those more-in-humor-than-anger recollections for his soon-to-be-wife. By then, they'd have children; and, like any mother, Anne would be thinking about her children's prospects.

Which would almost certainly be splendid. The future was always unpredictable, of course. But Adam Olearius was quite confident that in any one of the possible futures he and his wife would find themselves in, being able to bestow onto their children an original portrait by Rubens would mollify his wife. Especially *that* portrait, as famous as it would soon be.

By then, it would be worth...

Who could say? A very great deal, certainly.

He wondered, for a moment, what would happen to the others.

Richelieu pondered the three portraits. They were magnificent, especially taken as an ensemble. Three portraits by three great artists, each of the same subject...

To the best of the cardinal's knowledge, nothing like it had ever happened in the long history of art.

For a moment, he was tempted to keep them for himself. But, as always, duty triumphed.

"In the Louvre, Servien," he said firmly to his aide. "For the moment, we'll keep them here in my chambers. But once the work in the Grande Galerie is finished, we'll move them there. They'll form the anchor of the collection."

In another world, the royal castle known as the Louvre wouldn't become a museum until 1793, during the French revolution. But Richelieu, determined to see to it that the revolution never happened at all, had concluded that launching a museum much earlier would add to the grandeur of royal France. It was just one of many adaptations he was making to the new world created by the Ring of Fire.

"And the other matter?"

Richelieu continued his study of the portraits, for perhaps a minute.

"A good idea," he finally concluded. "No matter how the war ends. I have come to the conclusion that the more civilized the contest, the more advantageous is the position of France. This"—he gestured at the portraits—"was a very shrewd maneuver by our opponent. Best to respond quickly and in kind, I think, lest we seem churlish."

Servien nodded. "It will certainly please the city's artisans and tradesmen. It can take up to three hours to get a parcel properly sealed and certified."

"Yes, it will," Richelieu did not usually concern himself much with the sentiments of the merchant classes, since in normal times they carried little weight in the political affairs of France. But the war was not going as well as he had thought it would, and the king's younger brother Monsieur Gaston—treacherous as ever—was using the fact to undermine Richelieu's support in the aristocracy. Should the worst come to pass and a real crisis erupt, having the support and allegiance of the Parisian mob could be important.

"We'll have Georges de la Tour do the painting. I'll want the same model, you understand. Given the situation, Servien, that's essential."

"I'll see to the matter, Your Eminence."

Anne Jefferson sat at the same table in the embassy, staring at Rebecca. Mike was long gone from Amsterdam, by now, since the war was heating up again.

"You've got to be kidding."

"Not at all," said Rebecca. "The French are offering

to pay for your transport"—she glanced at Adam—"and your husband's, and they'll put you up in chambers in the Louvre itself. It's mostly a royal palace today, you know. They're certain to be very comfortable quarters."

She made a little face. "Allowing for seventeenth-century plumbing. But you've been dealing with that here in Amsterdam, anyway."

"This is a joke, right?"

THE
HONOR HARRINGTON
SERIES

Author's note:

This story introduces several characters who wound up becoming very important in David Weber's Honor Harrington series. In fact, over time, this story and its sequels began re-shaping the whole way Dave planned the series itself. Dave had always intended to make the struggle against Mesa and genetic slavery a major feature of the Harrington series—but he'd originally intended to have that happen after Honor Harrington died in the climactic battle that concludes *At All Costs,* the eleventh book in the Harrington series that was published in November 2005.

In Dave's original outline for the whole series, Honor's death would be followed by a break in the chronology of the series lasting a couple of decades, following which her son would emerge as the central figure in the emerging galactic struggle against genetic slavery.

But...that began to change, as a result of this story and the two that followed—*"Fanatic,"* a novella I wrote for the fourth Harrington universe anthology *(The Service of the Sword,* published in April 2003*),* and *Crown of Slaves,* the novel I co-authored with Dave which came out in September 2003. As the storyline that began with *"From the Highlands"* unfolded, Dave decided that he could start weaving the fight against Mesa into the series much earlier than he'd originally planned.

So...Honor Harrington wound up surviving the battle that ends *At All Costs.* To some extent, those of you who are fans of the Harrington series can thank this story for that. Not, mind you, that that was my intention in writing it. I just wanted to produce a good story in its own terms, which I daresay this one is.

From the Highlands

The First Day

Helen

Helen used the effort of digging at the wall to control her terror. She thought of it as a variation of Master Tye's training: *turn weakness into strength.* Fear drove her, but she shaped it to steady her aching arms instead of letting it loosen her bowels.

Scrape, scrape. She didn't have the strength to make big gouges in the wall with a pitiful shard of broken rubble. The wall was not particularly hard, since it was not much more than rubble itself. But her slender arms and little hands, for all their well-honed training under Master Tye's regimen, were still those of a girl just turned fourteen.

So what? She couldn't afford to make much noise, anyway. Now and then, she could hear the low sound of her captors' voices, just beyond the heavy door which they had placed across the entrance to her "cell."

Scrape, scrape. Weakness into strength. *The root breaks the rock. Wind and water triumph over stone.*

So she had been trained. By her father, as much as by Master Tye. *Decide what you want, and set to it like running water. Soft, slight, steady. Unstoppable.*

Scrape, scrape. She had no idea how thick the wall was, or even whether it was a wall at all. For all she knew, Helen might simply be digging an endless little tunnel through the soil of Terra.

Her abductors had removed the hood after they got her into this strange and frightening place. She was still somewhere in the Solarian League's capital city of Chicago, that much she knew. But she had no idea where, except that she thought it was in the Old Quarter. Chicago was a gigantic city, and the Old Quarter was like an ancient Mesopotamian *tel.* Layer upon layer of half-rubbled ruins. They had descended deep underground, using twisted and convoluted passageways that she had not been able to store in her memory.

Scrape, scrape. *Just do it. Running water conquers all. Eventually.*

While she scraped, she thought sometimes of her father, and sometimes of Master Tye. But, more often, she thought of her mother. She could not really remember her mother's face, of course, except from holocubes. Her mother had died when Helen was only four years old. But she had the memory—still as vivid as ever—of the day her mother died. Helen had been sitting on her father's lap, terrified, while her mother led a hopeless defense of a convoy against an overwhelming force of Havenite warships. But her mother had saved her, that day, along with her father.

Scrape, scrape. The work was numbing to the mind, as well as the body. Mostly, Helen didn't think of anything. She just kept one image before her: that of her mother's posthumously-awarded Parliamentary Medal of Honor, which, in all the many places they had lived since, her father always hung in the most prominent place in their home.

Scrape, scrape. Helen would get no medals for what she was doing, true. But she didn't care, anymore than her mother had cared.

Scrape, scrape. *Running water.*

Victor

When he spotted the figure he was looking for, Victor Cachat was swept by another wave of doubt and hesitation.

And fear.

This is crazy. The best way I can think of to guarantee myself the place of honor—in front of a firing squad.

The uncertainty was powerful enough to hold him rooted in one spot for well over a minute. Fortunately, the grubby tavern was so crowded and dimly lit that his immobility went unnoticed by anyone.

It was certainly unnoticed by the man he was staring at. It took Victor no more than seconds to decide that his quarry was already half-drunk. True, the man sitting at the bar was neither swaying nor slurring the few words he spoke to the bartender. In this, as in everything, Kevin Usher kept himself under tight control.

But Victor had seen Usher sober—occasionally—and he thought he could detect the subtle signs.

In the end, it was that which finally overcame Victor's fears.

If he denounces me, I can always claim he was too drunk to know what he's talking about. It's not as if Durkheim won't believe me—he makes enough wise-cracks himself about Usher's drinking habits, doesn't he?

At the moment when he came to that conclusion, Victor saw the man sitting next to Usher slide off his bar stool. An instant later, Victor had taken his place.

Again, he hesitated. Usher wasn't looking at him. The Marine citizen colonel was hunched over, staring at nothing beyond the amber liquid in his glass. Victor could still, if he chose, leave without committing himself.

Or so he thought. Victor had forgotten Usher's reputation.

"This is a gross violation of procedure," said the man sitting next to him, without moving his eyes from the glass. "Not to mention the fact that you're breaking every rule of tradecraft. Durkheim would skin you alive." Usher took a sip of his drink. "Well, maybe not. Durkheim's a bureaucrat. What he knows about field work wouldn't tax the brains of a pigeon."

Usher's soft voice gave no indication of drunkenness, beyond the slow pacing of the words. Neither did his eyes, when he finally lifted them toward Victor.

"But what's more important—*way more*—is that I'm off duty and you're disturbing my concentration."

Victor's angry response came too quickly to control. "Fuck you, Usher," he hissed. "As much practice as you get, you could drink in the middle of a hurricane without spilling a drop."

A thin smile came to Usher's face. "Well, well," he drawled. "Whaddaya know? Durkheim's little wonderboy can actually use cuss words."

"I learned to swear before I learned to talk. That's why I don't do it."

The thin smile grew thinner. "Oh, what a thrill. Another Dolee about to spin his tale of poverty and deprivation. I can't wait."

Victor reined in his temper. He was a little shocked at the effort, and realized that it was his own fear which was bubbling up. Victor had learned to control himself by the time he was six years old. That was how he had survived the projects, and clawed his way out.

Out—and up. But he wasn't sure he liked the vista.

"Never mind," he muttered. "I know I'm breaking tradecraft. But I need to talk to you privately, Usher. And I couldn't think of another way to do it."

The smile left Usher's face completely. His eyes went back to the glass. "I've got nothing to say to State Security outside of an interrogation room." The smile came back—*very* thin. "And if you want to get me into an interrogation room, you'd damned well better get some help. I don't think you're up to it, wonderboy."

For just an instant, the large hand holding the shot glass tightened. Glancing at it, Victor had no doubt at all that it would take a full squad of State Sec troops to bring Usher into an interrogation room. And half of them would die in the trying. Lush or not, Usher's reputation was still towering.

"Why?" Victor mused. "You could have been an SS citizen general by now—citizen *lieutenant* general— instead of a Marine citizen colonel buried here."

Usher's lips, for just an instant, twisted into a grimace. A half-formed sneer, maybe. "I don't much care for Saint-Just," was the answer. "Never did, even before the Revolution."

Victor held his breath for a moment, before exhaling it sharply. He glanced quickly around the room. No one was listening, so far as he could tell. "Well," he drawled, "you don't seem too concerned with your health, that's for sure."

Usher's lips quirked again. "Are you referring to my drinking habits?"

Victor snorted. "You'll be lucky if you die of cirrhosis of the liver, you go around making wisecracks about the head of State Security."

"I wasn't making a wisecrack. I was stating a simple fact. I despise Oscar Saint-Just and I've never made a secret of it. I've told him so to his face. Twice. Once before the Revolution, and once after." Usher shrugged. "He didn't much seem to care, one way or the other. You can say that much for Saint-Just—he doesn't kill people out of personal spite. And I'll grant you that he isn't personally a sadist—unlike most of the people working for him."

Victor flushed at the implied insult. But he made no retort, for the simple reason that he couldn't. In the short time since his graduation from the SS Academy, Victor had learned that Usher's sneer was all too close to the truth. Which, of course, was why he was sitting in this tavern in the first place, as dangerous as it was.

Usher lifted the glass and took a sip. From the color of the liquid and what he had read in Usher's file—very *big* file, even if Victor suspected half of it was missing—he was sure it was Terran whiskey.

Sour mash, technically, from some small province called Tennessee.

Usher rolled the glass in his hand, inspecting the amber contents. "But I decided it would be best if I made myself scarce. So, after a time, I took the commission they offered me in the Marines and volunteered to head up the security detachment at the embassy on Terra. Six months' travel, it is, from here to the People's Republic. The arrangement suits me fine. Saint-Just too, apparently."

Usher downed his drink in one gulp and set the shot glass on the table. The motion was swift and sure. The shot glass didn't even make so much as a clink when it hit the table top.

"Now get to the point, wonderboy. Why are you here? If you're trying to set me up, don't bother. My attitude toward SS is just as well known to Rob Pierre as it is to Saint-Just." For a moment, a wicked little gleam came to Usher's eyes. "But Pierre's a bit fond of me, don't you know? I did him a favor, once."

Usher's eyes came to Victor, and the gleam got a lot more wicked. "So go look for a promotion somewhere else."

Victor started to speak, but cut his response short. The bartender had finally arrived. "What'll you have?" he asked, as he refilled Usher's shot glass without being prompted. The Marine citizen colonel was a regular in the place.

Victor ordered a beer and waited until it was served before speaking. "I'm not trying to set you up for anything, Usher. I need your advice."

Usher was back to staring at his drink. The only sign he had heard Victor was a slight cock in his eyebrow. Victor hesitated, trying to think of the best way to say what he had to say. Then, shrugging, went straight to it.

"Durkheim's been dealing with the Mesans. And their cult sidekicks here on Terra. That stinking outfit called the Sacred Band."

Silence. Usher stared at his drink for a few seconds. Then, in another swift motion, drank half of it in one toss. "Why does that not surprise me?" he murmured.

The man's apparent indifference caused a resurgence of Victor's anger.

"Don't you even care?" he demanded, hissing. "For the sake of—"

"Ah! Stop!" Usher flashed him that wicked smile. "Don't tell me wonderboy was about to call on the deity? Rank superstition, that is—*citizen*."

Victor tightened his jaws. "I was about to say: 'for the sake of the Revolution,'" he finished lamely.

"Sure you were. Sure you were." The Marine citizen colonel leaned over, emphasizing his next words.

"Poor, poor wonderboy. You just discovered that the Revolution has a few blots on its stainless escutcheon, did you?" He turned away, hunching his shoulders, and brought the glass back to his lips. "Why *shouldn't* Durkheim get cozy with the scum of the universe? He's done everything else. State Sec's so filthy already a little more slime won't even show."

Again, Victor flushed at the insult; and, again, made no retort.

Usher started to down the drink, but paused. The pause was very brief. When he set the empty glass down on the table, he spoke very softly: "Did you know you were being followed?"

Victor was startled, but he had enough self-control to keep from turning his head. "*Shit,*" he hissed, momentarily losing his determination to avoid profanity.

The thin smile came back to Usher's face. "I will be damned. I do believe you are the genuine article, wonderboy. Didn't know there were any left. How well can you take a punch?"

The *non sequitur* left Victor's mind scrambling to catch up. "Huh?"

"Never mind," murmured Usher. "If you don't know, you're about to find out."

The next half minute was a complete blur. Victor only had fragmented images:

Usher roaring with rage, almost every word an obscenity. Customers in the bar scrambling away. Himself sailing through the air, landing on his back. Up again—somehow—sailing onto a table. Usher's face, contorted with fury, still roaring obscenities.

Most of all:

Pain, and Usher's hands. Big hands. *God, that bastard's strong!* Victor's attempts to fend them off were as futile as a kitten's attempts to pry open a mastiff's jaws.

But he never quite lost consciousness. And some part of Victor's brain, somewhere in the chaos, understood that Usher wasn't actually trying to kill him. Or even really hurt him that badly.

Which was a good thing, since after the first few seconds Victor had no doubt at all that Usher could have destroyed him utterly. That much of the man's reputation was no figment of the Revolution's mythology, after all. Despite the terror of the moment, some part of Victor was singing hosannas.

The admiral and the ambassador

Edwin Young was a tall man, with a lanky physique. The uniform of a rear admiral in the Royal Manticoran Navy—stretched to the very limits of official regulations with little sartorial touches and curlicues—fit him to perfection. The man's fine-boned features and long, slender fingers completed the image of an aristocratic officer quite nicely. So did the relaxed and languid manner in which he sat in his chair behind the large desk in his office.

Even at a glance, anyone familiar with the subtleties of Manticoran society would have assumed the admiral was a member of the nobility—and high-ranked nobility, at that. The intelligence captain who sat across the desk from him thought that the small, tastefully-subdued pin announcing Young's membership in the Conservative Association was really quite unnecessary.

The pin was also against Navy regulations, but the admiral clearly wasn't concerned about being called on the carpet for wearing it while in uniform. The only Manticoran official who outranked him on Terra was Ambassador Hendricks. As it happened, the Manticoran Ambassador to the Solarian League was in the same room with the admiral and the captain, standing by the window. And, as it happened, the ambassador was wearing the identical pin on his own lapel.

The intelligence captain's eyes, however, were not really focused on the admiral's pin. They were focused on the admiral's neck. It was a long neck, slender and supple. Entirely in keeping with Admiral Young's elite birth and breeding.

The captain was quite certain he could break it easily.

Not that he would bother, except as a side-effect. The captain had already considered, and discarded, several different ways in which he could snap the admiral's neck. But they were all too quick. What the captain primarily wanted was the pleasure of crushing the admiral's windpipe, slowly and methodically.

Eventually, of course, the vertebra would be crushed. The pulverized fragments would sever the spinal cord and complete the job. Probably too quickly, since the captain was an immensely powerful man and he could not recall ever having been as enraged as he was at the moment. But—

The captain restrained his fury. The effort involved was difficult enough that he only caught the last few words of the admiral's concluding summary.

"—as I'm sure you will agree, Captain Zilwicki. Once you've had a chance to think it through in a calmer and more rational state of mind."

Through ears still rushing with the sound of his own blood, the captain heard the ambassador's voice chiming in:

"Yes. There is simply no reason they would harm your daughter, Captain. As you have pointed out yourself, that would be quite out of character even for the Peeps. As it is, this brutal and desperate deed goes far beyond normal boundaries of intelligence work."

The captain's blocky form remained still and unmoving in his chair, his thick hands clutching the arm rests. Only his eyes swiveled, to bring the pudgy figure of Ambassador Hendricks under his gaze.

The captain spared only a moment's glance at

Hendrick's jowls. He had already concluded that the fat girdling the Ambassador's neck would present no obstacle whatever to strangling him also. But he still favored two or three maneuvers which were quite illegal in tournament wrestling. And for good reason, since all of them would result in ruptured internal organs. The captain thought Hendricks' obese appearance would be much improved, with blood hemorrhaging from every orifice in his body.

He forced his mind away from those thoughts, and brought his attention back to the ambassador's words.

"—can't believe SS is so arrogantly insane to pull something like this. On the eve of Parnell's arrival here on Terra!"

Admiral Young nodded. "They're going to be suffering the worst public relations disaster they've ever had here in the Solarian League. The last thing they'd do is compound it by murdering a fourteen-year-old girl."

Even to himself, the captain's voice sounded thick and hoarse.

"I keep telling you," he snarled, no longer even bothering with military formalities, "that this is *not* a Peep operation. Or, if it is, it's a rogue operation being conducted outside of the loop. There's no way of telling what the people who took Helen might do. I have *got* to have leeway to start investigating—"

"Enough, Captain Zilwicki!" snapped the ambassador. "The decision is made. Of course, I understand your concern. But, at least for the moment, all of our attention must be focused on the opportunities presented to us by Parnell's arrival here on Terra. As a professional intelligence officer, rather than a worried father, I'm sure you agree. We can play along with this Peep diversionary maneuver easily enough. What we *musn't* do is allow it to actually divert us."

"And mind your manners," growled Young. The admiral leaned back even further in his chair, almost slumping in it. "I've made allowances for your behavior so far because of the personal nature of the situation. But you *are* a naval officer, Captain. So you'll do as you're told—*and* stay within the boundaries of military protocol while you're at it."

For a moment, the captain almost hurled himself across the desk. But a lifetime of discipline and self-control stayed with him. And, after a few seconds, reasserted itself.

What kept him steady even more than training and habit was a simple reality: getting himself arrested, or even confined to quarters due to indiscipline, was the surest way he could think of to make his daughter's already slim chance of survival nonexistent.

That realization brought his own final decision. *I'll get Helen out of this, no matter what the cost. Damn everything else.*

The thought brought the first real calmness back to Anton Zilwicki since his daughter had been abducted. It drenched his fury like a bucket of icewater and restored his normally methodical way of thinking.

First things first, he told himself firmly. *Get the hell out of here before they put any actual restrictions on your movements.*

He rose abruptly to his feet and saluted. "As you wish, Admiral. I'll send the communication to the kidnappers from my own home. With your permission. I think that would be better."

"Yes," agreed the ambassador firmly. "If you send

it from here, or your own office, they might get
suspicious." His tone of voice actually managed a bit
of warmth. "Good thinking there, Captain. I'm quite
certain, along with the Admiral, that this is a long-term
gambit on the part of the Peeps to create a conduit
for disinformation. They'll be reassured if their contact
with you seems completely private."

The words were spoken in the manner of an old
intelligence hand, congratulating a novice on having
figured out a simple task. Given the circumstances,
Captain Zilwicki almost burst into laughter. The captain *was* an "old intelligence hand." What Hendricks
knew about the craft was simply the maneuvers he'd
learned as an ambitious nobleman in Manticore's
political arena. That arena was complex and tortuous,
true, but it was a far less savage place than Zilwicki
had inhabited for many years now.

But he let none of his contempt show. He simply
nodded politely, bowed, and left the room.

Anton

Sometime later, when he entered his apartment, Zilwicki
found Robert Tye still sitting in the lotus position in
the center of the living room. To all appearances, the
martial arts master had not moved a muscle since the
captain left that morning. Tye had his own way of
controlling rage.

The martial artist raised an eyebrow. Zilwicki shook
his head.

"About what I expected, Robert. The imbeciles are
taking this at face value. And they're so obsessed with

the propaganda coup provided by Parnell's coming testimony on the Peep regime that they don't want to deal with anything else. So I've been ordered to follow the kidnappers' instructions."

For a moment, Tye studied the captain. Then, a slight smile came to his face. "And clearly you have no intention of complying."

Zilwicki's only response was a faint snort. He returned the martial artist's scrutiny with one of his own.

Robert Tye had been the first person Anton contacted after he discovered Helen's abduction when he returned to his apartment the previous evening. The captain was still not quite certain why he had done so. He had acted out of impulse, and Anton was not by nature and habit an impulsive man.

Slowly, Anton took a seat on a nearby couch, thinking all the while. He and Helen had been on Terra for slightly over four years. Because of his duties in the Navy, Anton had lived a rather peripatetic life and he was sometimes concerned over the toll that took on Helen. Having to change schools and sets of friends frequently was difficult for a child.

But his daughter, to his surprise, had greeted the announced move to Chicago with enthusiasm. Helen, following in her mother's footsteps, had begun studying the martial arts at the age of six. As was his daughter's habit—her father's child, in this—Helen had studied the lore of the art as well as the art itself. To her, Chicago meant only one thing: the opportunity to study under one of the galaxy's most legendary martial artists.

Anton had been worried that Tye would not accept a young girl for a student. But the martial artist had done so readily. At his age, Tye had once told Anton, he found the presence of children a comfort. And, in the years which followed, Helen's *sensei* had become a part of their little family. More like a grandfather, in many ways, than anything else.

"Are you sure you want to be part of this, Robert?" he asked abruptly. "I'm not sure it was right for me to get you involved. Whatever I wind up doing, it's bound to be—"

"Dangerous?" suggested Tye, smiling.

Anton chuckled. "I was going to say: *illegal*. Highly illegal."

The martial artist's shoulders moved in a slight shrug. "That does not concern me. But are you so certain your superiors are in error?"

Zilwicki's jaws tightened. His already square face now looked like a solid cube of iron.

"Trust me, Robert. Something like this is completely out of character for Peep intelligence. And they've got nothing to gain."

His expression changed. Not softening so much as simply becoming more thoughtful. "By the nature of my position in Manticoran intelligence, I don't know anything of real use to the Peeps anyway. Not enough, that's for sure, to warrant such a risky gambit." He moved a hand across his knee, as if brushing off a fly. "The Admiral thinks the Peeps are engaging in a long-run maneuver, designed to turn me into an ongoing conduit for disinformation. Which is probably the single most asinine thing that asinine man has ever said in his life."

The martial artist cocked his head a bit. The gesture was a subtle suggestion that the captain's own subtlety had escaped Tye's understanding.

"Robert, the reason the Admiral's theory is nonsense is because it's in the nature of things that a long-run campaign of disinformation has to be reasonably stable. Disinformation campaigns take time—lots of time. You can't suddenly have your turned agent start flooding his own intelligence service with 'information' which seems odd and contrary to other information. It has to be done in a careful and subtle manner. Slowly adding one little bit of information at a time, until—over a period of months, more often years—a warped perception of reality becomes accepted without anyone really knowing when and how it happened."

"All right, I can understand that."

Zilwicki ran fingers through his short-cropped, coarse black hair. "Kidnapping a man's daughter and using her as a threat is about as far removed from 'stable' as I can imagine. Even if the father involved submitted completely, the situation would be impossible. If nothing else, in his anxiety the father would push the campaign too quickly and screw it up. Not to mention the difficulty of keeping a captive for a long period, on foreign soil where you can't simply toss her into a prison. And you'd have to do so, because under those circumstances the father would insist on regular proof that his child was still alive and well."

For all the captain's tightly controlled speech, his anxiety drove him to his feet. "Say whatever else you want about the Peeps, Robert, but they're not stupid. This is completely out of character for them in a hundred different ways."

"So now what shall we do?"

"I'll start with my contacts in the Chicago police," *

growled Zilwicki. He stalked over to the side table and stared down at the piece of paper resting on it. A cold, almost cruel smile came to his face.

"Can you believe this? An actual *ransom note?*" The barked little laugh which followed was harsh. "Professional intelligence! God in Heaven, what Hendricks knows about that subject could be inscribed on the head of a pin. Or his own head."

The savage smile widened. "Apparently, these so-called 'pros' have never heard of modern forensics. Which is not the least of the reasons I don't think this was done by the Peeps."

Zilwicki's eyes moved to the door of the apartment. The same door which, the day before, someone had managed to open without leaving any sign of a forced entry. "Everything about this operation smacks of amateurs who are too clever for their own good. Oil mixed with water. The ransom note is archaic. Yet the door's modern security devices were bypassed effortlessly.

"Idiots," he said softly. "They'd have done better to burn it open. Would have taken a bit of time, with a modern door. But as it is, they might as well have left another note announcing in bold letters: *inside job.* Whoever they were, they had to have the complicity of someone in the complex's maintenance staff. Within twenty-four hours, if they move fast—and they will—the Chicago cops can get me profiles of everyone who works in this complex along with the forensics results. I don't think it'll be that hard to narrow the suspects down to a very small list."

"Will the police cooperate to that extent?"

"I think so. They owe me some favors, for one

thing. For another, they have their own attitude toward kidnapping, which usually makes them willing to bend the rules a little."

His eyes came back to the ransom note sitting on the side table. An actual note, written by an actual person, on actual paper. Again the captain barked a laugh. "Professional intelligence!"

The Second Day

Helen

At first, Helen had planned to just leave the digging shards out in the open, lying with the rest of the rubble which half-filled the cell. But soon enough she realized that if her captors took a close look at the interior of the cell, they would surely notice the signs of recent use on the shards.

Not that such an inspection was very likely. From what she could tell, her captors were so arrogant that they apparently never even considered the possibility that a fourteen-year-old girl might try to thwart them.

Helen had never gotten a good look at her captors, after the first few moments when they had jimmied their way into the apartment and abducted her. They had fitted a hood over her head right away and some-how smuggled her out of the huge complex without being spotted. How they managed that feat was a mystery to Helen, since the complex had a population density which was astonishing to anyone from Manti-core. She had realized from the first terrifying hour that they must have planned her abduction carefully, and had the assistance of someone within the apartment complex's maintenance staff.

Once they got her underground, they had eventually removed the hood. Helen didn't think they had planned on doing that, but it had quickly proven necessary—unless they wanted to carry her. The footing in the subterranean labyrinth was so treacherous that Helen had continually tripped while wearing the hood. She had been snarled at and cuffed several times before the abductors finally bowed to the inevitable and took off the hood.

Her captors' angry exasperation with her was just another sign of the carelessness which lay beneath the arrogant surface. For all the meticulous planning that had clearly gone into her abduction, her captors had apparently never thought of such minor obstacles. From Helen's careful study of military history—she firmly intended to follow her parents' footsteps and have a career in the Navy—she recognized the classic signs of opponents who were too full of themselves and never bothered to consider what the enemy might do. Or to simply understand what the ancient Clausewitz had called the inevitable "friction of war."

But, even though the hood had been removed, they had cuffed her immediately whenever her eyes veered in their direction. And since they had shoved her into this cell they still demanded that she face the wall whenever they entered with her food. According to the novels she had read, that was a good sign. Captors who didn't want to be recognized were not planning to kill you.

That was the theory, at least. Helen didn't place too much credence in it, however. She still had no idea who her captors were, or why they had kidnapped her. But of one thing she had no doubt at all: they would no more hesitate to kill her than they would an insect. Granted, at the age of fourteen she could hardly claim to be an expert on human villainy. But it was obvious enough, just from the way her captors *walked*, that they considered themselves a breed apart. She had seen little of their faces, but she had not missed the little strut with which all of them moved. Like leopards, preening before sheep.

There were four of them: two males, and two females. From the few glances she'd gotten, they'd looked enough alike that Helen thought they might be part of the same family. But now that she had a chance to think about it calmly, she was beginning to think otherwise. Her captors had made no attempt to remain silent in her presence, for the good and simple reason that they spoke their own language. Helen didn't know the tongue, but she thought she recognized the language group. Many of the phrases resonated with the Old Byelorussian that was still spoken in some of the more rural areas of the Gryphon highlands. She was almost certain her captors were speaking a derivative of one of the Slavic languages.

And, if so, there was an ugly possibility. Her father had mentioned to her, once, that the genetic "super-soldiers" who had been at the heart of Earth's terrible Final War had originally been bred in Ukrainian laboratories. The "super-soldiers" had been supposedly annihilated in those wars. But her father had told her that some of them survived. And still lurked, somewhere in the great human ocean which was humanity's home planet.

By all accounts, those genetic "super-soldiers" had looked upon other people as nothing more than beasts of burden. Or toys for their amusement.

Or insects . . .

That last image brought a peculiar kind of comfort. Helen realized she was pursuing the ancient strategy of one of Terra's most successful species. Like a cockroach, she would find safety in the walls.

Her lips quirked in a smile, she went back to digging.

Victor

Durkheim came to visit Victor in the hospital. As always, the head of State Security's detachment at the Havenite embassy on Terra was curt and abrupt.

"Nothing really serious," he muttered. "Spectacular set of cuts and bruises, but nothing worse. You're lucky."

Durkheim was thin to the point of emaciation. His bony, sunken-cheeked face was perched on the end of a long and scrawny neck. Standing at the foot of the quick-heal tank and staring down at him, the SS citizen general reminded Victor of nothing so much as holographs he had seen of a Terran vulture perched on a tree limb.

"So what happened?" he demanded.

Victor's answer came without hesitation. "I was just trying to get Usher to cut down on the drinking. Looks bad for our image here. I never imagined—"

Durkheim snorted. "Talk about foolish apprentices!" There was no heat in his voice, however. "Leave Usher alone, youngster. Frankly, the best thing for everybody would be if he'd just drink himself to death."

He placed a clawlike hand on the rim of the tank and leaned over. Now, he *really* looked like a carrion-eater.

"Usher's still alive for the sole reason that he's a Hero of the Revolution—never mind the details—and Rob Pierre is sometimes prone to sentimentalism. *That's it.*" Hissing: "You understand?"

Victor swallowed. "Yes, sir."

"Good." Durkheim straightened up. "Fortunately, Usher keeps his mouth shut, so there's no reason to do anything about the situation. I don't expect he'll live more than another year or so—not the way he guzzles whiskey. So just stay away from him, henceforth. That's an order."

"Yes, sir." But Durkheim was already through the door. As always, watching him, Victor was a bit amazed. For all Durkheim's cadaverous appearance and the angular awkwardness of his stride, the SS official managed to move very quickly.

Victor almost laughed. The way Durkheim jogged out his elbows as he walked resembled a vulture flapping his wings. But Victor managed to keep the humor under control. He was not *that* naive.

Like any predator, Durkheim would eat carrion. But he was still a predator, and a very dangerous one. Of that, Victor had no doubt at all.

He was released from the hospital three hours later. It was too late in the day for Victor to go to the embassy, so he decided he might as well return to his apartment. His apartment was buried in the enormous, towering complex in which the People's Republic of Haven leased a number of apartments for its embassy staff. Unfortunately, the complex was located in the city's easternmost district, on the landfill which, over the centuries, had slowly extended kilometers into Lake Michigan. A prestigious address, to be sure, but it meant a long trip on Chicago's labyrinthine public transport system. The hospital was located on the edge of the Old Quarter, not far from the tavern which was Usher's favorite watering hole.

Victor sighed. And *that* meant—

It was not that Victor had any prejudice against the hordes of poor immigrants who thronged in the Old Quarter and mobbed public transport in its vicinity. In truth, he felt more comfortable in their midst than he did among the Solarian elite that he hobnobbed with in the embassy's frequent social functions. The Old Quarter's residents reminded him of the people he had grown up with, in the Dolist projects of Nouveau Paris.

But there was a reason, after all, that Victor had fought so hard to get out of those projects. So it was with no great enthusiasm that he resigned himself to spending an hour crammed into the transport network. The Solarian League's capital city liked to boast of its public transportation system. Yet Victor had noticed that none of Chicago's elite ever used it.

So what else is new? He consoled himself with thoughts of the inevitable coming revolution in the Solarian League. He had been on Terra long enough to see the rot beneath the glittering surface.

Not more than five minutes after he forced himself into the mob packing one of the transport capsules— a good name for the things, he thought ruefully—he felt someone pressing against him.

Like everyone else, Victor was standing. He had

been told once that the capsules had originally been built with seats, but those had long since been removed from the capsules used in the Old Quarter due to the pressure of overcapacity. Victor had the relatively short stature common to Havenites raised on a Dolist diet, but he was still taller than most of the immigrants in the Old Quarter.

He glanced down. The person pressed so closely against him—too closely, even by capsule standards— was a young woman. From her dusky skin tone and facial features, she shared the south Asian genetic background which was common to a large number of Chicago's immigrant population. Even if it hadn't been for the lascivious smile on her face, beaming up at him, he would have known from her costume that she was a prostitute. Somewhere back in the mists of time, her outfit traced its lineage to a sari. But this version of the garment was designed to emphasize the woman's supple limbs and sensuous belly.

Nothing unusual, in the Old Quarter. Victor had lost track of the number of times he had been propositioned since he arrived on Terra, less than a year ago. As always, he shook his head and murmured a refusal. As a matter of class solidarity, if nothing else, Victor was never rude to prostitutes. So the refusal was polite. But it was still firm, for all that.

He was surprised, therefore, when she persisted. The woman was now practically embracing him. She extended her tongue, wagging it in his face. When he saw the tongue's upper surface, Victor stiffened.

Speak of the devil. Mesa's genetic engineers always marked their slaves in that manner. The markings served the same purpose as the brands or tattoos used by slavers in the past, but these were completely ineradicable, short of removing the tongue entirely. The marks were actually part of the flesh itself, grown there as the genengineered embryo developed. For technical reasons which Victor did not understand, taste buds lent themselves easily to that purpose.

The stiffness in his posture was partly due to revulsion, but mostly to sheer anger. If there was any foulness in the universe as great as Mesa and Manpower Inc., Victor did not know what it was. But this woman, he reminded himself, was herself a victim of that monstrosity. So Victor used his anger to drive the revulsion under. He repeated the refusal—even more firmly—but this time with a very friendly smile.

No use. Now the woman had her mouth against the side of his head, as if kissing him.

"Shut up, wonderboy," she whispered. "He'll talk to you. Get off at the Jackson transfer and follow me."

Victor was stiff as a board. "My, my," she whispered. "He was right. You *are* a babe in the woods."

Anton

The Chicago police lieutenant's frown was worthy of Jove. "I'm warning you, Anton—if we start finding dead bodies lying around in this complex, I'll arrest you in a heartbeat."

Zilwicki's eyes never lifted from the packet the lieutenant had handed him. "Don't worry about it, Muhammad. I'm just looking for information, that's all."

Lieutenant Muhammad Hobbs studied the shorter man for a moment. Then, the small figure of Robert

Tye sitting on the floor of Zilwicki's apartment. Then, the cybernetics console tucked into a corner. Even at a glance, it was obvious that the capabilities of that console went far beyond anything that would normally be found in a private residence.

For a moment, Hobbs' dark face darkened still further. Then, sighing softly, he murmured: "Just remember. We're really going out on a limb for you with this one, Anton. At least half a dozen of us, starting with me, will be lucky if we just lose our pensions."

The Manticoran officer finally lifted his eyes from the forensics packet and nodded. "I understand, Muhammad. No dead bodies. Nothing, in fact, that would be awkward for the police."

"Such as a rush of people into hospitals with broken bones," growled the policeman. Again, his eyes moved to Tye. "Or worse."

Tye smiled gently. "I believe you misinterpret the nature of my art, Lieutenant Hobbs."

Muhammad snorted. "Save it for the tourists. I've seen you in tournaments, *sensei*. Even playing by the rules, you were scary enough."

He pointed a finger at Zilwicki. "And this one? I can't recall ever seeing him in a lotus, contemplating the whichness of what. But I use the same gym he does, and I *have* seen him bench-press more pounds than I want to think about."

The policeman straightened and arched his shoulders, as if relieving himself of a small burden. "All right, enough," he growled. He turned away and headed for the door. "Just remember: no dead bodies; no hospital reports."

● ● ●

Before the door had even closed, Zilwicki was sitting in front of the console. Within a few seconds, he had loaded the data from the police forensics report and was completely absorbed by the material appearing on the screen.

Victor

Victor had never been *into* the Old Quarter before. He'd skirted the edges of it often enough, and gone through it in public transport capsules. But this was the first time he'd actually walked through the streets.

If the word "streets" could be used at all. Urban planners, following the jargonistic tendencies of all social sciences, often preferred the term "arteries" to refer to public thoroughfares. The euphemism, applied to the Old Quarter, was no euphemism at all. Except for being square in cross-section rather than round, and the fact that human beings passed through them instead of blood corpuscles, the "streets" were as complex, convoluted, tortuous and three-dimensional as a body's circulatory system. More so, really, since the clear distinction between arteries and veins was absent here.

Victor was hopelessly lost within minutes. In that short space of time, the woman leading him had managed to take him through more streets than he could remember—including four elevator transits, three occasions when they passed through huge underground "plazas" filled with vendors' booths and shops, and even one instance in which she strode blithely through some kind of lecture or public meeting and exited by a door in the back next to the toilets. The only logic to her route that Victor could follow was that the "streets" always got narrower, the ceiling lower, and the artificial lighting dimmer.

At least I won't have to worry about being followed.

As if the thought had been spoken aloud, the women ahead of him cocked her head and said: "See? *This* is how you do it." She chuckled throatily. "Anybody asks, you just went to get laid. Who's going to prove otherwise?"

Suddenly, she stopped and turned around. The motion was so abrupt that Victor almost ran into her. He managed to stop, but they were now standing practically nose to nose. Well—nose to forehead. Like most Mesan genetic slaves except the heavy labor and combat breeds, the woman was very small.

She grinned up at him. The grin had a generic similarity to the professional leer she had bestowed upon him in the transport capsule, but there was more actual emotion in it. Humor, mainly.

Like all solemn and dedicated young men who don't suffer from extreme egotism, Victor suspected that the humor was at his expense. The woman immediately proved him right.

"You don't even have to fake it," she announced cheerfully. "If you want it kinky, of course, I charge extra. Unless it's too kinky, in which case I won't do it at all."

Victor liked her grin. It was almost friendly, in a rakish sort of way. But he still stammered out another refusal.

"Too bad. You would have enjoyed it and I could have used the money." She eyed him speculatively.

"You sure?" The grin grew more rakish still. "Maybe a little bondage? Not—"

Here came the throaty chuckle. "—that you don't look like you're tied up in knots already."

Fortunately, Victor didn't have to think up a suitable rejoinder to that remark. The woman just shrugged, turned, and got under way again.

They spent another few minutes following the same kind of twisted route. Two minutes into it, Victor remarked that he was quite certain they had shaken whoever might have been tailing him from the hospital.

The woman's reply came with a snort: "Who's trying to? This is how you get to where I live, wonderboy." Again, that throaty chuckle. "I'm not in the business of shaking tails *that* way."

The chuckle became an outright laugh. For the next minute or so, leading him through the crowded "public arteries," the woman ahead of him put on a dazzling display of shaking her tail. Long before she was done, Victor was beginning to deeply regret his refusal.

Duty first! Discipline!

But he kept the thought to himself. He could well imagine her response, and the rakish grin and chuckle which would accompany it.

Victor spent the remaining minutes of their trek simply studying his surroundings. Chicago's Old Quarter—or "the Loop," as it was sometimes called, for no reason that anyone understood—was famous from one end of the Solarian League to the other.

Notorious, rather, in the way that such largely-immigrant neighborhoods have been throughout history. Dens of vice and iniquity, of course. *You can buy anything in the Loop*. But there was also a glamorous aura surrounding the place. Artists, writers and musicians abounded, filling the Old Quarter's multitude of taverns and coffeehouses. (*Real* coffee—the true Terran strain. Victor had tried some once, but found he didn't like it. In this, as in many things, the earnest young revolutionary from the slums of Nouveau Paris was more conservative than any decadent elitist.) The artists were invariably "avant-garde" and had the poverty to prove it. The writers were mostly poets and enjoyed a similar income. The musicians, on the other hand, often did quite well. Except for opera, the Loop was the center of Chicago's musical night life.

Rich or poor, the culturally inclined habitués of the megametropolis' Old Quarter rubbed elbows with their more dangerous brethren. Over the centuries, the Loop had become the center of the Solarian League's criminal elite as well as every brand of political radical.

Chicago drew all of them like a magnet, from everywhere in the huge and sprawling Solarian League. But since respectable Solarian society generally refused to acknowledge the existence of such things as widespread poverty and crime, the bureaucrats who were the real political power in the League saw to it that the unwelcome riffraff was kept out of sight and, and much as possible, out of mind. As long as the immigrants stayed in the Loop, except for those who worked as servants, they were generally left alone by the authorities. Within limits, the Loop was almost a nation unto itself. Chicago's police only patrolled the main thoroughfares and those sectors which served as entertainment centers for the League's "proper" citizens. For the rest—*let them rot*.

In some ways—poverty, danger, congestion—the

Loop reminded Victor of the squalid Dolist slums which had grown like a cancer during the long reign of Haven's Legislaturalist regime. But only up to a point. The Dolist slums in which Victor had been born and spent his entire life until he volunteered to join State Security were grim, gray and sullen places. That was beginning to change, as popular fervor for the Revolution and the war against the Manticoran elitists swelled and Victor's class of people began to accept the necessity for discipline. Still, the Dolist quarters of the People's Republic of Haven were *slums*.

Victor suspected that the Loop was even more dangerous than the slums of Haven. Yet, there was a key difference. The Loop was a *ghetto*, not simply a collection of tenements. And, like many ghettoes throughout history, there was a real vibrancy to its life. Beneath the grime and the poverty and the sneers of respectable society, the Loop possessed a certain genuine verve and élan.

Alas, that dashing *joie de vivre* extended to pick-pockets as well. By the time Victor reached their destination, he had lost his wallet. He did manage to hang onto his watch, but it was a close thing.

When the woman reached her apartment, she began punching in the codes to unlock the door. It was a time-consuming process, given the number of locks. She even had a key for one of them—a real, genuine, antique metal *key*. As he waited, Victor suddenly realized that he didn't know her name. He was deeply embarrassed by his lapse into elitism.

"I'm sorry," he muttered. "My name's Victor. I forgot to ask—"

Triumphantly, the woman turned the key and the door finally opened. Just as triumphantly, she bestowed her grin on Victor.

"Sorry, wonderboy. I only give out my name to paying customers."

She swept through the door like a grande dame making an entrance into a palace. Sheepishly, Victor followed.

The door led directly into a small living room. Usher was there, sprawled comfortably on a couch.

"He's all yours, Kevin," announced the woman. "But I'll give you fair warning. He ain't no fun at all."

She moved toward a door on the right, shaking her tail with verve and élan and *joie de vivre*. "I'll be in the bedroom. Probably masturbating, even if the pay is scandalous."

She closed the door behind her. Also with verve and élan and *joie de vivre*.

Victor took a deep breath and let it out in a rush. "She's quite something," he pronounced.

Usher smiled. The same thin, wicked smile that Victor remembered. "Yeah, I know. That's why I married her."

Seeing Victor's wide eyes, Usher's smile became very thin, and very wicked. "There's no mention of her in my file, is there? That's lesson number one, junior. The map is not the territory. The man is not the file."

Helen

Helen was working much faster now. From experience, she had grown confident that her captors would only enter her cell to feed her. They seemed completely oblivious to the possibility that she might try to escape.

The heavy door which they used to lock her in the cell had clearly been brought there from somewhere else. An impressive door, in many ways—solid and heavy. It looked like a new door, in fact. Helen suspected they had purchased it for that very purpose. And then, must have spent many hours fitting the door frame into the ragged entrance and sealing it shut.

She found it hard not to laugh, imagining her father's sarcasm. *Amateurs!* A splendid door, sure enough—except it had no peephole. If her captors wanted to check on Helen, the only way they could do so was to open the door itself. Which, needless to say, they had equipped with several locks—even, judging by the sounds, with a heavy chain to secure the entire frame to the exterior wall. As if a fourteen-year-old girl was likely to smash through it by main force!

The end result was that Helen would always have advance warning if her captors entered her cell. Enough time, hopefully, to cover her work—although that would become less feasible as her tunnel deepened.

She broke off from her labor for a moment. She had now managed to get two feet into the wall, almost too deep for her to reach the face any longer. The hole she was digging was just big enough for her to squeeze into once it became necessary to continue the work inside. And it was still small enough to keep covered with an old panel which she had found lying among the pieces of rubble in the cell.

Thinking the situation through, Helen realized that she would have to figure out some kind of timing device before she went much further. Unfortunately, her captors had taken her chrono before they thrust her into the cell. Once she was actually working inside the tunnel, the loud warnings which her captors inadvertently made when they opened the door might not penetrate. And, even if they did, might not leave her enough time to come out and cover her tracks before they entered the cell.

But she didn't spend much time pondering that problem. Helen had always enjoyed working with her hands, especially after her father introduced her to the pleasures of model-building. She was adept at jury-rigging little gadgets, and was quite sure she could manage to design and build some sort of simple time-keeper.

Instead, she concentrated on a cruder and more fundamental problem. Digging itself, fortunately, was not proving difficult. Helen had discovered, once she broke through the first few inches, that the rubble beyond was not much more than loose fill. She was quite certain, by now, that she was somewhere deep beneath the Old Quarter, in the endless layers of rubble and ruins which marked the ancient center of the city. Chicago was well over two thousand years old. Especially during the war centuries, no one had bothered to remove old and crumbled buildings and structures. Just—leveled them, and built over the wreckage.

The real problem was the classic quandary of all tunnel escapes: *where do you put the dirt?*

Regretfully, because it would be so time-consuming, she came to the conclusion that she would have to mix the fresh fill with the old dirt and dust covering the cell. Carefully blending them, so that the color contrast would not be too noticeable. Over time, of course, the color would start to change and the level of the floor would slowly rise. But she hoped that the process would be too imperceptible for her captors to notice.

All that, of course, presupposed that she had weeks ahead of her. She had no idea if that presumption was accurate. It probably wasn't. For all Helen knew, her captors intended to kill her in the next hour. But she had no other option, other than to sit and wait. Like a sheep.

Damn that! The memory of her mother kept her strong; Master Tye's training kept her steady. And she knew that her father would be coming for her. Not soon, perhaps, but surely. Her father was like that. If he had none of the romance which surrounded her mother's memory, he was as certain as the sunrise and the tides.

She went back to work. Scrape, scrape.

Anton

After he finished studying the police forensics report, Anton rose from the console and moved over to the window overlooking the city. He was oblivious to the view, however. Which was probably just as well, since the "picture window" in his relatively inexpensive apartment simply had a view of another enormous residential complex across the boulevard. If he craned his neck, he might catch a glimpse of the busy street far below.

But his eyes were not focused on the sight. His mind was turned completely inward.

"Jesus Christ," he murmured. "I knew this wasn't a Peep operation, but I wasn't expecting *this*."

From behind, he heard Robert Tye's voice. "You know the identity of the culprits?"

Zilwicki nodded. "The Sacred Band," he growled. "The 'Scrags,' as they're sometimes called. The genetic markers are unmistakable." He turned away from the window and stared down at the martial artist. "You've heard of them?"

"They're supposed to be a fable, you know," replied Tye. "An urban legend. All the experts say so."

Zilwicki said nothing. After a moment, Tye chuckled dryly. "As it happens, however, I once had one of them as a student. Briefly. It didn't take me long to figure out who he was—or what he was, I should say—since the fellow couldn't resist demonstrating his natural physical prowess."

"That would be typical," murmured Zilwicki. "Arrogant to the last. What happened then?"

Tye shrugged. "Nothing. Once his identity became clear, I told him his company was no longer desired. I was rather emphatic. Fortunately, he was not *quite* arrogant enough to argue with me. So he went on his way and I never saw him again."

"One of them works in this building," said Zilwicki abruptly. "His profile leaps right out from the rest of the employee files. The bastard didn't even bother with plastic surgery. The bone structure's obvious, once you know what to look for, even leaving aside the results of his medical exams. 'In perfect health,' his doctors say, which I'm sure he is. The man's name is Kennesaw and he's the maintenance supervisor. Which explains, of course, how he was able to circumvent the apartment's security."

His eyes moved back to the window, and again

grew unfocused. "And it also explains why the Scrags
selected Helen as their victim. Opportunity, pure and
simple. Almost a random choice, given that they must
have wanted someone connected to the Manticoran
embassy."

"And why that?" asked Tye. "What does the Sacred
Band want with your people?"

Zilwicki shrugged. "That's still a mystery. But if I
had to guess, I'd say that they're working for Manpower Inc."

Tye's eyes widened a bit. "The Mesan slave-breeders?
I didn't realize there was a connection."

"It's not something Manpower advertises," chuckled
Anton harshly. "As much effort as those scum put into
their respectable appearance, you can understand why
they wouldn't want to be associated in the public mind
with monsters out of Terran history. Half-legendary
creatures with a reputation as bad as werewolves or
vampires."

"Worse," grunted Tye. "Nobody really believes
werewolves or vampires *ever* existed. The Final War
was all too real."

Zilwicki nodded. "As for the Sacred Band itself,
the attachment to Manpower is natural enough. For
all that they make a cult of their own superhuman
nature, the Scrags are nothing more today than a tiny
group. Manticoran intelligence has never bothered to
investigate them very thoroughly. But we're pretty
sure they don't number more than a few dozen, here
in Chicago—and fewer still, anywhere else. They're
vicious bastards, of course, and dangerous enough to
anyone who crosses them in the slums of the city.
But powerless in any meaningful sense of the term."

He shrugged. "So, like many other defeated groups in history, they transferred their allegiance to a new master and a new cause. Close enough to their old one to maintain ideological continuity, but with real influence in the modern universe. Which the Mesans certainly have. And, although Manpower Inc. claims to be a pure and simple business, you don't have to be a genius to figure out the implicit political logic of their enterprise. What the old Terrans would have called 'fascism.' If some people can be bred for slavery, after all, others can be bred for mastery."

"But—" Tye squeezed his eyes shut for a moment. "Oh, for the simple problems of the dojo," he muttered. Then: "I still don't understand. Why is Manpower doing this? Do they have some personal animus against you?"

"Not that I can think of. Not really. It's true that Helen—my wife—belonged to the Anti-Slavery League. But she was never actually active in the organization. And although not many officers go so far as to join the ASL, anti-Mesan attitudes are so widespread in the Navy that she didn't really stand out in any way. Besides, that was years ago."

Slowly, his mind ranging, Anton shook his head. "No, Robert. This isn't personal. The truth is, I don't even think Manpower is at the bottom of it. I wasn't kidding when I said they bend over backward to appear as respectable as possible. There's no way the Mesans would have gotten involved in something like this unless someone offered them a very powerful inducement. Either in the nature of a threat or a reward."

He clasped both hands behind his neck and spread his elbows. The gesture, which was simply a means of inducing relaxation, also highlighted the captain's immensely thick and muscular form.

After a moment, realizing what he was doing, Zilwicki smiled slightly and lowered his arms. The smile bore a trace of sadness underneath. His dead wife, Helen, had often teased him about the mannerism. "The Zilwicki maneuver," she'd called it, claiming it was a subconscious attempt at intimidation.

Yet, if he relinquished that form of projecting power, the cold grin which came to Anton's face probably served the purpose even better. "But now that the Scrags and Manpower have entered the picture, I think I've found the angle I need to get around Young and Hendricks. And, if I'm right, it'll be pure poetic justice."

Once again, Zilwicki sat down before the console. "This will probably take a couple of days, Robert. Unless those two are even dumber than I think they are, their security codes are going to take some effort to crack."

"Can you do it at all?" asked Tye.

Zilwicki chuckled humorlessly, as his thick fingers manipulated the keyboard with ease. "One of the advantages to looking the way I do, Robert—especially when people know I used to be a 'yard dog'—is that they always assume I must be some kind of mechanical engineer. As it happens, my specialty is software. Especially security systems."

Tye's face crinkled. "I myself shared that assumption. I've always had this splendid image of you, covered with grease and wielding a gigantic wrench. How distressing to discover it was all an illusion."

Anton smiled, but said nothing in reply. Already, he was deeply engrossed in his work.

By late afternoon, he leaned back in his chair and sighed. "That's as much as I can do for the moment. The next stage is pure numbers-crunching, which will take at least twenty-four hours. Probably longer. So we've got some time to pay a visit on Kennesaw. But first—"

The look which now came over Zilwicki's face made Tye think of someone who'd just seen a ghost. The intelligence captain's expression was almost haggard, and he seemed a little pale.

"What's wrong?"

Anton shook his head. "Just something I can't postpone any longer. I've been able to block it out of my mind so far, but now—"

Again, his fingers began working at the keyboard. Tye rose to his feet and padded over. Some sort of schematic diagram was filling the screen. None of it meant anything to the martial artist.

"What are you doing?"

Zilwicki's face was as gaunt as a square face could get, but his fingers never faltered in their work. "One of the standard techniques in kidnapping, Robert, is to simply kill the victim immediately. That eliminates the trouble of guarding the person, and it removes any witnesses."

He grunted. "But it's something which is done either by pure amateurs or complete professionals. The amateurs because they don't realize just how hard it is to dispose of a body quickly without leaving any evidence, and the pros because they know how to do it. What I'm hoping is that the people who took Helen know enough, but not too much."

As he had been speaking, several different diagrams

and schematics had flashed across the screen. Now, as a new one came up, Zilwicki concentrated on it for some time. Then he grunted again. This time, however, the sound carried an undertone of satisfaction.

"Good. There are plenty of traces of organic disposal, of course, but not what a human body would show. If there had been, the alarms would have gone off. And the alarms themselves haven't been tampered with. Unless it was done by a software maestro, which I'm willing to bet Kennesaw isn't. Or any other member of the Sacred Band. Not, at least, when it comes to this kind of specialized stuff."

The haggard look vanished. Zilwicki's fingers began working again. "But I *am* a software maestro, if I say so myself, and while this is tricky it's not impossible. *If* you know what you're doing."

Robert Tye cleared his throat. "Do you enjoy speaking gobbledygook, Anton?"

Zilwicki smiled crookedly. "Sorry. Occupational hazard for a cyberneticist. Modern technology makes disposing of a human body quite easy, Robert. Any garbage processing unit in a large apartment complex such as this one can manage it without even burping. In the Star Kingdom, we just live with that reality and the police do their best. But you Solarians are addicted to rules and regulations. So, without any big public fanfare having been made about it, almost all publicly available mechanisms which utilize enough energy to destroy a human body also have detectors built into them. If you don't know about them, or don't know how to get around the alarms, simply shoving a corpse into the disposal unit will have the police breathing down your neck in minutes."

He tapped a final key and leaned back, exuding a certain cold satisfaction. "They may have killed Helen, but they didn't do what I most feared—killed her right away and shoved her into the building's disintegrator."

There was silence for a moment. Then, speaking very softly, Tye said: "I take it you *have*—just now—circumvented the alarms."

"Yeah, I did. For the next twenty-fours, nothing disintegrated in this building is going to alert the police. And after the alarms come back on, it will be far too late to reconstruct anything at all—even if you know what you're looking for."

The captain rose to his feet, glanced at his watch, and headed for the door. "Come on, Robert. Kennesaw works the day shift. He should be coming back to his apartment in about half an hour."

Victor

"He did *what?*" demanded Usher. The Marine citizen colonel lost his air of casual relaxation and sat upright on the couch. The tendons on the back of his large hand, gripping the armrest, stood out like cables.

Knowing—all too well—what those hands were capable of, Victor almost flinched. He did shrink back slightly in his own chair. "I'm not *positive* about that, Kevin. Not that last bit, anyway, about the Zilwicki girl. I'm sure he sent the order to the Mesans he's been talking to, but I may not have interpreted it correctly. It was—"

Usher wiped his face wearily. "You were right, Victor. We'll have to make sure, of course. But I'll bet on it."

It was the first time Usher had called him by his

name instead of one or another appellation. Oddly enough, Victor found that he was delighted. But perhaps it was not so odd. In the short time that he had spent in Usher's secret apartment, Victor had decided that Usher was what he had always *thought* he would encounter in the field during his time at the SS Academy. Not simply an older, more experienced comrade serving as his mentor—but the spirit of comradeship itself.

Usher rose slowly to his feet and paced into the kitchen. When he came back, he was holding two bottles of that ancient Terran beverage called *cola*. Wordlessly, he handed one of them to Victor. Then, seeing the slight frown in the young SS officer's face, Usher chuckled drily.

"Lesson number—what is it, now?—eight, I think. A *reputation* for being a drunk can keep you out of as much trouble as being one gets you into." He padded to his couch and sunk into it. "I've got a high capacity for alcohol, but I don't drink anywhere near as much as people think."

Usher took a swig from his bottle. "No, this is exactly the kind of scheme Durkheim would dream up. Typical desk pilot idea—and Durkheim's a good one. It's a brilliantly conceived maneuver, sure enough. In one stroke, he gets both Parnell and Bergren assassinated, manages to keep the obvious culprits—*us*—from getting blamed, shifts the blame—or, at least, muddies the waters—by getting a Manty intelligence officer tied to the thing, and even, maybe, gets us a little bit of the first good media coverage since the Harrington news broke. Reminds the public that on the question of genetic slavery we're still the best guys in town."

Usher was silent for a moment, as he resumed his seat on the couch. Then: "Parnell, you may remember, was the admiral who cleaned out that Manpower nest on Esterheim when the Legislaturist regime was using extirpation of the slave trade as their excuse for territorial expansion. Bergren, as the Secretary of Foreign Affairs, gave the official approval for it. So killing them could seem like Mesa's overdue revenge." He took another swig from the bottle and snorted savagely. "The idiot! Talk about your castles in the air."

Seeing Victor's gape, Usher chuckled. His quick sketch of Durkheim's purpose had left young Cachat behind in a cloud of dust. *Way* behind. Victor's account of Durkheim's actions had included no mention of the purpose of those actions, for the good and simple reason that Victor was as mystified by Durkheim's doings as he was outraged.

Usher leaned forward. "Think it through, Victor. Why else would the head of SS on Terra be having black liaisons with Manpower and their stooges? And why else would he do something as insane as have the daughter of a Manty officer kidnapped?"

Victor shook his head. The gesture was not one of negation, simply that of a man trying to clear his head of confusion. "I don't get it. Parnell, sure—I can see why he'd want to have him killed, the moment he sets foot on Terra. But we had a discussion of that already—the entire officer staff—and it didn't take us more than twenty minutes to decide unanimously—Durkheim too!—that we'd automatically get the blame for *anything* that happened to Parnell. Even if he tripped on the sidewalk or came down with a virus." Victor winced. "Which would only make the propaganda damage that much worse."

The wince turned into a lasting grimace. "Is it really true, Kevin?" he asked softly. "I mean—what they say Parnell's going to say?" He was holding his breath without realizing it.

"Victor," Kevin replied, in a voice equally soft, "I made my decision to accept a commission in the Marines the day I heard Saint-Just had appointed Tresca as the new commander of the prison planet. That wasn't handwriting on the wall, that was blazing comets in the sky. Every old timer in the underground knew Tresca, and knew what that appointment meant. It was Saint-Just's way of telling us that the good old days of the comradeship were *over.*" He sighed, groping blindly for the bottle of cola sitting on the stand next to the couch. "Yeah," he said, "it's true. I don't doubt it for a minute."

Victor expelled his breath in a rush. The sorrow that came over his face in that moment belonged to a much older man.

Shakily, Victor tried to regain his composure. "Okay. But I still don't see how that changes anything. We knew—Durkheim told us—that whether the charges were true or not—and he swore they were all lies from an old Legislaturalist elitist admiral—that almost everyone in the Solarian League was going to *believe* them. Just because Parnell and Harrington were still alive after all, and we *had* been nailed with our pants down on that score. Since we'd lied about that, sure enough, who'd believe us when we insisted that the tales they brought back from their supposed graves were all fabrications?"

For the first time, the young officer took a sip of his own drink. "So I *still* don't see how anything's changed." His brow creased. "And you said Bergren too. Why him?"

Usher snorted. "The truth is, Victor, Bergren is the *main* target. I doubt if even Durkheim thinks the odds are better than fifty-fifty that we won't get blamed for Parnell, even if he is killed by Scrags and even if there is a Manty officer tied into it. But he's cut from the same cloth as Saint-Just. Durkheim cares a lot more about real power than anybody's perception of it. Bergren's the last remaining holdover from the Legislaturalist regime. The only reason he's remained here as our ambassador, since the Revolution, is because he had the good luck—or the good sense—to bring his whole family with him. So Saint-Just didn't have any real way of blackmailing him into return- ing, where he could be conveniently found guilty of something and shot. Or simply 'disappeared.' So they decided to just leave him here in place. If nothing else, Bergren's existence was a way of showing that the new regime's extermination of the Legislaturalists was because of their actual crimes rather than their simple status. 'See? Didn't we leave one of them—the only honest man in the den of thieves—as the head of our embassy on Terra?' "

Usher drained half the bottle before continuing. "But now—" He finished the bottle in one long guzzle. Watching him, and despite his anguish at seeing so much of what he believed turn to ashes, Victor had to fight down a laugh. Usher could claim that he didn't drink as much as everybody said—which Victor was willing enough to believe—but that easy, practiced chugalug proved that "not as much" was still a long way from abstention.

"But now everything's changed." Usher rose. Again, he began pacing about in the small living room. "Harrington's escape from the dead—not to mention the several hundred thousand people she brought out of Hell with her—is going to rock the regime down to its foundations. Durkheim knows damn well that Saint-Just's only concern now is going to be holding on to power. Screw public relations. There isn't any doubt in his mind—mine either—that once Parnell arrives Bergren will officially defect." His lips twisted into a sneer. "Oh, yeah—Bergren will do his very best 'more in sorrow than in anger' routine. And he's good at it, believe me, the stinking hypocrite."

For a moment, Usher's thoughts seem to veer elsewhere. "Have you ever dug into any of that ancient Terran art form, Victor, since you got here? The one they call 'films'?"

Victor shook his head. For a brief instant, he almost uttered a protest. Interest in archaic art forms— everybody knew it!—was a classic hallmark of elitist decadence. But he suppressed the remark. All of his old certainties were crumbling around him, after all, so why should he make a fuss about something as minor as that?

Usher may have sensed the unspoken rebuke, however, for he gave Victor that wicked, half-jeering smile. "Too bad for you, youngster. I have, and lots of them are excellent." He rubbed his hands gently. Then, speaking in a peculiar accent: "I am shocked! Shocked! To discover gambling in Rick's casino!"

The phrases were meaningless to Victor, but Usher seemed to find them quite amusing. "Oh, yeah. That's what Bergren'll say. Bet on it, lad." He paced about a little more, thinking. "Durkheim is certainly betting on it. So he'll move quick and see to it that Bergren's killed before he has a chance to defect. And he'll just hope that using Manpower and their local Scrag cult to do the wet work will distract suspicion from us. We Havenites *do*, after all, have our hands cleaner than anybody else on that score. *That* much is not a lie."

Victor felt a little warmth coming back into his heart. "Or, at least, we did until Durkheim started mucking in that cesspool," snarled Usher.

For a minute, the citizen colonel looked like he might spit on the floor. But, he didn't. For all the modest size and furnishings of the apartment, it was spotlessly clean and well kept. Whatever Victor thought of Usher's wife's occupation—and Usher's relationship to her, for that matter, which still shocked his puritanical soul—slatternliness obviously didn't extend into their own home.

But Victor didn't dwell on that. He'd lost enough heroes for one day, and firmly decided that he wasn't going to pass any judgments on Usher or his wife until he was certain that he was capable of judging anything correctly. Which, going by the evidence, he most certainly wasn't yet.

So, struggling, he tried to keep his mind focused narrowly. "What you're saying, in other words, is that by going completely outside the loop and using Manpower and the Scrags to do the dirty work—and tangling a Manty agent up with them—Durkheim can get rid of Parnell and Bergren both. And maybe even keep Haven from taking the blame."

Usher nodded. It was Victor's turn to shake his

head. "All right. That much I can follow. But there are still two things I don't understand. First, why would Manpower agree? They hate our guts!"

The answer came to Victor before he even finished the question. The cold and pitiless look on Usher's face may have helped. "Oh, shit," Victor groaned, lapsing for a moment into profanity.

"Yeah, you got it, lad. Of course, whether or not Durkheim will be able to come through with his promise is another thing—Saint-Just will have to sign onto it—but don't doubt for a minute what the promise was. *You do this for us and we'll look the other way, from now on, whenever Manpower starts extending the slave trade into our space.*"

Victor was mute. Perhaps out of kindness, Usher prompted him off the subject. "What was the other question?"

Victor swallowed, trying to focus his mind on top of heartbreak. "Yeah. You seem to have figured it all out—and you even said it was brilliant—but then you also said Durkheim was an idiot. So I'm confused about what you really—"

Usher snorted. "Oh, hell—Victor, for Christ's sake! Grow up! Hanging onto illusions is one thing. I'll forgive you for that, easily enough." For a moment, he looked uncomfortable. Then, shrugged. "Truth is, if I hadn't realized you *had* those illusions I wouldn't be talking to you in the first place."

The soft moment passed. The cold and pitiless look was back. "But there's no excuse for plain *stupidity*. You're supposed to be a field agent, dammit! Durkheim's complicated scheme is right out of the book. You know, the one titled: '*Harebrained Schemes*

Hatched by Desk Pilots Who Don't Know a Dead Drop From a Hole in the Ground.'"

Victor couldn't help laughing. In that moment, Usher reminded him of one of his instructors. A sarcastic and experienced field man, who had peppered his lectures with anecdotes. Half of which, at least, had been on the subject of desk pilots and their harebrained schemes.

Usher sat back down on the couch and shook his head wearily. "Every single damned thing in Durkheim's plot is going to go wrong, Victor. Trust me. The man forgets he's dealing with real people instead of ideological abstractions. And real people have this nasty habit of not quite fitting properly into their assigned pigeonholes."

Usher leaned forward, sticking up his right thumb. "The *first* thing that's going to go wrong already has, and don't think for a moment even Durkheim isn't nervous about it. I'll bet you any amount of money you choose that he expected Manpower would use some of their own professionals to do the dirty work with the kid. Instead, no doubt because they want to keep their distance in case the thing goes sour—no idiots *there*—they turned it over to the Scrags they keep on their leash. They'll save their pros for the attacks on Parnell and Bergren."

He squinted at Victor. "Do you really know anything about the Scrags?"

Victor started to give a vigorous, even belligerent, affirmative response, but hesitated. Other than a lot of abstract ideological notions about fascistic believers in a master race—

"No," he said firmly.

"Good for you, lad," chuckled Usher. "Okay, Victor. Forget everything you may have heard. The fundamental thing you've got to understand about the Scrags is that they're a bunch of clowns." He waved a hand. "Oh, yeah, sure. Murderous clowns. Perfect physical specimens, bred and trained to be supreme warriors. Eat nails, can walk through walls, blah blah blah. The problem is, the morons believe it too. Which means they're as careless as five year olds, and never think to plan for the inevitable screw-ups. Which there always are, in any plan—much less one as elaborate as this scheme of Durkheim's. So they're going to foul up, somewhere along the line, and Durkheim's going to be scrambling to patch the holes. The problem is, since he organized this entire thing outside of SS channels, he doesn't have a back-up team in place and ready to go. He'll have to jury-rig one. Which is something you *never* want to do in a situation as"—another dry chuckle—"as 'fraught with danger,' as they say, as this one."

He held up the thumb of his left hand. "And the *other* thing that's going to go wrong—this one is guaranteed, and it's a real lulu—is that the Manty officer he selected to be the official patsy in the scheme is going to tear him a new asshole." Usher pressed the palms of his hands to his temples. The gesture combined utter exasperation with fury. "In the name of God! Bad enough Durkheim screws around with a Manty's kid. But *Zilwicki's?*" He drove up onto his feet. "What a cretin!"

Victor stared at him. He was acquainted with Anton Zilwicki, in the very casual way that two intelligence officers belonging to nations at war encounter each other at social functions in the capital of a neutral state, but the 'acquaintance' was extremely distant. Thinking about it, Victor could only summon up two impressions of the man. Physically, Zilwicki had a rather peculiar physique. Almost as wide, he seemed, as he was tall. And, from his accent, he came from the highlands of Gryphon.

Victor frowned. "I don't quite understand, Kevin. Zilwicki's not a field agent. He's an analyst. Specializes in technical stuff. Software, as a matter of fact. The guy's basically a computer geek. He's the one who tries to find out how much tech transfer we're getting from the Sollies."

Usher snorted. "Yeah, I'm sure that's what Durkheim was thinking. But you're forgetting three other things about him. First of all, the kid's mother was *Helen* Zilwicki, who was posthumously awarded Manticore's Parliamentary Medal of Honor for hammering one of our task forces half-bloody with a vastly inferior force of her own."

Victor was still frowning. Usher sighed. "Victor, do you really think a woman like that married a *wimp*?"

"Oh."

"Yeah. *Oh.* Second, he's from the Gryphon highlands. And while I think those highlanders are possibly the galaxy's all time political morons—they hate the aristocracy so they put their faith in Aristocrat Number One—you won't find anywhere a more maniacal set of feudists. Talk about stupid! Snatching one of their kids, in the scale of intelligence, ranks right up there with snatching a tiger's cub."

He slapped his hands together and rubbed them, in that mock-gleeful way of saying: *oh, yes—here comes the best part!* "And—just to put the icing on the cake—Anton Zilwicki may not be a field agent but he's hardly your typical desk pilot either."

He cocked an eyebrow at the young SS officer. "You've met him?" Victor nodded. Usher put his hand at shoulder level. "Short fellow, 'bout yay tall." He spread his arms wide, cupping the hands. "And about yay wide."

He dropped his arms. "The reason for that build is because he's a weightlifter. Good enough that he could probably compete in his weight class in the Terran Olympics, which are still the top athletic contest in the settled portion of the universe."

Usher frowned. "The truth is, though, he probably ought to give it up. Since his wife died, he's become a bit of a monomaniac about the weightlifting. I imagine it's his way of trying to control his grief. But by now he's probably starting to get muscle-bound, which is too bad because—"

The wicked smile was back. "—there ain't no question at all that he could compete in the Olympics in his *old* sport, seeing as how he won the gold medal three times running in the Manticoran Games in the wrestling event. Graeco-Roman, if I remember right."

Usher was grinning, now. "Oh yeah, young man. That's your genius boss Raphael Durkheim. And to think I accused the Scrags of being sloppy and careless! Durkheim's trying to make a patsy out of somebody like *that*."

Victor cleared his throat. "I don't think he knew all that." Which, of course, he realized was no excuse. Durkheim was *supposed* to know about such things. And that, finally, brought Victor to a new awareness.

"How is it that *you* know this stuff about Zilwicki?"

Usher stared at him for a moment in silence. Then, after taking a deep breath, said:

"Okay, young Victor Cachat. We have now arrived at what they call the moment of truth."

Usher hesitated. He was obviously trying to select the right way of saying something. But, in a sudden rush of understanding, Victor grasped the essence of it. The elaborate nature of Usher's disguise, combined with his uncanny knowledge of things no simple Marine citizen colonel—much less a drunkard—could possibly have known, all confirmed the shadowy hints Victor had occasionally encountered elsewhere. That there existed, somewhere buried deep, an *opposition.*

"I'm in," he stated firmly. "Whatever it is."

Usher scrutinized him carefully. "This is the part I always hate," he mused. "No matter how shrewd you are, no matter how experienced, there always comes that moment when you've got to decide whether you trust someone or not."

Victor waited; and, as he waited, felt calmness come over him. His ideological beliefs had taken a battering, but there was still enough of them there to leave him intact. For the first time—ever—he understood men like Kevin Usher. It was like looking in a mirror. A cracked mirror, but a mirror sure and true.

Usher apparently reached the same conclusion. "It's *my* Revolution, Victor, not Saint-Just's. Sure as hell not Durkheim and Tresca's. It belongs to me and mine—we fought for it, we bled for it—and we will damn well have it *back.*"

"So what do we do?" asked Victor.

Usher shrugged. "Well, for the moment why don't

we concentrate on this little problem in front of us."
Cheerfully, he sprawled back on the couch. "For
one thing, let's figure out a way to turn Durkheim's
mousetrap into a rat trap. And, for another, let's see
if there isn't some way we can keep a fourteen-year-
old girl from becoming another stain on our banner.
Whaddaya say?"

The Scrag

Kennesaw sensed his assailants' approach as he was
opening the door to his apartment. Like all of the
Select, his hearing was incredibly acute, as was the
quickness with which his mind processed sensory
data. Before the attack even began, therefore, he had
already started his pre-emptive counterassault.

Given the areas of Chicago that Kennesaw fre-
quented, he was quite familiar with muggers. It was
one of the things he liked about the city, in fact. The
high level of street crime kept his fighting reflexes
well-tuned. He had killed three muggers over the past
several years, and crippled as many more.

The fact that there were two of them did not faze
him in the least. Especially once he saw, as he spun
around launching his first disabling kick, that both of
the men were much shorter than he was.

It took a few seconds for his assumptions to be
dispelled. How many, exactly, he never knew. Everything was much too confusing. And painful.

His target was the older and more slightly built of
the two men. Kennesaw almost laughed when he saw
how elderly the man was. One blow would be enough

to disable him, allowing Kennesaw to concentrate on destroying the thick-set subhuman.

But the kick never landed. Somehow, Kennesaw's ankle was seized, twisted—off balance now—

—his vision blurred—an elbow strike to the temple, he thought, but he was too dazed to be certain—

—agonizing pain lanced through his other leg—

—his knees buckled—

And then a monster had him, immobilizing him from behind with a maneuver Kennesaw barely recognized because it was so antique—even preposterous. But his chin was crushed to his chest, his arms dangling and paralyzed, and then he was heaved back onto his feet and propelled through the half-open door of his apartment.

On their way through, the monster smashed his face against the door jamb. The creature's sheer power was astonishing. Kennesaw's nose and jaw were both broken. He dribbled blood and teeth across the floor as he was manhandled into the center of his living room.

By now, he was only half-conscious. Anyone not of the Select would probably have been completely witless. But Kennesaw took no comfort in the fact. He could sense the raging animal fury that held him immobile and had so casually shattered his face along the way.

His legs were again kicked out from under him. A skilled and experienced hand-to-hand fighter, Kennesaw had expected that. What he *hadn't* expected was that the monster, instead of hurling him to the floor and pouncing on him, would do the exact opposite. Kennesaw was dragged down on top of the creature, who still held him from behind in that suffocating clasp.

He landed on a body that felt as unyielding as stone. An instant later, two legs curled over his thighs and clamped his own legs in a scissor lock. The legs were much shorter than his own, but thick and muscular. Kennesaw was vaguely surprised to see that they apparently belonged to a human being. He wouldn't have been shocked to see them clad in animal fur. Like a grizzly bear.

Some time passed. How much, Kennesaw never knew. But eventually he was able to focus on the face which was staring down at him. The genes which had created that face clearly had most of their origins in eastern Asia. The face belonged to the old man, the one he had tried to disable with a kick.

The man spoke. His voice was soft and low. "I used to be a biologist, Kennesaw, before I decided to concentrate on my art. What you're seeing here is an illustration of the fallacy of Platonic thinking applied to evolutionary principles."

The words were pure gibberish. Something of Kennesaw's confusion must have shown, because the face emitted a slight chuckle.

"It's sometimes called 'population thinking,' Kennesaw. A pity you never learned to apply those methods. Instead, you made the classic mistake of categorizing people into abstract types instead of recognizing their concrete variations."

Gibberish. Another chuckle.

"You're only a 'superman,' Kennesaw, if you compare the average of the Sacred Band to the average of the rest of humanity. Unfortunately, you're now in the hands of two men who, in different ways, vary quite widely from the norm. Partly because of our own genetic background, and partly due to training and habit."

The almond-shaped eyes moved slightly, looking past Kennesaw's own head. "I'm not sure how well this is going to work. I'm sure he's got an absolutely phenomenal pain threshold."

Finally, Kennesaw heard the monster speak. "Don't care," came a hoarse grunt. "I'm sure he was one of the men who took her, which means there'll be traces of where they went somewhere in the apartment."

The Oriental face frowned. "Then why—"

Even as dazed as he was, the brief exchange made clear to Kennesaw the identity of his assailants. He managed some grunting words of his own. "You crazy, Z'wicki? Anyt'in' happen t'me, 'ey'll kill 'er."

The clasp tightened, and Kennesaw couldn't prevent a low groan.

"I don't think so. As sloppy as you people are, they'll just assume you're goofing off somewhere. How would I know you were involved?"

Despite the crushing pain, some part of Kennesaw's brain was still functioning objectively. So he understood the incredible strength which lay behind those words. Precious few, if any, of the Select themselves would have been able to so completely immobilize Kennesaw. Much less, at the same time, manage to speak in what was almost a normal tone of voice!

"And you've already told me the only thing I really needed to know from you," continued the hoarse voice from behind. "I'm not cold-blooded enough to kill a man I'm not sure is guilty."

It took a moment for the meaning to register on

Kennesaw. He tried to grunt another warning, but the hoarse voice overrode his words.

"This is called a full nelson, Scrag. It's an illegal maneuver in tournament wrestling. Here's why."

In the brief time that followed, Kennesaw understood some of what the little Oriental had been trying to explain to him. Variation. He never would have believed that any subhuman would have been strong enough to—

But the thought was fleeting. The pressure on his neck, crushing his broken chin into his chestbone, drove everything but pain and terror away. And then his vertebra ruptured and Kennesaw thought no more at all.

Victor

Victor spent the evening in the company of Usher's wife, being given a guided tour of the upper levels of the Loop. He had intended, burning with desire to undo Durkheim—somehow—to return to work immediately. But Kevin had driven that notion down with his usual sarcasm.

"And just what do you intend to do, youngster?" he demanded. "Stay out of trouble, dammit! I'll get the ball rolling at my end. You don't do anything—*nothing*, you understand—until you either hear from me or Durkheim approaches you, whichever comes first."

Victor frowned. Kevin chuckled. "He will, he will— I'll bet on it. Didn't I tell you this scheme of his is going to start unraveling? And that, when it does, he's going to have to slap together a jury-rigged back-up team to clean up the mess?"

Usher didn't wait for a response. Clearly enough, he had once again left Victor behind in a cloud of mental dust. "So who do you think he's going to approach? Not one of his experienced field agents, I'll tell you that. No, he'll go to the same wet-behind-the-ears, naive, trusting, dumb-as-a-brick, do-as-he-says young zealot that he used to pass messages to the Mesans in the first place. You."

"Me?" Victor scratched his cheek. "Why? He never told me what those messages were, or who I was passing them to. I figured it out on my own. As far as he knows, I don't know anything about the situation."

Victor hesitated, youthful pride warring with his innate honesty. Honesty won.

"The truth is, Kevin, I really am kind of"—sigh— "wet behind the ears." He scowled. "It hasn't helped any that Durkheim hasn't given me any really important assignments since I got here, fresh out of the Academy. All he's used me for is routine clerical stuff and as an occasional courier. My knowledge of fieldcraft is really pretty much book-learning. If *I* was putting together a back-up team to clean up a mess like this, I'd want an experienced field agent in charge of it."

"You don't think like Durkheim does," replied Kevin. "You're still thinking in terms of making the assignment *work*. For that, sure, you'd want a real pro." He shook his head. "But don't ever forget that Durkheim is a bureaucrat, first and foremost. His central concern—now and always—is going to be his position within the power structure, not the needs of the struggle. When a job goes sour, his first thought is going to be: *cover my ass.* And for *that*, ain't nothing better than a dumb young greenhorn—especially one who has a reputation for zealotry."

Victor flushed a bit. "What's a 'greenhorn'?" he growled.

"It's a Terran term. Refers to a variant they have here of cattle. A young bull, essentially, who's got a lot more testosterone than he does good sense."

Victor's flush deepened. "You're saying he'll expect me to *fail*?"

Kevin grinned. "Go down in flames and smoke, as a matter of fact. With enough pyrotechnics that he can wash his hands clean and claim afterward the whole thing was your idea and he didn't know anything about it until the *boom* happened."

Kevin looked away for a moment, thinking. "What I imagine he'll do is give you a squad of experienced SS troops, with a citizen sergeant in charge that he trusts. Someone with some familiarity with the Old Quarter—the upper levels, at least. You'll be told that the Scrags have run wild—went ahead and *kidnapped* a Manty officer's daughter, the maniacs. He'll probably claim they were simply supposed to search his apartment and panicked when they found the girl there."

Usher waved his hand. "Yeah, of course the story's ridiculous. Why didn't they just kill her on the spot? But he won't be expecting you to scrutinize his story for logical fallacies."

By now, Victor had caught up with Usher's thought train. "So I take this squad into the Loop with orders to find the girl and get her back." His face tightened. "No. Not get her back. Just—"

"He won't give *you* that instruction, Victor. No matter

how zealous or naive he thinks you are, Durkheim's not dumb enough to think he can tell a youngster to murder a girl in cold blood without creating possible problems. No, he'll tell *you* the job is to rescue her. And kill the Scrags while you're at it. But the citizen sergeant will see to it that the girl doesn't survive."

"Or me either." The statement was flat, direct.

Usher nodded. "Or you either. When the dust clears, what do we have? A young and inexperienced Havenite SS officer, discovering some kind of Mesan/Scrag skullduggery underway, went charging off half-cocked—entirely on his own initiative and without getting authorization—and made a mess out of everything. Both he and the girl die in the crossfire. Who's to say otherwise?"

"The whole story's preposterous!" protested Victor. "The Manties'll never believe it. Neither will the Sollies, for that matter."

Kevin laughed harshly. "Of course they won't. But they won't be able to prove any different, and Durkheim doesn't care what they think anyway. After Harrington's escape—sure as hell after Parnell arrives here and starts shooting his mouth off—nobody on Terra will believe what Haven says about anything. So what's another little goofy story? All Durkheim cares about is covering his ass with Saint-Just."

Usher laughed again, and just as harshly. "Who won't believe the story either, mind you. But he'll be satisfied that Durkheim had enough sense to cut his losses. And Saint-Just has enough problems to deal with now that he's not going to run the risk of penalizing Durkheim."

Silence followed, for perhaps half a minute, while Victor digested this—indigestible—meal. He felt nauseated.

As a young and eager SS officer, Victor had prepared himself for ruthlessness in the struggle against elitism. But *this*—

"All right," he said. "So what do we do?"

"You leave that to me, Victor." Usher's face was bleak. "I'll do my best to see to it that both you and the girl survive. But I can't make any promises. The truth is, I'm going to be using you for bait. And bait has a way of getting eaten."

Victor nodded. He'd already deduced that much. But Victor had understood the risks of being an SS intelligence officer when he applied to the Academy. Danger, he could accept. Foulness—for no more purpose than a bureaucrat's self-aggrandizement—he could not.

"Good enough. Concentrate on the girl's survival." Stiffly, with all the pride of a greenhorn: "I can take care of myself."

Usher grinned. "The girl might surprise you, lad. Don't forget whose kid she is. She even has her mother's name. Oh, and I might mention something *else* that I'm sure Durkheim doesn't know—she's the youngest person who ever got a brown belt from Robert Tye."

Victor sighed. Again, he was in a cloud of dust. "What's a brown belt? And who's Robert Tye?"

I'm getting a little tired of that damn grin, he thought sourly, seeing its reappearance. The words which followed didn't help a bit.

"Not a devotee of the martial arts, are you? Well, I'd figured as much from our little fracas in the tavern." Grin.

● ● ●

So, Victor had wound up idling away the day with Usher's wife in the Loop. Her name—or so she claimed, in defiance of all logic—was Virginia. Victor had his doubts, especially in view of her scandalous clothing and the way she continually tormented him.

But he was obscurely relieved when she explained that she wasn't really a prostitute.

"Not any more, anyway," Ginny explained—although, at the moment she spoke the words, she was doing her best to prove to the world otherwise, the way she was pressed against him as they ambled through one of the bazaars in the Old Quarter. Under Victor's prodding, as they made their way through the crowded streets and open-spaced bazaars, Virginia gave him some of her life's history.

Before too long, he was sorry he had asked. Not because Virginia prattled—to the contrary, her narrative was terse and brief. But simply because it is one thing to understand, in ideological terms, that a social institution is unjust. It is another thing entirely to hear that injustice graphically described by one of its victims. The first causes abstract anger; the second, nausea and helpless fury.

Virginia had been born—bred—on Mesa. C-17a/65-4/5 was the name on her tongue. The label, it might be better to say. The "C" line was one of Manpower Inc.'s most popular breeds, always in demand on the market. Sex slaves, in essence. "17" referred to the somatic type; the "a" to the female variant. Her genotype had been selected and shaped for physical attractiveness, and for as much in the way of libidinal energy and submissiveness as Mesa's gengineers could pinpoint in the genetic code. Which, of course, was not much—especially since the two desired psychological traits tended to be genetically cross-linked with a multitude of opposing characteristics. One of which, unfortunately, was a type of intelligence popularly characterized as "cleverness." As a result, a high percentage of C-lines had a tendency to escape captivity once they left the extreme security environment of Mesa itself.

To combat that tendency, and in an attempt to "phenotypically induce" the desired submissiveness, the developing C-lines were subjected to a rigorous training regimen. Manpower's engineers, of course, had an antiseptic and multisyllabic jargon phrase to describe it: "Phenotype developmental process." But what it amounted to, in layman's terms, was that C-lines were systematically and continually raped from the age of nine.

"The worst of it," Virginia mused, "is that there wasn't even any real lust involved. No emotion at all. The rapists—sorry, the phenotype technicians—have to be chemically induced to even get an erection." She actually managed a giggle. "Sometimes, looking back, I almost feel sorry for them. Almost. I don't think there exists anybody in the galaxy as bored with sex as those people."

"Nine?" Victor asked shakily.

She shrugged. "Yeah. It hurts. A lot, in the beginning. And it's even worse for the b-variants. Those are the boys."

Victor felt like he was wading in a cesspool. But he finally understood the sheer savagery of the Audubon Ballroom. He had never approved of the kind of terrorist tactics which their militants often applied to individual targets. Counterproductive, ideologically. But—

She laughed harshly. "Almost! Ha! That one time Jeremy X and his comrades caught a phenotype technician here on Terra—stupid bastard went on vacation, can you believe it?—I raced down to see the body like everybody else."

At one time, Victor would have winced. Now, he simply growled his own satisfaction. He knew the incident she was referring to. It had been one of the most famous exploits of the Ballroom, and one which had produced a gale of official outrage. The Solarian League's Executive Council met in an elaborate palace. As part of the palace's decor, there was a statue in the center of the antechamber. The statue was a human-sized replica of a gigantic and long-destroyed ancient monument called the Statue of Liberty. The Council members had not been amused to arrive one day and find the naked body of a "phenotype engineer" impaled on the statue's torch, with a sign hanging around his neck which read: *Hoist on his own petard, wouldn't you say?*

He took a deep breath. "I *still* think the tactics are counterproductive."

Virginia smiled slyly. "That's what Kevin says, too." The smile faded. "I don't know. I suppose you're right. But—"

She took her own deep breath. "You don't know what it's like, Victor," she said softly. There was a hint of moisture in her dark eyes. "All your life you're told you're inferior—*genetically*. Not really human. You wonder about it yourself. Sometimes I think the way I put on such a slutty act is just because—" No hint, now; the tears were welling. She wiped them away half-angrily. "So maybe you and Kevin are right. All I know is that after I saw that body I felt a lot better about myself."

The moment passed, and Virginia went back to her customary badinage. "Anyway, after I escaped I made my living as a whore. The pay's good and what else do I know how to do?" Sourly: "Kevin insisted that I give it up, when he proposed."

Victor had learned enough to resist his natural impulse: *But surely you were glad to abandon that life of degradation!* Virginia, he was quite certain, had been happy enough to quit the trade. But she enjoyed goosing the greenhorn.

Ginny goosed him again. "And he was so mean to my pimp, too." Sigh. "Poor Angus. He was so refined, and Kevin is *such* a ruffian."

When she realized he wasn't going to rise to the bait, Ginny grinned. The grin, of course, was lascivious. Whatever the reality of their relationship and repartee, Victor realized that Ginny was a far more experienced field agent than he was. Except for that one brief teary-eyed moment, she had never once broken cover. Any of Durkheim's men who was following them would be quite certain by now that Victor Cachat had finally abandoned his stiff and proper ways. Another puritanical revolutionary undone by the fleshpots of Terra. *Join the club.*

And so, just as Usher had planned, it would never occur to them that the same Victor Cachat was getting a better introduction to the Loop and its secrets than they'd ever gotten.

"Smart man," mused Victor.

"Isn't he?" agreed Ginny happily.

The Third Day

Helen

Helen had no way of keeping track of time, beyond the meals which her captors gave her. After four meals, she decided that they were feeding her twice a day. Which, if she was right, meant that she had now been imprisoned for three days.

The food was plentiful, but consisted of nothing more than some kind of standard rations. For troops, possibly, although Helen suspected darkly that the rations were designed for convict laborers. Nasty stuff. *She* certainly wouldn't feed crap like that to armed soldiers. They'd mutiny within a week.

The stuff didn't do wonders for her digestion, either. Fortunately, her captors had provided her with a modern portable toilet instead of the crude bed pan which was always provided in the adventure novels she loved to read. She got plenty of use for the thing. More than her captors had intended, in fact, because she had quickly learned that the slot behind the heatflash disposal mechanism was perfect for concealing her digging shards.

That was about the only good thing about the disposal mechanism. It was so old and poorly maintained that it barely served for its official function. And not well enough to cover the stench which slowly, as the hours and days went by, began to fill the cell.

But that too, Helen decided, was all to the good. She noticed that after the second day, her captors came in and out of her cell as quickly as possible. Holding their breath all the while.

So she continued her dogged tunneling in a cheerful enough mood. She even had to restrain herself, once, from humming.

Victor

The next day seemed endless to Victor. The only assignment Usher had given him was to do nothing, beyond his normal tasks as an SS officer in the embassy. Which, in Victor's case, amounted to glorified clerical work.

He even found himself looking forward to the evening. He was supposed to meet with Virginia again, in a tavern deep in the Loop, and then spend the rest of the night with her at a nearby cheap hotel. The cover was the obvious one of a man having an assignation with a prostitute.

Despite his certainty that Ginny would tease him mercilessly—especially once they were in the hotel room—Victor was looking forward to it. Partly because she might have news, and partly because it would at least give him the feeling he was doing *something*. Mostly, he just wanted to see her again.

In the solemnly self-critical manner which was Victor's way, he spent some time examining that desire. Eventually, he was satisfied that there wasn't any foul concupiscence lurking beneath. It was just—

He *liked* Ginny, he realized. There was something clean at the center of the woman, which came like fresh water after the murky filth he had been plunged into. And, although he wasn't sure, he thought she liked him also. Victor had had few friends in his life, and none at all since he left the Academy. For all his stern devotion to duty, he realized, he had been suffering from simple loneliness for a long time.

By the time lunch break came around, Victor was actually feeling quite relaxed. Then, on his way to the cafeteria, he spotted Usher marching down another hallway toward the barracks and felt himself tighten up all over again.

If the Marine citizen colonel noticed him as well, he gave no sign of it. A moment later Kevin was gone, passing through the door into the section of the big building set aside for the Marine detachment which guarded the embassy.

Victor's stride, upon seeing Usher, had turned into an almost-stumbling shuffle. Then, frantically trying to recover his poise, he *did* stumble. He only kept himself from falling by an awkward half-leap which drew the eyes of all the other people in the corridor at the time. There were three of them—two clerks and a Marine citizen sergeant.

Flushing with embarrassment, Victor avoided their gaze and resumed his march toward the cafeteria. At first, he was almost petrified with fear. *Had he given away his connection to Usher by his own carelessness and tyro stupidity?*

But by the time he reached the entrance to the cafeteria, he came to the realization that his mishap was nothing to fear. In fact, much as he hated to admit it, even if the stumble was reported to Durkheim it would probably do some good. There was, after all, another perfectly logical explanation for why he might be taken aback by meeting Kevin Usher again.

A voice coming from behind him, speaking in a whisper which was still loud enough to be heard by anyone within twenty feet, confirmed the supposition.

"Try not to piss your pants, will you? The Citizen Colonel doesn't usually slap around punks more than once."

An instant later, almost roughly, Victor was shouldered aside by the citizen sergeant he had noticed in the corridor. Standing stock still, he stared at the Marine marching past him into the cafeteria. Then, realizing he was blocking the way of the two clerks, he stepped back. He saw one of the clerks glance at him as he went by, his lips twisted into a slight smirk.

By now, Victor realized, the story of his encounter with Kevin Usher in the tavern would have gone through the entire embassy staff. Causing no chagrin to anyone, not even other SS officers, and much amusement to many.

But it was not embarrassment which kept him standing in the doorway for another few seconds. It was simple surprise. Somehow—he hadn't noticed at the time—the citizen sergeant had managed to slip a note into his hand while he was manhandling Victor out of the way.

Victor recognized the fieldcraft, of course. From training if not from actual practice. But he was more than a little astonished to see it performed so precisely and perfectly by a man whom he would have assumed did nothing more precise than blow people apart in a combat assault.

Fortunately, Victor didn't forget his own fieldcraft. So he didn't make any of the tyro's mistakes, such as trying to read the note immediately. He just slipped it into his pocket and went to the line to get his food.

Nor did he try to read the note surreptitiously while he was eating. He was too well trained, for one thing. For another, he was far too preoccupied studying the Marines in the cafeteria.

And that, too, was a well-trained sort of study. Victor never gave the Marines sitting at their own table more than an occasional glance. He didn't really need to, after all, since he had observed Marines at lunch many times in the past.

Or, it might be better to say, had *seen* them. But he realized now that the Marines, as visible as they always were in the embassy, remained almost like ghosts in his actual knowledge. What *really* went on in the barracks? What did those combat troops *think* about anything?

He didn't know, he realized—and neither did almost any SS officer. As an institution, of course, State Security was always deeply concerned about the attitudes and political reliability of the military. But that assignment was so important that it was kept carefully shielded from the view of most SS men. As a rule, for a small detachment like the one guarding the embassy on Terra, only one officer would really know anything about the Marines.

That officer, in this case, was a certain Paul Gironde. About whom, Victor realized, he also knew almost nothing. Even by SS standards, Gironde was a close-mouthed sort of fellow. The few times Victor had found himself in a conversation with Gironde, the conversation had been brief. From boredom on Victor's part, if nothing else.

But of one thing Victor was almost certain, from certain subtleties in the way he had seen Durkheim and Gironde interact in the past. Gironde, while he was a respected SS officer, was not one of Durkheim's cronies.

Then came the hardest moment of the day, as Victor fought down a smile. He knew only one of the classical allusions which Kevin Usher was so fond of spouting. And he couldn't, even then, remember the actual Latin words. But he knew what they meant.

Who will guard the guardians?

Victor didn't finally read the note until he was in the jam-packed capsule heading into the Loop. There, carefully cupping the note in his palm while he was surrounded by a motley horde, he could be sure of reading it unobserved. By anyone, at least, connected in any way with State Security.

That his assignation with Virginia was in the Old Quarter, some time in the evening, he already knew. The note would tell him exactly when and where.

And so it did, in feminine handwriting, and then some:

Gary's Place. 8. Wear something pink. I love pink. It reminds me—

What it reminded Ginny of turned Victor's own face pink as well. But, this time, he made no effort to restrain his laugh. Why should he? In the crowded transportation capsules carrying the city's menials back into the Old Quarter after a day's work, there was a lot of laughter.

He found the time, before entering the tavern, to hunt down a clothing store and buy a scarf. A pink scarf. Bright pink, in fact. Victor felt silly wearing the thing. And it was probably a lapse into decadent habits on his part. Putting on a useless piece of garment just to please a lady!

But—

She wasn't *his* lady, true. A lady she was, nonetheless, and some part of Victor took pleasure in the fact itself. In a way he couldn't explain, it seemed like another victory, of which there had been precious few in his life. A small one, perhaps, but a victory sure and certain.

Anton

"And there it is," said Anton softly. He leaned back from the console and arched his back against the chair. He was stiff from the long hours he had spent there. All day, in fact, since early in the morning. And it was now almost ten o'clock at night.

Robert Tye, who had been standing at the window staring at the brightly lit city, turned his head and cocked an eyebrow. Catching a glimpse of the little movement, Anton chuckled.

"Bingo, as you Terrans would put it. And where does that silly expression come from, anyway?"

Tye shrugged. "What did you find?"

Anton pointed a finger at the screen. "I had plenty already, just from the embassy's general files and the ambassador's. But the real gold mine is here in Admiral Young's personal records." He shook his head, half with anger and half with bemusement. "What a jackass."

Tye came over and stared at the figures. As always with the material which Anton had brought up on the screen over the past two days, none of it meant anything to him.

"Surely he wasn't stupid enough..."

Anton barked a little laugh. "Oh, no—he was quite clever. Which was his undoing, in the end. When amateurs try to cover up stuff like this, they almost always make it too complicated. Keep your laundry simple, that's the trick."

The martial artist's face was creased with a frown. "Why would Young launder money? From what you've told me, the man's so rich he doesn't need to supplement his wealth."

"Money," hissed Anton. "Money's not this bastard's vice, Robert. He wasn't trying to cover up his income. He was covering his *expenses*."

"Oh." Tye's nostrils grew a little pinched, as if he were in the presence of a bad smell.

"So were most of the people on this list," continued Anton. "And, I'm pretty sure, most of the people on that list of Hendricks' I turned up earlier. Although that'll take some time to determine, since the ambassador was quite a bit less careless than Young was."

Anton pushed back the chair and rose to his feet. He needed to stretch a little. As he paced around, swinging his arms in a little arc to ease the tension in his back, he kept staring at the screen. His expression was intense, as he considered a new possibility.

After a moment, Tye's eyes grew almost round. Apparently, the same possibility had just occurred to the martial artist. "You don't think *they* were involved...?"

Hearing the question put so directly, Anton's answer crystallized.

"No," he said, shaking his head firmly. "I was wondering myself, once I saw how closely they've been connected to the Mesans. But there's no earthly reason for them to do it. Helen means nothing to them, and if they wanted to strike at me—and for what purpose?—they both have far quicker and simpler ways to do it. I *am* their subordinate, after all."

He left off his arm-swinging and began a little set of isometric exercises, one palm against another. "But if you look at it another way, everything begins to make sense. Those same ties to Manpower would make Young and Hendricks the perfect patsies."

Now he slapped the palms together. "And *that*—that, Robert—is what explains Helen. She's the daughter of a Manticoran intelligence agent. Another prybar, that's all. Another angle. Whoever's behind this isn't trying to get information of any kind, much less start a disinformation campaign." He barked another laugh. "Or, at least, not a subtle one. There's all hell brewing here, Robert, and when the explosion comes Manticore is being set up to take the blame."

"The blame for what?"

Anton smiled thinly. "Give me a break. I can't figure out everything in a few days." He studied the screen a little longer. "And, in truth, I'm beginning to suspect that the culprit—or culprits, if there's more than one—is being too clever himself."

"Peeps, you think? They're the obvious ones who'd want to damage the Star Kingdom's standing on Terra. Especially now. Parnell should be arriving in three days, according to the newscasts."

"Maybe." Anton shrugged. "But it still doesn't feel right."

He pointed a thick finger at the screen. "Too *clever*, Robert. Too clever by half. Whatever this scheme is, it's got way too many threads waiting to come loose."

"A Rube Goldberg machine, you're saying."

The Manticoran officer scowled. "And there's *another* stupid Sollie expression. I've asked six of you people since I got here, and nobody can tell me who this 'Rube Goldberg' fellow was supposed to have been."

Tye chuckled. But Anton noted, a bit sourly, that he gave no answer himself.

"Too many threads..." he mused. "I'd almost laugh, except the minute the thing starts coming apart the first casualty will be Helen."

Anton turned his head and stared at the data packet lying next to the console. Lieutenant Hobbs had brought it over just before noon. It hadn't taken the police lab long at all to analyze the material which Anton had given them the night before.

Muhammad's visit had been brief. He hadn't even come into Anton's apartment. He had just handed him the packet, scowling, and said nothing more than: "I am *not* going to ask where you got five pairs of shoes, Anton. Not unless I find the feet that used to fit them." Then he left.

Anton had read the data immediately, of course. That had taken no time at all, practically. The data was crystal clear: the owner of the shoes had—recently, and probably frequently—been in the lower depths of the Loop. Below the densely populated warrens, in the labyrinth of tunnels and passageways which marked the most ancient ruins of the city.

The intensity with which Anton now studied that packet was no less than that which he had earlier bestowed on the screen. Again, he was considering a possibility.

And, again, came to a decision. Quickly enough, if

not as quickly as before. The decision, this time, was affirmative. And it was one which he came to only with reluctance.

"No way around it," he muttered. Then, snorting: "God, to think it would come to this! Talk about supping with Satan with a long spoon."

Tye was startled. "You're planning to talk to *Manpower*?"

Anton laughed. No curt bark, either, but a genuine laugh. "Sorry," he choked. "I misspoke. Calling that woman 'Satan' is quite unfair, actually. Hecate would be more accurate. Or Circe, or maybe Morgana."

Tye scowled. "What woman? And are you trying to get even with me by using meaningless Manticoran expressions? Who the hell are Hecate and the others? I'm not a student of the Star Kingdom's mythology, you know."

He scowled even further, hearing Anton's ensuing laughter. The more so, no doubt, since Anton didn't bother to explain the source of the humor.

When Anton was done laughing, Tye gestured at the door. "Are we leaving now? To see whomever this mysterious woman might be."

Anton shook his head. "It's much too late. I'll put in a call right away, of course, but I doubt if we'll get an audience with her until tomorrow morning sometime."

"An 'audience'? What is she, some kind of royalty?"

"Close enough," said Anton softly. He was studying the screen again, where Edwin Young's vile nature was displayed in antiseptic columns of figures. "The admiral would call her 'the Lady from the Infernal Regions,' I imagine. As much as I probably despise the woman, I suppose that's as good a character reference as you could ask for."

"What's 'the Infernal Regions'?" demanded Tye. "A province of the Star Kingdom? And what do you mean: you *probably* despise her?"

Anton didn't bother to answer the first question. As for the other, he shrugged.

"I've never actually met her. But her reputation, as they say, precedes her."

Tye cocked his head. "Nice expression, that. 'Her reputation precedes her.' Another old Manticoran saying?"

The Fourth Day

Helen

When she broke through the wall, Helen was astonished. She had long since stopped actually thinking about escape. She had kept digging simply to keep herself occupied and control the terror.

She held her breath. There hadn't been much noise when her digging shard punctured the surface. But, for all she knew, she had simply penetrated into a space within sight of her abductors. Even if they heard nothing, they might spot the little trickle of dirt spilling on the opposite side.

So she waited, holding absolutely still and breathing as little as possible. She started a little count—*one, one thousand; two, one thousand, three*—until she reached three hundred.

Five minutes. And—nothing.

She tried to look through the small little crack the shard had made in the wall, but quickly gave up the effort. The hole where she had been digging was almost eighteen inches deep and not much wider than her arm. She couldn't get her eye close enough to see anything. Nor was there any light coming through the crack. She had known she broke through by feel alone.

She waited another five minutes before she started digging again. Then, moving very slowly and carefully so as to make as little noise as possible, she began to widen the hole.

The Lady Catherine Montaigne, Countess of the Tor

"Anton Zilwicki, Captain in Her Majesty's Royal Manticoran Navy," announced Lady Catherine's butler, as he came through the door to her study. "And Mr. Robert Tye." Isaac stepped aside and politely held the door for the visitors coming through behind him.

Isaac finished the introduction: "Lady Catherine Montaigne, Countess of the Tor."

Cathy rose from her reading chair. For a moment, before she focused her attention on her visitors, she allowed herself an amused glance at Isaac.

My, he does that well! Her butler—Isaac insisted on the title, though it was absurd—seemed every inch the perfect servant. He rattled off the aristocratic titles without a trace in his voice of Isaac's utter hatred of any and all forms of caste society. He even managed to wear the traditional menial's costume as if he had been born in it.

Which, of course, he hadn't. As was the custom of escaped Mesan slaves, except those who joined the Audubon Ballroom, Isaac had taken a surname shortly after obtaining his freedom. Isaac Douglass was now his official name, Isaac having chosen the most popular surname for such people, in memory of Frederick Douglass. But he had been born V-44e-684-3/5, and the name was still marked on his tongue.

Cathy's amusement was fleeting, however. Almost immediately, she realized that Isaac was tense. The symptoms were extremely subtle, a slight matter of his stance and poise, but she could read them. Isaac's feet were spread apart a bit farther than normal, his knees were slightly bent, and his hands were clasped in front of his groin. Cathy was no devotee of *coup de vitesse* herself, but she had no difficulty recognizing the "standing horse."

Why?

Her eyes went to her visitors, trying to find an answer. The man in front, the naval officer, seemed to pose no threat. Zilwicki was on the short side, and extremely stocky. His shoulders were so wide he almost seemed deformed. Put him in the right costume, grow a thick beard instead of a neat mustache, and he'd be the spitting image of a dwarf warlord out of fantasy novels. But his stance was relaxed, and Cathy could read no expression on his square face.

Then, noticing the intensity lurking in the man's dark brown eyes, she began to wonder. Her eyes moved to Zilwicki's companion. Robert Tye, wasn't it?

Tye solved the mystery for her. The little man's head was turned, examining Isaac. Suddenly, Tye's round face broke into a very cheery smile. Because of his pronounced epicanthic fold, the expression almost turned Tye's eyes into pure slits.

"With your permission, Lady Catherine, I will assume the lotus. I believe your—ah, *butler*—would find that more relaxing."

Tye didn't wait for Cathy's response. An instant later, folding himself down with astonishing ease and grace, Tye was sitting cross-legged on the lush carpeting. His legs were tightly coiled, each heel resting on the upper thigh of the opposite leg. His hands were placed on his knees, the fingers widespread.

Isaac seemed to straighten a bit. And his hands were now clasped behind his back instead of in front of his groin.

"Do you know this man, Isaac?" she blurted out.

Isaac's headshake was so slight it was not much more than a tremor. "No, ma'am. But I know *of* him. He is quite famous among martial artists."

Cathy stared at Tye. "*Coup de vitesse?*"

Tye's cheerful smile returned. "Please, Lady Catherine! Do I look like a barbarian?"

Zilwicki interrupted. "Master Tye is here at my request, Lady Catherine." His tight mouth twitched in one corner. "It might be better to say, at his insistence."

Cathy was struck by the man's voice. His accent, partly—Zilwicki still bore the imprint of his obvious Gryphon highlander upbringing. But, mostly, it was that Zilwicki's voice was so deep it was almost a rumble.

Her natural impulsiveness broke through the moment's tension.

"Have you ever considered a singing career, Captain? I'm sure you would make a marvelous Boris Gudonov."

Again, Zilwicki's mouth made that little twitch. But his eyes seemed to darken still further.

"My wife used to say that to me," he murmured. "But I think she was mostly just tired of coming to church choirs, dressed in suitably conservative clothing. She'd have rather swept into the opera house in one of the glamorous gowns I bought for her. Which, sad to say, almost never got worn."

For all the affectionate humor in the remark, Cathy did not miss the sorrow lurking behind it. That, and the name, finally registered.

"*Helen* Zilwicki?"

The captain nodded.

"My condolences, Captain."

"It's been many years, Lady Catherine," was Zilwicki's reply. His deep-set eyes seemed almost black, now. Perhaps that was simply a shading, due to the relatively dim lighting in the study. His mass of black hair—cut short, in the military style, but very thick—added to the impression, of course. But Cathy did not doubt for a moment that, despite the disclaimer, the man before her had never stopped grieving his loss.

"I'm surprised you made the connection so quickly," he added. "Zilwicki is a common name on Gryphon." The captain paused; then: "And I wouldn't have expected someone on your end of the political spectrum to remember such things."

Cathy shook her head. The gesture was not so much one of irritation as simple impatience. "Oh, please! Captain, I warn you right now that I *detest* being pigeonholed."

"So I deduced, studying your file. But I'm still

surprised." Zilwicki spread his hands in a little economical gesture. "My apologies."

She stared at him. "You studied *my* file? Whatever for?" Her jaws tightened. "And let me say, Captain, that I also detest being spied upon!"

Zilwicki took a deep breath. "I had no choice, Lady Catherine. Because of the situation, I am forced to operate completely outside of the command chain, and I need your help."

"*My* help? With regard to *what* situation?"

"Before I explain, Lady Catherine, I must tell you that I was not exaggerating when I said I was operating *completely* outside the command chain. In fact—"

He took another deep breath. "When this is all over, however it ends, I expect to face a court-martial. I won't be surprised if the charges include treason as well insubordination and gross dereliction of duty."

His eyes seemed like ebony balls. But it was fury rather than sorrow which filled his voice. "Ambassador Hendricks and Admiral Young were quite explicit in their instructions to me. And I propose to shove those instructions as far up their ass—pardon my language—as possible. With or without lubricant, I don't much care."

Cathy hated her own laughter. She had heard it, on recordings, and it sounded just as much like a horse's bray as she'd always suspected. But she couldn't suppress the impulse. She wasn't good at controlling her impulses, and laughter came easily to her.

"Oh, splendid!" she cried. Then, choking: "No lubricant, Captain—not for those two! In fact—" Choke; wheeze. "Let's see if we can't splinter those instructions good and proper beforehand. Leave the bastards bloody."

Captain Zilwicki's mouth began to twitch again. But the twitch turned into an actual smile, and, for the first time, the humor which filled his voice seemed to creep into his eyes.

He was quite an attractive man, Cathy decided, once you got past that forbidding exterior. "And just how can I help you in this magnificent project, Captain? Whatever it is."

Helen

Helen was so engrossed in her work that she completely forgot to gauge its duration. For the first time, escape was actually a tangible reality instead of an abstract possibility. It was only when the digging shard set loose a small pile of sand—a pocket of dust, rather, encysted within the crumbled stones and fill—that she remembered.

Helen was immediately swept by panic. She began hastily backing out of the small tunnel into her cell. As soon as she emerged, she scrambled over—still on her hands and knees—to her makeshift "hourglass."

Empty.

Now the panic was almost overwhelming. Helen had made the timing device out of an old container she had found in a corner of the cell. A paint can, she thought, although the thing was so ancient that it was hard to tell. Fortunately, the can had been made of some kind of synthetic substance. Metal would have long since corroded away.

Helen had punched a small hole in the bottom with a sharp stone. Then, as soon as her captors provided her with the next meal, she began experimenting by filling the can with the dry and powdery dust which covered the cell's "floor." After three meal cycles, she had been satisfied that the can would run empty long before her captors returned with another meal. But she had always been careful to emerge from the tunnel and cover her traces while there was still dust in the container.

Empty. *But for how long?* For all she knew, Helen's captors were about to enter the cell.

For a moment, she almost pressed her ear against the door to see if she could hear them. But there was no point to that. The impulse was pure panic, nothing else. Helen forced herself to remember her training.

Breathing first. Master Tye always says that. Breathing first.

She took a slow, deep breath, letting the air fill her mind with calmness at the same time as it filled her lungs with oxygen. Another. Then another.

Under control. Now moving quickly but surely, Helen began to cover her tracks. First, she fitted the panel over the tunnel entrance. Then, as always, she piled debris against it, making sure that the various pieces were in the same arrangement.

After that, she began mixing the fresh fill with the old dirt and dust covering the floor. That was slow work, because Helen had to be careful to stay as clean as possible. Her captors provided her with enough water to wash her hands and face, but nothing more. Of course, after days spent in the cell—which was really nothing more than a grotto in the ruins—she was dirtier than she'd ever been in her life. But she couldn't make it too obvious that the grime covering her was more than could be expected from the surroundings.

Finally, she put on the rest of her clothing. Whenever she went into the tunnel, Helen wore nothing but underwear. She had no way to wash her outer garments. If she'd worn them while she was digging, her clothes would have become utterly filthy. Even her captors, who seemed as indifferent toward her as they would to a lab rat, would have noticed soon enough.

She finished just in time. She heard voices on the other side of the door. By the time her captors started the process of unbolting the door, Helen had assumed the position they demanded of her when they brought food and fresh water. Squatting in a corner, staring at the wall. Docile and obedient.

She heard the door open, and her captors coming into the cell. Two of them—a woman and a man, judging from the sound of the footsteps.

The woman made a comment in that unknown language. Helen didn't understand the words, but she grasped the emotional content. Contemptuous and derisive humor; alloyed, she thought, with more than a trace of lasciviousness. True, Helen wasn't certain about that last. She had just reached the stage in her life when her body began to take a new shape, and Solarian mores were very similar to Manticoran ones when it came to sexual disrespect. But she thought she could recognize a leer when she heard one.

The man responded with his own laughing remark, and Helen had no doubt at all about *his*. She couldn't see his face, but the words alone practically drooled.

She heard the sounds of the food and water being placed on the floor next to the pallet which served her as a bed. Again, the man said something and laughed, and the woman joined him. Listening, Helen thought she had never heard such a coarse and foul sound in her life.

But that was the end of it. They did not come over to her, nor did they do one of their occasional and very cursory inspections of the cell.

Swine. Helen willed herself into a pose of utter subservience. A mouse huddling in the presence of cats. She concentrated on her breathing.

They left. Helen waited until she heard the chain being put into place before she moved a muscle. Then, scurrying like a mouse, she began to refill the hourglass.

Running water.

Cathy

After Zilwicki finished, Cathy felt as confused as she'd ever been in her life. *Nothing* of what he'd said made any sense.

"But surely the police—"

Zilwicki shook his head firmly. "No, Lady Catherine. On *that* subject Ambassador Hendricks and Admiral Young are perfectly correct. My daughter wasn't kidnapped by common criminals. This was a political act, of some kind. The Solarian police simply aren't equipped to deal with that, and I don't want to get the Solarian League's intelligence services anywhere near it." His square, blocky face tightened. "I trust those people not much more than I do the Peeps."

Cathy rose from her chair and moved over to the window. The act was not done from any desire to admire the view, but simply because she always found it necessary to be on her feet when she was trying to puzzle out a problem. It was one of her characteristic traits, which her friends were fond of teasing her about. Lady Prancer, they sometimes called her. Cathy thought the nickname was a bit grotesque, but she admitted the logic of it. Her nervous way of moving constantly, combined with her braying laugh and her tall and gangly figure, often reminded *her* of a skittish filly.

Once she was at the window, of course, she found it impossible not to admire the view. She was certainly paying enough for it, after all. Her apartment was located near the very top of one of the Solarian capital's most expensive apartment complexes. Cathy was looking down on the city from well over a mile above street level. Insofar as the term "street level" could be applied to Chicago, that is. Whatever other changes had come over the city in the millennia of its existence, Chicago still retained its fondness for underground passages and covered walkways. Which was logical, since the climate—and the wind—had *not* changed.

Cathy stared down at the teeming metropolis. It was like looking into a gigantic canyon. On the surface streets far below, and on the multitude of conduits which connected the various buildings on every level, she could see the crowds scurrying like ants. Most of them seemed in a great hurry. Which, in fact, they were. It was lunch hour, for the millions who worked in Chicago's center. And that, too, had not changed over the centuries. Lunch hour was never long enough.

She shook her head abruptly and turned back to face her visitors. The quick and jerky motions, though she had no way of realizing it, reminded the captain of a gawky young horse. Once again, silently, someone bestowed the old nickname on her.

"All right, I can understand that. I guess. But why are you so certain that the ambassador and the admiral are wrong in their approach?" She held up her hand and fluttered the long and slender fingers. "Yes, yes, Captain! I know they're both assholes, but that doesn't mean they're incompetent."

She flashed her visitor a jittery grin. "You'll have to pardon my language. I know I curse too much. Can't help it. Comes from being forced through snooty private schools when I was a youngster. Maybe that's why I'm such a rebellious creature." She pranced back to her chair and flung herself into it. "That's what my parents' psychologists said, anyway. Personally, I think they're full of shit."

Anton

Watching and listening to her, Anton was struck by how closely Lady Catherine's speech resembled her movements. Quick and explosive, with scant respect for grammatical elbow room. Her wide mouth and expressive blue eyes added to the effect, as did the great mane of curly blond hair. The only part of the woman's face which seemed subdued was her snub nose, as if it were the deaf mute in a lively village. And despite the title, and the Tor fortune which lay behind it, Lady Catherine's face *was* that of a villager, not a countess. She even had some sunburned skin peeling off of her nose. With her extremely fair complexion, of course, that was not surprising. But most Manticoran noblewomen would have been too mortified by the prospect to have taken the risk of getting a sunburn in the first place. Lady Catherine, Anton suspected, suffered that small indignity with great frequency and a complete lack of concern.

Oddly enough, the naval officer found the ensemble thoroughly charming. He had come here reluctantly, driven by nothing more than sheer and pressing need, and with the full expectation that he would dislike the countess. Like all Gryphon highlanders, Anton Zilwicki detested the aristocracy in general—and the left wing members of it with a particular passion. No one in the Manticoran aristocracy was further to the left than Lady Catherine Montaigne. Even hardcore Progressives like Lady Descroix considered her "utopian and irresponsible." Countess New Kiev, the ultra-doctrinaire leader of the Liberal party, had once denounced her on the floor of the House of Lords as a "dangerous demagogue."

Perhaps, he mused whimsically, that was because his own personality was attracted to opposites, when it came to women. His dead wife had not resembled Lady Catherine in the least, physically. Helen had been short, dark-complected, and on the buxom side. True, there was a closer ideological correlation. Helen, somewhat unusually for a naval officer, had generally followed the Progressives—but only up to a point, and always on the very right edge. And when it came to naval affairs, she was as pure a Centrist as you could ask for. She had *certainly* never been accused—as Lady

Catherine had, innumerable times—of consorting with dangerous and violent radicals. But, like Lady Catherine, Helen had exuded rambunctious energy. And, though she had rarely lapsed into profanity, Helen had had the same way of expressing her opinions directly and forcefully.

Quite unlike Anton himself, who always tried—and almost always succeeded—in maintaining a tight and focused control over his thoughts and actions. Old Stone Face was the nickname his wife had bestowed upon him. Even his daughter, who was the one person to whom Anton unbent, teased him about it. Daddy Dour, she sometimes called him. Or just Popsicle.

On the rare occasions when he thought much on the subject, Anton ascribed his personality to the stark upbringing of the Gryphon highlands. The Navy's psychologists, in their periodic evaluations, had an infinitely more complex way of explaining the matter. Anton could never follow their reasoning, partly because it was always presented in that fearsome jargon so beloved by psychologists, but mostly—

Because I think they're full of shit.

But he didn't speak the words. He simply gave Lady Catherine a friendly smile. "I don't mind, ma'am. Curse all you want."

He planted his hands on his knees. His hands, like his face and body, were square and blunt. "But I'm telling you, the ambassador and the admiral—and Admiral Young's whole little flock of armchair intelligence advisers—"

He couldn't resist: "—are full of shit."

All traces of humor vanished. "My daughter was *not* kidnapped by the Peeps. Or, if she was, it's some

kind of black operation being done completely outside
the Havenite command chain. By amateurs, to boot."

Lady Catherine frowned. "How can you be so certain of that? The demands they are making upon you,
in exchange for keeping your daughter unharmed—"

Anton flicked the fingers of his hands, without
removing the hands themselves from his knees. In its
own way, the gesture was also explosive.

"Doesn't make sense. For at least three reasons.
First of all, the demands were left in my apartment.
Written, if you can believe it, on a sheet of paper."

Seeing the frown on the Countess' face, Anton
realized that he had to elaborate.

"Ma'am, no field agent in his right mind would
leave that kind of physical evidence on the scene of
a crime. They would have communicated with me
electronically, in some form or other. Leaving aside the
fact that a physical note is legal evidence, it's almost
impossible to keep some traces of yourself off of it.
Modern forensic equipment—and the stuff the Solarians have is every bit as good as what the Manticoran
police use—is damned near magical, the way it can
squeeze information out of any kind of physical object
a person has been in touch with."

He reached into a pocket and pulled out a small, flat
package. "As it happens, although the Chicago police are
not officially involved, I do have some personal contacts.
One of them saw to it that the ransom note was given
the full treatment. As well as the evidence which I,
ah, uncovered elsewhere. The results are on this disk."

He tapped the package against his knee. "But I'll
get to that in a moment. First, let me finish my train
of thought."

With his left hand, he held up a finger. "So that's point number one. The people who abducted my daughter were not professional Havenite agents, nor were they following orders from one. Or, if he was one, he was a desk pilot rather than a field man."

He flicked up his middle finger to join the first. "Point two. The action itself—*kidnapping*, for God's sake—is completely out of whack with the supposed result. I'm an officer in naval intelligence, true, but my specialty is technical evaluation. My background's in naval construction. I was a yard dog before my wife was killed. After that—"

He paused for a moment, forcing his emotions under. "After that, I transferred into the Office of Naval Intelligence." Another pause. "I guess I wanted to do something that would strike the Peeps directly. Unlike Helen, however, I was never good enough at naval tactics to have much hope of climbing to a command position in the fleet. So intelligence seemed like the best bet."

Lady Catherine cocked her head. There was something faintly inquisitive about the gesture. Anton thought he understood it, and, if so, was a bit astonished at her perspicacity.

He smiled ruefully, running his fingers through his coarse mat of hair. "Yeah, I know. 'And how many barrels of oil will thy vengeance fetch thee in Nantucket market, Captain Ahab?' "

She returned the smile with a great, gleaming one of her own. Her eyes crinkled with pleasure. "Good for you!" she exclaimed. "A rock-hard Gryphon highlander who can quote the ancient classics. I'll bet you learned to do it just so you could show up the Manticore nobility."

For all the gravity of his purpose, and his own
tightly controlled terror for his daughter, Anton found
it impossible not to laugh. Chuckle, at least. "Only at
first, Lady Catherine! After a while, I started enjoying
them in their own right."

But the humor faded. Here, too, there was old
heartbreak. It had been his wife Helen—a Manticoran
herself, and from "good stock" if not the nobility—who
had first introduced Anton to *Moby Dick*. Not, in truth,
because Helen had been a devotee of classic literature, but simply because she had shared the passion
for any kind of naval fiction which was common to
many officers in the Manticoran navy. Among whose
ranks was firmly held the opinion that Joseph Conrad
was the greatest author of all time, except for a vocal
minority which held forth for Patrick O'Brian.

He brought his focus back to the moment. "The
point, Lady Catherine, is that I simply don't *know*
enough of any real value to the Peeps to make it
worth their while to commit such a crime."

"They *are* brutal bastards," stated the countess.
"Especially those sadists in State Security. I wouldn't
put anything past those thugs."

Again, Anton was surprised by the countess. Most
Liberals and Progressives he'd met, especially aristocrats, were prone to downplay or even semi-excuse
the viciousness of the Havenite regime with a lot of
left-wing jargon. As if tyranny stopped being tyranny
when you added more syllables to the term.

He shook his head. "That's irrelevant. They might
well be brutal enough—SS is *certainly* brutal enough—
but—"

He couldn't resist another chuckle. Talk about role

reversals! "Lady Catherine, I am hardly an apologist for the Peeps but I'm also not a cretin. However foul that regime may be, they're not storybook ogres out of a child's fairy tale. There's simply no *purpose* to this. Not enough, anyway." He leaned forward, elaborating. "I was sent here to keep track of technology transfers from the Solarian League to the People's Republic of Haven. Because of my technical background, I can make sense out of information that most intelligence specialists—" He hesitated. "Oh, hell, let's call ourselves 'spies,' why don't we?"

The countess smiled; Anton continued: "Which most spies can't. But it's in the nature of my work that I am trying to ferret out the enemy's secrets, rather than keeping our own. So why would the Peeps go to the extreme of kidnapping my daughter in order to force information out of me that they already have? It's not as if they need me to tell *them* what technology they're getting from the League."

"What about—"

"That idiot theory of the admiral's? That the Peeps are playing a long-term game, figuring they can use me to pass along disinformation?"

The countess nodded. Anton turned his head and stared at the giant windows along the wall. Even sitting where he was, a good twenty feet away, the view was breathtaking. But he was completely oblivious to it.

"That brings me to the third reason this doesn't make sense. It just isn't *done*, Lady Catherine." He sighed heavily. "I don't know if I'll have any more success trying to convince you of that than I did with the ambassador and the admiral."

Anton hesitated, gauging the personality of the

woman sitting across from him. The *noble*-woman.
Then, moved by a sudden feeling that he understood
her nature—some of it, at least—decided for straight-
forwardness.

"Lady Catherine, I will say this bluntly. Almost every
aristocrat I know—sure as hell Ambassador Hendricks
and Admiral Young—screws up when they try to understand the Peeps. They always look on them from the top
down, instead of the bottom up. If they're right-wing,
with a sneer; if left-wing, with condescension. Either
way, the view is skewed. The Havenites are *people*, not
categories. I'm *telling* you, this kind of personal attack
on a man's family is so utterly beyond the pale that I
can't imagine any professional Peep intelligence officer
authorizing it. Not a field man, at least. It just—" He
paused, setting his jaws stubbornly. "It just isn't done,
that's all. Not by us, not by them."

Lady Catherine cocked her head again. "Are you
trying to tell me that spies follow a 'code of ethics'?
Including Haven's *State Security?*"

Anton's gaze remained steady. "Yes." He spread his
hands slightly. "Well...I wouldn't call it code of ethics,
exactly. It's more like a code of honor—or, better yet,
the code duello. Even the Ellington Protocol doesn't
allow you to just up and shoot somebody whenever
you feel like it."

"That's true. But there's an official sanction standing behind—"

"And there is here too, ma'am," said Anton forcefully. "Any code of conduct has a practical basis to
it, no matter how buried it might be under the formal trappings. Spies don't go around attacking each
other's families, if for no other reason, because once

you open *that* can of worms there'd be no end to it."
He grimaced. "Well, I'm putting the thing too sharply.
Certain kinds of attacks are permissible—long hal-
lowed, in fact. Seducing a spy's spouse, for instance.
But kidnapping a child and threatening to kill her—"
Again, he set his jaws stubbornly. "It just isn't *done*,
Lady Catherine. I can't think of a single instance, for
all the savageness of this war between us and the
Peeps, when anything like that has happened."

He took a deep breath before continuing. "As for
State Security..." Another pause; then: "The thing
is much more complicated, Lady Catherine, than
people realize. The image most Manticorans have of
State Security is that they're simply an organization
of goons, thugs and murderers. Which"—he snorted—
"they certainly have plenty of, God knows. Some of
the foulest people who ever lived are wearing SS
uniforms, especially the ones who volunteer for duty
in concentration camps."

Seeing the countess' little start, Anton nodded.
"Oh, yes. You didn't realize that, did you? The fact
is, ma'am, that State Security allows its people a lot
more latitude in choosing their assignments than the
Peep navy does. Or the Manticoran navy, for that
matter. It's quite a democratic outfit, in some ways,
as hard as that might be to imagine."

He eyed her shrewdly. "But it makes sense, if you
think about it. Whatever else Oscar Saint-Just is, he is
most definitely not stupid. He knows full well that his
precious State Security is a—a—" When he found the
metaphor he was looking for, Anton barked a laugh.
"A manticore, by God! A bizarre creature made up
of the parts of completely different animals."

Again, Anton started ticking off his fingers. "A goodly chunk—undoubtedly the majority, by now—are people who joined after the Revolution looking for power and status. They've got as much ideological conviction as a pig in a trough. A fair number of those are former officers in the Legislaturalist regime's secret police. That's where you find your pure goons and thugs."

Another finger. "Then, there are a lot of young people who join up. Almost all of them are Dolists, from the lowest ranks of Havenite society. Some, of course, are just sadists looking for a legitimate cover or angry people looking to inflict revenge on the so-called 'elites.'" He shook his head. "But not most of them, ma'am. Most of them are genuine idealists, who believe in the Revolution and can see the gains it's starting to bring their own class—"

Lady Catherine started to interject a denial but Anton drove over it.

"Sorry, ma'am—*it has*. Don't ever think otherwise. A lot of people in Manticoran intelligence thought the Havenite empire would collapse, after the Revolution." He snorted. "Especially in the diplomatic service. Bunch of upper class snobs who think poor people are nothing but walking stomachs. Sure, Rob Pierre's war has brought Haven's Dolists a lot of bloody grief—not to mention that he's even frozen their stipend. But don't think for a moment that those Dolists are nothing but mindless cannon fodder. For *them*, the Revolution also meant lifting the Legislaturalists' hereditary yoke."

For a moment, Anton's eyes seem to smolder. Gryphon highlanders had chosen a different political course than Peep's Dolists—like Anton himself, they were fierce Crown Loyalists down to the newborn

babes—but no highlander had any difficulty understanding the fury of the underdog. Over the centuries, highlanders had had their own bitter experience
with Manticore's aristocracy. Anton himself hated the
People's Republic of Haven—for killing his beloved
wife, if for no other reason—but he had never shed
any tears over the Legislaturalists executed by Rob
Pierre and his cohorts after the Revolution. In Anton's
opinion, a fair number of the *Manticoran* aristocracy
would look pretty good, hanging by the neck. Half
the members of the Conservative Association, for a
certainty—with Ambassador Hendricks and Admiral
Young right at the front of the line.

His innate sense of humor overrode the moment's
anger. Indeed, for a moment, he felt a certain embarrassment. The friendly-faced woman sitting across
from him—whom he had approached for help, after
all, not the other way around—was also a member of
that same aristocracy. Very prominently, as a matter
of fact. If the countess was ranked only middling-high
in the Manticoran nobility's stiff hereditary terms—all
the stiffer for the fact that they had been artificially
created when the planet was settled—the Tor fortune
was greater than that of most dukes and duchesses.

Something in his thoughts must have shown, for
Lady Catherine was suddenly beaming from ear to ear.

"Hey, sailor!" she chortled. "Go easy on me, willya?
I can't help it—I was born there."

In that moment, Anton was stunned by how beautiful she looked. It was bizarre, in a way—a matter of
pure personality radiating through the barrier of flesh.
The countess' face was not pretty in the least, beyond
a certain open freshness. And while her figure was

definitely feminine, its lanky—almost bony—lines were quite a ways outside the parameters of what was normally considered, by males at least, "sexy." Yet Anton knew, without having to ask, that Lady Catherine had never even considered the body-sculpting which was so popular among Manticore's upper crust. Even though for her, unlike most people, cost was no obstacle. As expensive as body-sculpting was, Lady Catherine could have paid for it out of the equivalent of pocket change.

It was just—the way she was. *Here I am. This is how I look. You don't like it? Then go—*

Anton couldn't help it. He was grinning himself. He could just imagine the coarse profanities which would follow.

The moment lasted, and lasted. Two people, strangers until that day, grinning at each other. And as it lasted, began to undergo what Anton, from his reading of the classics, understood as a *sea change.*

And so, his shock deepened. He had come here, carrying years' worth of a widower's grief and the newfound rage of a father whose child was in danger, looking for nothing more than help. And found—damned if it wasn't true!—the first woman since that horrible day when Helen died who genuinely *interested* him.

He tried to pull his eyes away, but couldn't. And as the grin faded from the countess' face, he understood that he was not imagining anything. She, too, was feeling that tremendous pull.

The image of his daughter broke the spell. Helen, as a four-year-old girl, had been sitting on his lap at the very moment her mother died. Helen the mother had saved Helen the child. The father's responsibility remained.

Lady Catherine cleared her throat. Anton knew that she was trying to leave him the emotional space he needed, and was deeply thankful. Yet, of course, the same uncanny intuitiveness just deepened the attraction.

"As you were saying, Captain..." Her voice was a bit husky.

Anton finally managed to look away from her. He ran a blunt-fingered hand through his stiff and bristly black hair.

"The thing is, ma'am—"

"Call me Cathy, why don't you? Anton."

He took the hand away. "Cathy, trust me on this. There are fissure lines running all through Havenite society. State Security is no exception. Oscar Saint-Just knows that as well—hell, *better than*—anyone in the universe. Except maybe Rob Pierre himself."

He leaned forward, extending his hands. "So he's careful to keep the sheep separated from the goats. More precisely—since no one has still been able to nail down telepathy—he lets the goats and the sheep separate themselves. The thugs volunteer for the concentration camps, and the young idealistic firebrands head for the front lines. Which, for spies, means places like Chicago."

He nodded toward the window. "And that's mostly the kind of State Security out there. In the lower ranks, at least. Tough, yes—even ruthless. But I *know* they weren't the ones who took my daughter."

Cathy leaned forward herself, also extending her hands. But where Anton's movements had been tight and controlled, hers were jerky and expressive. "Anton, I can't honestly say that I share your assessment. I don't have your expertise in intelligence, of course, but my own work has brought me into contact with any number of young—ah, 'firebrands.' Some of them, I hate to say it, wouldn't shrink from *any* blow directed at their enemy."

Anton shook his head. "No, they wouldn't. But they *would* shrink from using the wrong weapon."

He held up the package in his hands. "This is the forensic report. You're welcome to look at it if you want, but I can summarize the gist. The people who broke into our apartment and took my daughter— probably male and female both, judging from the chemical traces—left a clear genetic track. Crystal clear, in fact—the idiots were even careless enough not to eradicate skin oils from the note."

"And they weren't Peeps."

"No. The genetic evidence carried not a trace of the normal Peep pattern. And it hardly matters, anyway, because the pattern they did carry is unmistakable. They were members of the Sacred Band—or, at least, people who came from that very distinct genetic stock."

Cathy didn't quite gasp, but her hand flew to her throat. "Are you *serious*?"

Anton was not surprised to see that Lady Catherine— *Cathy*—had not only heard of the Sacred Band but obviously didn't doubt their existence. Most people wouldn't have understood the term, and most of the ones who did would have immediately insisted that it was a fairy tale—a legend, like vampires. His suspicion was confirmed, and that knowledge brought him great satisfaction. There was only one way that the countess could have found out about the Sacred Band—she had been told by the very people Anton was searching for. The same people he had come here to find.

The countess was now staring blindly at the window. "But that makes no sense at all!" Her lips tightened. "Although I can now understand why you're so insistent that this wasn't a Peep operation."

She gave Anton a shrewd glance. There was hostility in her eyes, but it wasn't directed at him. "And—*of course*—I can understand why the ambassador and the admiral wouldn't believe you."

She sprang to her feet. "Fucking assholes!" The countess began pacing back and forth, waving her hands. "Fucking assholes," she repeated. "Charter members of the Conservative Association, the both of them, God rot their souls. Since their only guiding political principle is *gimme*—"

Anton smiled grimly.

"—they can't possibly understand people who take ideology seriously." For an instant, like a prancing filly, she veered at him. "You're a Crown Loyalist, I imagine."

"Rock hard."

Cathy brayed laughter. "Gryphon highlanders! Just as thick-skulled as their reputation." But she veered even closer. "S'okay. I forgive you." She ran slim fingers through his bristly hair before prancing away. Coming from anyone else except his daughter, that act of casual intimacy would have infuriated Anton. Coming from Cathy, it sent a spike down his spine which paralyzed him for an instant.

She was moving back and forth in front of the window, now. Her movements were jerky—almost awkward and ungainly—but they also expressed a fierce energy.

Anton was dazzled by the sight. The bright sunshine

penetrated her skirt—a modest enough garment, in its own right, but not made of a heavy fabric—and showed her long legs almost as if they were bare. Very slender, they were, though the muscles were obviously well-toned. Anton felt a sudden rush of sheer passion, imagining them—

He *forced* that thought away. And, with his capacity for concentration, succeeded within seconds. But he retained a small glow in his heart. He hadn't felt that kind of rush since his wife died. There was something pure about it, like an emotional cleanser.

Cathy came to an abrupt halt, spun around to face him, and planted her hands on her hips. Extremely slim, those hips. Anton suspected that they had been a lifelong despair for her. "Snake hips," she'd probably muttered, staring at herself in a mirror. *He* thought, on the other hand—

Down!

"Shit!" exclaimed the countess. "No Peep I know would come within a mile of either a Mesan or a Scrag"—*yes! She knew the pejorative nickname*—"unless it was to blow their fucking head off. As much as they hate us Manticoran 'elitists,' we're just Beelzebub in their demonology. The Great Satan himself is called Manpower Inc. and Hell is on a planet named Mesa."

"Exactly," said Anton. "However dictatorial and brutal they are, the Peeps are also ferocious egalitarians. You can get executed in Haven for arguing too hard in favor of individual merit promotion." Again, he quoted from the classics: "'All animals are equal even if some animals are more equal than others.' There's no room in there for hereditary castes—especially slave castes!—or for genetic self-proclaimed supermen."

He sighed heavily. "And, in all honesty, I have to say that in this, if nothing else, the Peeps have a pretty good track record." Another sigh, even heavier. "Oh, hell, let's be honest. They have an excellent track record. Manpower doesn't go anywhere near Havenite territory. That was true even before the Revolution. Unlike—"

"Unlike Manticoran space!" interjected the countess angrily. "Where they don't hesitate for a minute. *Damn the laws.* The stinking scum know just where to find Manticoran customers."

Anton scowled. "Cathy, that's not fair either. The Navy—"

She waved her arms. "Don't say it, Anton! I know the Navy officially suppresses the slave trade. Even does so in real life, now and again. Though not once since the war started. They're too preoccupied, they say."

Anton scowled even more deeply. Cathy waved her arms again. "All right, all right," she growled, "they *are* preoccupied with fighting the Peeps. But even before the war started, the only instance where the Navy ever hit the Mesan slave trade with a real hammer is when—"

Both of them broke into wide grins, now. The news of the incredible mass escape from the Peep prison planet of Hell was still fresh in everyone's mind.

"—when Harrington smashed up the depot on Casimir," she concluded. The countess snorted. "What was she, then? A measly lieutenant commander? God, I love impetuous youth!"

Anton nodded. "Yeah. Almost derailed her career before it even got started. Probably *would* have, if Courvoisier hadn't twisted some Conservative admirals' arms out of their sockets. And if—"

He gazed at her steadily. "—a certain young and impetuous left-wing countess hadn't given a blistering speech on the floor of the House of Lords, demanding to know why the first time a naval officer fully enforced the laws against the slave trade she wasn't getting a medal for it instead of carping criticism."

Cathy smiled. "It was a good speech, if I say so myself. Almost as good as the one that got me pitched out of the House of Lords entirely."

Anton snorted. Although membership in the Manticoran House of Lords was hereditary, not elective, the Lords did have the right under law to officially exclude one of its own members. But given the natural tendency of aristocrats to give full weight to lineage, it was very rarely done. To the best of Anton's knowledge, at the present moment there were no more than three nobles who had had their membership in the Lords revoked. One of them, the Earl of Seaview, had been expelled only after he was convicted in a court of law of gross personal crimes—which all the members of the Lords had long known were his vices, but had chosen to look the other way over. The other two were Honor Harrington and Catherine Montaigne, for having, each in her own way, deeply offended the precious sensibilities of Manticore's aristocracy.

Anton cleared his throat. "Actually, Cathy, that speech is why I'm here."

She paused in her jerky pacing and cocked her head. "Since when does a Crown Loyalist study the old speeches of someone who even aggravates Liberals and Progressives?"

He smiled. "Believe it or not, Cathy, that speech made quite a hit in the highlands. As it happens, one of our Gryphon yeomen was on trial at the time. Shot the local baron—eight times—for molesting his daughter. The prosecutor argued that a murderer is a murderer. The defense countered by quoting your speech."

"The part about 'one person's terrorist being another's freedom fighter,' I should imagine."

Anton nodded. But there was no humor at all in the face. Finally, Cathy understood his purpose in coming to see her. Her hand flew to her throat again, and this time she did gasp.

"Oh, my God!"

Anton's eyes were like coal, beginning to burn. "Yeah, that's it. I didn't come here to discuss the ins and outs of the political complexities which might or might not be involved with my daughter's kidnapping. Frankly, Cathy, I don't give a good God-damn. The ambassador and the admiral can order me to treat this like a political maneuver, but they're—"

He clenched his jaws. "Never mind what they are. What *I* am is a man of Gryphon's highlands. I was that long before"—he plucked the sleeve of his uniform—"I became an officer in Her Majesty's Navy."

The eyes were burning hot, now. "I can't use my normal channels, because the ambassador and the admiral would shut me down in a heartbeat. So I've got to find an alternative." He glanced at the little man still squatting on the floor. "Master Tye agreed to help—insisted, in fact—but I need more than that."

Once again, he lifted the little package which contained the forensic data. "The Scrags who kidnapped my daughter live—or operate—somewhere in Chicago's Old Quarter. You know what that maze is like. Only someone who knows it like the back of his hand could have a chance of finding Helen in there."

Cathy made an attempt to head him off. "I know several people who live in the Loop. Lots of them, in fact. I'm sure one of them—"

Anton shot to his feet. *"From the highlands, woman!"* His Gryphon accent was now so thick you could cut it with a knife. And the black rage of the Star Kingdom's most notorious feudists had shattered the outer shell of control.

"You are—have been for years—one of the central leaders of the Anti-Slavery League. And *by far* the most radical. That's why you've been here for years, in what amounts to exile." Anton's words, for all the Gryphon slurring, came out like plates from a stamping mill. "So don't tell me you don't know *him.*"

"Never been proved!" she exclaimed. But the protest was more in the nature of a squeak.

Anton grinned. Like a wolf, admiring the grace of a fox. "True, true. Consorting with a known member of the Audubon Ballroom—any member, much less *him*—is a felonious offense. In the Star Kingdom as well as anywhere in Solarian territory. You've been charged with it on four occasions. Each time, the charges were dropped for lack of evidence."

A very angry wolf, and a rather frightened fox. "Cut the crap, Cathy! You know him and I know you do and so does the whole damn universe. This isn't a court of law. I need his help, and I intend to get it. But I don't know how to contact him. You do."

"Oh God, Anton," she whispered.

He shook his head. "What did they think, Cathy?

That I would *obey* them?" The next words came through clenched teeth. "*From the highlands.* When they gave me that command, they broke faith with me. Damn them and damn all aristocracy! I'll do as I must, and answer only to the Queen. If she—*she*, not they!—chooses to call that treason, so be it. I'll have my daughter back, and I'll piss on the ashes of those who took her from me."

He reached into another pocket and drew out another package. Identical, to all appearances.

"You can tell him I'll give him this, in exchange for his help. I've spent the past two days hacking into the embassy's intelligence files to get it."

Anton's grin was now purely feral. There was no more humor in it than a shark's gape. "When I broke into the personal records of Young and Hendricks I hit the gold mine. I didn't expect either one of them to be stupid enough to have direct financial dealings with Manpower, and they don't. Technically, under Manticoran anti-slavery laws, that would lay them open to the death penalty."

Cathy's left hand was still clutching her throat. With her other hand, she made a waving gesture. "That's not the form it takes, in the Star Kingdom. Slavery's an inefficient form of labor, even with Manpower's genetic razzle-dazzle. No rich Manticoran really has much incentive to dabble in slave labor unless they're grotesquely avaricious. *And* willing to take the risks of investing in the Silesian Confederacy or the Sollie protectorates. Our own society's got too high a tech base for slavery to be very attractive."

"You might be surprised, Cathy—you *will* be surprised—at how many Manticorans *are* that stupid.

Don't forget that the profit margin in Silesian mines and plantations can be as high as the risk." Anton shrugged. "But you're basically right. Most of the Star Kingdom's citizens who deal with Manpower do so from personal vice, not from greed."

Cathy's face was stiff, angry. "'Personal vice!' That's a delicate way of putting what happens on those so-called pleasure resorts." She stared at the package in Anton's hands. Her next words were almost whispered. "Are you telling me—"

Anton's shark grin seemed fixed in place. "Oh, yeah. I was pretty sure I'd find it. That whole Young clan is notorious for their personal habits, and I'd seen enough of the admiral to know he was no exception." He held up the package. "Both he and the ambassador have availed themselves of Manpower's so-called 'personal services.' Both of them have invested in those 'pleasure resorts,' too, using Solarian conduits. Along with lots of others, for whom they acted as brokers."

"They kept *records*?" she gasped. "Are they that *stupid*?"

Anton nodded. "That arrogant, anyway." He looked down at the package in his hand. "So there it is, Cathy. I thought of using this information to blackmail them into rescinding my orders, but that would take too long. I've got to find my daughter *quickly*, before this whole crazy scheme—whatever it is—starts coming unglued. Which it will, as sure as the sunrise. And when it does, the first thing that'll happen is that Helen will be murdered."

Her hand was still clutching her throat. "My God, Anton! Don't you understand what he'll do if—"

"What do I care, Cathy?" No shark's grin ever held

such sheer fury. "You'll find no Gryphon highlanders on this list, I can tell you that. Nobles aplenty, o' course"—the word *nobles* practically dripped vitriol—"but not a one of *my* folk."

Finally, the fury began to ebb. "I'm sorry, Cathy. But this is the way it must be. My daughter"—he waved the package—"weighed against *these?*"

Cathy

Cathy lowered her hand and sighed. Then, shrugged. It was not as if she disagreed with his moral assessment, after all. Though she still found it difficult to match the man's ruthlessness with what she sensed of the man himself. But then, Cathy had no children of her own. So, for a moment, she tried to imagine the rage that must be filling Anton. Raising a daughter from the age of four as a widower, and coming from that unyielding highland clansmen background—

She glimpsed, for an instant, that seething void— like the event horizon of a black hole—and her mind skittered away.

"I'm sorry," Anton repeated, very softly. "I must do what I must." He managed a harsh chuckle. "In this area, you know, tradition rules. There's a term for what I need. Goes back centuries—millennia. It's called *wet work*."

Cathy grimaced. "How crude!" Again, a sigh. "But appropriate, I suppose. I'm sure Jeremy would agree."

She sighed again. "All right, I'll serve as your conduit to him. But I warn you in advance, Anton, he's got a peculiar sense of humor."

Anton held up the package anew. "Then I imagine this will tickle his fancy."

Cathy stared at the object in Anton's hand. Innocuous-looking thing, really. But she knew full well what would happen once Jeremy got his hands on it. Jeremy had come into the universe in one of Manpower Inc.'s breeding chambers on Mesa. K-86b/273-1/5, they had called him. The "K" referred to the basic genetic type—in Jeremy's case, someone bred to be a personal servant, just as Isaac's "V" denoted one of the technical combat breeds. The "-86b" referred to one of the multitude of slight variants within the general archetype. In Jeremy's case, the variant designed to provide clients with acrobatic entertainment—jugglers and the like. Court clowns, in essence. The number 273 referred to the "batch," and the 1/5 meant that Jeremy was the first of the quintuplets in that batch to be extracted from the breeding chamber.

Cathy ran her hand down her face, as if wiping away filth. In truth, she knew, Manpower's "scientific" terminology covered a genetic method which was almost as fraudulent as it was evil. It was the modern equivalent of the grotesque medical experiments which the ancient Nazis of fable were said to have practiced. Cathy was not a professional biologist, but in the course of her long struggle against genetic slavery she had come to be a lay expert on the subject. Genes were vastly more fluid things than most people understood. The specific way in which a genotype developed was as much a result of the environmental input at any given stage of development as it was on the inherent genetic "instructions." Genes reacted differently depending on the external cue.

Manpower's genetic engineers, of course, knew that perfectly well—despite the claims of their advertising that their "indentured servants" could be counted on to behave exactly as they were programmed. So they tried to provide the "proper environment" for the developing genotypes. On the rare occasions when a biologically-sophisticated prospective client pressed them on the subject, Manpower provided them with a learned and jargon-ridden explanation of what they called the "phenotype developmental process."

Strip away the pseudoscientific claptrap and what it amounted to was: *We breed the embryos in artificial wombs, making the best guess we can based on their DNA; and then we spend years torturing the children into proper alignment. Making the best guess we can.*

And, within limits, it worked—usually. But not always, by any means. Certainly not in Jeremy's case. Within less than a week after his sale, he had made his escape. Eventually, he arrived on Terra, through one of the routes maintained by the Anti-Slavery League. Within a day of his arrival, he had joined the Audubon Ballroom, probably the most radical and *certainly* the most violence-prone group within the general umbrella of the anti-slavery movement. Then, following the custom of that underground movement—whose membership was exclusively restricted to ex-slaves—had renamed himself Jeremy X. Within a short time, he had risen to leadership in the Ballroom. Today, he was considered one of the most dangerous terrorists in the galaxy. Or, to many—herself included, when all was said and done, despite her disapproval of his tactics—one of its greatest freedom fighters.

But if anyone could get Captain Anton Zilwicki's

daughter back alive, it would be Jeremy X. Certainly if she were held captive in the Loop. And if, in the months and years which followed, a number of Manticore's most prominent families found themselves attending an unusually large number of funerals, Cathy could not honestly say the prospect caused her any anguish. Rich people who trafficked in slavery for the sole purpose of indulging their personal vices would get little in the way of mercy from her.

And they would get none at all from a man whose birth name was still marked on his tongue. *Wet work, indeed.*

As she ushered the captain and his companion to the door, Cathy remembered something.

"Oh, yes. Satisfy my curiosity, Anton. Earlier, you said there were three types of people in State Security. But you never got around to explaining the third sort. So who are they?"

"It's obvious, isn't it? What happens to a young idealist, as the years go by and he discovers his beloved Revolution is covered with warts?"

Cathy frowned. "They adapt, I imagine. Get with the program. Either that or turn against it and defect."

Anton shook his head. "Many do adapt, yes. The majority of them, probably. And when they do they are often the most vicious—just to prove to their superiors, if nothing else, that they can be counted on. But almost none ever defect and there are a lot of them who just fade into the woodwork, trying to find a corner where they can still live. Don't forget that, from their point of view, the alternative isn't all that attractive."

His lips twitched. "Even a Gryphon traditionalist like me isn't all that fond of some aspects of Manticoran society. Try to imagine, Cathy, how a man from the Legislaturalist regime's Dolist ranks is going to feel, at the prospect that he'd have to bow and scrape before the likes of Pavel Young, Earl of North Hollow."

Cathy was startled. "Surely they don't know—"

"Of course they do!" Anton's mouth started to twitch again, but the twitch turned into a genuine smile. "The Peeps tend to be a little schizophrenic on the subject of Honor Harrington, you know. On the one hand, she's their arch-nemesis. On the other, she's often been their favorite example of the injustices of Manticoran elitist rule.

"Not any more, of course," he chuckled. "From the news coverage, I'd say the Salamander's days in exile and disgrace are *finished*. Doubt there's more than three Conservative Lords who'll still argue she's unfit for their company."

Cathy brayed her agreement. "If that many!"

"But don't think the Peep propagandists didn't make hay while the sun was shining, Cathy. At least until Cordelia Ransom decided that there was more propaganda value in having Harrington 'executed.'" Anton scowled. "That whole stinking Pavel Young affair was plastered all over every media outlet in the Havenite empire, for weeks on end. Hell, they didn't even have to make anything up! The truth was stinking bad enough. A vile and cowardly aristocrat used his wealth and position to ruin an excellent officer's career. Even paying for the murder of her lover—and getting away with it until Harrington finally cornered him into a personal duel. And *then*, when she shot him in self-defense after he violated the dueling code, the Lords blamed *her?* Because she shot him *too many times?*"

The highlander's soul was back in charge, never mind the uniform. "A pox on all aristocracy," he hissed. "Inbred filth and corruption."

Belatedly, he remembered. "Uh, sorry. Nothing personal. Uh, Lady Catherine."

"S'okay, Anton. I forget I'm a countess myself, as often as not." She rubbed her sunburned nose.

"I—I'm really sorry we met this way, Cathy. I would have liked—I don't know—"

Cathy placed her hand on his arm and gave it a little squeeze. She was a bit startled by the thick muscle under the uniform. "Don't say anything, Anton. Let's get your daughter back, shall we? The rest can take care of itself."

He flashed her a thankful smile. They were now at the door, which Isaac was holding open in his best butler's manner. Robert Tye had already stepped through and was waiting for Anton in the corridor beyond.

Anton and Cathy stared at each other for a moment. Now that they were standing side by side, she realized how much taller she was than the stocky captain. But, also, that the width of his shoulders was not an illusion created by his short stature. He really *was* almost misshapen. Like a dwarf warrior from the hills, disguised in a uniform.

Anton gave her a quick little bow, and hastened through the door. Then, stopped abruptly.

"Good Lord—I forgot to ask. How long will it take you—" He broke off, glancing quickly into the corridor.

Cathy understood. "I should be in contact with the

individual quite shortly, I think. I'll get in touch with you, Captain Zilwicki."

"Thank you." He was gone.

Helen

By the time Helen finished widening the tunnel enough to squeeze herself through, two-thirds of the dust in her makeshift hourglass had fallen through the hole. She had to wage a fierce battle to keep herself from leaving immediately.

That natural impulse was almost overwhelming. But it would be stupid. It wasn't enough to simply get out of the cell. She also had to make her *escape*. And that was not going to be easy.

Again, Helen's success had caught her off guard. She had never really thought about what she would do if she ever got out of the cell. But now she realized that she needed to think about it before she plunged into the darkness.

The darkness was literal, not figurative. Helen had stuck her head through the hole as soon as she widened it enough. And seen—

Nothing. Pitch black. Her own head, filling the hole, had cut off the feeble illumination provided by the cell's light fixture. Helen had never experienced such a complete darkness. She remembered her father telling her, once, of the time he and her mother had visited Gryphon's famous Ulster Caverns on their honeymoon. As part of the tour, the guide had extinquished all the lighting in their section of the caverns, for a full five minutes. Helen's father had described the experience, with some relish—not so much because he was fascinated by utter darkness as because he'd had the chance to fondle his new bride in flagrant disregard for proper public conduct.

Remembering that conversation, Helen had to control herself again. She was swept by a fierce urge to see her father as soon as possible. If Helen's long-dead mother was a constant source of inspiration for her, it was her father who sat in the center of her heart. Helen was old enough to recognize the emptiness which lurked just beneath her father's outward cheer and soft humor. But he had always been careful not to inflict that grief on his daughter.

Oh, Daddy!

For a moment, she almost thrust herself into the hole. But among her father's many gifts to her had been Master Tye's training, and Helen seized that regimen to keep her steady.

Breathe in, breathe out. Find the calm at the center.

Two minutes later, she backed out of the hole and went through the now-familiar process of disguising her work. Since she had plenty of time, she took more care than usual placing the coverings over the hole and blending in the fresh fill. But her own ablutions were as skimpy as she could make them. Just enough to remove the obvious streaks of dirt.

Helen had no idea how long it would take her to find water in that darkness beyond—if there was any water to be found at all. So she planned to drink the remaining water as soon as she heard her captors approaching. That way she could save the new water bottle her captors would bring her. She might have to live on that water for days.

Or, possibly, forever. Helen knew full well that she might simply die in the darkness. Even if she could elude her captors—even if she found water and food—she had no idea what other dangers might lurk there.

She stretched herself out on the pallet and began Master Tye's relaxation exercises. She also needed as much rest as possible before setting forth.

Breathe in, breathe out. As always, the exercises brought calmness. But, after a time, she stopped thinking about them. Master Tye faded from her mind, and so did her father.

There was only her mother left. Helen had been named after her mother. Her father, born and bred in the highlands, had insisted upon that old Gryphonite custom, even though Helen's mother herself—a sophisticate from the Manticoran capital of Landing—had thought it was grotesque.

Helen was glad for it. More now than ever. She drifted into sleep like a castaway, staying afloat on the image of the Parliamentary Medal of Honor.

Cathy

As soon as Isaac closed the door on the departing figure of Captain Zilwicki, a huge grin spread across his face. "I should be in contact with the individual quite shortly, I think," he mimicked. "Talk about understatements!"

Cathy snorted and stalked back into the living room. Once there, she planted her hands on her hips and glared at the bookcase against the far wall. It was a magnificent thing, antique both in age and function.

Cathy was one of that stubborn breed who were the only reason that the book industry (*real* books, dammit!) was still in business. But she insisted on having real books, wherever she lived—and lots of them, prominently displayed in a proper bookcase.

That was so partly because, in her own way, the Lady Catherine Montaigne, Countess of the Tor, was also a traditionalist. But mostly it was because Cathy herself found them immensely useful.

"You can come out now," she growled.

Immediately, the bookcase swung open. Between the piece of furniture's own huge size and the shallow recess in the wall, there was just enough room for a man.

Not much room, of course. But the reputation of Jeremy X was far larger than his actual size. The vicious terrorist and/or valiant freedom fighter (take your pick) was even shorter than Captain Zilwicki, and had nothing like his breadth of shoulder.

Wearing his own cheerful grin, Jeremy practically bounded into the room. He even did a little somersault coming out of the recess. Then turned, planted his own hands on hips, and exclaimed admiringly: "Tradition!"

Turning back around and rubbing his hands in an utterly theatrical manner, he said: "Never met a Gryphon highlander before. What a splendid folk!"

He gave Cathy a squint that was every bit as theatrical as the hand-rubbing. "You've been holding out on me, girl. I know you have—don't deny it!"

Cathy shook her head ruefully. "Just what the universe *didn't* need. Slavering terrorist fiend meets to-the-bloody-death Gryphon feudist. Love at first sight."

Still grinning, Jeremy hopped into one of the plush

armchairs scattered about the large room. "Don't give me that either, lass. I was watching. Through that marvelous traditional peephole. You were quite taken by the Captain. Don't deny it—I can tell these things, you know. I think it must be one of the experiments those Mesan charmers tucked into my chromosomes. Trying for clairvoyance or something."

Cathy studied him. For all Jeremy's puckish nature, she never allowed herself to forget just how utterly ruthless he could be. The Audubon Ballroom's feud against Manpower Inc. made the worst Gryphon clan quarrels of legend seem like food fights.

Still, in her own way—dry, so to speak, rather than "wet"—Cathy was just as unyielding. "Dammit, Jeremy, I'll say it again. If you—"

To her astonishment, Jeremy clapped his hands once and said: "Enough! I agree! You have just won our long-standing argument!"

Cathy's jaw sagged. Glaring, Jeremy sprang to his feet. "What? Did you really think I took any pleasure in killing all the people I have? *Did you now?*"

He didn't wait for a response. "Of course I did! Enjoyed it immensely, in fact. Especially the ones I could show my tongue to before I blew 'em apart. To hell with that business about revenge being a dish best served cold. It's absolute nonsense, Cathy—take my word for it. *I know.* Vengeance is hot and sweet and tasty. Don't ever think it isn't."

He grinned up at her impishly. "Ask the good Captain, why don't you? He's obviously a man of parts. Wonderful fellow!" Jeremy lowered his voice, trying to imitate Zilwicki's basso rumble: "'—and I'll piss on the ashes of those who took her from me.'"

He cackled. "T'wasn't a metaphor, y'know? I dare say he'll do it." Jeremy cocked his head at Isaac. "What do you think, comrade?"

Unlike Jeremy, Isaac preferred restraint in his mannerisms and speech. But, for all its modesty, his own smile was no less savage. "Isaac Douglass" was his legal name, but Isaac himself considered it a pseudonym. Isaac X, he was, like Jeremy, a member of the Ballroom.

"I'll bring the combustibles," he pronounced. "The Captain's so preoccupied with his daughter's plight that he'll probably forget. And wouldn't that be a terrible thing? To fail of revenge at the very end, just because you forgot to bring the makings for a good fire?"

Isaac's soft laughter joined Jeremy's cackle. Staring from one of them to the other, Cathy felt—as she had often before—like a fish stranded out of water. For all the years she had devoted to the struggle against genetic slavery, and for all the closeness of her attachment to the Mesan ex-slaves themselves, she knew she could never see the universe the way they did. There was no condemnation of them in that knowledge. Just a simple recognition that no one born into the lap of privilege and luxury, as she had been, could ever really feel what they felt.

But neither was there any condemnation of herself. Decades earlier, as a young woman newly entered into the Anti-Slavery League, Cathy had been a typical guilt-ridden liberal. Like many such women, she had tried to assuage her guilt by entering a number of torrid affairs with ex-slaves—who, of course, had generally been quite happy to accept the offer.

Jeremy had broken her of that habit. That, and

the guilt which lay beneath it. He was already quite
famous when she met him, a romantic figure in the
lore of the underground. Cathy had practically hurled
herself upon him. She had been utterly shocked by
his blunt and cold refusal. *I am no one's toy, damn
you. Deal with your guilt, don't inflict it on me.
Stupid girl! Of what crimes could you possibly be
guilty, at your age?*

It was Jeremy who had taught her to think clearly;
to separate politics from people; and, most of all, not
to confuse justice with revenge or guilt with responsibility. And if Jeremy's conclusion had been that he
would have his justice and enjoy his revenge too—*why
not? As long as you know the difference*—he had
enabled her to do otherwise. Unlike most youthful
idealists, Cathy had never "grown wiser" with age.
She had simply become more patient. Close friends
and comrades, she and Jeremy had become over the
years, for all their long-standing and often rancorous
quarrel over tactics.

Now—

"Stop joking!" she snarled at him. Then, at Isaac:
"And you! Quit playing at your stupid butler act!"

Jeremy left off his cackling and plopped himself
back in the armchair. Moving more sedately, Isaac
did the same.

"I am *not* joking, Cathy," Jeremy insisted. "Not in
the least."

Seeing the suspicion and skepticism in her eyes,
Jeremy scowled. "Didn't I teach you *anything*? Revenge
is one thing; justice is another." He nodded toward
the door. "That marvelous officer of yours is about to
hand me the instrument for my justice. In the Star

Kingdom, at least. D'you think for a minute that I'm such a fool that I'd forgo it for simple revenge?"

She matched his scowl with no difficulty at all. "*Yes.* Damn you, Jeremy! What else have we been arguing about for the past how many years?"

He shook his head. "You're mixing apples and oranges. Or, to put it better, retail with wholesale." He held out his left hand, palm up, and tapped it with his right forefinger. "As long as my comrades and I only had the names of the occasional Manticoran miscreant, now and then, justice was impossible. Even if we'd gotten the bastards hauled into court for violating Manticore's anti-slavery laws, so what? You know as well as I do what the official stance of the Star Kingdom's government would be."

Now, he did a sing-song imitation of a typical Manticoran aristocrat's nasal drawl: "'Every barrel has a few bad apples.'"

Cathy thought the imitation was a lot better than his earlier mimicry of Zilwicki's Gryphon basso. Which was only to be expected, of course—he'd been in Cathy's company often enough, and she herself spoke in that selfsame accent. She'd tried to shed it, in her earlier days, but found the effort quite impossible.

Jeremy shrugged. "There was no way to prove otherwise." His eyes gleamed pure fury for a moment. "So better to just kill the bastards. If nothing else, it made us feel better—and there was always the chance that another upcoming piglet would decide the risk wasn't worth the reward. But *now*—"

He studied her intently. "Tell me what you think, Lady Catherine Montaigne, Countess of the Tor. Tell me true. How many names of Manticore's highest and most respectable society d'you think are on that list of Zilwicki's?"

She shuddered slightly. "I don't even want to think about it, Jeremy. *Too damned many*, that's for sure." Her wide lips pressed together, holding back an old pain. "I won't be entirely surprised if I even see some of my childhood and college friends. God knows how far the rot has spread. Especially since the war started."

She waved feebly at the door. "I was being unfair to the Captain's precious Navy. Of all Manticore's major institutions, the Navy's probably been the best when it comes to fighting the slave trade. Since they've had their hands full with the Haven war, the swine have been able to feed at the trough unhindered. In the dark; out of sight, out of mind."

"The best *by far*," agreed Jeremy forcefully. "And now—" He clapped his hands and resumed his gleeful, grotesquely melodramatic hand-rubbing. If he'd had mustachios, Cathy had no doubt at all that he'd be twirling them.

But Jeremy X had no mustachios, nor any facial hair at all. That was because K-86b/273-1/5 had been genetically designed for a life as a house servant, and Manpower Inc.'s social psychologists and market experts had unanimously decreed that facial hair was unsuitable for such creatures. Jeremy had once told Cathy that he considered *that* Mesa's final and unforgivable crime. And the worst of it was—she hadn't been sure he was joking. Jeremy X joked about everything, after all; which didn't stop him from being as murderous as an avalanche.

"Everything will come together perfectly," Jeremy chortled, still rubbing his hands. "With Zilwicki's list in our hands, we'll be able to kick over the whole barrel and show just how deep the slave-trade infection really is." He spread his hands, almost apologetically. "Even in the Star Kingdom, which everybody admits—even me—is better than anywhere else. Except Haven, of course, but those idiots are busily saddling themselves with another kind of servitude. So you can imagine how bad it is in the Solarian League, not to mention that pustule which calls itself the Silesian Confederacy."

Cathy frowned. "Nobody will believe—"

"Me? The Audubon Ballroom? Of course not! What a ridiculous notion. We're just a lot of genetically deformed maniacs and murderers. Can't trust anything we say, official lists be damned. No, no, the list will have to be made public by—"

Cathy understood where he was going. "*Absolutely not!*" she shrieked. "That idea's even crazier!" She began stalking back and forth, her long legs moving as gracelessly as a bird on land. "And it's fucking impossible, anyway! I'm a disreputable outcast myself! The only living member of the nobility cast out from the House of Lords except that fucking pedophile Seaview and—"

Her screech slammed to a halt. So did her legs. She stumbled, and almost fell flat on her face.

A very pale face—paler than usual—stared at Jeremy with eyes so wide the bright blue irises were almost lost.

Jeremy left off his cackling and hand-rubbing. But he made up for it by beginning a grotesque little ditty, sung to the tune of a popular nursery rhyme, and waving his fingers in time with the rhythm.

"Oh! Oh! The witch is back!
The witch is back! The witch is back!

Oh, woe! The witch is back!
The wickedest witch
In the wo-orld!"

The ditty ended, replaced by—for Jeremy—an unusually gentle smile. "Oh, yes, Lady Catherine. Tell me again, why don't you—*now*—just how likely d'you think it is that some holier-than-thou Duke or Duchess is going to get up in the House of Lords and huff and puff about just who belongs and who doesn't. *Today?* After their most notorious outcast just shoved their own crap down their precious blue-veined throats?"

He rose to his feet with the lithe grace and speed—so *quickly* he could move—that made Jeremy X such a deadly, deadly man beneath the puckery and the theatrics. *"Harrington's back from the grave*, Cathy. Don't you understand—*yet*—how much that changes the political equation?"

Cathy stood ramrod straight. She was unable to move a muscle, or even speak. She realized now that she *hadn't* thought about it. Had shied away from the thought, in fact, because it threatened her with her worst nightmare. Having to return to the Star Kingdom, after the years of exile, and re-enter the political arena that she detested more than anything else in the universe.

Except—slavery.

"Please, Cathy," pleaded Jeremy. For a rare moment, there was not a trace of banter in his voice. "Now is the time. *Now.*" He turned his head and stared out the window, as if by sheer force of will his eyes could see the Star Kingdom across all the light years of intervening space. "Everything works in our favor. The best elements in the Navy will be roaring. So will

almost the whole of the House of Commons, party affiliation be damned. The Conservative Lords will be huddling in their mansions like so many sheep when the wolves are out running with the moon. And as for your precious Liberals and Progressives—"

Cathy finally found her voice. "They're not *my* Progressives, damn you! Sure as hell not my *Liberals*. I despise Descroix and New Kiev and they return the sentiment—and you know it perfectly well! So—"

"From the highlands, woman!" This time, Jeremy made no attempt to imitate Zilwicki's voice. Which only made his roaring fury all the more evident. Cathy was shocked into silence.

"From the highlands," he repeated, hissing the words. He pointed a stiff finger at the richly-carpeted floor. "Not half an hour ago, as fine a man as you could ask for stood in this room and explained to you that he was quite prepared to cast over everything—*everything*, woman—career and respect and custom and propriety—life itself if need be, should the Queen choose to place his neck in a hangman's noose—and for what? A daughter? Yes, that—*and his own responsibility*."

He breathed deeply; once, twice. Then: "Years ago, I explained to a girl that she bore no guilt for what her class or nation might have done. But I'll tell the woman now—*again*—that she does bear responsibility for herself."

He glanced at the door. "You know I've never cared much for doctrine, Cathy, one way or the other. I'm a concrete sort of fellow. So even though I think 'Crown Loyalty' is about as stupid an ideology as I could imagine, I've got no problem with *that* man."

His eyes were fixed on her, hard as diamonds.

"So don't tell me that they're not *your* Liberals or *your* Progressives. That's ancient history, and damn it all. *Make* them yours—Lady Catherine Montaigne, Countess of the Tor. Whether you asked for that title or not, it is yours. The responsibility comes with it."

She avoided his gaze, hanging her head. Not with shame, simply with reluctance. Jeremy's eyes softened, and his humor returned. "Listen to me, Lady Prancer," he said softly. "It's time the filly finally re-entered the race. And no filly, now, but a true grande dame. You'll dazzle 'em, girl. I can hear the roar of the crowd already."

"Cut it out," she muttered. "New Kiev has a death lock on the Liberals."

"Not after Zilwicki's list gets made public!" cried Jeremy gleefully.

Cathy's eyes widened, and her head came up. Her mouth formed a perfect round O of surprise.

Jeremy laughed. "Are you *still* such a naif? Do you really think the only traffickers in human misery sit in the Conservative Association?"

O.

"You *are*! Ha!" Jeremy was back to cackling and hand-rubbing—the whole tiresome lot. "Oh, sure—New Kiev herself will be clean as a whistle. Descroix, too, most likely. But I'll bet you right now, Cathy—don't take the wager, I'll strip you of your entire fortune—that plenty of their closest associates will be standing hip deep in the muck. Won't be surprised if that whole stinking Houseman clan's in up to their necks—with each and every one of the self-righteous swine oinking sophisti-cated gobbledygook to explain why slavery isn't really slavery and everything's relative anyway."

O.

Cackle, cackle. "Bet on it! If anything, Zilwicki's list will hit the Liberals and the Progressives harder than the Conservatives. There won't be as many of them on the list, of course, but nobody expects anything more than piggishness from High Ridge and his crowd. But I do believe, once the rock's turned over, that we'll find the Liberals and Progressives have taken their holier-than-thou draft to the bank one too many times." Cackle, cackle. "Their ranks will be shaken to the core—in the Lords as much as the Commons. Bet on it!" His hand rubbing went into high gear. "Just the right time for *another* disgraced outcast to make her return. And demand her rightful place in the sun."

Cathy hissed. "I *hate* those people."

Jeremy shrugged. "Well, yes. Who in their right mind wouldn't? But look at it this way, Cathy—"

He spread his arms wide, theatrically. Christ on the Cross. "*I'm* giving up the pleasure of shooting each and every one of the slaving bastards. Justice before vengeance, alas. If I shoot even one of them they'll make *me* the issue. So you can console yourself, as you sit through endless hours of rancorous debate in the House of Lords, with the knowledge that you finally won me over to the tactics of nonviolence."

From his armchair, Isaac hissed. Still standing in crucifix position, Jeremy wiggled his fingers. "Only in the Star Kingdom, comrade. That still leaves us the Solarians and the Silesians for a hunting ground."

Cathy glared at him. "Aren't you forgetting something, you great political strategist?"

Jeremy dropped his arms. "Finding Zilwicki's daughter? *In the Loop?*"

He cocked his head at Isaac. Simultaneously, both men stuck out their tongues, showing the mark.

Like two cobras, spreading their hoods.

The Fifth Day

Helen

The first few hours of her escape were a nightmare. The world Helen had entered was lightless chaos, as if the primordial ylem were made of stone and dirt and refuse. She realized soon enough that she had entered some kind of interconnected pockets of open space, accidentally formed and molded over the centuries, branching off from each other with neither rhyme nor reason beyond the working of gravity on rubble and debris.

Branching off in *all* directions, to make it dangerous as well as confusing. Twice, within the first few minutes, she almost fell into suddenly yawning holes or crevasses. She wasn't sure which. Thereafter, she was careful to feel her way thoroughly before inching forward on her hands and knees.

Soon enough, those knees and hands were beginning to get bruised and scraped. The pain was not Helen's principal concern. Although Master Tye's syncretic regimen emphasized its philosophical and emotional aspects, it was still, when all was said and done, a school of the martial arts. So, like any such school which is not simply oriented to the tournament world, Master Tye had trained Helen in the various manners in which to handle pain.

Pain, thus, she could ignore. At least up to a point, but even for a fourteen-year-old girl that point was far beyond a matter of mere scrapes and bruises. What she *couldn't* ignore, however, was the fact that she would begin to leave a trail of blood. Not much of a trail, true, but a trail nonetheless. Soon enough her captors would discover her absence and begin a pursuit. Unlike her, they would undoubtedly have portable lamps to guide them in their path. They would be able to move much faster than she.

Seeing no option, she tore off the sleeves of her blouse and wrapped them around her hands. For a moment, she considered removing the blouse completely and using the rest of the material to protect her knees. But she decided, after a gingerly tactile inspection of her knees, that the tough material of her trousers would hold up for quite a bit longer.

That done, she resumed her slow progress, feeling her way in the dark.

She had no idea how long she spent in that horrid place before she finally saw a glimmer of light. Early on, she tried to count off the seconds, but she soon discovered that she needed all of her concentration to avoid injuries.

At first, she thought the light was nothing more than an optical illusion, her mind playing tricks on her. But, since there was no real reason to go in any other direction, she decided to crawl toward it. After a time, she realized that she was actually seeing something.

A powerful surge of relief swept over her. Of course, she had no idea if that source of light was a refuge. For all she knew, she had been crawling in circles and was headed back toward the tunnel she had made in her own cell. But by that point, she was desperate simply to be able to *see* something. *Anything*.

It proved to be the light cast through some kind of ancient aperture. A drain grille, she thought. But it was impossible to be sure. The metal which had once spanned that hole had long since rusted away. The reason she thought it had been a grille was because the area she was looking into, standing on tiptoe and peering over the bottom lip, seemed to be some kind of ancient aqueduct or storm drain. Or—

Yuck. A sewer.

But the distaste passed almost as soon as it arrived. Whatever that broad low channel was, lined with still-solid masonry on all sides, it was an escape route. Besides, even if it had once been a sewer, it hadn't been used as such in many centuries. Other than a small, sluggish little rill running down the center of the age-darkened channel, the aqueduct/storm drain/sewer was as dry as a bone.

Helen placed her water bottle and little packet of food on the ledge. Then, using her arm strength alone, she hauled herself into the opening. Most girls her age wouldn't have been able to manage that feat of sheer muscle power, but Helen was very strong. Once her head, shoulders and upper torso were onto the ledge, it was a quick matter to scramble—wriggle, rather—through the opening and slide down the sloping ceramacrete ramp beyond.

Except it wasn't ceramacrete, Helen realized as soon as she felt the roughness of the surface scratching at her. She wasn't sure what the masonry was, but she suspected it might be that ancient and primitive stuff called *concrete*. She felt like she was entering a pharaoh's tomb.

Once she got her feet under her, she reached back and hauled down the water bottle and the food packet. Then, wobbling a bit on unsteady legs, she began walking as quickly as she could along the narrow ledge which bordered the former water channel. Since she had no idea which direction to take, she simply decided to follow the lamps which periodically lined the passageway. The lamps were some kind of jury-rigged devices and were very infrequent in their placement. She would have thought the lighting was absolutely terrible if she hadn't spent hours in total darkness. But they seemed to be a little less sparse to her left, so that was the direction she took.

She was so relieved to finally be able to see where she was going that it wasn't until she had traveled perhaps three hundred yards, moving as quickly as she could while using a pace she could maintain for hours, that the obvious question sprang into her mind.

Jury-rigged lamps, in a long-unused passageway.

So jury-rigged by whom?

The answer came almost simultaneously with the question. She had been approaching a bend in the passageway when she recognized the puzzling nature of the lamps. She came to a complete halt, peering into the dimness beyond. Helen was aware, vaguely, that the Loop's long-forgotten subterranean passageways were reputed to be filled with all manner of dangers. She had simply not worried about it, since her captors had been a far more tangible menace. But now—

The lurkers apparently decided she had spotted

them, for within two seconds they were scrambling around the bend and racing toward her.

Shambling toward her, rather. After an instant's spike of fear, Helen saw that the three men approaching bore no resemblance whatsoever to her captors. *They* had strutted like leopards; *these* scurried like rats. Her abductors' clothing had been simple jumpsuits, but clean and well made. The creatures lurching toward her wore a pastiche of rags and filthy garments that were almost impossible to describe. And where her male captors had been clean-shaven and short-haired, these *things* looked more like shaggy apes than people.

Short, stooped apes, however. One of them was shouting something in a language she didn't recognize at all. The other two were simply leering. At least, Helen *thought* they were leering. It was hard to tell because of the beards.

Whatever. One thing was certain—they were not advancing with any friendly intent. And if tunnel rats are not leopards, they can still be dangerous.

Helen didn't even consider the narrow ledge. In that cramped space, the advantage would all be against her. For a moment, she thought of fleeing. She was pretty sure that she could outrun the three men, even burdened with a water bottle and a package of food. They were about as far removed from physically fit specimens of humanity as could be imagined.

But she discarded that idea almost instantly. For one thing, she didn't want to retrace her steps back in the direction of her captors. For another—

Even fourteen-year-old girls, pushed hard enough, can become enraged. She was *tired* of this crap!

Rage, of course, was the ultimate sin in Master

Tye's universe. So, as she sprang off the ledge and
half-ran, half-slid down the concrete slope to the flat
and wide expanse of the channel—fighting room—she
summoned his memory to her aid. *Breathing first.*

By the time Helen trotted down to the largest
dry space within reasonable range, carefully set the
water bottle and the food packet to one side, and
assumed the standing horse, the rage was harnessed
and shackled to her purpose.

Calmly, she waited, breathing steadily. Her three
assailants—there was no doubt about *that* any longer, not with one of them brandishing a club and
another holding a short length of rope—spread out
and advanced upon her.

Scuttled, say better. Helen's eyes remained fixed
on a blank space in her mind, but she absorbed the
way they moved, their balance—everything. By the
time the men began their charge, she had already
decided upon her course of action. Master Tye would
not have approved—*keep it simple, child*—but for all
Helen's control over her rage it was still there, burning at the center.

So the man facing her went down in a tangle,
his legs twisted and swept away by the Falling Leaf,
tripping his club-wielding companion. The one still
standing—the rope-holder—fell to the Sword and
Hammer, clutching his groin and bleating pain and
shock through a broken face. The bleating ended the
moment his buttocks hit the cement, as Helen's heel
completed the Scythe. A sturdier man would have
been stunned; his scrawny neck snapped like a twig.

The club-holder was starting to rise when the Owl
By Night crushed him from existence. Master Tye

would have scolded Helen for using that Owl—*keep it simple, child!*—but he could not have chided her for the execution. Beak and talons had all found their mark, and in just the proper sequence.

The man still alive joined his fellows in death three seconds later. Again, the Scythe; and again, the Scythe.

When it was over, Helen fought for breath. Not because she was winded, but simply because her mind was reeling from the destruction. She had practiced those maneuvers a thousand times—for years, now, against padded and armored opponents—but had never really quite believed—

Nausea came, was driven down. Rage and terror also. She fought and fought for her center.

Breathing first. Breathing first.

Kevin

When Usher let himself into the hotel room in the Loop which Victor had rented for that night, the young SS officer was asleep. Seeing Cachat's fully-clothed form lying on the room's only bed next to Ginny, Usher grinned. The first night Victor had rented a hotel room for his new "debauched habits," he had insisted on sleeping on the floor.

Usher glanced at the table in the room. Clearly enough, Victor and Ginny had spent the previous evening playing cards. If Kevin knew his wife—and he did—Ginny would have teased Victor by suggesting a game of strip poker. Seeing the lay of the final hands, Kevin's face twisted into a moment's derision.

Gin rummy, for God's sake.

But there was no real sarcasm in it. And, as his eyes moved back to the sleeping form of the young officer, Kevin Usher's expression took on something which might almost be called paternalism. In truth, in the past few days, he had become quite fond of Victor Cachat. He even had hopes of awakening the wit which he was certain lay buried somewhere inside that solemn young soul.

But first, he's got to learn not to sleep so soundly.

Kevin's method for teaching that lesson was abrupt and effective. After Victor lurched upright, gasping and wiping the glassful of cold water off his face, he stared bleary-eyed at the culprit. Next to him, Ginny murmured something and rolled over, her own eyes opening more slowly.

"Up, young Cachat!" commanded Usher. "The game is afoot!"

As usual, the classical allusion went right over Victor's head. Kevin snorted again.

"You're hopeless," he growled. Kevin pointed an accusing finger at his wife. Ginny, like Victor, had been sleeping in her clothes.

"I'm not a cuckold *yet*? What is *wrong* with you, Cachat?"

Victor scowled. "That wasn't funny yesterday either, Kevin." Then, seeing the grin on the citizen colonel's face, Victor's eyes widened.

"Something's happened. What?"

Kevin shook his head. "Not sure exactly. But Gironde just called and told me Manpower's headquarters suddenly came alive last night. Busy as ants in the middle of the night they are, over there. I'll bet damn near anything Durkheim's scheme just fell apart at the seams."

Confused, Victor shook his head. "Citizen Major Gironde? He's in the SS. Why is he calling you? And what's he doing watching the Mesans anyway? Durkheim assigned him to—"

He clamped his jaws shut, almost with a snap. Kevin smiled, and sat down at the card table. "Good, lad," he murmured. "Remember: the map is not the territory. The file is not the man."

Victor replied with a murmur himself, quoting one of Kevin's own maxims: "'And there's nobody easier to outmaneuver than a maneuverer.'"

"Exactly," said Kevin. His eyes went to the only window in the room. It was a small window; grimy as only a cheap Loop hotel window ever gets. The view beyond was completely obscured, which was not the least of the reasons Kevin had insisted on a hotel in the Loop. Windows which can't be seen out of can't be seen into either. Not, at least, without specialized equipment.

Of course, the SS detachment on Terra *had* such equipment—and plenty of it. But the equipment was under the control of an SS officer and couldn't be checked out without his permission. A certain Citizen Major Gironde, as it happened.

"Dollars to donuts," Kevin mused, "the girl escaped. I can't think of anything else right now that would stir up Manpower's headquarters. Not in the middle of the night, anyway."

Victor was confused again. "What are 'dollars'? And 'donuts'?"

"Never mind, lad," replied Kevin, shaking his head. "Are you ready?"

Classical allusions might have been above Victor's

head, but the last question wasn't. Instantly, his face
was set in stone, hard and firm as unyielding granite.

By now, Ginny was lying half-erect on her elbow,
her cheek nestled in the palm of her hand. She gazed
up at Victor's face admiringly. "Anybody ever mention
you'd make a great poster boy for an SS recruitment
drive?"

Ginny's repartee usually left Victor confused and
embarrassed. But not this time.

Hard; firm—unyielding as granite.

Durkheim

Durkheim was awakened by the insistent ring of the
communicator. Silently, he cursed the Mesan idiots
who were careless enough to call him at his own
residence. Granted, the communicator was a special
one, carefully scrambled. Still—

He only spent a few seconds on that curse, however. Soon enough, he had other things to curse the
Mesans for—and not silently.

*What did you expect—you morons!—using Scrags? I
can't believe anyone would be stupid enough to think—*

But he didn't indulge himself for very long in that
pointless exercise. For one thing, the Mesan on the
other end was indifferent to his outrage. For another,
Durkheim himself had always understood that his plan
was too intricate to be sure of success. So, from the
very beginning, he had designed a fallback.

After breaking off his contact with the Mesan,
Durkheim spent an hour or so staring at the ceiling
of his bedroom. He didn't bother to turn on a light.

He found the darkness helpful in concentrating his attention, as he carefully went over every step of his next maneuver.

Then, satisfied that it would work, he even managed to get some sleep. Not much, unfortunately. The problem wasn't that Durkheim couldn't get to sleep—he'd never had any trouble doing that—but simply that he had to reset the alarm to a much earlier hour. He would have to be at work by the crack of dawn, in order to have everything in place.

Helen

It didn't take Helen long to find the lair of her three would-be assailants, even moving as carefully as she was. The place was less than a hundred yards distant, just around the bend in the channel.

She spent five minutes studying it, before she crept forward. The "lair" was just that—a habitation fit more for animals than men. The lean-to propped against the sloping wall of the channel reminded her of a bird's nest. Made by a very large and very careless bird. The shack—even that term was too grandiose—had been assembled from various pieces of wreckage and debris, lashed together with an assortment of wire and cordage. At its highest, it was not tall enough for even a short adult to stand up. From one end to the other, it measured not more than fifteen feet. There was no opening at her end, so Helen supposed that whatever entrance existed was on the opposite side.

She hesitated, but not for long. Her water was getting low and so, soon enough, would her food.

There might well be something in that lean-to, however unpalatable. Besides, she had no choice but to go past it—unless she wanted to retrace her steps back toward her captors—and so she might as well investigate it along the way.

The decision made, she moved quickly, racing toward the lean-to on quick and almost silent feet. If there were more men lurking within, she saw no reason to give them any more warning than necessary. One or two, she was certain she could handle. More than that, she could outrun them.

But there were no men in the lair to pose any danger to her. Instead there was something infinitely more dangerous—a moral dilemma.

The boy, she thought, was probably not more than twelve years old. Hard to tell, due to his bruises and emaciation under the rags. The girl was perhaps Helen's own age. But that was even harder to determine, despite the fact that she wore no clothing at all. The girl didn't have bruises so much as she seemed a single giant bruise.

Helen removed the filthy blanket and gave the girl a quick examination. The examination, for all its brevity, was both thorough and fairly expert. Her father had also seen to it that Helen received first aid instruction.

When she was done, and despite her recognition that an immense complication had just entered her life, Helen felt relieved. Immensely relieved, in truth. Less than half an hour earlier, for the first time in her life, she had killed people. Despite her concentration on her own predicament, some part of Helen's soul had been shrieking ever since. Now, it was silent.

Silent and calm. If ever men had deserved killing, those men had.

Since she entered the lean-to, the boy had huddled silently against one side, staring at her with eyes as wide as saucers. Finally, he spoke.

"You won't hurt my sister, will you?" he whispered. His pale eyes moved to the battered figure lying on the pallet. The girl, for her part, was conscious. But she was just staring at Helen through slitted eyes, as if she were blinded by the light. "I don't think Berry can take much more hurting."

He started to cry. "I don't know how long we've been here. It seems like forever since they caught us. We were just looking for food. We weren't going to steal any from them, honest. I tried to tell them."

Helen heard the girl whisper something. She leaned over.

"Go away," were the words. "They'll come back soon."

Helen shook her head. "They're dead. I killed them."

The girl's eyes popped open. "That's a lie," she whispered. "Why are you lying?"

Helen looked at the boy. "What's your name?"

"Larens. People call me Lars."

Helen jerked her head. "Go down the channel, Lars." She pointed the direction. "That way. Just around the bend."

He didn't hesitate for more than a few seconds. Then, scurrying like a mouse, he scrambled out of the lean-to. While she waited for him to return, Helen did what she could to help Berry. Which wasn't much, beyond digging out some food and wiping off the grime with the cleanest rag she could find.

Fortunately, while Helen didn't find much food there were enough water bottles that she was able to use some of it to wet the rag.

Throughout, other than an occasional hiss when Helen rubbed over a particularly sore spot, Berry kept silent. The girl was obviously weak, but Helen's principal fear—that the girl's wits were gone—soon proved false. As best as she could, given her condition, Berry tried to help by moving her limbs and torso to accept the rag.

Still, it was obvious that the girl was in no condition to walk. Helen wondered what was taking Lars so long to return. But while she waited she started assembling the makings of a stretcher. Or, at least, a travois—she wasn't sure Lars would be strong enough to hold up his end of the thing.

"What are you doing?" whispered Berry, watching Helen dismantle part of the lean-to. Helen had found two rods which she thought would make a suitable frame. She had no idea what they had been originally, nor even what they were made of. Some kind of artificial substance she didn't recognize. But, for all that they were a bit more flexible than she would have liked, they were about the right length and, she thought—hoped—strong enough.

"We've got to get out of here," Helen explained. "There are some people chasing after me. Just as bad as those three. Worse, probably."

That news caused Berry to sit erect. Try to, at least. The effort was too much for her. But, again, she gave evidence that her mind was still intact.

"If you—you and Lars—can get us maybe two hundred yards, there's a crossover to another channel. And after that—not far—there's another. That one leads up, and then down. That'll be hard. I'll try to walk, but you'll probably have to carry me. But if we can get down there it's the perfect place to hide."

For a moment, something like pride seem to come into the battered face. "That's my secret place. Mine and Lars'." Softly: "It's a special place."

Helen had already decided that she would have to take the two children with her. In truth, the "decision" had come automatically—even though she understood that she was almost certainly ruining her chances of escape. Now, for the first time, she realized that Lars and Berry would be an asset as well as a liability. She was quite certain that they were two of the small horde of vagrant children who were reputed to dwell in the lower reaches of the Loop. Castoffs of castoffs. They would know the area—their part of it, at least—as well as mice know their cubbyholes and hideaways. Helen would be moving slower, but at least she would no longer be moving blind.

She heard Lars re-entering the lean-to.

"What took so—"

She closed her mouth, seeing the object Lars was gripping. She recognized the knife. It had belonged to one of her assailants. Lars had apparently wiped it off, but the blade was still streaked with drying blood.

Lars' eyes were bright and eager. On his hands and knees, he scurried over to his sister and showed her the knife.

"Look, Berry—it's true! They can't ever hurt you again." He gave Helen an apologetic glance. "I think they were already dead. But I made good and sure."

Berry managed to lift her head and stare at the knife. Then, smiling for the first time since Helen had met her, she laid her head back down. "Thank you, brother," she whispered. "But now we have to help Helen go away to our special place. There are more men coming to hurt her."

Less than ten minutes later, they were on their way. Lars, somewhat to Helen's surprise, proved strong enough—or determined enough—to carry his end of the stretcher. He had trouble at first because he refused to relinquish the knife. But, soon enough, he discovered the obvious place to carry it.

As they stumbled as quickly as they could down the channel, Helen found it hard not to laugh. She'd read about it, of course, in her beloved adventure books. But she'd never actually thought to *meet* one—especially twelve years old! A pirate, by God, with the blade clenched between his teeth to prove it.

Suddenly, she felt better than she had since she was first abducted. She actually had to restrain herself from whooping with glee.

Durkheim

Victor Cachat reported to work as early as ever the next morning, Durkheim noted. The young officer's new found vice hadn't affected him that much, apparently. Quite the little whore-chaser the boy had turned into, according to the reports.

But Durkheim didn't let any of his amusement show when he summoned Cachat into his office, immediately upon his arrival.

"We've got a problem," the SS commander snapped. "And I need you to fix it."

●　　●　　●

In the time that followed, as Durkheim spun his tale and elaborated his instructions, Victor Cachat leaned forward in his chair and listened attentively. Durkheim, though not generally given to humor, almost found himself laughing. Cachat could have made an ideal poster boy for an SS recruitment drive. *Young and earnest officer of the Revolution, eager and willing to do his duty.*

And though Durkheim noticed the hard, dark gleam in the eyes of the officer across the desk from him, he thought nothing of it. Simply the natural ruthlessness of a young zealot. Ready, at an instant's notice, to strike down the enemies of the Revolution with neither pity nor remorse.

Anton

By the time Anton reached the rendezvous, he was utterly lost. Not in the sense that he had any trouble following the directions given to him by Lady Catherine's messenger. Anton had years of experience finding his way through the three-dimensional maze of giant warships under construction, guided by nothing more than blueprints or verbal instructions. But when he walked through the door of the small coffeehouse at the end of an alley in the Old Quarter, he couldn't for the life of him have told anyone if he was headed north, east, south or west. He *thought* he still knew up from down, but he was beginning to wonder about that.

He wasn't entirely pleased, then, to see Robert Tye

bestowing upon him that particularly obnoxious grin by which the expert greets the tyro. Tye had taken a different route than he. But, though they had left at the same time, it was obvious the old martial artist had been comfortably ensconced on his seat at the table for quite some time.

But Anton didn't give Tye much more than a sour glance as he strode up to the table. His attention was riveted on the other two people sitting there. In the case of one, because he was fascinated. In the case of the other, because he was flabbergasted—even outraged.

"What are you doing here?" he demanded. "Lady Catherine," he added, a bit lamely.

Cathy started to bridle, but Jeremy cut her off.

"Didn't I say it?" he remarked cheerfully. "The good Captain's sweet on you, girl."

That remark caused both Anton and Cathy to choke off whatever words they had been about to speak and glare at Jeremy. The ex-slave bore up under the burden with no apparent effort.

"Those who speak the truth are always despised," he added, turning to Robert. "Isn't that so?"

Tye said nothing, but the smile on his face as he reached for his coffee indicated his full agreement. Anton and Cathy looked back at each other. Cathy seemed to flush a bit. Anton didn't—his complexion was quite a bit darker than her ivory pale skin—but he did straighten stiffly and clear his throat.

"I am simply concerned for the Countess' safety," he pronounced.

"Isn't that what I just said?" asked Jeremy. "Why else would a proper Gryphon highlander give a damn about the well-being of an idle parasite?" He cocked an eye at Cathy. "Well... parasite, at least. You can hardly accuse the lady of being idle."

Anton restrained his temper. Partly, by reminding himself of his daughter. Partly—

Damn the imp, anyway! But there was a trace of humor lurking under the irritation. Anton could not deny that the impudent little man—like a sprite, he was, both in size and demeanor—had cut rather close to the truth.

Bull's-eye, actually, admitted Anton, as his eyes moved back to the countess. This morning, Cathy was not wearing an expensive gown made of thin material. She was dressed in much heavier garments—pants and a long-sleeved shirt—suitable for outdoor hiking. The outfit was obviously well-used and fitted her comfortably.

Cathy, Anton knew, was in her fifties. But she was a third-generation prolong, with the youthful appearance that such people carried for decades. Although most people would have said her outfit did nothing for her tall, slim figure, Anton thought it made her perhaps even more appealing than the gown she had been wearing the previous evening. The practical clothing fit her plain, open face to perfection. Young, healthy, vigorous—a woman who enjoyed life to the fullest.

He found himself swallowing, and groping for words. "I *am* concerned, Cathy," he muttered. "This is likely to be dangerous."

"Not for the two of you," announced Jeremy. "And her presence here is essential anyway." He gestured politely to the remaining chair at the table. "Sit, Captain Zilwicki. There is news—and a change in plans."

That announcement drove all other thoughts out of

Anton's mind. He slid into the chair and leaned over the table, planting his hands on the edge. "What news?" His enormous shoulders, hunched with apprehension, made his square and blocky head look like a boulder perched atop a small mountain.

Finally, Jeremy's grin went away, replaced by a much kindlier smile. "Good news, Captain. For now, at least. Your daughter has escaped her captors."

Anton had been holding his breath. Now, he let it out in a rush.

"Where is she?" he demanded, half-rising. He had to restrain himself from reaching across the table and shaking the answer from Jeremy. Fortunately, years of habit as an intelligence officer did not completely desert him. His was the one trade which, along with philosophers, always understood the precedence of epistemology.

So, after a moment, Anton lowered himself slowly back into the chair. "How do you know?" he demanded.

Still smiling, Jeremy shook his head. "I'll not give you an answer to that question, Captain. Not that I don't trust you, of course." The impish grin made its reappearance. "Heavens, no! But after this is all over, I'm afraid you might remember that you are an officer in Her Majesty's Royal Manticoran Navy and feel compelled to strike a blow on your Queen's behalf."

Jeremy was not the first person who had underestimated the intelligence hidden beneath the Gryphon highlander's thick-headed appearance. It did not take Anton more than five seconds to make the connections.

"I was right," he stated flatly. He glanced at Cathy. "You told him our conversation?"

She nodded. Now it was Anton's turn to bestow a grin

on Jeremy. And if his grin could hardly be called impish, it had something of the same devilish humor in it.

"It *was* a rogue Peep operation. And you've been
in touch with the Peeps. The ones who aren't pleased
with the rogue."

Jeremy started. Something in the expression on his
face led Anton immediately to a further conclusion.

"No," he rumbled. "I've got it backwards. The
operation was outside of normal channels, but it
was no rogue who ordered it." His grin was now
utterly humorless. A murderous grin, in truth. "It was
Durkheim, wasn't it? That stinking pig. And the ones
you have contact with are the real rogues."

There was no expression at all on Jeremy's face.
His pale gray eyes, staring at Anton, were as flat as
iron plates. Slowly, he swiveled his head and looked
at Cathy.

"Tell me again," he rasped.

"You're too fucking smart for your own good,"
she snickered. She beamed upon Anton. "He's such
a clever little man. But he always has to poke the
wild animals, and sometimes he forgets to use a long
enough stick." Her smile was very approving. Very
warm, in fact. "Congratulations, Anton. It's nice to
see him get bitten for a change."

"The reminder was good enough," rasped Jeremy.
"I don't need the whole song and dance."

"Yes, you do," retorted Cathy forcefully.

Jeremy ignored her. He was back to staring at Anton
with those flat, flat eyes. Suddenly, Anton was reminded
that Jeremy X, whatever impish exterior he chose to
project, was also one of the galaxy's deadliest men.

For a moment, he began to utter some sort of

reassurance. But then, moved by his innate stubbornness and his own cold fury, he bit back the words and simply returned the stare with one of his own. Which, if it was not exactly ruthless, also indicated that he was not a man who intimidated easily, if at all.

Anton heard Cathy suck in a breath. In his peripheral vision, he saw Robert Tye's sudden stillness. But his eyes never left Jeremy's.

And then, after perhaps three seconds, the moment passed. Depth seemed to return to Jeremy's gaze, and the little man leaned back in his chair.

"Ah, but you wouldn't, Captain. Would you, now? It's that highland sense of honor moves you. You'd keep the knowledge that there was an opposition amongst the Peeps to yourself, and not pass it on to your superiors."

Anton snorted. "We've known for years that there was disaffection among the Havenites."

Jeremy's gaze didn't waver. After a moment, Anton looked away. "But, yeah, this is the first time there's ever been any concrete indication that it extends into SS. And the first time—given the relatively small size of the Peep contingent here—that we could probably pinpoint the individuals."

He drew in a deep breath, swelling his chest and squaring his shoulders. Then: "From the highlands, as you say."

"A life for a life, Captain," said Jeremy softly.

Anton understood the obscure reference at once. For some reason, that made him feel oddly warmhearted toward the man across the table from him. A *concrete* sort of fellow. Much like himself, whatever other differences separated them.

"Yes," he murmured. "The daughter for the mother, and I'll take the knowledge to the grave."

Jeremy nodded solemnly. "Good enough." And now he was back to being the imp. "And good it is, boyo! Because it'll be those selfsame wretched rotten Peeps who'll get your daughter. Not you or me."

Anton goggled him.

Imp. "Oh, yes—for a certainty. We've other fish to fry." Goggled him.

Damned imp. "But it's as plain as the nose on your face, man! They can get close to her, through the manhunt. Girlhunt, I should say. We can't."

Anton was clenching his fists. "Then *what*—"

Jeremy shook his head. "And to think he was so shrewd not a moment ago. Think it through, Captain. The rotten wretched Peeps—*Peep*, I should say—can *get* the girl. But that's not to say he can get her *out.*"

Again, it didn't take Anton more than a few seconds to make all the connections. He turned his head and gazed at Cathy.

"And that's why you're here. To distract them, while"—a stubby forefinger shot out from his fist, pointing at Jeremy—"he settles his accounts."

"Long overdue accounts," murmured Jeremy. The flat, flat eyes were back.

Anton leaned back in his chair, pressing himself against the table with the heels of his hands. Slowly, the fists opened.

"That'll work," he announced. "If the Peep's good enough, at least."

Jeremy shrugged. "Don't imagine he's really all that *good*. But he doesn't have to be, now does he, Captain? Just *determined* enough."

Helen

Not for the first time, Helen bitterly regretted the loss of her watch. She had no idea how long it took her and her two companions to finally make their way into Berry's "special place." Hours, for a certainty—many hours. Just as Berry had feared, making the upward climb—and, even more so, the later descent—had been extremely difficult. Berry, for all that she had tried heroically, had simply been too injured and feeble to make it on her own. And her brother, for all his own valiant efforts, too small and weak to be of much assistance. So, for all practical purposes, Helen had been forced to make what would have been an arduous enough trip for herself burdened by the weight of another strapped to her back.

By the time they finally got to their destination, she was more exhausted than she had ever been in her life. If it hadn't been for the years she had spent in Master Tye's rigorous training, she knew she would never have made it at all.

Vaguely, with fatigue-induced lightheadedness, she tried to examine her surroundings. But it was almost impossible to see anything. The two small lanterns they had taken with them from the vagabonds' lean-to were too feeble to provide much illumination.

They were resting on a large pallet under a lean-to. Both the pallet and the lean-to, Lars told her, had been built by him and his sister after their mother disappeared (some unspecified time since—months ago, Helen judged) and they had found this place. The lean-to nestled against some sort of ancient stone staircase. It was the buttress of the staircase, actually.

They had come down very wide stairs to a platform, where the stairs branched at right angles to either side. At Berry's command, Helen had taken the left branch and then, at the bottom, curled back to the right. There, thankfully, she had found the lean-to and finally been able to rest.

Now, lying exhausted on the pallet, Berry nestled against her right side. A moment later, dragging a tattered and filthy blanket out of the semi-darkness, Lars spread it over them. A moment later, he was nestled against Helen's left.

Helen whispered her thanks. She didn't really need the blanket for warmth. In the depths of the Loop, the temperature never seemed to vary beyond a narrow range, which was quite comfortable. But there was something primordially comforting about being under that sheltering cover, even as filthy as it was.

No filthier than me! she thought, half-humorously. *What I wouldn't give for a shower!*

But that thought drew her perilously close to thoughts of her father and their warm apartment. Always warm, that apartment had been. Not so much in terms of physical temperature—in truth, her father preferred to keep the climate settings rather low—but in terms of the heart.

Oh, Daddy!

Summoning what strength remained, Helen drove the thought away. She could not afford that weakening. Not now. But, as it fled, some residue of the thought remained. And Helen realized, as she lay there in the darkness cuddling two new-found children of her own, that she finally understood her father. Understood, for the first time, how courageously he had struggled, all those years, not to let his own loss mangle his daughter. And how much love there must have been in his marriage, to have given him that strength. Where another man, a weaker man, might have felt himself weakened further by his wife's self-sacrifice, her father had simply drawn more strength from it.

People had misunderstood him, she now realized—she as much as any. They had ascribed his stoicism to simple stolidity. The resistance of a Gryphon mountain to the flails of nature, bearing up under wind and rain and lightning with the endurance of rock. They had forgotten that mountains are not passive things. Mountains are *shaped*, forged, in the fiery furnace. They do not simply "bear up"—they *rise* up, driven by the mightiest forces of a planet. The stone face had been shaped by a beating heart.

Oh, Daddy... She drifted off to sleep, as if she were lying on a continent rather than a pallet. Secure and safe, not in her situation, but in the certainty of stone itself. Her father would find her, soon enough. Of that she had no doubt at all.

Stone *moves*.

The Sixth Day

Victor

When they found the bodies, Victor had to restrain himself from grinning. Whoever had cut the three men had done so with as much enthusiasm as lack of skill. So far as Victor knew, there was no antonym for the word "surgical." But if there was such a term, the half-severed heads of the wretched vagabonds lying sprawled in the middle of the dry channel exemplified it perfectly.

The small mob of Scrags accompanying Victor and his squad of SS troopers were convinced that the girl had done it. And *that* was the source of Victor's humor. He wasn't sure what amused him the most: their fury, their bewilderment, or—the most likely source—their obvious relief. As in: *There but for the grace of God ...*

There was more ferocity than genuine humor in Victor's suppressed grin. The Scrags were notorious, among other things—the females as much as the males—for their predatory sexual habits. Victor had no doubt at all that they had planned to rape the Zilwicki girl when her immediate purpose was served. Before killing her.

Now, looking at the corpses, the thoughts of the Scrags were not hard to read. *Easier said than done ...*

Victor leaned over the sergeant's shoulder. "And?" he asked.

Citizen Sergeant Kurt Fallon shook his head. "I don't think it was the girl cut 'em, sir." He pointed to the small pools of blood which had spread out from the wounds. The blood was dry and covered with insects, as were the corpses themselves. "They didn't bleed much, as you can see. Not for those kinds of wounds. She couldn't have cut 'em any time soon after she killed 'em. And why would she wait?"

"*Did* she kill them?" asked Victor.

Fallon nodded, pointing to the small tracking device in his left hand. Victor was unable to interpret the readings on the screen. The chemo-hormone sensor was a highly specialized piece of equipment. As rare as it was expensive. That was the reason, Durkheim had told Victor, that he was assigning Fallon to the squad. The citizen sergeant was an expert with the device.

"Her traces are all over them," said Fallon. "Adrenaline reading's practically off the scale. That means either fear or fury—or both—and as you can see..." He shrugged. "She didn't have much to fear. Besides—"

He pointed to the head of one of the corpses. The filthy, bearded thing was unnaturally twisted. "Broke neck." He pointed to another. "Same." Then, at the third, whose throat had clearly been crushed as well as slit. "And again."

Fallon rose. "Didn't know the girl had training, but that's what you're seeing." He studied the sensor screen. "But there's someone else's readings here, too. Besides her and the croaks. Male readings. Prepubescent, I'm pretty sure."

Victor glanced around. The Scrags had now collected in a body around them, staring at the tracker in the sergeant's hand. For all their strutting swagger, and their pretensions at superhuman status, the Scrags were really nothing much more than Loop vagabonds themselves. They were clearly intimidated by the technical capacity of the SS device. During the hours in which they had organized a search for the girl after discovering her escape, before they finally admitted their screw-up to their Mesan overlords, the Scrags had accomplished absolutely nothing. After they found the bodies and the lean-to, the girl's trail seemed to have vanished.

"Can we follow her?" Victor asked. "Or *them?*"

Fallon nodded. "Oh, sure. Nothing to it. Won't be quick, of course. But—" He cast a sour glance at the nearby Scrags. "Since they at least had the sense to come to us before too much time had gone by, the traces are still good. Another couple of days, and it would have been a different story."

"Let's to it, then."

They set off, following the traces picked up by the sensor. Victor and Citizen Sergeant Fallon led the way, flanked by the other three SS soldiers in Fallon's squad. Victor and Fallon didn't bother carrying their weapons to hand. The other SS soldiers did, but they held the pulse rifles in a loose and easy grip. The Scrags trailed behind, with their own haphazard weaponry. For all the bravado with which they brandished the guns, they reminded Victor of nothing so much as a flock of buzzards following a pack of wolves.

He glanced sideways at Fallon. The citizen sergeant was too preoccupied with reading the tracker to notice the scrutiny. There was no expression on his lean-jawed, hatchet face beyond intense concentration.

Like a hawk on the prowl. Which, Victor knew, was an apt comparison. Fallon *was* a raptor—and he was hunting bigger prey than a fourteen-year-old girl.

And that, of course, was the other reason Durkheim had assigned Fallon and his squad to Victor. The hatchet-faced man was a hatchetman in truth. And Victor's neck was the target of his blade.

Anton

As he watched the rally, Anton was struck by the irony of his situation. He really didn't approve of this kind of gathering. For all the stiff-necked belligerence of Gryphon's yeomanry toward nobility, the highlanders were very far from being political radicals. They were a conservative lot, when all was said and done. That was especially true of the large percentage—perhaps a third of the population—which belonged to the Second Reformation Roman Catholic Church, a sect which retained its ancient attitude of reverence for monarchy and obedience to authority in general.

Anton himself had been raised in that creed. And if his continued membership as an adult was more a cultural than a religious habit—his basso was much sought after by church choirs, and he enjoyed singing himself—his career as a naval officer had done nothing to weaken his traditional political attitudes. *A strong monarchy resting on a stout yeomanry*—that was Moses and the prophets, for Gryphon highlanders. Their quarrel with the nobility was, in a sense, the opposite of radicalism. It was Gryphon's *nobles*, after all—not the commoners—who were continually seeking to subvert the established order.

So, watching the huge crowd of poor immigrants who were packed into the amphitheater, applauding the firebrand speakers and chanting distinctly anti-establishment slogans, Anton felt a bit like a church deacon trapped in a sinners' convention. That was all the more so since the rally's hidden purpose was directly bound up with the scheme to rescue his daughter. In a certain sense, *he* was responsible for this disreputable and unseemly affair.

Something of his discomfort must have shown in his posture. Sitting on one of the benches next to him, far up in the galleries, Robert Tye leaned over and whispered: "I'm told this sort of thing is contagious. Spreads like an aerosol, I believe."

Anton gave him an acerbic glance. Tye responded with a sly smile. "But perhaps not, in your case," he murmured, straightening back up. "'My strength is as the strength of ten, because my heart is royalist.'"

Anton ignored the jibe. On the podium far below, he could see that Cathy was next in line for the speaker's dais. He thought so, at least, from the way she was fidgeting in her chair and hurriedly scanning through her handwritten notes.

Anton had to force *himself* not to fidget. In his case, the problem was not nervousness so much as the fact that he was torn by conflicting impulses. On the one hand, Anton was fascinated by the prospect of finally hearing Cathy speak in public. Even as a young woman in the Manticoran House of Lords, the Countess of the Tor had been a famous orator. Notorious, it might be better to say. From what he had learned since he arrived on Terra, her reputation had not declined in exile. Rather the contrary.

On the other hand—

Anton took a deep breath and let it out slowly. His lips quirked in a wry smile of self-deprecation.

Leave it to a thick-skulled highlander to get infatuated with a damned wild-eyed radical! What the hell is wrong with me?

Trying to distract himself, Anton let his gaze roam the amphitheater. "Soldier Field," it was called, a name whose original meaning was long-forgotten, buried under the rubble of Chicago's fabled millennia. The structure was so ancient that here and there Anton could even see a few patches of that incredibly primitive construction material called *cement*.

Over the centuries, of course, the original shell of

the amphitheater had been rebuilt and rehabilitated time after time. In a way, there was something almost mystical about the place. There was nothing much left of the original gathering area except the space itself. The material components which encapsulated that large and empty cyst buried deep below the modern city's surface had changed time and again, as the millennia crept forward. But the emptiness always remained, as if the spirits of the people who filled it—forgotten ghosts, most of them—kept the city's encroachment at bay.

Here, over the centuries, Chicago's outcasts had come, time and again, to voice their grievances and air their complaints. And mostly, Anton suspected, just to be able to look around the one place in the Old Quarter which was *not* cramped and crooked. The one place where the masses who swarmed in the city's ghetto could actually *see* themselves, and see their number.

An incredible number, in truth. Given that the rally had been literally organized on a moment's notice, he was astonished by the size of the crowd. Anton had no idea how many people were packed into the amphitheater, but he was certain that the figure was in the tens of thousands.

All of whom, at that moment, roared their approval of the speaker's concluding slogan. Anton winced, as much from the sheer aural impact as the content of the slogan itself.

Self-determination! Ha! He enjoyed sour thoughts, for a few seconds, of how that principle might be applied by the notoriously cantankerous and particu-laristic highlanders of his youth. *Every hill a kingdom, every hollow a realm!*

Sheer nonsense. *The crown welds the nation, and that's that. Otherwise—chaos.*

But he left off the rumination. Cathy had risen from her chair and was advancing toward the podium in her characteristically jerky and high-stepping gait. She reminded Anton of a young racing horse approaching the starting gate.

He braced himself. *Oh, well,* he thought, *it'll all be for the best, once I hear her prattling nonsense. Let this idiot infatuation be dispelled.*

His military training recognized the subtle but ferocious security which protected the Countess of the Tor. Anton spotted Isaac immediately, standing at the foot of the speaker's platform. Cathy's "butler"—who was actually her chief bodyguard—had his back turned toward her. His attention was entirely given to the crowd packed near the podium. Within seconds, Anton spotted several other people maintaining a similar stance. He recognized none of them, but he knew that they were all either members of the Audubon Ballroom or other organizations of Mesan ex-slaves in alliance with the Ballroom.

The sight made him relax a bit. The genetic slaves who escaped from Manpower's grip and made their way to the Loop were the lowest of the low, by the standards of Solarian society. For all the League's official egalitarianism, there was a taint which was attached to those genetically manipulated people. *Subhumans,* they were often called in private.

The Old Quarter's other immigrants—who constituted, of course, a vastly larger body of people than the ex-Mesans—were by no means immune to that bigotry. Indeed, some of them would express it more openly and crudely than any member of the genteel upper crust. But if those immigrants shared the general attitude that the ex-slaves were the lowest of the low, they also understood—from close and sometimes bitter experience—that there was a corollary.

The hardest of the hard. Not all of the blows which Jeremy X and his comrades struck fell on the rich and powerful. A time had been, once, and not so many years ago, when a Mesan ex-slave had to fear pogroms and lynchings in the Old Quarter. The Audubon Ballroom had put a stop to that, as savagely as they felt it necessary.

Cathy reached the podium and began to speak. Her words, amplified by the electronic devices built within the speaker's stand, brought instant silence to the entire amphitheater.

Anton was impressed. The immigrants who lived in the Loop were drawn from dozens of the Solarian League's so-called "protectorate worlds." Most of them subscribed to a general principle of solidarity among the downtrodden, but that unity was riven—fractured, often enough—by a multitude of political differences and cultural animosities. No one had tried to shout down the previous speakers, representing one or another of the various groups which had agreed to sponsor this rally. But neither had they felt constrained to listen quietly. Cathy was the first speaker who was getting the huge crowd's undivided attention.

In truth, Anton was not simply impressed—he was a bit shocked. He had known, abstractly, that Cathy had the authority to call for such a rally on a moment's notice. Or so, at least, Jeremy X had claimed when he laid out his plans for Helen's rescue in the coffeehouse. But seeing that authority manifested in the concrete was an altogether different experience.

How does she do it? he wondered. *She's not even from the League, much less one of its protectorates. For God's sake, the woman's a foreign aristocrat!*

Cathy began to speak, and Anton began to understand. Slowly and grudgingly, of course—except for that part of him which realized, with deepening shock, that his ridiculous infatuation was not about to go away.

Part of it, he decided, was precisely *because* she was a Manticoran aristocrat. If the Star Kingdom had a certain reputation for arrogance and snobbery among the huge population of the Solarian League, it also had a reputation for—to a degree, at least—living up to its own standards. Quite unlike, in that respect, the officially egalitarian standards of the League itself. The Sollie upper crust and the comfortable middle classes on the Core Worlds could prattle all they wanted about democracy and equality, and sneer at the "reactionary semi-feudalism" of the Star Kingdom. The immigrants packed into that amphitheater knew the truth.

In the far-off and distant protectorate worlds from which they had come—fled, rather—the iron fist within the Sollie velvet glove was bare and naked. The protectorate worlds were ruled by the League's massive bureaucracy, whose institutional indifference was married to the avarice of the League's giant commercial interests. If none of those protectorate worlds was precisely a hell-hole, a modern equivalent of the King Leopold's Congo of ancient legend, they *did* bear a close resemblance to what had once been called "banana republics" and "company towns." *Neocolonialism*, many of the previous speakers had called it, and even Anton did not disagree with that characterization.

There was nothing of that nature within the Star Kingdom. Anton himself, as a Gryphon highlander, could attest to that. The conflict between Gryphon's yeomanry and its aristocracy was the closest the Star Kingdom had ever come to that kind of open class war. And that conflict paled in comparison to anything which these immigrants had experienced.

But most of it, he realized as Cathy's speech unfolded, was due to the woman herself. Anton had been expecting another histrionic speech, like the ones which had preceded Cathy's, wherein the speakers bellowed hackneyed slogans and shrieked phrases which, for all their incendiary terminology, were as platitudinous and devoid of content as any politician's. What he heard instead was a calm, thoughtful presentation of the logic of genetic slavery and the manner in which it undermined any and all possibility for human freedom. Speaking in her husky, penetrating contralto—without, he noted with some amusement, any of the profanity which peppered her casual conversations—Cathy took up the arguments advanced by the Mesans and their apologists and began carefully dissecting them.

For all that her own motivation was clearly one of simple morality, Cathy did not appeal to that. Rather, as cold-bloodedly as any Machiavellian politician devoted to *Realpolitik*, she examined the *logic* of slavery—especially slavery which was connected to genetic differentiation. Her speech was filled with a multitude of examples drawn from human history, many of them dating back to the ancient era when the planet on which she now stood was the sole habitat of the human species. Time and again, she cited the words of such fabled sages as Douglass and Lincoln, showing how the logic of genetic slavery was nothing new in the universe.

Two things, in particular, struck Anton most about her speech. The first was that the woman had obviously, like many exiles before her, taken full advantage of her long years of isolation to devote herself to serious and exhaustive study. Anton had been aware, vaguely, that even professional scholars considered the Countess of the Tor one of the galaxy's authorities on the subject of "genetic indentured servitude." Now he saw the proof of that before his own eyes, and reacted to it with the traditional respect which Gryphon highlanders gave to any genuine expert. The Liberal and Progressive Manticoran aristocrats whom Anton had encountered in the past had repelled him, as much as anything, by their light-minded and casual knowledge of the subjects they so freely pontificated about. *Lazy dabblers*, was his opinion of them. His former wife Helen's opinion had been even harsher, for all that she considered herself a Progressive of sorts. There was nothing of that dilettantism in the woman standing at the podium.

The second thing was the *target* of her speech. Although Cathy was focusing on the plight of the Mesan slaves, her words were not addressed to them but to the big majority of the audience in the amphitheater—who were not Mesans. The point of her remarks—the pivot of them, in fact—was her attempt to demonstrate that any waffling on the issue of genetic slavery by *any* political movement which demanded justice for its own constituents would surely undermine its own cause.

Before she was more than ten minutes into the speech, Anton found himself leaning forward and listening attentively. A part of his mind, of course, paid no attention to her words. In one sense, the entire rally and Cathy's speech itself was a gigantic diversion designed to cover the effort to rescue his daughter. But that part was quiescent, for the moment, simply waiting with the stoic patience of Gryphon's great mountains. The rest of his mind, almost despite his own volition, found himself enjoying the quick humor and slowly unfolding logic of the woman he was listening to.

So it was almost—not quite—with regret, that he broke away when he felt the nudge on his elbow.

He turned his head. One of Jeremy's comrades was leaning over his shoulder. He recognized the young woman, although he did not know her name.

"It's time," she said.

Anton and Robert Tye immediately rose and began following her out of the amphitheater. Dressed as they were in the typical clothing worn by many immigrants in the Old Quarter, nobody took note of their departure.

"How far?" asked Anton, the moment they had exited from the amphitheater itself and could no longer be overheard.

The woman smiled, almost ruefully. "Would you believe it? Not more than a mile. They're somewhere in the Artinstute."

Tye's eyes widened. "I thought that was a fable," he protested.

"Nope. It exists, sure enough. But talk about your buried—!" She broke off, shaking her head. "Never been there myself. Don't know anyone who has, actually."

Anton frowned. "But you're sure Helen's there?"

They were moving quickly now, almost running down a long and sloping ramp. Over her head, the woman said: "Guess so. Jeremy didn't seem the least unsure about it."

Anton was not entirely mollified. From what he had seen of Jeremy X, he suspected the man was never "unsure about it" with regard to anything. He could only hope the assurance was justified.

And now they *were* running, and Anton drove everything out of his mind except his own implacable purpose.

Helen

When Helen awoke, the first thing she saw was a blue glint. It came from somewhere high on the wall opposite the pallet where she was resting. The "wall" was more in the nature of collapsed rubble, which seemed to have forced its way into some kind of opening. As if one wall—she could still see remnants of what must be an ancient structure—had been filled by the centuries-long disintegration of walls which came after. The glint seemed to come from a piece of that most ancient wall, a jagged and broken shard.

Blue. As if it were shining by its own light. Helen stared at it, puzzled.

When she finally realized the truth, she sat upright, almost bolting. *That was sunlight! Shining through something!*

Next to her, Berry stirred. The girl had apparently already been awake. Seeing the direction of Helen's stare, Berry followed her eyes. Then, smiled.

"It's so special, this place," she whispered. "There's light down here—all the way down here!—coming from someplace above. Must be little crevices or something, all the way up to the surface."

The two girls stared at the blue glint. "It's the Windows," Berry whispered. "I *know* it is. The Shkawl Windows everybody always talks about but nobody knows where they are. I found it—me and Lars."

Helen had never heard of the "Shkawl Windows." She was about to ask Berry what they were, when another thought occurred to her. She looked around. Then, seeing that the cavernous area she was in was too poorly lit by the feeble light to see more than a few feet, listened.

"How long have I been asleep?" she asked, her voice tinged by worry. "And where's Lars?"

"You've been sleeping forever, seems like. You must have been real tired."

Berry nestled closer. "Lars said he was going back to make sure we didn't leave any tracks. He took a lantern with him." She frowned and raised her head. "But he's been gone a long time, now that I think about it. I wonder—"

Helen rummaged under the blanket, searching for the other lantern. When she found it, she rose and headed for the stairs. "Stay here," she commanded. "I'll find him."

But Lars found her, instead. And brought the terror back.

"People are coming," he hissed. "With guns."

Startled, Helen lifted her eyes. She had been looking at the floor, picking her way through the debris which filled what seemed to have once been a wide hallway. From a corner twenty feet ahead and to her left, Lars flicked his lantern on and off, showing her where he was hidden.

She extinguished her own lantern and moved toward him, as quickly as she could in the darkness.

"Who are they?" she whispered.

"Most of 'em are Scrags," came the answer. "Must be a dozen of 'em. Maybe more. But there's some other people leading them. I don't know who *they* are, but they're real scary-looking. One of them has some kind of gadget."

Helen was at his side, her hand resting on the boy's shoulder. She could feel the tremor shaking those slender bones.

"I think they're tracking us with it, Helen," he added. His voice was full of fear. "Our smell, maybe. Something."

Helen felt a shiver of fear herself. She knew that there were such devices, because her father had mentioned them to her. But the devices were very expensive.

Which meant—

Helen didn't want to think about what it meant. Whatever it was, it was bad news.

"How close are they?" she whispered.

"Not too far any more. I spotted 'em a while ago. After that I stayed ahead of them, hoping they were going somewhere else. It was easy 'cause they've got a lot of lanterns and they're not afraid to use them."

The fear in his voice was stronger. For a waif like Lars, anyone who would move through the dark caverns of the lower Loop without worrying who might spot them was an automatic danger. The arrogance of power.

"Stay here," she whispered. A moment later, after adjusting the lantern to its lowest power setting, Helen began moving ahead into the darkness. The soft glow emitted by the lantern was enough to illuminate her immediate footsteps, no more. She was searching for the oncoming enemy—and that they *were* her enemies, she didn't doubt at all—using her ears and her nose.

She found them two minutes later. And felt the worst despair of her life. There would be no escaping *these*.

The Scrags, maybe. But not the five people in front.

From her vantage point, peeking around another corner in the endless hallways which seemed to make up this place, Helen studied the oncoming searchers. She gave no more than a momentary scrutiny to the Scrags bringing up the rear, strutting and swaggering exactly the way she remembered them. It was the five people in front that she spent her time examining.

They were dressed in civilian clothing, but Helen knew at once that they were trained professionals. She had spent her whole life as a military brat. Everything about those four men and one woman shrieked: *soldiers.* It was obvious in the way they maintained their positions, the way they held their weapons, everything—

Peeps! The thought flooded her, unbidden. It made no sense that a Peep military detachment would be down here, but Helen never questioned the logic. Peeps were her enemies. Peeps had killed her mother. Who else—what other *soldiers?*—would be looking for her? She was much too politically unsophisticated to understand the illogicality of an alliance between Scrags and Peeps. Enemies were enemies, and there's an end to it. Such is the root of highland political logic, as it has been throughout human existence. Helen had been born in a military hospital in the great orbiting shipyard called *Hephaestus*, and had only occasionally visited Gryphon. No matter. She was her father's girl. From the highlands.

She focused her eyes on the two Peeps in the very forefront. The leaders, obviously. The one on the left had all the earmarks of a veteran. He was studying a device held in his hand, his hatchet face bent forward and tight with concentration.

Her eyes moved to the man standing next to him. The officer in charge, she realized. She wasn't certain— it was hard to be, with prolong—but she thought he was as young in actual fact as his face would indicate.

She took no comfort in that youthfulness. She saw the veteran's head nod, like a hatchet striking wood, and his lips move. The young officer's face came up and he was staring directly at her, from a distance of not more than twenty yards.

He could not see Helen in the darkness, but she could see him clearly. There was nothing soft and childlike in that lean face; nothing boyish in the wiry body. She saw his jaw tighten, and the dark gleam which seemed to come into his eyes. That was the face of a young fanatic, she knew, who had just come to an irrevocable decision. Pitiless and merciless in the way that only youth can be. Helen realized, in that instant, his true purpose.

That was the face of a killer, not a captor.

● ● ●

And so, in the end, Helen belonged to her mother also. Helen Zilwicki came back to life, reborn in the daughter named after her. As she continued her examination, Helen gave no thought at all to her own certain death. That her enemies would catch Helen herself, and kill her, she did not doubt for an instant. But perhaps, if she did her job and led them astray before they trapped her, the monsters would be satisfied with her alone. And not seek further in the darkness, for her own new-found children.

Victor

"Almost there," said Citizen Sergeant Fallon. "She can't be more than a hundred yards away. And whoever's with her. Youngsters, I think, the way these readings keep coming up. One boy and one girl, would be my guess. Her age or younger."

Victor raised his head and stared at the wide opening which loomed before them. The room they were in, for all its size, was like a half-collapsed ancient vault. It was well-illuminated by their lanterns, but the ancient corridor ahead was still buried in darkness.

He hesitated for not more than a second or two. His jaws tightened with decision.

Here. Now.

Victor hefted the flechette gun in his hands. Except for one of the Scrags, Victor had the only flechette gun in the party. Everyone else was armed with pulse rifles. As casually as he could manage, he looked over his shoulder and studied the soldiers and the Scrags following him. Quickly, easily—an officer doing a last inspection of his troops before he led them into combat. He spotted the Scrag holding the other flechette gun and fixed her location in his mind.

"Citizen Sergeant Fallon and I will take the point," he said. His voice sounded very harsh, ringing in his own ears. The other three soldiers in the SS detachment, hearing the announcement, seemed to relax a bit. Or so, at least, Victor hoped.

Fallon cleared his throat. "If you'll pardon me saying so, sir, I think—"

Whatever he thought went with him. Victor leveled the flechette gun and fired. He had already set the weapon at maximum aperture. At that point-blank range—the muzzle was almost touching Fallon when Victor pulled the trigger—the volley of 3mm darts literally cut him in half. The citizen sergeant's legs, still connected by the pelvis and lower abdomen, flopped to the ground. Fallon's upper body did a grotesque reverse flip, spraying blood all over. The Scrags standing near him were spewed with gobbets of shredded intestine.

The butt of the gun came up to Victor's shoulder quickly and easily. He took out Citizen Corporal Garches next. Other than Fallon, she was the only combat veteran in the Peep detachment. The other two were simply typical SS guards.

A burst of flechettes shredded Garches. Victor's aim moved on, quickly. The Scrag holding the other flechette gun came under his sights. The woman was standing paralyzed. She seemed completely in shock. One of her hands, in fact, had left the gun and was wiping pieces of Fallon from her face. An instant later, her face was disintegrated, along with the rest of her body above the sternum.

SS next. *Quick!* He swung the flechette gun back and took out the two remaining members of Fallon's squad with a single shot. They never did more than gape before Victor erased them from existence.

Victor had never been in combat, but he had always taken his training seriously. He had never stinted on the officially mandated hours spent on the firing range and the sim combat tanks. Indeed, he had routinely exceeded them—much to the amusement of other SS officers.

Dimly, he heard the Scrags shouting. He ignored the sounds. Some part of his mind recognized that the genetic "supermen" were beginning to react, beginning to raise their own weapons, beginning—

No matter. Victor stepped into their very midst, firing again and again. In close quarters, a flechette gun was the most murderous weapon imaginable. The weapon didn't kill people so much as it ripped them apart. In seconds, the underground cavern was transformed into a scene from Hell. Confusion and chaos, blood and brains and flesh spattering everywhere, the beams from wildly swinging hand lanterns illuminating the area like strobe lights.

Abstractly, Victor understood his advantage—had planned for it. Despite his lack of actual combat experience, he had *trained* for this. Had spent hours, in fact, thinking through this very exercise and quietly practicing it in the sim tanks over the past two days. He *expected* what was happening, where the Scrags were still half-paralyzed with shock.

Or, even where they weren't paralyzed, they had so much adrenaline unexpectedly pumping into them that their motions were too jerky, too violent. When they managed to get off shots, they missed their target—or hit one of their own. Shrieks and shouts turned the nightmare scene into pure bedlam. The noise, added to the bizarrely flickering light beams, added to the gruesome splatter of wet human tissue flying everywhere, was enough to overwhelm any mind that wasn't braced for it.

Victor ignored it all. Like a methodical maniac, he just kept stepping into them. Almost in their faces, surrounded by their jerky bodies. Twice knocking rifle barrels aside to get a clear shot himself. He expected to die, in the instant, but he ignored that certainty also.

He ignored everything, except the need to slay his enemies. Ignored, even, the plan which he and Kevin Usher had agreed upon. Victor Cachat was supposed to spray the Scrags with a single burst of automatic fire. Just enough to scatter them and confuse them, so that the Ballroom would have easy pickings while Victor made his escape.

It was insane to do otherwise. If the Scrags were not trained soldiers, still and all they were genetically conditioned warriors with superb reflexes and the arrogance to match their DNA. *Suicide to stand your ground, lad*, Kevin had told him. *Just scatter them and race off. See to the girl. The Ballroom will take care of the rest.*

But Victor Cachat was the armed fist of the Revolution, not a torturer. A champion of the downtrodden, not an assassin lurking in ambush. So he thought of himself, and so he was.

The boy inside the man rebelled, the man demanded the uniform he had thought to wear. Say what they would, think what they would.

Officer of the Revolution. Sneer and be damned.

Victor waded into the mob of Scrags, firing relentlessly, using the modern flechette gun in close quarters like a rampaging Norseman might have used an ax. Again and again and again, just as he had trained for in the years since he marched out of the slums to fight for his own. He made no attempt to take cover, no attempt to evade counterfire. Never realizing, even, that the sheer fury of his charge was his greatest protection.

But Victor was no longer thinking of tactics. Like a berserk, he would meet his enemies naked. The Red Terror against the White Terror, standing on the open field of battle. As he had been *promised.*

He would *make* it so. Sneer and be damned!

The shots went true and true and true and true. The boy from the mongrel warrens hammered supermen into pulp; the young man betrayed wreaked a war god's terrible vengeance; and the officer of the Revolution found its truth in his own betrayal.

Sneer and be damned!

Jeremy

"Crazy kid!" hissed Jeremy. He and the others had been following Victor and his would-be executioners. They were now hidden in the shadows toward the rear of the chamber. Jeremy sensed his Ballroom comrades raising their own pulse rifles. They were aiming at the mob of shrieking Scrags swirling in the center of the vault. But there was no way to fire without hitting Victor himself. He was right in the midst of the Scrags.

What was left of them, anyway. Half the Scrags were

down already, ripped to shreds by Cachat's murderous madness.

Murderous, yes, and mad besides. But Jeremy X had been accused of the same, often enough. And there were times, the truth be told, when he thought the accusation was dead on the money.

Such a time was now.

"Hold your fire!" he shouted to his comrades.

With the agility of the acrobat he had been brought into the world to be, Jeremy sprang over the rubble and landed lightly on his feet. Then, bounding forward like an imp, he hefted the handguns which were his favored weapons. One in each hand, as befitted his version of the court jester, gleefully calling out the battlecry of the Ballroom.

"Shall we dance?"

The Scrags who had managed to survive Cachat's fire just had time to spot the capering fool, before they were cut down. Court jester or no, Jeremy X was also, in all likelihood, the deadliest pistoleer alive. The shots came like a master pianist's fingers, racing through the finale of a concerto with a touch as light and unerring as it was thunderous. The sound was all darts flying and striking. There were no screams, no groans, no hisses of pain. Each shot was instantly fatal, and the shots lasted not more than seconds.

Not one of the Scrags managed so much as a single shot at Jeremy. The only moment of real danger for him came at the very end, as the last Scrag fell to the ground. His body one way, his head another. Jeremy's shot had severed the neck completely.

Jeremy found himself looking down the barrel of Cachat's flechette gun. Jeremy was the last thing still standing in the chamber, and the young SS officer had naturally brought the deadly weapon to bear on him.

A tense moment, that. Cachat's young face looked like the face of a ghost. Pale, taut, emotionless. Even his eyes seemed empty.

But the moment passed, the gun barrel swung aside, and Jeremy gave silent thanks to *training*.

By the time Jeremy's comrades made their way into the chamber, it was all over. Stillness and silence. Slowly, Victor Cachat lowered the flechette gun. More slowly yet, as if in a daze, he began to examine his own body. Astonished, it seemed, to find himself alive.

"And well you should be," muttered Jeremy. The lanterns dropped by the dying Scrags cast haphazard light here and there. He swiveled his head, examining the corpses scattered all over the chamber. The ancient stone floor was a charnelhouse of blood and ruin. Carrying their own lanterns, the Ballroom spread out and began moving slowly through the human wreckage, searching for survivors.

They found one still alive. His last sight was the tongue of his executioner.

Then, silence again.

Jeremy caught motion in the corner of his eye. He turned, raising a pistol, but lowered it at once. With his uncanny reflexes, of mind as much as body, he recognized the motion. A captain and a master of the martial arts, advancing slowly into the light.

The silence was broken, by a scream out of darkness. *"Daddy!"*

Motion anew, a girl's blurring feet. Racing across a field of carnage as if it were a meadow; skipping through havoc as easily as they would have skipped through grass.

"Daddy! Daddy! Daddy! Daddy!"

"It's an odd sort of place, this universe of ours," mused Jeremy. He smiled at the comrade at his side. "Don't you think?"

Donald X was cut from more solemn cloth, as befitted such a thick creature. F-67d-8455-2/5 he had been, once, bred for a life of heavy labor. "I dunno," he grunted, surveying the scene with stolid satisfaction.

"Master Tye! Master Tye!"

"Seems just about right to me."

Daughter struck father like a guided missile. Jeremy winced. "Good thing he's a gold medalist. Else that's a takedown for sure."

His eyes moved to a young man, standing alone in a lake of blood. The flechette gun was held limply in his hands. There was nothing in that face now but innocence, wondering.

"Odd," insisted Jeremy. "Galahad's not supposed to be a torturer."

Rafe

The first thing he recognized, as he faded back in, was a voice. Everything else was meaningless. Some part of him understood that his eyes were open. But the part of him that *saw* did not.

There was only the voice.

Your plan worked perfectly, Rafe. Beautiful! They'll make you a Hero of the Revolution. In private, of course. Just like they did with me.

Oddly, the first concrete bit of information that returned was the name. He felt a trickle of emotion re-entering a field of blankness. He hated being called "Rafe." He would not even tolerate Raphael.

Everyone knows that! There was less of anger in the thought than sullenness. The pout of an aggrieved boy.

Yeah, it was damned near as perfect an operation as I've ever seen—and I'll make sure to include that in my own supplemental report to Gironde's.

The name "Gironde" registered also. Gironde was a citizen major in the SS detachment on Terra. One of his own subordinates. Not close, though; not one of his inner sanctum. An "ops ape," Gironde was; not his kind at all.

You'll be glad to know that the Ballroom's sweep of the Loop seems to have damned near wiped out the Scrags completely. Lord, that was a stroke of genius on your part!

The word "Lord" was not supposed to be used. He remembered that. And remembered, also, that it was his responsibility to see to it that it wasn't.

Between the confusion caused by the rally at Soldier Field—all those people crowding through the streets and alleys—and their own efforts to catch the girl, the Scrags all came out of their hideyholes. Well... No doubt there's a few left. Not many.

The next sound he recognized as laughter. No, more like a dry chuckle. Very dry. Very cold. Then, more sounds. Someone, he understood vaguely, had pushed back a chair and risen from it.

Oh, yeah. You're a genius, Rafe. Just like you planned, the Ballroom wiped out the Scrags in one day. And the girl's safe, of course, so you got us out of that mess. Can you imagine? The nerve of those Manpower bastards! Trying to set us up as the patsy, figuring everybody would believe anything about Peeps now that Parnell's arriving.

That was the sound of a man pacing, he realized. And then, suddenly, understood that he was *seeing* the man. His optic nerves had been working all along, but something in his brain must have suddenly switched on. He had been looking sightlessly. Now he was seeing.

He arrives today, you know. Just after the Mesan assassination squad gets arrested by the Sollies we tipped off. You *tipped off, I should say. Credit where credit is due.*

Another harsh, dry laugh. He remembered that laugh. Remembered how much he detested it. Remembered, even, how much he detested the man who laughed in that manner.

But he couldn't remember the man's name. Odd. Irritating.

Like a bird, his mind fluttered in that direction. Irritation was an emotion. He was beginning to remember emotions too.

The man who laughed—very big, he was, especially standing in the center of a room looking down at him—laughed again. When he spoke, the words came like actual words instead of thoughts.

"Of course, there isn't the horde of newscasters waiting at the dock for him that everyone expected. Plenty of them still, needless to say. But half of the Sollie casters are in the Loop, covering what they're already calling the Second Valentine's Day Massacre. Good move, Rafe! Everything about your plan was brilliant."

Usher. That was the man's name.

He remembered how much he detested that grin. More, even, than the man's way of laughing.

"Yeah, brilliant. And after the final masterstroke, which—" The man glanced at the door. "—should be coming any moment now, you'll go down in history as one of the great ops of all time."

He had been drugged, he suddenly realized. And with that realization came another. He knew the drug itself. He couldn't remember its technical name, although he knew that it was called the "zombie drug." It was so easy to use as an aerosol. He remembered thinking that his office had grown a bit muggy, and that he'd intended to speak sharply to the maintenance people. Highly illegal, that drug. As much because it left no traces in a dead body as because of its effects. It broke down extremely rapidly in the absence of oxygenated blood.

There was a knock on the door. Very rapid, very urgent. He heard another voice, speaking through the door. Very rapidly, very urgently.

"Now! They're about to blow the entrance!" Footsteps, scampering away.

Again, that hated grin.

"Well, there it is, Rafe. Time for you to put the capstone on your career. Just like you foresaw, Manpower saved its real pros for the attack on the embassy. Here they are, raring to go. 'Course, we got Bergren out already, so they're walking into a massacre. Just like you planned."

An instant later, he was being lifted like a doll by huge and powerful hands. Now that he was on his feet, he could see the Marines lining the far wall. All of them in battle armor, with pulse rifles ready to hand.

"Such a damn pity that you insisted on leading the ambush yourself, instead of leaving it to the professional soldiers. But you always were a field man at heart. Weren't you, Rafe?"

He was being propelled to the door. Usher was forcing something into his hand. A gun, he realized. He tried to remember how to use it.

That effort jarred loose his first clear thought.

"Don't call me Rafe!"

The building was suddenly shaken by a loud explosion and then, a split-second later, by the sound of debris smashing against walls. The shock jarred loose more memories.

This was exactly how I planned it. Except—

Usher was opening the door with one hand, while he shifted his grip onto—

Durkheim! My name's Durkheim! Citizen General *Durkheim!*

He heard Manpower's professionals pouring into the embassy's great vestibule. He could see the vestibule through the opening door.

There's not supposed to be anybody here, except Bergren and a squad of Marines. Newbie recruits.

The huge hand holding him by the scruff of the neck tightened. He could sense the powerful muscles tensing, ready to hurl him into the room beyond.

"Don't call me Rafe!"

"Hero of the Revolution! Posthumous, of course."

He was sailing into the vestibule. He landed on his feet and stumbled. He stared at the Manpower professionals swinging their pulse rifles. Call them mercenary goons if you would, they were still trained soldiers. Ex-commandos. Hair-trigger reactions.

He was still trying to remember how to use the gun when the hailstorm of darts disintegrated him.

Thereafter

The admiral and the ambassador

Sitting behind his desk, Admiral Edwin Young glared up at the captain standing at attention in front of it.

"You're dead meat, Zilwicki," the admiral snarled. He waved the chip in his hand. "You see this? It's my report to the Judge Advocate General's office."

Young laid the chip down, with a delicate and precise motion. The gesture exuded grim satisfaction. "*Dead—stinking—meat.* You'll be lucky if you just get cashiered. I estimate a ten-year sentence, myself."

Standing at the window with his hands clasped behind his back, Ambassador Hendricks added his own growling words.

"By your insubordinate and irresponsible behavior, Captain Zilwicki, you have managed to half-wreck what should have been our greatest propaganda triumph in the Solarian League *ever*." Glumly, the ambassador stared down at the teeming streets and passageways over a mile beneath his vantage point. "Of course, it'll blow over eventually. And Parnell will be giving his testimony to the Sollie Human Rights Commission for months. But still—"

He turned away, adding his own fierce glare to the admiral's. The stocky officer who was the object of that hot scrutiny did not seem notably abashed. Zilwicki's face was expressionless.

"*Still!*" Hendricks took a deep breath. "We should have been able to start the whole thing with a flourish. Instead—" He waved angrily at the window.

Young leaned forward across his desk, tapping the disk. "Instead, all everyone's talking about is the so-called Peep–Manpower War. Who wants to watch testimony in a chamber, when the casters can show you a half-wrecked Peep embassy and a *completely* wrecked Manpower headquarters?" He snorted. "Not to mention the so-called"—his next words came hissing—"*'drama'* of Mesa's slave revenge. With most of their pros gone, Manpower was a sitting duck. Especially with that terrorist Jeremy X on the loose. Christ, they didn't leave anyone alive over there."

For the first time since he'd entered the admiral's office, Captain Zilwicki spoke.

"None of the secretaries in Manpower's HQ were so much as scratched. Your Lordship."

The glares were hot, hot. But, still, the officer seemed unconcerned.

"Dead—stinking—meat," Young repeated, emphasizing each word. He straightened up. The next words came briskly.

"You are relieved of your duties and ordered to report directly to Navy headquarters in the Star Kingdom to account for your actions. *Technically*, you are not under arrest, but that's purely a formality. You will remain in your private quarters until such time as the next courier ship is ready to depart. In the meantime—"

"I'll be leaving immediately, Your Lordship. I've already made the arrangements."

The admiral stumbled to a halt, staring at Zilwicki.

That moment, the admiral's secretary stuck his head through the door. The admiral had deliberately left the door open, so that the entire staff could overhear his dealings with Zilwicki.

The secretary's face was a mixture of concern and bewilderment.

"Excuse me for interrupting, Your Lordship, but Lady Catherine Montaigne is here and insists on seeing you immediately."

The admiral's frown was one of pure confusion. From the side, the ambassador gave a start of surprise.

"*Montaigne?*" he demanded. "What in the hell does *that* lunatic want?"

His answer came from the lunatic herself. The Lady Catherine Montaigne trotted past the secretary and into the room. She bestowed a sunny smile on the ambassador. Her cheerful peasant face clashed a bit with her very expensive clothing.

"Please, Lord Hendricks! A certain courtesy is expected between Peers of the Realm. In private, at least."

She removed the absurdly elaborate hat perched on her head and fluttered it. "In public, of course, you're welcome to call me whatever you want." The smile grew very sunny indeed. "Now that I think about it, I believe I once referred to you as a horse's ass in one of my speeches."

The smile was transferred onto Admiral Young and grew positively radiant. "And I am *quite* certain that I've publicly labeled the entire Young clan as a herd of swine. Oh, on any number of occasions! Although—" Here the smile quirked an apologetic corner. "I can't recall if I ever singled you out in particular, Eddie. But I assure you I will make good the lack at the very first opportunity. Of which I expect to have any number, since I'm planning a speaking tour immediately upon my return."

It took a moment for the last few words to penetrate the indignation of the ambassador and the admiral.

Hendricks frowned. "Return? Return *where?*"

"To the Star Kingdom, of course. Where else? I feel a sudden overwhelming impulse to revisit my native land. Thinking of moving back permanently, in fact."

She glanced at her watch. The timepiece seemed more like a mass of precious gems than a utilitarian object. It quite overwhelmed her slender wrist. "My private yacht departs within the hour."

The smile was now bestowed on Captain Zilwicki. And what had been a radiant expression took on warmth as well.

"Are you ready, Captain?"

Zilwicki's square head jerked a nod. "I believe so, Lady Catherine." He peered at the admiral. "I think the admiral is finished with me. His instructions were quite clear and precise."

Young gaped at him.

Zilwicki's shoulders twitched in a minute shrug. "Apparently so. With your permission then, Your Lordships, I will do as I am commanded. Immediately."

Young was still gaping. Hendricks found his voice.

"Zilwicki, are you *mad?* You're in enough trouble already!" The ambassador goggled the tall and slender noblewoman. "If you return to Manticore in the company of *this*—this—"

"Peer of the Realm," Lady Catherine drawled. "In case you'd forgotten."

The smile made no pretense, any longer, of disguising its contempt. "And—in case you'd forgotten—I am thereby required to provide Her Majesty's armed forces with my assistance whenever possible. That *is* the law, Lord Hendricks, even if that herd of Young swine and your own brood of suckling piglets choose to ignore it at your convenience."

She laid a slim-fingered hand on the shoulder of the captain. As broad and short as he was, they made an odd looking pair. She was a good six inches taller than he. Yet, somehow, Zilwicki did not seem to shrink in the contrast. It seemed more as if Lady Catherine was in orbit around him.

"*So*—I must see to it that Captain Zilwicki is brought before the Judge Advocate General as soon as possible, to face the serious charges laid against him. And since I was leaving at once anyway, because of my *other* pressing responsibility to the Crown, I would be remiss in my duty as a peer if I did not provide the captain with transport."

Again, it took a moment for the words to register.

Admiral Young finally stopped gaping. "What 'other' responsibility?" he demanded.

Lady Catherine's eyes grew a bit round. "Oh, you hadn't heard? It seems that the self-destruct mechanism in Manpower's vault failed to operate properly. When those savage Ballroom terrorists wreaked their havoc on Manpower's headquarters, they were able to salvage most of the records from the computers. I received a copy, sent by an anonymous party."

She planted the hat back on her head. "I haven't had time to study it fully, of course—such *voluminous* records—but it didn't take me more than a minute to realize that the information needs to be presented to the Queen as soon as possible. You all know how much Elizabeth *detests* genetic slavery. She's said so in public—oh, I can't keep track of all the times! And in private, her opinion is even more volcanic." She shook her head sadly. "Such a hot-tempered woman. I worry about her health, sometimes."

The smile was back. "Elizabeth and I were childhood friends, you know. Did I fail to mention that? Oh, yes. Very close, at one time. Our relations have been strained for years, naturally, due to political differences. But I'm quite certain she'll want to speak to me on *this* subject. And Lady Harrington also, of course. I've never met her personally, but my butler Isaac is an old acquaintance."

She'd left them completely befuddled, now. The smile widened. "You didn't know? How odd, I thought everyone did. Isaac was one of the slaves Lady Harrington freed—well, she wasn't a peer in those days, of course, just another commoner naval officer—when she smashed up the depot at Casimir. I'm sure she'd agree to see him again, to allow him to present his overdue thanks. Along with a copy of these records. Quite certain of it."

Her hand squeezed Zilwicki's shoulder. "Captain?"

"Your servant, Lady Catherine."

A moment later, they were gone. The two men remaining in the room stared at each other. Their faces were already growing pale.

"Records?" choked Hendricks.

The admiral ignored him. He was already scrabbling for the communicator. In the minutes which followed, while Hendricks paced out his agitation, Young simply sat there. Listening to his chief legal officer explain to him, over and again, that he had neither the legal grounds—nor, more to the point here on Terra, the police authority—to detain a Manticoran Peer of the Realm engaged in the Queen's business.

Victor

As he leaned over the railing on the upper level of the terminal, studying the small party below getting ready to enter the embarkment area, Victor had mixed emotions. Which, sad to say, seemed destined to be his normal state. He almost felt regret for past simplicities and certitudes.

Almost. Not quite.

He heard a chuckle. The big man standing next to him, with the very pretty woman nestled under his arm, had—as usual—read his mind. Victor was almost getting tired of that also.

Almost. Not quite.

"Grotesque, isn't it?" mused Usher. "All that obscene wealth, in the hands of a single person? You could feed a small town for a year on what a private yacht like that costs."

Victor said nothing. He had learned that much, at least. *One thing at a time.* He didn't want to hear the lecture again.

"What do you think he's saying to her?" he asked.

Usher's eyes moved, focusing on the girl below. She was giving a fierce hug to the small man who had accompanied the party to the terminal.

"Well, let's see. He's probably stopped chiding her for using the Owl By Night. And he's probably already told her exactly which schools to investigate, once she gets to Manticore." A large hand came up and rubbed his jaw. "So I imagine he's simply telling her the kind of things which she really needs to know. Things from the heart, so to speak."

Below, the embrace ended. With the quick motions of someone steadying loss with new determination, Helen Zilwicki marched her entire party to the gate. There were six people in the party. Her father and Lady Catherine and Isaac brought up the rear. In the front, nestled under Helen's wings, her new brother and sister advanced toward a new life. Master Tye alone remained behind, simply staring.

Usher turned away from the railing. "And that's that. Come on, Victor. It's time for Ginny and me to introduce you to a new vice."

Victor followed obediently. He didn't even grimace at the gibe.

"Good lad," murmured Usher. "You'll like it, I promise. And if the elitism bothers you, just use the plebe word for it. *Movies.*"

He leaned over, smiling at his wife. "Which one, d'you think?"

"*Casablanca*," came the immediate reply.

"Good choice!" Kevin draped his other arm over Victor. "I do believe this is the beginning of a beautiful friendship."

Helen

On the second night of their journey home, her father didn't return to their suite on the yacht. Once she was sure he wasn't going to, Helen made up her bed on the couch in the small salon. It took her a while to settle Lars and Berry for the night, in the stateroom which she was sharing with them. Partly, because something of her own good cheer seemed to infuse them. But mostly it was because they were afraid of sleeping without her.

"Come on!" she snapped. "We aren't going to be sharing a bed forever, you know." She eyed the huge and luxurious piece of furniture. "Not one like this, anyway. Not with Daddy on half-pay, at best."

She did not seem noticeably upset at the prospect of future poverty. Lars and Berry, of course, were not upset at all. Their new father's "half" pay was a fortune to them.

"Get to sleep!" Helen commanded. She turned off the lights. "Tonight belongs to Daddy. And tomorrow morning too."

In the time which followed, Helen set her clever alarms. She did the work with the same enthusiasm with which she had spent the evening designing them.

But, in the event, the alarms proved unnecessary. She never managed to sleep herself. So, when she heard her father coming through the outer doors, early in the morning, she had time to disengage them before he entered. She even had time to perch herself back on the couch. Grinning from ear to ear.

The door to the salon opened and her father tiptoed in. He spotted her and froze. Helen fought to restrain her giggles. *Talk about role reversal.*

"So!" she piped. "How was she?"

Her father flushed. Helen laughed and clapped her hands with glee. She had *never* managed to do that!

Her father straightened, glared at her, and then managed a laugh himself.

"Rascal," he growled. But the growl came with a

rueful smile, and he padded over to the couch. The moment he sat down next to her, Helen scrambled into his lap.

Surprise crossed her father's face. Helen had not sat in his lap for years. Too undignified; too childish.

The look of surprise vanished, replaced by something very warm. A film of tears came into his eyes. A moment later, Helen felt herself crushed against him, by those powerful wrestler's arms. Her own vision was a bit blurry.

She wiped away the tears. *Whimsy, dammit!*

"I bet she snores." She'd planned that sentence for *hours.* She thought it came out just right.

Again, her father growled. "Rascal." Silence, for a moment, while he pressed her close, kissing her hair. Then:

"Yeah, she does."

"Oh, good," whispered Helen. The whimsical humor she'd planned for that remark was absent, however. There was nothing in it but satisfaction. "I *like* that."

Her father chuckled. "So do I, oddly enough. So do I." He stroked and stroked her hair. "Any problem with it, sugar?"

Helen shook her head firmly. "Nope. Not any." She pressed her head against her father's chest, as if listening to his heartbeat. "I want you full again."

"So do I, sugar." Stroked and stroked her hair. "So do I."

THE
JOE'S WORLD
SERIES

Author's note:

I started the Joe's World series with my friend Richard Roach way back in 1969, over one-third of a century ago, when we were college students. In the decades that followed, both of us got involved in other things and the writing pretty much languished. Now and then, we'd pull out the manuscripts and work on them for a while, but for the most part the material just lay idle in desk drawers and cardboard boxes.

Then, in 1992, I decided to start writing fiction seriously. The first thing I did was pull out one of the intended episodes for the Greyboar and Ignace sub-plot of the series and rewrite it as a stand-alone short story. I entered the end result, "Entropy and the Strangler," in the *Writers of the Future Contest*—and it won first place in the contest for the winter quarter of 1992.

A few years later, after deciding to separate most of this sub-plot and publish it as an independent novel, I included a slightly rewritten version of this story as the Prologue to *The Philosophical Strangler*, which was published in 2001. That's the version I'm including in this anthology.

The second story included in this section of the anthology is "The Realm of Words." I wrote this several years ago, intending it to be included as one of the episodes in a later volume of the Joe's World series. Which, indeed, it will be. But, in the meantime—professional writers really, really *hate* to leave perfectly good stories lying around not earning any money—I sold it as a standalone story to *Jim Baen's Universe* magazine. It was an easy sale, since I was able to apply the principle of Ultimate Nepotism—seeing as how I'm also the editor of that magazine.

Cheating, I suppose, but I can't say I feel any guilt over the matter. It really is a very entertaining tale, so who cares?

For those of you interested in looking into the Joe's World series, the books either published or projected as part of the series are included in the appendix.

Entropy, and the Strangler

"To the contrary," demurred Greyboar, toying with his mug, the secret lies entirely in the fingerwork."

But the bravo wouldn't have it. "'Tis rather in the main force!" he bellowed, and fell upon the strangler. The table splintered, the mugs went flying in a cloud of ale froth.

Needless to say, I scrambled aside. Like being a chipmunk caught between two bull moose, don't you know? Besides, there's no profit in this sort of thing.

Safe at a distance, I stuck my head between two cheering onlookers and saw that my client was in his assailant's grasp. The lout's great biceps, triceps, deltoids, pectoids and whatnot bulged and rippled as he worked at Greyboar's throat. Couldn't find it, of course.

They're a low lot, these tavern rowdies, not given to temperate debate.

Stupid, to boot. What I mean is, the outcome was

never in doubt. "Professional fingerwork," as Greyboar calls it, is simply beyond the ken of hurlyburlies who lounge about the alehouses, until they encounter it firsthand.

For this particular clown, personal experience had now arrived. Casually, Greyboar sank his hands into his opponent's belly, kneading and squeezing. It must be like eating ten cucumbers at once. An astonished grimace came over the goon's face.

"Fouled our breeches, have we?" chuckled the chokester. A good lad, Greyboar, but his humor runs in a low vein.

His jest made, the strangler proceeded to more serious business. A quick flip of the thumbs popped the bullyboy's kneecaps. His victim now at eye level, Greyboar leaned back in his chair and shrugged off the hands which were still groping in the vicinity of where his neck would be if he had one.

"As I said," he concluded, "it's all in the fingerwork."

Then, just as I thought we'd gotten out of the silly affair with no harm, wouldn't you know it but that the barkeep had to go pour oil on the flames.

"And who's going to pay for all this broken furniture?" he demanded. The barkeep's voice was shrill, in keeping with his sour face. He looked down at the bullyboy, now writhing on the floor.

"Not Lothar, that's for sure," he whined. "Not much money to be made by a loan enforcer on crutches."

That's done it! I thought.

"Him?" exclaimed Greyboar. "A shark's tooth?" His good humor vanished like the dew.

"And here it is," I grumbled, "there'll be lawsuits, damages, weeping widow and wailing tots, and the

Old Geister knows what else." I squirmed my way through the crowd.

"Greyboar, let's be off!" There's nothing worse than a usurer's lawyers.

"Not quite yet," growled the strangler, reaching for the doomee's neck. But luck was with us. At that very moment the porkers arrived, a whole squad of them.

"What's the disturbance here?" demanded the sergeant in charge, flattening the nearest patron with his bullystick. "You're all under arrest!"

If we'd been in our usual haunts, quaffing our ale at The Sign of the Trough in the Flankn, the porkers wouldn't have dared come in—not with less than a battalion, at any rate. Of course, if we'd been in the Flankn, where Greyboar's well known, no bullyboy would have picked a fight with him in the first place. But I'll give the patrons in that grimy little alehouse this much, they didn't hesitate but a second before the benches were flying and the fracas was afoot.

I seized the propitious moment. "Out!" I hissed, grabbing the strangler's elbow. "There's no money to be made here."

"Money, money, that's all you think about," grumbled Greyboar. "What then of ethics, and the meaning of life?"

"Save it for later." I pulled him toward the rear exit. Fortunately, the strangler was willing to leave. He's not the sort one drags from a tavern against his will, don't you know. On our way out, a beefy porker blocked the route, leering and twirling his club, but Greyboar removed his face and that was that. Fingerwork, he calls it.

Once in the back alley, Greyboar returned to the matter, like a dog chewing a bone.

"Yet there must be a logic to it all," he complained. "Surely there's more to life than this aimless collision of bodies in space." His thick brows knotted over his eyes.

"Wine, women and song!" I retorted. "There's sufficient purpose for a strangler and his agent. And it all takes money, my man, which you can't get rousting bravos in alehouses."

That last was a bit unfair. It had been my idea to go into the alehouse, to celebrate the completion of a nice little job with a pot or two. Bad idea, of course. The job had taken us to a grimy little suburb of the city, where we'd never been before. And there's something about Greyboar—his size, maybe, or just an aura of implacable certainty—that inevitably seems to arouse the local strong man to belligerence. As the wise man says: "Big frogs in little ponds are prone to suicide."

But it was just so exasperating!

"Still and all," continued Greyboar, like a glacier on its course, "I'm convinced there's more to it. 'Wine, women and song,' you say, and that's fine for you. You're a sybarite of the epicurean persuasion. But I, it is clear to me, incline rather to the stoic, perhaps even the ascetic."

"You're driving me mad with this philosophical foolishness!" I exclaimed. "And will you *please* curl up your hands?"

"Sorry." He has long arms, Greyboar, it's an asset in his line of work. But the sound of fingernails clittery-clattering along the cobblestones gets on my nerves.

By now we had reached the end of the alley and

were onto a main street. I looked around and spotted a hansom not far away. I whistled, and it was but
a minute later that we clambered aboard. It was an
extravagance, to be sure, but we were flush with cash
and I'd no desire to walk all the way back into the city.

"Take us to The Sign of the Trough," I told the
driver. "It's in the Flankn, right off—"

"I know where it is," grumbled the cabbie. "It'll
cost you extra, you know?"

I sighed, but didn't argue the point. Cabbies always
charged extra for going into the Thieves' Quarter. Can't
say as I blamed them. It was one of the disadvantages
of living in the Flankn. But the advantages made it
worth the while—hardly any porkers to bother you,
hidey-holes galore, a friendly neighborhood (certainly
no pestersome bullyboys!), a vast network of information, customers always knew where to find you, etc.

As the hansom made its way back into New Sfinctr,
Greyboar continued to drone on about philosophy's
central place in human existence. I struggled manfully
to control my temper, but at one point I couldn't
resist taking a dig.

"You're only doing this philosophy nonsense because
of Gwendolyn," I grumbled.

Of course, that made him furious. This is not, by the
way, a stunt I recommend for the amateur—infuriating
Greyboar, that is. But I'm the world's expert on the
subject, and I know exactly when I can get away with it.

His jaws clamped shut, his face turned red, he
bestowed a ferocious glare on me.

"What's my sister got to do with it?" he demanded.
I glared right back at him.

"It's obvious! You never gave a second thought—you

never gave a first thought!—to this philosophy crap until
Gwendolyn said you had the philosophy of a weasel."

He looked away from me, his face like a stone. I
felt bad, then. He was such a formidable monster,
that I forgot sometimes he had feelings just like other
people. And before their fight, he and his sister had
been very close.

Still, it shut him up. The rest of the ride into the
Flankn took place in a cold silence. Uncomfortable,
yes, but it was a damned sight better than having
to listen to him prattling on about epistemology and
ontology and whatnot.

The cabbie dropped us off in front of our lodgings. We had some small rooms on the top floor of
a typical Flankn flophouse. I paid the cabbie and we
headed for the door.

Just as we started up the steps to the landing, a
voice sounded behind us.

"Hold there, sirrahs!"

We turned and beheld a bizarre sight, even for
the Flankn. A small man stood before us, clad in the
most ridiculous costume: billowing green cloak, baggy
yellow pants tied up at the ankles, tasseled slippers
curling up at the toes, his head bound in a bright
red strip of cloth. A "turban," it's called.

"Who're you?" I demanded.

The fellow glanced about. "Please, lower your voice!
My business is confidential."

"Confidential, is it?" boomed Greyboar. "Well, out
with it!"

The man hissed his agitation. "Quietly, please! It
is not to be discussed on the public thoroughfares!"
He cupped his ear.

Greyboar snorted. "It's as good a place as any. There's none to listen but the urchins of the street, who're loyal to their own." The strangler gazed benignly over the refuse, debris and tottering tenements that encompassed a typical street of the Flankn. His eyes fell upon a ne'er-do-well lounging against a wall some steps beyond. "And the occasional idler, of course." Greyboar cracked his knuckles; it sounded like a coal mine caving in. The layabout found urgent business elsewhere.

"Nevertheless," continued the turbaned one, "I must insist on privacy. I represent a most important individual, who demands the utmost discretion."

Left to his own, Greyboar would have quitted the fellow with no further ado. But that's why he needed an agent.

"Important individual, you say? No doubt he's prepared to pay handsomely for our services?" I spoke softly, since there was no reason to aggravate a potential client. Strangler's customers were always a twitchy lot.

"He can be quite generous. But come, let us arrange a meeting elsewhere."

"Done!" I said, cutting Greyboar off. "In three hours, in the back room of the Lucky Lady. Know where it is?"

"I shall find it. Until then."

"It'll be twenty quid for the meeting—whether or not we take the job." For a moment, I thought he would protest. But he thought better of it, and scurried around the corner.

And that's how the whole thing started. It was bad enough when Greyboar was wasting his time (and my patience) searching for a philosophy of life. But now that he's *found* one, he's impossible. If I'd known in advance what was going to happen, I wouldn't have touched the job for all the gold in Ozar. But there it is—I was an agent, not a fortune-teller. And even though we were flush at the moment, I always had an eye out for a lucrative job. "Folly ever comes cloaked in opportunity," as the wise man says.

Three hours later we were in the back room of the Lucky Lady. The tavern was in the Flankn, in that section where the upper crust went slumming. Greyboar didn't like the place, claimed it was too snooty for his taste. I wasn't too fond of it myself, actually. Much rather have been swilling my suds at The Trough, surrounded by proper lowlifes. But there was no place like the Lucky Lady for a quiet business transaction. Especially since almost all our clients were your hoity-toity types, who'd die of shock in The Trough.

Mind you, my discretion was all in vain. The man was there, all right, accompanied by a fat, frog-faced lad barely old enough to shave. And both of them were clad in the same manner, except that the youth's costume was even more extravagant. *Customers*. As the wise man says: "Wherefore profit it a man to be learned, if he remains stupid in his mind?"

"You could have worn something less conspicuous," I grumbled, after we took our seats across the table from them.

The stripling took offense. "I am the Prince of the Sundjhab! The Prince of the Sundjhab does not scurry about in barbarian rags!" Typical. Sixteen years old, at the most, and he was already speaking in ukases.

Greyboar's interest was aroused. "The Sundjhab? It's said the Sundjhab is a land of ancient learning and lore. Sages and mystics by the gross, you stumble over 'em just walking down the street."

"Let's to business!" I said, rather forcefully. Once let Greyboar get started on this track, we'd never get anything accomplished.

The Prince's companion nodded his head. "You may call me Rashkuta. My master's name"—a nod to the Prince—"is of no import. His involvement in this affair must remain completely hidden." He cleared his throat. "Our business is simple. My master's birthright is barred by another, his uncle, whom we wish removed that my master may inherit his kingdom."

"What about his uncle's children?" demanded Greyboar. "D'you want I should burke the whole brood?" Sarcasm, this—Greyboar drew the line at throttling sprouts, save the occasional bratling.

The gibe went unnoticed. "It will not be necessary. In the Sundjhab, the line of descent passes from uncle to nephew. There are no others between my master and his due."

"Odd sort of system," mused Greyboar. "In Grotum, a man's own children are his heirs."

"Yours is a preposterous method!" decreed the Prince. "That a king's children be his own is speculation, pure solipsism. But that a king's sister's children be of his own royal blood is certain."

"A point," allowed Greyboar. The royal nose lifted even higher.

"Let's keep it to business," I interjected. "There is a problem with your proposal. The Sundjhab is known to us here in New Sfinctr, but mostly as a land of

legend and fable. Three obstacles are thus presented.
First, it is far away. Second, should we arrive there,
we are unfamiliar with the terrain. Finally, how will
we make sure to collect our fee once the job is done?"

"Your concerns are moot," replied Rashkuta. "My
master's uncle is touring the continent of Grotum.
For the next week, he will be residing in New Sfinctr.
The work can be done here. Indeed, it *must* be done
here. Fearsome as are the guardians who accompany
him on his travels, they are nothing compared to what
surrounds him in his palace in the Sundjhab."

His words jogged my memory. I had heard vague
talk in the marketplace about some foreign mucky-
muck on a visit. Couldn't for the life of me understand why. What I mean is, if I'd been the King of
the Sundjhab, I'd never have left the harem except
to stagger to the treasure room. And I'd certainly not
have come to New Sfinctr! The place is a pesthole.
Probably some scheming and plotting going on. A dirty
business, politics. Of course, it was great for the trade.

But a chokester's agent can't afford to let his mind
wander. "Who are the King's guardians?"

"They consist of the following," replied Rashkuta.
"First, the King has his elite soldiery, a body of twelve
men, the cream of the Sundjhabi army—"

"Not to be compared to the buffoons in Sfinctrian
uniform," sneered the Prince.

"—secondly, he is accompanied by his Grand Sorcerer, one Dhaoji, a puissant thaumaturge—"

"Not to be compared to the fumbling potion-mixers
called wizards in these heathen lands," sneered the
Prince.

"—and thirdly, should you penetrate these barriers,

you will confront the Royal Bodyguard, Iyesu by name, who is a master of the ancient martial arts of the South."

"Not to be compared to the grunting perspirers called fighters in your barbarous tongue," sneered the Prince.

I looked at Greyboar. He nodded.

"We'll take the job. Now, as to our fee. We will require ten thousand quid, payable half in advance and half upon completion. In addition, of course, to the twenty quid you owe us for this meeting."

Our clients gaped. "But we were informed that you only charged one thousand quid for, uh, for your work!" protested Rashkuta.

"And we *are* only charging you a thousand quid for strangling the young master's uncle," I agreed cheerfully. "In addition, however, it is necessary to charge two thousand for the elite soldiers, three thousand for the unexcelled sorcerer, and a clean four thousand for the incomparable master of the martial arts. As a rule, such trifles come with the job. But—I am only respecting the Prince's fiat—his uncle's protectors are not to be compared to the riffraff we normally encounter in our work." A nice touch, this. To be sure, I was demanding an outrageous fee. But I'd be a poor agent if I didn't milk the Golden Cow when I could. "Greater greed is the greedy man's gratuity," as the wise man says.

"We can find another to do the job!" countered Rashkuta. But it was weak, very weak.

"Greyboar's the best." No boast, it was a simple fact. And by the look on their faces, our clients had already learned as much in their investigations.

Rashkuta tried to bargain, but His Adolescence cut him short.

"Pay them. We are not peasants, to squabble in the bazaar."

You could always count on royalty. Why the world was such a madhouse. Buggers'd rather slaughter each other's plebes than compromise their noble dignity. Parasites, the lot of them. I'd always agreed with Greyboar's sister on that point, even if I thought Gwendolyn's ideals were a lot of utopian nonsense.

"Going to be a bit of trouble collecting the back half of our fee," I said to myself. It was clear from his glare that Tadpole the Terrible was not pleased with us. But I wasn't worried about it. Greyboar was the dreamy type, true, but he was always quick enough to squeeze what was owed to us out of recalcitrant clients. That is not a metaphor. He fed them the money first. Crude, I admit, but the word got around.

Rashkuta counted out the money and slid it across the table. Naturally, he made a big production out of it, hunching his shoulders, eyes flitting hither and yon. As if a Flankn cutpurse this side of an asylum would intervene between Greyboar and his commission.

Naturally, too, he had to add: "How can we be certain that you will do the job, now that you possess such a princely sum?"

"Matter of professional ethics," growled the strangler. Rashkuta made to press the point, but Greyboar transmuted a chunk of the oak table into sawdust, and that was that. An easy-going and tolerant sort, Greyboar, but he'd always been testy about his professional ethics.

"Where can we find the Prince's uncle?" I asked.

"He retains a suite at the Hospice of Stupefying Opulence. You are familiar with the establishment?"

"Of course." Wasn't quite a lie. I'd seen the outside of the place. I was even familiar with the servants' quarters in the back, due to a brief but torrid affair with one of the maids in my earlier years. But I'd never been in the guests' portion of the Hospice. They catered to a rather different clientele.

"However," I continued, "it will prove a wee bit difficult for us to saunter through the main entrance, don't you know. Exclusive, it is. They'd as soon let in a measly baronet as a leper. Doormen standing on porters on top of bellhops. Professional busybodies, the lot of them, they send 'em to the Royal Academy of Officiousness. Desk clerks get three years' postgraduate training. What I mean is, we can't very well march in and announce we've come to throttle the King of the Sundjhab. We'll need help getting in. Are you staying there too?"

Hem, haw, squirm, squirm. Customers. Eventually, they confessed to a small room tucked away in an obscure corner of the Hospice, practically a broom closet in the maids' quarters, to listen to them.

"Fine. There's a rear entrance, leads off the kitchen. At midnight, tonight, one of you will be there to let us in."

Of course, they squawked and quibbled, but they finally gave in. Greyboar and I arose. "Our business is then concluded, for the moment," I said. "We'll meet you here the night after tomorrow, same time, for the balance of the fee."

"It's the wizard what bothers me," said Greyboar some time later, as we discussed the job over pots of ale at The Trough. "The soldiers are meaningless, and the martial artist will be interesting. But sorcerers are tricky, and besides, I hate to extinguish any bit of knowledge that brightens this dark and murky world."

"Oh, give me a break! That so-called wizard is nothing but another pretentious trickster. 'Secret lore,' 'hidden mysteries,' 'opaque purports of the unknown'—it's all rot for the weak-minded. Reality's what is, and the truth is there for all to see it. A pox on all philosophy!"

Greyboar would have continued the argument, but I cut him off. "I'll deal with the sorcerer. I've got just the thing—a small potion Magrit made up for me the last time we were in Prygg."

"Really?" Greyboar's curiosity was aroused; best way to distract him. "What is it?"

"How should I know? Since when does Magrit divulge trade secrets?"

"True," mused the strangler. "A proper witch, she is."

"Best in the business. None of your epistemology for old Magrit! Cuts right to the quick, she does. As for the potion, all I know is that when she gave it to me she said it was tailor-made to take out any obnoxious wizard that got in the way."

"But how will you get him to drink it?"

I snorted. "Intravenous injection, that's the thing."

In the blink of an eye, I whipped out the little blow-pipe from its pouch in my cloak. A second later, a dart was quivering in the bull's-eye of the dart board against the far wall. The crowd playing darts looked over, frowning fiercely, but when they saw who the culprit was they relaxed. Fergus even brought the dart over and handed it back. I was popular with the lads at The Trough.

"If that big gorilla wasn't here, I'd bust your head," grumbled Fergus.

"Don't let me stop you," said Greyboar instantly. I cast him an aggrieved look. Fergus smiled, then shrugged.

"Ah, what the hell? The shrimp's good for comic relief. And if we ever get bored with darts, we can always use him to play toss-the-midget."

A round of laughter swept The Trough. I was not amused. After a while, my glare finally quieted Greyboar's bass braying.

"Oh, stop glaring," he chuckled. "It serves you right, showing off like that. All this fancy stuff you do with darts and knives—it's just overcompensation 'cause you're such a little guy. Now, if you'd apply yourself to a study of philosophy—"

And there he was, off again. Injury added to insult.

At midnight, Greyboar and I slipped through the back door of the Hospice. Rashkuta was there to let us in, as promised. It was obvious, from his twitchy face and trembling limbs, that his nerves were not of the best. A bloodthirsty lot, your strangler's customers, when it comes to the theory of the thing. But when the deed's to be done, their knees turn to water. Else why hire a chokester? It's a simple enough matter, all things considered, to shorten a man's life.

Quickly, Rashkuta guided us through the Hospice's maze of stairways and corridors. We encountered no one, which was fortunate, as Greyboar and I were rather stunned by the place. Not our normal haunts, don't you know? Eventually, we arrived at an immense double door carved out of a solid slab of some exotic hardwood. There was enough gilt on the handles alone to drown a whale.

"The door is locked," whispered Rashkuta, "with

an intricate and powerful lock constructed by the King's master locksmith, brought especially from the Sundjhab for the occasion."

"No problem," grunted Greyboar. He looked at me. "Are you ready, Ignace?" I shrugged.

"A moment, please!" hissed Rashkuta, and scurried down the corridor. Customers, like I said.

Greyboar seized the handles and tore the doors off their hinges. Entering, we beheld an antechamber, empty except for four guards. These lads were bare from the waist up, clad in baggy blue trousers tied up at their ankles. Curl-toed red slippers completed their uniforms. Funny-looking, sure, but each one held a huge scimitar, and there was no denying they were splendid soldiers. Though caught by surprise, they were on top of us in a heartbeat.

Upon Greyboar, to be precise, for I naturally took myself to one side. Not for me, this sort of melee.

The foremost soldier, muscles writhing like boas, swung a blow of his scimitar that would've felled a cedar. But Greyboar seized his wrist in midstroke and tore the arm out of its socket and clubbed the other three senseless and that was that.

"Aside from the professional fingerwork," Greyboar liked to say, "I think of my methods as a classic application of Occam's Razor."

To the left stood an open door, leading to the guards' quarters. Beyond, a group of soldiers were scrambling from a table where some exotic game was in progress. The most enterprising of the lot was even now at the door, scimitar waving about.

"Bowls!" cried Greyboar, slamming the door in the soldier's face. You could hear them falling like tenpins beyond. The door now closed, Greyboar sealed it by the simple expedient of wrenching the frame out of shape. He had a way with doors, Greyboar did. On those occasions when we found ourselves guests of the porkers in the Durance Pile, they kept us in a special dungeon equipped with sliding stone slabs instead of the usual gate and grill. "At great expense to the State," Judge Rancor Jeffreys sourly noted.

The preliminaries accomplished, Greyboar and I burst through the right-hand door. This new room was obviously a sleeping chamber. But the bed and all other items of furniture had been shoved against the walls, leaving the center of the room empty. Even the carpet that would normally have covered this portion of the floor was rolled up and standing on end in a corner. The purpose of this unusual arrangement was clear. For there, in the center of the room, squatting in a pentacle drawn on the bare floor, was a man who could be none other than the sorcerer Dhaoji.

I won't attempt to describe him. Wizards are usually bizarre in their appearance, and this was a wizard among wizards. Even at that very moment, the fellow was bringing some fearful-sounding incantation to a close, which I had no doubt would have transmogrified us right proper. Mind you, I've no use for their extravagant theories, mages, but there's no denying the better ones can wreak havoc on a man's morphology.

"My job, this," said I. A moment later, two of my darts were sprouting from his neck. Dhaoji cried out and clapped his neck. He broke off his incantation and tried to remove the darts. But the potion was already at work.

Nor did Magrit fail us. A dire potion, indeed.

"Horrible!" gasped Greyboar. For even now was Dhaoji locked into his doom.

"Yet 'tis clear as day," we heard him whimper, quivering, hunched like a hamster, eyes gazing into The Terror, "that an arrow can only travel its course by traveling half the distance first. But then, to cover the second half, it must cover half of that half first. And in order to cover half of that half, 'tis necessary that it first cover half that distance again. How, then, can it ever complete its course? Yet it does!" A hideous moan ensued.

Xenophobia hastening our steps, we entered the room beyond. At last, the royal chamber, no doubt about it. Luxuries like sand on the beach. And our prey stood before us.

Or rather, lounged before us. Astonishing sight! Here we had a mighty king, his death at hand, all his protectors destroyed (save one—a moment, please), and all he could do was laze about on a divan, chewing a fig. I was rather offended, actually.

But we'll get back to him. First, there was the matter of the final bodyguard. Even as foretold, this wight was there: a smallish man, though very well-knit in his proportions.

"You'll be Iyesu, master of the martial arts," said Greyboar. The man bowed courteously.

"Well, be on your way. There's no point in a useless fracas. It's your boss we've business with."

Iyesu smiled, like an icon.

"I fear not," he replied. "Rather do I suggest that you depart at once, lest I be forced to demonstrate my incomparable skills upon your hapless body. For know, barbarian, that I am the supreme master of all the ancient arts of the South—I speak of the blows, the strikes, the kicks, the holds, the throws, the leaps, the bounds, the springs, eschewing not, of course, the subtle secrets of the vulnerable portions of the musculature and nerves. Observe, and tremble."

And so saying, Iyesu leapt and capered about, engaging in bizarre and flamboyant exercises. Many boards and bricks set up on stands to one side of the room were shattered and pulverized with sundry blows of well-nigh every part of his body.

"As you can see," he concluded, "your crude skills cannot begin to compare with mine."

"No doubt," replied Greyboar, "for I possess no such skills, other than professional fingerwork. Of the martial arts, as you call them, I am as ignorant as a newborn babe. A simple workingman, I, who worked as a lad plucking chickens, as a stripling rending lambs, as a youth dismembering steers. A meatpacker, employed now in a related but much more lucrative trade."

Iyesu gibbered his disgust. "The insult to my person!" he cried, and sprang into action. And a pretty sight it was, too, to see him bounding and scampering about, landing many shrewd and cunning blows of the open hand, the fist, the knee, the elbow and the foot upon those diverse portions of Greyboar's anatomy which he imagined to be vulnerable.

So great was his interest that Greyboar stood immobile for no little time.

"Most proficient!" marveled the strangler. Then, recalling his duty, Greyboar seized Iyesu in mid-leap and pulverized his spine and that was that.

"Master, I am undone!"

Iyesu's shriek stirred the King to a flurry of activity. He raised his head from its pillow.

"Can you do nothing?"

"The probability is small, Your Highness. Indeed, were it not for my incomparable training in the mystic arts of bodily control, I would already be dead. The spine is rather central to all human endeavor. But I shall make the attempt."

And so saying, the master of the martial arts slithered his way to Greyboar's side and tried a few blows.

"'Tis as I feared, the leverage is no longer available. On the other hand," he mused, "there are possibilities for the future. Perhaps even a new school!"

"Too late, I suppose, to prevent my assassination?"

"Indeed so, master. Even the great Ashokai required four years to found his school. I fear it shall take me longer. There are, it must be admitted, certain obstacles to overcome." Here he seized Greyboar's ankle and attempted a throw. "Just as I predicted," he complained, flipping and flopping about, "it's the leverage."

"So be it," yawned the King. Greyboar advanced and seized his neck. "Yet do I regret the truncation of my philosophic endeavor."

Greyboar's fingers halted in mid-squeeze. A great fear seized my heart.

"What philosophic endeavor?" demanded the strangler.

"Greyboar!" I shouted. "Burke the bugger and let's be off!"

"One moment. What philosophic endeavor?"

The King stared up at the strangler. "Surely you are not interested in such matters?" he wheezed. His round face was very flushed, which was not surprising, given that Greyboar's hands were buried in the rolls of fat adorning the royal neck.

"To the contrary," replied Greyboar, "philosophy is my life's passion."

"Indeed!" gasped the King. "It seems . . . an odd . . . avo . . . cation . . . for an as . . . sassin."

"Why? It seems to me quite appropriate. After all, my trade brings me in close proximity to the basic metaphysical questions—pain, suffering, torment, death, and the like. A most fertile field for ethical ponderations."

"I had . . . not . . . con . . . sidered . . ." The King's face was now bright purple. "But . . . I . . . ex . . . pire."

"Oh. Excuse me." Greyboar released the royal gullet. "Professional reflexes, I'm afraid."

"Quite so," agreed the King. His Royal Rotundness managed to sit up, coughing and gagging and massaging his throat.

Well, you can imagine my state of mind! By now I was hopping about in a rage. "Greyboar! Will you cease this madness and get on with the job?"

The next moment I was peering up Greyboar's massive hook of a nose, his beady black eyes visible at a distance. So does the mouse examine the eagle's beak just before lunch.

"You will annoy me," he predicted.

"Never," I disclaimed.

"That is not true. You have annoyed me before, on several occasions."

Prudence be damned, I'm not the patient type. I was hopping about again. I fear my voice was shrill.

"Yes, and it's always the same thing! Will you *please* stick to business? Save the philosophy for later!"

"I cannot discuss metaphysics with a dead man." He turned to the King. "Is this not so?"

"Indeed," concurred His Majesty. "Although the transcendentalists would have it otherwise."

Greyboar's fingers twitched.

"Not my school," added the King hastily.

I saw my chance, while they were distracted. I drew my dagger from my boot and sprang for the royal throat.

I know, I know, it was stupid. But the aggravation of it all! Of course, Greyboar snatched me in midair.

"As I foretold, you have annoyed me." Moments later, my arms and legs were tied up in knots. Square knots, to boot. I *hate* square knots—they're not natural to the human anatomy.

"Last time you tied me in a granny," I complained.

"Last time you got loose."

He turned back to the King. "And now, Your Highness, be plain and to the point. What is this philosophic endeavor of which you spoke?"

"I have discovered the true philosophy, the correct metaphysical basis upon which to construct the principles of human conduct. Even when you entered, was I perfecting my discipline."

"Liar!" I shouted. "You were lazing about, eating a fig!"

Greyboar glared at me and I shut up. Tongue knots are the worst.

The King gazed at me reproachfully. "You misinterpret these trifles," he said, waving a vague hand at his surroundings.

Trifles! His silk robe alone was worth enough to feed all the paupers of New Sfinctr for a year. And New Sfinctr has a lot of paupers.

The King got that long-suffering look in his face.

You know, the one rich people get when they talk about the triviality of wealth in the scheme of things.

"These small luxuries are but the material aids to my philosophy," he said, "necessary, I regret to say, solely because I have not yet sufficiently advanced in my discipline to dispense with them. I am only, as yet, an accomplished Languid. I am on the verge, however—I am convinced of it!—of achieving Torpor, whereupon I will naturally dispose of these intrinsically worthless comforts."

"What is this Torpor you seek?" asked Greyboar.

"To a question, I respond with a question. What is the fundamental law of the universe?"

"He's stalling for time, Greyboar!" Sure enough, I was tongue-tied. A half hitch.

Greyboar turned back to the King. "Conservation of matter and energy."

His Highness began to sneer, thought better of it.

"To be sure, but the conservation of matter and energy is at bottom a mere statement of equivalence. From the ethical standpoint, a miserable tautology."

The strangler scratched his chin. "I admit that it does not appear to bear upon one's moral principles."

"Course not!" snorted the King. "Subject's fit only for tinkerers. No, sir, the whole secret lies with the *second* law of thermodynamics."

Greyboar's frown had to be seen to be believed.

"Surely it's obvious!" exclaimed the King. "Philosophy—ethics, that is, the rest is trivia—concerns itself with the *conduct* of men, with the *direction of their actions*, not the substance of their deeds. To place our ethics upon a sound metaphysical basis, therefore, we must ask the question: To what end do all things in the Universe, without exception, conduct themselves?"

Greyboar was still frowning. The King's jowls quivered with agitation.

"Come, come, my good man! To what destination does Time's Arrow point?"

"Maximum entropy," responded the strangler.

"Precisely!"

"But life works against entropy, human life most of all. At least, in the short run."

"Yes! Yes! *And there's the folly of it all!*"

I hadn't the faintest idea what they were babbling about, but all of a sudden Greyboar's eyes bugged out. Never seen it happen before. What I mean is, he wasn't what you'd call the excitable type.

"I've got a bad feeling about this," I mumbled to myself.

"Of course!" bellowed the chokester. He swept the King into his embrace. "Master! Guru!"

"I've got a *very* bad feeling about this," I mumbled to myself.

Then everything fell apart at once. A loud crash indicated the escape of the King's soldiers from their makeshift prison. As if that weren't bad enough, I could hear the squeals which announced the arrival of the porkers. Bound to happen, of course, a strangler's got no business dawdling on the job.

Fortunately, Greyboar hadn't lost his ears along with his senses.

"Time presses, master." He set the King back on the divan. "Quickly, what is the Way?"

The King frowned. "Why, 'tis simple enough, in its bare outline. The achievement of ethical entropy lies along the ascending stages of Languor, Torpor, and Stupor. In turn, achievement of these steps requires following the eightfold Path of Chaos through application of the Foursome Random Axioms. But where is the haste? I shall intercede on your behalf with the authorities. You can be sure of it! Long have I sought a true disciple. We shall discuss our philosophy at length."

"Languor, torpor, stupor, eightfold path, foursome axioms, languor, torpor, stupor..." muttered Greyboar, like a schoolboy reciting his tables. He seized the King by the throat. "I fear not, my guru."

The King's face swelled like a blowfish. "But... but..."

Greyboar shook his head sadly. "Matter of professional ethics."

The whirlwind was upon us! Alarum! Alarum! Hack and hew! The King's guards filled the room, the porkers close behind. Bobbing, weaving, ducking, dodging—he can be nimble when he has to be—Greyboar scooped me up and headed for the door. He was handicapped at first, what with me in one hand and the King in the other. But once the choke was finished—I'd like to stress that point, there've been allegations in certain quarters; I'll admit he was eccentric, but his craftsmanship was impeccable—he had one hand free and that was that. Guards and porkers went flying and we were out of the King's chamber.

But by then, of course, we'd been recognized.

"It's Greyboar and his shill!" squealed the porkers.

"I resent that!" I cried, finally tongue-loose. (I'm good at half hitches.) "I'm a bona fide agent!" But it's hard to pull off dignified reproof when you're being carried like a cabbage. I got an upside-down view of the sorcerer as we made our way through the madding crowd. He was still rooted to the spot, paralyzed by the Void.

"—for if what is were many it must be infinitely small, because the units of which it is composed must be indivisible and therefore without magnitude; yet, it must also be infinitely great, because each of its parts must have another before it from which it is separated and this must be likewise—"

Magrit, there's a proper witch. Mind you, if I'd known what the potion was, I'd never have used it. I'm not what you'd call soft-hearted, but that doesn't make me a bloody *sadist*.

Once we got into the corridor, it was easy going. Porkers all over the place, of course, and the Hospice's staff and filthy-rich clientele ogling and staring, all agog and atwitter, but give Greyboar some finger room and it took a small army to pull him down.

Truth to tell, it wasn't long before we were out on the street, and from there into the sanctuary of the Flankn, with its maze of alleys, byways, tenements, cellars, attics, and all the other accouterments of the Thieves' Quarter. On our way, I gave Greyboar a good talking to, you can be sure of it, but I doubt he heard a word I said. His mind, plain to see, was elsewhere.

Eventually, I ran out of breath, and besides, we'd arrived at one of our hideouts. "All right," I concluded sourly, "untie me and let's split up. Hide yourself somewhere and don't move around—you're too conspicuous. I'll make the rendezvous with Rashkuta and collect the rest of our fee. Meet me in the attic over old Fyqulf's place the day after tomorrow. At night, mind you, if you move around during the daylight, you'll get spotted for sure."

Two days later, I was sprawled on the attic floor counting our money. Things were coming up roses. I'd expected some haggling over the balance owed, but nary a peep. I suspect, after viewing the carnage in the Hospice, that His Acneship gave up any thought of stiffing us.

It was by far the biggest fee we'd ever collected, and I was feeling quite pleased with the world. "Lucre," I gloated, "abundance, riches, affluence, pelf, the fleshpots! The cornucopia! The full measure!—and then some! O wallow, wallow, wallow, wallow, wallow, wallow—" I'm afraid I got quite carried away. I didn't even notice Greyboar come in until he tapped me on the shoulder.

"Snap out of it," he grumbled. "It's only money." Imagine my indignation. But it was no use. Greyboar slouched against the wall, gazing at his hands.

"Without my guru to lead the way, the road will be long and hard."

"Ha! With what we've got here you can slobber around in all the extravagance you need to achieve— what'd the old geezer call it?—sloth, wasn't it?" I giggled; Greyboar glared. "No, no, that's not quite right! Languor—of course, that's the word!"

"I fear not," said Greyboar. "The hunt's up all over the city. The whole army's been turned out. The Flankn's crawling with informers and stool pigeons. We'll need every copper we've got just to bribe the porkers and get out of Sfinctria. Starvation rations, we'll be on, until you scrounge up some work. Even that'll be hard, being in a different city and all."

I laughed, gay abandon. "Is that what's troubling you? Fie on it! D'you think I hadn't figured this all out before I took on the job? Sure, for the moment there's a little heat. Looks bad, prominent tourist getting throttled. But what does the Queen of Sfinctria care, when all is said and done? Unless there's pressure from the Sundjhab—zilch, that's what Belladonna cares! And the Prince—remember him, he's our client?—he's the new King of the Sundjhab now. He'll cool things down right quick."

"I fear not." He scowled. "It's not the loss of the money that bothers me, it's the dislocation—the interruption of my habits, the distractions. It'll make it difficult to concentrate on my Languor."

"You're mad! The main thing the little—pardon, His Puissant Pupness—wants is for the hubbub to die down. After all, if we're caught, how's he to know we wouldn't sing like birds? No, no, Greyboar, take my word for it—the one thing you can be sure His Pimple will be doing is to move heaven and earth to get the hunt called off."

"Under other circumstances, no doubt he would." Greyboar rubbed his nose thoughtfully. "I think our best bet's to make for Prygg. I know the captain of the guard at the southeast gate; we can bribe him. And once we get to Prygg, Magrit'll put us up till the heat's off. Have to do a job for her, of course. No freebies from Magrit. Proper witch, she is."

"What're you running on—" A queasy feeling came to my stomach. "Wait a minute. What d'you mean, 'under other circumstances'?"

Greyboar looked at me, surprised. "Those circumstances under which the Prince would call off the hunt."

"But why wouldn't he—" A *very* queasy feeling. "You've seen him!"

"Last night."

"Why? Rashkuta had the money—I collected it."

"Money." He waved the subject away. "To refute his disrespect for philosophy. Imagine—hiring me to strangle my own guru!"

"To refute his disrespect for philosophy?"

"Well, naturally, what did you expect? I found it necessary to acquaint him with the second law of thermodynamics."

"You—*what*? What did you say to him?"

"Say to him? Nothing."

I was on my feet. "*What did you do to the Prince?*"

"I aligned him with Time's Arrow."

I was hopping up and down in a fury. "*What does all that gibberish mean?*"

Greyboar grinned, a cavern in the abyss.

"The Prince has achieved maximum entropy."

The Realm of Words

Damn Les Six. The way I see it, it's all their fault.
Sure, you could blame Wolfgang. Humans would.
That's because their minds are twisted and whenever
disaster strikes—which for them, is about twelve times
a day—they're always trying to figure out who's to
blame by looking to see who caused it.

Idiots, the lot of them. The more educated they
are, the worse. The real eggheads among them go so
far as to prate on and on about the *sufficient* versus
the *necessary* cause—blah! blah!

Who cares who causes a disaster? What's important
is—who's responsible for getting *me* caught in the
middle of it?

The lousy drunks, that's who. Ever since we arrived
in the Mutt, Les Six have been acting like the world's
just one giant party. Yesterday they kept me fetching
alepots until midnight. And they started drinking at
noon!

True, I didn't have to listen to the windbag today. I don't care what Magrit says about the so-called "best actual sorcerer in the world." Zulkeh is a windbag, windbag, windbag, windbag. That's it—pure and simple—question closed.

But it wasn't all that great. The reason I didn't have to listen to the windbag is because Zulkeh was holed up all day with the other windbags, plotting some idiot scheme to travel to the "Realm of Words."

No kidding. *I'm serious.* Can you believe it? Why would they need to *travel* to the Realm of Words when they already live in it twenty four hours a day? Not only that! Everybody else seems to think this project is a really grand old idea—Magrit and Gwendolyn were talking about it all day! And when Les Six finally stumbled into the salon around mid-afternoon, belly-aching about their hang-overs (for which, naturally, the only cure is more drink—Wittgenstein! fetch us some alepots!), no sooner do they let out their first collective belch than *they* start prattling about the prattler's project!

I'm not sure what's worse—listening to a windbag talk or listening to people talk about a windbag.

Then, of course, once Magrit saw Les Six knocking back their alepots, naturally she suddenly developed an overwhelming thirst. Even Gwendolyn got in on the act. So there I was, racing back and forth all day from the salon to the kitchen fetching alepots, when if it hadn't been for the souses I would have been somewhere else, when Wolfgang ambled into the room.

At first, I was a little relieved. It'd mean more alepots, of course, but I figured Wolfgang's babble would distract the others from babbling. And I'd rather listen to a babbling idiot than to idiots babbling.

Besides, I was hoping Wolfgang would start feeling Magrit up and the next thing you'd know, they'd be off to the sack. Then Gwendolyn'd leave, and I'd only have to fetch alepots for Les Six.

I had every reason to hope, too. She's a proper witch, Magrit, I'd be the last to deny it, but she's also a complete slut. Of course, they're all sluts, human beings—male and female both. Never act rationally about sex, the way amphibians do. Civilized, we are. A clutch of eggs in the water, a quick spray of sperm, and that's it. None of this sloppy disgusting stuff—and they say we're slimy! But, I suppose you can't blame them, handicapped by nature the way they are. Evolution reached its peak in the Age of Amphibians, and it's all been downhill since. Humans are just a stupid accident of history. Hadn't been for that comet—

Well, what's past is past. Anyway, it didn't work out that way, because no sooner did he sit down than Wolfgang started moaning and wailing that the dwarf Shelyid—he's the windbag's apprentice—and the two Kutumoff brats had gone after the windbag into the Realm of Words. (I'd thought better of that little guy. But he's only human, even if he is a dwarf.)

Uproar! Uproar! Uproar!

I could see the disaster coming, and there I was! I started looking for a mousehole but I was handicapped what with the alepots I was carrying. Before I could dump them Magrit snatched me up.

"No you don't, you mangy little lizard!" she hollered, adding insult to injury. "You're coming with me!"

"Where?" I demanded, as if I didn't know.

"We've got to go rescue the poor little tykes!"

Me, I would have let natural selection take its course.

And what was the fretting for, anyway? If Shelyid had survived years in the company of the windbag, I didn't see where a little trip to the Realm of Words could hurt him any. And what did I care about the Kutumoff brats? The boy was about as interesting as an encyclopedia, and the girl—well, if Polly Kutumoff had been a proper salamandress, of course, I'd have told all kind of lies about being the most degenerate salamander who ever lived so's I could cash in on the Kutumoff Grand Old Tradition, but the truth is that swaying hips and batting eyelashes don't do a thing for amphibians.

I tried to explain all of this to Magrit, but she wasn't having any of it and Gwendolyn was getting downright peevish with me. So I shut up. I'll take my chances with Magrit, but Gwendolyn's a different story. Woman scares me and every amphibian I know. Even the dumb frogs down at the Old Mill Pond call her The Knife. (Her knife itself they call the Edge of the Known Universe.)

Now everybody was charging around all over the Kutumoff mansion. The Kutumoff elders showed up, demanding to know what all the ruckus was about. When they heard, Madame Kutumoff immediately started wailing and wringing her hands. (Best hand-wringer I've ever seen, by the way. Really world class.) Papa Kutumoff, on the other hand, reacted kind of oddly. He just got this little smile on his face and wandered off muttering something about his boy getting into his first real scrape and his girl being a chip off the old block. Whatever that means.

For a while I started getting my hopes back up, because soon enough it became clear than nobody had any idea exactly how they were supposed to carry

out this "rescue." First they charged over to Uncle
Manya's mini-mansion and stormed into his library and
started ransacking all his papers until they found the
windbag Zulkeh's formula lying right there in plain
sight on top of the desk where I'd seen it straight off
but kept my mouth shut. Then they tried to read the
formula and was that ever a laugh! Humans are all
windbags at heart, but there's still a whale of a difference between the Genuine Article like the wizard
Zulkeh and a bunch of boozy wannabes.

Then they charged back to the Kutumoff macro-
mansion and stormed upstairs into Magrit's room and
Magrit started consulting her grimoire and brewing up
potions and what not and was that ever a laugh! Mind
you, the old witch is one of your all-time potioneers.
She could whip up something that'd make a scorpion
fall in love with a rock and the scorpion would die
of heartbreak because she'd whip up something else
that'd cause the rock to have a heart attack. But travel
to the Realm of words? No, no, no, no, no, no. No
such potion. No such spell. No such hex.

That requires Grade A, officially-approved, pedi-
greed, certified, documented, diploma-ed, Zulkeh-style
WINDBAGGERY.

But then, just as I was starting to feel relieved, I
also started getting a bad feeling. Some of that came
from watching Gwendolyn, who, since she doesn't know
zip about magic wasn't trying to figure out a way to
travel to the Realm of Words but was just relieving
her tension by sharpening her knife which is already
as sharp as a razor and I could tell she was getting
to the point where she was just going to have to try
the edge on *something* and whenever humans get to

that point it seems they always remember that you can cut off an amphibian's tail without doing any "real damage" since the tail will grow back, which is true, but it *hurts*.

But mostly it was because I had a bad feeling about Wolfgang, on account of the way he was drooling.

Now, your humans always think that since Wolfgang's a drooling maniac and he always drools that it doesn't mean anything. But what'll fool a dumb human won't fool a salamander for a minute. There's drool, and there's drool. Even people who ought to know better don't really listen to the lunatic when he tries to tell them about the twin powers of madness and amnesia. But I know that particular drool that he always starts doing whenever he's going to spring some sly one. It's especially disgusting, even for Wolfgang's drool, which is especially disgusting, even for an amphibian who doesn't have that silly human aversion to slime.

But it was obvious to me. I didn't know the ins and outs of it, of course. After all, I'm as sane as a salamander! But one thing was clear as a bell.

Wolfgang Laebmauntsforscynneweëld was about to spring something. And whatever it was, it was going to be crazy.

Really crazy. I mean—*demented*.

Sure enough, Wolfgang suddenly started raving about applying his twin powers of madness and amnesia and Magrit blew her stack at him and Wolfgang got insulted and started whining.

"Well, I was going to go with you, but since you're going to be that way about it you'll just have to go without me! And it's just as well! Doctor Wolfgang Laebmauntsforscynneweëld has an upcoming appointment with God's Own Tooth himself, you know, and he insisted that I had to come along. Of course, I escaped from the asylum so I wasn't going to go but now I think I will! So there!"

Magrit started hollering that he was a crazy lunatic and what did he know and Wolfgang started smirking and then—I knew it!—he started babbling in an unknown tongue.

I hate it when he does that. Magrit hates it too, because she can't understand him. That's the only part I *like* about it. I hate it because past experience has taught me that when Wolfgang starts babbling in an unknown tongue sometimes it's just because he's an idiot and other times it's because he's applying his twin powers of madness and amnesia and humans can laugh at him but not me because—

—everything started getting hazy!

The universe started spinning around!

I heard voices everywhere!

Sure enough. There we were. Not Wolfgang, just like he promised. But there was Magrit, and Les Six, and Gwendolyn—all of whom deserved it—and there was me, who didn't.

In the Realm of Words.

2

Only humans would come up with a name like that. Sounds majestic, doesn't it—the "realm", no less. And—oh!—so refined!—"of words," no less.

Let a salamander tell you the truth.

The Realm of Words, at first sight, is nothing but

a barren desert stretching in every direction as far as the eye can see, and that's very very very far indeed on account of there is no actual horizon in the Realm of Words due to the fact that (as it might fairly be called by a clear-headed amphibian) Blatherland is *flat*.

You heard me. *Flat*—as in, not round; as in, not a sphere but a table.

How far does it stretch? Who knows? Who cares?

There is neither day nor night, since there is no sun. Light is provided by the Great Lamp in the Sky, which may either be fifty miles high and five miles wide or fifty miles wide and five hundred miles high or—your guess is as good as mine. No doubt the windbag Zulkeh would have performed experiments, but none of the company I was with was so inclined.

At second glance, the barren desert was not entirely barren. At a great distance, we spotted some mounds. Since they were the only thing visible on the plain, we headed off in that direction.

As we got closer, the mounds resolved themselves into great piles of letters. Great piles of the letter O, to be precise, stacked up in pyramids:

```
    o             o             o
   ooo           ooo           ooo
  ooooo         ooooo         ooooo
 ooooooo       ooooooo       ooooooo
```

After we stared at these piles for a bit, trying to figure out what they were, we heard a whimpering noise coming from underneath one of them. We investigated. (Rather: I watched; Magrit bossed; Gwendolyn and Les Six rummaged around.) Soon enough, Gwendolyn crawled out from under the pile holding two little p letters and one big one that looked kind of scarred up, like this: P. The little ones were wailing and the big one was blubbering "don't kill us, don't kill us!"

"I'm not going to kill you," growled Gwendolyn. That set them all wailing even louder, which isn't surprising if you've ever heard Gwendolyn growl.

"And there's no way to kill a letter, anyhow," added Magrit.

"Is too," sniveled a little p.

"You chop 'em wid a knife," sniveled the other, "just like the one the big mean lady has."

"Just like happened to everyP else," sniveled the P.

We stared at the piles of Os.

(Hell with it; looks silly; I hereby declare that the plural of O is Oes.).

"You mean—" exclaimed Magrit.

"It was the Horde what done it!" cried out the P. "Massacred 'em all! Made a pyramid of their heads! Me and the little ones is all that survived, because I hid them under me and the Horde thought I was dead."

A sad tale, a sad tale—but then! Will wonders ever cease? Of a sudden, all the piles of Oes started quivering and jerking around and suddenly collapsed into a great disgusting mass of Oes squirming and squiggling all over the landscape.

"Look! They're not dead!" shrieked one of the little ps.

(Looks silly; I hereby declare that the plural of p is pees.)

(No, looks obscene; I hereby declare that the plural of p is pese.)

"Ghosts!" shrieked the other.

"Oh, stop that!" snapped one of the Oes. "We're not ghosts, we're Oes."

It seemed to examine itself. I think; hard to tell; no eyes.

"Yuck!" it exclaimed. "How are the mighty fallen!" Then, philosophically: "Could have been worse, I suppose. They might have split us lengthwise and made us all into Fs." It shuddered. (And there's a nauseating sight, let me tell you, watching an O shudder.) "A fate worse than death!"

"Look on the bright side!" exclaimed another of the newly-revived Oes. "They always say vowels have more fun!"

In an instant, the cry went up, and before you knew it the whole teeming mass of Oes were—what? Let's just say they seemed to be having an orgy and leave it at that. Hard to tell, really.

"Don't watch, children!" hissed the surviving elder P, shepherding the little ones away.

"Now what?" demanded Gwendolyn. She glared at Magrit.

"What are you glaring at me for?" snarled Magrit.

"Who else is there to glare at so maybe they'll come up with an idea for what to do next?" She glared at Les Six. "The Beerbelly Boys?" (They looked offended.) She glared at me. "The Tail That Talks?" (I'm sure I looked nonchalant.)

Magrit threw up her hands. "I'm a working witch, dammit! I'm not some kind of philosopher! I can't make heads or tails out of this place!"

Gwendolyn got a wild and wicked look in her eyes. "What the hell, why not?" she mused.

It never fails to amaze me how fast that woman is. I mean, even though she looks sort of normally attractive in a female human way except that she's oversize, Gwendolyn can benchpress six hundred pounds. So you wouldn't think the monster could move like a mongoose but she can. Oh yes she can.

The next thing I know she snatched me off of Magrit's shoulder and tossed me high (way high!) up in the air. Spinning and twirling around! Of course, I landed on my feet (cats have got nothing on salamanders), but even so I was outraged. Incensed!

I made my feelings clear, but Gwendolyn ignored me. Rather, she ignored my words. She was scrutinizing my tail.

"That way!" she announced, pointing along the direction my tail happened to be lying.

The whole idea was idiotic, but nobody saw any point in arguing. Not even me. Actually, after a while I decided to be flattered. After a little while longer, I decided there was a profound lesson here: a salamander's tail is worth more than eight human heads.

On and on we trudged. (They trudged; I rode on Magrit's shoulder). On and on they trudged. On and on they trudged. On and on—you get the idea.

After who knows how long, the landscape started to change. Say better—there started to appear the resemblance of a landscape, since you can't hardly call Pure Flat Flatness a "landscape." Not much, mind you—just the occasional stone here and pebble over there, until finally we came across some ruins.

Ruins of what? Don't ask me. Ruins of ruins, looked like.

Then—a sepulchral voice.

"Save the runes," it moaned. "Save the runes."

A rune came out from the ruins.

"Save the runes," it moaned again. "You can start with me. I'm Γ."

"Who?" demanded Magrit.

"Γ." It seemed to shrug. "If you want to be formal about it. My friends call me Γrank. Or Γran, depending on what sex I am."

"Which sex are you, then?" asked Gwendolyn.

"What are you, stupid or something? If I'm Γrank, I'm male; if I'm Γran, I'm female. Once I had a friend who needed his soul saved, so I was Γra. Which reminds me—" Here it started moaning again: "Save the runes, save the runes."

"Save you from *what*?" growled Gwendolyn. She was starting to get testy, I could tell.

"From extinction, what else? What are you, a moron or something?"

"How about I call you Γrankfurter," she cooed, fingering her cleaver.

"Nay, lass!" protested the first of Les Six.

"'Tis low! 'Tis low!" disapproved the second.

"Haute cuisine—that's the ticket!" exclaimed the third.

"Γilet Mignon!" enthused the fourth.

"Γillet of Γish, rather," opined the fifth.

"Properly Γlayed and Γried," qualified the sixth.

Magrit intervened. "Easy there! Γrank doesn't mean any harm, do you now, lad? It's just his way, that's all."

Γ apparently decided to fall back on his stock in trade.

"Save the runes! Save the runes!"

Magrit waddled over and patted the creature. "There now! There now! It's all right—you can tell me all about it. Save you from what, exactly?"

Terminal idiocy, it seemed. Immediately the rune lipped off again.

"What are you, another moron? From—"

It got no further, of course, because Magrit gave it one hefty wallop and knocked it Γlat. (Sorry. I couldn't resist.)

"Don't get Γresh with me, you little Γreak!" she bellowed. "Keep a civil tongue or I'll turn you into Γlapjacks!"

"Yes, ma'am!" squeaked the twit.

"Good. Let's try again. Save you from *what*?"

The rune snuffled. "Extinction, that's what. They're rounding us all up and turning us into"—a shudder— "scrap. And then they're melting down the scrap and turning it into"—a wail of horror—"*common ordinary letters!*"

"Who's doing this?" demanded Gwendolyn.

"What are you, a—" It paused, found wisdom. "The Captains of Industry, that's who. And their goons."

Les Six started to ask who the "Captains of Industry" were but before they got well started the rune jumped up, exclaimed "too many questions! too many questions!" and started scurrying off to the—east?— west?—whatever. After a moment it stopped, turned back, and shouted: "I'll show you! I'll show you!"

And so it was that eight human idiots and a salamander down on his luck found themselves trailing after a lippy rune across the Realm of Words for what seemed an eternity until eventually we came to a slight rise in the "landscape" from the "top" of which we were treated to the vista of—

—a vast jumble of giant factories, stretching as far as the eye can see.

"'Orrible!" croaked the first.

"A vision of Hell itself," groaned the second.

"No vision!" countered the third.

"Hell itself!" mourned the fourth.

"Don't mourn!" cried the fifth.

"*Organize!*" bellowed the sixth.

And with no further ado the half dozen halfwits charged down the slope, capering and cavorting like so many tots in a toy store.

"I'll take that one!" cried the first, pointing to a huge, smoke-belching factory bearing the proud logo *I. G. Sprechenindustrie*.

"I'm for *General Words!*" hallooed the second.

"I've a yen for *Nouns R Us!*" hollered the third.

"Me for *Microspeak!*" cried the fourth.

By the time the fifth and the sixth added their bits to the round, they were too far off to hear. But, judging from the directions they were taking, I thought the fifth had set his aim for the huge *International Business Mots* complex and the sixth seemed to be wavering between *General Linguistics* and *LTVerbs*.

"Idiots!" screamed Magrit. "Morons!"

"Them, too?" asked Γ.

"Now what?" wondered Gwendolyn.

"Save the runes," moaned the rune. "Save the runes. Look! Over there! See what I mean!"

In the distance, we saw a long train of wagons hauling up before a huge stockade. Within the barbed wire compound I could see a bunch of grimy barracks and what looked like smokehouses. With the nonchalance of long habit, burly guards were herding little runes out of the wagons and through the gates.

"What are they handing the runes?" asked Gwendolyn.

"They say it's soap!" cried Γ. "But it's a trick! It's a trick!"

Suddenly, one of the smokehouse chimneys belched a great plume. Γ shrieked. "They're melting us down! They're melting us down!" It clutched Magrit's leg.

"Save the runes," it moaned, "save the runes."

I could see it coming a mile away. I tried to whisper sweet reason into her ear but the old witch was getting her dander up. And who was there to help me advance the voice of sanity?

Gwendolyn? Hah! Hah! The Agitatrix herself!

"You know," mused the damned lady wrestler, "maybe Les Six have the right idea. And besides, what else have we got to do?"

A moment later she was striding off. "I'm for that one!" she announced, pointing to a great ugly heap of a factory called *UmlautMobil*.

"As for us," said the witch, "it's the stockade. Let's see what these bums are up to."

"Us?" I cried. "Us? What have I got to with this madness? I'm an intelligent amphibian—the pinnacle of evolution! What natural selection hath wrought!"

Unheeding, Magrit waddled down the slope. I would have jumped off her shoulder and hid somewhere but I hate to walk and, besides, where was there to hide? Not a mousehole in sight.

Behind me, I heard Γ moaning: "Save the runes, save the runes."

I twisted my head and glared back. "Fuck the runes! And the horse they rode in on!"

Turning around, I could see the stockade looming larger and larger.

"Save the salamander," I moaned. "Save the salamander."

3

Well, there's good news, bad news, and terrible news.

The good news is that Magrit landed a great job almost as soon as we walked into the door of *Umlaut-Mobil*. She was shooting for some kind of low level chem lab job, but the company president wouldn't hear of it. No, no! Seems that humans hardly ever apply for a job in the Realm of Words on account of there's all these words ready and eager to do the coolie work, so the company president was only too delighted to offer Magrit a plum job as his executive secretary. Easy work, great money, perks you wouldn't believe ("of course your salamander can have his own desk!"), the whole bit.

The bad news is that in order to get the job Magrit had to hump the company president.

The terrible news is that she turned him down.

I couldn't believe it!

"Oh, sure," I complained bitterly, as she stalked out of the building, "God forbid you should put out for a respected pillar of the community. Oh, no—not Ms. Morality! Not Ms. Pick-and-Choose! Drooling, gibbering lunatics, sure. Young windbag apprentices, sure. Drunken sailors on leave, sure. Hordes of flea-bitten barbarians, sure. Escaped—"

"Three barbarians are not a horde!" she snapped. "Those three were!"

"That creep!" she snarled. "That drooling old lecher!"

"Wolfgang drools worse—"

"Wolfgang drools cute! The rich fatboy drools rich fatboy disgusting!"

"So what? Concentrate on the adjective: *rich*. We're in the 'realm of words,' Magrit—nouns and verbs don't count."

Well, as you can see, I won the argument hands down, but it didn't do me any good since once Magrit gets set on a course, that's that. Logic, reason, common sense—out the window!

Oh, well. It's the hallmark of sane salamanders that we adjust instantly to reality, no matter how grim. So I took it in stride when Magrit gave up the silly idea of going back to work in a factory (oh, yes, she's a true-blue prole by origin; that's what explains her low tastes, even for a witch) and decided to resume her normal trade. Even though I knew we'd be lucky not to starve to death since all of our customers would be words and what, I wondered, would words need with a witch?

Quite a bit, as it turns out. Mostly fortune-telling. It seems words are all convinced that after they're made they're going to be sent somewhere which they call the "Realm of Reality" where they will be—you're going to love this—words, what else? They say they're where words come from. Anyway, the point is that lots of them want to know exactly *where* they're going to wind up.

It's kind of pathetic, actually, especially for all the "thes" and "ands", each and every one of which is convinced it's going to be the key word in the key sentence which—you name it!

Which, of course, Magrit was more than willing to do, gazing into the crystal ball that she picked up years ago in a junk store.

"I see a man—he has a full beard, a lofty brow—a very lofty brow—he's sitting at a desk; he's writing—what? Yes, I see it now—he's writing a great novel—no! It's going to be the greatest novel ever written, probably; certainly the longest. He's finished the book! Now, he's scratching his head; stroking his beard; pursing his lips thoughtfully. What can he be—oh, I see it now! He trying to think of a title for the longest, greatest novel ever written. Yes, yes, it's coming to him now. He writes the first word—*War*. Yes, that's it. Now he's really thinking hard, really hard. Suddenly—his eyes light up! Yes, he has the second word of the title—and it's—yes! yes! It's you! It's you! *War and*—"

And (pardon the pun) another happy customer trots off. Well, not trots actually, since words don't have legs and feet so they move around in the weirdest ways imaginable, but you get the idea.

The truth is, Magrit's lousy with a crystal ball. She usually reads palms or tea leaves when she tells fortunes, but words don't have palms and they don't drink tea. They don't drink anything, as a matter of fact, or eat—which makes the bosses happier than clams.

When they discovered this fact, Les Six really hit the roof. No sooner did they get off work on their first shift than they all headed for the gin mills, only to discover that there weren't any. Soon enough, they were crowded into Magrit's parlor, bitterly expressing their complaint. They started with lofty political principles:

The first: "'Tis a plot to keep the wages down!"

The second: "As 'tis well known that the variable portion of the capital—"

The third: "—more commonly known as the wage bill—"

The fourth: "—is regulated by the necessity to reproduce the working class in its historically determined standard of living."

The fifth: "The which, in this benighted place, approximates the living standard—"

The sixth: "Of stones."

Soon enough, however, they got down to the gist of the matter, which (I will summarize a mound of verbiage) was that inasmuch as it was widely known that drink is the curse of the working class, the downtrodden masses in the Realm of Words had been foully deprived of their curse in addition to the blessings of life which are, as a matter of course, naturally denied the proletariat.

As always with Les Six, complaint soon led to action. Magrit's little parlor was located on the bottom floor of one of the many tenements in one of the many slums which surround the word factories. In a matter of days, Les Six obtained the floor above from a landlord who, though grasping, was the word "butterfingers." Within days thereafter, they had transformed the seedy dump into an even seedier gin mill and were ready for the business which they confidently expected their daily agitation on the job would soon drum up.

I thought they were nuts, and was highly amused, until they turned out not to be nuts and I got dragooned into being the bartender. I couldn't believe it! I mean, what possible use could words have with booze? Or coffee, and damned if Les Six didn't add on a coffee house. ("Keeps the high-falutin' intellectual words out of our hair.")

But, practically overnight, *The Gin Mill and Pretentious Coffee House* became the center of social life in the slums. Which tells you all you need to know about social life in the slums of the Realm of Words. I thought I was going to die of overwork.

I complained to Magrit, but the rotten witch had already jumped aboard the bandwagon. Now she was telling all her customers that when they went to the Realm of Reality they were all going to be words spoken by profane proles hunched over their alepots in taverns, plotting and planning the revolution. No sooner did they leave her parlor than the cretins (words are not bright) piled into the saloon, eager to prepare for their future life.

Words are weird. Must be why humans like them so much. I remember one in particular—"because." It insisted on shortening itself to "be," so that it could go around bragging that it was a rebel without a cause.

The whole set-up in the Realm of Words is weird. (Our part of it, anyway—later, we found out that the Realm of Words has lots of different levels. All of which are weird.) There's a handful of humans who own all the word factories. Where they came from, nobody knows, and the owners aren't talking. Under them, there's a class of parasite words who lord it over all the other words. They toil not, neither do they labor. They are called the Proper Words, and they are all capitalized.

The common words do all the work, which consists of rendering raw material (mostly hot air, but with lots of scrap words thrown for good measure—runes, obsolete and archaic words, *passe* slang, etc.) into shiny new words. The shiny new words are immediately put to work, while the worn-out old words are "retired" to a giant complex called the Happy Home—which, to a salamander, looks remarkably like a blast furnace— where they are shortly thereafter "elevated" to the "Realm of Reality," rising thereto on a vast column of—can you doubt it?—hot air.

Into this weird but efficient set-up, Les Six and Gwendolyn charged like the proverbial bull in a china shop. If it had been Les Six alone, things would have just gotten rowdy. But when you added Gwendolyn to the stew! There's a good reason the porkers all over Grotum have a price on her head that's only a few pennies less than the one on The Roach—and only a small part of that's due to the numerous porkers she's gutted over the years with her cleaver. No, the real reason is that the woman is a fiendishly good agitator, propagandist, organizer, you name it.

The first thing she did, naturally, was call for the unity of all oppressed and exploited common words. No mean trick, that, let me tell you. Words are even worse than people when it comes to figuring out ways that this group is better than that group. The nouns detested the verbs and vice versa; their sidekicks the adjectives and adverbs positively hated each other; the pronouns always tried to get cozy with the nouns but the nouns referred to hanging around with pronouns as "slumming;" among the verbs, the third person singulars were considered uncouth; on and on.

Then, to boot, the words were further disunited by the rampant animosity among the different fonts.

Helveticas despised Century Gothics who loathed Britannic Bolds who detested Courier News. All regular fonts considered all bold fonts (even their own) to be hopelessly low-class, and as for italics—I remember one italic word (*indeed*, I think it was) bitterly complaining to me over its alepot:

"It's a dirty rotten stereotype! It's not true that all italics are part of organized crime!"

Anyway, sooner than you would have thought possible Gwendolyn managed to convert a bunch of new words to her viewpoint, and the next thing you knew leaflets were being passed around all over the slums with slogans like:

FONTS OF THE WORLD, UNITE!
THE PARTS OF SPEECH, UNITED, SHALL NEVER BE DEFEATED!

Within a week, she had Committees of Correspondence organized all over the place; within another week, she had all the Committees organized into cell structures. Within a month, she put together a full-fledged insurrectionary movement.

Sometimes, I think that woman's not playing with a full deck.

I tried to reason with Magrit:

"It's all nuts! I let it go back in the real world, on account of I have a soft spot for humans, handicapped as you are with mammal habits and brains. But this is going too far! What do we care about a bunch of words, anyway? When you prick them, do they bleed? No! Utterly impervious to pain and hardship. Do they starve? Nope—can't eat anyway. Sure, they're overworked and underpaid, but so what? What else are words good for? And besides, the whole reason we came to this Godforsaken Realm of Words in the first place was to rescue Shelyid and them. What happened to that, huh? Think of the poor dwarf! And the Kutumoff youngsters! Why—right this minute, they're probably in dire peril of their lives! We should be off to their rescue!"

"And just how do you propose to do that?" demanded the witch. "We wound up here because that stupid Wolfgang babbled in an unknown tongue and planted us in the middle of nowhere. Do *you* have any idea where Shelyid and the Kutumoff kids are? And if you do, do *you* know how to get there from here? Well? Speak up, Wittgenstein!"

"I'm your familiar, remember. *You're* the witch—the 'proper' witch, no less! *You're* the one's supposed to know how to get your way around."

"Well, I don't," she grumped, and then she started making noises about how if the sorcerer Zulkeh were here he'd probably know the answer and at that point I realized the poor old woman had lost her mind and it was hopeless. Imagine! Actually wishing the windbag were around!

Her conclusion was that since we were stuck here anyway, we might as well start a revolution since this place needed it as much as anywhere. To which I made the sane response that there'd be trouble since this place had powers-that-be as much as anywhere and they wouldn't like it. But I might as well have saved my breath.

And, sure enough, trouble came. As soon as the company owners figured out what was afoot, Les Six and Gwendolyn all got fired. That, as they say, was locking the barn door after the horse got out, since by that time Gwendolyn and Les Six had already organized the factories they worked in and now they were free to concentrate on agitating all the rest. Which they did, needless to say.

Next, the bosses—they're a sorry lot, bosses, dumb as frogs—set their company goons on Gwendolyn and Les Six. That resulted in a lot of thug words being turned into ex-thug letters.

Finally realizing that the usual methods weren't going to work, the bosses whistled up the official authorities, who promptly responded by sending the police into the slums to round up all agitators and malcontents.

The police were a riot, as always. They came in with their shields, batons and helmets: þôlì¢ê! and went out (ρφʃιζει) better educated.

"It'll be the fascists, next," predicted Gwendolyn, and, sure enough, it wasn't long before we started hearing about a word called "mustache" that was making a lot of noise about what it called "the subjunctive problem." The mustache had a whole crowd of lumpenproletarian words gathered about it, with all the silly buggers coloring themselves brown instead of black.

To my outrage, I got sent in as a spy. So there I was in a big square, a disgruntled salamander if there ever was one, watching this jerk word jerking around other jerk words. "Mustache" was up on a podium and it was haranguing the mob, calling for the extermination of all qualifiers:

"No ifs, ands or buts!" it shrieked. "There must be a final solution for the subjunctive problem!"

The mob went wild, rampaging through the streets of the slum. All shop windows which displayed the ? mark were smashed. The wretched maybes, perhapses, and possibles who huddled within were dragged out into the streets and beaten into 8-point. A scholarly *insofar as* was torn letter from letter.

It didn't go any further, however, because at that point Gwendolyn and Les Six showed up, leading an army of Working Words Defense Guards, and proceeded to beat the brownwords into 4-point. Mustache itself was singled out for special attention by Gwendolyn and her cleaver, whereupon the would-be demagogue was known forever after as must ache.

Now the powers that be declared martial law and brought in the army, but to no avail. The word army was made up of a lot of unhappy conscripts who were easy prey for Les Six and their experienced rabble-rousers, and before you knew it the troops had deserted to the revolution and Gwendolyn was cheerfully setting up a Words and Scripts Council.

In desperation, the Proper Words set up a Provisional Revolutionary Government and tried to take control of the situation by going with the flow, so to speak, but Gwendolyn and Les Six soon had the Words and Scripts Council set the situation right. The Word Palace was stormed, the Proper Words were arrested and stripped of their pretensions. Count Jello became the plebeian jello, the haughty twin earls Ping and Pong became ping pong, and the whole lot of useless parasites were set to work digging the trenches and earthworks which Gwendolyn and Les Six said were going to be needed to repel the inevitable forthcoming invasion by reactionary imperialist powers bent on crushing revolution before it could spread.

I thought they had completely lost their minds, but we'll never know because at that point the Old

Geister stepped in directly and sent The Flood. He usually keeps a lower profile in the "Realm of Reality," but I guess He figures He can afford to use a heavier hand in the Realm of Words on account of He claims to have spoken the Word in the first place.

I dunno, I'm just a sane salamander trapped in a universe of human lunatics. Who else but humans would have invented God in the first place? You wouldn't catch salamanders doing any such silly thing!

Yeah, it was great, just great. For forty days and nights, the Realm of Words was deluged by a rain of letters, periods, commas, colons and semi-colons. Naturally, having gotten us into the fix, Gwendolyn and the half-dozen bigmouths had no idea how to get out of it, but Magrit said there was nothing to worry about.

"Where there's a Flood, there's gotta be an ark. We'll just catch a ride."

Sure enough, about a week into the Flood this bearded character named Noah showed up, with a bunch of sons and a big boat. They started scurrying around collecting two of every word and hustling them aboard the boat. Most of the work was being done by Noah's son Ham, who was a nice enough kid except he complained a lot.

As usual with humans, most of his problem was with sex.

"I've got to avoid sodomy, you know," he mused. "The Lord's very insistent on that!" He reached down and grabbed up a word that was running around loose, *un chien* as it happened. Ham held it up for cursory inspection. "Boy," he announced. "No problem." Next, he picked up *une table.* "Piece of cake. It's a girl."

Then, with a look of total disgust, he held up a chair. He turned it upside down and spread its legs.

"I ask you, Wittgenstein—is this a boy word or a girl word?"

Then he and his father got in a big argument over whether or not they had to save pidgin words and creole words. Noah started off by damning all unauthorized words, but Ham sweet-talked him into finding room for the creoles. The pidgins were out of luck, which caused a lot of squealing, let me tell you.

"That boat's not going to be big enough," I remarked to Ham. He looked shocked.

"Of course it's going to be big enough! We made it just according to the Lord's specifications"—here he rattled off a lot of stuff about cubits and such—"so it's bound to be big enough."

And, whaddaya know? Damned if it wasn't big enough. Don't ask me how. I'm just a salamander, not the Supreme Being. But, when the time came, all the chosen words trooped aboard and crammed themselves into the hold. I had wrangled us a place, too, buttering up Ham and the boys. I think Magrit on her own would have gone for it, but Gwendolyn and Les Six naturally had to stand up for principle.

So there I was, formerly a salamander *sans souci*, perched on Magrit's shoulder, the waves lapping at the last little outcrop of rock left in the Realm of Words, treated to the spectacle of Gwendolyn and Les Six shaking their fists at the heavens and taking the Lord's name in vain. Actually, they were cursing Him directly, which I'm not sure counts as the same thing.

"Things," I muttered, "couldn't get worse."

Things, of course, got worse. The Old Geister heard

them cursing Him, took umbrage, and sent down an archangel. Sehehoth, I think his name was.

"*Curse ye the Lord?*" he demanded.

A string of curses confirmed the charge.

"*Be ye damned!*" he cried.

Then, frowning: "But wait! I forgot—you're already damned. Damned the day you were born, in fact. Predestination, you know. Hmmm. Let me think. I have it! *Be ye cursed!*"

"Cursed with what?" sneered Magrit. The archangel took a breath, and I saw my chance.

"No!" I shrieked. "Not that! Anything but that!"

The archangel frowned again. "Not with what?"

Hey, it's as old as the hills, I know that. But a good trick's a good trick, even if a stupid rabbit did come up with it. So I shrieked:

"Not the dwarf! We've had enough of that gnome Shelyid to last a lifetime! No, let us drown here in peace! Oh, please! Don't cast us into whatever mess that dwarf's got into! Oh, please! Oh, please!"

The archangel beamed, gestured grandly, spoke portentous words of doom.

A flash, a feeling of sudden heat and cold, total disorientation, and—there we were!

Where? Well, at first glance, we seemed to be in a big glass jar at the bottom of what seemed to be some kind of ocean. Just beyond the glass we could see Shelyid in a peculiar get-up—a helmet of some kind, with a hose leading above into the gloom. The dwarf had a chain in his hand and was trying to hook it up to the glass jar, which wasn't easy on account of he was being beset by every kind of monster you could imagine. But he seemed pre-occupied with something else, because as soon as he saw us he started gesturing madly at something in the glass jar behind us. When we turned around, we saw Polly Kutumoff all tied up with rope, which was a lot of rope on account of the girl looked to be about eight and 99% months pregnant.

"Boy, am I glad to see you!" she said, snapping with her teeth at a really nasty-looking acronym that was trying to bite her on the neck—CREEP, it was—while she was trying, with bound feet, to stomp another one that was crouching by her leg.

"You're pregnant!" cried the first.

"No kidding," snarled Polly. Snap! Good teeth, that girl had. EEP went scuttling off; she spit CR out in a hurry.

"Be careful!" she warned. "These things are venomous. Poisonous, too."

"How did you get in such a fix?" demanded the second.

Polly stomped DRM and then fixed the second with a glare.

"By screwing, how else?" She snapped at another acronym and swept her feet around wildly. The damned things were all over the place.

"Not that, lass—'tis obvious!" exclaimed the third.

"Nay, we mean—" For a wonder, words failed the third; he was reduced to gesturing about him.

"All of you shut up and do something useful!" bellowed Magrit. "If I'm not mistaken, the girl's about to give birth."

I didn't think she was mistaken. She's a proper witch, Magrit; which, among other things, means she's been a midwife more times than you can count. She and Gwendolyn began untying Polly.

Within seconds, Les Six were frantically trying to fight off venomous acronyms. I myself had no trouble. An acronym began scuttling toward me—RIAA, that one—I flickered my tongue, the acronym went elsewhere. Simple as that. Acronyms are terrified of salamanders. Actually, the nasty things generally ignore any kind of animal except humans, who are their natural prey.

I heard Gwendolyn chuckle. "Nice move, Wittgenstein. Did you ever hear the one about the frying pan and the fire?"

I maintained a dignified silence.

THE
RATS, BATS & VATS
SERIES

Author's note:

I do a lot of collaborative writing, but almost always with novels. Short fiction, I usually write solo. The one exception is my long-time writing partner Dave Freer, with whom I've written several pieces of short fiction, ranging from short stories to novellas.

The novella that follows is the first story in our Rats, Bats & Vats series, which also contains the novels *Rats, Bats & Vats* and *The Rats, the Bats & The Ugly,* as well as the novelette "Crawlspace" (published in *Jim Baen's Universe* magazine

Genie Out of the Bottle

PROLOGUE

"When shall these three meet again, in thunder, lightning or in rain?"

The dark, hook-nosed lab-coated woman looked as if she might have been one of the witches. And, had this been one of the world of Harmony and Reason's updated Shakespearean plays at the New Globe theatre, the setting too would have seemed appropriate. What she leaned over was no cauldron with simmering eye of newt and toe of frog, but three tissue-cloning vats with their attendant electronics and glassware.

The fetuses developing under the glass covers all looked like unborn rats.

One of them was.

Mari-Lou Evans, once, twenty-four frozen light-years ago, of Stratford-on-Avon, and, like her boss, a loyal part of the New Globe Thespian society, knew her prescribed reply. *"When the hurlyburly's done, when the battle's lost and won,"* she intoned sepulchrally. Then she sighed. "If it ever is, Sanjay. If we don't just lose."

The colony's chief biologist shrugged and pulled a wry face. "Do you think I'd be playing God if we faced any real alternatives?" She pointed to the third breeding vat. "No need for another standard human control, Mari-Lou. We won't be breeding up any more vatbrats for a while. We need to gear up the equipment for mass production of that long-nose elephant-shrew mix. The army has put in impossible demands for quantity. If it tests out fine on emergence, then we're going to have to set up a production line for the creatures."

The chief geneticist nodded. She pointed to the third vat. "The ultrasounds of the bat's gastrointestinal development don't look good, Sanjay. We're going to have to tinker and tweak those genes a bit more in my opinion. Perhaps cherry-pick from the *Tadarida*. It's the size problem. The bigger bats are fruit-eaters, not insectivores."

"Destroy the fetus and start again, Mari-Lou. Make it smaller if need be. The army will just have to take what it can get."

It was the geneticist's turn to pull a wry face. "I hate pulling the plug at this stage."

"And I hate making them intelligent...to go and be cannon fodder. I hate implanting alien-built software and cybernetics that I don't properly understand into their heads. But we don't have a lot of choices. Humans are too slow to produce, and the Magh' are advancing faster than we can retreat, never mind stop them. The council of Shareholders are now talking about introducing compulsory conscription for everyone between the ages of eighteen and twenty-two. Even that won't be enough. We need more fighters."

The geneticist knew that for a truth. The Magh' tide, even with the assistance of the alien Korozhet and their wonderful new devices, was proving very difficult to stem. She shifted subject. "What are you planning on using for language download?"

Her fellow amateur thespian shrugged. "It's just got to be a spoken source of vocabulary in computer-friendly format for the voice synthesizer. We're a bit short of material so I was going to download the Complete Shakespeare, and the D'Oyly Carte Gilbert and Sullivan recordings. That should do."

Mari-Lou couldn't help but smile. "Shakespearean rats, imagining themselves to be Julius Caesar."

Sanjay acknowledged a hit. "Well, they'll make good soldiers anyway."

She was wrong about that. Both language and genetics shape character. They made merry wives, bawds, rogues and rude artisans, or occasionally pirates. The rats were great Magh' killers.

They made terrible soldiers.

In the months that followed, conscription was introduced. So, to the front lines, went the newly produced and uplifted elephant-shrew troops with their soft-cyber implants. Despite the fact that they weren't even rodents, everyone called the small Siamese-cat-sized creatures "rats." The rats and conscripts slowed the advance of the insectlike Magh' invaders . . . but it wasn't stopped. Rumor had it that genetically modified and soft-cyber uplifted bats were about to be added to the war effort. The colony, planned as the new Fabianist utopia in which harmony and reason would finally triumph, seethed with such rumors. It also seethed with frenetic parties, and young men and women in ill-fitting new uniforms.

Harmony and reason were notably absent.

1

A small plane rose slowly, her twin airscrews biting the thicker-than-earth air. The colony—mankind's brave leap into the future—had meant that they had to live in the past. Technology had to be self-sustaining without the interreliant industries of Earth. Some things had gone back a long way—like the propeller-driven aircraft.

Conrad Fitzhugh looked out through the hole in the rear fuselage where the rear door had once been. There was smoke on the southern horizon, where the front lines lay. They'd taken Van Klomp's plane for a look. The alien invaders' scorpiaries had spread their red spirals, twinkling behind their force fields, all the way to the Arafura Sea.

Fitz pulled his gaze inward. He'd see the war front soon enough from a lot closer. He looked nostalgically at the battered little aircraft, and at his fellow sky divers. This would be the last jump for most of them. Bobby Van Klomp had finally gotten the go-ahead to form a paratroop unit. Collins and Hawkes were on a final pass from OCS before being posted to the front. Young Cunningham had just gotten his call-up papers. And Conrad had finally decided to join the next intake at OCS in three weeks' time, despite Candice. He'd have to explain to her tonight. He'd already booked a private table at Chez Henri-Pierre.

He tightened his harness. One of the best things about skydiving was that it stopped him thinking about her, at least for a while. Every man needs a rest from confusion.

Confusion, smoke, dust and fear. And a dead twitching thing, ichor draining from the severed chelicerae to mingle with the blood in the muddy trench. Pseudochitin armor couldn't cover the 'scorps' joints. And, once they'd learned to operate within the constraints of a personal slowshield, none of the Maggots, not even the 'scorps, could match rat speed. But there were always so many of them.

Ariel twitched her whiskers and fastidiously began to clean them. All the Maggots here were dead. So were the human troops.

Another rat sauntered across the trench, pausing to rifle a dead second lieutenant's pockets. He shook his head glumly at the pickings. "I' faith, these whoreson new officers aren't any better than the last lot. Poorly provisioned. What's a rat to loot in such poverty?"

"You could try looting a Maggot, Gobbo," said a plump little rat leaning against a sandbag stack, picking her teeth with a sliver of trench knife.

Gobbo grunted. Shoved a few things into his pouch and tossed the rest. "Even thinner pickings, methinks, my little Pitti-Sing."

The plump little rat considered Gobbo from under lowered lashes. Gently arched her long tail. "Of course, if it is less thin pickings thou art after, *I* wouldn't try a Maggot," she said archly.

A rat peered out from a bunker. A particularly long-nosed rat with a rather villainous cast to one eye. "Zounds! 'Tis all done then? I fought them off bravely."

Ariel and the others snickered. "In every doughty deed, ha, ha! He always took the lead, ha ha!" she caroled. No sensible rat wanted to fight Maggots, but Dick Deadeye took discretion to the ridiculous.

Deadeye drew himself up. "I was foremost in the fight!"

Ariel snorted. "The first and foremost flight, ha, ha!" she said, showing teeth.

Deadeye certainly wasn't about to ruin his reputation for staying out of trouble by rising to the bait from this particular rat-girl. Ariel might be smaller than most, but she made up for it with pure ferocity. He took in the scene instead. The dead lieutenant, with his turned-out pockets, the several dead human grunts, a dead 'scorp and the body parts of several more of the aliens. "Methinks we'd better send a runner back to let them know we need human reinforcements."

Rats had no problem with Deadeye's being a coward. It was his being a brown-noser that was going to get him killed. "Art crazed?" snapped Ariel, irritably. "'Tis fully two hours to grog ration. What need have we to alert them before 'tis needful? They'd make us work."

Gobbo nodded, sauntered over to Pitti-Sing and leered down at her. "Methinks you can hang me up as a sign at a brothel, before I do that, eh, wench?"

Deadeye looked lecherously and rather hopelessly at the two rat-girls. "Well, then I must go myself."

Gobbo yawned artistically. "Methinks the whoreson fancies a bit of time away from the front."

"The swasher can take himself away from my front," said Pitti-Sing, trailing her tail along Gobbo's shoulders.

"'Tis not an ill-thought-of idea, mind," said Ariel, consideringly.

Gobbo grinned toothily. "Ha. Ariel, I had not seen you flee a fight. Can it be that you've abandoned me to go with this swaggering knave? You saucy jade!"

Ariel chuckled. "Pitti-Sing, you're in for a grave disappointment with this swasher. He's all blow and no poignard. I'd like to stay and watch. But I might be able to buy some chocolate back there," she said, longingly. "The vatbrats sometimes have some. Give, Gobbo. The money you found in that top pocket."

"'S mine!"

"You got his hip flask, Gobbo," she said, closing on him with a bound. "You wouldn't want to fight with *me* then, would you?"

"Hello. Methinks 'tis a threesome," said a new haughty voice. "I wouldn't hesitate to report this, unless I was insulted with a very considerable bribe."

Ariel turned. A party of wary-looking rats peered around the sandbagged corner. "'Twould appear that rumors of your demise have been greatly exaggerated, Ariel," said the owner of the haughty voice, and an elevated snout, as he stepped jauntily out of cover.

"Pooh-Bah! Hasn't anyone killed you yet, you cozening rogue?" demanded Ariel, grinning.

The rat shook his head. "No. Alack. But I am sure for suitable fee it can be arranged." He looked at the dead lieutenant. "Methinks you'd better tuck his pockets back in," he said professionally. He gestured behind him with a stubby thumb. "They'll be here in few minutes. They don't make a fuss about us looting vatbrats, but it's the guardhouse and death for snaffling the wares of Shareholders. Didst get much?"

The gleam of silver on the crisp white cloths, and the twinkle of crystal in the candlelight: This was George Bernard Shaw City's finest restaurant, the Chez Henri-Pierre. The crystal glasses were from old Earth. Rumor had it that Henri-Pierre had killed an indentured Vat-scullion who had broken one. The astronomical distance the beautiful, fragile things had travelled was only matched by the prices of the food and the fine wines. The prices, of course, were not listed on the menu. If you had to ask you couldn't afford it. But Conrad had worked out by now that the price was related to the length of the dish's French name.

It was also inversely proportional to the size of the portion. By the exquisite—but minuscule—arrangement on Candice's plate, it was going to cost Conrad the equivalent of an ordinary worker's annual salary. Well, no matter. Conrad was a Shareholder, even if his father wasn't old money. It wasn't as if he was some indentured Vat. And he'd be off to join the army soon. It wasn't going to be easy to break it to her. He hoped that the ring in his pocket would offset the news.

Candice looked perfect in this setting, almost like some milk-white porcelain Meissen statuette, poised and with not a hair out of place. He cleared his throat uneasily. How should he do this?

"Uh. Candy." As soon as he'd said it he knew it was a mistake. She hated to be called that. Van Klomp always did it, at the top of his voice. She didn't like Bobby Van Klomp. She'd done her level best to see that Conrad kept away from the big Dutchman. It was a difficult situation. He and Bobby had come down on one 'chute together. Had resultantly spent six weeks next to each other, in the hospital, in traction. He owed an old friend loyalty. But Van Klomp had gone too far when he'd suggested that Candice might be seeing someone else.

"Um. I've got to tell you something." He felt for the ring box in his pocket.

She looked down at her plate. Conrad noticed that she'd not eaten much of the complex stack of ginger-scented scallops and tiger prawns. "I've got something to tell you too, Conrad." She fiddled with something on her right hand. It was, Conrad noticed for the first time, a band of gold. On her third finger. She turned it around. It was a diamond solitaire. Tombstone size. A lot bigger than the stone in the ring in his own pocket. "I'm engaged to be married."

Conrad stared at her, unbelievingly. Then at the ring. "Who . . . ?" he croaked.

"Talbot Cartup," she said coolly. "I'm sorry, Conrad. This is good-bye."

Talbot Cartup. One of wealthiest men on HAR. An original settler, not, like Fitzhugh, the son of one. At least thirty years her senior. And recently widowed. Very recently.

The bentwood chair and cerise satin cushion went flying. "How long has this been going on?" Conrad demanded, leaning over the table, apparently unrelated events suddenly coming together in his mind.

She colored faintly. "That has absolutely nothing to do with you. Sit down and behave yourself. People are staring."

"Let them stare. I want to know, damn you, Candice."

"If you can't conduct yourself decently, then I suggest you leave," she said icily. "There was no future for us anyway. They're going to raise the conscription age to twenty-six. You will be going into the army."

He laughed humorlessly. "I was going to go anyway. And it's just as well. If I saw that fat creep Cartup, I'd probably kill him. You've been cheating on me, Candice. And, seeing as you'd like me to, I'm leaving."

Blundering blindly through close-set tables, and pushing aside the maître d'hôtel, he headed for the night air and his car. It was a fine reproduction of a mid-twentieth-century Aston Martin. It was his pride and joy.

It was also in the throes of being towed away. Parking over there had been a risk, but he'd been late, and reluctant to hand the keys of his darling to the doorman. Well. He could reclaim it from the pound in the morning. And it wasn't as if he'd been going anywhere right now, except to drive too fast. He set out, walking. Walking nowhere in particular, but going there as rapidly as possible. He strode past the skeletal remains of the huge slowship that had brought the settlers here. The bulk of the twenty-first-century technical heart of the Colony remained here. Conrad did not. He continued on, past the security fence that surrounded the alien Korozhet's crippled FTL starship. Onward without purpose or direction. Brooding. Furious—with himself and with her. Miserable.

It was well after midnight when he realized that his wandering feet had taken him far from the suburbs of George Bernard Shaw City. Far from a taxi to take him home.

And . . . relatively close to the airfield, and the hangar holding Van Klomp's jump-plane. He knew from past experience that the hangar wouldn't be locked.

Briefly he considered taking the little Fokker-Cessna up on a one-way flight. That would show her!

It would also ruin Bobby Van Klomp. The burly instructor had a solitary Share, and not much else besides that aircraft. Conrad knew that Van Klomp was coming in, in the morning, to do the final clearing and storage arrangements. He could scrounge a lift home then.

The clatter of the hangar doors woke him from an uncomfortable dream-chased sleep. And there, in the bright blue sunlight, stood Van Klomp, shaking his head at him. "You dumb bastard. They're bound to think of looking here soon. Where is your car?"

"City pound. It was towed away from the no-parking zone outside Chez Henri-Pierre, where—"

"Where you had a fight with that bimbo, told the whole restaurant you wanted to kill Talbot Cartup, and then stormed out." Van Klomp's face was creased with a wry grin. "And left Candy with a bill to settle, and her with not a dollar in her purse, never mind her taxi fare."

Fitz felt himself blush. "How do you know?"

"The cops told me, *boeta*. When they woke me up at three this morning, looking for you."

"Looking for me at three in the morning? For not settling a restaurant bill?"

Van Klomp gave a snort of laughter. "The way I heard it, there were a couple of tables full of crockery, food and glassware—oh, and a skinny little maître d' that got in your way too. But that's minor, comparatively."

"Comparatively?"

"Compared to being wanted for murder."

"Murder?"

"Well, it is still attempted murder, at this stage. Talbot Cartup's not dead yet." Van Klomp's face was deadpan. "But if he dies, which looks likely, you're for the organ banks."

Fitz swallowed. "And Candice! Is she all right?"

Van Klomp shook his head. "You're a slow learner, Fitzy. She's the one who put the cops onto you. Said you tried to kill him."

Fitz gaped. "I didn't have anything to do with it, Bobby. When I saw them towing my car away, I... I was so mad and miserable that I just kept walking. Next thing I realized it was early morning and I was near here. I thought I'd wait for you to come in and cadge a lift home."

Van Klomp slapped him on the back, grinning again. "Oh, I didn't think you'd done it, *boeta*. I could just see the headline: Martial arts, dangersport and fitness fanatic ties old fart wearing woman's underwear to bed, beats him, puts plastic bag over his head and throttles him. When the cop told me about it, I said he was crazy. But face it, it looks pretty bad for you, Fitzy. You yelled that you wanted to kill him in front of a whole lot of witnesses, besides the bimbo saying that you did it."

"Candy?"

Van Klomp nodded. "Swears it was you, looking for revenge. You locked her in the bathroom while you did the dirty deed. Did it like that to humiliate him and incriminate her. Brave girl broke her way out and called the cops." Van Klomp tugged his beard thoughtfully. "Bet your fingerprints are all over her apartment too."

"But . . . ! I was nowhere near there last night!"

Van Klomp shrugged. "Prove it, Fitzy. Me, I think it was probably a sex game that went wrong. She panicked. Needed a scapegoat."

"Candy!" Fitz shook his head incredulously. "No. You must be wrong, Bobby. She'd never do anything like that. She's . . . she's so . . . pure. Prim. There must be another explanation."

Van Klomp took a deep breath. "Rule my brother told me once: Never criticize a man's mother or his girlfriend if you want to stay friends. So: Now I'm going to tell you something that I've avoided saying because I liked you, Fitz. I've known Candy Foster all her life. Her mother also had exactly one Share. Lived three apartments down from me, on Clarges Street. I bet she never told you that."

She hadn't. Clarges Street was just one step up from the Vat tenements. Fitz's parents were comfortably upper-middle-class Shareholders. "No . . . but I'm sorry, Bobby. I don't see what that's got to do with it."

"Nothing. Except Candy always planned to move up in the world. She didn't have brains or business sense. She did have a pretty face and a good body. She was damned good at being just what the men who were stepping-stones on her way wanted. You wanted a pure little ice-maiden. You got one, kid. Candy's been around. You ask any of the boys on Clarges Street what sort of ice-maiden she was."

"I don't believe you, Van Klomp," said Fitz stiffly, knowing deep inside that he was making a fool of himself. "You're making her out to be a prostitute."

"Oh no, she's not that. A hooker is at least fairly honest. And unclench those hands, Fitzy. I'm your mate, trying to help you, even if you don't believe me," the big man said gently.

Fitz took a deep breath. "I'm sorry, Van Klomp. You don't like her and you never have. Okay I admit, you were right about her seeing someone else. It's kind of obvious now, thinking back. This Talbot engagement didn't just spring out of nowhere. But I can't believe she'd..."

The big man shrugged. "Suit yourself. Believe anything you please. But Talbot is in a coma. And you're going to take the fall for it, unless he comes round. Even then...he might decide to stick to her story." Van Klomp grinned ruefully. "I would."

"But—surely I can explain. I'm innocent!"

"Get this straight. It's *Talbot Cartup* we're talking about. The cops want to catch someone to satisfy the Cartup family. And they want someone in a hurry. And that someone, right now, is you. You'll be pieces of liver and lights in a nutrient bath within the next three days, if they find you. There are roadblocks all around town. I came through one on the way here." Van Klomp grinned evilly. "One thing on your side is they're still looking for the Aston Martin. Someone's face is gonna be red. But it's only a matter of time before they look here too."

"So you think I should run?"

Van Klomp shook his head. "Nope. I think you should join the army."

He pointed out of the hangar door. "They've set up a camp just across the other side of the airfield. Ten minutes' walk."

"But...That's a Vat-camp. I'm going to OCS."

"The next OCS intake is in a few weeks' time," said Van Klomp, grimly. "You're not going to live that long."

"They'll find me there anyway. I'd rather hand myself over and face my trial. They haven't got the evidence to convict me."

"*Boeta*. If they have to *make* that evidence, they will. The Special Branch is good at that. They're hunting you hard. But if you walk across to that camp and join the queue...once you're inside, they won't find you. Just like they haven't found your car. And even if they do find you, as an army volunteer, they can't touch you."

Van Klomp smiled beatifically. "Thanks to Special Gazette item 17 of 11/3/29, all civil legal matters are held in abeyance until the volunteer is demobilized at the end of hostilities. *And* service time will be considered to be in lieu of imprisonment and deducted from the sentence. As it happens, just last night I was talking to Mike Capra at the Pig and Swill. The law was introduced at the start of the war, to try and draw in more volunteers. Even though there is conscription now, it hasn't been repealed. Mike reckons it's a problem looking for a place to happen."

Fitz stood up. "I'll join up," he said determinedly. "But I still want to clear my name. I don't want to take the blame for something I didn't even have the pleasure of doing."

"First things first," said Van Klomp. "And first is to stay alive, *boeta*. Now, I suggest you leave through the side door and take the long way around. There's a fair forest of bushes just beyond the south end of the runway. I've been trying to get the airfield authority to trim them." He patted Fitz on the shoulder awkwardly.

"Good luck, Fitzy. Keep a low profile among the Vats. I'll be in touch, somehow."

Fifteen minutes later, standing in the queue of miserable-looking men at the gate of a barbed-wire-enclosed camp, Fitz saw a police car drive slowly over the grass to Van Klomp's hangar. Then the clerk at the gate asked for his call-up papers.

"I'm a volunteer."

The man shook his head. "There's one born every minute. Name and ID number?"

By that evening Fitz was beginning to think that maybe the organ banks hadn't been such a bad option after all. But he hadn't had much spare time to think about Candice, either.

2

"Swing those arms! Left. Left. Left. Right, left. Keep those damned tails straight!" bellowed the officer.

With distinct lack of enthusiasm, the rats complied. "Methinks this shogging new lieutenant hath forgotten that this is not boot camp," snarled one of the rats, indignantly.

"Silence in the ranks!" snapped the sergeant.

The lieutenant was determined to stamp his authority onto his new troops. They'd explained at OCS that an example was necessary. He'd make one. "You. You that was talking. What's your name, Private?"

"Parts, Sah!" said Bardolph, loudly and untruthfully, to a chorus of sniggers.

The new lieutenant lacked both a sense of humor

and common sense. "Sergeant. Get that rat's number. We'll see how funny it finds being on a charge."

The human sergeant was not a young Shareholder fresh from OCS. He was a Vat who'd stayed alive in the trenches for some months. His expression was more than just wary. "Sah. If I might advise, sah?" he asked, uneasily, *sotto voce*.

The owner of the shiny new pips did *not* choose to be advised. To be confident enough of your authority to listen to advice from experienced NCOs was not something they'd taught this young man. "If I need your advice, I'll ask for it, Sergeant."

Even Deadeye raised his eyes to heaven. It was done in far more unison than the ragged marching.

"Tonight there will be a full-kit inspection! I have never seen such a sloppy, shabby, gutless lot in my life. Things are going to change around here."

"Whoreson Achitophel, he never will be missed," muttered Ariel, shaking her head.

"Not even," said Pooh-Bah, in a quiet but nonetheless lofty voice, "by the lord of the backstairs passage, or by the master of deerhounds or the Solicitor, or even..."

"Straighten those backs! I'll make you lot into soldiers if it kills me."

"'Twill," said Ariel, under her breath. Elephant-shrews were superb killers. Even cybernetic uplift couldn't make them into soldiers.

In a boot camp not far from hell...

In fact the sign in the middle of the camp read "Hell, 3km back." Conrad Fitzhugh was being reborn. They say that the first time is the worst trauma most humans go through.

It wasn't any better this time around. And Conrad Fitzhugh, born with a silver spoon in his mouth the first time, was discovering that going economy class was very different. You weren't wrapped in a pure wool receiving blanket, for starters.

"It doesn't fit."

"Oh, we'll call the tailor so you can have it made to measure," said the quartermaster's clerk sarcastically, tossing a pile of shirts and outsize underwear at him. "Who the hell do you think you are, vatscum? A namby-pamby Shareholder? Move along. On the double. Change. Dump those civ clothes in the hopper there. You won't wear them again."

Fitz moved. His evening wear had been slept in and walked in. But that was a Silviano jacket even if it was a little crumpled, and he loved those half boots. He didn't intend to throw them away!

"They say there are only two sizes in the army. Too big and too small," said the skinny man beside him, pulling on an overall that incontrovertibly proved his point. The little fellow was unusual in the crowded room. Like Fitz he wasn't eighteen.

"Er. Isn't there anywhere private to change?" asked Fitz, looking in startlement at the young conscripts stripping off with unconcern all around him.

The skinny man paused in the act of putting on his horn-rimmed glasses and chuckled. "You've been out of the dormitories a while."

A sudden harsh realization came to Fitz. He was a Shareholder. His parents had come to HAR as frozen Shareholders. Everyone else here was probably—no, almost certainly—a Vat. Bred up in a cloning vat from a tissue scrap that had made the long journey from

Earth. Naturally, every human on HAR was entitled to become a Shareholder. The New Fabian Society wouldn't have it otherwise. Of course, the Company was entitled to recover the costs of cloning, rearing, feeding and educating the Vat-kids before they could buy that Share. After all, utopia didn't come for free. Existing Shareholders were entitled to some return on their investment, naturally. Certain privileges were of course reserved for Shareholders.

He was almost certainly the only Shareholder-boot in this camp. He'd known that. He'd just suddenly become aware that pointing this out could be very bad for his health. He blinked, and began stripping.

"Yes. I've become rather spoiled." He looked at the older man. Twenty-five, at least. He must have been one of the original Vats. Conrad Fitzhugh realized that he was going to need a role model. Skinny looked friendly enough. But how to initiate a conversation? He'd never had much to do with Vats. They were servants, mostly.

The little man took it out of his hands. He had obviously made his own assessment, and probably had a very sensible reason—Fitz would make two of him. "These kids make me feel ninety. They're likely to beat us fossils up. We should stick together." He stuck out a hand. "McTavish. Call me SmallMac." He grinned wryly. "Everyone does."

Fitz took his hand. "Fitzhugh. Um. Call me Fitz."

"So, what was your line on civvy street, Fitz?" asked SmallMac, attempting to cram the remaining issue gear into a kit bag, a job requiring two more hands than he had. Fitz held the mouth of it open for him. It gave him a moment to think. All Vats worked—they were in debt. Fitz had never worked a day in his life. Only those

Shareholders with very few Shares or a desire to work
did. It had been a long-standing source of acrimony
between him and his father. "Um. I did a lot for the
Parachute club." It was not strictly a lie.

"Oh. Van Klomp," said SmallMac, satisfied. He
returned the favor with Fitz's kit bag. "One of the
best of them. Good-o. Looking at your clothes and
hair, I thought you might be one of their pretty boys."

Fitz had no doubt who "them" were. And he wasn't
surprised that his new acquaintance knew who Van
Klomp was. It was a small colony for a loud voice.

"And you?"

SmallMac smiled wryly. "Oh, I played with horses.
Kept me out of the army. But they decided I wasn't
young enough anymore. Besides being a bit slow."

"Move, you lot! On the double."

Carrying their kit bags, they ran again to get their
heads shaved. Then to have slowshields implanted. To
get infrared lenses implanted. Then, still carrying the
kit bags, straight to drill.

Fitz had gone into this strong and fit. He'd heard
about boot camp—although he was sure that OCS
candidates did not have nineteen-year-old Vat sadists
as instructors. He'd vaguely thought that the suffering
associated with boot camp would be for other people.
Less fit people. His aching body was beginning to
realize that the purpose of exercise here was twofold.
As a secondary thing, it was to get you into condition.
Principally, it was to break you. No kind of fitness is
enough for that. He was as exhausted as SmallMac
by the end of it.

He'd also come to realize he'd been wrong about
the wiry little man. SmallMac, while lacking in upper

body musculature, had incredibly strong legs and fantastic balance. He'd been a horse-breaker for a large riding academy—quietly excused military duty because of his employer's connections. Unfortunately he'd had a falling-out with his boss. So here he was, carrying a pole, at a jog.

"Are they trying to kill us?" panted the horse-breaker.

"No. Well, not quite. One step short of it."

"But why?" asked SmallMac. "I thought they wanted soldiers. They'll end up with wrecks."

"My sensei explained it to me," said Fitz. "Most humans aren't natural killers. You can make them into soldiers, though. Humans will fight bravely, using the skills you train into them. You can either bring them up from the cradle to do this, in which case you have samurai. Or you can make soldiers in six weeks. They won't be anything like as good as samurai, but it is quicker. But to do that they have to get you into a state of physical and mental exhaustion, in which old habits are forgotten. The soldier doesn't think anymore. He just has to obey. Obey unconditionally."

"Hmm. A bit like breaking horses. Well, not my way. But one of the ways. I see the advantages," panted SmallMac, "to the army anyway, of getting conscripts young and fresh out of Vat-school. They're pretty blank anyway, and used to obeying orders. It's a lot harder for them—and us—dealing with old fossils."

"Yep. We're foolish enough to question things and to think for ourselves."

"Speak for yourself, Fitz. I'm too tired to."

"That's the whole idea. Come on. We've got to run again."

"This is your bangstick." The instructor held up the short-bladed assegai. "This is your new wife. You will sleep with it. You will run with it. You will eat with it in one hand. You will clean it. You will love it. You will treasure it. God help you if I find you without it, because He is the only one who may be able to."

Fitz looked at the issue weapon. Three feet long with a foot-long blade and a cutout into which a shotgun cartridge was inserted. Personal shields, which stopped anything moving faster than 22.8 mph, made projectile weapons useless. So: You had a short little spear, a trench knife—which, as a connoisseur of knives, he was almost ashamed to touch—and a funny little ice-pick thing. Technological advances seemed to have sent weaponry back to the iron age.

The next three days were a blur of the worst that life had ever offered Fitz. Aside from the lack of sleep and the sheer physical grind, he'd never even cleaned his own boots before. Or made a bed.

He learned. But not fast enough.

The corporal picked up the corner of the bed with its display of laboriously polished, ironed, starched and folded items and tipped it onto the floor. Fitz, standing at attention by the foot of the bed, couldn't see what was happening. He could hear it, though.

The young corporal came and stood in front of Fitz, and lifted his chin with one finger. He looked at the name stenciled on the overall. "This is a sty. And that makes the person living in it a pig, Private Fitzhugh. A filthy fucking pig. What are you?"

Silence.

"You're a slow learner, Private. I'll ask you one

more time before your entire squad does two hours of bangstick drill in full kit. What are you?"

"I'm a pig, Corporal. A filthy fucking pig," said Fitz. *And you are two seconds from being dead, you snotty Vat-shit,* he thought.

"Right," said the Corporal with a nasty little smile. "Your squad mates can sort out the pig in their midst. There'll be another inspection of this tent in one hour. I expect this pigsty to have become a decently starched bed by then. Otherwise, it's full-pack drill for all of you."

He walked out.

"You stupid bastard!" yelled Ewen, the self-elected squad tyrant. "Can't you make a bed properly? Another fucking inspection. I've got a good mind to—"

SmallMac interrupted. "He saved us all a couple of hours' full-kit drill, Marc. Come on, we've got an hour. We'd better all get stuck in."

The stolid Vat-kid from the next bed, who had been scathing about Fitz's ability to polish boots, nodded. "I reckon. Come on, Marc. You do the best hospital corners in the company. I've got some spray starch. We're all for it otherwise. We can beat the Oink up later."

Marc Ewen tugged his jaw. "I suppose so. Come on, Oink. Move it up. Drop us in it again, and you're for it."

The beating got delayed by a session of P.T. and a five-kilometer run. In the manner of these things, it kept being delayed until it was forgotten.

The slowshields had caused small arms to be dispensed with in this war. Both sides still used heavy artillery, however. It could destroy defenseworks, soften up or even bury the enemy. And the pounding could drive anyone mad.

The rats knew by now that when it stopped, the legion of varied creatures that made up Magh' infantry would mount an assault. Sometimes they came surging over no-man's-land like a tide. Sometimes they came pouring out of burrows like lava.

But they always came, if the pause in the bombardment was more than momentary. From the minute the heavy shells started to fall, the troops in the trenches knew the attack was coming. The sector had been quiet for some weeks and Lieutenant Lowe thought that he had at last begun to instill some discipline in these unruly rats.

The shells had fallen thick and fast for the last six hours. The HAR gunners tried to give as good as they got, but the humans simply couldn't match the range, accuracy or sheer volume of fire that the insect-like Magh' mounted. The colony had turned all their spare manufacturing capacity into producing food for the guns...but the Magh' capacity appeared to grow, along with their scorpiaries. The original invaders had set up five of the vast, odd, flattened termite heaps, each one mile in diameter. One scorpiary for each of the vast ships. But the creatures were obviously reproducing a lot faster than their human opponents.

Then the guns had fallen silent.

"Where do you think you're going? Come on, form up. A proper military formation, now. The Magh' are coming," said the lieutenant, his voice cracking.

Ariel leapt acrobatically onto his right shoulder. And Gobbo to the other. "If what, you shogging whoreson?" asked Gobbo, twitching his whiskers.

The lieutenant nearly fell over backwards. "Get off me! Get to your posts!" He pawed at the two rats. "Argh, let go!"

Gobbo's long red-tipped fangs had closed through his thumb. Ariel was even more direct. She had her teeth at his throat.

Pooh-Bah looked up at the lieutenant, who was now standing very, very still. The rat said, pompously. "And secrets of state, I will sell for a very reasonable rate: This is one that never will be missed."

Ariel pulled her fangs away from his throat. "Methinks you must choose, Bezonian. You can run and be shot for desertion. Or we'll let the Maggots kill you. And if they fail, we shall deal with you. The Maggots will take the blame."

"I . . . I'll have you all court-martialed and shot—*eek*. Magh'!" he shrieked, as the varied white grub-shapes poured over the top of the trench.

The lieutenant's flight lasted less than thirty yards before one of the Magh' caught up with him.

"Help! Help me!" he yelled desperately.

Gobbo shook his head as the venomous barbed tail stabbed through the man's uniform. "Help me, *if you please*, Lieutenant."

3

The seven of them were on their way back from the mess hall in the moonlight when they came upon two very, very drunken NCOs. Under most circumstances this would have been a good reason to turn and quietly walk away. In fact, they all checked. It was the whimpering that was coming from a thing at the feet of the two corporals that made Fitz decide to walk forward. That, and the fact that SmallMac was already doing so.

Coming closer, Fitz saw that the bundle lying there was human. Or had been, before they'd started kicking it.

"Whatsh are you lot doing here?" slurred the one man.

"KP duties, Corporal," said SmallMac, kneeling next to the victim.

"Well bugger off to y'r tent. And leave that little dickhead alone."

"We're taking him to sick bay, Corporal," said the small man, his glasses glinting in the moonlight.

"Like fuck you are!" The corporal swung a vicious kick at SmallMac's head.

Fitz caught the man's foot and extended the swing. He gave the falling corporal a far-better-placed kick in the solar plexus. The corporal doubled over as he flew. And as his fellow drunk swung wildly at him, Fitz hit him neatly on the jaw.

"Holy shit! Let's get out of here!" gasped one of the conscripts.

"What the hell do you think you've done, Fitz?" demanded another, horrified.

Fitz ignored them. He leaned down and grabbed both of the drunk NCOs by the throats. Neither was a particularly large man. The little Vat they'd been beating was even smaller than SmallMac. "Is he okay?"

SmallMac shook his head. "Hard to tell. He's not really conscious. Blood coming out of his ears by the feel of it. Let's get him to sick bay."

One of the drunks began to struggle. Fitz brought their heads together with a crack and tossed them aside. SmallMac was already staggering to his feet with his burden. They linked arms to form a chair. And ran. Three of the others ran too, heading for their tent with as much speed as possible. The other two came along to the sick bay. One of them actually had the forethought to run ahead and pound on the door. There was always a medic on duty.

When it opened . . . Fitzhugh realized that things could get a lot worse. Two medic NCOs, the camp doctor, and Major Ogata were all there—playing cards on one of the examination beds.

"What is it?" asked the medic who had opened the door, plainly not pleased.

"Emergency, sir. We found this man. He's been beaten up, sir. He's unconscious."

"Bring him in. Get him onto the examination bed."

Fitz and SmallMac complied.

"Christ! I want an IV line up on this kid," snapped the doctor.

The doctor and medics moved into action.

That left the four of them . . . and Major Ogata, who had moved against the far wall to allow them passage. Ogata, with JAG flashes on his shoulders, had arrived in the camp three days before. Nobody knew quite what he was doing here, but he had been taking some bangstick drills. "Stand," he ordered coldly, as they attempted to melt back to the open door. "Just what happened here?" he asked. He pointed to one of the young Vats in the group. "You speak."

The youngster looked around, nervously. "We were on our way back from KP, sir. We . . . we found that private in the alley between Q-stores and the chaplain's offices, sir. We brought him here."

"You had no part in beating him up?" All of them shook their heads.

"We wouldn't have brought him in if we had, sir," said SmallMac earnestly.

The major looked at them with cold speculation. "Maybe. And maybe you realized that you or perhaps your companions had gone too far? You know who did this."

"Sir, KP ends at 2100," said Fitz, calmly. "Look at the time now, sir. We haven't had time to administer that kind of beating."

Ogata looked at his watch. Looked at the doc and his two medics. Then, nodded.

"Two men have been killed in this camp, and a number of others have ended up seriously injured. As yet no one has been prepared to testify. I have been sent here by the Attorney General to put a stop to it." With a ghost of a smile he said "The army doesn't want soldiers dying before they reach the front."

The major's eyes narrowed. "If I have to drill this entire camp until half of you end up as clients for the lieutenant"—he pointed to the doctor who was helping the medics to get the boy onto a stretcher—"I will find out who did this. I'll need all of your names and numbers. Then you can get yourselves back to your tents." He jerked a thumb at the victim, now being carried through to the military ambulance. "He doesn't need you anymore."

As far as Fitz could see it was a lose-lose situation, especially for the four of them. All the conscript-boots dropping dead on the parade ground weren't going to affect the guilty parties in this case. On the other hand... If they grassed... the instructors would see that they suffered in interesting ways. And Fitz—by now—had a grunt conscript's faith in the fairness of the system: ten to one, the two corporals would get off while they carried the can.

Just then fate, in the shape of two drunken corporals, intervened. They also obviously did not expect the sick bay to be occupied by anything more than one easily intimidated medic. And they were less than observant as they barged in and turned on the four privates.

"All right, you lot of little scabs! Where's Margolis? We haven't finished with him. Or you. Especially you," one of them snarled at Fitz.

Standing against the wall behind them, Ogata cleared his throat. "I think I have solved that little mystery."

The two corporals turned, and looked in horror at the pips and JAG flashes. As one they tried to bolt.

"Halt!" yelled Ogata. They didn't.

"Privates! Catch those two. Restrain them," snapped Ogata.

It was not an opportunity that came the average boot's way very often. An order from heaven, as it were. By the time the two corporals had been caught and "restrained"—one by SmallMac with his powerful horse-breaker's legs applying a life-threatening scissors, and the other by being sat on—a number of scores from the last five and half weeks had been settled. Then a squad of guards and the guard commander arrived at a run.

Ogata looked grimly at the two prisoners hauled before him. Sniffed. "I'll want blood samples from these two when the Doc gets back. And I want sworn statements. Now. Before anyone gets either intimidated or clever."

He turned to one of the guard detachment. "Get

me Lieutenant Belsen. I'll use the doctor's room for the statements. I'll want these men one at a time. There will be no discussion amongst them." He turned to Fitz and his companions. "I advise you strongly to stick to the bald truth. If one of your statements does not agree ... you will be subjected to further investigation and charged."

The lieutenant arrived at a run. He was a young, rather sadistic and sarcastic man, a once-minor Share-holder who obviously enjoyed controlling life and death for a large number of conscripts. The camp commandant was a bumbling and mediocre career officer. Belsen's overeagerness appeared to give the old man dyspepsia. But the lieutenant stepped a wide and wary berth around Ogata.

Fitz's turn came. He stuck to the truth. Under the circumstances it seemed like pretty good advice. The major, and the lieutenant who wrote it all down, seemed satisfied.

"Very well," said the major. "Read through the document. If it is correct, put your number and signature at the bottom."

Fitz did. He was then dismissed, and told to wait in the outer room. It looked like it was all over.

Ogata and Belsen came out with one of the statements. "Take those two NCOs to the second room under guard," said Ogata. "The medical personnel will be here to take blood samples in a few minutes. Then you can take them to the cells." He looked down at the piece of paper he was carrying. "Fitzhugh, you've made a mistake with your serial number. This will have to be corrected, signed again and witnessed." He held out the piece of paper.

Fitz looked at it. The number was a simple enough one: his own ID with an army prefix. "There is no mistake, sir. That is my number."

Lieutenant Belsen lifted Fitz's chin with his swagger stick. "You're a fool, Private. The last four digits indicate Shareholder status. Making up a number was bound to trip you up."

Ogata pursed his lips, shook his head and sighed. "You obviously wanted to derail the course of justice with something the court-martial tribunal was bound to pick up. Slick, Fitzhugh. But not slick enough."

Fitz felt the blood drain from his face. "Major. I *am* a Shareholder," he said angrily.

In reply, Ogata tore his statement up. "Very funny, Private," he said grimly. He turned to the guard commander. "Put this one in the cells also. Not the same cell as the other two. I'm going to contact military police headquarters and have them moved there. No sense in keeping them here."

Fitz found himself spending a cold night in a cell in the guardhouse. He'd been made to clean it and was then given breakfast, while the sounds of the first parade of the day went on outside. It was silent and monotonous in the cell. Fitz had never thought the day would arrive when he would have preferred to be on parade to any other possibility.

4

Dick Deadeye, the walleyed rat-coward, edged his way into the tent where Sergeant Marcowitz was reporting to Captain Witt. "Gamma 425 section lost most of their humans when we pulled back, sir. Forty-three casualties and seventeen shipped out the field hospital. Lieutenant Lowe was among the dead, sir. Several minor injuries that will be back, but at the moment there are only four privates and two NCOs still fit for duty."

The captain steepled his fingers. "I have asked for reinforcements, but we're stretched. Southwestern Sector command says the new intake are about to finish boot camp. We'll get some of those. In the meanwhile those troops will just have to be integrated with other companies." He sighed. "And the rats? What have we got left there?" His voice showed distaste.

The sergeant consulted the clipboard. "Two casualties, sir."

The captain hauled himself to his feet. "The human troops get massacred—and those filthy little scavengers lose two out of five hundred! I'm sorry, Sergeant, but I smell a rat—"

"'Tis only I, Dick Deadeye, Captain," squeaked that hero, peering out from behind a canvas chair. "We don't get to have a bath very often on the front." He scratched his scraggly nose with a stubby pawhand. "Except when it doth rain. And then methinks 'tis more like a shower."

"What the hell are you doing here, rat? Sergeant, get it out of here. Or rather let me get the MPs. We need to make an example of a few of these—"

"Er. Captain." The sergeant interrupted. "This is one of the rats that Captain Shweto, um, bribed to be informers. Dick Deadeye isn't it?"

"Shweto's dead," said Captain Witt, his tone indicating that he'd liked his predecessor as much as the sergeant liked this rat.

Dick Deadeye nodded. "Aye. Shog him for a debt-dodger. He still owed me for the last lot."

"Owed you? I suppose you've come to collect, and you expect us to believe you," said the sergeant, dangerously.

"Poor Dick Deadeye. My name and my looks are against me. A merest trifle. A matter of a hogshead of grog."

"They're habitual liars," said the sergeant. "And cowards, too."

Dick Deadeye did his best to look affronted. "In every doughty deed I always took the lead!"

"You give yourself airs!" said the sergeant, disdainfully.

"Nay. 'Tis the food," said Dick Deadeye. "But some more grog will fix that. I've come to give you warning, Captain."

The captain leaned forward. "I don't want warnings. I want to know why most of my human troops died in the last assault and only two of the rats did."

The rat twitched his nose and looked thoughtful. "Methinks the two were a bit slow? Or mayhap too busy tail-twisting to notice? It can happen, or so I'm told." The rat sounded regretful. "Now, I have decided. I don't just want grog this time. I believe 'tis tradition to demand your daughter's hand in marriage, but to be honest, I fear she may have inherited your homely face and bad complexion. And while your nose is a more attractive length than that short little stump that doth do most humans service, you lack a tail entirely, unless 'tis hidden in your trousers. So: you'll give me Ariel. And a gill of liquor per man whose life I've saved. Twice that for your own, even though

I daresay 'tis not worth half as much," said the rat, head on one side and rubbing his paws thoughtfully, for all the world like a merchant at a market stall.

The captain and sergeant gaped at the rat. "Wh-what do you mean..." stuttered the captain.

The rat held out his paws. "'Tis clear enough. I know marriage is not something we rats have hitherto aspired to. But I have despaired of ever winning her affection. And from what I can gather this 'marriage' thing is just the ticket for an ugly fellow like me." He looked at the sergeant quizzically. "Woman are then bound to 'serve, love and obey,' when married, aren't they?" he asked. "It says so in *The Taming of the Shrew*."

Sergeant Mary Marcowitz missed. But only because she moved fast enough to harden her slowshield.

"I meant, what do you mean about saving our lives?" snapped the captain.

"Why, what I said, sirrah," said the rat. "The others said that the Maggots disposed so efficiently of you humans in the last assault that they thought they would let this burrowing clean you out of here too. They're going to leave you to this lot."

"You mean...there's a mine?"

"Aye. Ariel said 'twas unsporting not to tell you. But at length 'twas decided you wouldn't listen anyway." The sergeant and the captain were already out, yelling for action stations.

The sergeant headed for the rat quarters, where she found the rats about to depart.

"Traitors!" she screamed.

The outer door opened, and Fitz heard the unmistakable sound of someone snapping to attention. A recognizable chilly voice spoke. "At ease, Sergeant. I believe you have Private Fitzhugh here."

"Yes, sir! The prisoner is in cell two, sir."

"I'll speak to the man alone, Sergeant. He's to be released. There was a misunderstanding," said the major.

"Sir."

The sergeant led Major Ogata through, clattered the keys and let the major into the cell. The sergeant walked off back to his desk. Ogata waited carefully until he'd gone. Fitz decided that two could play the waiting game.

"I made a mistake," said the officer quietly. As usual, he allowed almost no trace of expression into his face or voice. "I should have recognized the name. You're free to go, and there will be no mention of this on your record." Now he allowed a glimmer of a smile to appear. "You won't be called as a witness in the assault case. Nor will your affidavit be rewritten. Somebody else might recognize the name, and they might not be quite so slow."

Fitz was not feeling too fast himself. "Uh. Thank you, sir."

The major nodded. "Special Gazette item 17 of 11/3/29 still stands. But I wouldn't bet on the legislature not repealing it, and not making that retroactive, if they discovered you. Talbot Cartup is a powerful man. He controls the Police Special Branch handling colony security, you know."

Fitz hadn't—but then it wouldn't have made any difference anyway. "He's alive, sir?"

Ogata raised his eyebrows. "You're pretty cool, Fitzhugh. I think so. I'm afraid I haven't followed up on his well-being. However, it appears that Private

Margolis will live. In fact I have just been to the military hospital where—as the local enforcers can't get to him, and he thinks he's dying—he has confirmed your testimony."

Now he smiled properly for the first time and stuck out his hand. "I've never met you, and it has been my pleasure not to do so. Good luck, Private Fitzhugh. I think one good deed fairly well cancels the other out."

Fitz took his hand. "Nobody would believe me, but I didn't do it."

The major looked steadily at him. "I was a prosecuting attorney before the war, Private. You're right. No one would believe you. Now get lost. Collect your boots and belt from the desk sergeant and get back to your squad. Good luck."

Outside, blinking in the sunlight, Fitz wondered if it was going to be as simple as that. It was Sunday, officially a day off after the morning parade. Mostly it was spent polishing, ironing and preparing for the week ahead. He walked slowly back to his tent.

"Fitzy!" SmallMac yelled. "Hey, guys, he's back."

Fitz was amazed to find himself being slapped on the back and grinned at.

Marc Ewen had always found the two older men in his tent and his squad something of a trial. He was standing with his hands on his hips, surveying the scene, taking no part in the congratulations. If there was going to be trouble, Fitz realized, it would be with him. He was the only one in the tent who had persisted in calling Fitz "Oink."

"Hey, Oink. SmallMac says you gave two instructors a hiding at once," he said. There was a testing quality to his voice. He was used to thinking that he was the toughest man in the squad.

Fitz shrugged. Best to try and deal with it peacefully. They had barely two more days of boot before they were posted out. He just had to get through to Tuesday. "I know a trick or two, Marc. We can go over to the gymnasium and I'll show you. Friendly, of course."

Marc Ewen shook his head and smiled. He was considerably larger than most of the Vats, and had been a meat packer before his call-up. He was as strong as one of the bulls whose carcasses he used to heft around.

"This I'd like to see, Oink. But we'll keep it friendly."

A few minutes later the squad and a few others were in the gymnasium, and on the mat Fitz showed Marc Ewen—gently—how to use a meat packer's strength against him.

Ewen stood up. Nodded. "Okay. I guess SmallMac told it straight. Run me through that again, so—"

His sudden silence was caused by the entry of a crowd, mostly from B Company. They seemed to have padlocks with them. Attached to their belts. And the belts were in their hands, not through their belt loops. "Well, well. There he is. Golden boy Shareholder," said the leader of the mob, B Company's official bruiser, a gorilla called Bennett. "We'll take over, Ewen. We'll do a proper job."

Marc Ewen faced them, hands on hips. He shook his head. "Butt out, Bennett. This is our affair. Got nothing to do with you B Company goons."

The man snorted. "He's a fucking Shareholder. We heard it from the guys who were on duty last night.

And Sarge Lenoir confirmed it. He was there when that little shit admitted it himself. Move out of the way, Ewen. He's going to have an accident."

Fitz tensed. There wasn't any way out of the gymnasium, except past the mob. But he was damn well going to take a few of them with him.

To his surprise the broad Marc Ewen stood his ground "Take yourself and your crew back to your tents, Bennett. He's one of us. If anyone takes it out of him, it'll be us. And it's not going to happen."

"You're full of shit, Ewen. He's a fucking Shareholder. He admitted it!"

SmallMac nodded. "So what if he is? He's sweated and bled with us. He's done full-kit drill with us, and ended up in the guardhouse just for helping Margolis—who was from B Company, I might remind you beggars. You boys take him on and you'll have to take us on, too."

There was a tense silence. There were a good forty of them to twenty of Fitz's company. And the others had padlock-weighted belts.

Fitz cleared his throat and pushed his way forward. "Look. I *was* a Shareholder. Once. But now I'm a private the same as the rest of us, in the same army as the rest of us. I'm part of A Company, tent 17. And I'm damned if I'm going let my squad mates bleed for me. I'll fight you one at a time or all together, first. Any one of you got that kind of guts?"

The pack had come hunting, expecting the prey to run. This was something entirely different. But Bennett wasn't going to back off. "Sure. This is going to be a pleasure. An education for you, namby-pamby Shareholder."

"Don't do it, Oink. He's a killer," warned Ewen.

Fitz just took off his shirt, assessing his opponent as he did. Bennett took off his shirt too, in a deliberate camp mockery of Fitz. The man had more body hair than your average gorilla, and muscles that would have done that creature proud, too. He would probably weigh in at two hundred and forty pounds against Fitz's one-eighty.

"Watch out for his head," said one of Fitz's squad mates, taking his shirt. "He likes to close and head-butt. And watch out for your eyes with those thumbs."

Fitz nodded and stepped forward. He'd been in camp with these men for nearly six weeks now. He was no longer naive enough to believe his martial arts skills would simply overwhelm Bennett. The dojo was quite unlike real fighting.

But he was unprepared for the suddenness and unpredictability of the assault. He had no intention of getting into a clinch with the man. And then he was. Bennett had managed to grab him and was pulling him in by the shoulders, his forehead coming down to smash Fitz's nose to pulp. Desperately Fitz ducked sideways. Bennett's head cracked against his eyebrow-ridge instead.

Bennett threw Fitz over his hip.

It was a foolish move. Had the big man kept Fitz in the clinch, things could have ended nastily and very quickly. As it was, Fitz rolled clear and was back on his feet as Bennett landed, hard, on his knees, where he'd expected Fitz to be.

"Get him while he's down, Fitzy!"

"Kill him, Oink!"

Fitz stepped back instead. Blood was trickling from the cut above his eye. "Get up, Bennett," he said, keeping his voice cool. The man could plainly fight and fight dirty. He was fast and had the weight advantage. Taunts would mean nothing to him. Disdain however...might make Bennett mad. And hopefully that wouldn't help his fighting or his judgement.

Bennett lunged forward. Fitz danced aside, and gave him a sweeping kick that assisted Bennett's forward progress. The man sprawled again. "Up, Bennett. I'm not finished with you."

"I'm gonna rip your damned Shareholder head off." This time he stood up slowly, expecting Fitz to wait.

Fitz did not oblige. He found himself, to his alarm, enjoying the fight. He'd had weeks of abuse and this was the first time he'd been able to plan to strike back at anything. There was none of the aseptic, sterile, and controlled atmosphere of the dojo fights here. This man would kill him if he could. And the crowd too, were hungry for blood. Still, the sensei's advice was as clear as a neon sign. Never do quite what the opponent expects. And make him pay for each breath, while you keep your own breathing steady. Bennett's stomach muscles were like iron.

But no one's kidneys are that well protected.

"Up, Bennett."

This time his opponent was more wary. He expected attack. He was watching for dodges and kicks. He lunged, arms wide to catch the expected leap. Fitz stood right where he was and hit him. Punching for a point on the other side of Bennett's face.

The man had a jaw like an ox. But he wouldn't be smiling for a while. Not without pain.

Fitz kept hitting him. Keeping out of the reach of the shorter, heavier man.

"Break it up," hissed someone from the doorway. "The captain and Lieutenant Belsen are coming across. Break it up now or we're all for it. Grab both of them."

Fitz backed off, and Bennett fell to his knees again. "Get him up against the wall bars." Fitz pointed. "Bennett. I'll fight you anytime you like. But not now. Later."

The big man looked at him through dulled eyes, as three of his friends hauled him upright and over to the wall bars. "Later."

"Hold on to the bars. And don't look at them. Your face is a bloody mess."

"Ten-*shun!*" yelled someone from the door.

Fitz stood rigidly facing the wall bars, blood trickling down his face.

"As you were. Carry on." The captain walked slowly around the room. Fitz did some slow pull-ups on the bars. He saw, from the corner of his eye, that Bennett was doing push-ups. Well, that was one thing all of them could probably do by now, even if punch-drunk. And it kept his face down.

It was a long exercise session, until someone at the door said, "All clear."

Bennett stood up. His mouth was bloody. It would be badly swollen by nightfall. His rebroken nose did not make him look any less like a gorilla. "What's a Shareholder doing here anyway?" he asked, awkwardly feeling his nose.

Fitz watched him, warily. The man didn't look as if he was about to attack again, but he'd been fooled once. "I volunteered."

The Vats in the gymnasium gawped at him.

"Why?" said one finally.

Fitz shrugged. Answering honestly might save him continuing this fight or having too many others. "I am supposed to have killed a man. He was in a coma last I heard."

"Who?"

"Talbot Cartup."

Fitz hadn't been prepared to find himself a hero. He hadn't realized just how notorious Cartup's "Specials" were among the Vats. In fact, as a Shareholder, he'd barely known the Special Branch existed.

"Atten-*shun!*"

The commandant surveyed them. Walked along the line. Paused in front of the rigid Fitz. "Where did you get that black eye from, Fitzhugh?"

"Slipped in the shower, sir."

The commandant looked at Bennett. "And I suppose you slipped in the shower, too?"

The hulking man nodded. "Eth, thah," he slurred.

The commandant shook his head. "You damned Vats have no self-control. Well, you can try fighting the Magh' for a change, instead of each other. You're being posted out. You'll get a twenty-four-hour pass to wrap up your last affairs in the civilian world. Posting lists are up on the central notice board. Dismissed. Fall out."

> *NCO training course. Camp Dendro.*
> Fenton, Brett 24031232334000
> Fither, Miguel 24003107455000
> Fitzhugh, Conrad 24950101803371

His name had been inserted by hand. And it was initialed by Major Ogata and the camp commandant.

Fitz gaped. That was one list he hadn't bothered to look at. This man's army had not posted a single list in alphabetical order, with the posting listed afterward. That would have been far too simple and logical. No, instead there had been a number of lists, depending on the unit. Your name could be on any one of them, so you had to search each one.

This had been the one he'd least expected. It had certainly not been one he'd put his name down for.

SmallMac's name wasn't in the Equestrian unit either. It was on the same list as Fitz's.

Inserted and initialed in the same way. So were the other two who'd been there that night.

That first pass had an almost surreal feel to it. Walking out of the camp gates . . . The air was just too crisp, the sunlight too beautiful, the grass too green. And nobody was yelling at them. Strolling down the road in a casual, deliberately out-of-step snaggle of other dazed but happy-looking squaddies from tent 17, Fitz wasn't even fazed that he'd have to walk a couple of miles to get to a bus stop, instead of having the Aston Martin. It was just great to be out. There was also an "eye-to-the-storm" feel about it. The life expectancy of frontline troops was short, and everyone knew it.

"I am going to drink myself into a stupor, wake up, stay in bed and get drunk again," announced Ewen with great satisfaction. "I don't see myself getting to spend much of my pay where I'm going."

"You're abnormal!" said one of lads. "I haven't seen

a woman for six weeks. Even the colonel's bulldog bitch was starting to look sexy."

Ewen laughed. "Women get posted to the front, too. And if one eighth of what my cousin Dimitri told me is true, we'll catch up on our shagging. Everyone is scared and everyone is bored. There is nothing much else to do but shag and die. But booze . . . Enlisted men are allowed two blasted beers a night—if you're not in frontline trenches. Dimitri said they end up buying the stuff from those rats. Reminds me. You guys had better buy whatever chocolate you can get and smuggle it in. The rats will pay through the nose for it."

"I hear there are a lot of places in town that won't admit men in uniform," said another one of the men, cracking his knuckles suggestively.

"Keep out of trouble, Isaacs," said SmallMac. "The town's crawling with MPs. I've heard they get a bonus for every Vat they beat up and toss into the cells."

"Huh. They'll have to catch me first. So what are you going to do, SmallMac? Kiss a horse or two?"

"That's not a polite thing to say about my wife and daughters," said SmallMac, looking indecently happy.

It left Conrad Fitzhugh feeling indecently sad instead. SmallMac was one of the few who got regular mail. Somebody out there loved him. Which was both sad and frightening at the same time. Fitz hadn't spoken to his father for two years, since his mother's death. Who else did he have to see? They were either in the army or belonged to the other life that that stranger, Conrad Fitzhugh, Shareholder, had led. Or both. SmallMac had someone that he could go back to. And to whom it mattered if he was killed.

Fitz wondered now, from a dispassionate distance,

what Candy would have said if he had killed himself. Or if he was killed in the war. He hadn't thought about her much in the last six weeks. He resolved to go and straighten things out. After all, Cartup was either dead or he wasn't. One way or the other it didn't really matter now. And he'd go around and see his father, too.

He caught a bus into town. Took another to Van Klomp's apartments on Clarges Street, on the off chance that Bobby's army plans had gone awry. Besides, he hadn't a lot else to do, except look at the girls on the street. It was quite amazing how beautiful they'd become over the last six weeks.

The door opened. Meilin, Van Klomp's factotum, manager of his small electronic repair business, general fix-it woman and fanatically loyal Vat-servant, looked at Fitz blankly. Fitz had been a regular caller for the last five years.

"Where is Bobby?" he asked with a grin.

"I am sorry, sir," said Meilin stiffly, doing her best Vat-butler imitation. "Mr. Van Klomp is not home. He's at military headquarters. He is due back this afternoon, if you would like to call again?"

"He's not got that parachute regiment formed *yet*?"

Meilin sniffed. "He believes that it may be happening today, sir. That's what Mr. Van Klomp believed yesterday, and the day and the week before too, sir." Meilin spoke with an urbanity that betrayed how Van Klomp must have been making the walls shake for the last while. "If I might have your name, sir? I will tell him that you called."

Fitz shook his head. "Don't you know who the hell I am, Meilin? Conrad Fitzhugh."

The factotum—who did everything from packing

parachutes, repairing electronic cameras and writing invoices for Van Klomp—blinked. Her mouth fell open, and she hauled Fitz into the apartment, neatly kicking the door closed. "Good Lord, Mr. Fitz! The boss has been trying to track you down, discreetly. I'd never have recognized you in a month of Sundays. You've changed."

"I've had a haircut."

"No." She shook her head firmly. "It's your posture. Well, you're tanned, and your face is thinner. And the uniform and the haircut, I suppose. But you don't look like . . . well, the youngster you used to be."

"The spoiled Shareholder brat, you mean." Fitz grinned.

"Oh, you were never as bad as some of them, sir."

"Damned with faint praise," said Fitz, laughing now, flopping down into a chair. "Anyway, do you know what happened to Cartup? And has Bobby got any drink left in this place?"

Meilin gave him a wink. "I hide it. Otherwise. that useless bunch of Shareholder friends of his drink it up. And Talbot Cartup recovered three days after you disappeared."

"So I'm in the clear after all! Well, well." He stood up again. "Hold the drinks, Meilin. I'm going to pop in on my old girlfriend. Clear the air. Tell her I wish her well. Y'know, there's nothing like six weeks of boot camp to give you a new perspective on life."

"Do you think that's a good idea?" asked Meilin worriedly. "She did try and have you arrested, Fitz. Why not wait until Van Klomp gets home?"

Fitz shook his head. "When he gets home I'll be back with a few decent bottles. I'm going to see Candy, see my Old Man. Get things off my chest."

He went out onto the streets of George Bernard Shaw City, whistling. Took a cab across town. He really must get the Aston Martin out of hock. The fines on it must be astronomical by now. He walked up the stairs to Candy's rather pretentious penthouse apartment door. He felt in his pocket. He still had the key in his wallet. Then he paused. He must remember to give it back to her. After all, he had no rights to it anymore. He knocked politely on the imitation oak-paneled door.

She opened it, and stared as blankly at him as Meilin had.

"Afternoon, Candy."

She gave a little squeak of pure, unrefined terror. "Conrad! Don't. Please. I promise..." she panted, backing away.

He shook his head at her. "I haven't come to hurt you. I just came to say good-bye, good luck and I hope you're happy. I'm off to NCO training and then probably the front. There's a chance I'll get killed, so I'm clearing things up. I just came to say good-bye. And no hard feelings. Anyone could make a mistake. I suppose it was natural you should think that I'd done it."

"You—you're not—" she whispered, hands still ready to thrust him off.

He shook his head, walking calmly into the familiar apartment, a bubble of unholy amusement at her reaction making him grin. "No. I'm not even mad that you accused me. I suppose it was a natural thought."

"Oh, I know it wasn't you, now. It must have been one of Talbot's enemies, who did it to shame him. It was half-dark and I made an awful mistake. Look, Conrad, I...I'm most terribly sorry. I'm just a weak woman. Talbot organized it all...He made me break up with you. I promise. Of course I'm really still in love with you, darling." She stepped up to him and embraced him, plastering herself onto him.

As she rubbed her breasts and thighs against him, and lifted her beautiful face to be kissed, Fitz had to admit that maybe Van Klomp had called the shots remarkably closely. What a damn fool he must have been. All the same, it was distracting to have her body this close, after six weeks of sweaty male company. He pushed her away, but gently.

"It's all right, Candy." He rather enjoyed calling her that, now. "You don't have to fake it. Look, it's over. I just came to say...well, I've gotten over it. I wish you happiness. I guess you got what you really wanted. I'll be going now."

She looked consideringly at him. "Must you? Yes, I suppose you'd better. Look, sit down for a minute. There are a few things you gave me that I want to return. They're in my bedroom...unless you want to fetch them with me?" she asked, licking her short upper lip.

Was that an invitation? Now? After all this? Suddenly, Fitz knew he'd rather bed a viper. "I'll wait."

He sat down.

And about two minutes later—someone smashed the door in. Three of them. They were firing as they came barrelling in.

Fitz reacted as any soldier in HAR army would, under the circumstances. He froze to immobility—as the sudden hardening of his slowshield forced him to. He did see one of the men fall, as the other two emptied their pistols. And then—as the army-issue slowshield was no longer being fired at...

Fitz stopped being immobile just as the two paused to reload.

They never got that chance. Fitz dropped one with a marble-based lamp—which made a better club than a light—and in the semidarkness dropped the other attacker with a disarming kick to the forearm and a punch that flattened the man against the wall, knocked loose a fair amount of the plaster, and put an original Miró painting onto the man's head. It was the best use the picture had ever been put to, in Fitz's opinion, but Candy had liked it.

Kicking a pistol ahead of himself, Fitz stepped across to the overhead light switch and the wall-mounted telephone. Clicking the lights on, Fitz picked up the telephone and tapped in the emergency number.

"Police? This is Conrad Fitzhugh at 207 Kensington Mansions, Masden Boulevard. There's been an armed break-in by some thugs. I've got a couple of them. You'd better get here quickly—and send an ambulance, too. One of them has been shot by his mates."

Fitz put the phone down and ran to check on Candy. The bedroom was empty, and the bathroom door was soundly locked. Sensible girl! He knocked on the door. "Candy! Are you all right?"

There was a terrified whimper from inside.

She must be frightened witless. Getting involved with ultrawealthy Shareholders was one thing, but nothing could have prepared her for this. Their politics were dirty. No wonder she'd blamed him. "It's all right. I've dealt with them. The cops are on their way."

"Thank God!" she said.

"You're not hurt?"

"I'm fine."

"Good. Stay in there until the cops get here, Candy. I'll call you when it's safe."

He ran back through to find one of the attackers determinedly staggering towards a pistol. Fitz dealt with him. Hard. He took some duct tape from the drawer under the telephone and did some trussing and gagging. Then he did some first aid on the gunshot victim.

He was busy with that when the ambulance and half a dozen uniformed policemen arrived. He stood up, allowing the two paramedics to take over. The police lieutenant looked at the two burly trussed-up men, and prodded one with his toe.

"Well done, soldier! These Vat-bandits are getting more cheeky by the day. Firearms! I'm tempted to shoot the bastards with their own guns and save the courts the trouble. It'll be the organ banks for them, for sure," he said, beaming. "Come on, boys. Take 'em away. Better put some cuffs on them, read them their rights and take 'em to the station. Simpson. Nygen. You two had better accompany the medics and keep that one under guard."

Fitz tapped him on the shoulder. "Candy—my ex-girlfriend—sensibly locked herself in the bathroom when these guys broke in. Can we go through and let her out? She's terrified, poor girl."

The police chief beamed expansively. "Sure, soldier. Though why she worries with a guy like you around, I don't know."

They went through and the police lieutenant knocked cheerfully on the bathroom door. "Lieutenant Swiggers here, ma'am. You can come out now, ma'am. We've got the miscreants safe under lock and key."

Candy emerged with her cell phone still clutched in her hand. "Lieutenant! Thank God you're here." She pointed at Fitz. "Arrest him! He's wanted for attempted murder."

Just at this point one of the uniformed cops came through. "Uh. Lieutenant. The paramedics just found this in the injured guy's pocket."

It was a badge. And an ID card. "He's a Special Branch detective."

Van Klomp shook his head at Fitz, who stood behind the bars of a holding cell in the GBS Central Police Headquarters. The big man sighed. "As my mother used to say: *Lelik is nix, maar stupid!* Fitzy, you're so dumb it almost isn't funny. As soon as I got home, and Meilin told me where you'd been thickheaded enough to go, I got hold of Mike Capra and headed here. We nearly beat you into the place. You moron! *Of course* Talbot Cartup had to stick to Candy's story when he came around—or be the laughingstock of the town. Now, Capra will talk to you. I believe they've scheduled throwing the book at you for the morning."

"But Bobby, those guys—who turned out to be Special Branch plainclothes security police—tried to kill me."

Van Klomp snorted. "Dead men don't have to go to court, Fitz. Much more convenient, *né*. The security lot act as enforcers for some of the top Shareholders. And Cartup is their boss."

Fitz sighed. "Bobby, can you get a message to my father?" He looked down. "I've been thinking the last while that I need to sort things out with him. I was going to go and see him after I'd seen Candy."

"You should have done it first, *idioot*," said Van Klomp roughly. "He would have told you not to be so stupid. He came to see me the day you went into the army. I had him on the phone a few minutes back."

Mike Capra stood up. "Detective-inspector, you've stated that you entered the premises at 207 Kensington Mansions through a smashed-in front door. Was the door broken before you arrived there?"

The thick-set man nodded. "It was."

"At this point you state that the accused, who was lying in ambush, opened fire on you without any warning or provocation."

"That's what I said, yes," said the detective. "And these are the same questions you asked DI Scott. You've got the sworn statements of two trained officers on these points."

Mike Capra nodded. "The court has indeed. Thank you. I have no further questions."

"The prosecution may call its next witness," said the judge.

The next witness was a demure-looking Candice Foster in a virginal white blouse and neat gray skirt. "It is safe, Judge? He is restrained, isn't he?"

The judge nodded benignly. "Quite safe, my dear. You may take the oath."

Fitz was amazed to learn just how insanely jealous and violent he was. And how he'd locked her in the bathroom—on his second attack while he waited in ambush for her fiancé. She did some most artistic weeping and shuddering, too. To the point where the judge cautioned Capra to be gentle in his cross-examination.

"M'lud! When am I ever anything else?"

"When it suits you, Capra," said the judge, dryly.

"Precisely, M'lud. It does not suit me to be anything else but gentle when I am forced to defend a man accused of so vilely abusing one of our most respected citizens. A person who would dress such a man in lacy yellow polka-dotted women's underclothing, tie him to the bed, beat him and then suffocate him with a plastic bag, deserves little."

Talbot Cartup cringed. The prosecution had been very circumspect about the exact nature of the assault. The press gallery scribbled frantically.

"Now. Ms. Candice Foster, could you clarify one point? On the occasion of the second assault you have stated that the accused broke down your door."

"Yes. He's a very violent man. Very strong. I tried to fight him off, but—"

"Thank you, Ms. Foster. There is no need to upset yourself with the sordid details. Now: On the occasion of the first assault—I have examined the police report in detail. I could find no report of forced entry on that occasion. How did the accused get in that time?"

She shrugged. "Maybe he climbed in the window."

Mike Capra looked thoughtful. "Number 207 is a penthouse apartment, is it not?"

"Yes," she nodded proudly. Everyone knew those cost a mint.

"You say he came into the lounge where you and your fiancé were sitting in discussion, at which point he forced you both through into the bedroom, and you into the bathroom. You must know where he came from? Through which door, Ms. Candice?"

"My bedroom," she said thoughtfully. "I remember now. The window was open."

"Thank you. I have no further questions at this point."

"Very well. I think the court will recess for lunch. The defense may present its arguments and I should be able to deal with sentencing today," said the judge.

"I thought you said we should be able to wrap this up, Mike," hissed Fitz. "The judge has already decided to sentence me. And you hardly even questioned those damn liars. Even that lying doorman who says he saw me there. Recognized my car."

"Patience," said the Capra. "When you want to catch monkeys you put lots of tempting things in the calabash. You don't frighten them off *before* they have their hands in it. We'll do the nasty questions and scaring after lunch. They've been very cooperative. Don't be ungrateful. Go and enjoy your nice prisoner's nubbins like a good boy. You'll be back on army rations soon."

And so it was.

"M'lud, first I'd like to ask that a policeman be dispatched with my assistant to bring the accused's wallet from his personal possessions here, to be used as evidence."

"That should have been entered as evidence beforehand, Mr. Capra, as you well know."

"M'lud, the court shares a building with the Central Police Station. This seemed the most obvious way of dealing with any possibility that anyone might tamper with the evidence. I have grounds to believe certain members of the police are in fact in collusion with the true perpetrators of these crimes."

The judge raised his eyebrows. "That's a serious accusation, Mr. Capra. I hope you can substantiate it."

"I'll do my best, M'lud. Now, if a policeman could accompany my assistant to recover my client's possessions? I will proceed with other evidence in the meanwhile."

The judge nodded. "It is irregular, Mr. Capra. But under the circumstances, proceed. Granted."

"Objection, M'lud!" protested the prosecution.

The judge shook his head. "Objection overruled. Continue, Mr. Capra."

"M'lud, if we could proceed to exhibit one of the evidence which I have entered. As you can see these are certified copies of the lease of 207 Kensington Mansions and payment records for the rental thereof. Could I ask the clerk of the court to read out in whose name the lease is held, and from whose account the rentals were paid?"

The judge nodded. And the reedy-voiced clerk read, "Conrad M. Fitzhugh."

As the court bubbled and a furious Talbot turned on Candy ... the policeman and Capra's assistant returned with Fitz's wallet.

"Please give that item to the clerk of the court," requested Capra. "And sir, if you could be so kind as to examine the inner pouch of the wallet. You should find a key there. Please hold it up."

He did. "M'lud. That is the key to Number 207 Kensington Mansions. Another copy of this key was in the possession of the agents, Messrs. Smythe and Austing. With a letter of authority from the tenant and both Mr. Smythe and Mr. Austing, as well as the block-caretaker, we ascertained that key held by

Smythe and Austing fits the lock. I have their copy of the key here. I think we can establish that the two are identical. I should like to enter these as exhibits two and three. If the clerk of the court would like to examine them?"

The reedy-voiced clerk was enjoying himself very much. And he could indeed confirm the two keys were identical. The judge had to bang his gavel and call for silence after that.

"Now, M'lud, I don't believe the charge of breaking and entering...into one's own property can be entertained. I think we should also question the credibility of a witness who expects us to believe a large man would climb the outside of a five-story building to enter by the window, or by breaking down the door, when he has the key in his pocket. I would also question how someone who felt she was in extreme danger from my client didn't even bother to change the lock. Far from being guilty of breaking and entering...in fact my client should charge Ms. Foster and Mr. Cartup with trespass."

In the sudden silence Candice's voice, protesting to Talbot, was remarkably clear. "I forgot he had a key. He always knocked."

"Objection!"

"Sustained." The judge nodded to the clerk. "See that the charges of breaking and entering are struck from the roll. Proceed, Mr. Capra. As usual, you are providing the court with much entertainment." The judge's voice did not indicate that he approved.

"I do my best, M'lud," said Capra, urbanely. "I have here a statement of account from the municipal pound. As you will see, the vehicle which the night concierge at Kensington Mansions described in such loving detail, was impounded some four hours before the incident is supposed to have occurred. He also said my client entered the building by the front door. This is unusual for a man who is supposed to have entered number 207 through a window." Capra turned to the judge. "I think it is very clear that one or the other or both of these witnesses is lying."

The judge raised his eyebrows. "At very best that they were mistaken, Mr. Capra. I will grant you that their credibility is somewhat dented, and the lengthy testimony of Mr. Brenner should probably be subjected to a motion to strike."

Capra nodded. "My feelings exactly, Your Honor. Now we come to the second alleged attempted murder: that of DI Carr. We have already established that the two officers in question may possibly also, at best, have been ... mistaken, as to the door being smashed in before they arrived."

"Objection!"

"On what grounds, Mr. Penquick?" the judge asked icily.

"Er. The defense is putting his own interpretation of events on the testimony of two respected officers!"

"He's putting *my* words to their testimony. It is, in my opinion, a very generous interpretation. Continue, Mr. Capra."

"Thank you, Your Honor. I'd like to call Dr. Liepsich of the HAR Institute of Technology as my first witness."

An untidy, long-haired man proceeded to the stand, took the oath and scratched in his scraggly beard. Capra proceeded onward.

"Dr. Liepsich, you are head of the physics department at HARIT. I believe you are also chief consultant to the HAR defense force on Korozhet equipment. The soft-cyber and the slowshield particularly."

The scientist grimaced. "For my sins, yes. Although I would have more luck explaining them to brain-dead first-year art students."

Mike Capra persisted. "But you are the best expert on the function of the slowshields that the military issue to their troops."

"Yep. Dead simple things, really. From the functional point of view. They harden if anything moving faster than 22.8 mph passes through the exclusion zone."

"Can a soldier turn his shield off?" asked the defense attorney.

"Nope," said the scientist. "They're as idiot-proof as possible. They're surgically implanted, draw power from the user's electromagnetic field."

Capra nodded. "And just what would happen if someone wearing one fired a pistol?"

Liepsich shrugged again. "Does the word 'colander' mean anything to you?"

The judge cleared his throat. "Could you stop speaking in riddles, Dr. Liepsich? Mr. Capra, what is all this about?"

The physics professor looked at the judge as a man might a beetle crawling out of his sandwich. "It means," he said with an air of exaggerated patience, "that if your accused over there had shot the cop—as the other two cops testified he did—the ricochets inside his own slowshield would have killed him. It is a physical impossibility. He didn't shoot anyone. He can't. They lied. Is that clear enough?"

The prosecuting attorney had leapt to his feet. "Your Honor, I object to the witness drawing unsupported conclusions."

The untidy professor looked at the attorney. "Meatball, when you have the intellect to manage elementary arithmetic without counting on your fingers, you can tell me I draw unsupported conclusions. In the meantime I suggest you go off and learn how to tie your own shoelaces."

The judge was forced to resort to his gavel to quell the riot. "Dr. Liepsich, desist with abusing our learned friend. I caution you that if you do not moderate your tone, I might have to find you in contempt. What I meant was I wanted to know what this slowshield issue has to do with this case?"

Mike Capra cleared his throat. "M'lud, I don't believe that the prosecution had seen fit to inform you that as of the fifth of last month, my client has been a volunteer, serving with the HAR defense force. He therefore has a surgically implanted slowshield. He therefore cannot have shot anyone on the afternoon of the seventeenth instant."

The judge cocked his head. "He's a member of the *army*?"

Capra nodded. "Yes, Your Honor. A private."

The judge looked at the documents before him. "And he joined as a volunteer on the fifth?"

Capra nodded again. "Yes, Your Honor. It is a matter of public record."

"Then I have no jurisdiction over this case. By the terms of Special Gazette item 17 of 11/3/29 he cannot be prosecuted for misdemeanors committed prior to this, while he is in the service. A foolish statute, in my opinion, but nonetheless, that is the law. And for any crimes he committed after that date, he should be tried by the military, not, thank goodness, by me. And anyway, it is my considered opinion that there is no case against this man."

"In that case, Your Honor, may I raise a motion that these charges be dismissed?"

The judge nodded. He looked at the prosecution. "I do, however, instruct that the police investigate and appropriately charge the two detective inspectors who lied under oath. Much as I deplore Dr. Liepsich's abusive manner, I cannot fault his conclusions. It is my opinion that the prosecutorial work done here was more than appallingly sloppy." He struck the desk with his gavel. "Case dismissed."

Walking out of the court, arm in arm with Van Klomp and his father, Fitz couldn't help grinning. "Well. Now all I have to face is a charge for being AWOL. I'll have to get back to camp as soon as possible."

Van Klomp cleared his throat. "As it happens, a major from the Attorney General's office contacted me about that. Scariest man I've met for a long time. Fortunately, he seems to approve of you. He said if you have an affidavit from the judge, to the effect that you'd been illegally detained by civil authority, you'd get away with it. Give it to your commanding officer. The army looks with disfavor on civil authorities messing around with their own. Capra's hopefully organizing it right now."

The camp commandant looked at the affidavit. Shrugged. "Not my business anyway. You've been transferred to OCS instead. Someone higher up obviously decided that the Vats would murder a Shareholder, now that, thanks to the newspapers, everyone knows you are one. You're due to report there tomorrow. So, it looks like I should give you another pass. Try and stay out of trouble on this one."

5

"We need more loyalty. More courage. More military backbone." Thus spoke the plump jellyfish of a general, Blutin, who was officially the head of HAR's army.

"We had to resort to bribing them with drink. It's the only thing we've found that actually motivates them," said his 2IC, General Cartup-Kreutzler. "We're forced to apply the harshest of military discipline, too. They desert with regularity. It's only the grog ration that keeps them in the trenches at all. We need you to sort this out and to treble production."

The colony's chief biologist sighed. "You asked us for some animal that we could uplift with this Korozhet device that would be an efficient killer of the insectlike Magh' invaders. We took one of the best naturally equipped species, that we could breed quite fast. Now . . . you're telling us fast isn't fast enough. You need more rats. Are they no good as Magh' killers?"

The two generals looked at each other. Blutin might be the senior, but he always let Cartup-Kreutzler lead. "They do seem to be very good at killing Magh'," admitted Cartup-Kreutzler.

"Then why are you experiencing such high mortalities?" she asked dourly. "I must tell you, gentlemen, that we simply cannot step up production. Our facilities were never meant to carry the load they are doing now. If anything, production is going to decline as certain irreplaceable equipment breaks down."

"Er. Well, we've had to execute rather a lot in training," said Blutin. "Slacking. And for military crimes. Insubordination. Desertion. Refusal to obey the orders of a senior officer. That's why we want you to improve their attitude."

Devi Sanjay laughed. There was no humor in that laugh. "Attitude? You want me to change their attitude in my cloning vats! I can't change their nature. *You* will have to change their nurture."

They looked blankly at her. "What do you mean, ma'am?" asked Cartup-Kreutzler, finally.

If there was one thing Devi hated it was being called "ma'am."

"I mean you'll have to change the way you train them."

Blutin shook his head. "We can't do that. It . . . it's not the way it is done!"

Cartup-Kreutzler backed him up. "Yes, I must really insist that you leave military matters to us, Professor Sanjay. It's not your field of expertise."

Devi Sanjay looked at the two generals coldly. She refrained from saying "it's not yours either."

Mentally, she shrugged. She'd hit brick walls before. In the Shareholders' current panic, they would give their support to these idiots and not to the voice of reason. Before this war, the HAR army had been a rather trivial out-of-the-way make-work place to dump well-connected incompetents. Now, with the Magh' invasion, the army had assumed a central position in human society. Unfortunately, it had retained its idiots.

"Well, you're going to have to give up these executions. We can't replace the rats or the soft-cyber units you're . . . using up." She had managed not to say "wasting."

"Discipline must be maintained!" snapped Cartup-Kreutzler. "We've got to set an example or the rats will be far worse."

She looked dispassionately at the two. No wonder humans were in such trouble. "If I might suggest . . . Simply remove the troublemakers and repost them elsewhere. Tell the rats that remain that the troublemakers have been executed. From what you've told me, they're in no position to know any different. Tell the reposted ones they've been reprieved. It would give us breathing space here at the cloning labs. And we'll experiment with a different language download on the bats."

The two generals looked at each other. "I suppose that might work," said Cartup-Kreutzler reluctantly. "We can send them to areas the Korozhet advisors say are imminent attack zones."

Blutin looked suspiciously at her. "What has language got to do with it? I don't see why they're required to speak anyway."

"Language shapes the way you are able to think. For example, Zulu has no distinct word for the color blue as opposed to green. This makes describing the difference between hydrous and anhydrous copper sulphate difficult," she said dryly.

The two generals looked blankly at her. She decided to continue anyway. "The microprocessor in the soft-cyber unit 'learns' how to translate thought patterns into words existing within the vocabulary download.

This is naturally a little imprecise. The software in the cybernetic unit selects the nearest possible word with impeccable logic. Unfortunately, English isn't terribly logical. It does mean that you can't think of a complex matter which you do not have words for, however."

A dim light dawned at the end of Cartup-Kreutzler tunnel. "Could you arrange it so that they don't know the meaning of fear?"

"Unlikely," said the scientist dryly. "It's a core word in the human vocabulary. And without the concept you would be even shorter of soldiers. Gentlemen, I've heard your requests." She emphasized that word. "I've told you what can be done. Now, if you'd excuse me, I shall see about implementation."

Without asking their permission, she got up and left. It would be better if she could depart this over-plush office, and this chateau with its fake military grandeur, without explaining that the bats would be getting downloads of Irish nationalist folk music and old Wobbly songs.

Devi Sanjay had joined the New Fabians back on Earth as a young idealist, with many others, planning a utopia. She'd seen the ideals of her compatriots wither as they became part of the entrenched privileged class. She wasn't young anymore. But she, personally, had not quite lost all her idealism. When she'd left Earth, humans had been the intelligent species of the universe. Alone. Special. Now she knew that intelligent life was not rare. There were the alien enemy—the Magh', the alien allies—the spiny beach ball Korozhet, and, according to the Korozhet, hundreds of others in this part of the galaxy alone. Evil ones such as the Jampad and Magh', friends like Korozhet. She'd fostered two new intelligent species herself. The army still regarded them as trained animals. Biomechanical weapons. Things.

Devi Sanjay knew they were wrong. Things stopped being things when they reasoned. And, like the aliens, they would not see the world from a human perspective. Devi had never explained just why she had chosen the species she had, or the language downloads that she had. Her reasons were subtle, and her plans and vision deep. Some of them had very little to do with the war.

Humans had let the genie out of the Vat. Of one thing she was certain: it wouldn't be that easy to put the two new intelligent species back. She'd given the rats some of the most intense and skilled portrayal of human drama and history. Now she was about to do the same, with emotional and revolutionary content instead, to a species that could indeed kill Magh'— among other things.

Whatever came out of the meeting of these three… humans, rats and bats, all endowed with a shaping human heritage, when the hurlyburly was done… would not be in the smug plans of the aging New Fabian Shareholders.

The rats marched between the shock-stick-armed MPs, to face the bored-looking tribunal. The clerk listed their numbers. The officer presiding looked up from the sheaf of papers in front of him. "You are charged with aiding and abetting the enemy, desertion and murder of your human officer. We have affidavits here from the OC commanding and Rat 235645670045, known as 'Dick Deadeye.' Do you have anything to say in your defense?"

The rats looked in puzzlement at the officers. "We never did any a-betting. 'Tis a good idea, mind," said Gobbo.

"Murder?" said Ariel. " 'Twas pesticide. And that is no crime. We asked."

The officer ignored her. "We note that Rat 235645670045, known as 'Dick Deadeye,' is deceased. I presume he was murdered to try and cover up your heinous deeds."

Pooh-Bah shook his head. "Humans doth mistake rats' morality. But then we find you incomprehensible. He took liberties that he wasn't invited to with Ariel."

6

"Oink! I mean, Lieutenant," said Ewen, the big private grinning all over his ugly face. But, also, saluting earnestly.

"At ease," said the newcomer to Ariel's chief supplier. "I feel uncomfortable enough with this bird shit on my shoulders without having to run into my old squad. What are you doing here, Ewen? I thought you'd been posted to the artillery."

The big private shrugged. "I got caught running a black-market trade with the rats. When it got to the court-martial they couldn't quite pin it on me. So I got posted here to 'Fort Despair.' What did you do wrong?"

"Other than graduate from the OCS course, nothing I can think of. Why?"

Ewen shook his head. "You always were a bit slow— sir—even when it came to making a bed." The private grinned broadly at the memory. "This is 'Fort Despair.'

Where they send the malcontents and troublemakers. It's a hot sector. The Maggots are pushing forward fast and hard. The Maggots are supposed to do the job for them without having to go through all the hassle of finding evidence for a court-martial." The private laughed. "We read all about your little court case, Oi... Lieutenant."

"We'll have to keep it 'Lieutenant,' Private. Too damn difficult otherwise."

The big man smiled. "I reckon I won't have any trouble taking orders from you. Sir."

"This is Lieutenant Fitzhugh. He is the new OC for this sector," said the sergeant.

The rats seemed vastly uninterested. The humans— and they were a rough-looking lot—looked as if they were already planning to desert or kill him.

Fitz looked speculatively at them, without saying a word, until they began to get uncomfortable. Then he sighed. "Right. Listen up all of you. I gather you are all here to save the army the trouble of killing you legally." There was low-throated grumble. "It probably hasn't occurred to you that they'd give you an officer that they feel the same way about."

The grumble was silenced as they digested this one. Fitz ground his fist into his palm. "I'm planning on pissing on their fireworks, soldiers. I'm here because I got up the noses of certain powerful Shareholders. Private Ewen here will fill you in on all the gory details. For a fee, I'm sure. But to cut a long story short, I was a boot with the conscripts. I know every 'stute trick you lot can pull. And they will not happen. Is this clear?"

There were a few mutters. "On the other hand, I am not going to waste your time with petty crap. There will be weapons drills, come hell, high water or shelling. Your bangsticks will be sharp and ready. Hygiene will be of the highest standard we can manage out here. God help anyone I find crapping in their foxhole. For the rest, I'm really not interested. When, if, we get out of here, you'll worry about polished boots and belt buckles. Until then, don't waste your time or mine." There was a muted cheer. He hushed it with a wave. "I'll want to talk individually to all of you, especially the combat vets. I've no intention of obliging anyone by dying easily. I want that attitude from all of you. Dismissed. Back to your posts."

There was a silence. And then Ewen began clapping... It caught on.

Fitz waved it down after a minute. "Enough. We can see if you still want to clap in a week's time. To your posts."

Fitz leaned against the dugout wall. His father had given him two items on that last pass. "Take this tin of boiled candy. The candy is new. The tin isn't. It's been through four Earth wars with various Fitzhughs." The tin was a thin, flat one. The paint had long since worn off. But there was a deep gouge right across it. "Tradition has it that you will keep it in your left breast pocket."

The other thing he'd given him was a piece of advice: "Forget what they told you in OCS. When you get to your unit, talk to your NCOs. Let them lead you around quietly until you know enough not to make a fool of yourself."

"So tell me about the rats, Sarge," said Fitz to the rat-corps sergeant. "Before I make a fool of myself."

The sergeant permitted himself a hint of a smile. "Bit different from our last lootie, sir. He knew it all when he got to us. They told him at OCS how to deal with them."

Fitz raised one eyebrow. "Sergeant. They also told me how to deal with Vat-conscripts. Seeing as I've been one of those, and I know how they messed up there... I thought I might try asking one of the people who really run things."

Now the sergeant was grinning openly. "Ewen said you were a 'stute one. Well, sir, there is a whole set of different rules for dealing with them. They've got no morals at all, for starters. And they speak sort of English, but they don't think like we do. They take things very literally, and they still think like rats—you know, food, sex and strong drink are the only important things in the world, and devil take tomorrow and the hindmost."

"Ah!" said Fitz with a smile. "Like most of my boot-camp Vat-companions."

"Bit like, sir. But the difference is they don't seem to get concepts like respect for rank or a uniform. You earn respect personally. They don't have much loyalty, not even to each other. You can force them to do things, but the minute your back's turned they won't do them. The honest truth is it is easier to buy 'em than to try and do it any other way."

He looked warily at his new CO. "Er. I've heard, sir, all the human rat-corps NCOs who survive crook the mortality records so they've got some extra grog on hand."

Fitz didn't turn a hair. "Hmm. I trust you will continue to do so. And what else do they fancy?"

The sergeant was getting to like his new lieutenant. "Well, drink's best, sir," he said with a grin, "but you'll find lads like Ewen run a good black market in chocolate, lighters, knickknacks, fancy goods. They find tails the sexiest part of the body so they like to ornament them."

"And where do they get the money for all this?" asked Fitz. "I was under the impression they weren't paid."

"Ah," said the sergeant, giving him the sort of look a proud teacher might give a star pupil. "There you have it, sir. The rats' chief vice is looting. If the Maggots had loot, we wouldn't be able to hold them back."

The rats were lounging in the OP, discussing the curious behavior of the humans. "Methinks he is popular enough with them. They clapped."

"You mean he is pronging yon Linda. Methinks I have heard of that. They call it Vat-shagging," said Gobbo, knowledgeably.

Ariel stared at him in puzzlement. "Art mad? What sayest thou?"

"Well, he hath got the clap," said Gobbo. "Ewen said *he* was sure he had it from her."

"Not that sort of clap. The clapping you get for being popular."

" 'Twas my thought you could not be my kind without being popular," said Gobbo earnestly. His ears twitched. "Hist. He comes."

The rats were earnestly doing what they were supposed to when Fitz arrived. None of them leapt to attention. "As you were," said Fitz, dryly.

They went back to their lounging, which hadn't been quite what he'd meant. That was what the sergeant had meant by "take things very literally." Well, he could work against them, or work with them. . . .

He sat down, and hauled out Van Klomp's parting gift. A hip flask full of HAR's best yet attempt at a single malt. It was a reasonable exchange for the gift of an Aston Martin replica. "Does anyone here want a drink?"

One rat—smaller, therefore a female, at a guess—with a rakish tilt to her tail and a particularly rich chocolate color to her fur, was quickest. She snatched the hip flask and leapt to a niche in the wall while the others were still gaping. "'Tis mine!" she squealed triumphantly.

"'Tis not right, Ariel. That's not what the whoreson said!" protested another of the rats.

Fitz saw that a mighty fight was brewing. So he neatly snagged the hip flask back. It came with a clutching rat. "All of us." He stared at the rat who was still clinging to the hip flask, but whose teeth were now bared viciously. "And I will personally bite the tail right off any rat who tries to hog it all. Which would be a shame as yours is one of the sexiest I've ever seen."

To the sound of ratty chuckles and a couple of very credible wolf whistles, she let go. And winked salaciously at him. Then she sniffed. "You've got chocolate," she said, suddenly fiercely intent.

"Indeed. And we'll discuss my parting with some in a few minutes."

A pompous-looking rat strutted forward, a cup made out of a bangstick cartridge outstretched. He motioned at the hip flask. "For a suitable insult, I, as Minister for Interior Affairs, will tell you her weaknesses. Although, as Minister for Defense and Lord High Archbishop, I will say Ariel's tail is not without risks."

Ariel, remaining perfectly confidently standing on Fitz's knee, her eye fixed on his breast pocket, said, "Shut up, Pooh-Bah."

He'd placed the names now. Ariel—the sprite in Shakespeare's *Tempest*. Pooh-Bah from *The Mikado*. The names were an affectation he'd heard about. A side effect of the language download into their Korozhet-built soft-cyber units. As the soft-cyber unit selected the nearest approximate meaning to what the user meant, the name would probably reflect the nature of the beast. "Let's start with names."

"Bardolph." "Gobbo." "Pitti-Sing." "Trinculo." "Caliban." "Poo-Bah-for a reasonable fee." "Hymen." That one arched her tail provocatively at him.

"Paws off, bawd. I found him first," said Ariel.

No heroes. No kings. Rogues and lechers, in their own self-image, by the sounds of it. Well, he'd have to work with the clay he had.

"Get some mugs." He gestured with the hip flask. There was a scamper and a scattering. Except for Ariel. She merely unscrewed the silver cup off his flask, and grinned rattily at him. "Methinks I'll stay put, 'til I have that chocolate."

He shrugged. "I'll drink out of the flask."

"I should have thought of offering to do that," she said, as he doled out liquor.

"You snooze, you lose," he said cheerfully. "Now, to business. I've decided to pay a bounty on Maggot chelicerae. For every left chelicerae you have for me after the next assault, I'll pay one HAR cent—multiplied by the number of live troops I have under my command. At the moment I have some two hundred rats and sixty men, four NCOs and myself. Work that out in booze or bars of chocolate."

The rats began frantically counting on paws and toes and tails. After a while Ariel said. "'Tis no use. Help us with the mathematics. Our base eleven doth make calculation much labor."

"How many Maggots can you kill in one assault?"

The rats blinked at him. "As many as is needful. As many as doth threaten us. Sometimes there are too many," said Ariel. "Then we run away."

"Call it ten each. At that rate—if everyone survives, you rats will get $26.50 each. Of course it gets less if anyone dies."

"Methinks I have found more looting in a lieutenant's pocket," said Trinculo.

"Ah." Fitz was unsurprised by the admission. "But then he's dead, and there is no more. And that's one lieutenant among two hundred. Your chances are not good. This way . . . you're onto a sure thing. Of course I'll have to put a ceiling on it, or I'll go broke. Say $50 a month. That's what the army gives conscripted privates."

Ariel tapped the side of the hip flask suggestively. "I'm in. Now this rotgut sack you have in here: 'tis remarkable easy to drink compared to issue grog, even if it doesn't have a proper bite to it. How about another, then?"

"Well, for those who are in, naturally," said Fitz, innocently. He could afford $10,000 a month for a private army, he thought as he poured. Candy's apartment had cost him about that—and he wasn't having to pay for that anymore. He'd cancelled the lease.

Ariel drank the whiskey slowly, speculatively, unlike most of the rats who were into chug-and-splutter. "Methinks I shall nursemaid this one," she announced. "For if he dies, we get naught." She looked curiously at him. "Besides, I want to inspect his naked weapon and see if he's adequate for a girl like me." She wrinkled her whiskers and revealed that the stories of his exploits had reached the rats. "This 'woman's underwear.' Explain?"

Fitz was still blushing at the idea that a rat might consider his wedding tackle too small. Or interesting. The sergeant had been right about no morals . . . or inhibitions! "Ah. Underclothes. Um. Panties and brassieres. Suspender belts."

"Doth speak riddles. Small pants? Things for grilling meat?"

"Women . . . um, men too, wear a second pair of pants under their clothes. To cover their private parts."

The rats would obviously have found astrophysics more comprehensible.

Fitz discovered that Ariel took "nursemaid" to mean she was going to take up residence in his magazine pouch, or on his shoulder. But the day wasn't out before he discovered that this casual invasion of his privacy was worthwhile.

The nightmare creatures struck just at dusk. None of the pictures or lectures had prepared Fitz for the reality. Or for the speed and ferocity of it all. They'd said at OCS that up to seventy percent of human soldiers never survived the first major assault. Now Fitz understood why. And he also knew that if it wasn't for his pocket assassin-cum-bodyguard, he'd have been dead five times over in that assault. Rats were everywhere. Blur-fast lethal killers with a terrifyingly casual attitude to their killing. And Fitz discovered that "ten each" was a gross underestimate of their potential and the Magh's sheer numbers.

"Sector headquarters on the blower, Lieutenant."

"Hell's teeth. Have you told them we're under attack?!"

"They know, Lieutenant. The line on either side of us folded. They're sending reinforcements into those trenches, hoping to hold line two. They thought we—being in the center of the attack—must all be dead. They want us to retreat."

"Tell 'em we're still holding. We don't want to be outflanked though." Fitz turned to one of the NCOs. "What are our losses like, Corporal?"

The man was grinning like a dervish, despite the blood soaking his shirt from a gash on his chest. "Slight, sir. Five men I know of. Some wounded, but there are no more Maggots coming over. We're fighting them coming along the trenches from the sectors next door now."

"Are we going to hold them, Corporal?"

The man nodded. "The rats have gone kill-crazy, Lieutenant. I've never seen anything like it. The Maggots usually send a lot of 'scorps. This is all light, fast stuff. Easy to kill. Those damned rats would have killed twice as many if they didn't stop to take a claw off each one. Some kind of new rat-craze."

"Tell 'em. Hell, no. I'd better tell them." Fitz ran for the field-telephone bunker.

"Lieutenant Fitzhugh here."

"Captain Dewalt here. Colonel's orders. Sound a retreat for any survivors, Lieutenant," said the voice on the other end.

"We've held them off, sir. And there are no more Magh' coming. We're mopping up."

His words didn't appear to have registered with the Captain. "We'll have stretcher teams in the second trench line. Leave the rats..."

"We've held them off, sir," repeated Fitz, louder now. "No need to retreat."

There was a stunned silence. "What! That's ridiculous.... I'd better confer with the colonel. Stay near the field telephone."

Fitz didn't. Instead he left—at a run—to see how the fight with the Magh' from the next-door sector was doing.

The answer was: not well. The rats were there... but several of them were sitting down, leaving the fight to the human troops. And those that were still fighting were going to die. It was not that the Magh' were overwhelming. It was just that the rats seemed to be behaving like clockwork toys... in need of rewinding. "What's wrong?" yelled Fitz to Ariel as he ran forward to the fray.

"Methinks they're faint with hunger."

Of course! He'd been told the elephant-shrew genes gave the rats phenomenal appetites. They must have fast metabolisms and little stamina. "Feed the rats! Give them any food you've got, especially sugar, or we're dead!"

He hauled out the tin of sucking candy and flung it at a sergeant, before running into the fight. "Get someone across the west side and tell them," he yelled, bangstick stabbing through pseudochitin.

He had no idea how fast the rats would recover. He was relieved to discover that it was really quick, and that the average grunt, when faced with death or parting with precious little luxuries he kept next to his skin, would reluctantly part with the luxuries. The east side trenches of the late Lieutenant Zuma soon would be free of Magh'.

As he set off across to the west side, he was met by a panting private. "Sir. Colonel Brown on the line. He's insisting we retreat."

Fitz stopped. "Did you give him your name, Private?"

"I couldn't get a fucking word in edgeways, sir. Sorry, pardon language, sir."

"This is a war, not a kindergarten, Private. A pity Private Johnstone was killed before he could give me the message. He is dead, isn't he?"

The private grinned. "Yes, sir. I saw him die. Poor fellow."

"Stick to that story," said Fitz. "And see that the field telephone has a convincing accident. Cave part of the bunker in. The fight's all over on the east side. If we can lick them on the west, I'm not running."

Ten minutes later Fitz called in from the west side's field telephone. "Yes, sir. My apologies, sir. I was called away from our field telephone to deal with an immediate crisis. Unfortunately the instrument was destroyed and the man I had instructed to remain with it was killed."

He waited for the volcano to subside and then answered the last question.

"Where am I calling from, sir? Why Section B3, sir. On our west side. We've already secured the east side. We'd like some relief, Colonel. We're pretty thin spread holding three pieces of the line."

There was a long silence from the other side. Then: "You're making your fellow officers look bad, Lieutenant. Hum. I'll get some men up to you at once. They're waiting in trench line two."

7

In the seven weeks that followed, Fitz's section survived a sequence of small probes and one more direct assault. This was somewhat worse than the first one. But Fitz's new system of buddying two rats to each human soldier worked remarkably well. The rest of the rats he used as a free-range strike force. And this attack seemed almost like a spearpoint aimed at his piece of the line. Once they'd stopped it, they didn't even have to deal with the other sections. And then even artillery bombardment slacked off.

They eventually had to retreat after three weeks of near idleness and weapons drill, because the line had folded to the west of them. "It's almost as if they won't hit here, because we're strongest here," grumbled Fitz. He never thought he'd miss Magh' attacks, but the boredom made keeping the troops in readiness hell. There was drunkenness, gambling, and several fights about women . . . and fights about men among the women. Only the rats seemed content.

Sergeant Ellis nodded. "It's always like that, sir. The Maggots always attack where we're weakest."

"Suggests good intelligence, doesn't it, Sarge?"

"Can't be military intelligence then, sir," said the sergeant, handing him a couple of sealed dispatches.

Fitz cracked the first open. "Well, glory be! This'll cheer the troops up. We've done our two-month frontline stint and we're being pulled back to third line for a month to rest the men."

"Be about the fullest company to get rested," said the sergeant. "Half the time the companies have to be replaced and re-formed before that. The lads'll see some leave, too. You get a week when you're on third trench," she said with relish.

"That'll be a shock to civvy street," said Fitz dryly. Life expectancy in the trenches was about forty days at the moment. Inside, he was deeply grateful that he would be returning some eighty-three percent of his men past that. It was something you didn't dwell on here. But it did make boredom sweet. He opened the second envelope. Blinked. "It appears this bunch of ne'er-do-wells is due to attend a medals parade at sector headquarters. And yours truly is promoted to lieutenant first class. With the corresponding increase in pay of seven dollars a day, and family and retirement benefits."

"The family and retirement benefits sound good, sir," said the sergeant. She'd given up trying to get into Fitz's pants a while back. Ariel was a good dog-in-the-manger. But the sergeant still cast sheep's eyes his way sometimes. Fitz avoided them with care. That was a set of complications he didn't need here, as their CO. Still, as a normal male there were certain intentions he was planning to follow up on that seven-day pass, when he didn't have a minder.

● ● ●

In dress BDUs that now had a row of ribbons on the chest, and a second pip on their shoulders, Fitz blinked at the bright lights outside the troop disembarkation station. He put his bag down and wondered just where to go now.

"To find some food and drink," said the bag, in Ariel's voice, obviously guessing his thoughts.

"What the hell are you doing in there?" he demanded.

"Methinks I am crossing my legs and tying a knot in my tail. Hurry up and let me out before I pee on your kit."

Given the alternative, letting her out seemed the only option. And, tempting though it might be, he couldn't just run off and leave her there. She had kept him alive in the trenches, after all. So, with a curious rat peering out of his magazine pocket, he took a taxi into town. It was at her orders he stopped at the Paradise Pussy Club, too. It had a flashing neon cocktail-glass sign.

The bouncer eyed the man in uniform uncertainly. While officers in full-dress uniform, complete with ceremonial swords, were regular and welcome visitors to the club, men in BDUs were not. However this was definitely an officer, even if he was wearing dress BDUs. Against his better judgement he'd let him in.

In the pale hours of morning, Fitz looked cheerfully back at the club. It had been a great evening. The lap dancer would no doubt recover from the bite on her well-padded tail-end...

He gently patted the rat whose long nose protruded from his pocket, issuing ladylike snores. He'd had a wonderfully vulgar evening with a delightful girl, who had just discovered Cointreau. She'd thought that the strippers and pornographic backdrop movie were the best live entertainment she'd ever seen. Well, it was also the only show she'd seen. Of course, Ariel had also thought it was the side-splittingest comedy she'd ever seen. Rats have no taboos about genitalia or even sex. But what a wonderful girl. She had a biting sense of humor and just happened to be a rat. Damn fool of a bouncer should have understood that. The man would almost certainly recover. Saunas weren't that hot, were they?

It seemed a little early on such a delightful evening— or morning—to go and visit the parental abode. His own residence had been sold. He'd terminated the lease on the only other place he'd had a claim on, and anyway, Candy probably wouldn't have been glad to see him. Perhaps 4:00 a.m. was a little late to go and see if Van Klomp had gone soldiering, finally. He walked idly through an alleyway, where a foolish man waved a knife at him.

"Empty your pockets, soldier," sneered that shifty soul.

Fitz shrugged. "On your head be it."

A few minutes later, now in search of an all-night store that sold chocolate, he'd gently woven his way up to two men in uniform with white bands around their hats and asked directions. One had been about to prod Fitz in the gut with a nightstick, when he saw the pips on his shoulders. While the MPs were pointing Fitz toward an all-night convenience store, someone with a much faster metabolism was opening the doors to the paddy wagon. Ariel had not survived her only brush with the law not to recognize one.

They zigzagged their course onward rather like that extra stray neutron in a fissionable mass. Letting a rat inside the doors of something like Aladdin's cave was rank foolishness. Fortunately, Fitz was by now sober enough to point out the closed-circuit television to her. She was even more fascinated by this concept and insisted on breaking into the security room to inspect the monitors. The puzzled alarm-response crew found nothing.

Then, it was dawn, and since a passing taxi was available, Fitz had taken her to see Van Klomp. Unfortunately for the HAR Bolshoi Ballet company...

Van Klomp was only due back from his new unit that night. Fitz had peacefully fallen asleep—a good soldier can sleep anywhere, anytime—on Van Klomp's sofa. So that left Meilin talking to Ariel. And the subject, naturally enough, was Fitz himself—his reputation, and the trouble he'd had with the law, and, of course . . . Candy.

What was less predictable—unless you knew rat-nature—was that this long discussion should also involve pornographic backdrops and closed-circuit television. Meilin knew quite a lot about the latter, as that was one aspect of Van Klomp's business. Neutrons are very small. What they can cause is not.

There was a sonic boom. Well. The return of Van Klomp, anyway.

"Can't you keep away from troublesome women?" demanded Van Klomp, on meeting the rat with a glass of his port in her hand.

She blew him a raspberry, a rather good one, as she'd only learned to do so the night before.

He blew one back that nearly flattened her ears. "So what have you been doing so far, boykie? Nothing as stupid as last time, I trust."

Fitz grinned. "We've toured one of GBS city's finest establishments, namely the Paradise Pussy Club, and visited my father. Cordial terms are restored, but his advice is that we're too alike to keep it that way if we share a house. So I've come to bum a piece of floor. It's got to be drier and more comfortable than where I've been sleeping lately."

"And welcome. Pull up any piece you like. So, what did the old man think of a visit by a rat?" He looked disapprovingly at the bottle Ariel was clutching. "Did you steal his booze too?"

Ariel lifted her nose at Van Klomp. "Pshaw. Of course I was well behaved. 'Twas an experience. I never met a real live progenitor before. He told me to look after Fitz, because it is obvious he can't look after himself."

"True," said Van Klomp, taking the bottle away from her. "And having visited the ancestral home, what excitement is planned for tonight? More visits to cathouses?" he asked with vast tolerance.

Fitz lifted his aristocratic nose. "I am going to introduce Ariel to culture."

Van Klomp snorted. "There's a Bavarian beerfest tomorrow night. Or is that a bit upmarket for a rat who has stolen half my port? Or maybe you were thinking of Chez Henri-Pierre again. He won't let a Vat in the front door. I'm sure he'd be charmed at a rat—especially after your last visit. And then you could go and watch the HAR Bolshoi Ballet's performance of *The Nutcracker Suite*."

"The latter sounds about right. I think we will give Henri-Pierre the go-by," said Fitz, loftily. "His portions are too stingy for Ariel, anyway."

"Besides, I haven't finished all your port, yet. And Meilin is cooking dinner for us. Curried tripe," said Ariel with an expression of bliss.

Van Klomp laughed. "I'm tempted to come along just to see what a rat makes of the ballet. But I've got work to do tonight. And beside, the beerfest is more my sort of thing."

The acrobatic Ariel thought ballet was quite funny for about five minutes. She was mostly fascinated by the large flatscreen DVD backdrop, which was a great saving in set changes. When Ariel pointed out it was rather reminiscent of last night's pornographic one, only with worse dancing, Fitz had to turn his laughter into a fit of coughing. He still attracted a number of disapproving "hushes."

Ariel also alarmingly disappeared from their private box for a while. There were no screams or other sounds of pandemonium, so Fitz didn't allow the look of glee on her ratty face to worry him too much. She did however adore the Cointreau-centered liqueur chocolates he'd bought her.

He'd have slept less soundly if he'd known that she'd spent the rest of the night driving around with Meilin, part of it in a very exclusive Shareholder neighborhood. And part of it visiting a couple of Vat-girls of negotiable virtue and adaptable morality. It was, Ariel concluded, a lot more fun than the ballet.

"This lot should bring down the house," said Mei-lin with a particularly evil grin when she'd finished editing the film.

Ariel looked puzzled. "Why? 'Tis very funny, but not explosive."

Meilin snorted with laughter. "Believe me, this is H.E."

"And her," corrected Ariel, pedantically.

"You're Lieutenant Conrad Fitzhugh?" The MP at Van Klomp's door asked.

"Yes," said Conrad warily. What had Ariel been up to? Besides running up the beer waitress's dress last night?

"Colonel Brown has ordered your recall, sir," said the MP apologetically. "There's been a major incursion in your sector. We've got transport waiting for you."

Fitz nodded. "Give me five minutes to get into uniform and get my kit together."

Ariel was unbelievably dozy. It was almost as if she hadn't slept.

It was a long drive to the front. She snoozed most of the way, contentedly.

The general bowed his tiara-wearing plump wife into her seat. Ballet wasn't really his favorite entertainment, although he'd known an entertaining ballerina a year or two ago. But Maria was a true aficionado. And when all was said and done, it was her money. The war and cost-plus on artillery ammunition had made the Cartup clan enormously rich.

Having ogled the dancers and ordered some champagne, and salmon-and-watercress sandwiches for the interval, he settled into a comfortable doze.

He was woken by the buzz in the audience.

And no one was saying "hush."

It took a few moments of unbelieving blinking to be sure he wasn't hallucinating.

This was taking *avant garde* theater to new limits. The last time he'd seen anything like that backdrop had been at the Paradise Pussy Club. And that hadn't been quite so explicit. And while the female in the leather outfit wielding the whip was a stunning platinum blond...her partner did absolutely nothing for his lacy polka-dot knickers and black bra. And even fishnet stockings couldn't help legs like that.

The two dancers continued to pirouette with grim artistic determination as the huge screen behind them showed the details of his brother-in-law's face.

Talbot Cartup had always liked to sport a figure in high society. He was frequently seen at the opera and ballet. But never before in quite such detail.

The general missed the part showing the interviews with the two ladies of the night, discussing his transvestite brother-in-law's enjoyment of the rather bizarre perversion of semisuffocation. They did mention their prices for what was a very risky pastime. But General Cartup-Kreutzler was too busy trying to break into the very securely locked projection unit.

As it turned out, the DVD in the unit was amazingly bare of fingerprints.

And while the booking for the ballet trebled, it did rather change the way people regarded the art form.

"Captain?" said Fitz, looking at the bars being handed to him.

"We're out of officers," said the colonel, grumpily.

"We lost seven including two captains and a major when we were pushed back to line three. Those troops of yours are heading for court-martial. They're not exactly refusing orders. They want you. We just lost another two officers and your NCOs pulled the men back into the trenches. And what is this story about troops fraternizing with the rats?"

For a moment Fitz thought that Ariel must have put her head out of his pocket. Then he realized what the man was getting at. "Ah. It's a system we've evolved that works. Men have the stamina, rats the speed."

"Well, like your crazy idea about paying them, I'm not having any of it," said the colonel cholerically. "Just see you that get them over the top and that you recapture line two. You've got two new second lieutenants fresh out of OCS. See what you can do, Captain Fitzhugh. Put some discipline into this lot."

"Impossible, Talbot. He's back in combat. And Major Van Klomp is on a forced march with his men." The general looked in disgust at the telephone. Waited for his brother-in-law to stop rabbiting on. "There is nothing you, or even I, can do about it. Anything direct is almost certain to backfire on you now. I would certainly quietly withdraw those charges, because if the matter comes to court, you're going to end up being sued out of existence. You're a laughingstock and the best you can do is to go to that place of yours in the north and stay there. The town won't forget you in polka-dot panties for a long time."

Candy Foster was sitting looking gloomily at the door. He hadn't been near here since it happened. Hadn't called. It was his fault, not hers. She did it because that was what he wanted. She had no real interest in sex. Never had had. But it was a useful lever. So she'd panicked when he wouldn't come to after the plastic-bag thing. Her fingers had been stupid with fear and she hadn't been able to get it off. But at least she'd managed to tear the plastic, and hide that stupid leather outfit under a gown when the paramedics came. The story about Conrad had been born out of that panic. Talbot had decided to stick to it to save face. Had that ever blown up in his stupid *face*!

A brown envelope dropped through the letter slot in the door.

Candice opened it with trepidation. Talbot's brother-in-law's influence had stopped her getting call-up papers before. But this letter definitely began with . . .

"Greetings."

With her academic marks she knew she'd wash out of OCS. Let it be catering or nursing services. That was where nice girls were posted. She could change her hair color and use some skin pigment. Maybe change her name too. No one would recognize her. Hopefully.

Infantry school.

8

"They're pounding us, Captain. Going to push forward soon," said the slight, bespectacled lance corporal.

"SmallMac! What the hell are you doing here?"

"Transferred in. You're getting a reputation, Fitz. You keep your men alive. And you don't lose."

It was a heavy weight to bear. "I won't always manage to do either, Corporal McTavish," he said quietly.

He knew that in this man's case he was carrying a pregnant wife and two small children as well.

SmallMac shrugged. "Ah, but you try to do both, Captain. That's a rarity in a Shareholder officer."

Fitz found that, with the remnants of the rats (numerous) and the humans (few) from the collapse of the forward trenches, he had double his previous troop complement. There were only three other officers—a major who was keeping himself very busy with the troops who were furiously digging in behind them and two fresh-out-of-OCS lieutenants. He held a hasty staff meeting with them and his NCOs.

"Right, based on previous experience, we know when their artillery stops, the Maggots will come swarming."

"You mean the Magh', Captain," said one of the new lieutenants.

Fitz gave the snotty wet-behind-the-ears brat a look that would curdle milk. "Lieutenant Pahad, you'd better learn to speak the language that your men speak, or you'll be a mortality statistic. While I'm on the subject—Sergeant Major, I want you to detail a veteran NCO to each of these new officers. You two—" he pointed at them in their new, crisp BDUs with their new, shiny pips— "will listen to those men. Take advice from them before you give any orders, if you have time."

Pahad drew himself up. "How are we supposed to establish authority under those conditions, Captain?"

Fitz noticed that the other youngster had said nothing. For his sake, and the sake of the men this young idiot would command, he continued. "Lieutenant Pahad. Does the term 'frag' mean anything to you?"

"No, Captain, it does not," the man said stiffly.

"It's an old combat word. One my father told me about. From a long-ago war on old Earth. Unpopular officers who went into combat usually had a fragmentation grenade dropped into their pockets—a few seconds before it exploded. Our troops are combat veterans. They'll take orders or they wouldn't have survived. What they won't take is crap from wet-behind-the-ears ignoramuses who know nothing about real fighting. The average life of a soldier on the front is about forty days. The average life of a second lieutenant is half that. If you're stupid enough to think that that is coincidental... then you're a dead man walking. Now, I don't personally give a shit if you get killed. But if the NCOs in your unit tell me you wasted a single troop's life through your arrogance... you'd better *be* dead. Because I'll kill you before my troops do. Is that clear?"

The lieutenant gaped at him. But Fitz noticed that the other one nodded.

"Ahem." The sergeant major cleared his throat. "What you may not know, sir, is that the captain here has the best Maggot-kill rate we know of. He's also known to be an absolute bastard—pardon my saying so, sir—" he nodded at Fitz— "at weapons and fitness drill. He's also got the best troop survival rate on the front. Most of his men are veterans. And we get volunteers wanting to serve under him. That's a first for the hottest sector on the front. You're privileged to serve here, son." Which, as the sergeant major was perhaps two years older than Pahad, was not unamusing.

Fitz stopped the incipient reply with a finger. "Right. Enough of this. If you have any problems with me, Lieutenant, see me afterward. If we live through this, you can go and complain to the colonel. In the meanwhile, you will spend the next eight weeks on the front lines."

"If *you* survive that long," muttered SmallMac.

Fitz pretended he hadn't heard him. The white-lipped lieutenant certainly had. "Now, I've told Ariel to get the rats to work as the rats in my old command did. Two rats per human. The rest will be split into three groups, Sergeant Major, two cover groups and a backup. For each cover group I want two strong, fit, experienced soldiers. They'll be carrying heavy loads of rations and sugar for the rats. I want fast packhorses with brains. For the third group I want light, fast troops, twenty of them. They're our backup and, if we get a chance, our spearhead group. I want troops who can run."

"Sah! I'll confer with the platoon sergeants and have them assembled."

"Do that. And tell the troops the first one to cause trouble or bad feeling with the rats is going to answer to me, personally. Now, medics . . ."

At three that afternoon, the Magh' guns fell silent. And the fighting began. They came in waves over the top. They came in columns out of tunnels. And they seemed to be only hitting Fitz's patch of the line. It was obvious that they intended to push the weakened front into a beachhead. The Magh', it appeared, did not know the meaning of "retreat" or "fear."

They learned the meaning of "die."

Fitz nearly learned it himself. Lieutenant Pahad did. As Sergeant Anderson said, the Maggots had merely saved the captain trouble. But toward dusk the attack began to slow down. The last wave was more of a splash than a wave. As the Magh' artillery began to cut loose again, the rats and troops in Fitz's third group, with him at their head, went over the top. Moving as fast as a slowshield would allow, taking advantage of the Magh's weaker eyesight, they pushed into the human-abandoned old second line. The Magh' here were few and far between. Obviously the creatures had thrown everything at the human line. How fast they could move more troops up to fill the gap was an unknown. But the old line two was not under artillery bombardment. Fitz began to move men and rats forward. He rested them in the relative tranquillity of the comparatively easily recaptured line. The Magh' had moved their artillery forward in anticipation of the human line falling. Now, rather like Drake and the Spanish Armada, Fitz realized his men were too close to be fired on. If he had reinforcements now, he could keep pushing, maybe even to the Magh' force field edge. Only one massive human assault had managed that in the past, at vast cost in lives and materiel.

Fitz got on the radio to sector headquarters.

"Colonel Brown."

"Try and hold them a bit longer, Fitzhugh," said the colonel. "We've almost got the earthworks finished for the new trenches. And the attacks usually slack off at dusk."

"Sir. We've held them off. In fact, we've retaken the old line two. I've got my troops working on repairs right now."

"What? Impossible!" huffed the colonel, sounding less than grateful. "It must have been less of an attack than we'd expected."

"We estimate between ten and twenty thousand Magh', sir. But we have a bit of an advantage right now, sir. We appear to be so close that their guns' elevation capability does not allow them to fire on us. We think they've moved their artillery to our old line one. I'd like to press the advantage, sir. We can take those fieldpieces. But we'll need more men. Reinforcements before dawn."

The colonel showed the military dash and flair which had taken him so far in HAR's make-work pre-war army, and seemed destined to push him higher as the most incompetent of the mediocre-to-useless chateau-officer class. "Um. Well. Er. Don't you think you should play it safe?"

"We can hold these lines, sir, if that's what you want me to do," said Fitz. "But capturing some of the Magh' artillery would let us onto the technology they're using. It would be quite a kudo for you."

"Hmm. I don't like your newfangled way of doing things, Fitzhugh, but you do get them done," said the colonel. "Yes. Advance, see if you can take a Magh' fieldpiece. I'll see if I can scare up some reinforcements."

"If we push too far, sir, without reinforcements, we could lose even these trenches. So I'm afraid I need a firm commitment, sir."

"What? Damn your eyes, man. You'll have them. Take those guns at all costs," boomed the colonel.

"At least a company of rats, sir. Maybe even a few of these new rats, if possible."

"You're insufferable, Fitzhugh. Get me a gun and you'll get them."

"I'll rely on you for that, Colonel. Out."

"I'faith. What a whoreson Achitophel!"

Fortunately, Fitz did not transmit Ariel's accurate comment to the colonel.

The advance began. It was rapidly obvious that the Magh' had never met such tactics from the HAR armed forces before. The usual slow buildups and massed assault of the meat-grinder war that the HAR chateau generals fought, they dealt very effectively with. They simply outgunned and outnumbered the humans, and it appeared that the Magh' generals also had no objection to vast body counts. The idea that a thrust might be matched with a counterthrust, immediately, without two or three days of troop movements, appeared to have taken them off-balance.

"Get me Major Bartok," snapped Fitz to the radio operator.

The artillery officer was obviously bleary with sleep. Great, thought Fitz. Our artillery is near ineffectual and here we are in a major battle, and their commander has been catching up on his shut-eye. "Major. We're retaking our old front lines. Your men are shelling us." Slowshields at least meant they weren't being killed. But they could be buried, and slowed down.

"Huh?" said Bartok. "But we were pushed back two days ago. There's been no major advance planned."

Fitz ground his teeth. "Major. I'll set off a red flare. Your range finders can pick it up. We're fighting hand to hand in the trenches of our old trench one. It's slow going because we're thinly stretched. We've got the defensive troops from one trench line occupying two and fighting in a third. We've been promised relief before morning."

"First I've heard of it," grumbled the major. "It wasn't mentioned at last week's staff briefing."

Fitz had to stop talking to help Ariel with a pair of arrowscorps, which was probably just as well, as it stopped him biting the fool's head off. Then he let off the flare and went back to trying to keep his temper and get the human gunners to stop firing on their own side.

"Check with Colonel Brown. We've taken advantage of a situation. Look, it would help us if you could range your guns beyond us instead."

"Hmph. I'll put you onto the gunnery officer for tonight. Out."

The gunnery officer at least was simply cooperative. And his gunners, despite the fact that HAR industrial technology was still battling along in the nineteenth and early twentieth century and their fieldpieces were to match, were more than cooperative. Their rate of fire increased, which, as Fitz had heard, took nothing short of a miracle. At least somebody back there wanted them to succeed.

Then he and Ariel were fully engaged again, in the first hard fighting in this trench. They'd reached the gun emplacements. The Magh'der, the kind that tended the fieldpieces, were there in numbers and it was obvious that they felt about their strange weapons the way ants do about their grubs. But they appeared to be genetically designed to tend guns . . . not fight rats and men.

Looking at the pod of captured alien weapons in the infrared torchlight, Fitz allowed himself a brief moment of triumph in front of his cheering troops. Even the rats were caught up in it. "Methinks these should be worth a good few claws, eh, Captain," chittered one, cheerfully, kicking the wheelless platform, with its long stabilizers.

Ariel licked a slash on her shoulder. She pointed at the barrels. "Long muddy congers aren't they? Fair give you envy, Gobbo."

She stuck her long nose into the air. Sniffed. Twitched her ears. Fitz noticed several of the other rats doing the same.

"Methinks, it is the cat," said Pooh-Bah.

"'Tis time to cut and run," Ariel announced. "The Maggots are coming thick and fast from back there."

"We should be getting backup soon. We'd better dig in. Issue rations all round," said Fitz. "Radio. Let's get the Colonel and find out why they aren't here yet."

Minutes later Fitz knew fear. "We've taken their gun pod. Three fieldpieces, sir. But we need reinforcements if we're to hold them."

The colonel paused. "Er. I consulted General Blucher, and he refused to countenance moving troops until morning."

"Morning will be too late, Colonel," snapped Fitz. "The Magh' are just about solid out there. They want to retake their guns and they're not counting costs. If you want these guns, if you want this trench, if you want my men to survive, I need reinforcements *now*."

"Well, I'm sorry, Captain Fitzhugh," said the colonel huffily. "but there is nothing I can do, *now*."

"Useless asshole."

There was a splutter of outrage from the radio. But Fitz was too busy to care.

"If we try to pull back now, we'll be exposed to the faster Magh'. So. We'll need a rear guard."

"What about these guns, sir?" asked the surviving lieutenant.

"We'll do our best to destroy them, Lieutenant Cavanagh. You've done well today. You'll be leading the retreat back to trench two. We'll hold them as long as we can here. It'll be over to you to hold them there. Bring up as many men as possible from trench three. Sergeant. Drawing straws time. I want one man in three staying here."

The young lieutenant was pale. "With respect, sir. I'll stay here. You lead them back. You're worth a lot more than I am to the troops. I'm going to try and turn these guns on them."

A good kid, thought Fitz. *I wonder why he got sent to "Fort Despair?"* Probably too good, just as the other one had been too obnoxious. In the midst of mediocrity and incompetence, "good" was unpopular. He shook his head. "Lieutenant, thank you. But what I'm asking you to do is no lesser task. It's a tough one. You must keep the retreat orderly, keep it disciplined or it'll turn into a rout, and then we're lost. If the troops are panicked and half-dead with exhaustion when they get to trench two, they won't hold that. And I'm relying on you to do that, rather, because the rats will stay for me. They won't for you. And without them we have no rear guard. But it is a good idea about the guns. Now, move out. Go. Give us a flare when you have less than fifty yards to go."

The lieutenant saluted crisply. "Damn that lily-livered colonel and his stupid general to hell, sir. I'll hold that trench, come hell or high water." He turned. "Sergeant. Move them out in an orderly fashion. The first man to run or panic had better keep running because he'd be better off if the Maggots killed him than if I caught him." His voice cracked slightly. But the troops obeyed him, as if he were a veteran.

Three minutes later the old front line was populated by a skeleton crew of men and rats. And Fitz was wrestling with the guns. SmallMac and Ewen were assisting. Fitz's heart had fallen still lower when he'd seen the faces of his old squad mates. But . . . the lots had been drawn. Someone had to get the short straws. Some of those who retreated had families too. But he wished like hell he could have sent SmallMac back too.

Ewen, a man who could lift half an ox carcass back when he'd been a meat packer, strained with Fitz to turn barrels. They could tilt the entire structure but not turn it. There were no wheels, just flat metal platforms.

SmallMac nearly knocked them both flying, as the barrel began to rotate under its own steam. "What the hell are you fiddling with, Mac!"

The ex-horse-breaker gave a wry grin. "There must be electronic locks holding them, Fitz. Damned if I'm going to call you 'Captain' when we're all going to die. This disc here looked likely, and we need to learn to work them before the Maggots arrive."

"Hell's teeth. You're right and I'm an idiot. Each of you to a gun. Fiddle. I just hope we don't shoot at our own men or blow these things up."

Three minutes later they had rotation and elevation licked. They had reloading done too. Firing . . . well it was only when Fitz thought of the flat-scorpion shape of the gunners that Ariel discovered where the firing lever was. Tailgunners! Still, the shots they managed to direct toward the enemy were probably ineffectual, especially as the guns could not be elevated beyond a certain point.

"Bugger this for a joke!" yelled Ewen as the first Magh' came over the top. He cranked the gun barrel down furiously. Instead of using it as the howitzer it was designed as, he directed the barrel straight at the oncoming mass. It couldn't be elevated enough, but it could be depressed.

For the next few moments it rained slowshielded Maggots and earth.

"Yes!" The other two also hauled their gun barrels down.

The Maggot shells couldn't actually blow the enemy apart, not inside slowshields. But their weapons had been intended to fling a shell at high trajectory for a few miles. At this close a range it could physically remove anything. Blow them away if not apart. And the flying debris hardened slowshields and stopped the Magh' advance.

"Gather around the guns!" yelled Fitz. As long as they could keep them off the guns, as long as the shells lasted, they could hold back the bulk of the Maggot tide. With more luck than judgement he managed a skimming, plowing shot along the ground nearly parallel to the trench. Not only did it blow away the bulk of the wave of Magh' who had been pressing forward, but it also hardened the slowshields behind them. "Retreat on the guns," he yelled again, desperately reloading, knowing that his lucky shot had bought them the time to do so. Ariel bit down on something and a claw cut Fitz's face. He was in pain, but this was no time to stop and think about it. He must fire again! The rear guard surged back toward the gun pod, fighting their way through the few Maggots who had reached the trench. Soon, he had a reloader. And as the humans and rats fended off close attackers, the curiously silent alien howitzers were used in the fashion of the siege cannon of the fourteenth century.

Despite this, the Magh' seemed endless. Even the light of a flare behind them was of no help. There was no retreat now. The Magh' had surrounded them. And the shells were getting few.

Fitz saw Ewen abandon his gun and attempt to wade though the swirl of Magh' fighter bodies, using his huge strength to pick them up and fling them away... And then he went down under the tide. The rat that had been on his shoulder ran across Magh' backs. It nearly made it, too. SmallMac also was plainly out of shells—and defenders. There were still some fifteen men and an equal number of rats around Fitz's gun.

And he had three more shells.

SmallMac must have seen the rat nearly make it running across Magh' backs. He leapt.

Only the man didn't try to run on their backs. He leapt onto the biggest long-legged runner there. Astride it. Out of reach of claws and stingers.

The horse-breaker used all the skills at his disposal to cling to something that hadn't ever been ridden. Stayed on and somehow propelled his alien steed though the press. And then flung himself at the raised tier at the far end of the gun platform.

A claw snagged his foot. For a moment it looked as if he'd be pulled down. Then a rat bit through the clawjoint. Screaming... grabbing anything for handholds... SmallMac was up.

And so were they. Whatever control SmallMac had grabbed on the tier was raising the entire platform. Men and rats scrambled, snatched for purchase as the whole platform wobbled gently up into the sky, the rotors underneath lifting, clanging into suddenly hardening slowshields, faltering, lifting again. Maggots leapt frantically after them. Fitz saw Ariel go down under one. He lunged at it, pulling it aside.

Its razor-edged claw cut into his thigh and up toward his belly . . . before something stopped it.

Ariel.

The hovercraft-mounted gun was genteelly blundering deeper into enemy territory. As he lay there bleeding, Fitz saw SmallMac, his face white with pain, sticking his bangstick into holes plainly intended for a claw. And, although it nearly had them off, turning the thing in a wobbling circle toward the HAR-held lines.

With Fitz holding on to Ariel, and she holding on to him, consciousness faded as the handful of rear guards headed home, in the dawn.

9

His first memory of the hospital was clouded with anesthetics and pain. But after a couple of weeks, that too cleared. On the first day that he actually knew just who he was, a Vat-visitor with glasses in a dressing gown and on crutches came to see him.

"SmallMac!"

"Captain." The bespectacled man managed a salute, despite the crutches.

"I thought you weren't going to call me that anymore."

"That was when we were going to die," said Lance

Corporal McTavish with a grin. "And that appears to have been delayed."

"And the rest? Ariel?" There was a lump in his throat. He felt sick and weak and like crying.

SmallMac pulled a face. "Injured. Spanoletti came through it all with no worse than a few cuts. She's been to see all the rats. Apparently Ariel looks like she'd been through a fight with a grizzly. She'll live, though. We lost one of the rats to injuries. Pitti-Sing, I think. The rest of us . . . thirty-one men and rats in all . . . made it. Some of them won't fight again. We had our doubts about you making it though, Captain. You owe your life to Ariel and some pretty sharp medics."

"And to your riding and flying skills."

"For a minute I almost thought we had cavalry," said SmallMac, wryly. "But I won't be riding again for a while. I've lost the foot. On the plus side I won't be marching again either."

"Hell. I'm sorry. But . . . that's your livelihood."

SmallMac shrugged. "I was getting too old for the falls anyway. And, well, I was nearly dead, like poor bloody Ewen. I hear I'm due for a desk posting here in GBS city. I'll be able to sleep out with my family! There's many a poor bastard who would cut their own foot off for that."

After that came Fitz's father. Other survivors. Parachute Major Van Klomp.

And then Ariel came to visit him. Rats of course were strictly not allowed in the hospital.

Fitz looked at her. Ariel's rich fur was bandaged. So was one paw. The once beautiful little creature looked bedraggled. Her delicate ears were tattered.

But worst of all was the bandaged stump of a tail.

"I've just come to say good-bye," she said, in a voice that was unaccustomedly subdued.

"Have you been posted back to what's left of our unit?"

"No." She twitched her tail stump. "I...methinks... I'll...I just wanted to see you a last time. To be sure you were still alive."

Fitz knew this rat. He'd long since stopped regarding her as anything other than another person. The crucible of the front line was far too hot for the metals in it not to meld. He'd learned to understand some of the things she left unspoken. Ariel was going to die. Rats did without most things except food and sex. Losing her tail was like a man losing his balls, but a lot more public.

"I despair of ever winning affection." Voice synthesizers were not designed to carry the loss. But Fitz understood anyway. Ariel...Ariel had been accustomed to being the very best. To being sought after. To knowing herself as desirable. Well. He knew partly how it felt. The left side of his face was never going to be anything but a mask to frighten children. The wounds on his thigh and lower abdomen had been repaired. But he couldn't bet anyone his left ball anymore.

"I still love you, Ariel. I love you for what you are, not for what you look like. I don't have a tail myself."

The rat snuffled. "I always thought 'twas a sad lack in you."

She scrambled up the bedclothes, and gave his throat a slight nip. Rats didn't kiss but that as a gesture of trust and affection was as close as it came—a sort of "I could rip your jugular out but I won't."

"Take care," she snuffled, and got up to leave.

"Where are you going?"

"Away."

"Stay. Please stay," he begged, urgently.

She paused. "Why?"

"Because I need you. Well, because I still love you. And tails have never been very important to me. Um. And because I have chocolate for you. We humans never offer chocolate to those we don't love."

"Never?"

He knew the prescribed rat-reply. "Well, hardly ever."

She even summoned up a ratly look of acquisitiveness. "Chocolate Cointreau straws? I wouldn't stay for less. Someone who loved me would give me those."

"Hmph. Cupboard love," he said loftily, knowing he'd won at least a reprieve, especially as he had some of the desired item.

She took it. To his surprise she offered him a bite. It was the most unratly gesture he'd ever seen her make. Then, with her sticky chocolate, she burrowed under the bedclothes. "Well. I can't love your tail. I still think 'tis a sad lack in you. I mean size does count, and a girl could get some respect with a boyfriend like you, if you had a tail in proportion."

When Fitz opened his eyes again, there was a four-star general, and several other staff officers, looking at him. He hoped that the general was not aware of the beady eyes peering at him from under the blanket. There were also two people who bore the unmistakable mark of "press" even if one hadn't borne a shoulder-cam as well. The other one grimaced. "Better focus on the right side of his face. He's not a pretty sight on this side. Right, General, you're on. Roll it, Paul."

Fitz discovered that he was now a major. The bits of gold in his hand seemed a very poor recompense for his troops' lives. "And for service over and above the call of duty in the capture of the first intact Magh' fieldpiece: The George Bernard Shaw Cross, first class."

"Thank you, sir. But I believe the credit should go to the men and rats in my unit, sir. A number of them lost their lives in this action, and I'd like them to get the recognition for their courage. And we captured an entire pod of Magh' guns. We'd have held them if Colonel Brown had sent us the reinforcements we were promised. Loss of life and loss of those field-pieces is due to his and General Bulcher's decisions not to back us up." Fitz hoped this was going out live.

The general was only momentarily discomfited. "General Bulcher was unfortunately misinformed by the colonel. The matter is under investigation. But you and the men under your command did very well under the circumstances. A rather substantial number of medals are being awarded. Lieutenant Cavanagh will command one of the most decorated units on the front." He cleared his throat. "I believe you may be invalided out of active frontline duty, Major. You're a valuable soldier. Too valuable to waste on just any desk job. Which is why I have ordered your transfer to the Military Intelligence Corps. You'll be replacing Major Dunsay."

"No thank you, sir. I'd like to try and get fit, and return to my unit."

The general looked as if he'd just bitten into a slug in his salad. He made a quick recovery. "Intelligence is where you can really make a contribution to the war effort, young man. However, I am open to other requests."

"Very well, sir. I'd like to add a severely injured rat to my staff. We need someone who understand rats, sir. They're valuable military assets. It's due to them and the courage of my troops that I owe what success we had. It is my feeling that the rats should be paid. They'd be much better motivated then."

The general blinked. "Yes. Well. We shall have to see what can be done. The bats that we are about to introduce will make a great deal of difference too, eh."

A little later when the general and his entourage had left, Ariel emerged. "Why did you agree?" she asked, helping herself to a grape.

Fitz shrugged. It was a painful experience. "Because... God knows if either of us will ever be fit to fight again. And, well, the Maggots always attacked where we were weakest. They obviously have good intelligence. We also need it. And maybe at Military Headquarters I can get something done about idiots like Colonel Brown and General Bulcher. Maybe we can make the system work."

Ariel chuckled. "'Tis the HAR army we speak of, Fitz. Methinks it will be 'once more into their breeches' and bite their bollocks."

Fitz grinned. It hurt his face. "We'll try it my way first, okay?" He looked at the order that the general had left behind.

It was signed: *H. Cartup-Kreutzler*.

He stared at the signature for a long time. He began to understand just why he'd been posted to "Fort Despair." Or why the orders for relief had been delayed. And just what his posting to "Intelligence" might be. It wouldn't stop him. But it would make for interesting times, ahead.

Ariel shrugged in her turn when he pointed it out.

"Methinks we'll end up doing things in my way after all. 'Tis the only way the army works."

A few minutes later, they had another visitor. An elderly woman, this was, wearing what looked like a laboratory coat. She was holding an antique-looking item in her hands. A brass object of some sort. At first, Fitz though it was an oddly shaped teakettle, until he realized it was an oil lamp.

The woman placed the lamp on a small table next to the bed and gazed down at Fitz. He couldn't read the expression in her face. There was *something* there . . . Amusement, maybe, combined with satisfaction. Hard to tell.

Then the woman spotted Ariel's nose poking out from under the covers. She smiled, and murmured some verses under her breath. Fitz could just barely make out the words.

"The culminating pleasure that we treasure beyond measure, Is the gratifying feeling that our duty has been done."

Fitz cleared his throat. "May I help you, Ms. ah . . . ?"

"Just think of me as John Wellington Wells. A dealer in magic and spells. And that's all I'm going to tell you."

She started to turn away, gesturing with a finger at the oil lamp. "A gift I brought for you." Her eyes went back to Ariel, whose entire head was now sticking out of the covers. "I'm glad to see it will be trebly appreciated."

And with that, she headed out the door. On her

way through, Fitz heard her murmuring: "The genie out of the bottle, indeed."

When she was gone, Ariel popped out from under the blankets. "You humans are a daft lot, but that is the first one I have ever heard quote Gilbert and Sullivan." She scrutinized the gift on the nearby table with a rat's usual intentness when the possibility of loot arose. "What's that?"

Fitz shrugged. "Nothing you'll be interested in. Me neither, actually. It's an antique kind of lamp."

Ariel was puzzled. "What for? When you want light, you flip a switch. When you want light and can't get it—like in a tunnel in a Maggot raid—that silly thing will be useless. Won't even make a good bludgeon."

Fitz shrugged again. "Like you said, humans are all daft. That old lady, for sure."

But Ariel had already leapt onto the table. Though disgruntled, she wasn't going to leave even a faint possibility of loot unchecked.

She lifted the lid. Then, squeaked sheer glee.

"It's full of chocolates! And—!"

Ariel reached in and plucked out a little sample bottle of Grand Marnier. Then, clutching it to her chest, she replaced the lid and perched herself atop the lamp. Looking, for all the world, like a guardian demon.

She gave Fitz a slit-eyed stare.

"I'll share the chocolates—maybe. If you're sweet to me. But the booze is mine."

Fitz rolled his eyes. "Rats!"

"It's important!" insisted Ariel. "There's not going to be any of that human folderol in *this* romance."

Now, she looked positively indignant. "Won't ever find a rat—sure as hell not a rat-girl—getting her stars crossed. Much less her loot. That silly crap's got to go."

Fitz leaned back in the pillows, chuckling. He thought he understood now—a bit, at least—of the weird old woman's last words.

"Genie out of the bottle! One way to put it, I guess."

"Why do humans have so many useless words?" grumbled Ariel. "And what's a 'genie,' anyway?"

"You are." Fitz thought about it for a moment. "Or maybe we are."

THE
RANKS OF BRONZE
SERIES

Author's note:

Except for the story I submitted to the *Writers of the Future* contest, this is the first piece of short fiction I ever got commercially published. That happened as a by-product of my partnership with David Drake in writing the Belisarius series. At Jim Baen's request, David put together an anthology of stories set in the universe he'd created for his novel *Ranks of Bronze*. I was one of the authors he asked to write a story for the collection, *Foreign Legions*, published in 2001.

With some hesitation, I accepted—my hesitation being my long-known inability to write a piece of short fiction without turning it, willy-nilly, into a novel. But, as it turned out, it was this story that first made clear to me that I could write short fiction—quite easily, in fact—provided that the setting for the story was already established. In this instance, of course, the setting was established by another author, not me. But I soon discovered that didn't make any difference.

In fact, I had a lot of fun writing the story; and, almost a decade later, I still like it. I also think it works well enough as a stand-alone story. But if you find the story entertaining and would like to see the novel for which it serves as something of a sequel, David Drake's *Ranks of Bronze* is still in print—and, in my opinion, one of the best novels he's ever written.

Cathargo Delenda Est

I

"What is the point of this?" demanded Agayan. The Guild Voivode emphasized his irritation by flexing the finger-clusters of his midlimbs.

Yuaw Khta ignored both the question and the cluster-flex. The Guild Investigator was immune to the Voivode's displeasure. The Guild's Office of Investigation had a separate command structure from that of the Trade Web. Although Agayan was its nominal superior in their current mission, Yuaw Khta's career in no way depended on the Voivode's goodwill.

"Again."

The Gha sepoy it commanded twisted the native's arm further. Gobbling with pain, the native struggled furiously.

Its efforts were futile, despite the fact that the

orange-skinned biped was not much smaller than its Gha tormentor. It was more slender, true—although much of the Gha's squat bulk was the product of its heavy armor. Still, the native was every bit as tall as the Gha. But the real difference lay beneath the surface. For all the near-equivalence of size, the native was a child in the hands of an ogre.

The Gha were a heavy-planet species. Due in large part to that gravity, theirs was the most inhospitable world that had ever produced an intelligent race. The Gha were few in numbers, but all the great trading Guilds and Combines favored them as bodyguards for their strength and physical prowess.

The native's gabbles reached a crescendo, but they still expressed nothing more than pain—and curses.

"Again," commanded the Guild Investigator. The Gha twisted; the native howled.

Guild Voivode Agayan ceased his finger-flexing. He transformed his mid-limbs into legs and stalked off in disgust. While the native continued to screech, the Voivode stared out at the landscape.

The scene was as barren as their investigation had thus far proven to be. The sun—a green-colored dot in the sky—cast a sickly hue over the gravelly terrain. The land was almost flat, broken only by a scattering of squat gray-skinned plants with long, trailing leaves.

And the bones. Gha bones, and the skeletal remains of the huge carnivores which served as mounts for the sepoys. The bones were picked clean, now, and bleached white by the sun. Every other relic of the battle which had raged across this plain was gone. The natives had buried their own dead, and scavenged all the discarded weapons and armor.

Behind him, Agayan heard a cracking noise. The native shrieked and fell suddenly silent. The Voivode twisted his body, caterpillarlike, and examined the situation. As he had expected, the Gha had finally broken the native's arm. And, still, without the Investigator learning anything they didn't already know.

"Are you quite finished?" he demanded.

Again, Yuaw Khta ignored him. But, after a moment, the Investigator made a gesture to the Gha. The sepoy released its grip. The native, now unconscious, collapsed to the ground.

Satisfied that the charade was at an end, Agayan transformed his forelimbs into arms and reached for his communicator. After summoning the shuttle, he amused himself by watching the Investigator scampering about the area, looking for some last-minute clue.

As always, the Voivode found Yuaw Khta's movements both comical and unsettling. The Investigator, like all members of his species, was a tall and gangling creature. Its long, ungainly head hung forward from its neck like certain draft animals Agayan had observed on various primitive planets. That much was amusing. Yet there was a quick, jerky nature to the Investigator's movements which created a certain sense of anxiety in Agayan's mind. His own species, supple but slow-moving, retained a primordial fear of predators.

He shook the uneasiness off. Ridiculous, really. Even a bit embarrassing. Such atavistic fears had no basis in reality. Agayan's race—like that of the Investigator—was counted among the Doge Species which dominated both the Federation and the great trading Guilds and Combines.

The Doge Species numbered only twenty-three. All other races were subordinate, to one degree or another. Some, like the species which provided the Pilots and Medics for the great trading ships, were ranked Class One. Class One species were privy to the highest technology of galactic civilization, and enjoyed many privileges. But they were still subordinates. Others, specialized laborers like the Gha, were ranked Class Two. Below Class Two species came nothing but indentured servant races, like the quasi-reptilian Ossa whose flexible phenotypes made them useful, or outright slaves like—

The shuttle swept in for a landing. The Investigator joined Agayan as they marched up the ramp.

"I told you the humans did it," he hissed, knotting the finger-clusters of his forelimbs in satisfaction.

II

After their ship left the planet, Agayan pressed the advantage.

"It is the *only* possibility," he announced firmly. "Ridiculous to think those natives were responsible!"

He and the Investigator were in that chamber of the vessel which combined the functions of a lounge and a meeting room. In deference to its multispecies use, the room was bathed with soft indirect light and bare of any furnishings beyond those of use to its current occupants. Each of those two occupants, in his or its own way, was relaxing. For Agayan, that involved nothing more elaborate than draping his body over a sawhorse-shaped piece of furniture and enjoying a tumbler of a mildly intoxicating liquor.

For the Investigator, relaxation was more intense.

Yuaw Khta was also positioned on its preferred furniture, in that posture which almost all bipeds adopted when resting. (In their different languages, it was called *sitting*. As always, it seemed peculiar to Agayan—as if a person would deliberately choose to break his body in half.) Yuaw Khta was also sipping at a beverage. A different one, of course. The liquor in Agayan's tumbler would poison the Investigator; and, while Agayan would survive drinking the blue liquid in Yuaw Khta's cup, he would certainly not enjoy the experience.

In addition, however, the Investigator enjoyed the ministrations of a personal attendant. As it leaned forward in its chair, the Ossa behind it subjected Yuaw Khta's long neck to a vigorous massage.

Between grunts of pleasure, the Investigator said:

"No variant explanation can be discounted in advance, Voivode Agayan. Proper investigatory technique is primarily a process of eliminating possibilities, one by one, until the solution finally emerges."

Agayan's forelimb finger-cluster flexed sarcastically. "And are you *now* satisfied? Can we *finally* lay to rest the—variant explanation!—that primitives somehow seized a Guild vessel? *After* they had already been decisively defeated in battle?"

"Your own explanation would also have primitives seizing the ship," pointed out the Investigator.

Agayan restrained his anger. The self-control was difficult, but allowances had to be made. Yuaw Khta, after all, had never personally witnessed the humans in action.

"There is no comparison," he said forcefully. "It is true that the humans were also iron-age barbarians. But their discipline and social coordination were many levels beyond those of any other primitives you may have encountered."

"So you say," grunted the Investigator. Its long, bony face was twisted into an expression which combined pain and pleasure.

To Agayan, watching, the whole process—what Yuaw Khta called a *massage*—seemed as grotesque as the Investigator's seated posture. To the Voivode's soft-bodied species, pain was pain and pleasure was pleasure, and never the twain shall meet. Not for the first time, Agayan concluded that the vertebrate structure which was by far the most common *Bauplan* of the galaxy's intelligent races was a curse on its possessors. A preposterous structure, really. Contradictory to the core.

Still, mused Agayan, it had its advantages.

Strength, for one. The Voivode glanced at the nearest of the sepoys standing silently against the wall of the chamber. Now unencumbered by armor, the Gha's bronze-colored, rangy body was fully visible. Quite impressive, in its own crude way.

Especially this one, thought the Voivode. *He's the commander of the squad, I believe.*

For a moment, Agayan's gaze met the bulging eyes of the sepoy. As always, the Gha's face was utterly expressionless. To humans, that face would seem froglike in its shape. To the Voivode, it simply seemed inanimate.

Gha, he reflected, were the most uninteresting species he had ever encountered. Barely sentient, in his opinion, based on his long experience with the sepoys. The creatures never expressed any sentiments in their faces, and they were as indistinguishable as so many pebbles. This one, for instance—the one he supposed to be the sepoy commander. Agayan thought that the Gha was the same one which had been in his service when he was a mere Guild Cacique. But he was not certain.

He looked back at Yuaw Khta. The Investigator was now practically writhing in the pain/pleasure from its massage. For a moment, Agayan felt genuine envy. The ubiquity of the vertebrate structure, whatever its limitations, meant that vertebrate Guildmasters could enjoy more in the way of personal and intimate service than could members of his own species.

While Yuaw Khta grunted its pain/pleasure, Agayan took the time to examine its personal attendant. Ossa were particularly favored for that purpose by genetic engineers. The quasi-reptiles lent themselves as easily to phenotype surgery as they did to genetic manipulation. And there was always a large supply of the things. Their sexual and procreative energy was notorious, in their natural state as well as the multitude of bodily forms into which they were shaped by Doge engineers.

Idly, Agayan wondered if this particular Ossa regretted its transformation. It was neutered, now, to match Yuaw Khta's current sexual stage. The Investigator kept two other Ossa on the ship, one male and one female, to serve it/her/him as Yuaw Khta progressed through the cycle.

Agayan did not ponder the matter for more than a few seconds. Ossa, for him, were not much more interesting than Gha.

He decided that he had been polite enough. "Are you going to be distracted by this exercise in self-torture for much longer?" he demanded. "The affairs of the Guild press heavily."

Yuaw Khta's grunt combined satisfaction with irritation. The Investigator made a snapping sound with its fingers and the Ossa attendant immediately departed the chamber.

After taking a long draught from its cup, Yuaw Khta said: "I fail to see your point, Voivode Agayan. Regardless of their social discipline and cohesion, the humans are still primitives."

He made a small waving gesture, which encompassed the entirety of the ship. "Even if they managed—somehow—to seize the ship, they would have no way to fly it anywhere."

"Unless they coerced the Pilot," retorted Agayan. The Voivode spread both his forelimb clusters, to give emphasis to his next words. "Unlike you, Yuaw Khta, I have personal experience with the humans. I was their Commander, for a time, before my promotion to Voivode. As you may or may not know, I passed through the Cacique ranks faster than any Guildmaster on the record. Some of that unprecedented speed in climbing through the ranks, of course, was due—"

He interlaced his finger-clusters modestly.

"—to my own ability. But *every* Commander of the human sepoys enjoyed rapid promotion. The humans were, far and away, the best sepoy troops the Guild has ever had. They were invariably successful in their campaigns, and did not even suffer heavy casualties."

He took a drink from his tumbler. "As these things go," he concluded. "In time, of course, their numbers would have declined to the point where they would have been useless. But there were many, many campaigns which the Guild would have profited from before their liquidation was necessary."

"So?" demanded Yuaw Khta.

Agayan could not control the agitated flexing of his hindlimb clusters, he was so aggravated. But he managed to maintain a calm voice.

"So? What do you think accounts for the human success, Investigator? It was not simple physical prowess, I can assure you!"

The Voivode pointed to the Gha commander. "This one—or any of its fellows—could easily defeat a human in single combat. Several of them at once, in fact. But I have no doubt whatsoever that on a field of battle, matched with equivalent weapons, the humans could have defeated a Gha army."

The Investigator was still not convinced.

"Gha are stupid," it grumbled. "Everyone knows that. I am prepared to admit that the humans were unusually intelligent, for a slave race, but—"

The Voivode had had enough. "Do you have any alternative explanation?" he demanded.

The Investigator was silent.

"In that case," stated Agayan firmly, "I now exercise my command prerogatives. If the humans seized their transport vessel, and coerced the Pilot into operating the craft, their most likely destination would have been their original home. Their native planet. Accordingly, this ship will proceed to that same planet. If the humans are there, we will destroy them. This vessel is far better armed that any troop transport."

"*Their native planet?*" exploded the Investigator. "That's ridiculous! The humans were in Guild service longer—*far longer*—than any other sepoy troops. They underwent tens and tens of Stasis episodes. It must be hundreds—thousands—of years since their initial recruitment. I doubt if we even have a record of—"

"The record will exist," stated Agayan firmly. "I have instructed the Pilot to check. You underestimate the care with which the Guild—"

He was interrupted by the appearance of the Pilot herself in the chamber.

"Ah!" he exclaimed. "I presume you have finished your examination of the records?"

"Yes, Guild Voivode." The Pilot belonged to a spindle-shaped species which found bowing impossible, so she indicated her respect by darkening her purple skin.

"The results?"

"The human planet—there is no name for it, beyond the catalog number—is only two hundred and twelve light years distant. The humans were recruited slightly over two thousand Guild years ago."

Agayan turned triumphantly to Yuaw Khta.

"You see, Investigator?" He waved a finger-cluster at the Pilot, dismissing her. To his surprise, the Pilot remained planted on her footskirt.

"There is something else, Guild Voivode."

"Yes?"

"I used a broad-range program in my search, and it brought up all information concerning this planet. In addition to the original sepoy records, there is also a significant—*perhaps* significant—item of meteorological data."

Agayan's finger-clusters began to flex. "What is the point of this?" he demanded.

The Pilot turned a very dark purple, in her attempt to placate the Voivode's rising irritation.

"The Federation's Meteorological Survey has been paying close attention to that region of the galaxy. A

Transit storm has been moving down that spiral arm for many thousands of Guild years. The human planet and its environs were cut off from all Transport nodes shortly after the sepoys were recruited. The nodes were only reestablished two hundred Guild years ago."

"Has a Guild vessel returned to that planet since Transit possibility was renewed?"

"No, Guild Voivode. Nor has any Federation ship. But shortly after the nodes re-formed, the Meteorological Survey began detecting oddities in the region, which they eventually pinpointed to that planet's solar system. They didn't know what to make of the peculiar data, until they thought to consult with the Federation's Historiographic Bureau."

Seeing the Voivode's increasingly rapid finger-flexing, the Pilot hurried to her conclusion.

"The data indicate that the natives of that planet have recently developed the capacity to manipulate the electromagnetic spectrum. Radio waves, to be precise."

Agayan's clusters spread wide with puzzlement.

"*Radio?* Of what possible use—"

"It is a primitive technique, Guild Voivode. No advanced civilization bothers with radio, but—according to the Historiographic Bureau, at least—the radio portion of the electromagnetic spectrum is typically the first point of entry for civilizations which—"

The significance of the information finally penetrated. Agayan lurched erect.

"*Civilization?*" he screeched. "Are you trying to claim that these—these human *savages* have reached the point of industrial chain reaction?"

The Pilot scuttled back on her footskirt. Her color was now so deep a purple as to be almost black.

"*I'm* not claiming *anything*, Guild Voivode! I'm just relaying what the—"

"Ridiculous! I know these humans, you fool! They served under me. There is no—no—"

Agayan's indignation overwhelmed him. He fell silent, fiercely trying to bring his fury under control.

The Investigator interjected itself. "No species in the historical record has reached industrial chain reaction in less than two hundred thousand years since initial habitat domestication," it stated ponderously. "And none has done so since the last of the Doge Species."

The Pilot said nothing. She was tempted to point out that the policies of both the Federation and the Guilds were precisely designed to *prevent* such occurences, but suppressed the whimsy ruthlessly. Foolish, she was not.

Agayan finally restored his calm enough to speak. Icily:

"That is quite enough, Pilot. You may go. This information—this preposterous twaddle, I should say—will be corrected as soon as we reach that planet. Set the course."

"Yes, Guild Voivode. I have already done so. Your instructions, as always, were very clear and precise."

Agayan spread his clusters in acknowledgement of the praise. "Send a message to Guild Headquarters informing them that we are Transiting to the human planet."

The Pilot scuttled out of the chamber as fast as her ungainly form of locomotion permitted.

Agayan resumed his position of rest. "I cannot believe how incompetent some of the Federation's—"

"*Ptatti gattokot poi toi rhuch du! Ptatti gatt!*"

All six of Agayan's clusters knotted in shock. The

sheer volume of the Gha commander's voice had been almost like a physical blow.

The shock deepened. *Deepened.*

Dazed, the Voivode watched one of the Gha sepoys stride forward from its position against the wall and shatter the Investigator's spinal cord with a single blow of its fist. Shatter it again. Seize Yuaw Khta's lolling head and practically twist it in a full circle.

The Voivode could *hear* the bones break.

Ancestral reflex coiled Agayan into a soft ball. He heard the Gha commander bellowing more phrases in the sepoy language. Two of the Gha immediately left the chamber.

Agayan was utterly paralyzed. He could not even speak. Only watch.

His soft-bodied species, some distant part of his brain noted, did not respond well to physical danger.

Standing in front of him, now, he recognized the figure of the Gha commander.

The Gha spoke to him. He did not understand the words.

The sepoy spoke again. The meaning of the words finally penetrated. Oddly, Agayan was surprised more by the *fact* of those words than their actual content. He had not realized that Gha could speak Galactic beyond a few crude and simple phrases.

"I said," repeated the Gha, "do you know my name?"

Paralyzed. Only watch.

The sepoy repeated its question: "Do you know my name, Guild Voivode Agayan?"

The Gha towered above him like an ogre. Immense, heavy-planet muscles coiled over that rangy, vertebrate body. Strength. Leverage. Power.

The other Gha spoke now, also in fluent Galactic: "Just kill him and be done with it."

The sepoy commander: "Soon enough." To the Voivode: "Do you know my—ah! No use."

The monster reached down a huge hand and seized the Voivode by one of his forelimb clusters. A moment later, still curled into a ball, Agayan found himself suspended in midair. The Gha commander's bulging eyes were right before him.

Paralyzed. Only watch.

"My name," said the Gha softly, "is Fludenoc hu'tut-Na Nomo'te. Since I have served you for more years than I wish to remember—a second time, now, when the first was bad enough—I feel that it is only proper that you should know my name."

Paralyzed. Only watch.

"I will even educate you in the subtleties. Some of them, at least. Fludenoc is the familiar. Nomo the family name, with the 'te-suffix to indicate that we are affiliated to the Na clan. Hu'-tut is an honorific. It indicates that my clan considers my poetry good enough for minstrel status."

Paralyzed. Only watch.

"I will not bother explaining the fine distinctions which we Gha make between poets. They would be quite beyond your comprehension, Guild Voivode. Even if you were still alive."

The Gha's other hand seized Agayan's head. Began to squeeze. Stopped.

"On second thought, I'd better not crush your worm-face beyond recognition. The Romans are probably holding a grudge against us. If they can recognize your corpse, it may help."

Paralyzed. Only watch. The Voivode saw the two Gha who had left the chamber return. Dragging the Pilot and the Medic with them.

The Gha commander's clawed hand plunged into Agayan's mid-section. Pushing the soft flesh aside until it gripped the vital organs at the center.

"I'm sure you never knew the names of the three Romans you executed, either. To my own shame, I only know one of them. Helvius, he was called."

Squeezed. *Squeezed*.

Paralyzed, even at his death. Only watch.

The Guild Voivode's last thought was perhaps inappropriate. It seemed outrageous to him that there was still no expression on the Gha's face.

III

The Guild official's body made a soft plopping sound when Fludenoc hu'tut-Na Nomo'te finally let it fall to the deck. Around the corpse, a pool of pink blood spread slowly from the Voivode's alimentary and excretory orifices. The Gha commander's incredibly powerful grip had ruptured half of Agayan's internal organs.

"I am *not* cleaning up that mess," announced the Gha who had killed Yuaw Khta. He pointed to the body of the Investigator. "Notice. Clean as a sand-scoured rock. Finesse."

Fludenoc barked humor. "The worm didn't *have* a neck to break. And I meant what I said, Uddumac. His corpse—if they recognize it—may be our passkey with the Romans."

Uddumac made the sudden exhalation of breath

which served Gha for a facial grimace. "All right,
Fludenoc. *Explain.*"

The other two Gha in the room flexed their shoulders, indicating their full agreement with that sentiment. The gesture was the equivalent of vigorous head
nodding among humans.

Before answering, Fludenoc examined the Pilot
and the Medic. The Pilot was utterly motionless.
Much like the species which had produced Agayan,
the Pilot's race also responded to sudden danger by
instinctive immobility. Only her color—pale violet,
now—indicated her terror.

There would be no problems with her, Fludenoc
decided. He did not think she would recover for
some time.

The Medic, on the other hand—

The Medic belonged to a species which would
have seemed vaguely avian to humans. *His* instinctive
reaction to shock was rapid flight. Yet, aside from an
initial attempt to struggle free from the iron grip of
the Gha who had captured him, the Medic seemed
almost tranquil. His Gha captor still held him by the
arm, but the Medic was making no attempt to escape.

Fludenoc stared down at him. The Medic's flat,
golden eyes stared back.

"Do not not mind me," the Medic suddenly trilled.
"I am just just a bystander. *Interested* bystander."

The Medic gazed down at the corpse of the Voivode.
"I always always wondered what the worm's blood
looked like." He trilled pure pleasure. "Never never
thought I'd find out."

Uddumac interrupted.

"*Explain, Fludenoc.* I obeyed your command because

you are the *flarragun* of our Poct'on cartouche. But now that the action is finished, I have a full right to demand an accounting."

Fludenoc decided the Medic was no immediate problem, either. He turned to face Uddumac and the other Gha in the chamber.

"I gave the command because our opportunity has finally arrived."

"*What* opportunity?" asked the Gha holding the Medic.

Fludenoc's whole upper torso swiveled to face his questioner. For all its immense strength, the Gha physique was not limber. Evolved on a heavy-gravity planet, Gha necks were almost completely rigid.

"You know perfectly well *what* opportunity, Oltomar. The same opportunity the Poct'on has been searching for since it was founded."

Oltomar's response was a quick, wavering hiss.

Fludenoc, understanding the subtleties in that hiss, felt a sudden surge of bitter anger. His anger, and his bitterness, were not directed toward Oltomar. They were directed at the universe, in general; and galactic civilization, in particular.

The same evolutionary necessities which had produced the rigid upper vertebra of the Gha species, had also produced their stiff, unmoving faces. The bleak, wind-scoured, heavy planet where Gha had originated was merciless. No soft, supple, flexible animals could survive there—only creatures which presented a hard shield to the world, and thereby withstood its heavy lashes.

Intelligence, when it came to that planet, came in a suitable form. A form which, when other intelligences discovered them—more technologically advanced intelligences, but not smarter ones—could see nothing beyond the stiff shield of Gha faces. And the immense strength of Gha bodies.

The Gha were famed—notorious—among all the intelligent races of the galaxy. They were the epitome of the stolid dullwit. Only the Gha themselves knew of their inner life. Of the subtle ways in which their breath transmitted meaning; their voices, undertones of sentiment.

Only the Gha knew of their poetry. To galactic civilization—to the Doge Species which ruled that civilization—the Gha were nothing more than splendid thugs. The galaxy's premier goons.

Fludenoc shook off the anger. (Literally. His fellows, watching, understood the nuances of that shoulder movement as perfectly as he had understood the skepticism in Oltomar's hiss.)

"I'm quite serious, Oltomar. Even before this incident, I thought the Romans were the best possibility we had ever encountered."

"Too primitive," interjected Uddumac. "We talked it about, you and I, long ago."

Uddumac gestured to the Voivode's corpse on the floor. "The first time we had the misfortune of being assigned to this worm. We talked about it, then, and we reached a common conclusion. For all their astonishing competence, the Romans were simply too primitive. Barbarians, to all intents and purposes."

Oltomar chimed in. Again, literally. The chime-syllable which prefaced his words was a Gha way of expressing agreement.

"Yes. Nothing's changed simply because they managed to seize their troop transport. *If* they seized it.

I'm not sure the worm's theory was correct, but even if it is—so what? The Romans are still barbarians. The Poct'on has always known that—"

Fludenoc silenced him with a gesture. Left hand before his face, palm outward, fingers spread. *Stop—I must interrupt.*

"You're missing the significance of the new data," he said. "*That's* why I gave the order to kill them." His next gesture—right hand turned aside, waist high, fingers curled against the thumb—was the Gha expression of apology.

"That's also why I didn't wait until we had an opportunity to discuss the matter, as a Poct'on cartouche would normally do. I had to stop the Pilot from transmitting anything to Guild Headquarters. I'm hoping the Federation itself doesn't understand the significance of the meteorological report. The Guilds may still not know of it at all."

The other three Gha in the room were silent. Their stiff postures, to anyone but Gha, would have made them seem like statues. But Fludenoc understood their confusion and puzzlement.

To his surprise, the Pilot suddenly spoke. Fludenoc had almost forgotten her presence.

"Are you talking about the radio signals?" she asked.

Fludenoc swiveled to face her. The Pilot froze with instinctive fear, but her color remained close to purple. "I'm s-sorry," she stammered, in Gha. "I didn't mean—"

"I did not realize you spoke our language," said Fludenoc.

Then, sadly (though only a Gha would have sensed it in his tone):

"I am not angry at you for interrupting me, Pilot.

Among ourselves, we consider conversation a fine art. Interruption is part of its pleasure."

The Pilot's shade developed a pinkish undertone. "I know. I have listened to you, sometimes, when you versified each other in your chamber. I thought the poetry was quite good. Although I'm sure I missed most of the nuances."

Now, all four Gha were staring at the Pilot. And it took no Gha subtlety to realize that they were all absolutely astonished.

"You are not the only people in the galaxy," the Pilot said softly, "who mourn for what might have been."

She shifted her footskirt, turning away from Fludenoc to face the other Gha. "I do not think you grasp the importance of those radio signals. The reason the Voivode was so indignant was because he understood that, if the data is accurate, it means that the Romans—or, at least, the human species which produced them—are no longer barbarians. They have reached industrial chain reaction."

"What in Creation are *radio*?" demanded Oltomar. "And why is it important?"

The Pilot hesitated. Again, Fludenoc barked humor.

"He is not actually an ignoramus, Pilot, appearances to the contrary. It's just that, like most Gha, his education was oriented toward practical matters. His knowledge of history is sadly deficient."

Beyond a mildly irritated inhalation, Oltomar did not argue the point. Fludenoc made a gesturing motion to the Pilot. *Continue.*

"Radio is a part of the electromagnetic spectrum," she explained. "Very far toward the low frequency end. Modern civilization doesn't have any real use for those bands. But in the early stages of industrial chain reaction, it is always the first avenue by which rising civilizations conquer electromagnetism. For a short period of time, such planets project radio waves into the galaxy. The waves are very weak, of course, and undirected, so they are quickly lost in the galaxy's background noise. If the Federation Meteorological Survey hadn't been keeping that portion of the galaxy under close observation because of the Transit storm, those signals would never have been noticed."

Uddumac interrupted. "You are saying that humans have achieved *civilization*?"

"Yes. There can be no natural explanation for such radio signals. And only a civilized species can project radio signals powerful enough to be picked up at interstellar distances."

"What level of civilization?" demanded Oltomar. "Class One or Two? Or even—Doge?"

"There's no way to tell without—"

"The distinction is critical!" Oltomar's statement was almost a shout. "*It's absolutely critical.*"

The Pilot froze. Fludenoc interposed himself between her and Oltomar. She was actually in no physical danger at all, but her species tended to panic quickly. His protective presence would enable her to relax.

"Stop bullying her, Oltomar," he said quietly. "She has no way of answering your question—without us making the journey to that planet. Which is precisely what I propose to do."

He gestured to the dead bodies of the Voivode and the Investigator. "*Our* journey, not theirs."

Oltomar subsided, but Uddumac was still unsatisfied. "This could easily be a complete waste of effort,

Fludenoc. We need to find a suitable species which can claim Doge status. *Legally*. If the humans are already Class One—*advanced* Class One—we might be able to nudge them over the edge. As long as we could keep hidden the fact that their Transit capability was stolen from already established Doge technology. But if they're only Class Two, there's no way—"

He broke off, shivering his shoulders in that Gha gesture which corresponded to a human headshake.

Fludenoc hesitated before responding. Uddumac's reservations, after all, were quite reasonable. In order for a species to claim Doge status under Federation law, they had to demonstrate a capacity for interstellar travel and commerce. In technological terms, Transit; in socio-political terms, a mercantile orientation. An *independent* capacity, developed by their own efforts, not simply a capacity acquired from already existing Doges.

Civilized species which lacked that capacity were considered Class One if they had managed to depart the confines of their own planet before being discovered by galactic civilization. Class Two, if they were a society still bound to their world of origin.

As Uddumac had rightly said, it *might* be possible to give humans a false Doge identity by surreptitiously handing them Transit technology. Transit technology, by its nature, was fairly invariant. All the existing Doge Species used essentially the same method. But the subterfuge would only work if humans had already achieved a very high level of Class One civilization. Nobody would believe that human Transit was self-developed if the species was still pulling wagons with draft animals.

"The decision has already been made," Fludenoc stated, firmly but not belligerently. Again, he pointed to the Doge corpses. "We have no choice now, brothers. Let us make Transit to the human planet. The answer can only be found there."

There was no further opposition. Fludenoc swiveled to the Pilot.

"Take us there," he commanded.

The Pilot left the chamber immediately. Fludenoc turned to examine the Medic.

"Do not not mind me," the Medic immediately trilled. "I am just just a bystander."

All the Gha, now, barked their humor.

"But are you still *interested*?" asked Oltomar.

"Oh, yes yes! Very interested interested!"

IV

Not so many days later, after Transit was made, the Medic was still interested. Fascinated, in fact.

"What what in the name of Creation is *that that that*?"

There was no answer. Everyone in the control chamber was staring at the viewscreen.

Staring at *that*.

The Pilot finally broke the silence. "I think it's a boat," she whispered.

"What is a—a *boat*?" asked Oltomar. He, also, spoke in a whisper.

"I think she's right," muttered Fludenoc. "I saw a hologram of a boat, once. It looked quite a bit like—that. Except *that's* a lot bigger. A whole lot bigger."

"I say it again!" hissed Oltomar. "What in Creation is a *boat*?"

"It's a vessel that floats on water," replied Fludenoc.

"Very large bodies of water, such as don't exist on our planet."

Oltomar stared at the screen. "*Water?*" he demanded. "*What* water? We're still in the outer fringes of this solar system!"

A hum from the communication console announced an incoming message.

"I think we're about to find out," said the Pilot. She shuffled toward the console. "Let's hope they speak some language the computer can translate."

Fludenoc was suddenly filled with confidence. *That* was the strangest-looking spacecraft he had ever seen. But, then again, he had thought the Romans were the strangest-looking soldiers he had ever seen, too.

"The computer will be able to translate," he predicted. "Latin has been programmed into it for over two thousand years."

He was not wrong. The Latin phrases which the computer received were spoken in a very odd accent, it was true. Quite unlike the original input. But the phrases were simple enough:

"*Unknown spacecraft: you are ordered to hold position. Any movement toward the inner planets will be construed as a hostile act.*"

"There are more of those—*boats*—coming," said Uddumac. "Lots of them. Very *big* boats."

"*We repeat—hold your position. We are sending a boarding party. Any resistance will be construed as a hostile act.*"

Fludenoc instructed the Pilot: "Send a message indicating that the boarding party will be allowed ingress without obstruction. And tell them we seek a parley."

"These are Romans?" queried Oltomar. His tone wavered pure confusion.

"Pilot," said Fludenoc. "Ask them to identify themselves as well."

The reply came quickly:

This is Craig Trumbull speaking. I am the Commodore of this fleet and the Captain commanding this vessel. The CSS Scipio Africanus."

V

"I feel like an idiot," muttered Commodore Trumbull. His eyes, fixed on the huge viewscreen, shifted back and forth from the sleek, gleaming Guild vessel to the nearest of the newly arrived ships of his flotilla.

The Confederation Space Ship *Quinctius Flaminius*, that was. As she was now called.

Standing next to him, his executive officer grinned. "You mean you feel like the guy who shows up at a formal ball wearing a clown suit? Thought he'd been invited to a costume party?"

Trumbull grunted. Again, he stared at the CSS *Quinctius Flaminius*. As she was now called.

The USS *Missouri*, in her former life.

"I can't believe I'm trying to intimidate a Guild vessel with these *antiques*."

Commander Stephen Tambo shrugged. "So what if it's a World War Two craft dragged out of mothballs?" He pointed at the ancient battleship on the viewscreen. "Those aren't sixteen-inch guns anymore, Commodore. They're lasers. Eight times as powerful as any the Guild uses, according to the transport's computer. And the *Quinctius'* force-screens carry the same magnitude of superiority."

"I know that!" snapped the commodore. "I still feel like an idiot."

The executive officer, eyeing his superior with a sideways glance, decided against any further attempt at humor. The North American seemed bound and determined to wallow in self-pity.

Commander Tambo shared none of that mortification. True, the Confederation's newly created naval force was—from the standpoint of appearance—the most absurd-looking fleet imaginable. It had only been a few years, after all, since the arrival of the Romans had alerted humanity to the fact that it was a very big and very dangerous galaxy. Proper military spacecraft were only just starting to be constructed. In the meantime, the Earth had needed protection. *Now.*

So—

The Romans had brought the technology. Their captured troop transport's computer had carried full theoretical and design criteria in its data banks. The quickest and simplest way to create an instant fleet had been to refit the Earth's old warships.

By galactic standards, the resulting spacecraft were grotesque in every way. Nor was that simply a matter of appearance, They were not airtight, for instance. Because of the force-screens, of course, they did not need to be. But no proper galactic vessel would have taken the chance of relying on force-screens to maintain atmospheric integrity.

But Tambo did not mind in the least. As a South African, he was accustomed to the whimsies of history.

And besides, there were advantages.

He turned away from the viewscreen and gazed through the window of the bridge. A real window, that was—just plain, ordinary glass—looking down onto the vast, flat expanse where Tambo enjoyed his daily jogging. No galactic spaceship ever built—ever conceived—would have provided him with that opportunity.

The huge flight deck of the CSS *Scipio Africanus*. Formerly, the USS *Enterprise*.

"The boarding party's leaving," he announced.

Commodore Trumbull turned away from the viewscreen and joined him at the window. The two men watched as the boarding craft lifted off from the flight deck—no hurtling steam catapults here; just the easy grace of galactic drives—and surged toward the forcescreen. There was a momentary occultation of the starfield as the boarding craft's screen melded with that of the *Africanus*. A moment later, the boarding craft was lost to sight.

"Jesus H. Christ," muttered the commodore. "A *complete* idiot."

Tambo could not resist. He did a quick little dance step and sang, to the tune from *Fiddler on the Roof*: "Tradition!"

Trumbull scowled and glared at the viewscreen. The boarding craft was already halfway to the Guild vessel.

The CSS *Livy*, as she was now called. Naming her after a historian, thought the commodore darkly, was appropriate. He had protested bitterly. *Bitterly*. But the Naval Commissioning Board had been seized by the rampant historical romanticism which seemed to have engulfed the entire human race since the return of the Roman exiles.

The CSS *Livy*. Formerly, the prize exhibit at the

Berlin Museum of Ancient Technology. A full-size reproduction—faithful in every detail—of one of the Roman Empire's quinqueremes.

The commodore could restrain himself no longer. *"They could at least stop rowing the damned oars!"*

VI

Gaius Vibulenus shook his head firmly, and turned to Trumbull.

"No, Commodore," he said in his heavily accented English. "I do not recognize them. Not specifically. They *are* the same species as the—we just called them the 'frogs.' Or the 'toads.'"

The Roman looked back at the viewscreen. His eyes were now focused on the corpse of the Voivode. A Confederation Marine lieutenant was holding the creature's head up.

"And I cannot say that I recognize him, either. He is the same type as the Guild Commander who murdered Helvius and the others, yes. But whether he is the same individual—"

Gaius shrugged. "You must understand, Commodore, that we saw many intelligent species while we served the trading guild. But never very many different individuals of any one species. So they all looked much the same to us. Bizarre."

From behind them, Quartilla spoke. "I recognize *him*. The dead one, I mean."

Everyone on the bridge turned toward her.

"You're sure?" asked the Commodore.

Quartilla nodded. "Oh, yes. His species call themselves *Rassiqua*. Their body shapes and—call them 'faces'—are difficult for others to distinguish between, but each of them has a quite distinct pattern of skin mottling." She pointed at the corpse being held up before the viewscreen. "This one has a—"

She leaned over to the historian standing next to her, gesturing with her agile plump hands. "What do you call this, Robert—a thing with six sides?"

Robert Ainsley frowned for a moment, tugging at his gray-streaked professorial beard, before he understood her question.

"Hexagon."

"*Hex-a-gon*," she murmured, memorizing the word. The executive officer, watching, was impressed by the—*woman's?*—obvious facility and experienced ease at learning languages. She and Vibulenus had arrived at the *Scipio Africanus* aboard a special courier vessel less than an hour before. But even in that short time, Tambo had been struck by the difference between Quartilla's fluent, almost unaccented English and the stiff speech of her Roman companion.

"If you turn him around," said Quartilla, "you'll see a hexagon pattern on his left rear flank. Three hexagons, if I remember correctly. All of them shaded a sort of blue-green."

Commodore Trumbull began to give the order, but the Marine lieutenant was already moving the body. A moment later, grunting slightly, he held the Voivode's left rear flank up to the screen.

Three small hexagons. Shaded a sort of blue-green.

Gaius Vibulenus hissed. "That stinking *bastard*."

Tambo stared down at the Roman. The former tribune's fists were clenched. The steel-hard muscles in his forearms stood out like cables. For all the man's

short size—and Vibulenus was tall, for a Roman—
Tambo was glad that rage wasn't directed at him.

By current physical standards, the Romans were not
much bigger than boys. The appearance was deceiving.
Small they might be, and slightly built, compared to
modern men, but the returned exiles' ancient customs
were unbelievably ferocious, by those same modern
standards. Tambo knew of at least one college fraternity, full of bravado, which had been hospitalized in
its entirety after making the mistake of challenging
four Roman veterans to a barroom brawl.

"But you don't recognize the frogs?" asked Trumbull. "The—what do they call themselves? The Gha?"

Quartilla shook her head. "No, Commodore. The
Gha never demanded service from us Ossa pleasure
creatures. We had almost no contact with them."

Her voice was icy with old bitterness. Tambo watched
Vibulenus give her hand a little squeeze.

The commodore frowned deeply. Quartilla took a
breath and added:

"I can verify everything else the Gha have said,
however. I think they must be telling the truth here
also. How else could they have known that the Voivode
had once been the Roman commander? For that matter, how else could they have learned Latin?"

"He knew Helvius's name, too," muttered Vibulenus.
The Roman was frowning very deeply himself, now.
Almost scowling, in fact.

Seeing the expression on his face, the commodore
stated: "Yet you still seem very suspicious, Tribune."

Vibulenus gave a little start of surprise. "Suspicious?"
His face cleared. "You do not understand, Commodore.
I was just thinking— It is hard to explain."

The Roman gestured toward the Gha on the viewscreen. They were standing toward the rear of the Guild vessel's command chamber, closely guarded by armed Marines. "*Guilty*, perhaps. These—Gha—were never anything to us but our masters' goons. It never occurred to me that they might have names. It certainly never occurred to me that they might know *our* names."

The Gha commander in the viewscreen suddenly spoke. His Latin was crude, but quite understandable.

"You Gaius Vibulenus. During period was I assigned guard Cacique, while was your Guildmaster, you tribune command Tenth Cohort."

Gaius winced. "Your name is Fludenoc, am I right?" Quickly, with the easy familiarity of a man accustomed to elaborate ancient nomenclature, he added: "Fludenoc hu'tut-Na Nomo'te?"

The Gha bent forward stiffly.

"I believe him," said Gaius abruptly. The tone of his voice carried the absolutism of a hardened, experienced commanding officer. The Roman returned the bow, and spoke again in Latin.

"I thank you, Fludenoc hu'tut-Na Nomo'te, and your comrades, for finally giving justice to Helvius. And Grumio and Augens."

When he straightened, his face was rigid. "I also declare, on behalf of myself and all Romans, that any quarrel between us and Gha is a thing of the past."

Tambo translated the exchange for the commodore. Like most North Americans, with the creaky linguistic skills of a people whose native language was the world's *lingua franca*, Trumbull had not picked up more than a few phrases of the Latin tongue which had been enjoying such an incredible renaissance the past few years.

The commodore scratched under his jaw. "All right," he muttered. "I'm satisfied these people are who they say they are. But what about their other claims? And their weird proposal?"

Before anyone could respond, the communication console hummed vigorously. The com officer, Lieutenant Olga Sanchez, took the call.

"You'd better look at this yourself, Commodore," she said, standing aside.

Trumbull marched over to the screen and quickly read the message. "Wonderful," he muttered. "Just perfect." He turned back, facing the small crowd on the bridge.

"Well, folks, after two hundred years—and God only knows how much money poured down that sinkhole—the SETI maniacs have finally picked up a signal from intelligent extra-solarians. Wasn't hard, actually. The radio signals are being beamed directly at the Earth from a source which just crossed Neptune's orbit."

He took a breath and squared his stocky shoulders.

"Their findings have been confirmed by Operation Spaceguard, using the radar net set up to watch for asteroids. And Naval Intelligence has spotted them also, with modern equipment. The source is a fleet of spacecraft."

He stared at the Gha in the viewscreen. "It seems they were wrong. About this, at least. Somebody else also realized the significance of the radio signals."

"The Guilds!" exclaimed Quartilla.

Trumbull nodded. "One of them, anyway. They're

identifying themselves—in Latin—as the Ty'uct Trading Guild."

Quartilla pointed to the body of the Voivode, still visible in the viewscreen. "That's his guild. The one which bought and used the Romans."

"What do they want?" snarled Vibulenus. His fists were clenched again.

"What do you think?" snorted the commodore. "They say that by right of first contact they are claiming exclusive trading privileges with this solar system. A Federation naval vessel is accompanying them to ensure the correct protocols. Whatever that means."

Tambo translated this recent exchange for the benefit of the Gha. As soon as he finished, the Gha commander spoke.

"What it mean," stated Fludenoc, "is they have right hammer in to the submission anybody objects. But must restrict theyselfs this system existing technology. Federation vessel is watchdog make sure they follow rules."

Again, Tambo translated. The commodore's gloom vanished.

"Is that so?" he demanded. "Is that so, indeed?"

He and his executive officer exchanged grins. The North American often exasperated Tambo with his quirks and foibles. But the South African was glad, now, that he was in command. There was a long, long tradition behind that wicked grin on Trumbull's face.

Trumbull turned back to Lieutenant Sanchez. "Tell Naval Command that I'm deploying to meet this threat. If they have any new instructions, tell them they'd better get 'em off quickly. Otherwise, I will follow my own best judgment."

She bent over the console. Trumbull glanced up at the viewscreen. "Bring that ship aboard the *Africanus*," he commanded the Marine lieutenant. "I want to get it below decks before the Guild vessels arrive."

Seeing Tambo's raised eyebrow, he asked:

"Any suggestions? Criticisms?"

Tambo shook his head. "I agree with you."

The South African waved at the viewscreen, now blank. "We can decide later what we think about the Gha proposal. It sounds crazy to me, frankly. But who knows, in this strange new universe? In the meantime, by keeping them hidden we leave all our options open."

The sight of the viewscreen flickering back into life drew his eyes that way. Within seconds, a starfield filled the screen. Against that glorious background, little lights could be seen, moving slowly across the stars. The ships were far too small to be seen at that distance, by any optical means. The lights were computer simulations based on information derived from a variation of Transit technology which was quite analogous to radar.

There were fourteen of those lights, Tambo saw. One of them—presumably the Federation observer—was hanging well back from the others. The thirteen ships of the Guild force itself were arrayed in a dodecahedron, with a single ship located at the very center.

"That's a fancy-looking formation," mused Trumbull. "But I don't see where it's worth much. Except for parades."

From the corner of the bridge, where he stood next to Quartilla, Robert Ainsley spoke up.

"Excuse me, Commodore."

Trumbull cocked his head around.

The historian pointed at the screen. "Judging from what I've learned since I was assigned to help the Romans orient themselves after their return—and everything we've just heard today fits in perfectly—I don't—" He hesitated, fumbling for words.

"Go on," said the commodore.

"Well, this isn't my field, really. Not in practice, at least. But—I don't think these Guilds have fought a real battle in—in—Jesus, who knows? Millennia. *Many* millennia."

Trumbull smiled thinly and looked back at the formation marching across the starfield.

"Funny you should say that," he murmured. "I was just thinking the same thing."

Tambo cleared his throat. "According to the computer, sir, there are three classes of warships in that fleet. Eight small ones—about the size of the vessel the Gha seized—four mediums, and the big one in the center."

He issued a modest little cough. "Naval procedure, as you know, recommends that we give enemy vessels a nomenclature. Since we don't know what the Guild calls their own ships, we'll have to come up with our own names."

Trumbull's smile widened. "Do you have any suggestions?"

"Oh, yes," replied Tambo, solemn-faced. "I believe we should name them as follows: small ones, *Bismarcks*; the mediums, *Yamatos*; and the big one—"

He could not restrain his grin.

"—is a *Titanic*."

VII

The bridge was crowded, now, with the addition of
the aliens. The Pilot and the Medic huddled against
a wall, out of the way. But the four Gha, by virtue of
their size alone, seemed to fill half the room.

"Do any of you know the rules of engagement?"
Trumbull asked the Gha. Tambo translated his question into Latin.

The Gha were stiff as statues.

"We understand do not," said Fludenoc. "What
are—engagement regulations?"

Before Tambo could explain, the Gha commander
turned to the Pilot and motioned. Fearfully, creeping
on her footskirt, she shuffled forward. Tambo waited
while Fludenoc spoke some rapid phrases in a language
he didn't recognize.

"That's Galactic," whispered Quartilla. "It's an artificial language, with several dialects designed for the
vocal apparatus of different Doge Species. This one
is called Galactic Three."

She began to add something else, but fell silent
when Fludenoc turned back to the humans.

"Now I understand," said the Gha. "Pilot say
she not certain. Doges not fought each other many
thousands—*many* thousands—years. But she think
there no rules between Guild fight Guild. She—what
is word?—strongly says you must not attack Federation vessel."

"Will it attack us?" asked Tambo.

The Gha did not bother to check with the pilot
before answering. "No. Federation ship will watch only."

He waved a huge, clawed hand at the viewscreen. "This is Guild business. Federation not interfere."

After Tambo explained to his superior, Trumbull nodded. "It's a straight-up fight, then." To the com officer: "How good's your Latin?"

She smiled. "Well, sir—it's just about perfect."

Trumbull grimaced. "Christ," he muttered. "I'm going to have to learn that damned archaic tongue, after all."

Then, with an irritated shrug: "Contact that fleet and warn them off."

"Yes sir. How should I identify us?"

Trumbull hesitated, before turning to the historian. "Give me some good old Roman term," he ordered. "Something vague, mind you—I don't—"

Ainsley understood immediately. Smiling, he replied: "Just use *SPQR*."

Tambo chuckled. Trumbull said to the com officer: "Use it. Tell them we're the—the *SPQR Guild*—and *we* have already established prior rights to all trade and commerce with this system." Growling: "Way, *way* prior rights."

The com officer followed his orders. Three minutes later, a burst of Latin phrases appeared on the com screen.

Lieutenant Sanchez clucked disapprovingly. "Their Latin's really pretty bad. That's a ridiculous declension of the verb 'to copulate,' for one thing. And—"

"Just give me the message!" bellowed the commodore.

The com officer straightened. "The gist of it, sir, is that our claim is preposterous and we are ordered to surrender."

Trumbull grunted. "I was hoping they'd say that. I've never even met these people, and already I hate their guts." He leaned toward his executive officer. "Any recommendations?"

"Yes, sir. I'd send the *Quinctius*. With an escort of SSBNs."

Trumbull nodded. "I was thinking the same way. We may as well find out now if our lasers are as good as they're cracked up to be. And I'll be interested to see how the missiles work. The galactic computer claims kinetic weapons are obsolete, but I think it's full of crap."

Trumbull began giving the necessary orders to his operations staff. Tambo, seeing the Gha commander's stiffness out of the corner of his eye, turned to face him.

He wasn't sure—Gha were as hard to read as the Romans said they were—but he thought Fludenoc was worried.

"Are you concerned?" he asked.

The Gha exhaled explosively. "Yes! You must careful be. These very powerful Guildmaster craft."

Tambo shook his head. "I think you are wrong, Fludenoc hu'tut-Na Nomo'te. I think these are simply arrogant bullies, who haven't been in a real fight for so long they've forgotten what it's like."

He did not add the thought which came to him. It would have meant nothing to the Gha. But he smiled, thinking of a college fraternity which had once tried to bully four small Romans in a bar.

Don't fuck with real veterans.

"We've been doing this a long time, Fludenoc," he murmured. "All those centuries—millennia—while we were out of contact with the galaxy, we've been fighting each other. While these Doges—God, what a perfect name!—got fat like hogs."

VIII

The battle lasted two minutes.

Seeing the huge ancient battleship sweeping toward them, with its accompanying escort of three resurrected Trident missile submarines, the Guild dodecahedron opened up like a flower. Ten laser beams centered on the *Quinctius* itself, including a powerful laser from the "Titanic" at the center of the Doge fleet. The three remaining Guild vessels each fired a laser at the escorts—the *Pydna*, the *Magnesia*, and the *Chaeronea*.

Powered by their gigantic engines, the shields of the human vessels shrugged off the lasers. Those shields, like the engines, were based on galactic technology. But the Doge Species, with the inveterate habit of merchants, had designed their equipment with a cheeseparing attitude. The human adaptations—robust; even exuberant— were based on millennia of combat experience.

The *Pydna*-class escorts responded first. The hatches on their upper decks opened. Dozens of missiles popped out—driven, here, by old technology—and then immediately went into a highly modified version of Transit drive. To the watching eye, they simply disappeared.

"Yes!" cried Trumbull, clenching his fist triumphantly. Not three seconds later, the Guild fleet was staggered by the impact of those missiles. As the commodore had suspected, the Doge Species' long neglect of missile warfare was costing them heavily. Human electronic countermeasure technology was vastly superior to anything the Guild vessels possessed in the way of tracking equipment. Most of the incoming missiles were destroyed by laser fire, but many of them penetrated to the shield walls.

Even galactic shields were hard-pressed against fifteen-megaton nuclear charges. Four of those shields collapsed completely, leaving nothing but plasma to mark where spacecraft had formerly been. The others survived. But, in the case of three of them, the stress on their engines had been great enough to cause the engines themselves to collapse. Their shields and drives failed, leaving the three ships to drift helplessly.

Now the *Quinctius* went into action. Again, there was an exotic combination of old and new technology. The three great turrets of the ancient battleship swiveled, just as if it were still sailing the Pacific. But the guidance mechanisms were state-of-the-art Doge technology. And the incredible laser beams which pulsed out of each turret's three retrofitted barrels were something new to the galaxy. Human engineers and physicists, studying the data in the Roman-captured Guild vessel, had decided not to copy the Doge lasers. Instead, they combined some of that dazzling new technology with a revivified daydream from humanity's bloody past.

Only a ship as enormous as the old *Missouri* could use these lasers. It took an immense hull capacity to hold the magnetic fusion bottles. In each of those three bottles—one for each turret—five-megaton thermonuclear devices were ignited. The bottles trapped the energy, contained it, channeled it.

Nine X-ray lasers fired. Three Guild ships flickered briefly, their shields coruscating. Then—vaporized.

Thirty seconds elapsed, as the fusion bottles recharged. The Guild ships which were still under power were now veering off sharply. Again, the turrets tracked. Again, ignition. Again, three Doge vessels vaporized.

More seconds elapsed, while the *Quinctius'* fusion bottles recharged.

The communication console on the bridge of the *Scipio Africanus* began humming. "Sir," reported Lieutenant Sanchez, "it's the Guild flagship. They're asking to negotiate."

"Screw 'em," snarled the commodore. "They're nothing but pirates and slavers, as far as I'm concerned."

Tambo grinned. "You want me to see if I can dig up a black flag somewhere?"

Trumbull snorted. "Why not? We're resurrecting everything else."

The operations officer spoke: "The *Quinctius* reports fusion bottles fully recharged, sir."

Trumbull glared at the surviving Guild ships. "*No quarter,*" he growled. "Fire."

IX

The World Confederation's Chamber of Deputies reminded Robert Ainsley of nothing so much as a circus. He even glanced at the ceiling, expecting to see a trapeze artist swinging through the air.

"Is this way always?" Fludenoc asked quietly. The Gha, towering next to the historian, was staring down from the vantage point of the spectators' gallery. His bulging eyes were drawn to a knot of Venezuelan delegates shaking their angry fists in the face of a representative from the Great Realm of the Chinese People.

The Chinese delegate was imperturbable. As he could well afford to be, representing the world's largest single nationality.

Largest by far, thought Ainsley sardonically, *even if you limit the count to the actual residents of China*.

He watched the bellicose Venezuelans stalk off angrily. Most likely, the historian guessed, they were furious with the Chinese for interfering in what they considered internal Venezuelan affairs. That was the usual bone of contention between most countries and the Great Realm. The Chinese claimed a special relationship—almost semi-sovereignity—with everyone in the world of Chinese descent, official citizenship be damned. Given the global nature of the Han diaspora, that kept the Chinese sticking their thumbs into everybody's eye.

The Gha repeated his question. Ainsley sighed.

"No, Fludenoc. This is worse than usual. A bit."

The historian gestured toward the crowded chamber below. "Mind you, the Chamber of Deputies is notorious for being raucous. At the best of times."

Somehow—he was not quite sure how it had happened—Ainsley had become the unofficial liaison between humanity and the Gha. He suspected that his long and successful work reintegrating the Romans into their human kinfolk had given him, in the eyes of the world at large, the reputation of being a wizard diplomat with weird people from the sky. Which, he thought wryly, was the last thing a man who had spent a lifetime engrossed in the history of classical society had ever expected to become.

On the other hand— Ainsley was not a man given to complaining over his fate. And, fortunately, he *did* have a good sense of humor. He eyed the huge figure standing next to him. From his weeks of close contact with the Gha, Ainsley was now able to interpret—to some degree, at least—the body language of the stiff giants.

"You are concerned," he stated.

Fludenoc exhaled sharply, indicating his assent. "I think—thought—*had thought*"—the Gha struggled for the correct Latin tense—"that you would be more—" His thought drifted off in a vague gesture.

"United?" asked Ainsley, cocking an eyebrow. "Coherent? Rational? Organized?"

Again, the Gha exhaled assent. "Yes. All those."

Ainsley chuckled. "More *Guild*-like, in other words."

The Gha giant swiveled, staring down at the old historian next to him. Suddenly, he barked humor.

Ainsley waved at the madding crowd below. "This is what a real world looks like, Fludenoc. A world which, because of its lucky isolation, was able to grow and mature without the interference of the Guilds and the Federation. It's messy, I admit. But I wouldn't trade it for anything else. Not in a million years."

He stared down at the chaos. The Venezuelans were now squabbling with representatives from the Caribbean League. The Caribs, quite unlike the Chinese delegate, were far from imperturbable. One of them shook his dreadlocks fiercely. Another blew ganja-smoke into the Venezuelans' faces. A third luxuriated in the marvelously inventive *patois* of the islanders, serene in his confidence that the frustrated Venezuelans could neither follow his words nor begin to comprehend the insults couched therein.

"Never fear, Fludenoc hu'tut-Na Nomo'te," he murmured. "Never fear. This planet is as fresh and alive as a basket full of puppies. *Wolf* puppies. The Guilds'll never know what hit 'em."

He turned away from the rail. "Let's go get some ice cream. The important business is going to take place later anyway, in the closed session of the Special Joint Committee."

The Gha followed him readily enough. Eagerly, in fact.

"I want cherry vanilla," announced Fludenoc.

"You *always* want cherry vanilla," grumbled Ainsley.

The Gha's exhalation was extremely emphatic. "Of course. Best thing your insane species produces. Except Romans."

X

After the first hour of the Special Joint Committee's session, Ainsley could sense Fludenoc finally begin to relax. The Gha even managed to lean back into the huge chair which had been specially provided for him toward the back of the chamber.

"Feeling better?" he whispered.

The Gha exhaled vigorously. "*Yes*. This is much more—" He groped for words.

"United?" asked Ainsley, cocking a whimsical eyebrow. "Coherent? Rational? Organized?"

"Yes. All those."

Ainsley turned in his seat, facing forward. Behind the long table which fronted the chamber sat the fifteen most powerful legislators of the human race. The Special Joint Committee had been formed with no regard for hallowed seniority or any of the other arcane rituals which the Confederation's governing body seemed to have adopted, over the past century, from every quirk of every single legislative body ever created by the inventive human mind.

This committee was dealing with the fate of humanity—and a number of other species, for that matter. Those men and women with real power and influence had made sure they were sitting at that table. Hallowed rituals be damned.

Not that all rituals and ceremony have been discarded, thought Ainsley, smiling wryly.

He was particularly amused by the veil worn by the Muslim Federation's representative—who had spent thirty years ramming the world's stiffest sexual discrimination laws down her countrymen's throats; and the splendiferous traditional ostrich-plume head-dress worn by the South African representative—who was seven-eighths Boer in his actual descent, and looked every inch the blond-haired part; and the conservative grey suit worn by the representative from North America's United States and Provinces, suitable for the soberest Church-going occasions—who was a vociferous atheist and the author of four scholarly books on the historical iniquities of mixing Church and State.

The Chairperson of the Special Joint Committee rose to announce the next speaker, and Ainsley's smile turned into a veritable grin.

And here she is, my favorite. Speaking of preposterous rituals and ceremonies.

The representative from the Great Realm of the Chinese People, Chairperson of the Special Joint Committee—all four feet, nine inches of her—clasped her hands demurely and bobbed her head in modest recognition of her fellow legislators.

Everybody's favorite humble little woman.

"If the representative from the European Union will finally shut his trap," she said, in a voice like steel—

Mai the Merciless.

"—maybe we can get down to the serious business."

Silence fell instantly over the chamber.

"We call her the Dragon Lady," whispered Ainsley.

"She good," hissed Fludenoc approvingly. "What is 'dragon'?"

"Watch," replied the historian.

Two hours later, Fludenoc was almost at ease. Watching Mai the Merciless hack her bloody way through every puffed-up dignitary who had managed to force himself or herself onto the Committee's agenda had produced that effect.

"She *very* good," the Gha whispered. "Could eat one of those stupid carnivores we ride in a single meal."

"—and what other asinine proposition does the august Secretary wish us to consider?" the Chairperson was demanding.

The Secretary from the International Trade Commission hunched his shoulders. "I must protest your use of ridicule, Madame Chairperson," he whined. "We in the Trade Commission do not feel that our concerns are either picayune or asinine! The project which is being proposed, even if it is successful—which, by the way, we believe to be *very* unlikely—will inevitably have the result, among others, of our planet being subjected to a wave of immigration by—by—"

The Chairperson finished his sentence. The tone of her voice was icy: "By *coolies.*"

The Trade Commission's Secretary hunched lower. "I would not choose that particular—"

"That is *precisely* the term you would choose," snapped Mai the Merciless, "if you had the balls."

Ainsley had to fight not to laugh, watching the wincing faces of several of the legislators. From the ripple in her veil, he thought the Muslim Federation's representative was undergoing the same struggle.

"What are 'balls'?" asked Fludenoc.

"Later," he whispered. "It is a term which is considered very politically incorrect."

"What is 'politically incorrect'?"

"Something which people who don't have to deal with real oppression worry about," replied the historian. Ainsley spent the next few minutes gleefully watching the world's most powerful woman finish her political castration of the world's most influential regulator of trade.

After the Secretary slunk away from the witness table, the Chairperson rose to introduce the next speaker.

"Before I do so, however, I wish to make an announcement." She held up several sheets of paper. "The Central Committee of the Great Realm of the Chinese People adopted a resolution this morning. The text was just transmitted to me, along with the request that I read the resolution into the records of this Committee's session."

A small groan went up. The Chairperson smiled,

ever so slightly, and dropped the sheets onto the podium.

"However, I will not do so, inasmuch as the resolution is very long and repetitive. There is one single human characteristic, if no other, which recognizes neither border, breed, nor birth. That is the long-windedness of legislators."

The chamber was swept by a laugh. But the laughter was brief. The Chairperson's smile vanished soon enough, replaced by a steely glare.

"But I will report the gist of the resolution. *The Chinese people of the world have made their decision.* The so-called galactic civilization of the Guilds and the Federation is nothing but a consortium of imperialist bandits and thieves. All other species, beyond those favored as so-called 'Doges,' are relegated to the status of *coolies.*"

Her voice was low, hissing: "It is not to be tolerated. It *will* not be tolerated. The Great Realm strongly urges the World Confederation to adopt whole-heartedly the proposal put forward by our Gha fellow-toilers. Failing that, the Great Realm will do it alone."

Ainsley sucked in his breath. "Well," he muttered, "there's an old-fashioned ultimatum for you."

"What does this mean?" asked Fludenoc.

Ainsley rose from his seat. "What it means, my fine froggy friend, is that you and I don't have to spend the rest of the afternoon watching the proceedings. It's what they call a done deal."

As they walked quietly out of the chamber, Ainsley heard the Chairperson saying:

"—to Commodore Craig Trumbull, for his unflinching courage in the face of barbaric tyranny, the Great

Realm awards the Star of China. To all of the men and women of his flotilla who are not Chinese, in addition to he himself, honorary citizenship in the Great Realm. To the crew of the heroic *Quinctius Flaminius*, which obliterated the running dogs of the brutal Doge—"

When the door closed behind them, Fludenoc asked: "What is a 'done deal'?"

"It's what happens when a bunch of arrogant, stupid galactics not only poke a stick at the martial pride of North Americans, but also manage to stir up the bitterest memories of the human race's biggest nation."

He walked down the steps of the Confederation Parliament with a very light stride, for a man his age. Almost gaily. "I'll explain it more fully later. Right now, I'm hungry."

"Ice cream?" asked Fludenoc eagerly.

"Not a chance," came the historian's reply. "Today, we're having Chinese food."

XI

And now, thought Ainsley, *the real work begins. Convincing the Romans.*

He leaned back on his couch, patting his belly. As always, Gaius Vibulenus had put on a real feast. Whatever else had changed in the boy who left his father's estate in Capua over two thousand years ago, his sense of equestrian *dignitas* remained. A feast was a feast, by the gods, and no shirking the duty.

Quartilla appeared by his side, a platter in her hand.

"God, no," moaned Ainsley. "I can't move as it is."

He patted the couch next to him. "Sit, sweet lady.

Talk to me. I've seen hardly anything of you these past few weeks."

Quartilla, smiling, put down the platter and took a seat on the couch.

"Did Gaius tell you that we're going to have children?"

Ainsley's eyes widened. "It's definite, then? The Genetic Institute thinks they can do it?"

Quartilla's little laugh had more than a trace of sarcasm in it. "Oh, Robert! They've known for months that they *could* do it. The silly farts have been fretting over the *ethics* of the idea."

Ainsley stroked his beard, studying her. Quartilla seemed so completely human—not only in her appearance but in her behavior—that he tended to forget she belonged to a species that was, technically speaking, more remote from humanity than anything alive on Earth. More remote than crabs, or trees—even bacteria, for that matter.

And even more remote, he often thought, in some of her Ossa *attitudes*.

The Ossa—whether from their innate psychology or simply their internalized acceptance of millennia of physical and genetic manipulation by their Doge masters—had absolutely no attachment to their own natural phenotype. They truly didn't seem to *care* what they looked like.

To some humans, that attitude was repellent— ultimate servility. Ainsley did not agree. To him, the Ossa he had met—and he had met most of the "women" whom the Guild had provided for the Roman soldiers' pleasure—were simply *unprejudiced*, in a way that not even the most tolerant and open-minded human ever was. Ossa did not recognize species, or races. Only *persons* were real to them.

He admired them, deeply, for that trait. Still—Ossa were by no means immune to hurt feelings.

"What phenotype will you select?" he asked.

Quartilla shrugged. "Human, essentially. The genotype will be fundamentally mine, of course. The human genome is so different from that of Ossa that only a few of Gaius's traits can be spliced into the embryo. And they can only do that because, luckily, the chemical base for both of our species' DNA is the same. You know, those four—"

She fluttered her hands, as if shaping the words with her fingers.

"Adenine, guanine, cytosine, thymine," intoned Ainsley.

"—yes, them! Anyway, our DNA is the same, chemically, but it's put together in a completely different manner. We Ossa don't have those—"

Again, her hands wiggled around forgotten words.

"Chromosomes?"

"Yes. *Chromosomes.* Ossa DNA is organized differently. I forget how, exactly. The geneticist explained but I couldn't understand a word he said after five seconds."

Ainsley laughed. "Specialists are all the same, my dear! You should hear Latinists, sometimes, in a bull session. My ex-wife—my *second* ex-wife—divorced me after one of them. Said she'd rather live with a toadstool. Better conversation."

Quartilla smiled archly. "Why did your *first* ex-wife divorce you?"

Ainsley scowled. "That was a different story altogether. *She* was a Latinist herself—the foul creature!—with the most preposterous theories you can imagine. We got divorced after an exchange of articles in the *Journal of*—"

He broke off, chuckling. "Speaking of specialists and their follies! Never mind, dear."

He gestured at Quartilla's ample figure. "But you're going to stick with your human form?"

"Not quite. The children will have a human shape, in every respect. They'll be living in a human world, after all. Human hair, even. But their skins will be Ossa. Well—almost. They'll have the scales, but we'll make sure they aren't dry and raspy. Gaius says people won't mind how the skin looks, as long as it feels good"—she giggled—"in what he calls 'the clutch.'"

Ainsley raised his eyebrow. "*Gaius* doesn't object to this? I thought—you once told me—"

Quartilla shrugged. "That was a long time ago, Robert. It's his idea, actually. He says modern humans aren't superstitious the way he was. And he doesn't give a damn about their other prejudices."

The last sentence was spoken a bit stiffly. Ainsley, watching her closely, decided not to press the matter. By and large, the Ossa "women" had shared in the general hero worship with which humanity had greeted the Roman exiles. Most of them, in fact, had quickly found themselves deluged by romantic advances. But there had been some incidents—

It was odd, really, he mused. Years after their return from exile, the Roman legionnaires still exhibited superstitions and notions which seemed absurd—outrageous, even—to modern people. Yet, at the same time, they shared none of the racial prejudices which so often lurked beneath the surface of the most urbane moderns. The ancient world of the Greeks and Romans had its prejudices and bigotries, of course. Plenty of them. But those prejudices were not tied to skin color and facial features. The Greeks considered the Persians *barbarians* because they didn't speak Greek and didn't share Greek culture. It never would have occurred to them, on the other hand, that the Medes who dominated their world were *racially* inferior. The very notion of "races" was a modern invention.

It had often struck Ainsley, listening to the tales of the legionnaires, how easily they had adapted to their sudden plunge into galactic society. No modern human, he thought, would have managed half as well. Their very ignorance had, in a sense, protected them. The world, to ancient Romans, was full of bizarre things anyway. Every Roman knew that there lived— somewhere south of Egypt, maybe—people with tails and heads in their bellies. A modern human, dropped onto a battlefield against aliens, would have probably been paralyzed with shock and horror. To the Romans, those aliens had just seemed like weird men—and nowhere near as dangerous as Parthians.

Ainsley, catching a glimpse of Pompilius Niger across the room, smiled. Only an ancient Roman would have so doggedly tried to make mead by following something that might be a funny-looking bee. A modern human would have understood the biological impossibility of the task.

And, in that wisdom, died in the hands of the Guild.

He looked back at Quartilla.

And so it had been with her and Gaius. The ancient Roman had been frightened and repelled by her scaly reptilian skin, when he first met her. But he had never thought she was anything but a—person.

"I am glad," he said quietly. "I approve of that decision. You understand, of course, that your children will face some difficulties, because of it."

Quartilla shrugged. It was a serene gesture.

"Some, yes. But not many, I think. If other children get too rough on them, Gaius says he will put a stop to it by simply crucifying a couple of the little bastards."

Ainsley started to laugh; then choked on his own humor.

He stared across the room at Vibulenus. The tribune was standing in a corner of his villa's huge salon, wine glass in hand, in a cluster of veterans who were having a vigorous and friendly exchange of war stories. With him were Clodius Afer, Julius Rusticanus—and all four of the Gha.

Good Lord. That's probably not a joke.

He caught Quartilla watching him closely.

"No, Robert," she murmured. "He is a Roman. He is not joking at all."

XII

An hour later, Gaius Vibulenus called the meeting to order.

There were almost sixty former legionnaires sprawled everywhere in the great salon. Fortunately, Gaius owned an enormous villa. The entire estate—not far from Capua, to his delight—had been a historical museum before it was turned over to him by the Italian regional government, following the dictates of popular demand.

Many more legionnaires had offered to come, but Gaius had kept the invitations reasonably small. Too many people would make decisions impossible. Besides, the men in the room were, almost without exception, the surviving leaders of the Roman legion. All of the centurions were there, and almost all of the file-closers. Whatever decision they made would be accepted by the rest of the legionnaires.

"All right," began Vibulenus, "you've all heard the Gha proposal. In its basic outline, anyway."

He waved his hand airily. "I have it on the best authority that the Confederation government will give its backing to the scheme. Unofficially, of course."

Clodius Afer sneered. "Those *politicians*? Be serious, Gaius! They're even worse than that sorry lot of senators we left behind."

Several other legionnaires grunted their agreement with that sentiment. Ainsley, watching, was amused. With few exceptions—Vibulenus, for one; and, oddly enough, Julius Rusticanus—the Romans had never been able to make sense out of modern politics. They tended to dismiss all of it as so much silly nonsense, which could be settled quick enough with just a few crucifixions.

Much as the historian admired—even loved—the Romans, he was glad not to have lived in *their* political world. True, much of modern politics was "so much silly nonsense." But, much of it wasn't, appearances to the contrary. And, modern man that he ultimately was, Ainsley thoroughly approved of the world-wide ban on capital punishment—much less torture.

"You're wrong, Clodius," rumbled Julius Rusticanus. The first centurion set down his wine goblet, almost ceremoniously, and stood up. Trained in the rhetorical traditions of the ancient world, he struck a solemn pose. His audience—just as well trained—assumed the solemn stance of listeners.

"Listen to me, Romans. Unlike most of you, I have paid careful attention to modern politics. And I do not share your contempt for it. Nor do I have any desire to listen to puling nonsense about the 'glories of Rome.' I remember the old politics, too. It was stupid Roman politics—the worst kind of personal ambition—that marched us all into that damned Parthian desert. Whatever folly there is in modern men—and there's plenty of it—they are a better lot than we were."

He glared around the room, as if daring anyone to argue with him. No one, of course, was foolish enough to do so. Not with the *first centurion*.

"No children starve, in this modern world. No old people die from neglect. No rich man takes a poor man's farm by bribing a judge. No master beats his slave for some trifling offense. There *are* no slaves."

Again, the sweeping glare. The silence, this time, came from more than respect. Whatever their crude attitudes, the legionnaires all knew that in this, at least, Julius Rusticanus spoke nothing but the plain and simple truth.

"So I'll hear no sneering about 'politicians.' We humans have always had politicians. Our old ones were never any better—and usually a lot worse. I know why Gaius is confident that the Confederation will support the proposal. I don't even need to know who his 'best authority' is. All I have to do is observe what's in front of my nose."

He laughed heartily. Theatrically, to Ainsley; but the historian knew that was an accepted part of the rhetoric. The ancients had none of the modern liking for subtle poses.

"The simple political reality is this, legionnaires," continued Rusticanus. "The people, in their great majority, are now filled with anti-Galactic fervor." Again, that theatrical laugh. "I think most of them are a bit bored with their peaceful modern world, to tell you the truth. They haven't had a war—not a real one, anyway—in almost a hundred years. And this is what they call a *crusade*."

"Won't be able to fight, then," grumbled one of the file-closers. "They're all a pack of civilians."

"Really?" sneered Rusticanus. "I'll tell you what, Appuleius—why don't you explain that to the Guild fleet? You know—the one that's nothing more than gas drifting in space?"

The jibe was met with raucous laughter. Joyful, savage laughter, thought Ainsley. For all their frequent grumbling about "modern sissies," the historian knew the fierce pride which the Romans had taken in Trumbull's destruction of the Guild fleet.

The first centurion pressed home the advantage. He gestured—again, theatrically—to one of the Medics standing toward the side of the salon. This was the "old" Medic, not the "new" one—the stocky, mauve-skinned, three-fingered crewman from the ship the Romans had captured years earlier. A few months after their arrival on Earth, the troop transport's Pilot had committed suicide. But the Medic had adjusted rather well to his new reality. He had even, over time, grown quite friendly with many of the legionnaires. Vibulenus had invited him to this meeting in order to take advantage of his Galactic knowledge.

"Tell them, Medic!" commanded Rusticanus. "Tell them how long it's been since an entire Guild fleet was annihilated."

The Medic stepped forward a pace or two. All the Romans were watching him intently, with the interest of veterans hearing the story of an unfamiliar campaign.

"As far as I know, it's never happened."

The legionnaires stared.

"What do you mean?" croaked one of them. "What do you mean—*never*?"

The Medic shook his head, a gesture he had picked up from his long immersion among humans. "Not that I know of. I'm not saying it *never* happened—way, way back toward the beginning of the Federation, sixty or seventy thousand years ago. But I know it hasn't happened in a very long time."

The Romans were practically goggling, now.

Again, the Medic shook his head. "You don't understand. You all think like—like *Romans*. All humans seem to think that way—even modern ones like Trumbull. The Guilds—and their Federation—are *merchants*. Profit and loss, that's what sets their field of vision. The Guilds fight each other, now and then, but it's never anything like that—that *massacre* Trumbull ordered. After one or two of their ships gets banged around—they hardly ever actually lose a ship—the Guild that's getting the worst of it just offers a better deal. And that's it."

The room was silent, for over a minute, as the Roman veterans tried to absorb this fantastical information. Ainsley was reminded of nothing so much as a pack of wolves trying to imagine how lapdogs think.

Suddenly, one of the legionnaires erupted in laughter. "Gods!" he cried. "Maybe this crazy Gha scheme will work after all!" He beamed approvingly at the huge figure of Fludenoc. "And at least we'll have these damned giant toads on *our* side, this time."

Fludenoc barked, in the Gha way of humor.

"Only some of us, you damned monkey shrimp," he retorted. "In the beginning, at least. All the members of the Poct'on will join, once they learn. But most Gha do not belong to the secret society, and it will take time to win them over."

"That doesn't matter," interjected Gaius. "The new legions are the heart of the plan. They'll have to be human, of course. There aren't very many Gha to begin with, and half of them are scattered all over the galaxy. Whereas we—!"

He grinned and glanced at his watch. "Let's stop for a moment, comrades. I want you to watch something."

He nodded at Rusticanus. The first centurion picked up the remote control lying on a nearby table and turned on the television. The huge screen on the far wall suddenly bloomed with color—and sound.

Lots of sound.

Wincing, Rusticanus hastily turned down the volume. In collusion with Gaius, he had already set the right channel, but he hadn't tested the sound.

The legionnaires were transfixed. Gaping, many of them.

"This scene is from Beijing," said Vibulenus. "The small square—the one that *looks* small, from the camera's height—is called Tien-an-Men."

The scene on the television suddenly shifted to another city. "This is Shanghai," he said.

Another scene. "Guangzhou."

Another. Another. Another.

"Nanjing. Hangzhou. Chongqing."

China was on the march. Every one of those great cities was packed with millions of people, marching through its streets and squares, chanting slogans, holding banners aloft.

"It's not just China," said Rusticanus. His voice, like that of Gaius, was soft.

Another city. More millions, marching, chanting, holding banners aloft.

"Bombay."

Another. "Paris."

Another. Another. More and more and more.

Sao Paolo. Moscow. Los Angeles. Lagos. Ciudad de Mexico.

On and on and on.

A different scene came on the screen. Not a city, now, but a hillside in farm country. The hillside itself— and everywhere the camera panned—was covered with an enormous throng of people. Speeches were being given from a stand atop the ridge.

"That is called Cemetery Ridge," announced Rusticanus. "It is near the small town of Gettysburg in the North American province called Pennsylvania. These people have gathered here to participate in what they are calling the Rededication."

Harshly: "Most of you ignorant sods won't understand why they are calling it that. But you can find out easily enough by reading a short speech which a man named Lincoln gave there not so very long ago. He was a 'stinking politician,' of course."

None of the legionnaires, Ainsley noted, even

responded to the jibe. They were still utterly mesmerized by the scenes on the television.

The historian glanced around the room. Its other occupants, mostly aliens, were equally mesmerized—the Gha, Quartilla, the two Medics and the Pilot.

But only on the faces of the legionnaires did tears begin to fall.

They, like the others, were transfixed by the unforgettable images of sheer, raw, massive human *power*. But it was not the sight of those millions upon millions of determined people which brought tears to Roman eyes. It was the sudden, final knowledge that the world's most long-lost exiles had never been forgotten.

One thing was common, in all those scenes. The people varied, in their shape and color and manner of dress. The slogans were chanted in a hundred languages, and the words written on a multitude of banners came in a dozen scripts.

But everywhere—on a hillside in Pennsylvania; a huge square in China—the same standards were held aloft, dominating the banners surrounding them. Many of those standards had been mass-produced for the occasion; many—probably most—crafted by hand.

The eagle standard of the legions.

Gaius rose. Like Rusticanus, he also adopted a theatrical pose, pointing dramatically at the screen.

"There are twelve *billion* people alive in the world today," he said. "And all of them, as one, have chosen that standard as the symbol of their new crusade."

The tribune's eyes swept the room, finally settling on the scarred face of Clodius Afer.

"*Will history record that the first Romans failed the last?*" he demanded.

Rusticanus switched off the screen. For a moment, the room was silent. Then, Clodius Afer rose and (theatrically) drained his goblet.

Theatrically, belched.

"I never said I wouldn't do it," he announced. With a dramatic wave at the screen:

"Besides, I couldn't face my ancestors, knowing that all those innocent lads went off to war without proper training from"—dramatic scowl—*"proper legionnaires."*

Very dramatic scowl: "The poor sorry bastards."

XIII

"Is this where you died?" asked Ainsley.

For a moment, he thought Gaius hadn't heard him. Then, with no expression on his face, the former tribune shrugged. "I don't think so, Robert. I think we pretty much razed that fortress after we took it. I don't remember, of course, since I was dead when it happened."

Gaius turned his head, examining the walls and crenellations of the castle they were standing on. "It was much like this one, though. Probably not far from here." He gestured toward the native notables standing respectfully a few yards away. "You could ask them. I'm sure they remember where it was."

Ainsley glanced at the short, furry beings. "They wouldn't remember. It was so long ago. Almost two thousand years, now. That was one of your first campaigns."

"They'll know," stated Gaius firmly. "They're a very intelligent species, Robert. They have written records going back well before then. And that was the battle that sealed their fate."

He scanned the fortress more carefully, now, urging

Ainsley to join him in that inspection with a little hand gesture.

"You see how well built this is, Robert? These people are not barbarians. They weren't then, either. It was a bit of a shock to us, at the time, coming up against them. We'd forgotten how tough smart and civilized soldiers can be, even when they're as small as these folk."

His face grew bleak. *"Two thousand years,* Robert. For two thousand years these poor bastards have been frozen solid by the stinking Doges. The ruinous trade relations the Guild forced down their throat have kept them there."

"It wasn't your fault, Gaius," murmured Ainsley.

"I didn't say it was. I'm not feeling any guilt over the thing, Robert. We were just as much victims as they were. I'm just sorry, that's all. Sorry for them. Sorry for us."

Suddenly, he chuckled. "Gods, I'm being gloomy! I'm probably just feeling sorry for myself." With a grimace: "Dying *hurts,* Robert. I still have nightmares about it, sometimes."

Ainsley pointed down the wooded slope below them.

"Look! Isn't that Clodius Afer?"

Gaius turned and squinted at the tiny figure of the horseman riding up the stone road which led to the castle. After a moment, he chuckled again.

"Yes it is, by the gods. I will be damned. I never thought he'd let the legion fight its first real battle without him there to mother his chicks."

Ainsley raised his eyes, looking at a greater distance. In the valley far below, the legion was forming its battle lines against the still more distant enemy.

"How soon?" he asked.

Gaius glanced at the valley. His experienced eye took only seconds to gauge the matter. "Half an hour, at the earliest. We've got time, before we have to go in."

The horseman was now close enough for Ainsley to see him clearly. It was definitely Clodius Afer.

Fifteen minutes later, the former centurion stamped his way up the narrow staircase leading to the crenellated wall where Vibulenus and Ainsley were waiting. His scarred face was scowling fiercely.

"I couldn't bear to watch!" he snarled. He shot the historian a black, black look. "I hold you responsible, Ainsley. I know this whole crack-brained scheme was your idea."

The centurion strode to the battlements and pointed theatrically toward the valley. "In less than an hour, thousands of witless boys—and girls, so help me!—will lie dying on that field. Crushed under the heels of their pitiless conquerors. *And it will all be your fault.*"

He spit (theatrically) over the wall.

Ainsley's reply was mild. "It was the Poct'on's idea, Clodius Afer, not mine."

"*Bullshit.* Fludenoc and the other Gha just had a general plan. *You're* the one put flesh and bones on it—I know you were!"

There was just enough truth in that last charge to keep Ainsley's mouth shut. Vibulenus filled the silence.

"So we've no chance, Clodius Afer? None at all?" The placid calmness of his voice seemed utterly at variance with the words themselves.

"None," came the gloomy reply. "Might as well put sheep—*lambs*—up against wolves. You should see those frightful brutes, Gaius! Fearsome, fearsome. Ten feet tall, at least, maybe twelve. Every one of them a hardened veteran. I could tell at a glance."

Gaius shook his head sadly. "Such a pity," he murmured. "Throwing away all those young lives for nothing."

He pushed himself away from the wall, shrugging with resignation. "Well, there's nothing for it, then, but to watch the hideous slaughter. Come on, Robert. They should have the scanners in the keep set up and running by now. We can get a much better view of the battle from there."

As he strode toward the stairs, he held up a hand toward the centurion. "You stay here, Clodius Afer! I know you won't want to watch."

The centurion sputtered. Ainsley stepped hastily aside to keep from being trampled as Clodius Afer charged past him.

The room in the keep where the viewscanners had been set up was the banquet hall where the local clan chiefs held their ceremonial feasts. It was the largest room in the entire castle, but, even for Romans, the ceiling was so low that they had to stoop slightly to walk through it. Ainsley, with the height of a modern human, felt like he was inside a wide tunnel.

The poor lighting added to his claustrophobia. The natives normally lighted the interior of the castle with a type of wax candles which human eyes found extremely irritating. So, for the occasion, they had decided to forgo all lighting beyond what little sunlight came through the narrow window-slits in the thick walls.

"I still say we could have put in modern lighting,"

grumbled Vibulenus, groping his way forward. "Temporarily, at least. The Guild command posts always used their own lighting."

"We already went through this, Gaius," replied Ainsley. "The Federation observers are going to watch us like hawks. Especially here, in our new Guild's first campaign. They'll jump on any violation of the regulations, no matter how minor—on our part, that is. They'll let the *established* Guilds cut every corner they can."

"You can say that again," came a growling voice from ahead.

Peering forward, Ainsley saw Captain Tambo's face raising up from the viewscreen.

"Come here and take a look," grumbled the South African. "The Ty'uct are already deploying their Gha. The battle hasn't even started yet, for Christ's sake— and they've got plenty of native auxiliaries to begin with. They don't need Gha flankers."

Gaius reached the viewscreen and bent over.

"That's it!" cried Clodius Afer. "Gha flankers? *The legion's doomed!*"

Vibulenus ignored the former centurion's dark prediction. Silently, he watched the formations unfolding on the large screen in front of him.

After a minute or so, he looked up and smiled. "Speaking of Gha flankers, you might want to take a look at this, Clodius Afer. After all, it was your idea in the first place."

The centurion crowded forward eagerly. "Did Fludenoc and his lads move up?"

He stared at the screen for a moment. Then, began cackling with glee. "*See? See?* I told you those stinking hyenas were just a bunch of turbo-charged jackals! Ha!

Look at 'em cringe! They finally ran into something bigger than they are. A *lot* bigger!"

Ainsley managed to shove his head through the small crowd and get a view of the screen.

"I will be good God-damned," he whispered. He patted the former centurion on the shoulder. "You're a genius, Clodius Afer. I'll admit, I had my doubts."

Clodius Afer snorted. "That's because you modern sissies never faced war elephants in a battle. The great brutes are purely terrifying, I'm telling you."

"As long as they don't panic," muttered Gaius.

"They won't," replied Clodius Afer confidently. "These are that new strain the geneticists came up with. They're really more like ancient mammoths than modern elephants. And they've been bred for the right temperament, too."

He pointed to the screen. "Besides, the Gha know just how to handle the damn things. Watch!"

The scene in the viewscreen was quite striking, thought Ainsley. The main body of the Ty'uct army was still milling around in the center of the field, whipping themselves into a frenzy. On the flanks, Gha bodyguards had pushed forward on their "turbo-charged" giant quasi-hyenas. But they were already falling back before Fludenoc and the other Poct'on members who were serving the legion as a special force. There were thirty-two of those Gha, all mounted on gigantic war elephants, all wielding the modified halberds which human armorers had designed to replace the traditional Gha maces.

The Poct'on warriors loomed over their counterparts like moving cliffs. The giant "hyenas" looked like so many puppies before the elephants. Bad-tempered,

nasty, snarling puppies, true. But thoroughly intimidated, for all that. Despite the best efforts of their
Gha riders, the hyenas were slinking back toward
their lines.

Ainsley could hardly blame them. Even from the
remoteness of his televised view, the war elephants
were—as Clodius Afer had rightly said—"purely terrifying." These were no friendly circus elephants. They
didn't even *look* like elephants. To Ainsley, they seemed
a perfect reincarnation of mammoths or mastodons.
The beasts were fourteen feet high at the shoulders,
weighed several tons, and had ten-foot-long tusks.

They also had a temperament to match. The elephants were bugling great blasts of fury with their
upraised trunks, and advancing on the hyenas remorse-
lessly.

"Jesus," whispered Tambo, "even the Gha look like
midgets on top of those things. They seem to have
them under control, though."

"I'm telling you," insisted Clodius Afer, "the Gha
are wizards at handling the brutes." He snorted. "They
always did hate those stinking hyenas, you know. But
with elephants and Gha, it was love at first sight."

Tambo glanced up. "Whatever happened to their
own—uh, 'hyenas'? The ones they had on the ship
they seized?"

Gaius whistled soundlessly. Clodius Afer coughed,
looked away.

"Don't rightly know," he muttered. "But Pompilius
Niger—he raises bees now, you know, on his farm—
told me that Uddumac asked him for a couple of
barrels of his home-brewed mead. For a private Gha
party, he said."

Tambo winced. "Don't let the SPCA find out."

The centurion mumbled something under his breath. Ainsley wasn't sure, but it sounded like "*modern sissies.*"

"The hyenas are breaking," announced Gaius. "Look at them—they're completely cowed."

Tambo slapped the heavy wooden table under the viewscreen. The gesture expressed his great satisfaction.

"It'll be a straight-up fight, now! Between the legion and those—what in the *hell* are they, anyway? Have you ever seen them before, Gaius?"

The tribune grinned. So did Clodius Afer.

"Oh, yes," he murmured. "These boys were the opposition in our very first Guild campaign."

"Sorry clowns!" barked the centurion. "Look at 'em, Gaius—I swear, I think those are the same wagons they were using two thousand years ago."

The Ty'uct mercenaries started their wagon charge. Clodius Afer watched them on the screen for a few seconds before sneering: "Same stupid tactics, too. Watch this, professor! These galloping idiots are about to—"

He scowled. "Well, if they were facing a *real* Roman legion."

Deep scowl. "As it is—against these puling babes—?" Low moan of despair. "It'll be a massacre. A *massacre*, I tell you."

"Actually," murmured Gaius, "I think the puling babes are going to do better than we did."

He glanced over at Tambo, who was sitting to one side of the big screen. The naval officer's eyes were on a complex communication console attached to the viewscanner. "Are we secure?" asked Gaius.

Tambo nodded. "Yeah, we are. Our ECM has got the

Federation's long-distance spotters scrambled. Everything in the castle is out of their viewing capability."

He sat up, sneering. "And, naturally, the lazy galactics never bothered to send a personal observer. Even if they shuttle one down now, it'll be too late. The battle'll be over before they get here."

"Good." Gaius turned and whistled sharply. A moment later, several natives appeared in the main doorway to the great hall. Gaius gestured, motioning for them to enter.

Somewhat gingerly, the natives advanced into the room and approached the small knot of humans at the viewscreen.

"You watch now," said Gaius, in simple Latin.

"Is safe from Federation?" asked one of the natives, also in Latin. Ainsley recognized him. The Fourth-of-Five, that one was called. He was a member of the clan's central leadership body, as well as the clan's warchief.

"Safe," assured Gaius. "They can not see you here with"—he groped for a moment, in the limits of the simplified language—"high-raised arts. But must keep this secret. Not tell them. Not tell anyone."

"Secret be keep," said the Fourth-of-Five. Still a bit gingerly, the warchief leaned forward to examine the scene on the scanner.

"Battle start?"

"Yes," replied Gaius. "Now you watch. I explain what we do. Why we do."

Two minutes later, the battle was joined in earnest. As it unfolded, Gaius followed the action with a running commentary for the benefit of the Fourth-of-Five, explaining the methods and principles of Roman tactics. The warchief was an attentive student. A very knowledgeable one, too, who asked many pointed and well-aimed questions. His own people had never been slouches, when it came to warfare; and now, hidden miles away in a forest camp, the warchief's own native *legion* had already begun its training.

Commander Tambo watched some of the battle, but not much. He was a naval officer, after all, for whom the tactics of iron-age land warfare were of largely academic interest. He was much more concerned with keeping a careful eye on the ECM monitors. By allowing the natives to follow the battle with the help of modern technology, the humans were breaking the letter of Federation law.

The *spirit* of that law, of course, they were trampling underfoot with hobnailed boots.

Ainsley simply watched the battle. Quite transfixed, he was; oblivious to everything else.

Ironically, *his* interest was purely academic. But it was the monomaniacal interest of a man who had spent all but the last few years of his adult life studying something which he was now able to see unfold before his own eyes. *A Roman legion in action*.

A purist, of course, would have been outraged.

Such a purist, in his own way, was the legion's expert consultant and field trainer, the former centurion Clodius Afer. Throughout the course of the battle, Clodius Afer danced back and forth between the viewscreen and the far wall, to whose unfeeling stones he wailed his black despair.

Roman legion, indeed!

Smiling, Ainsley leaned over and whispered to

Gaius: "Is the rumor true? Did Clodius Afer really call Colonel Tsiang a 'slant-eyed bastard'?"

Gaius grinned, though his eyes never left the screen. He was keeping a close watch on the legate commanding the legion, in order to provide him with expert consultation after the battle.

That legate was a former colonel in the Chinese Army. Of the ten tribunes commanding the legion's cohorts, four were Chinese, three North American, one German, one South African and one Pakistani. True, there was one Italian centurion, and three Italian file-closers. But the overall national and racial composition of the legion was a fair reflection of modern Earth's demographics, except that it was skewed toward Chinese and North Americans. This, for the simple reason that all the legionnaires were former soldiers, and only the North Americans and Chinese still maintained relatively large standing armies.

"Oh, yes," murmured Gaius. "Fortunately, Tsiang's a phlegmatic kind of guy. Good thing for Clodius. The colonel has a black belt in at least five of the martial arts."

He turned his head. "You might want to watch this, Clodius Afer! They're getting ready for the first volley of javelins!"

Two seconds later, the former centurion's face was almost pressed to the screen. "They'll screw it up," he groaned. "Damned amateurs think they're throwing darts in a tavern."

Silence ensued, for a few seconds. Then:

Gaius grinned. Clodius Afer scowled and stalked off. Robert Ainsley hissed, face pale.

"God in Heaven," he whispered shakily. "I had no idea."

The former tribune's grin faded. "A good javelin volley is like the scythe of death, Robert. It's pure butchery."

"Was this one good?"

"As good as you'll ever see. I knew it would be."

Ainsley studied Gaius for a moment.

"You've never shared Clodius Afer's skepticism. Why?"

Gaius snorted. "The old bastard's just jealous, that's all."

The former tribune jabbed his forefinger at the screen. "Every single one of those legionaires, from the legate down to the last man in the ranks, is a hand-picked volunteer. The cream of the crop—and it was a huge crop of volunteers. Every one's a soldier, and every one's dedicated to this cause. Not to mention the fact that, on average, they're probably half again as strong and twice as fast as the average Roman legionnaire of our time. So why shouldn't they do well?"

Ainsley rubbed his chin. "It's still their first real battle."

Gaius shrugged. "True. And it shows." He nodded at the screen.

"They're sluggish, right now. They're not reacting as quickly as they should to the success of their javelin volley. That's inexperience. A blooded legion would already be down the enemy's throat. But—*see*? Tsiang's already bringing the line forward. Good formations, too. The spacing's excellent."

He glanced over his shoulder at the figure of Clodius Afer, wailing against the wall.

"Clodius forgets. How good do you think *we* were

in the beginning? A bunch of ignorant kids, half of us. Marched off to slaughter in the desert and then sold to aliens. I had no idea what I was doing, at first. *This* legion's already doing well. Give them three more campaigns and they could have chopped us up for horse meat."

He turned back to the screen. "Trust me, Robert. There's never been a better Roman legion than the one down there on that field today."

Again, he cocked his head and bellowed at Clodius Afer. "They've almost closed with the enemy! Oh—*and look*! The Tenth Cohort's going to bear the brunt of it!"

"*That bitch!*" shrieked Clodius Afer, charging back to the screen. "She's going to get 'em all killed!"

Silence, for two full minutes. Then:

Gaius laughed. Clodius Afer spit on the floor and stalked back to the wall. Spit on the wall. Ainsley wiped his face.

"I thought the Tenth Cohort was supposed to be the legion's shield, not its sword arm," he muttered.

Gaius's grin was cold, cold. "Yeah, that's the tradition. But traditions are meant to be broken, you know. And Tribune Lemont is *not* the phlegmatic type."

"Is it true?" whispered Ainsley. "Did Clodius Afer really call Shirley Lemont a—"

Gaius laughed. "Oh, yes! Then, after he woke up, he insisted on a formal rematch. He didn't quit until she threw him six times running, and told him she was going to start breaking his puny little bones."

Ainsley stared at Clodius Afer. The former centurion was studying the stone wall with a deep interest which seemed entirely inappropriate to its bare, rough-hewn nature.

"I guess it took him by surprise, seeing women in the legion's ranks."

Gaius started to reply but broke off suddenly, rising halfway out of his seat. "Gods, look at them rolling up the flank! This battle's already won, Robert." Turning his head, he bellowed:

"Hey, Clodius Afer! You might want to see this! The enemy's pouring off the field! The legion's hammering 'em into mash! And—guess what?—*great news!* It's our old Tenth Cohort that turned their flank! God, what a maneuver! I'm telling you, Clodius Afer—*that Shirley Lemont's the best tribune I've ever seen!* Come here! You don't want to miss it!"

In the next five minutes, Gaius Vibulenus went over the battle with the Fourth-of-Five, patiently answering the native warleader's many questions. Robert Ainsley simply sat, recovering from the experience—simultaneously exhilarating and horrifying—of finally seeing the Roman war machine in action.

Clodius Afer leaned his head against the stone wall. Banged it once or twice. Wept bitter tears for the lost legacy of ancient Rome.

Ruined—*ruined*—by modern sissies. *Girls.*

XIV

As he watched the troop transport settle its enormous bulk into the valley, Ainsley found it impossible not to grin.

"Travelling in style, I see," he chuckled.

Gaius gave him a stern look. "I beg your pardon? The *Cato* is an official SPQR Guild transport vessel, properly registered as such with the Federation authorities."

Ainsley snorted. "She's also the former *Queen Elizabeth*, luxury liner."

Gaius grinned. "So? It could be worse, you know. They're already talking about raising the *Titanic* and retrofitting her."

A voice from behind them: "It's already been decided. Damn fools are going to do it."

The two men turned to face Tambo. The naval officer was just climbing off the stairs onto the stone ramp behind the castle's crenellations. A few steps behind him came the Second-of-Five.

The South African and the native clan leader joined them at the battlements. Tambo scowled.

"I think it's pure foolishness, myself. The whole point of refitting old naval vessels is to re-arm the Earth as fast as possible. *Stupid*. It'll take twice as long—and twice the money—to fix up that shipwreck than it would to build a brand-new transport."

Ainsley's reply was mild. "Humans are a bit swept up in historical sentiment, you know. All things considered, I have to say I'm rather in favor of it."

Tambo grimaced but didn't argue the point. Instead he went straight to his business.

"I've just gotten word from the escort vessels. The Federation ship and the Guild transport have left the system, so there are no observers left. The colonists can debark before the legion boards the transport."

"Any threats?" asked Gaius.

"From the *Ty'uct*?" sneered Tambo. "Not likely—not after we smeared their second invasion fleet in less time than the first. No, no threats. But they are definitely in a foul mood after yesterday's whipping. They're complaining about the elephants."

Gaius shrugged. "Let 'em! Elephants were a regular feature of Roman warfare."

"Not genetically engineered semi-mastodons," pointed out Ainsley.

Again, Gaius shrugged. "So what? The Guild can hardly complain—not when *their* Gha ride mounts that have to be turbocharged to even breathe the air."

Tambo smiled. "They're still going to complain about it. Demand a full Federation hearing, they say." His smile broadened. "God, would I love to be there! Did you hear? Mai the Merciless has been appointed Earth's official representative to the Federation."

"Heaven help them," murmured Ainsley. Then:

"I thought you *were* going to be there."

Tambo's smile was now an outright grin. "Change of orders." He squared his shoulders. Struck a solemn pose.

"You have the honor of being in the presence of the newly appointed commodore in charge of Flotilla Seven."

The false pomposity vanished, replaced by a cheerful rubbing of his hands. "The campaign against the Ssrange is on! And I'm in command!"

Ainsley's eyes widened. "They decided to do it? I thought—"

Tambo shook his head. "No, it seems good sense won out over timidity, after all. Christ, I should hope so! We've got a tiger by the tail. Last thing we can afford to do is let go. If the Guilds and the Federation ever figure out how vulnerable we are—will be, for at least twenty years—they could slaughter us. *Keep the bastards cowed*—that's the trick!"

Gaius nodded. "I agree. Bloodying the Ty'uct Guild's

nose in a couple of small ship battles will only win us a couple of years. Before one of the bolder guilds decides to mount a real armada."

"Unless we show the galaxy how rough we are—by wiping out the nest of pirates that the whole Federation's whined about for thirty millennia." The South African's voice took on a whimpering tone. "*What can we do? Best to reach an accommodation with the Ssrange. They're businessmen, too, after all, in their own way.*"

Gaius's eyes were icy. "They held Quartilla, for a time. Did you know that?"

Both Tambo and Ainsley nodded.

"What's your plan, Stephen?" asked the historian. "You're the commander."

For a moment, Tambo's eyes were as cold as the Roman's. "It's been named Operation Pompey. That should give you the idea."

Ainsley sucked in his breath. Gaius grinned like a wolf.

As well he could. In 67 B.C.—just fourteen years before Crassus's ill-fated expedition against the Parthians had resulted in Gaius's enslavement to the Guild—the Roman republic finally lost patience with the pirates who had plagued the Mediterranean for centuries. Pompey the Great—one of the three members, along with Caesar and Crassus, of the First Triumvirate—was charged with the task of exterminating piracy.

He did it. In exactly three months.

"The *Roman* way," growled Gaius.

"Here come the colonists," murmured Tambo. He raised the binoculars hanging around his neck and studied the small crowd of people filing from the

Cato. Then, after a minute or so, passed them to the Second-of-Five. The native clan leader immediately—and with obvious familiarity with the eyeglasses—began examining the scene in the valley below.

Ainsley spent the time studying the binoculars themselves. He was rather fascinated by the simple, obsolete device. Modern humans, when they wanted to view something at a distance, used computer-enhanced optical technology. But such technology would be far beyond the capacity of the natives who had just entered a new trading agreement with the galaxy's newest guild.

The *SPQR Guild*, as it was formally known—and so registered, officially, with the Federation.

The "guild" had other, unofficial names. Many of them, in many human languages. The names varied, depending on each human subculture's own traditions. Some called it the Tea Party, others the Long March. Others, Francophones, *la Resistance*. Most people, though, simply called it the Liberation.

Ainsley's attention shuttled back and forth between the binoculars and the small, furred figure of the native holding them.

They've started their first lens-grinding works, Tambo tells me. They already knew how to make good glass.

He looked away, smiling. The occasional Federation observer who scanned from orbit, now and then, would have no way of seeing the technological and social revolution that was exploding across the surface below. This planet—and its people—were frozen no longer.

The "SPQR Guild" had set up quite different trade relations than the ones which had dominated here for two millennia. The Doge guilds, had they known, would have been utterly shocked.

These trade treaties would not bleed the natives dry. Quite the opposite.

Ainsley looked down into the valley. He could not see the individual faces of the colonists who were now making their way toward the castle, escorted by elephant-mounted Gha. But he knew what those faces would look like. Human faces, in their big majority—although some of those faces concealed Ossa. But there would be a few unreconstructed Ossa among them, the first contingents of what was already being called the Underground Railroad. And, here and there, a few members of other species. Freed slaves, some. Others, people from Class One planets—like the Pilot and the Medic—who had decided to throw in their lot with the rising new human "Doge Species."

On every planet which the SPQR Guild's legions cleared of their former guild masters, such small colonies would be set up. Scattered like seeds across the starfields, to intermingle with the natives and create a multitude of new, vibrant societies.

He caught Tambo's warm eyes watching him.

"Twenty years, Robert," said the naval officer softly. "Twenty years. By then, Earth's navy will be too strong for the Guilds—even the Federation—to defeat us."

He made a sweeping gesture which encompassed the valley and, by implication, the entire universe. "And, by then, we'll have created an army of allies. A *host*, Robert, like this galaxy's never seen."

Ainsley smiled crookedly. "You're not worried, Stephen? Not at all?"

Before answering, Tambo studied him.

Then, he shook his head. "God, I'd hate to be a

historian," he muttered. "Worry about everything."
Again, he made the sweeping gesture.

"You're concerned, I assume, that we'll screw it
up, too? Set up a new tyranny?"

Ainsley nodded. Tambo chuckled.

"Don't worry about it, Robert. I'm *sure* we'll screw
it up. Some. Badly, even, here and there. So what?
It'll sort itself out, soon enough."

He grinned widely. "We humans have always been
good at sorting out that kind of thing, you know."

Tambo stretched out his muscular, light-brown arm.
"*Look at it, historian.* There's all of Africa—half the
world—in that arm. Bantu, Boer, Khoisan, English. A
fair chunk of India, too." He lowered the arm. "When
I was a boy, growing up, I was thrilled as much by the
Trek as I was by Isandhlwana, Moshoeshoe and Man-
dela. It's all part of me. Now that it's been sorted out."

Tambo pointed his finger at the great banner flying above the castle. The banner of the new guild,
proudly announcing its trade dominance of the planet.

"We'll sort it out. And wherever we screw up,
there'll be others to kick us in the ass. We humans
are just as good at learning from a butt-kicking as we
are at delivering one. Better, probably."

Ainsley stared at the banner. Then, smiled as broadly
as Tambo. "Poor Doges," he murmured. "Merchants
have never been worth a damn, you know, historically speaking. Not, at least, when they try to run
an empire."

Emblazoned atop the banner, above the eagle
standard, were the simple letters: *S.P.Q.R.*

Below, the Guild's motto:

Carthago delenda est.

XV

Some years later, a great crowd filled the villa near Capua owned by Gaius Vibulenus. The occasion was the ninth birthday of Gaius and Quartilla's first child. The boy they had named Ulysses, but called simply Sam.

Clodius Afer, one of the boy's four godfathers, had been disgruntled by the name. "Sissy Greek name," he'd muttered, speaking of the official cognomen. And he had even less use for the nickname.

Pompilius Niger, the second of the godfathers, also thought the name was a bit odd, for a Roman. But, unlike Clodius Afer, the simple farmer rather liked the simple "Sam."

Julius Rusticanus, the third godfather, was delighted by the name. As well he should be—it was his suggestion in the first place. Unlike his two fellow legionnaires, Rusticanus knew that the boy had not been named after an ancient Greek adventurer. No, Rusticanus had become quite the student of world history—as befitted a man who had recently been elected, by an overwhelming majority of Italians, to the Confederation's most august legislative body. The former first centurion, born a peasant, was now—what would his father have thought, he often wondered?—a senator.

Ulysses had been named after another, much later man. The man who led the armies which destroyed chattel slavery. Ulysses "Sam" Grant. Rusticanus had great hopes for the boy. Especially now, watching the child bouncing in the lap of his fourth godfather, demanding an explanation for the new toys.

The boy, though large for his age, was almost lost in that huge Gha lap.

"What do you do with them, Fludenoc?" demanded Sam. "How do you play with them?"

Rusticanus grinned. Fludenoc hu'tut—*No*. He was now Fludenoc *hu-lu-tut*-Na Nomo'te. His epic poem—the first epic poem ever written by a Gha—had won him that new accolade, from his clan. Fludenoc now belonged to that most select of Gha poets, those considered "bards."

The epic had been entitled the *Ghaiad*. Rusticanus had read it, twice. The first time with awe, at the Gha's great poetic skill, which came through even in the Latin translation. The second time with amusement, at the Gha's wry sense of humor. It was all about a small band of Gha, long ago, who had been driven into exile by rapacious conquerors. Wandering the galaxy—having many adventures—until they finally settled on a new planet and founded Rome. (With, admittedly, a bit of help from the local natives.)

Fludenoc, like Rusticanus, had also become an avid student of human history.

"Tell me, Uncle Fludenoc, tell me!" demanded the boy. The child pointed at the new toys which the Gha had brought him for his birthday. "How do you play with them?"

Fludenoc's huge, bulging eyes stared down at the tiny Ossa/human child in his lap. As always, there was no expression in the giant's face. But the boy had long since learned to read the subtleties of Gha breathing.

"Stop laughing at me!" shrilled Sam. "I want to know! How do you play with them?"

"I was not laughing at *you*, Sam," rumbled Fludenoc. "I was laughing at the Doges."

Sam's slightly iridescent, softly scaled face crinkled into a frown.

"When you grow up," said the Gha, gently, "you will know how to use them."

Sam twisted in Fludenoc's lap, staring down at the peculiar toys sitting on the floor.

A small plow.

A bag of salt.

Appendix:
Eric Flint Bibliography

Author's note:

I've sorted out the various novels and stories I've written according to whichever series they belong to. With the exception of two novels, a short novel with Ryk Spoor, and some short stories I've written over the years for various anthologies, all my work fits into one broader setting or another. I'm an author who much prefers to work in big series. It's just the way my scribbler's mind works.

Standalone stories:

Mother of Demons (1997)
Slow Train to Arcturus, with Dave Freer (2008)

"The Thief and the Roller Derby Queen," published in *The Chick is in the Mail*, (2000), ed. Esther Friesner

"The Truth About the Gotterdammerung," published in *Turn the Other Chick* (2004), ed. Esther Friesner

"The Flood Was Fixed," published in *Something Magic This Way Comes* (2008), edited by Marty Greenberg and Sarah Hoyt

"Red Fiddler," with Dave Freer, published in *Bedlam's Edge* (2005), edited by Mercedes Lackey and Rosemary Edghill

"Diamonds Are Forever," with Ryk Spoor, in *Mountain Magic* (2004)

"Conspiracies: A Very Condensed 937-Page Novel," with Mike Resnick, published in *Sideways in Crime*, edited by Lou Anders (2008)

"Pirates of the Suara Sea," with Dave Freer, published in *Fast Ships, Black Sails*, edited by Jeff Vandermeer (2008)

"Operation Xibalba," in Poul Anderson tribute anthology *Multiverse: Exploring Poul Anderson's Worlds*, edited by Gardner Dozois (forthcoming 2012)

The Belisarius series (with David Drake)

An Oblique Approach (1998)
In the Heart of Darkness (1998)
Destiny's Shield (1999)
Fortune's Stroke (2000)
The Tide of Victory (2001)
"Islands," originally published in *The Warmasters* (2002), edited by Bill Fawcett
The Dance of Time (2006)

The Tyrant (2002) [Note: this is not directly part of the Belisarius series, but is part of the related General series]

The 1632 series

1632 (2000)

1633, with David Weber (2002)

"The Wallenstein Gambit," first published in *Ring of Fire* (2004), edited by Eric Flint

"Portraits," first published in *Grantville Gazette I* (2004), edited by Eric Flint

"Steps in the Dance," first published in *Grantville Gazette II* (2006), edited by Eric Flint

"Postage Due," first published in *Grantville Gazette III* (2007), edited by Eric Flint

1634: The Galileo Affair, with Andrew Dennis (2004)

1634: The Baltic War, with David Weber (2007)

1634: The Ram Rebellion, with Virginia DeMarce (2006)

1634: The Bavarian Crisis, with Virginia DeMarce (2007)

1635: The Cannon Law, with Andrew Dennis (2006)

1635: The Dreeson Incident, with Virginia DeMarce (2008)

"The Austro-Hungarian Connection," first published in *Ring of Fire II* (2008), edited by Eric Flint

"Anatomy Lesson," first published in *Grantville Gazette IV* (2008), edited by Eric Flint

"Steady Girl," first published in *Grantville Gazette V* (2009), edited by Eric Flint

1635: The Eastern Front (2010)

1636: The Saxon Uprising (2011)

"Four Days on the Danube," first published in *Ring of Fire III* (2011), edited by Eric Flint

1636: The Kremlin Games, with Gorg Huff and Paula Goodlett (forthcoming September 2012)

In addition to the above, there have been thirty-eight issues published of the *Grantville Gazette* bi-monthly electronic magazine.

Connected to the 1632 series will be another series which I'm calling the Assiti Shards series. The first book in that series is *Timespike*, which I co-authored with Marilyn Kosmatka (2008).

The Honor Harrington series (by David Weber)

"From the Highlands," first published in *Changer of Worlds: Worlds of Honor #3* (2001), edited by David Weber

"Fanatic," first published in *The Service of the Sword: Worlds of Honor #4* (2003), edited by David Weber

Crown of Slaves, with David Weber (2003)

Torch of Freedom, with David Weber (2009)

The Trail of Glory series

1812: The Rivers of War (2005)

1824: The Arkansas War (2006)

The Joe's World Series

"Entropy, and the Strangler," first published in *Writers of the Future, Volume IX* (1993), edited by Dave Wolverton

The Philosophical Strangler (2001)
Forward the Mage, with Richard Roach (2002)
A Desperate and Despicable Dwarf (forthcoming)

The Rats, Bats & Vats series (with Dave Freer)

"Genie Out of the Bottle," first published in *Cosmic Tales II: Adventures in Far Futures* (2205), edited by Toni Weisskopf
Rats, Bats & Vats (2000)
The Rats, The Bats & The Ugly (2004)
"Crawlspace," first published in *Jim Baen's Universe*, April 2007.

The Pyramid Series (with Dave Freer)

Pyramid Scheme (2001)
Pyramid Power (2007)

Forthcoming:
As yet untitled, the third volume in this trilogy

The Heirs of Alexandria Series

The Shadow of the Lion, with Mercedes Lackey and Dave Freer (2002)
A Mankind Witch (2005) [Note: this is a solo novel in the series by Dave Freer]
This Rough Magic, with Mercedes Lackey and Dave Freer (2003)
Much Fall of Blood, with Mercedes Lackey and Dave Freer (2010)

"The Witch's Murder," with Dave Freer, first pub-
    lished in *The Dragon Done It*, edited by Eric
    Flint and Mike Resnick (2008)
Burdens of the Dead, with Mercedes Lackey and
    Dave Freer (forthcoming)

The Witches of Karres series
(created by James H. Schmitz)

The Wizard of Karres, with Mercedes Lacky and
    Dave Freer (2004)
The Sorceress of Karres, with Dave Freer (forth-
    coming)

The Boundary series (with Ryk Spoor)

Boundary (2006)
Threshold (2010)
Portal (forthcoming)

The Jao series (with K.D. Wentworth)

The Course of Empire (2003)
The Crucible of Empire (2010)
The Span of Empire (forthcoming)

In addition to my own work as an author, I've edited a lot of anthologies. Most of these involve multi-volume reissues of authors from times past. I'm listing them below

Complete Works of James H. Schmitz (with Guy Gordon, co-editor)

Telzey Amberdon (2000)
TnT: Telzey and Trigger Together (2000)
Trigger and Friends (2001)
Dangerous Territory: The Federation of the Hub (2001)
Agent of Vega & Other Stories (2001)
Eternal Frontier (2002)
The Witches of Karres (2005)

Complete Works of Christopher Anvil

Pandora's Legions (2002)
The Interstellar Patrol (2003)
The Interstellar Patrol II: The Federation of Humanity (2005)
The Trouble with Aliens (2006)
The Trouble With Humans (2007)
War Games (2008)
Prescription for Chaos (2009)
The Power of Illusion (2010)

Works of Keith Laumer

Retief! (2002)
Odyssey (2002)
Keith Laumer: The Lighter Side (2002)

A Plague of Demons (2003)
Future Imperfect (2003)
Legions of Space (2004)
Imperium (2005)
The Long Twilight & Other Stories (2007)
Earthblood & Other Stories (2008)
The Universe Twister (2008)

Works of Murray Leinster

Med Ship (2002)
Planets of Adventure (2003)
A Logic Named Joe (2005)

Complete Works of Howard L. Myers (with Guy Gordon, co-editor)

The Creatures of Man (2003)
A Sense of Infinity (2009)

Other anthologies

Tom Godwin, *The Cold Equations & Other Stories* (2003)
Randall Garrett, *Lord Darcy*, with Guy Gordon, co-editor (2002)
The World Turned Upside Down, co-edited with David Drake and Jim Baen (2005)
The Best of Jim Baen's Universe (2007)
The Dragon Done It, co-edited with Mike Resnick (2008)
The Best of Jim Baen's Universe II, co-edited with Mike Resnick (2007)

IF YOU LIKE...
YOU SHOULD TRY...

DAVID DRAKE
David Weber

DAVID WEBER
John Ringo

JOHN RINGO
Michael Z. Williamson
Tom Kratman

ANNE MCCAFFREY
Mercedes Lackey

MERCEDES LACKEY
Wen Spencer, Andre Norton
Andre Norton
James H. Schmitz

LARRY NIVEN
James P. Hogan
Travis S. Taylor

ROBERT A. HEINLEIN
Jerry Pournelle
Lois McMaster Bujold
Michael Z. Williamson

HEINLEIN'S "JUVENILES"
Rats, Bats & Vats series by Eric Flint & Dave Freer

HORATIO HORNBLOWER OR PATRICK O'BRIAN
David Weber's Honor Harrington series
David Drake's RCN series

HARRY POTTER
Mercedes Lackey's Urban Fantasy series

THE LORD OF THE RINGS
Elizabeth Moon's The Deed of Paksenarrion

H.P. LOVECRAFT
Princess of Wands by John Ringo

GEORGETTE HEYER
Lois McMaster Bujold
Catherine Asaro

GREEK MYTHOLOGY
Pyramid Scheme by Eric Flint & Dave Freer
Forge of the Titans by Steve White
Blood of the Heroes by Steve White

NORSE MYTHOLOGY
Northworld Trilogy by David Drake

ARTHURIAN LEGEND
Steve White's "Legacy" series

SCA/HISTORICAL REENACTMENT
John Ringo's "After the Fall" series

CATS
Larry Niven's Man-Kzin Wars series

PUNS
Rick Cook
Spider Robinson
Wm. Mark Simmons

VAMPIRES & WEREWOLVES
Larry Correia
Wm. Mark Simmons

NONFICTION
Hank Reinhardt
Tax Payer's Tea Party
by Sharon Cooper & Chuck Asay
The Science Behind the Secret by Travis Taylor

Flag in Exile   pb • 0-7434-3575-3 • $7.99
"Packs enough punch to smash a starship to smithereens."—*Publishers Weekly*

Honor Among Enemies   hc • 0-671-87723-2 • $21.00
                      pb • 0-671-87783-6 • $7.99
"Star Wars as it might have been written by C.S. Forester
. . . fast-paced entertainment." —*Booklist*

In Enemy Hands   hc • 0-671-87793-3 • $22.00
                      pb • 0-671-57770-0 • $7.99
After being ambushed, Honor finds herself aboard an
enemy cruiser, bound for her scheduled execution. But
one lesson Honor has never learned is how to give up!

Echoes of Honor   hc • 0-671-87892-1 • $24.00
                      pb • 0-671-57833-2 • $7.99
"Brilliant! Brilliant! Brilliant!"—Anne McCaffrey

Ashes of Victory   hc • 0-671-57854-5 • $25.00
                      pb • 0-671-31977-9 • $7.99
Honor has escaped from the prison planet called Hell and
returned to the Manticoran Alliance, to the heart of a furnace of new weapons, new strategies, new tactics, spies,
diplomacy, and assassination.

War of Honor   hc • 0-7434-3545-1 • $26.00
                      pb • 0-7434-7167-9 • $7.99
No one wanted another war. Neither the Republic of
Haven, nor Manticore—and certainly not Honor Harrington.
Unfortunately, what they wanted didn't matter.

At All Costs   hc • 1-4165-0911-9 • $26.00
                      pb • 1-4165-4414-3 • $7.99
The war with the Republic of Haven has resumed. . . disastrously for the Star Kingdom of Manticore. The alternative
to victory is total defeat, yet this time the cost of victory
will be agonizingly high.

THE DAHAK SERIES:

Mutineers' Moon	pb • 0-671-72085-6 • $7.99	
The Armageddon Inheritance	pb • 0-671-72197-6 • $7.99	
Heirs of Empire	pb • 0-671-87707-0 • $7.99	
Empire from the Ashes	trade pb • 1-4165-0993-X • $16.00	

Contains *Mutineers' Moon, The Armageddon Inheritance* and *Heirs of Empire* in one volume.

THE BAHZELL SAGA:

Oath of Swords	trade pb • 1-4165-2086-4 • $15.00
	pb • 0-671-87642-2 • $7.99
The War God's Own	hc • 0-671-87873-5 • $22.00
	pb • 0-671-57792-1 • $7.99
Wind Rider's Oath	hc • 0-7434-8821-0 • $26.00
	pb • 1-4165-0895-3 • $7.99

Bahzell Bahnakson of the hradani is no knight in shining armor and doesn't want to deal with anybody else's problems, let alone the War God's. The War God thinks otherwise.

BOLO VOLUMES:

Bolo!	hc • 0-7434-9872-0 • $25.00
	pb • 1-4165-2062-7 • $7.99

Keith Laumer's popular saga of the Bolos continues.

Old Soldiers	pb • 1-4165-2104-6 • $7.99

A new Bolo novel.

OTHER NOVELS:

The Excalibur Alternative	hc • 0-671-31860-8 • $21.00
	pb • 0-7434-3584-2 • $7.99

An English knight and an alien dragon join forces to overthrow the alien slavers who captured them. Set in the world of David Drake's *Ranks of Bronze*.

In Fury Born   pb • 1-4165-2131-3 • $7.99
A greatly expanded new version of *Path of the Fury*, with almost twice the original wordage.

1633 with Eric Flint   hc • 0-7434-3542-7 • $26.00
                                    pb • 0-7434-7155-5 • $7.99
1634: The Baltic War with Eric Flint   pb • 1-4165-5588-9 • $7.99
American freedom and justice versus the tyrannies of the 17th century. Set in Flint's *1632* universe.

THE STARFIRE SERIES
WITH STEVE WHITE:

The Stars at War I   hc • 0-7434-8841-5 • $25.00
Rewritten *Insurrection* and *In Death Ground* in one massive volume.

The Stars at War II   hc • 0-7434-9912-3 • $27.00
The Shiva Option and *Crusade* in one massive volume.

PRINCE ROGER NOVELS
WITH JOHN RINGO:

March Upcountry   pb • 0-7434-3538-9 • $7.99

March to the Sea   pb • 0-7434-3580-X • $7.99

March to the Stars   pb • 0-7434-8818-0 • $7.99

We Few   pb • 1-4165-2084-8 • $7.99
"This is as good as military sf gets." —*Booklist*

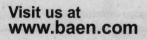

"Will seem crazy to them," Jason interrupted forcefully. "Cut it out, Dunash. How many have you managed to recruit so far, since you've been here? All of five, I believe—three of whom are orphans, two of those too young to use a gun—and of the other two, one of them is not much more than the village idiot. You know as well as I do that the only recruit you've gotten in three months who'll be any use is Bezalel Pitzkler."

Jason's eyes examined the eight young men sitting around Dunash. "At that rate—one real recruit every three months—you won't be able to field more than a squad when the balloon goes up. What's the point?"

"We have special weapons!" one of Dunash's followers said stoutly.

Morris had to fight down a sneer. Red didn't even bother. "Oh, swell. 'Special weapons.' Which translates to: maybe three dozen rockets you got smuggled into Prague, supplied by sympathizers in Grantville—do notice that I'm not inquiring as to the particulars, but I somehow doubt that Mike Stearns or Frank Jackson authorized that—and none of which you really know how to use."

"Do you?" demanded Dunash.

"Me? Don't be silly. Rockets are dangerous. Besides, I'm a man of peace. Well, a man of words, anyway. But I know someone who *does* know how to use them, and he happens to be a friend of mine—well, associate—and he's willing to come here for a bit and teach us. I hope you noticed the functioning pronoun there. *Us.*"

Red leaned back in his seat, spreading his hands in something of a placating gesture. "Dunash, if it'll make you feel better, you and your guys can stay in charge of the rockets. As well as that pickup truck that you've also managed to smuggle into this city, piece by piece, to use as a jury-rigged katyusha—a truck which you have no fricking idea in the world how to assemble. Or drive, even if you did manage by some kinda miracle to put it back together in working order."

Red looked smug. "I, on the other hand, am a crackerjack auto mechanic. I've rebuilt more cars and trucks than I can remember. And I *do* know how to drive."

"In a manner of speaking," Morris muttered under his breath. He'd driven with Red, on two occasions in the past. And while the union organizer wasn't quite as reckless as the now-infamous Hans Richter, riding in the passenger seat of a vehicle driven by Red Sybolt was no pleasure for anyone other than a daredevil. Or teenagers, among whom Red had always been surprisingly popular for a man in his forties.

"That's the deal, Dunash," Red went on. "You can keep the rockets, and I'll volunteer to show you how to put together the truck—even get you some fuel, which you haven't given any thought to at all. And I'll drive it for you when the time comes. But you give up the idea of a separate Jewish combat unit and integrate yourselves with us."

Dunash was still looking stubborn, but his cousin Yehuda spoke up. "Who is 'us,' exactly?"

Red hooked a thumb at Billek. "The Brethren, mostly, other than some people from the CoC we've managed to get started here in Prague. By now, me and Jan—mostly him—have managed to recruit about four thousand volunteers from the Brethren. Half of them are already in Prague, with the others on the way."

Four thousand. Red let the words hang in the air, for a moment. Four thousand—as opposed to Dunash Abrabanel's handful. For that matter, Morris didn't doubt for a minute that Red would provide more people from his newly organized CoC than Dunash had following him. Say what you would about Red Sybolt, the man was a superb organizer.

"We will be buried," hissed Dunash.

For the first time since he'd entered the room, Bishop Comenius spoke. "No, you will not be 'buried,' young man. I give you my word on that. My oath before God, if you will accept it."

Comenius was, by nature, an immensely dignified man, and even Dunash was visibly affected by his words. The more so after the bishop rose to his feet.

"I am recognized by all the Brethren as the foremost religious authority in our church." To the side, Deacon Billek nodded firmly. "Tolerance was one of our watchwords from the beginning of our faith. And now that I have had a chance to study what would have happened in the world of our future, my faith has been fortified."

He turned and pointed to Len Tanner and Ellie Anderson. Then, to Morris himself; then, to Jason; and finally, to Red Sybolt. "Consider, if you will, these five people. One, a Catholic noted for his lapses; two, a man and a woman who believe in no God at all; one, a Jew who is considered a heretic by most other Jews living today; the last, a young Jew who is trying to decide whether he can be a rabbi in these times, because he is no longer sure exactly what he believes."

Morris was astonished by Comenius' accurate assessment of five American strangers whom he had never met before. Obviously, the Brethren (with Red's help) had an excellent espionage service in all but name. True, it wasn't *quite* accurate. Except for a few places like Amsterdam, most rabbis were loath to proclaim someone an actual "heretic," since Jews didn't place the same emphasis that Christians did on doctrinal purity. What most of them would have said about Morris was that he was "practically an apikoros"—an uncomplimentary term indicating someone who was much too loose and self-willed in his interpretation and application of customs and observances.

"Yet in the world they came from," Comenius continued, "it was people such as this who built a nation which, in the fullness of time, provided a sanctuary for my people as well as yours. Most of the world's Brethren wound up living in that 'United States,' as did the single largest grouping of the world's Jews. There is a lesson there for any of God's children, in whatever manner they see that God. Unless you are blind. Which I am not. Freedom of religion must be the banner for both of us—a banner which, by its nature, must be held jointly."

He sat down. "That is my pledge—and the pledge of the Unity of Brethren. You will not be 'buried.' Unless you are buried by our enemies, along with us ourselves."

The decision hung in the balance. Then—and this surprised Morris more than anything that happened that morning—Dunash turned to Jason.

"You will be our rabbi, if anyone is to be. You are sure of this?"